FORGOTTEN MASTERS V

RIPENING OF FATE

SCOTT M. SWAINE

Primix Publishing
East Brunswick Office Evolution
1 Tower Center Boulevard, Ste 1510
East Brunswick, NJ 08816
www.primixpublishing.com
Phone: 1-800-538-5788

Published by Primix Publishing: 11/06/2024

ISBN: 979-8-89194-150-2(sc)
ISBN: 979-8-89194-257-8(hc)
ISBN: 979-8-89194-151-9(e)

Library of Congress Control Number: 2024907434

CONTENTS

Chapter 1.   Trailblazers 1
Chapter 2.   Remotely Interested 61
Chapter 3.   The Lost Ones 105
Chapter 4.   Forward Momentum 252
Chapter 5.   Of Gods and Orcs 303
Chapter 6.   Containment Procedures 332
Chapter 7.   Ruminations of Guile 410
Chapter 8.   Outpatient 524
Chapter 9.   Coming of Age 576
Chapter 10. Breaking New Ground 616

Chapter 1

TRAILBLAZERS

In a seemingly abandoned mining camp, a group of refugees were
struggling to make repairs to a series of defunct vehicles scavenged
from the crumbling remains of their former home, a city located just
east of their hideout.

The Daanen-Aryku survivors of the holocaust that destroyed their
home were working to refit the old hover-trucks they found in one of
the industrial buildings with axels and wheel assemblies. The vehicles
were not normally made for wheels, being a technological design to
hover above the ground. But due to the dilapidated condition and
age of the equipment, nothing worked any more.

The disaster that destroyed their city was an attack by the native
orcs of the world, with the primary body of them occupying a large
village just east of the city, opposite the mining camp where the
survivors found refuge. The orcs didn't know of the survivors, and
seemed occupied with other things, therefore they never discovered
their hideout.

The group was led by a surviving member of the local militia,
Captain Tudorin Lapäli, and further assisted by a number of
individuals who were participating in the recovery and restoration
of their lives…what little they had.

The vehicles had been dragged out of a storage garage in the city, which once belonged to the Civil Utilities service. Lumberjacks using crude axes had cut down a number of trees from the woods further west of the mine, along a small range of mountains. These were then used as rollers to move the vehicles out of the city, hauling them along the streets and through the fields back to the work yard in front of their mine hideout. Once there, they began to fashion new platforms for the vehicles, along with cranes to lift the trucks onto the axels. But without any kind of engine or other power source, they would need to use manual labor to haul them to any work site.

Sulíma Tad'vaal was one of the lead members overseeing the restoration effort. As the weeks passed by, she supervised the repair and refitting of the vehicles. Between her and a close friend, Petrith Girhani, they had plans for a long-distance expedition to retrieve a collection of equipment left behind by their long-time enemies, the Suuden-Aryku, who had taken sides with the orcs and were using conveyor devices to relocate the orcs off-world. The equipment they hoped to retrieve included a series of solar panels, a water pump and storage tank, a utility box that housed a cooling system and electrolysis unit, a high-pressure tank, a mini fusion reactor, and a rift generator, along with their associated connecting pipes and conduits.

They were able to salvage four different vehicles, two large ones and two smaller ones. One of the smaller vehicles would be used for the solar panels, which should stack neatly inside, while the other would carry a crane assembly for use on-site to aid in the loading of the larger components.

The large transports would carry the heavier items, the worst of which was expected to be the reactor itself. This unit alone might take up most of the payload space of a single truck, leaving the second one to load up the remaining large pieces. For this reason, it was decided to give them six wheels for added support. In addition, the undercarriage would need to be heavily reinforced with extra bracing, which meant creating metal supports for it. They also needed spikes and nails to hold things together.

The refugees had to be thrifty with their resources, as a lot of it was collected as salvage from the city. They also had to be very cautious about the smoke they raised, so as not to be noticed by the orcs. Despite all this, it still became necessary to consider some simple forging, so they built a primitive forge inside one of the buildings in the work yard and used it only at night, hiding the light of the fires within the building, and the smoke behind the veil of darkness.

Sulíma had been selecting her crew, pulling together nearly a hundred people to take on this trip, which included scouts, defenders, and laborers. By this time, the vehicles had been outfitted with wheel assemblies, along with towbars affixed with rows of crossbar handles for a labor crew to drag the transports like teams of shackled thralls hauling their master's treasure wagons. Bags of tools had been assembled and tied down in the rear of one of the smaller vehicles, along with some replacement parts in case something breaks down. They also packed ropes and supplies for the trip, and the disassembled parts for a crane to use once they arrive.

"Captain, we're ready with the transports," Sulíma reports. "How does the situation in Camp Three look?"

"So far, clean. The most recent reports tell of nothing bigger than a few prairie cows passing through. The conveyor still seems operational, which is rather amazing for what we're considering to be the last time someone might have been out there to look at it. Other than that, I think you might be on the nose with the idea of the Suuden-Aryku leaving it to rot. It just goes to show you how much they care about the trash they leave behind."

"Their trash will be our treasure, though."

"It certainly will, but I still want you to be careful out there. Don't get cocky, and if you see trouble, run."

"Yes Sir!" she smiles. "We'll have a lot of people riding along with us, for defense as well as relief labor to haul the vehicles. So, unless they come at us with an army, I shouldn't think it would be so bad."

"Maybe. But if you do find trouble, and are forced to fight, don't allow any of them to run and call for reinforcements. Then, depart the area as fast as you can, and try not to leave any tracks they can follow."

"Sounds good enough."

"Finally, I want you to make use of our relay network as you go along to send in reports on your progress. I want to know what's happening, every step of the way."

"Yes Captain."

"And as you come back in, I think we'll start reeling in the network from that side. I see no sense in keeping our people out there spying on wild animals and open fields. If the orcs are all gathering at Camp One, it's not likely they'll be heading back out that way."

"But you'll send word to us if you see anything, right?"

"Absolutely, you can be sure about that."

"Petrith, how do you feel about the electronics side of it?"

"The Captain and I went over as much detail as he can recall on reactors and the shutdown procedures. Assuming they still use any of the standard design layouts, it should follow a predictable pattern."

"Let's hope so, but for all the design changes and new tech they've apparently been making since we left..."

"Yes, well, worst case scenario is we could try unplugging the solar panels and draining the water tank to starve the thing. This should cause it to go into a failsafe mode, but the trouble with that is getting it started again. We're not sure how they're configuring these things."

The Captain was browsing a crude hand-drawn map of the region, reviewing the course they'll take on the way to and from Camp Three, which was located far to the southeast.

"You'll have to circle around the western side of these mountains behind us," he begins. "It's the safest way since the orcs are using the river canyon on the other end. Except for all the underbrush in the jungle region, most of the terrain is reasonably smooth heading into the grasslands and prairies, at least until you get further south. There you have a series of hills, but you won't be going that far."

"And once on the other side of these mountains," Sulíma considers. "It's mostly travelling to the east through those grasslands. Camp Two is way off to the south from us, but if the area is mostly clear, we shouldn't need to worry about seeing anything along the way."

"There are a few elevation contours in your path…that'll slow you down…and several rivers, but nothing too bad. But you'll probably need to build some kind of bridge to get over them."

"Good thing we have a little bit of experience with that now, after redesigning the one out near the pond."

"Yeah, that old strip of dead wood we were using before would never support running a truck over it. You'll need to use local resources, but with the workforce at hand, you should be able to do this. The only thing after that is to pick up the cargo and return home the same way."

"What about the migration paths for the orcs?"

"You'll be below that on the route you'll be taking. Our scouts tell us they've all clustered in a number of camps just south of the mountains from Camp One, and more to the east. There's nothing else spilling into them from further south where you'll be."

"Good, so we'll go in, passing around behind their lines, pick up the conveyor, return home, and then get to the real work of repairing some of our equipment."

"I think we'll set up the reactor on the other side of the pond out there, since we need water for it anyway. This will keep it out of our way, but we'll need to run some conduits back into the yard for the workshops."

"All right, you can get that organized while we're out loading it up."

"You'll be out there several months, at least," he notes. "No doubt you'll have a lot of obstacles in your path. There aren't any roads out there…it's all rough terrain."

"Fallen logs and tree branches, rocks and boulders…" she reminisces. "Yeah, but we'll manage."

With the final pieces in place, they all travel outside to the trucks, which had been lined up to begin rolling out. The first team of laborers was in position on the towbars with the rest of them standing by. Some were riding on the trucks while others would walk the first shift. Sulíma and Petrith climb up on the first vehicle and settle into a perch fashioned as a driver's box.

"All right, Captain," she shouts. "We're ready. Wish us luck."

"You got it," he replies. "May the cu'Nar watch over you. Try to keep yourselves out of trouble. I'll keep in touch via the relay. If we see any changes at Camp Three before you arrive, we'll let you know."

"Thanks."

She gives the order for the team to pull the vehicles away and begin crossing the bridge into the western fields. A team of a dozen laborers were pulling each of the large vehicles, with eight on each of the smaller ones. Together, they slowly made their way across the field, heading off to the end of the hills where they would turn south towards the grasslands and forests on the other side.

The Captain and his officers watched as they pulled away into the distance.

"It's almost demeaning to watch that," he relents. "For all the history and progress our society has made over so many hundreds of millennia."

"Yes," a Lieutenant responds quietly. "But it's progress, maybe also a bit nostalgic, like reliving an ancient moment in history, and starting over from scratch. And it's certainly better than sitting on your tail all day."

"You're right, and afterwards we'll have a chance at rebuilding something…I hope."

✦✦✦

"May I have the attention of the classroom, please? Thank you."

Aerlie was giving an opening lecture for the Third Circle mage studies class. It was the start of the spring season, and Relissa, Marelle, and Haran were all attending the same class together. They had become very close during their time in study, and worked together as a group to help each other with their lessons.

"As you enter into the Third Circle," she continues. "The demands of your study will place additional emphasis on your need for discipline during this and future lessons. The need to respect the powers you will be wielding increases with each Circle, and since the craft is a licensed art, you will need to demonstrate increasingly higher standards of responsibility for your use of it as you progress."

She shuffles around behind the desk at the head of the class, assessing their attentiveness before continuing.

"To make an example of how important it is to develop your focus and discipline, I will tell you a little story of a student who once attended the academy in these same studies. This was back in the early days of the Elixir of Visions, where so much of this became apparent, at least as much due to the rapidity of the lessons, as to the craft itself."

"That was a while back, if I reckon it right," Relissa notes. "And we still talk about it?"

"Indeed. It is not as important how long ago it was, but rather the lesson that was learned and why it is so essential. The craft is a delicate one, and she was young and ambitious, but also inexperienced in many ways. She aspired to make a strong impression, and was maybe a little too anxious at times. In those days, our studies arranged the hierarchy of spell groupings differently from today, and she was just receiving instruction on the Lightning Bolt spell in her Fourth Circle."

"Isn't that a much higher spell circle now?" Haran inquires.

"Yes, as a result of our combined experience, we rearranged the groupings over the years as a means of assigning spells with higher potential into the more appropriate Circles of study. But in her Fourth Circle, perhaps due to her ambition, she should have learned better these basic rules of discipline I mentioned."

"Something tells me she flubbed up, right?" Relissa surmises.

"She did, and in a very embarrassing way. In the old days, Thaelyn would select a handful of students for some field exercises. This was during a time when we still had a lot of hazards roaming around out there, such as orcs, goblins, gnolls, and other things. The exercises would serve two functions. First was to give our people some practice, and second was to help patrol the region to keep the dangers under control."

"And I'm guessing he chose her for one of these patrols?" Marelle muses.

"He most certainly did," she smiles softly. "Her time came up on one occasion, and she accompanied him with a group of other students, including fighters and some young clerics. This was a standard formation for the day. The practice was for each support member to line up with a fighter, offering their service, either offensive or defensive on his behalf. For instance, a mage will attack his target, aiding him in combat, while the priest would give blessings of health or augmentation to support his combat style."

"Sounds like a nice arrangement. Do we still do this? I seem to recall something when that demon came to town."

"Yes, we do, at least in one form or another. The formations have evolved over the years, but the emphasis is usually to focus on one fighter as your support target."

"I see, so what happened on this occasion?"

"On this day, the group came upon a party of orcs. The team formed up and made ready to fight. All was proceeding according to their study. This young lady lined up with her champion in front and started sending out offensive spells at his target. But then, in the heat of battle, she heard a loud war cry. It was the orcish leader making his charge. She was in the process of conjuring her first combat lightning bolt spell when she was distracted by the sound."

"Gracious," Haran mutters. "That's not a good sign already."

"Indeed, and the orc was charging directly at Thaelyn, as he recognized him to be the leader of the group. Worse, the orc was on the opposite side of Thaelyn from where this girl stood."

"Criminy," Relissa mumbles. "So, where did the lightning go after this?"

"Her distraction placed her new focus on the approaching orcish leader, just as her lightning spell was letting go. It flew out and struck Thaelyn square in the back. She was mortified at the error."

"Buggers, I'll bet he wasn't happy about that!"

"Fortunately, due to at least a few factors, it wasn't quite as bad as it could've been. Her skill was still kind of low, his armor also protected him from part of it, and his own skill in mage craft allowed him to resist a fair portion of it. This is another skill we learn here, by the way. And finally, being Aasimar, they also have a kind of natural resistance factor that plays into it."

"Sounds fair, but what happened to the girl?"

"Although Thaelyn was briefly stunned, he was still able to throw a shoulder-butt at the orc to knock it down, giving him time to turn to the girl and remind her, as any good instructor would, that her fight was on the other side, and to refocus herself. He then returned to finish the orc."

"I'll bet that girl was horrified at what she did," Haran remarks. "And to Thaelyn on top of everything else."

"Oh, she was, you can be sure of that. She had a few friends who tried counseling her, telling her to refocus herself on her studies, and saying accidents can happen, even to the best of us. This is a school after all, and nobody is perfect. Still, she couldn't help but to feel she had failed somehow, and she tried to avoid Thaelyn whenever she saw him passing by in the halls."

"How long did this continue?"

"Actually, not very long. Thaelyn realized she was feeling so poorly, and he didn't want to see her falling behind in her studies, especially when you factor in the Elixir. So, he called her into his office one day, had a nice little chat to restore her confidence, and encouraged her to carry on."

"You would never see that kind of support with any of the instructors we had in our old academy in Rolsklinde. They would simply scream at you and throw you out the door."

"Based on the stories you've given us, I'm sure of it. But in this case, if you can believe it, Thaelyn actually congratulated her for being the first to hit him with a lightning bolt."

"What?" he balks. "He congratulated her for it?"

"This is partly his way to disarm the tension levels. In his time, after training so many people, he's taken more than a few accidental hits, though none of them using lightning. So, this would make for a rather curious initiation moment."

"Curious, indeed!" he chortles.

"This is also when we realized the lessons for the different Circles had to be reworked a little in order to accommodate for the hurried pace of study when using the Elixir of Visions. Practice and discipline became much more important, and so the stronger spells had to be moved into higher Circles to compensate."

"Ah, so this is the reason."

"It was a simple mistake, by comparison, but an important one to learn and correct."

"Whatever happened to her?" Marelle inquires. "Did she finish her studies?"

"Oh, she did!" Aerlie replies cheerfully as she wraps up. "She graduated with honors, made many new friends, and even set a new standard for some of her class choices. And finally, she went on to become married. Now she teaches others about her error in the hopes they don't make the same mistake."

Aerlie gives a polite wave as she leaves the class to the other instructors. The three friends gazed at each other in disbelief.

"Marelle," Relissa groans. "I think we've just been had again, and by the same peeps that keep hitting us with all these floozy tales."

"It must be a cultural thing," she shakes her head.

✦

Thaelyn and his officers were meeting in the tactical office in the village of Firstfall with the Daanen'kai High Commander to compare notes on a new activity they were testing.

"Your Lordship," Kailen begins. "I've pulled together a number of people, very discreetly of course, for these interviews with Lady Aerlie. These are mostly low-ranking laborers from various professions that shouldn't be noticed if they take a minor leave of absence from their duties, just in case that spy is watching anything."

"Very good, Commander, and even if Darumon is still watching, all he should gather from this is a simple exercise for a bit of cultural exchange. Aerlie will take it from there. Then we will have Aelwyn conduct some testing of this Prodigy skill to see what, if anything, we can gain from it."

"I would be truly amazed to see if anyone else can do this, but I'm also a little uncertain of how we might use it. I guess the only way to know is to work it slowly and test the limits, just like with Kaliya."

"And so far, Kaliya is demonstrating herself to be quite functional. I hear she will be entering a new stage of her training shortly. I wonder what sort of results she might have."

"It all still seems a little too fantastic to me. My little sister parading around the place as a projected image," he ruminates.

"But the possibilities available to us can be rather remarkable."

"Well, anyway, I sent a group to B.T. to meet with the Lady. This should get us started."

"Most excellent, then we shall give her some time to process them and wait for a result."

The meeting continued onto other topics, including the reconstruction efforts occurring around the land after the war with Marshal Darumon and his Suuden-Aryku loyalists. But in the city of Bya'an Tamoranth, Aerlie was in her office in the city temple preparing to interview the first of a line-up of people from the Naarg uy'Sodrad for this new testing.

"Good greetings," she announces politely. "Please sit down."

A young Daanen'kai female had just been called into the office for her interview. She was neatly attired in a shirt and pants, and a dress coat, appearing as if she was applying at an employment office for a new job. She took up seating in front of the desk as Aerlie was reviewing a paper with her personal information on it.

"Your name is Navina Lar'akan, correct? According to my information, the Commander selected you because you expressed an interest in this new project we are working on."

"Yes, Ma'am...um, Your Ladyship," she blushes almost immediately for the error.

"It's quite all right," Aerlie soothes. "Your society isn't accustomed to working with someone in a royal station, so I'm not going to be too critical for it."

"Thank you," she sighs. "The Commander tried to instruct me on my language and terms, but some of it seems…um, well, unusual."

"Perhaps you would like to use the word alien?" she smiles gently.

"Well, while it might serve, I think it wouldn't be appropriate, and I'm trying to make a good impression," she returns the smile.

"Of course. This is fair enough, but now, moving on. Did he mention to you precisely what sort of work we're hoping to accomplish here?"

"Not really. He said something about a review of skills for some kind of special project. He mentioned we're going to be working together much more in the coming months and years, and we'll likely find opportunities for new occupations to develop ourselves along the way. So, I'm curious as to what kinds of opportunities might be out there, and if any would be available for me."

"This is a very fair statement. What is it you do now?"

"I'm currently working as an assistant cook in the Naarg uy'Sodrad's cafeteria."

"Is this your primary profession?"

"In recent times, yes. I've bounced between a few occupations, as we had to juggle our workforce due to the constant attacks outside and so many of us taking injury along the way. We couldn't keep anyone in one profession for very long before having to call them into another to fill in for our losses."

"That sounds like a very difficult life for you. What did you do before this?"

"Back home on Ruuki uy'Daan, I worked in a machine shop assembling circuit boards for our electronics industry."

"How interesting. Have you ever considered any professions besides industrial?"

"Up until the time of the attack, no. I had hoped our lives were finally turning for the better…at least until those horrid Suuden-Aryku found us again," she frowns intensely.

Aerlie was studying her, not only for her words, but also for her emotions, trying to employ a passive telepathic scan to understand her thoughts while not precisely invading her mind. And at this moment, she could feel a strong revulsion and pain of loss welling up inside the woman.

"How old are you?"

"Twelve centuries."

"That's still rather young for your race. Were you born on Ruuki uy'Daan?"

"Yes, part of the first new generation there."

"Would this be alongside such as Lieutenant Lapäli, perhaps?"

"Yes, actually, although he's a little older than me."

"I see. This is interesting, to learn of these progressions. But what happened to you during the attack? I feel you hold something especially bitter…that is, more so than some."

"I lost my whole family…everything, including my new husband and my child."

"Oh wow. I'm terribly sorry. From the stories I've heard; that attack was an especially devastating one. How old was your child?"

"Only four decades. She was in school at the time. My husband too, for that matter. He was a science teacher. No one from the school made it to the ship, so we have to assume they were all lost."

"That's a terrible pain to suffer, and I can feel it in you all the way over here. Have you ever considered a military career, perhaps one that could allow you to take your fight back to the one who started it all?"

"The one?" she puzzles. "They're ALL responsible. Our history tells us they come at us again and again, mercilessly attacking and destroying our homes. We were hoping that wild jump to Ruuki uy'Daan finally evaded them, but I guess nothing helps. Well, at least not until you people showed up. I still can't believe you were able to chase them away."

"But Navina, you do realize the one who is most responsible is Sargeras…or perhaps I should say two, as we now know of Darumon."

"I've heard talk about this new one. He was supposedly the one leading this military, right? But to lead something, don't you still need people who are willing to follow you?"

"Yes, this is most often the case, unless you are also well-known to use propaganda and misinformation to delude them."

"Delude? How can you delude someone to treat others like target practice?"

"While this is surely a reasonable question to ask, and I'm not precisely sure what he did over there, but we have some new information on our side that suggests he must've been very devious on multiple levels to deceive your people into believing many things that were simply wrong."

"Wrong? Like what?"

"Well, first, I'm sure it goes without saying that your departure from Azgarén would probably give him an excuse to pursue you. We believe he wanted you, all of you, to follow him for some ultimate purpose. For any of you to disobey his wishes would surely make him angry."

"Oh really! So, we don't have the right to use our own minds? Cu'Nar help us. And as a result, he chases us all over the place, hitting us just enough to move somewhere else so he can hit us again."

"Navina, his kind is an ancient race that likes to play with others as toys. So, as for a mind of your own, no, you're not permitted this. His kind truly has a god complex in the most literal sense of the word. And he's probably using the rest of your people as tools to do his work for him."

"Tools to do his work!" she snaps. "How can anyone with half a horn choose to do this kind of work?"

"Choose? This is an interesting statement, but to answer this, we need to reflect on some recent information we've been collecting, but keeping a careful secret in case he's still spying on us."

"Wait a minute, STILL spying?" she yips.

"Yes. We believe he was following you during your chase, impersonating one of your own, and this is how they found you each time. You were never a mystery to them. And your wild jump wasn't so wild. It was probably planned, as he must've owned that world for much longer."

"Why do you say this?" she asks tenuously.

"Those orcs once arrived on our world many millennia ago, likely as part of an early invasion effort, but they would need help even to find us. We also have the local races on Therinë who just happened to find that world, migrating away from Tae'Eladar, and this would also require help, as none of them should be able to find a world in another universe."

"Uh oh…"

"There was also mention of a strange portal being used along the way, and once we found it, we saw it could not be native to anyone local. This means someone much older and with very specialized knowledge came to Tae'Eladar and conducted all this behind our backs."

"Who?"

"Darumon, it has to be. He is attempting a revenge attack on his old rivals, the Estelar. But doing so very quietly, and using others to do most of his work for him, and most of THAT is without any proper explanation of WHY they are doing anything at all."

"All right, but can you give me an example of how he can make people do something without a proper explanation?"

"Most likely, as we saw so often on Therinë, he lies and fabricates stories to keep them in line. For instance, Thaelyn found a lost trans-com in the city of Rolsklinde once. It had to belong to Darumon as he was impersonating their local Governor. It linked to their command base, and this allowed Thaelyn to speak briefly to the Suuden'kai High Commander. The Commander explained how he believed they were on this grand crusade to return some stolen property, or some such, and you were all in league with his enemies."

"Oh! So that's it! We're in league with people we never heard of before."

Aerlie giggles softly and shrugs as she continues.

"And apparently, with no proper background information on his side to confirm or deny any of this, they chose to follow it, likely with the promise of this great wisdom waiting as their reward."

"Oh wonderful, so he promises the secrets of the universe if only we blow it up for him in the process."

"Ironically, yes," Aerlie smirks tenderly. "And this is generally where we stand on it by now. But the story gets complicated here, because now we need to involve the cu'Nar."

"The cu'Nar," she emits cautiously. "Why, what role do they play in all this?"

"They are apparently spies working for someone who was watching Sargeras during this time. We believe that ship of yours was no accident, and instead a planned incentive to take you away, with the cu'Nar passing a message for you to bring to us."

"Huh?" she winces. "We were carrying a message for you?"

"We believe you were evacuated intentionally. Furthermore, it was likely expected for Darumon to give chase, as he would need to return back here regardless, since this is where his enemies are found...or at least the most immediate ones."

"Uh huh, and I'm starting to regret coming in here now. And this message?"

"The word they used to describe him. Very few races in existence by now would associate the word Titan, at least in the context being used here. Thaelyn and I represent one such example, along with the other Celestial races and the Estelar themselves."

"Oh dear cu'Nar, and literally so," she murmurs. "Suddenly, this is getting very complicated...like you said."

"This new information being revealed to us is by someone dropping clues that are designed to lead us in a specific direction of realization of a much longer history than what we might see on the surface. The existence of a being that should no longer exist, his observation by some third party, likely as a plot against him, and we who are apparently being arranged as a counterforce to what he created. Then we have you and your message to bring it together. Now, we must take it back to him."

"Take it back..." she whispers distantly.

"Navina," Aerlie continues. "This interview isn't for some simple position as a cook or other common laborer. We have a special need to test our applicants to see if they possess a very unusual skill. This skill could be a turning point for us in our battle against a creature who should not otherwise be alive."

"Why...um, that is, why is he not actually supposed to be alive? I recall it said the cu'Nar mentioned something about a dead race, but..."

"His kind are ancient enemies to the Estelar. THEY are the reason the others are dead."

"In all the nether-space!" she shouts. "Yeah, now I really am sorry for coming in here."

"The two of them are leftovers from an ancient battle that destroyed the rest. We think these two must've escaped at some moment and went into hiding. Further, if they are hiding so deeply, they will not likely hold still if the Estelar themselves should go in search of them. Therefore, it falls to us, who might not stand out in their eyes as a threat. They don't hold very high esteem for...little things," she smirks.

"Oh, little things, is it? Those same little things they like to blast whenever their tail itches?"

"Exactly. And then we have your people. Among us is one we call Adalon the Silver. She is a very powerful prophetess. She wrote a long series of prophecies about our world, our people, where we came from, where we're going, and what we'll do when we arrive there. Right now, our scholars are studying a final chapter where she apparently speaks of your people."

"A prophetess..." she grimaces. "You know, we don't usually fall into such things as, um..."

"...Mysticism?" Aerlie finishes. "Yes, we already went through this a few times with your people, even though your metaphysics faction IS about mysticism, in a classic sense of the word, as it is surely not an empirical science."

"Oops. I guess that exposes something."

"Indeed," she grins mildly. "So you will need to check your horns to make sure they're firmly attached."

"Thanks. But I may need to visit the medical lab before this is done to repair any fractures. Um, can you tell me a little about what she says about us?"

"She tells us a very curious story of how you came to be, and then of Sargeras and Darumon arriving on your world, taking control of your government, probably by corrupting them to their whims, and how you and your people, under the guidance of Velen, fled at the instruction of the cu'Nar."

"In all the nether-space…" she mumbles. "If that doesn't twist my horns."

"It continues up to where we are now with your message, but then we have even more detail we are still studying. The next in sequence seems to suggest building a fighting force, and we think it involves this strange skill we are now investigating."

"A skill…what sort of skill? Keeping in mind, I'm just a laborer in a kitchen. And even that industry I was working once before was generally a routine employment."

"Perhaps, but this is no ordinary skill you might discover by assembling a circuit board or cooking dinner. This one is special, and it will require some very special testing. We're also keeping it a highly classified secret for now, in case Darumon is still spying on us. We certainly wouldn't want HIM to know what we're doing!"

"Oh, sure! After all, if you're hoping to sneak up on a god with little things like us, why would you advertise!" she chuckles ironically.

"Naturally!" Aerlie smiles mischievously. "And this is where YOU come in, assuming you're not thinking of dashing out of the room and possibly missing out on the greatest opportunity in your life to liberate a world full of…how do you describe it…dull-horns who do not know how to ask the right questions at the critical moment."

Navina glared at Aerlie and raised her brow prominently. She felt her face beginning to pucker giddily, and she rolled her eyes around the room as she pondered the statement.

"Now I know why you're the Queen of this world. You know how to inspire people to follow you. You and that high-spirited husband of yours, for all the stories I've heard of him."

"Absolutely! So, how many hooves would you wish to jump in with, one or both?"

"Oh, and thank you for plagiarizing one of our most popular expressions," she grins.

"Now, I should temper this with the fact that we can't be absolutely sure who among you might show this ability. But we suspect it might be widely available…you just don't know it yet."

"I don't know it yet…" Navina muses. "That certainly sounds mysterious. And just when WILL I know of it?"

"We have someone who will conduct the testing, but this will need to occur after I finish my interviews. We're actually still learning about it, ourselves."

"And what will I use it for? What sort of employment are you actually suggesting for me here?"

"Military. But at this point, it might be a very specialized service. Do you know Kaliya Nazég? You will be joining alongside of her."

"Did she do this testing as well?"

"She did, and she is currently aiding us in our further development of its potential. But we need to assemble a team now."

"A team…" she contemplates as she leans forward. "I've heard a few things about her studies over here. Magic…among other things. Would I be involved in this as well?"

"I believe so, and probably the same or a very similar program as what she's running right now."

"I never trained as a soldier. Um, I suppose I wouldn't be against it, but exactly who are we fighting here? If the Suuden-Aryku are essentially innocent of anything other than being dull-horns to the extreme, am I going to be one of those…" she coughs softly, "…little things, rushing up to a god?"

"We might not be specifically rushing up to him proper, but we will certainly want to turn things around for Darumon and his propaganda machine. Among other things, he's apparently using devices to control that military of his. So, dull-horns or no, they may not have much choice in it, and we need to disarm this component."

"Devices! I know the stories of how they behave like machines, but…"

"Right. When Thaelyn had that opportunity to speak with the Suuden'kai High Commander, he learned a few things. The Commander was clearly under a control effect, as was evidenced in his voice, and he also admitted to having a control chip in his brain of a military design."

Navina grimaced at the depiction.

"He would actually admit to this? That might instead sound like a leak. This sort of thing isn't what I would expect someone to simply come out and reveal openly."

"I may have to agree, but since we already knew of it from your Med-tech Tad'vaal and her studies, I guess it was no longer a secret."

"I suppose."

"We are also aware from our own spy efforts where Darumon admitted himself and Sargeras to be the last known survivors of a society of what he calls Overseers. Therefore, between this and Darumon's lies, we are looking at beings who like their position of power over others who do not otherwise ask questions, and this carries its own meaning to us."

"Great…" Navina surmises. "So, he uses devices and tells them stories, and denies them to ask questions as they blast whole worlds apart. Cu'Nar help us all. Honestly, dull-horns or otherwise, I don't know who to accuse the most, because in my opinion, you still need to hold some responsibility, no matter what you do. Is this to say it's all his work, or our people back home for being so dull-horned that they allowed it."

"I suppose you do carry a point," Aerlie muses. "It can certainly be disparaging, and I would imagine many of them would feel just as badly if they were ever to realize the error. But under these conditions, we can't truly blame them for their actions if they're being forced into it."

"Maybe," she sighs despondently. "But it's a really bitter pill to swallow, listening to this when you lost everything dear to you because of it."

"I understand, and I'm sure you're not the only one."

"And we put ourselves in the crosshairs simply because we wouldn't bow down and kiss his hooves, like all the rest."

"He probably wanted all of you to behave like his puppets as he made his plans of revenge on the Estelar. Our space was apparently the last pocket of their former holdings, and our spy reports tell us their society experienced a long decline. So, he must hold a deep revulsion against them, and therefore has such strong desires to take this action, even though he is alone. And he needs servile minions, not people asking why they're destroying something outside their personal concern."

"Yes!" she emphasizes with a finger. "And this makes perfect sense, as we certainly wouldn't do this on our own. But then, what are these plans to take it back to him? How do you hope to find Azgarén? Last I heard, our nav computers were wiped."

"We think we have an alternate route available to us, but we're going to need people like you to lead the way."

"Like me..." she ponders uncertainly. "And no doubt using this skill I don't know about, and likely will NOT know about until AFTER you test me for it, and only THEN to learn what I'm supposed to do with it, alongside of Kaliya, of all people, and the reputation SHE developed during these past three and a half centuries with our Elder Council."

"Oh, come now. She's made a few improvements since then."

"Uh huh, sure... And then, here you are propositioning me to be a savior to a world full of dull-horns. You know, I think my horns ran out the door already, but I'll admit one thing. If I still had my husband and child, I might want to take the easy path...you know, to raise my new family."

"Of course..." Aerlie nods.

"But for where I find myself now, I may simply have to jump in with both hooves and go fight a god. After all, how many times do you get to do THAT in your lifetime?"

"Especially one as long as yours!"

"That's right! So, what do I have to do?" she smiles gently.

◆ ◆◆◆ ◆

"Are we there yet?" Sulíma whines mockingly.

"You asked that question just a short while ago," Petrith complains.

"I'm just trying to be annoying," she grins.

"And doing a very good job of it," he returns back.

"I am getting very bored, however. You can only sing the same songs and play the same games just so many times before it gets extremely monotonous."

"I agree, but you wanted this reactor, and I suppose the rest of us do too, so we have to put up with it until we get the work done."

"I just wish we could go a little faster."

"It'll probably be worse on the way back, carrying all that equipment."

"Well, at least we won't have to fill in all these potholes and ditches twice," she admits. "If we follow the same course on the way home, that much should already be done."

"And building these bridges over the rivers we cross."

"Yeah, that part is slowing us down more than anything."

"So long as we keep the scouts running ahead of us to give us a heads-up on what's coming, we can send some workers to take care of it. This can save us from having to stop for a long time."

"I'm glad most of this central section is flat, though. Just think if we had to cover a lot of hills between here and there."

"Yeah, and it could cut our rate of travel in half, I'll bet," he winces.

Sulíma sighs audibly. The long journey across the central plains had been dragging out for nearly two months. The trip had been mostly uneventful. No orcs were seen in the area, either as local residents or migrations from more distant camps. Some local wildlife had been spotted, and the hunters would go out to collect food for the group.

The teams pulled the vehicles with a methodic march. The work was difficult, but in time they became used to it, and it strengthened their bodies. Relief teams would rotate in periodically, and scouts would run alongside keeping watch for trouble. Several scouts were sent ahead to check for deviances in the landforms, such as ditches, soft soil from burrows, old logs, and other debris. Work teams would then go clear the path and fill in the holes so the haulers could keep up their stubborn pace. At the occasional river, they would search for local wood harvests and build a crude bridge for a water crossing.

Petrith carried a copy of the hand-drawn map the Captain was using, trying to track their progress. From time to time, a scout would be sent to find the local relay outpost to deliver a status report, which would then be sent to the hideout in the mine. They would also pick up news of the latest events back home.

"According to this last report from home," Sulíma announces. "The orcs in Camp One are still receiving a few reinforcements, but the camps south of those mountains are clearing out. Everything is moving into one place. If this keeps up, the only orcs to be found anywhere will be found only in Camp One."

"Those Suuden-Aryku will be the death of them as a race soon."

"I'm actually starting to feel a little sorry for them. They probably don't even know what's waiting for them on the other side."

"Assuming it's a quick death," Petrith suggests. "We were also considering if they're just filling an empty space."

"Maybe, but I think the other idea holds more merit. If they were filling in a space, they could do it from their local conveyors, and then converge if they need to on the other side. Why move everyone to a single point on this side just to jump through a conveyor if they're simply relocating to another world. There's something special about this one point, and I don't think it could be a land grab."

"You know, Suli, you have a good point there. A land grab would make more sense if to spread it out where you have more land to grab. Sending everyone to one place, unless we're talking about building a big city, which doesn't fit with their normal lifestyle, wouldn't make as much sense."

"So, they're being spent, like we said before. Right down to the last."

The journey continued as they crossed more open territory. They were nearing the end of the second month when one of the scouts reported in after her survey of the terrain ahead.

"Suli, I've spotted something just on the horizon. It looks like the remains of a camp with several bright white objects sticking out of it."

"Finally!" she cheers. "Then it might be just another day or so to reach it. If I had any wine, I'd be popping it open right now."

"Are you actually old enough to drink?" Petrith smirks.

She whaps him on the arm and sneers at him teasingly.

"Hey! I'm an adult, I'm liberated, and I'm out here in the middle of nowhere with no rules or restrictions. I just wish I actually had some wine now. Does anyone know how to make that stuff?"

"Well, don't get too excited yet, Suli," Petrith cautions. "Save it until after we get there and see if we can actually load it up."

"Party pooper… All right, I can wait one more day."

The labor teams pressed forward. The news filled them with renewed vigor, but the day was wearing on into evening. Even though they wanted to continue, they knew it was better to make camp, and start fresh in the morning.

When the sun rose the next day, they loaded themselves up and began moving again. A morning run to the nearby scout station sent word that the camp was in sight, and all was well so far. They were expecting to reach it possibly by midday. The hours passed and the teams rotated their shift to a fresh crew, continuing their course until the camp came into view just a few miles ahead.

"People," Petrith announces. "It looks like we have another river to cross before we can reach it. Let's get out there and build a bridge."

A work crew picks up tools from one of the vehicles and rushes out to a grove of trees they spotted to the north. It was a small, forested area located only a moderate distance away, not too excessive, but they would still need to carry the logs all the way back, and this would take time.

The teams brought the vehicles near the river's edge and stopped.

Sulíma and Petrith both jumped off and looked for a passable area through the water. They found a shallow section and waded across.

"Here you go, Petrith," she directs. "This is where you come in."

He walks up to the condenser unit and begins examining it while Sulíma strolls over to look at the solar arrays a short distance upstream. She also finds a water pump immersed in the river.

"I need some people over here," she calls. "We should be able to pull these out while Petrith works on those other things. They shouldn't be too heavy, but they look delicate, so be careful."

She studies the cabling and the plug attachments under the panels and starts testing one to see how hard it is to remove. After a few attempts, she discovers the plug needs to be twisted and then pulled.

"Here, like this," she demonstrates to the others.

She notices hinges on the panels where wing segments folded out to expand the surface area. She tries folding one in to see how they pack down.

"And this too, these fold in to make it smaller. Those Suuden-Aryku thought of everything, lucky for us. Let's pack them up and carry them across. And bring some tools over here for these pipes."

Petrith was examining the condenser unit. He found an access panel, but it apparently needed a key of some sort to turn a latching screw.

"I need something over here to open this," he shouts. "It's some kind of five-pointed screw head. Do we have anything like that?"

Sulíma walks over to take a look.

"I've never seen one like that before. This could be tricky, but maybe we can wedge something in there to turn it. We'll work on making up a tool for it when we get home."

She calls over one of the other workers with a bag of tools and pulls out a few items to test on the screw. She ends up using the flat edge of a small chisel to turn the screw and release the latch.

Petrith opens the panel to find the controls for operating the condenser. The device was fairly simple in design with some status displays for the power input, electrolysis conversion rate, and a pressure gauge leading to the output tank. There was also a very clearly marked power switch. He flips the switch and the humming fades. The fan slows to a stop and the status readouts zero out.

"That was easy. Let's close these valves to preserve the fuel we already have. I'll take a look at the reactor."

"We should also drain the water tank," Sulíma suggests. "No sense in hauling a full tank around. That would be heavy."

Petrith nods as he steps around to the reactor and begins searching for a similar panel. He locates one on the side of the box underneath the spherical fusion chamber.

"I need that tool again," he notes. "We have another of those screws here."

"At least they're consistent."

"Consistent, yes. Secure, no. If it were me, I'd put a key lock on it, not simply a screwhead. But then if you're an orc, I suppose it doesn't matter, it's all the same."

Sulíma hands the tool across, and he wedges the end inside the screwhead. He carefully turns the latch and opens the access door. He looks inside to see a display panel with statistical details of the fusion reaction, power output, a load meter, and fuel consumption. To one side he sees a large red button.

"Well, I have to admit, they may have made a few advancements, but it's still a familiar design to our own. The Captain suggested they might do this. See this button here? This looks like a shutdown switch."

"You'd better be sure of that, Petrith," Sulíma winces. "After all, this is a fusion reactor…emphasis on the fusion part. I'd like you to be a little more certain than just 'it looks like…' "

"All right, how about this label saying 'Scram' on it?"

"I might do that regardless," she snickers.

He looks around briefly at the other equipment, including the rift generator and the swirling vortex inside the ring, and takes a deep breath.

"Well, this is it. Ready, Suli?"

She gazes at him hesitantly.

"I have to admit, I'm a little scared about this."

"Yeah, but this is what we talked about once before. If we tried cutting off the fuel, or anything else, it might go into a fail-safe mode, but we can't be sure what sort of protocols it uses to re-enable it. Following a procedural shutdown might be the most predictable method."

"All right, then hit it, and let's pray to the cu'Nar we're still here to talk about it after."

He nods and presses the button.

A flashing light appears on the panel, accompanied by a beeping sound. Cold chills run down both of their backs as they watch the display readings fluctuate. The normal humming of the reactor is now accompanied by a brief whirring, followed shortly after by the cycling of popping sounds which seemed to be occurring within the projections sticking out of the sphere itself.

"These must be some sort of control rods to draw power from the reaction inside," Petrith suggests.

"And the whirring?"

"That sounded like it was at the bottom, maybe a control valve for the fuel input."

"I love your definitive evaluation, Petrith," she chuckles feebly.

Another few moments pass, and the humming begins to fade, allowing the two attendants to breathe a sigh of relief. The shutdown of the reactor also brings the rift generator offline, and the aperture closes.

"Well, Suli, I guess today is your centennial. Congratulations, you have a new toy to play with."

She squeals with excitement and calls the crew over to begin the disassembly.

"My Lord," the page calls out. "The General desires your attention to a matter just received in Firstfall."

Thaelyn was inspecting the early construction efforts in Rolsklinde of the new academy and military buildings when the announcement came. The upper district of the city was coming alive again with new civic buildings, market centers, and inns. The flow of workers, as well as civilian travelers and merchants from other cities, including those on Tae'Eladar, was bringing a much-needed influx of revenue to the local economy.

"What is it, page?" he replies.

"He only told me to fetch you, my Lord. He didn't say what the reason was, but it sounded rather urgent."

"Very well, I suppose we should go investigate."

Thaelyn and the page stroll across the plaza to the recently completed city portal hub. It had addressing runes to the other local cities and to Firstfall. They step through as the wheel turns to their preferred destination.

They arrive in the village and the page moves off to his reserve station, while Thaelyn walks across the village square towards the tactical office.

"General, you called for me?"

"My Lord, we have a most curious turn of events. I just received word that Portal Three has closed. We have no obvious explanation for it, however."

"There were no observations of activity in the window before this?"

"No, my Lord, they did not notice anything pass in front of the portal window. Therefore, my guess, for lack of a better reason, might be equipment failure."

"I suppose this is to be expected after a while. How long do you suppose those conveyors might have been in operation without supervision? Certainly long enough for some manner of wear to finally settle in. I now wonder about the other two."

"Surely, if this is the beginning of a failure cycle, they cannot be too long behind."

"I would still desire to keep our garrison active, however, just for reassurance. Until we find our way there personally, I think it would be unwise to take anything for granted."

"Of course, my Lord…"

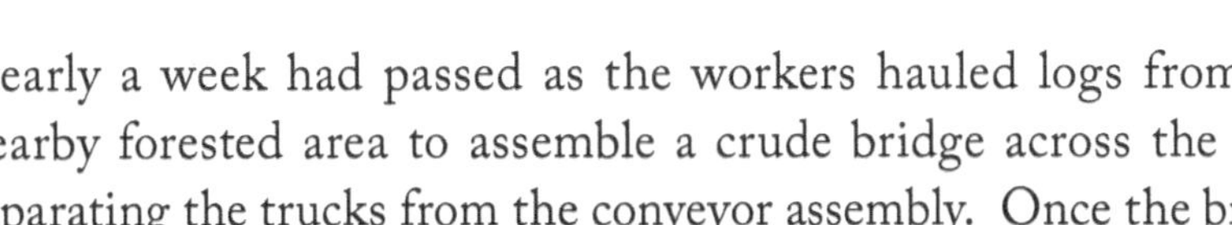

Nearly a week had passed as the workers hauled logs from the nearby forested area to assemble a crude bridge across the river separating the trucks from the conveyor assembly. Once the bridge was complete, they towed the trucks across and began loading up the equipment, securing it with ropes and padding between the more delicate components. When the work was finished, they turned the vehicles around and slowly made their way back home.

Word was sent along the scout relay camps of their success, and instructions were given to pull back the outposts as the team moved along their return route.

Captain Lapäli called together a new work team in the assembly room at the mine to give an announcement.

"We have word that Suli is coming home with a new fusion reactor. This will put us in a position to start repairing some of our equipment and allow us to get back on our hooves. But it won't be easy, as there are a lot of dead machines out there to be repaired. One thing we need to do is start scavenging anything we can find that could possibly be useful, either as repairable items or replacement parts."

Among those participating in the review was Túfula Vankkar, another prominent member of the advisory council offering her opinions and support to the team.

"Captain," she asks. "Where will we put all this stuff? Are we going to set up shops outside, and what about the orcs?"

"The orcs are on the other side of the city and seem to have their minds on other things. So long as it stays that way, we're in good shape."

"All right, so what should we be looking for?"

"Old tools, measuring equipment, arc welders, plasma torches; whatever you can find that's still in one piece. Even if it's not in one piece, take it anyway as we might be able to use it for parts. Check the old workshops at schools, civic buildings, industrial repair shops and manufacturing facilities. If it's small enough to lift, bring it home. Just keep in mind to watch for that odd orcish patrol and the mutants. Travel in groups, no less than three each."

"What about the larger pieces?"

"We'll need transports to pick those up, and last I heard, they're currently in use, so we'll have to wait."

Another week passes, and a message comes in from the scout relay network. The messenger arrived to find Captain Lapäli reviewing a list of objectives with one of his lieutenants, summarizing the work orders to be carried out once the reactor was installed.

"Captain, we have news on Camp Two."

"What is it, Cadet?"

"The camps that were feeding into it have finally depleted, and the remainder of the western camp has picked up and merged with Camp Two."

"I guess this means the end of that camp soon."

"Yes Sir, but we also saw a group of orcs detach and form a migration party heading north. It appears to carry families. We think they're probably going to join Camp One, like so many others have recently."

"All those orcs in Camp One pulling in their kids, and now more of them from out there at Camp Two dragging them across... Wait a minute, are they already moving?"

"Yes Sir, since the time this report was sent."

"Wonderful..." he groans as he pulls up his map of the region. "We have our people heading in, and them coming up. With travel times as they are, we're coming very close to an intersection. We can't let our people cross paths with those orcs. Send word and tell them to take action, maybe divert to the south. The orcs will continue north, and our people can circle around behind them."

"Yes Sir, we'll get the word out to them."

✦✦✦✦✦

"Suli, what is that?" Petrith observes.

"I picked it up a while back and I'm carving it out."

"A piece of an old log... Are you really that bored now?"

"Well, yes, but I have a plan. And besides, would you rather I ask if we're there yet fifteen times a day?"

"Actually no, keep it up, whatever it is."

"It's going to be a drum once I get something to put on top of it. One of the hunters suggested a piece of leather, but the thing is we need a way of tanning it. Túfu was able to do this in her lab, but of course that's all the way back home. So, unless I want to send away for it, well..."

"And why do you need a drum? Yet another way to annoy me?" he smirks.

"Sure," she chirps. "After all, if I'm going to be a world-class pest, I need to diversify."

They share a round of laughter, joined by some of the others in the vehicle.

"Suli, a runner is coming," calls one of the scouts walking alongside the team.

The messenger was carrying a note from the Captain, the message itself being in transit for a week since he sent it. The scouts have been passing it along on their daytime runs from relay to relay until it finally arrived at the convoy.

Sulíma takes the note, thanking the runner and inviting her to sit for a while to rest. She begins to read.

"Uh oh, we have trouble up ahead. Petrith, send some scouts up there, but be careful of orcs. There's a migration party of some kind coming out of Camp Two heading north. At the rate we're going, we might bump into them."

"What kind of party? We haven't seen any of those coming out of there before."

"The note mentions a family that he thinks is going to join Camp One."

"A family?" he muses. "So, that means Camp Two may be empty by now. The reports we were getting from our earlier runs told us they send family parties as the final stage of abandoning the camps. Suli, maybe we should go check it out while we're in the area."

"I'm not so sure the Captain would like us going off and getting ourselves into trouble."

"Let's put it this way, if we have orcs crossing our path up ahead, we need to either stall or divert ourselves to avoid them, and I'd much rather keep moving than to stop. If we go around, that just puts us on a new path to come closer to that camp. It's a long walk to come back here, and if we're already out here…well, what do you think?"

"All right, we need to turn south anyway, according to this note. Let's see where it takes us, but I don't think we should take any big chances. You know how he is on protocol."

Another week passes after they diverted to a southwesterly route, arcing around in the direction of Camp Two. The scouts reported the passage of the migration party moving north-northeast, apparently in the direction of the river canyon within the mountains east of the city towards the orcish camp. Another set of scouts were dispatched to find Camp Two for a status update. Sulíma and her team found themselves on a new course that took them out of easy range of the scout relay posts they were following, but as they came nearer to Camp Two, they would rejoin the line of outposts in that direction.

"Suli," reports a scout returning from an extended run. "We found Camp Two. It's maybe a week ahead if we're measuring right. It's not completely empty, though. We still saw a small number of orcs inside."

"Dammit," Petrith mumbles. "But if it's only a few…"

"Petrith, what are you thinking?" Sulíma demands apprehensively. "You're not thinking of going over there and 'helping' them leave, are you?"

"Maybe," he replies modestly. "Suli, look at us. We're this close. We have the element of surprise on our side. We can hit them at night to catch them off-guard. We'll be in and out before anyone knows we're there. And these are the last orcs in the region."

"And how will we explain this to the Captain?"

"We'll just tell him the area is clear, no more need for our scouts to run all this way, and no more orcs to worry about from this side."

"We could wait, too, and the problem will take care of itself."

"And we'll be halfway home and have to trudge all the way back out here to shut down the other reactor. I wonder if we have space for two of them in here," he looks over his shoulder at the vehicle's cargo segment.

"It would be twice as heavy."

"The reactor is the worst of it. But if we repack things to distribute the weight better..."

"And these poor guys out here who need to haul it?"

"I know. But again, one trip instead of two, if we pack it right," he offers. "And even if we can't, we could still shut it down and the next crew only needs to take it apart and load it."

"You have a point. Then we could go home and hire a new team for the next run. I'm sure I'm going to regret this someday, but all right, let's take a look...but carefully."

✦✦✦✦✦✦✦

"Kaliya," Aelwyn instructs. "I will have you practice outside today with your new skill. Recall the lessons you have learned this past week and make a few simple rounds outdoors. Maybe, if you should see Relissa out in the courtyard again, you could stop in for a brief visit."

"This will be fun," she grins. "And then I report back on my results, right?"

"Yes, same as before."

Kaliya was already in her projected form when she left the room to go outside. She made her way through a side exit of the guild onto a walkway, pausing momentarily to take in the sights before engaging her new skill.

Relissa, Marelle, and Haran were once again comparing notes and discussing school affairs, along with some other conversation in the guildhall courtyard.

"I did a little looking ahead," Haran notes. "The studies we're receiving in this course are starting to move ahead of those I had in our old academy in Rolsklinde. They didn't teach us much over there, not that it surprises me…they didn't want us to know that much. But even for the number of years I spent there, the rate of study here is so much more intense, especially when you consider it's delivered in a standardized format as a learning curriculum."

"Aye," Relissa admits. "I remember you always complaining about your old instructors bashing you whenever you asked for better assignments. Here, you get it all just by being in class."

"I think by the time I get into the Fourth Circle; I'll probably be well ahead of whatever they kept even for their more privileged Masters."

"I'm wondering just how far I actually want to go in this," Marelle considers. "It's fun to learn, and I'm sure it can be useful, but I also need to consider where I'm going with it. I'm still hoping Thaelyn will give me a chance to learn to fly those aircraft things."

"Jiggers, Marelle," Relissa moans. "Are you serious with that? I'm still trying to get over the joyride you gave us coming out of that mine the dwarves were digging up."

"But we did it, Relissa. Can you deny it? We did it, and we did it well."

"Aye, I can't say no to that," she grins sheepishly. "We had a wee bit of help from Lieutenant Lapäli, and it was fun by a fair bit, but it still sent the jitters through me."

"If I can learn to do it properly, it'll be a lot different, I'm sure. But that's for later. I have a long way to go before then."

"And you'll need to go take lessons from the Daanen-Aryku for it, too. Maybe by then we'll see some new toys come out of the research teams to go with it."

In the sky overhead, a large raven was circling around looking for a suitable landing site. It spies a likely candidate and swoops down, perching neatly on Relissa's head.

Relissa and the others recoil in surprise at the strange visitor, with the young elf trying to duck away as the errant bird settles into place.

"Ay, what do I look like, a park statue?" she complains. "Little fellow, I hope you're not thinking of pulling up the bedding for your new nest."

"Hey, Relissa," Marelle jibes. "I like your new hat. Did you get it on special?"

"Aye, they were just flying out the door!"

The group ushers up a brisk laugh.

"I hear those birds can be very bold on occasion," Haran observes. "But this one seems downright determined on something."

"I think he just likes her," Marelle teases.

"Personally, I'll go with the park statue idea. She always sits in the same place."

"Maybe he heard she's in the ranger study and came to check out the new kid."

"All right you two, are you finished?" Relissa growls as she reaches up to the bird. "Little guy, come down here where I can see you."

She lifts up her arm and scratches her wrist to entice the bird to jump across. The bird seems to follow her motion and perches calmly in place. She then brings it down for a better look.

"There now," she ushers gently. "You're a cute one. Where did you come from, I wonder?"

The bird gazes at her curiously and makes a squawk as it studies her face. She brings up a finger to caress its breast. The bird seems content to receive the attention, turning its head to-and-fro as it looks around at the group.

"Wow, Relissa," Marelle remarks. "You sure got him wrapped around your finger quick."

"Technically, he's wrapped around her wrist," Haran corrects.

Marelle discreetly twists her arm around to whap Haran in the chest, being careful not to disturb the bird with any sudden motion.

"Look at you," Relissa coos. "You're a pretty one, all gleaming and such."

The bird makes another squawking sound, now softer in tone.

"I'm sorry I don't have anything to give you today, but maybe if you come back tomorrow, I can sneak out a few breadcrumbs for you."

"Actually, I'd prefer a steak, some roasted vegetables, and maybe a pint of dwarven ale," the bird suddenly announces in a squeaky voice.

The group turns an astonished stare at the strange anomaly.

"Did that thing just talk?" Marelle whimpers.

"Gracious, Sis," Haran gasps. "I'm glad it wasn't only me hearing it."

Relissa stares at the bird while trying to find her voice, hoping to cough up a response.

"'Ere now, who's inside there!" she demands.

"I'll give you a hint…it's no bulbous-headed door-knocker!" the bird cackles.

"Jiggers! Kaliya! Is that you? In all the bleedin' hells, how did you do that?"

"I'll tell you, it wasn't easy," she squawks in a bird-like manner. "I started a while ago to learn how to study detail in other bodies. They had me visit an art class to take a few lessons on observational study. You know, how to take notice of fine details, as if you were going to paint or sculpt a replica."

"That's a very interesting way to approach it," Haran nods.

"Yeah, and it helped me learn ways of seeing things such that I could create my own. But rather than sculpt something out of clay, I'm doing it with my projection."

"And that's a very strange way to apply it, but I can surely see how it could be useful."

"Finally, I spent time studying an actual raven in a cage. I studied how it looks, how it sounds, its behavior, and so on. I spent all last week on it. Then, I practiced making my own. This is my first official time out. What do you think?"

"This is getting a little too creepy," Marelle whines.

"But you have to admit, Sis," Haran states. "She had us all fooled. The appearance, the behavior, and even the sounds. Just think if she went out on assignment like this."

"Gods' pity, she's getting dangerous with this thing."

"Let me look at you," Relissa solicits. "Hold out your wings."

Kaliya, in her bird form, extends her wings for Relissa to examine.

The elf runs her fingers across them, feeling the soft plumage. She further runs her fingers along its back.

"Open your mouth, let me look inside."

"Isn't it actually a beak?" Haran cites timidly.

Kaliya opens her beak and angles up for Relissa to peer inside.

"Do you see her in there?" Marelle jests.

"Nah, too dark…" she replies with a humorous glare. "Girl, you got this one down real good," she admits. "Will you be trying any others out?"

"Eventually," Kaliya nods. "But I need to study each one carefully. I don't think I'll try a large number, but at least a selection for different sizes and applications."

"Are you actually able to fly in that form?" Marelle asks.

"She was up there a little while ago," Haran notes.

"It took some practice, but yeah," Kaliya admits. "Although the landings are still a little rough…you should've seen me on my first attempt."

"Oh? What happened?" Marelle inquires.

"Boom is what happened. I came down and went splat, and then tumbled. Fortunately, I don't feel any pain in this form. But I figured it out after a few runs."

"How do you fit all of you inside that little thing?"

"Um, I had to squeeze really hard?" she chuckles. "But in truth, size isn't really an issue in this form. Anything goes."

"Amazing. So, you could change into anything from a small fly to a huge beast."

"And mingle with the rest without anyone knowing the better," Haran adds.

"The perfect spy…"

"Well, I need to report back," Kaliya declares. "Thanks everyone for the fun."

She takes off in a flutter and rises into the air, soaring off across the courtyard, circling once around a corner spire on the wall, and away down the side of the guild compound.

The three companions look at each other and shake their heads, then return to their previous conversation.

✦✦✦✦✦✦

"What's the situation over there?" Petrith asks of a returning scout.

"They look like they're settling in for the night," she responds.

"How much longer, do you think?"

"I saw several of them already going into their huts, and a few more sitting around the campfire. I might say another hour, two at most."

"We should wait, just to be sure. Maybe more towards midnight, that'll put them to sleep. Then we'll move in. How many did you count?"

"I'm guessing fifteen to twenty, not that many, and we surely outnumber them."

"Petrith?" Sulíma whispers. "Are you sure about this? You've never actually fought a battle before, much less killed anything."

"Every soldier starts out that way, Suli, but there has to be that first time, and this is it. We'll take them down, and that'll be the end of this group. Then we'll take a look at that reactor. I think we can squeeze it in if we're careful."

"A lot of our people will have to give up their space for it. We'll all be walking home after this."

"Better than making another trip hauling those transports all the way back here."

"Yeah, you're right. I just want you to be careful."

"Suli, it's nighttime," he affirms. "We'll make a surprise hit after they all go to sleep. I think we'll have this one in the bag, we just need to move silently as we go in."

"What about the campfire? We should put it out first. It'll give us more cover that way."

"Yeah, we'll send in some of the scouts to check on things while the rest of us move into position. They can put out the fire, and then we attack."

"All we have are these spears and a few bows. Will that be enough?"

"I think if you're asleep in a bed and someone comes up and impales you with a long stick, that should be enough. One thing I'd recommend, however, is that we move in and take our positions before we strike. Then we hit them all at once."

Sulíma and her team had approached Camp Two, but not within visible sight. The vehicles had been brought up behind a row of trees some distance away and a troupe of armed cadets moved in on foot. It was after sunset, and they hid in the underbrush waiting for darkness.

A scouting patrol had been sent in to observe and monitor the orcs inside the camp. Some had already gone to bed for the night while a few stayed up, telling stories around the campfire. As the last of them turned in, the scouts reported back.

Petrith was in charge of this operation as the de facto commander of the military aspect of the group, while Sulíma was the technical advisor for retrieving the equipment. Nevertheless, she was concerned about this operation, so she tagged along for moral support. They continued to wait a while longer into the night before moving out.

Petrith motioned to the others to remain silent. This included their hoof steps in the grasses, as well as communication. They had all been briefed on the plan, and now it was only a matter of performing their function.

The scouts, all female, moved on ahead, sneaking up to the edge of the camp, while the larger males lumbered along slowly to keep the rustling of their movements to a minimum. The scouts reached the camp to observe that the orcs had nestled quietly on the mats in their huts. They cautiously crept up within range of the campfire and began scooping mounds of dirt in their hands to toss into it, dousing the flames.

The males took this as a sign to move forward, breaking formation and heading off in the direction of the various huts, coming alongside just beyond the tent flaps with their spears ready in hand.

Sulíma moved in closer for a better view. She was nervous, as this was her first combat scene. She watched as Petrith moved in front of one of the huts and raised his hand, preparing to give the signal. He drops it and the team lurches forward through the flaps to make their kills.

The sound of groans and shrieks filled the air as the orcs felt the stab of the spears through their chests, but then quickly subsided when they met the cold embrace of death, and the team emerged from the huts bearing the stern countenance of war.

Sulíma stood up and rushed forward to meet Petrith, who was walking through the camp examining their handiwork.

"That was quick. Much more so than I would've thought. Why can't we do things like this all the time?"

"Suli, I think if we were to put together a proper military, we probably could. Just between you and me, the Sentinels is nothing more than a civilian law enforcement agency, not a full military. If we're going to survive in this world, we need to beef it up…a lot."

"And the Captain? He's the boss around here, you know."

"I have nothing against the Captain, and I'm sure he knows the score. But we're not in a position to take things lightly. Remember that talk we had a while back? If we're to survive, we can't be sitting on our tails for it. We need to make a stand, and this is it. You once asked if I had in mind to fight a world full of orcs. Well, that world is all inside Camp One right now. That's not much of a world anymore."

"No, it's not, but on the other hand, do we actually NEED to fight that 'world' if they're all jumping through that hole in space. They won't represent much of an opponent soon. And, well, if we're right about the Suuden-Aryku and whatever they're doing on the other side, do we want to be any more responsible for their destruction as what's happening with those conveyors?"

"I don't know if I could give you a proper answer to that, Suli," he sighs. "If they're all in Camp One, we might have a lot of space for ourselves. And if the rest of them jump through, it might not be our decision anymore. We'll inherit this world by default."

"Maybe. Anyway, this part is done, so let's take a quick look at that reactor."

They walk over to the side of the reactor assembly. As before, Sulíma calls for help to unplug the solar arrays and remove the pump from the local stream. She was carrying a bag of tools from the truck, and Petrith pulled out the same chisel he used before to unlatch the panel on the condenser so he could turn it off. He then moved to open the panel for the reactor.

"Here we go again, Petrith," Sulíma chirps. "Let's hope this one goes down as nicely as the other one."

Petrith nods and looks inside the compartment to find the shutdown button. He reaches in to press it, but halts just before making contact. Sulíma notices his reaction.

"What's wrong?" she asks, feeling a slight tremor.

"Nothing, I'm thinking of something."

"Thinking of what? What can you possibly have going on now? You've already killed the orcs, and we're clear to take this home with us. We'll just tell the Captain we saw an opportunity and took it. No big deal. No one got hurt, we have TWO reactors to play with, and life is good."

"That's right, Suli, life is good, and I want them to know about it."

"Them? Them who?" she mutters as she watches him get up and walk away. "Where are you going, Petrith?"

He walks back around to one of the huts and drags a body outside. He then pulls out a crude blade they once fashioned back home in their makeshift forge. It was basically a cut piece of sheet metal hammered around the edges to give it shape. It wasn't a true knife, but it was good enough to cut with. He proceeded to draw a line across the orc's neck.

"Petrith!" she shouts. "What in the cu'Nar's name are you doing? Ew, yuk!"

He continues hacking away at the orc's body, cutting away its head. It was a gruesome process, mostly due to the dullness of the blade's edge. Sulíma could no longer watch, and so she turned away from it.

When he finally finished with his macabre deed, he turned and walked back in the direction of the equipment, sidelong to the rift aperture.

"Suli, get ready to hit that button," he directs.

"Just what are you doing, Petrith?!" she demands.

"Sending a message... They're leaving this world and we don't want them coming back."

"Do you actually think they'll come back? What about all that talk we just had? You know, things like the Suuden-Aryku spending them on something, maybe relocating them somewhere..."

"Yes, Suli, but I'm also thinking of something new. Expendable or not, relocating or not, I want to give the impression that the locals are turning against them. If the Suuden-Aryku still hold an interest in orcs, maybe that interest will fade if they think they've lost control. And the rest will get the message that no more will be joining them in this relocation, or whatever it is they're doing."

"Losing control?"

"Call it an insurance policy. If the Suuden-Aryku have been coming here and doing anything at all with these orcs, they shouldn't have any further interest after this."

"But wait a minute. What if they behave with them like they do to us, and try blasting them out of existence?"

"Blasting, as opposed to sending them to their potential death on the other side?"

"Um, all right, I suppose you have a point there. But what about the other idea, a relocation effort?"

"Relocating people who WANT to relocate, maybe. But if we suggest an uprising of those who choose otherwise, what can you do about that if you no longer control them?"

"Blast them?"

"I suppose it's possible, but blasting THEM, not us, assuming it's worth the trouble to begin with. This world was full of them. One little camp, by comparison, probably isn't worth taking aim."

"Should I remind you about the Suuden-Aryku and us?"

"You can if you like, but should I also remind you of that talk relating to Sargeras and us running away. Maybe he really didn't like the idea, but the orcs may not be as critical. Still, it's them, not us."

"All right, I'm having a hard time fighting your logic."

"Petrith," calls one of the scouts. "Not that I want to add any fuel to the fire, but what is your ultimate objective here? By the sound of it, do you hope to send a message that no more are going to just give themselves up for it? What about Camp One? They're still doing it."

"Yes, we still have that..." he nods. "But this could possibly point to a beginning, in case one day we find an opportunity for that one also."

"All right, but this simply leads me to the next question. Are WE to kill them instead of the Suuden-Aryku, clearing the last of them from this world? Or is this an effort to save them FROM the Suuden-Aryku. And then, what about us and them, if we should ever come face-to-face again? Will they be thankful for it, or attack again?"

"Yeah, Petrith," Sulíma adds. "We might have these ideas, but how do you convince THEM about it?"

"This is something I can't answer right now," he concedes. "Maybe there isn't an easy answer, for what we have to work with. But as for what's on the other side, if they're expecting full loyalty, we need to break that image. Maybe we can work on the rest at another time."

"Petrith, the hero," Sulíma smiles gently. "Trying to save lives of people we wouldn't otherwise want to save, for all they did to us. But I think I need to agree. I don't want to be responsible for their complete destruction, and neither do I want to see someone else do it. I may not like them, but I don't not-like them to the point of wanting them all dead just for being there."

"Good, Suli. This may be the way of our people, with or without making a stand for ourselves. Who knows if we can see this through to a proper result, but we can't just, well, sit on our tails and watch someone else do it."

"All right, so what are you going to do, throw that through the conveyor?"

"Yeah, and they'll see it on the other side. If there are orcs over there, they should probably get the message right away."

"And if it's someone else?"

"If we say Suuden-Aryku, I think it should be as we discussed. At the very least, you might have a rogue band parading around… somewhere…attacking loyalist orcs. How do you track something like that if you don't know where it came from? Otherwise, if it's someone completely different, well, they might still take it as a message of one orc to another. After all, they shouldn't know of us any more than the orcs do."

"Cu'Nar's pity, Petrith… Where did you learn to debate like that?" she chuckles. "All right, toss it in and I'll hit the button. But we'd better hurry up and clear out after this."

Petrith swings the head around towards the rift generator. He tosses it in, and it vanishes through the vortex.

Sulíma hits the button as soon as she sees the object disappear. The same flashing light and beeping sounds engage as the reactor shuts down, followed by the whirring and popping sounds, until all goes quiet.

"Petrith, I hope you're going to wash your hands now. You're not coming anywhere near me like that."

Petrith strolls up and playfully reaches out at her, forming his hands into malignant claws. She flinches and slaps him on the arm, grinning as he passes by to wash in the stream.

"I think we'll pack it up in the morning," he states. "It's nighttime and the trucks are at distance and hidden. We can check the place in the morning to see if anyone is stomping around, but personally, I doubt anyone will."

"I hope you're right."

"For now, let's get some rest."

"My Lord! You're not going to believe this!" the General shouts as Thaelyn rushes into the tactical office.

Thaelyn had been called away from his morning meal by a messenger sent by the General, who was also pulled from breakfast as the result of an urgent note received from one of the garrisons.

"General, although I am not against the urgent summons, the timing of it has me somewhat disturbed. What happened?"

"My Lord, my deepest apologies for disrupting your meal, but we just got a note from the camp at Portal Two. The portal has closed, but not without a rather unpleasant delivery."

"A delivery? What sort of delivery?"

"A severed orcish head, my Lord! It came through just before the portal closed."

"A severed head?" he winces. "This is indeed most curious as well as disturbing. This sort of thing would represent some form of message."

"I am at a loss at this time, perhaps due to the shock of it."

"Wait. Let us think calmly a moment. Obviously, heads do not simply fall through portals by themselves."

"Oh, but of course, my Lord," he attempts a chuckle. "But for one to come flying out would suggest some sort of activity on the other side...a rather gruesome one."

"Yes, but I think we cannot suggest it to be a message for us, especially as it is orcish and we are at war with them anyway. They cannot know we are on this side...unless the Suuden-Aryku passed word of it. Even so, I cannot see the reason for this as a message to us, so this might represent an act of defiance. Can it be as the result of a clash between two orcs?"

"Maybe. On occasion, orcs do experience disputes, and they're also known for contests of dominance, with the loser sometimes losing his life. But to send his head through the portal? What purpose would that serve?"

"Probably none for the local group..."

Thaelyn paces a few times in deep thought.

"What if it was some manner of dispute against a ruling clan member, a kind of uprising and this is a message to their brethren on the other side that no more will be joining? Or perhaps to the Suuden-Aryku if they believe them to be watching."

"A most curious proposal," the General admits. "This is to say this band of orcs are turning rebel, and they might think their own people are receiving it."

"Yes, and furthermore, consider this. Sargeras has likely been absent from them for a long enough time for some of them to lose faith. If this could be interpreted as a rebellion of some sort, I wonder if it might spread to other areas."

"But my Lord, it could not be much of one. The last we saw was only a small pittance in that camp. If they try to spread this around, they may be facing an uphill climb to be heard."

⁓✦⁓

"Hey, Petrith, look what I found!" Sulíma shouts as she comes out of one of the huts.

Sulíma was holding an orcish war drum left behind by the orcs they killed the night before. It was in good condition and made a solid drumbeat.

"Skip that piece of junk I've been working on, I'll take this," she continues.

"Suli, you and your toys... Sometimes I wonder if you ever actually grew up."

"Hey, I'm entitled, especially after what you did last night. I need a little relief."

"So, do you plan on starting up a new music group?"

"Ooh, yeah! We can call it Suli and the Orc-heads."

They let out a loud roar of laughter at the thought.

"Suli," Petrith wonders. "Where do you come up with these things? All right, fine, put it in the truck and let's finish up here."

They were in the process of disassembling the second conveyor and loading it onto the transports. The vehicles had been brought around earlier in the morning and the crane assembled to help lift the heavy equipment into the cargo compartments. Some of the pieces from the first unit were removed in order to reposition the items to better balance the load. It became apparent that there would be just enough room for both conveyors if they used all available space from all the vehicles. This would leave the crew with no seating space, but it was a sacrifice they felt was worthy if only to avoid a second trip into the region.

"What are we going to do with these bodies?" Sulíma wonders. "Are we just going to leave them here?"

Petrith relaxes from helping move one of the pieces to consider the prospect. He makes a cursory inspection of the camp to peek inside the huts at the bodies still lying on their mats, and the decapitated body he covered with a piece of animal skin he found.

"I mean, honestly," she continues. "We shouldn't just leave them out here. We're not animals, not like they are."

"No, we're not," he agrees. "But they didn't care as much to bury our dead after the attack if you remember. Many of those bodies were left to rot in the streets. We were too young to do anything about it, so it was up to the surviving adults to try to clean it up and give our people a proper burial."

"I know, but look at it this way. If we take these bodies away and bury them, not only can we say we did what we believe is right, but we can also hide the evidence of what we did in case anyone comes around looking."

"Good point, so if any other orcs, or even the Suuden-Aryku come back here to check on things, it won't be quite as obvious. And this will confuse them even more. But I don't think we should bury them anywhere nearby. Let's move them up along those hills to the north, near the trees. And we can use the local underbrush to conceal the mounds."

"Sounds good to me, then we can go home and start setting up the reactors."

Petrith calls over some extra help to drag away the bodies and assign a burial detail. They finish loading the vehicles with the new equipment and reassemble themselves to set off again.

⋆ ◆◆◆◆ ⋆

Thaelyn had gathered his officers for a morning meeting in the tactical office in Firstfall. On this occasion, he also called in Commander Nazég to participate. The topic of the meeting was the turn of events at Portal Two.

"The possibility of an orcish uprising on Ruuki uy'Daan is an interesting one, Your Lordship," Kailen notes. "But if it comes from such a small outpost, as you suggest from your observations, I find it unlikely to take on much momentum if it should reach the larger camp coming out of Portal One."

"While this may be the case," Thaelyn suggests. "I would like to point out another detail we were able to determine after a more careful review with our troops at the garrison. It was apparently at night. Our people say it was dark and they saw the flickering of the local campfire through the window. This has become the traditional representation from their observations during the course of time in that outpost."

"So, this was a nighttime assault?"

"If this were a typical uprising, it could not have been an outright protest, which would more likely occur during the daytime. This is further complicated by the fact that one of our guardsmen reported catching a glimpse of a sudden change in the lighting, as if the campfire, which was apparently in full burn, quickly went out. This now suggests a surprise attack."

"But then, by whom? Not the orcs within the camp, they would all be asleep by then. This sounds like an outside job."

"This is my thought, as well. One possibility may be a dissident group of orcs parading around taking on other camps. And this now makes me wonder about Portal Three, but there are a few complications imposing themselves on my mind here."

"You said Portal Three closed before this something like a month ago, wasn't it? And it was showing up as an abandoned camp on the other side."

"Yes, and this is one of those complications. Why attack an abandoned camp? Are they simply going about destroying these conveyors as a sign of protest? And now we need to ask ourselves about the timing of it. This is where I need your support."

"All right, what do you need?"

"Do you have any old maps of Ruuki uy'Daan, or can you recall enough detail to draw one? I would like to see what sort of landforms we have over there, and if we can make a few guesses as to the placement of these camps. The timing between Portals Two and Three was approximately one month. If we calculate the average walking speed and distance, as well as take into account our assumptions that each of these portals was clearing out an independent region, perhaps we can speculate on their placement, and whether this theory could be plausible."

"I can certainly see what we have available, and I'm sure some of us can draw something up from memory also. But what about these other complications you were mentioning?"

"A surprise attack preceded by dousing a campfire indicates a stealth operation. Orcs, in my experience, are not as likely to use a tactic like this. Rather, they are just as likely to start more fires, burning the whole camp to the ground."

✦

Kaliya had been in careful study for the last couple of weeks after her exhibition as a bird. Aelwyn conferred with Thaelyn on the matter, and they decided to have her study a selection of items, either in replica form or as taxidermy examples…whichever might be the most convenient for her to carry.

The specimens she had been given so far included a squirrel, a tiger, a hawk, a small flying insect, and a tree. She would often study these items in her free time after her practice sessions, and during her weekend hours. It was one such weekend, and she was sitting on the bench in the courtyard when Relissa and the others arrived.

"Are you still gawking at these things, girl?" Relissa asks as she sits down.

"I need to understand every little detail, Relissa, especially if I'm going to make a convincing example."

"Aye, but what are you going to use them for, that's the big one on my side of it."

"Consider this as part of my training. One of these days, I'll be on assignment, and one or more of these could come in handy as cover."

"So you go in, make like a tree for a bit to listen in on the local chatter, then buzz off as a bug and get yourself in trouble with something nasty, so you turn into a hawk, or maybe a tiger to chase it off, then run up the nearest tree as a squirrel and collect your nuts for the winter. Is that about the size of it?"

The group engages in a friendly round of laughter at the strange assignment routine.

"Well, I kind of doubt it'll work out quite like that, but to have the different options, and practice to get it just right, could offer me a few choices depending on the situation."

"I just hope you remember who your friends are," Marelle submits. "I'd hate to be on the other end of that tiger encounter."

"Does that bug bite?" Haran asks. "I just hate whenever I get bitten. It itches for days afterwards."

"Aye," Relissa infers. "And just think if she's the one doing it, you can be sure she'll get you in a really sensitive spot."

"Relissa!" Kaliya winces. "That's actually… Well, maybe it's not such a bad idea when you think of it," she grins.

"Ay, are you taking that for real on me?"

"The problem here is being swatted. I'm not sure what that'll do to me."

"It'll make you much flatter than how you started," Marelle smirks.

"Can you actually be killed in this form?" Haran asks.

"I doubt it since I'm not corporeal. In a traditional spirit projection, like what some people describe as an astral projection, you are always connected to your body by what they call a silver cord. This is the link you follow to go home to your physical body. If this should break, your spirit can become lost, and your body dies. But this is only while you are in the astral realm and affected by another entity there. They might be able to attack the cord."

"And what about the type of projection you're doing here?"

"Having something happen to me in this type of projection, like to be swatted as a bug, should not be the same as having the cord broken. The cord should still be there. At worst, it's only a disruption of my projected form due to an external influence, and it's questionable if an external influence can actually affect my projection in this way."

"So, if someone sticks you with a blade," Relissa suggests. "It wouldn't cut a hole in you where you start to bleed?"

"I can't see how, really. But something like this would make for good study, just to learn what might happen. I suppose I could also make my projection transparent to any interaction. If I can make it tangible, I should also be able to make it intangible."

"Now that's an interesting thought," Marelle offers.

✦ ✦ ✦◆✦ ✦ ✦

"Your Lordship," Kailen notes. "If we consider the placement of our city, as well as the arrangement of the orcish camps, at least how we recall them while we were on Ruuki uy'Daan, they should occupy most of this area to the east, and virtually everything to the south, at least to this line here..."

Once again, Thaelyn and his officers, along with Commander Nazég, were convening in the tactical office, this time reviewing a set of maps pulled from one of the data systems in the Naarg uy'Sodrad, and further marked with the recalled memories of the Commander and a few of his officers of significant features and orcish settlements. The maps showed a topographical display of the continental geography, including mountains, forests, jungles, rivers, and lakes.

"Your city was here in the northwestern quadrant," Thaelyn observes. "And we are assuming, at least from your last known studies, there were no other orcish settlements further to the west from there. Of course, this could have changed in your absence."

"Yes, it could. There were once a few in that area, but our activities in the region caused them to move to other areas further south."

"Then you have this row of mountains just below you. The region to your east is jungle, and this makes a good starting point for us to consider Portal One, as we can see a jungle environment on the other side through the window. The others were apparently grasslands and prairies, and you say this region midway down included those."

"Correct, but below this line, you go into a subarctic zone, much the same as you found here where there were no orcish settlements. We found the same conditions on Ruuki uy'Daan in that area."

"This would make sense for their environmental preferences," the General considers.

"Indeed," Thaelyn continues. "Now, if we consider that we had three portals opening into this world from Ruuki uy'Daan, we may be looking at a triangular configuration. With your city in the upper quadrant here, this leaves the northeast and the south on both sides."

The Commander studies the map in the lower regions.

"You said Portal Two showed some rocky hills and Portal Three was a flat prairie by a river? Hmm, in the south below us, here on the west, you have plenty of hills, so anything is possible down there. But if we're considering a centralized location in the southeast, we have a large prairie there. There are a few rivers that cross the region, so any of those could be it."

"We may find ourselves travelling along some of those rivers, perhaps to their full length to find our mark. But at least we have a general idea of placement. If we make some rough estimates, drawing a line from a suspected source for Portal Three to a suspected destination for Portal Two, how far would you say that is?"

"We could be talking anything from eight hundred to over a thousand miles."

"It would seem the upper portion of this continent is rather narrow. Let us restrict our numbers from nine hundred to an even one thousand. In the space of one month…"

Thaelyn makes some calculations on a scrap of paper to estimate walking speeds and timing for the distance.

"For an orc," he continues, "if simply walking, this looks to be slightly outside our timing. However, this is native turf for them, which grants them familiarity for quicker movement. And if they have a sustained purpose, it is well within the potential of our previous hypothesis."

"So, you think it might be an uprising?" Kailen asks. "But where did they come from, in this case? If we say Portal Three is in the east, and it went down first, then to say Portal Two is in the west, and it went down a month after, then these orcs had to come from somewhere either on the eastern side, or from the jungles to the north."

"And if we further assume Portal Three has already emptied the eastern side, this leaves only the area around Portal One in the jungle, which is still active."

"Suggesting there is no dissention in that region."

"And if we reverse it, with Portal Three in the west and Portal Two in the east, we still have a discrepancy, as the northwest presumably has no orcs in which to launch the attack, unless of course they reestablished themselves during this time."

"That's the only answer I can come up with, given these conditions. Someone in the northwest launched the attack."

"We need eyes in the region to confirm some of this," Thaelyn admits. "Kaliya is very close to being permitted her first venture to Ruuki uy'Daan. I will see about giving her a few assignments to investigate some of these locations and report back what she finds. I think our first objective should be to identify the portal in this jungle. This will give us an idea of what to look for in the further regions."

"May I offer a suggestion? There was an orcish camp just east of the city. This is where they established themselves shortly after our arrival as part of our early interactions. It's also where they launched their main attack on us. Start there and continue east, if necessary. Kaliya should know the way. She never actually went out there, but she knew about it."

✦ ✦✦✦ ✦

"All right, let's try this again from the top," Sulíma calls out to the assembly.

"Suli, are you really going to do this?" Petrith groans. "And how many times do we have to rehearse it?"

"Until we get it right, I want to put on a good show when we get home. It's only a few more days."

"I still can't believe I actually let you talk me into this."

"Didn't you ever take a theater class?"

"No, that wasn't one of my topics."

"Still, just think, maybe there's a spot for you on the next vid-com concert!"

"First, we need a vid-com that works. Then we need the production facilities and broadcasting relay to deliver it. I hope, by that time, no one will remember this," he chuckles.

Sulíma and Petrith sat on the hood of the lead transport. They had been practicing a marching work song while she beats on her new orc drum. The rhythmic tune paces along with their stride as the laborers hauled the heavy vehicles. They had been travelling for almost three weeks while she worked on inventing the lyrics and an appropriate musical beat. Ahead of them was the line of mountains where they would circle around a set of low hills and through a valley on the western side. After that, it was a straight run home.

The addition of music offered a pleasant distraction to the workforce hauling the vehicles. Rather than the monotony of trudging forward in silence, now they had a musical beat to inspire them along. Their victory over the orcs in Camp Two, however small it might seem, encouraged them into a new sense of recovery, and now they looked forward to returning home with their bounty.

Several more days pass, and they perfect their routine. Sulíma, in her classic mischievous style, had envisioned a homecoming worthy of remembering. They worked their way across the fields on the last leg of their journey, now coming within sight of their goal. She calls out to the people to begin their song, shouting out in unison while she stood on the hood beating her drum.

The chorus begins singing. The laborers hauling the vehicles raise their voices as they trudge along to the beat of the drum. The scouts and relief workers following behind added their chants and wails as a background rhythm. The song echoes across the field at the work yard in front of the mine hideout.

Several people had been busy in the work yard sorting through the salvage they had been collecting from the city. When they heard the strange disturbance resounding from outside, they poked their heads out to see a mass of bodies surrounding the four transport vehicles, all moving in their direction and singing a bold melodic song.

"It's Suli!" shouts one of the workers.

"In all the nether-space," calls another one. "What are they doing out there?"

"I don't know, but they're coming home! Someone, go find the Captain!"

"I got it!" a young female shouts as she hurries off. "But for the cu'Nar's sake, that's not something you see every day!"

"And Tana," he calls after her. "Call everyone out here. Let's give them a nice Welcome Home party."

The girl nods and makes a quick trot inside the hideout to deliver the news.

"Captain," she shouts as she enters the room. "Suli is coming in…and they're singing!"

"Singing? What do you mean?"

"It's probably that little tail-yanker," she jibes. "She's got the whole group marching along and singing something. You need to come out and see this."

"I swear. That troublemaker is always getting crazy ideas inside her head."

"Well, on this occasion, she might have a good one to spice things up."

The Captain gets up from his table and follows the girl outside. Tana waved at the assembly of other people sitting around the room to join in, and the announcement soon spread throughout the hideout until the major portion of the people started moving outside to observe the ceremony.

They step outside the mine and walk down the ramp into the work yard. The Captain hears the noise and looks out onto the field to see the parade of laborers led by the team of haulers pulling the first vehicle, with Sulíma standing proudly on the hood of the truck banging a drum.

"I don't believe this," he shakes his head. "Where did she find that?"

The laborers followed the beat with the plodding of their hooves, an image no doubt recalled from their ancient history when servants were employed as manual labor to haul wagons for their feudal lord. Occasional shouts and hollers sounded out from the scouts strutting alongside the teams, giving orders like taskmasters on a slave train. The rising and falling of the song delivered a sense of inspirational harmony, while the overall scene recalled the nostalgia of a forgotten moment in their ancestral lore.

"Suli… Dear little Suli," the Captain mutters softly. "If only your parents could see this. I wish I had a camera to take a photo of it."

The people gathering in the work yard sounded out an uproar of applause and cheers as the teams made their way across the bridge and into the yard to park the vehicles. As the last of them arrived, the song wrapped up into a final verse, bringing the ballad to an end as the team came to a rest.

"Would you mind explaining what all that was about, Miss Sulíma Tad'vaal?" the Captain calls out to the girl as she steps down from her perch.

"Just a little homecoming, Captain, we're all so happy to be back."

"Uh huh, right," he glares at her. "Well, I'm happy to have you back, and more so to see you in one piece. That was a long trek you made, and I'm sure it was a hard one. Welcome home, everyone. But now, what did you bring us?"

"We have two full conveyor assemblies in the back, ready to put to good use."

"Just a moment, did you say two? Where did the other one come from?"

"Well, we swung by Camp Two after receiving your orders to divert south, since we were coming so close to it anyway. It was just sitting out there, all alone," she declares with a gloomy frown.

"Oh, I'm so sorry to hear about that. So, I guess you wanted to give it a new home? But, what about the orcs in that camp? Last I heard, we still saw a few inside there. At least at the time you were passing by."

"Well, it's true we did pass by that migration party, but we kept at distance. As for the camp, well..." she rolls her eyes away to meet with Petrith. "There really wasn't anything...serious...to worry about."

"Uh huh..." he eyes her suspiciously. "Is that before or after you arrived?"

"Um..." she coughs subtly and turns away.

"I see. So, did anyone get hurt from it?"

"Captain," Petrith steps up. "As the military leader of that operation, I felt it necessary to make a field decision. We were too far away for a convenient relay of our ideas, and it presented an opportunity to close our interests in the region."

"Is that so. All right, so what do you have to report on it?"

"There were only a small number of them compared to what we had, and we hit them at night. We rushed in and took them down by surprise. It was over before we could even break a sweat. Then we packed up the reactor and came home."

"Really. How many are we talking about?"

"We tallied up a total of eighteen. And we hit them while they slept."

"All right, I suppose this is war, in a manner of speaking, and anything goes. Although I'll admit, I'm not one who would take pleasure in hitting someone while they're asleep. But then again, considering what they did to our people…"

"I would agree to this, but we had to make a series of decisions out there. First, to come home, only to have to go back out again for the next camp and the conveyor, which seemed like an extra effort. Second, if they were clearing out the camp anyway, and if we're right about a death march, it probably doesn't matter how they die, they're still going to die."

"This does present a rather resolute, if also morbid, conclusion. But what if it's a relocation effort instead? Can you justify yourself for that case?"

"Well, sort of…" he coughs. "Um, we left a piece of what we'll call evidence behind."

"Oh! Evidence, he says," Sulíma blurts ironically. "That's a new one."

"Right…" the Captain raises his brow. "And what was this… evidence?"

"Um, well," Petrith begins. "If we can avoid the gory details, I left a message for any other orcs who might be interested that there's a mysterious uprising of protest to continue following Sargeras."

The Captain glared at him, with his eyes opening wide, and further to survey Sulíma and the other team members.

"I simply need to ask this now," he shakes his head. "How does this protest appear and why?"

"Captain," Sulíma interjects. "Before we continue, Petrith and I had this debate, along with one of the scouts. His logic seemed very sound to me. I would also like to say, he showed a very noble attitude, if also a bit strange for the circumstances. Where it takes us, I don't know, but it leaves a possibility or two open if we can work it right."

"All right, I'll take this into consideration. But now, as to the explanation?"

"I considered several things here," Petrith replies. "First, we want the orcs on the other side to know that no more will be following, and my…evidence…was a message of a feud on this side to stop their migration, at least as far as Camp Two is concerned. But this could offer a later spillover effect if the…rebellion…should one day grow to include Camp One."

"I see, but how do we interpret this from the other side?"

"If it's orcs receiving it, they should know not to expect any more reinforcements. If it's the Suuden-Aryku calling a death march, or even a relocation, and THEY see it, the message would be they lost control on this side. If they should do to them as they've done to us so many times, I guess there's not much we can do about it. But it's orcs they'll be shooting at, not us."

"All right, so far, so good, I guess."

"If it's anyone else on the other side, like again that death march, they wouldn't know who WE are, and will probably again interpret it as orcs leaving a message to other orcs."

"I suppose they would, at that. But as for Camp One?"

"There may not be anything we can do in the immediate term, and if they all jump across before then, we might inherit a world for ourselves. But Suli and I, and in fact I think all of us feel we don't want to be responsible for the destruction of a race, even if indirectly. If the Suuden-Aryku told them to jump into a trap, I would hope one day we might find a way to stop it somehow. What reaction the orcs might have to it is another thing, but if to find a way to close that other conveyor, we could save lives."

The Captain gazed tenderly at Petrith. He nodded silently and patted him on the shoulder.

"I'm sure your parents would be proud of you, young man. By the way, what did you do with the rest of the bodies?"

"We buried them, Sir. We moved them out of the camp and away into a wooded area to give us cover; just in case anyone should pass by."

"Interesting, and very good. This gives us a little bit of protection. Now, as to the reactors… We've been gathering up as many pieces of hardware as we can find in the city. We're going to be very busy for the foreseeable future putting things back together. I've had talks with some of the former teachers who were involved in the science and technology shops. Since you kids didn't finish your classes properly, it's time for a little refresher course, hands-on style. We don't have any technicians or engineers with us to do the delicate work, so we'll need to start over."

"This sounds like it's going to be hard," Sulíma asserts. "But that's fine by me, so long as I can finally fix something that stays that way."

"We're going to need you to go pick up some of the larger pieces still in the city. You'll need the trucks for it. As always, keep watch for anything dangerous. We still don't want the orcs to find us. Not until we're ready."

Chapter 2

REMOTELY INTERESTED

"Kaliya," Kailen begins. "You remember that orcish camp east of the city, right?"

"Yeah, it was a long time ago, but I remember it was just outside the city."

"Good. Your first mission for us is simple reconnaissance."

"Keeping in mind," Thaelyn adds. "You should stay out of sight and use an alternate form as cover. A bird, for instance."

"Of course, I understand," she nods.

Thaelyn had convened a meeting in the tactical office with Commander Nazég, Med-tech Tad'vaal, and Aelwyn, for a briefing with Kaliya on her first official mission to Ruuki uy'Daan. She had progressed far enough with her studies to take on a simple assignment, and the need for information was pressing.

The meeting had been called to give her the details for her primary objectives, which included observing the orcs and locating the conveyors. The medical technician also had a few interests on her mind.

"We will have you investigate this one first," Thaelyn continues. "If you do not find your target there, then search for others in the local region. But if you do discover it, you should make a close inspection and report back on the details."

"Your Lordship," Ankhia submits. "I'd also like to ask for something."

"Yes, Med-tech, you have been waiting patiently for us during this briefing. What do you wish?"

"I have a list of things, actually. There is so much I'd like to accomplish since we have this opportunity, but I realize we can't possibly do it all at once. To begin with, if you remember those first days, when you helped us fight the Suuden-Aryku, and I had a chance to study their bodies, I started to form my opinions that they were using these biotech seeds to augment themselves."

"Yes, I recall that."

"From what Kaliya told me of her first encounter with her mother, I'm wondering about what really happened over there during the attack. We've always thought the orcs used some of this crazy magic of theirs to harm our people. But with the Suuden-Aryku apparently donating their technology into the equation, I'm now thinking they used something else, and I'd like Kaliya to help me confirm this."

"Something else, meaning more of these biotech seeds?"

"Yes, perhaps a weaponized version of it, as disgusting as it sounds. But the problem I'm having now is how it might have been applied. They attacked us at range, so I need to assume it was something launched at us, like a projectile. I don't know if we'll ever discover what it was, especially after so long a time, but maybe if Kaliya could make a close examination of her mother, perhaps take a few photos, and bring them back to me, it could give me some ideas."

"Do you have a camera device for her to use?"

"Yes, I do, right here..." she pulls out a camera from her pocket and slides it across the table. "A few photos, front and back, maybe a close-up of the impact center, would be wonderful."

"And Kaliya," Aelwyn advises. "This will be your first venture to Ruuki uy'Daan. I know the others will place many demands on you, but keep in mind to practice your skills along the way. Each new environment you enter may behave differently, so you must always test yourself to understand the demands you will face."

"I will," she affirms as she picks up the camera. "I'll admit, I'm a bit nervous, also anxious to try this out officially, maybe also a little excited to be serving this new role. Is there anything else?"

"We will limit ourselves to this for now," Thaelyn offers. "And then decide on the rest after we have this new information. Since the Med-tech's request will have you carrying an item, I might suggest you attend to that first, then return to drop it off in order to free your hands for the next part."

"Good point. All right, wish me luck. Here I go."

Kaliya was already in her projected form during the meeting. Once the initial briefing ended, she closed her eyes to focus herself on the old but familiar sights of her hometown on Ruuki uy'Daan. Since her first stop would be to visit her mother, she concentrated on the street curbside just in front of her house, and in her traditional manner, she vanished in a puff.

It was early morning on Ruuki uy'Daan. The timing of this occasion was not accidental. Observations through the window of Portal One suggested this might be a good time of day when there would be enough light to see, but the orcs might not be fully active.

She initially arrived on the street just in front of her house. The scene was eerily quiet, as a city long dead. The house looked old and dilapidated, stained from centuries of neglect, and covered with vines and leafy foliage.

Kaliya examined herself. She appeared fully formed and distinct as her natural adult image, but then a thought came to her. The last time she visited her mother, she took the form of a young child. The image she used on that occasion was likely the result of old memories bringing up past horrors which manifested themselves during the ritual she took as the result of her failed Spirit test. She considered the prospect briefly and decided to make a change to keep herself consistent. Her mother has never seen her adult form, and therefore may respond better to the child image.

She recalls her youth and the image she once took, if only by accident during that first visit. She manipulates her form to replicate herself as a young girl. She once again checked her image to ensure it was solid and well-defined. Lastly, she examined the camera in her grip, peering through the viewfinder at the small status icons to ensure it was functional. When she was ready, she moved forward up the stairs to the front porch and peeked through the gap in the double doors.

Just as before, the doors were leaning against the framework, having been apparently kicked in at some moment and no longer attached to the hinges. There was only enough space for her to stick her head through on this occasion, but this would not stop her. Using her new skills, as Aelwyn always suggested, she folded herself to the space just inside the doors. There was no need for her to actually squeeze through or move anything. Once inside, she walked through the foyer and into the main room, which once served as the family's gathering place during their home life here.

"Mother?" she shouts optimistically. "It's me, Kali. I'm back."

She waits for a response, which seems to stall. Then a thud echoes softly in the rear part of the house, followed by the clopping of heavy hoof steps through the hall. The sounds grow until the hulking form of Kaliya's mother appears at the edge of the hallway.

"Mother! It's me!" Kaliya smiles brightly as she turns to see the large form.

"Kali? Kali come back?"

"Yes, I'm back, and I'll be coming back more, too. I've learned how to do this."

"Kali dream walk?"

"Yes, and I'm getting good at it. I have a teacher and she's helping me learn."

"Kali learn? Good Kali! Kali learn dream walk. Me happy!" her mother bounces.

Kaliya rushes over to give her mother a firm hug.

"Mother, I have a lot of work to do. The people I work for have me going out to find the orcs so we can watch them."

"Kali go look at orcs? Kali say people fight orcs. People fight orcs more?"

"No more on our world. Now we're coming here, but I'm here to find them and learn what they're doing."

"Kali people come here? Wait, me not understand. Kali say ship hurt, yes?"

"Yes, but we're not using the ship. We're using me. I'm learning things that can help our people. We're not ready yet, maybe not for a while, but I want you to know we didn't forget, and we're going to try to help you and the other people here."

"Kali people… No, Kali people no help me. Me hurt, orcs hurt people here, Kali people no help."

"Mother, we have ideas on what they did. We need to learn more. Do you see this in my hand?" she shows her the camera. "I need to take some photos of you for Med-tech Tad'vaal. She's doing research to learn what happened here."

"Take what? Who?"

"Med-tech… Ankhia, do you remember Ankhia Tad'vaal? Kailen's wife…and Sulíma's older sister."

"Ank… Ankhia, yes, long time, me remember. Ankhia good girl, help sick people."

"She's a med-tech now. She asked me to take photos, you know, to show what you look like. Like those on the table over there."

Kaliya points at the display table in the corner where she once stood to examine some old family photos on her previous visit.

"Oh. Kali make picture. Me understand. Kali, no, me ugly, no make picture."

"Mother, no argument, the medical technician needs this to see how you look so she can study what the orcs did to you."

"Kali people try learn what orcs do? How orcs make hurt-people?"

"Yes. We think it was not magic. Instead, the Suuden-Aryku gave them something to do this. Now we need to find a way to undo it. So, will you help me, or do I have to get rough," she smirks.

Her mother attempts a cautious smile through her distress at being photographed in her gruesome condition.

"Kali… Yes, make picture," she agrees hesitantly. "Kali not give to father. No let father see. No let Kailen see."

"Kailen needs to see you, he's the High Commander now, but I'll tell him to keep it away from Father until we can learn more, all right?"

She reluctantly grunts in agreement. Kaliya steps back for a better view, but the room seems dark in the early morning sunlight. She looks around at the windows, most of which were very dirty.

"We need more light. Can we go outside?"

"Yes, go outside, make picture, come back."

They walk back towards the front door. Her mother begins moving the pieces out of the way to allow passage, and they continue outside onto the porch. Kaliya takes another look to size up the image.

"This is good, hold still," she instructs as she snaps the first image. "Now, turn around, let me see the back."

"Kali, back hurt, back ugly. Little Kali not good to look."

"I'm not actually little, Mother, I'm a grown woman. I'm only in this shape because I thought it would be better for you."

"What Kali say? Kali not little? Kali look little."

"Mother, I can change my shape. I can be a woman, a girl, an animal, a tree, anything I want. I just need to think about it, and I change into it."

"Kali dream walk other things?" she perks up.

"Lots of things, but it takes time to learn."

"Kali, me look. What Kali do?"

Kaliya sets the camera down on the porch decking and moves out into the yard just in front of the house. She takes up a comfortable position and begins recalling some of the shapes she's been practicing so far. She first morphs herself into a hawk, then into a squirrel. Her next choice is the tiger image, and then a tree. Her mother watches in astonishment at the many shapes.

"How Kali do this? Kali learn?"

Kaliya changes back to the small girl image again so she can interact.

"Yes, the people I work for understand what this is, and they're teaching me to do it."

"Oh Kali, me want learn. Me head not good, me sad."

"Well, Mother, that's why I'm here, to take these photos so we can see if we can help you. Now turn around for me."

The woman turns around slowly for Kaliya to see her back. In the lower right quadrant is a clear impact site for what she interprets to be the core of the biotech seed. It glistened as a grotesque infestation growing out of the woman's body, spreading tendrils both above and below the skin.

"Cu'Nar's grace," she emits softly and winces. "If I thought my memories of it were bad, this is a hundred times worse."

She retrieves the camera and takes several photos from different angles and distances before calling the job complete.

"All right, I'm done. You're right, it's really ugly. I hope we can learn something from this."

"Me ask Kali, no tell father," she responds as she turns back to face the girl.

"I understand. Mother, I love you very much, and I want you to know I'll come back more, but right now I have more work to do."

Kaliya steps forward to give the woman another big hug.

"Kali good daughter. Kali go work, help people," she accedes. "Kali, wait. Me ask, how Kali look now?"

"What do I look like now?" she smiles. "All right, Mother, you deserve this."

Kaliya brings her mind back to her natural adult form, changing her shape to represent her true self more appropriately. The image of the child blurs and alters, redefining itself as a fully mature adult female. Her mother stares intently as the transformation takes place. Tears begin welling up in her eyes as she sees her daughter for the first time as a grown woman.

"Kali?" she calls, her voice trembling slightly.

"It's me, Mother," she declares tenderly. "This is who I am now."

Kaliya steps in closer, taking her mother's hands and looking deep in her eyes.

The woman studies her daughter's graceful form, the neatly curved horns and soft lines of her face, the trim physique, and well-toned legs.

"Kali look strong. Kali go run more?"

"I'm a soldier, Mother. I practice a lot of things."

"Kali fight? What Kali fight?"

"Well, right now, I'm training in an academy. But later, we'll be taking our fight back to Azgarén…back to Sargeras."

"What?" she yelps as she jerks back. "Kali go fight Sarg-us? Fight Suuden'kai? No! Kali no fight Suuden'kai. No fight Sarg-us."

"Mother, you don't understand. This is bigger than just us. Sargeras is a creature from a long time ago. His kind is supposed to be dead, but this one is not. These people we met know who and what he is. Someone has been watching him…and us too. Our long travel brought us to them to give a message that he's out there."

"Huh? Kali wait, me head not good. Me think now… People run, Suuden'kai come. People run more…erm…ship hurt now. Kali finds new friends…"

"Right, and these friends are old enemies of Sargeras and his kind."

"Sarg-us ene…enem…enemimies…enem…" she shakes her head in frustration.

"It's alright, Mother, I understand. Anyway, we MUST go back to Azgarén and stop him. It's not a choice for us. He is dangerous to a lot of people."

"But Sarg-us big…and Suuden'kai…"

"…Are also victims, Mother. They're not the real enemy. You think you're hurt? Well, they're also hurt."

"Suuden'kai hurt?"

"Yeah, so we need to help them, also."

"How Suuden'kai hurt?"

"Like you, in a way," she points at the seed entity. "It's old tech from a long time ago. Do you remember the name Darumon? He came to us with Sargeras."

"Who? Wait, me think. Dar-mon…yes, long time, me remember Dar-mon. Why Kali ask?"

"He's the one chasing us. He's the one controlling the Suuden'kai military. And he's hoping to go fight his old enemies. But we learned about this, and he ran away from us when he learned who our new friends are."

Her mother simply glared at Kaliya for the strange remark, trying to imagine anyone who might be big enough to frighten Darumon and Sargeras, to say nothing of who these old enemies of theirs might be.

"Dar-mon run?" she intones curiously. "Now Kali go fight?"

"Mother, we must fight if we want to live. I know you don't like to fight…you never did. This is part of our problem…none of us likes to fight. Therefore, we become victims instead. But this is bigger than just us…our people, and also the Suuden-Aryku. Entire worlds can die because of him. So, we are putting together an army. Our purpose will be to save lives and protect people. Our new friends are teaching us many new things, including magic."

"Kali learn magic?" she inquires enthusiastically.

"Our friends understand magic, much more than the orcs. They study it like we study science, and now they're teaching us."

"Oh…" she croons. "Kali friends teach Kali dream walk, teach Kali magic, teach Kali fight. Me want see Kali friends."

"Someday you will, I hope. We need to take things one at a time. I still have more to learn, and then we can come help you."

"Yes, Kali go learn. Learn good! Me wait, Kali come back, talk more."

"I will, Mother, you can be sure of it."

Kaliya lays a soft kiss on her mother's cheek, and they separate to go their different ways. She draws in her focus and folds herself out of the local space back to the tactical office to deliver the camera. When she arrives, she sets the camera on the table for Ankhia.

"I don't wish to complain," Ankhia asserts curiously. "But did it actually take that long to snap a few pictures?"

"Well, other than trying to get her to cooperate for her disfigurement…"

"Oh, is she doing that now?" she smirks delicately.

"Yeah, you know my mother. Aside from that, no, but I had to say hello and share a little conversation. After all, she's all alone over there in that house."

"Of course, I'm sorry," she slaps her forehead. "Naturally, you need time to visit. I'm just not used to this."

"It's alright, Ankhia. For all we've been through, we can't remember how to be people anymore. But now back to work. Oh, and she asks you not to share these photos with Father. She's very uncomfortable with her condition and doesn't want him to know."

"I understand. I'll keep it confidential."

Kaliya once again closes her eyes, this time envisioning a location downtown where she can begin her surveillance duty. She vanishes from the room and later reappears on a street near some civic buildings.

She had visited this place before in her youth. It was also where she returned during her first visit while taking her ritual. From here, she would be able to easily navigate her way to observe the orcish settlement east of the city. She began by morphing herself into a hawk and taking off into the air.

During her training sessions, she had refined the practice of flying. She soared over the streets and buildings of the city into the outer residential areas, finally to cross the city limits into the jungle. She kept herself high in the air so as not to draw the attention of the orcs, knowing how they often liked to catch birds and use their feathers as decoration. She didn't care to be the next headdress.

She passed over the dense foliage of the jungle, eventually taking notice of the orcish habitation below. The camp was big, much more so than she remembered when it was described to her as a child. She could see two clearly defined campsites with many huts surrounding them. Then she noticed some oddly white pieces of equipment which appeared anything but orcish.

She circled above the camp, using her elevated vantage point to study the white objects. There were no trees within the village, having been long since cut down for firewood. This was good for visibility, but bad for a landing site, as there was nowhere to settle for a closer look, and the orcs were beginning to move around in the morning light of the camp. She passed her glance around the general scene of the jungle, catching a glimpse of something shiny on the hillside to the southeast. She glided over for a better look.

She found a series of solar panels, along with an exposed stretch of pipe leading into a small lake. She swooped lower to see the pipe appearing to connect to something submerged in the water.

"A pump," she thinks to herself. "And the solar panels must be providing power to something in the camp."

She noticed the pipe angled in the direction of the camp, so she followed it back, returning to her higher vantage again. The pipe became lost in the underbrush, but she found it again reemerging within the camp leading into an upright cylindrical tank.

"Water storage," she considers silently.

She knew there could be only just so much she could accurately determine from this altitude. To learn more, she would need to go lower, but to simply swoop into the camp like this could be dangerous. Instead, she diverted to a stand of trees to the north of the camp, choosing that side after studying the arrangement of buildings and a convenient access to the equipment through a channel between the two camps and a set of buildings lined up back-to-back. She lands high in one of the trees.

From this location, she figured it should be a straight run across the ground, between the buildings and up to the equipment. She morphed herself into a squirrel, taking note if there might be anything larger in the area that looked hungry. She needed to be quick and silent if she wanted to get in there, otherwise she might discover what it feels like to be eaten.

She ran down the tree to the ground and dashed underneath the bushes to the edge of the camp. She peeked out from under a set of leaves to see that the coast was clear, and made a quick jump across between the first set of buildings. As she progressed, she stopped and checked at each intersection to make sure no one was looking. When she arrived at the large water tank, she paused to study the arrangement of pipes leading out to the next item, which was a tall rectangular box. She could hear humming, and recalled from her aerial observation that it seemed to have a fan on top.

"A cooling unit?" she muses silently. "What for?"

She cautiously moved between the tank and the box to see the other items, noticing a pipe from the box to a horizontal tank.

"More storage…gases, probably compressed."

She turned to the next item. It was an oddly shaped apparatus, box-like on the bottom with a spherical shape on top studded with projections. She studied it for several moments until a thought came to her.

"That looks like a miniature fusion reactor," she declares silently in her mind. "Incredible…it's tiny! So, this tank must be for fuel… hydrogen, taken from the water…an electrolysis reaction, then cooling and compressing it for storage."

She finally gazed at the upright rift generator, with the power conduit leading in from the reactor.

"And this is Portal One," she considers again in her thoughts. "How do you do, people, I'm the girl from the other side of the fence."

She studies the various pieces for a few moments longer until she hears sounds approaching from the side. Believing she may be very close to becoming someone's breakfast, she vanishes in a puff back to report.

✦✦✦✦✦

"This is a rather interesting configuration," Thaelyn muses.

"A disturbing one, if you ask me," Kailen suggests. "A mini fusion reactor, and that rift generator sounds like a different design than what I recall of the stories from back home. It looks like the Suuden-Aryku have made a few changes to their technology over the years."

"This should not be so surprising. First, if to consider how long it has been, and second if you consider whatever influence Darumon may have had."

"Sharing advanced knowledge with them like he did the orcs

and portal magic," Kaliya notes. "But in all honesty, I think I would agree with Kailen. That mini fusion reactor would be an amazing technological breakthrough, but can it actually power a rift generator by itself, or did he apply a little…magic…to it," she grins impishly.

Both Thaelyn and Kailen glare at her before turning to each other.

"I may actually have to admit," Kailen offers. "She could be right. This fusion reactor simply looks too small to be a fully functional unit without some extreme tech inside to actually make it work."

"Maybe so, Commander," Thaelyn nods. "If he initiated a private project, as we have been doing lately, and applied a little arcanic knowledge into it, since it would be deployed in this environment anyway, and if we also consider he seems to have no interest in recovering old equipment, it could be no more than a fire-and-forget solution to his immediate concerns."

"Could this also afford us a solution to the low maintenance idea?" Kaliya asks.

"Possibly. If the orcs are not intended to maintain it, and the Suuden-Aryku might only check to ensure the power flows are still operational, it could be largely self-maintaining. Then we have these solar panels and the pump to supply water and energy for the support equipment. This could also power whatever maintenance apparatus, leaving the core to focus on the more imperative needs."

"So, it could probably continue for quite some time," Kailen considers.

"But for our interests, we must ensure it does not. We should then consider the most efficient manner in which to disable this equipment. If we recall that reactor in the Governor's basement, this ought to have a shutdown feature of a similar sort, should it not?"

"Yes, it should, and probably clearly marked in case of an emergency. Although, I'm not sure who would be conducting the shutdown if there aren't any Suuden-Aryku in the area at the time."

"Perhaps, but if we assume a predictable design schematic, it should be there."

"All right, we'll keep this in mind. Then we have the cooling system and electrolysis separator for the hydrogen in the water.

This may be nothing more than a simple piece of industrial-grade equipment with a standard power switch. There is probably a control panel, maybe behind a door, and if it were me, it would use some kind of lock or a latching screw to keep it safe from the orcs tampering with things."

"This would certainly make sense."

"I recall we observed screw latches on some of the equipment we confiscated during our engagement with the Suuden-Aryku. They used a five-pointed key fitting. Kaliya, do you think you could create one of those to open the panels?"

"I think that should be easy enough," she responds as she examines her finger. "Just change this into a tool for turning screws."

Kailen studies her and winces at the thought of a finger transforming into a screwdriver.

"Yeah, easy for you to say... All right, once you get inside, the electrolysis unit should be easy. Just hit the switch, and I would further suggest closing the panel afterwards, if you have time for it, to prevent them from going back in there to fool with things."

"Good point; we don't want them turning it back on."

"Yes, indeed," Thaelyn affirms. "And at the very least, this will eventually starve the reactor, even if we are unable to shut it down directly. But I would still desire to see it shut down sooner rather than later, if only to preserve lives and allow us to relax our position somewhat."

"I would agree," Kailen accedes.

"And so this would take care of Portal One. But the next question must be if the orcs understand how to correct the situation. Might the Suuden-Aryku, or even Darumon himself, have taught them how to turn it back on."

"Unfortunately, I can't answer that. The only way to know is to try it and see."

"Indeed. Then we should prepare ourselves. Kaliya will need the means to get in there with little or no interference, and long enough to accomplish all this."

"She'll need to move quickly," Kailen cautions. "I doubt she can do it in the form of a bird or a squirrel, and if she shows up as herself…well, I think the outcome there will be obvious."

"You're right," she agrees. "I'll need to study the situation carefully before making my move. One thing that comes to mind already is I'll need a cover to get in there."

"It would need to be something familiar and expected within the camp," Thaelyn muses. "But for this, we also need to acquire it, and for this we might need some manner of distraction."

"And after that," Kailen adds. "You'll need to improvise a lot, I'm sure."

The weekend had arrived, and Kaliya was visiting Relissa and her friends in the courtyard of the guildhall. She had decided to take time out of her training to relax and enjoy some recreation time, a treat she didn't often afford herself for all the demands placed on her. The conversation jumped from one topic to another, including her recent scouting exercise, where she took special delight in being a part of something again, now with a role where she could provide such an important purpose to the war effort.

Thaelyn was returning to the guild after a morning inspection of the new construction in Rolsklinde. He notices the gathering of young women and strolls up to greet them. When they catch sight of his approach, they quickly jump to their feet and offer a polite salute, as is the tradition for cadets in the Order.

"At ease, Cadets," he announces. "This is an informal occasion. It is a weekend, a warm pleasant day, and I am enjoying it as much as the rest of you. How are we doing today?"

"We're doing very well, my Lord," Marelle offers. "Are you just making your rounds again? You seem to like that."

"It relaxes me and offers me something to ease my mind from so many other tensions."

"Sounds very nice… How are things going in Rolsklinde these

days? I hear they're making progress on the new barracks and the academy over there."

"It is coming along nicely. I think the finished product will be worthy of a good mention."

"That's great. I can't wait to see it."

"My Lord," Kaliya asks. "Do we have any plans yet for that orcish camp? I recall you said we would need a disguise. Is there anything else?"

"Indeed there is. It occurs to me that between finding and acquiring a disguise, we may have other demands. For instance, I would imagine you will be encountered at some moment and need to interact in some way, at the very least as part of your act to stall for time. For this, you will need to become much more proficient in orcish. I still recall the day of our first meeting," he grins.

"Oh no, not that one," she winces. "I remember that…me trying to speak orcish and nearly losing my head for it."

"Oh, it would not have gone that far, but you did demonstrate a severe lack of fluency. We should sign you up for a special class, and considering the demand, it should be made a priority."

"All right, so I learn orcish…on top of everything else," she sighs. "Then it's just a question of how long before they notice me, and how much I can get done before then. How long does this orcish class take?"

"First, we must arrange a special tutoring session. We will replace your combat class on alternating days with this language course, but I will also have you contribute an additional two hours to it, making your afternoon schedule six hours rather than four."

"So, I'll need to drink a six-hour elixir instead of the usual four-hour one on those days, right?"

"Correct. The orcish language is not as complex as ours, and so it should not take as long to study. In addition to the weekday classes, if you can also offer some time during the weekends, I think the course should be complete within five to six weeks. Then we should be ready. In the meantime, I had another thought," he smiles playfully.

"Buggers," Relissa grumbles. "Every time you put that shine on your face, you have something bouncing hard between your ears."

"But Relissa," he replies cheerily. "It is such a lovely day; how could it be so bad."

"Right, a lovely day it is. So, what do you have for us?"

"Very simple, and you might even enjoy it. With all the hard work you have been struggling through, have any of you had the opportunity to visit Shescellaie's grove?"

"Ay now, there's one! I completely forgot about that. I remember promising I'd go take a look at it, but that was a while ago now."

"Then, by all means, you should go see it. Take some time this afternoon to make a visit. Simply follow the Gateway links through to the Grove District. Walk around, sample some of the local atmosphere, be sure to patron the offering stand, and then step into the grove to pay your respects. Perhaps even sit a while and relax, it is such a peaceful setting."

"Sounds right and dandy, so what's the catch?"

"A catch?" he responds harmlessly. "Do you, dear Child, suspect me of foul play? Nonsense! But while you are there..."

"Here it comes," she cites expectantly.

"Kaliya, I would like for you to pay special attention to the little pixies that flutter about amongst the trees. Very... Close... Attention..." he smiles and pats her on the arm, and then casually strolls away.

The group studies him as he calmly leaves the courtyard through one of the side entrances of the academy, all of them puzzled by the meaning of his last statement.

"I wonder," Haran states as he considers the suggestion. "Were we just invited to visit the grove, or given an assignment to do so."

"I don't know about the rest of you," Kaliya mumbles. "But I think I just got some new homework."

Relissa, Kaliya, and their friends arrived in the Grove District just after lunchtime to visit the dryads. The grove was a fully mature arrangement of a mother tree surrounded by six daughter trees in a grassy circle. The entire plaza was a scene of botanical delight, with trees and small shrubs lining the sidewalks and extending throughout the quaint marketplaces and taverns. The entire district was organic in design, and seemed to mingle with the natural foliage rather than to supplant it.

The district was a unique neighborhood located across town to the north of the guildhall and below the foothills. A retaining wall lined the area to delineate the plaza bounds from the surrounding neighborhoods and hillside terraces, encapsulating the area into a neat, well-defined nook for visitors, tourists, and shoppers to stop in and sample the local culture.

On one side of the plaza was a local druid temple, where the caretakers of the grove would assemble in their worship and offer lessons to visitors about the nature of the dryads and their role in keeping the balance of the natural world.

The Tree of Life in the grove stood well above the local buildings with a broad canopy of leaves resembling a large umbrella. The smaller daughter trees shared similar characteristics, but on a lesser scale and with narrower canopies. On occasion, the dryads would emerge from their trees to interact with worshipers and patrons who made offerings at a special altar inside the circle.

The offerings were purchased from a nearby market stand and consisted of various scented flowers, sprigs of pungent herbs and bark, and large seeds, all arranged into a bowl fashioned out of twigs and leaves.

"Right. Now, Haran," Relissa recounts sternly. "If you can hold back some of that human pessimism of yours and give this a chance to sink in, you might actually learn something."

"I won't argue, Relissa," he admits. "I've spent enough time here to know there's more to it than I originally thought from those early days. I'm just a little nervous about walking out there among all those half-naked spirits."

"Aye, well, try to keep it in your pants. They might be spirits of life and love, but we're not here for that," she grins.

"Relissa," Kaliya calls hesitantly. "I don't know about Haran, but how would they respond to someone like me?"

"You're as much a creation of nature as the rest of us. I'd say, don't worry about it."

Relissa leads the group over to the market stand to buy one of the offerings. It was a standard arrangement for a flat fee. The bowl was shallow and smaller than an average dinner plate, but for all the people who visited the grove, it was more than enough to admire and provide fulfillment to the spirits. Once she had the offering in hand, they walked back around to the path leading up to the tree.

"Remember peeps," she recalls. "This is holy ground, so drop your shoes here. It looks like they set up some cute little shelves for us to stack them up."

"Um…" Kaliya mumbles as she studies her hooves.

"Well, that's for the rest of us. You're good, Kaliya."

They removed their shoes and set them on the racks just to the side of the path before going in. Relissa goes ahead to demonstrate to the others how to proceed along the path, bowing penitently as they move forward.

As each member stepped within the circle, they felt a sensation like being wrapped in a warm fuzzy blanket. Even Kaliya sensed this as the waves of comfort rippled up through her hooves and into her body. She had never felt anything like it before.

Haran, with all his years of picketing the druidic faith, couldn't help but notice the same cozy warmth as the rest of them.

"Gracious, Relissa," he notes. "It almost feels improper. Is it right for someone like me to be here?"

"Relax, Haran. We all feel it. There's nothing wrong with feeling the love of beings who take delight in the pleasures of life."

Relissa brings her offering up to the altar and kneels. The others follow her motion in a moment of reverence before she leads them off to the side to recline in the serene setting of the trees at close range.

In the canopy overhead, Haran catches the motion of small

creatures flitting through the branches. They appeared slightly luminescent, almost like bugs at a distance, until several came down to investigate the visitors. They were feminine in form, tiny in proportion, and carried by gossamer wings.

"What in all the…" he begins.

"These are pixies, Haran," Relissa affirms.

"Do they bite?"

"Nah, don't worry about that. Besides, I doubt you'd taste very good," she jokes.

"Thanks, I'll take that as a compliment, in this case."

"They look like little female…er, things," Marelle observes.

"They are, sort of," Relissa admits. "They gather around mature groves, like this one. They're a part of it, budding off the trees like… well, maybe like seedlings in a way, but more spirit-like."

"Fascinating," Kaliya whispers as she studies their delicate forms. "Such a unique form of life. Do they interact with people?"

"A little bit, but they don't talk, if that's what you're asking. They can be playful little rascals, dancing around you, darting in and out."

"Could I get one to land in my hand so I can look at it closer?"

"Maybe, if you hold real still. You could try scratching your palm with a finger to see if you can entice one closer."

Kaliya tries the suggestion, holding up a palm and gently scratching with a finger near one of the dancing creatures. At first, the pixie simply circles around observing the gesture, but eventually it glides in slowly to check the action at close range, finally to settle in her palm.

Kaliya holds herself motionless as she examines the fragile female form resting in her palm. It appeared very much like a tiny person, but with wings and thin antennae that curled at the tips. The curious sight caused Kaliya to smile, and she noticed a similar reaction in the pixie's face. The little female then started acting up playfully, weaving her arms in a sideways motion as she tilted left to right, then standing up and pirouetting in a little dance.

"Do you see this?" she whispers softly. "Look at her. She's performing a little act for me."

"Didn't I tell you they like to play?" Relissa twitters.

The pixie continued her routine of bobbing and twirling a few moments longer, and finally flew up to Kaliya's face, planting a tiny kiss on her nose before darting off into the trees again. Kaliya held herself stoically for the occasion, and then watched as the small figure moved away. She felt as though her spirit was soaring among the clouds at the gesture.

"I think she likes you, Kaliya," Marelle jests. "I didn't know you had it in you."

"Does this sort of thing happen often?"

"I know they like to play," Relissa considers. "But to get this close must mean something special. Maybe it's some of that positive energy you have from that cu'Nar blessing."

"Kaliya," Haran mentions. "Did you manage to get a good enough look at her, like Thaelyn asked?"

"Yeah," she nods confidently. "I got a real good look, from all sides. I think I can do that."

✦✦◆✦✦

"How is it going out there, Suli?" the Captain asks.

"It's hard work, but we're making progress. The biggest problem is that you can't fix A without fixing B, and you can't fix B without fixing C, and sometimes you need A to fix C. And then we worry about raising smoke and making a lot of noise."

"Well, as far as the noise goes, I think we're far enough from the orcs that the sound won't carry the distance. And if we do the part that makes the smoke only at night, the cover of darkness will hide it. We just need to keep pushing forward. For now, time is working for us."

"Fine, but for how much longer. So far, I think we've been lucky to get this much done."

"Maybe, so let's hope that luck holds out."

"One thing that's going to be a big problem for us is repairing or building anything that takes something we can't get as salvage. We can recycle most forms of metal by melting it down and reforging it, or casting it into a mold. But nonmetals, like silicon, need a special industry to produce."

"If we could ever get that machine out there running again," he considers. "It might help with the reprocessing of scrap, but we might just have to settle for a lower rung on the tech tree for now. Some of the old industry equipment in the city might help, but to put it back into service means to go in and reclaim those buildings."

"Not simply that, but we need power too…BIG power."

"The old fusion reactor we had once, I know. But for that, we also need fuel, and I think these little electrolysis units wouldn't be sufficient even to tickle the tail on that beast. We would need to refurbish the old hydro-processor plant up there on the coast, along with the old solar collector array to go along with it."

"Repairing A to repair B, which goes to fix C, and so on…" she sighs. "It's like we have to put everything back together the way it once was. But working on those facilities will definitely make noise AND smoke. And then we have the issue of the mutants in our way."

"We'll work on that later. Let's just get the small stuff done so we can better prepare ourselves."

"Do we have anything new on the orcs out there?"

"Last word was the final stage of abandoning the outer camps on the other side of the mountains to the east. This leaves a big gathering of them in Camp One, several thousand at last estimate, and a lot of them appear to be families. So, they must've already sent most of their scar-faced warriors through with only a smaller set holding back as local protection and hunting parties."

"Do you think they might send the rest through? They've cleared out everything else by now, so what's left for them?"

"I don't know," he muddles. "We haven't really noticed the family units passing through, as their numbers are still high. Maybe once the younger ones are old enough, or maybe they're waiting for word on when it's safe to bring them to the other side."

"Captain, do you remember when we were talking a while back about the Suuden-Aryku spending them? Well, Petrith and I spoke on this a bit while we were out on our expedition, and I think that idea holds a lot more merit than them moving into an empty space."

"How do you figure this?"

"Let's call it a type of land grab. This is how we described it before. If they're moving in to take up space, it would make more sense to use ALL the conveyors to take up more space across a wider area, not to focus on one spot on the map."

"What if they're just building a large settlement on the other side?"

"Captain, when was the last time you saw orcs building a large metropolitan city? They use wood poles, animal skins, and other primitive materials to build simple huts, not high-rise apartment buildings. And we're talking about what could be hundreds of thousands of them, at least, if you consider the full continent on this side."

"All right, good point," he chuckles. "So, it's more like they're focusing on whatever is on the other side of Camp One's conveyor, pulling in from the outlying areas to concentrate all their efforts in one place."

"Something happened on the other side, and the orcs are being told to move everything to that one location. If the Suuden-Aryku are using them as expendable labor, they must be throwing them away over there. And since there's no way for anyone on this side to know what's over there, I'd hate to see the result once they pop through."

"Maybe so."

"So, unless we should see the families going through, it could be simply to produce kids and send them through once they're old enough."

"Suli, that's a very cruel scenario, but if you're right, Camp One could be setting itself up as a feed simply to torment someone."

"And this just brings us back to the original question. What do we do about that conveyor? If they should all file through, we might be able to move in and take it. But if it's simply a feed, do we just sit back and watch? And for how long before we try to show a little sympathy for their own misfortune?"

"That's a good question, Suli, but at the same time, I doubt they'll just sit down and listen to us preaching some new religion. If they're actually following Sargeras as a kind of god figure, he might hold a bigger image than anything we could produce. Meanwhile, I'm going to wait till we can build ourselves up a little more and see how things go out there. For as long as they stay over there, I think we should bring ourselves into a position of self-sufficiency with a strong defense."

"All right, I suppose I can't argue with that. And speaking of watching them, who is on patrol today?"

"Um…" he references the work orders on his desk. "That would be Tana Lar'akan."

"She's taking a lot of these missions lately. She must like to get dirty," she giggles.

"She certainly doesn't seem to mind wearing plants as her clothing."

"She doesn't have much else by now. Her old clothes gave way a couple centuries ago…like with most of us. So, except for a few scraps of leather, she's almost naked these days."

"This is one of those things we'll need to correct. You kids need to remember we're a society that tends to behave a little more like civilized people, not savages."

"Captain, I wouldn't mind a nice new dress, but the way I see it, if this is all we're given, we need to make the best of it. And besides, how am I supposed to torment the boys if I can't show off a little."

"Just leave something for the rest of them," he grins.

◆◆◆

"Are you ready, Kaliya?" Thaelyn asks.

"Yes, my Lord. I think I have everything now. Kailen explained a few things about reactors to me, and I've studied an example of that screw latch fitting. I should be able to replicate that with no trouble."

"And now that you are better practiced at speaking orcish, you can find your way through their ranks without causing too much suspicion. That is, until you start poking around in places where you might not otherwise be welcome," he grins.

"And don't forget, Kaliya," Ankhia states. "Our study of those photos tells us they must've used a launcher of some kind. Although it might be hopeless at this time, but if you get a chance, look for an instrument, maybe something like a rifle. At least this much would be proof, even if there is no more of the actual ammunition available for study."

"My personal guess, in this case," Thaelyn considers. "Might be to check the shaman huts, as they are most likely the ones to make use of something like this, considering it would be a gift of the Suuden-Aryku and represent something from their so-called god."

"I'll do what I can," Kaliya affirms.

"But try not to start any significant wars along the way, just in case we need live specimens for later interrogation."

Kaliya makes a brief chuckle as she prepares herself for her mission. She had finished her orcish language study and was now in the final briefing before her mission to contend with the conveyor in the orcish camp. If all went well, this should mean an end to Portal One and the outpour of orcs from that direction. And so, she draws in her focus and fades from the local scene.

In the jungle just north of the orcish camp outside the city, a lone scout is watching from her favorite hiding place amongst the ferns. The position afforded her a safe vantage with a decent view of the camp through the trees. From here, she could see both sides of the settlement, including many of the buildings, the campfires, and a large number of orcs moving around as they conducted their business.

Tana was a frequent observer in the area, having learned her way around over the course of her lifetime exploring the woodlands, and more recently scouting the orcish camp. She knew the terrain, the best places to hide, and what other dangers might be lying in wait, which were very few as the orcs had already cleared the area of anything hostile.

During her lifetime, she felt comfortable in the wild, having grown up as a girl making runs through the woods to collect wild fruits and herbs. She became familiar with many of the local plants, learning which roots were edible, which leaves might hold medicinal value, and how to prepare and apply poultices as soothing and healing agents. Some of this had been learned from the orcs, both before the attack when she might watch them during their peaceful interactions, and later by observing them from hidden locations as they went out to collect these items for themselves.

On this occasion, it was late morning, and she had recently settled in for her daily observation. The scene was typical of her routine. The orcs generally kept inside their camp, only to move outside briefly to relieve themselves, but otherwise mostly sitting around the campfires chatting, or involved in some manner of craft. Many of the hunters had gone out for the day, either moving off to the east or through the river valley to the south, as that's where most of the wild game could be found.

She watched the orcs in the settlement from between the fronds of a leafy fern. She was well concealed, using the native foliage as covering, and a homemade concoction of natural pigments to paint her face and body in dark camouflage colors. If not for the fact that she came from a society of scholars and scientists, one might instead think she grew up with tribal mystics.

Above her, a stray bird flies overhead, landing discreetly in one of the nearby treetops. She didn't take notice of this, as her focus was on the camp, and birds were mostly outside her concern. The bird, in this case, which was entirely alien to the local wildlife, also appeared interested in the activity below.

Kaliya perched in the tree, her bird form peering down into the camp, studying the motions of the orcs, and planning her approach. She sees one moving around to the near side of the western campfire, apparently bored, and looking for something to do. With this, she spies her opportunity. She applied herself to bring forward a new image she recently learned, and morphed into an unusual shape.

The orc wandered around the campfire. He was looking for new activity as the morning wore on. Earlier in the day, he had been in conversation with a group sitting around the campfire, but now he dreamed of the hunt and bringing home a trophy from a great beast. Other orcs had gone out on the hunt today, but he had to stay home and watch the camp.

As he comes around to the northern edge of the camp, he feels the call of nature. He struts over to a line of bushes, ready to attend to his needs when he catches sight of an unusual creature fluttering down from the treetop. It appeared to be glowing softly with delicate wings and a strangely feminine form. He had never seen anything like it before.

He paused in his actions to watch the small figure flying in circles and loops. It frolicked amongst the ferns, tempting him to move closer for a better look. He began to step forward, pushing away the leafy foliage to make a path.

Kaliya dodged and twirled in her new pixie form, enticing the hapless orc with her graceful dance, and leading him further away from the camp and into the jungle.

Tana also noticed the movement of the lone orc outward from the camp. He seemed mesmerized by something flying in the air just in front of him. She could see a shape of something odd, resembling an insect by some proportions, but uniquely different. Still, she had to duck low in her hiding place to keep out of sight, as it seemed the orc and his quarry were moving in her general direction.

The orc continued following the small airborne creature, amused by the spirited acrobatics and the casual game it seemed to be playing with him. Then it dove into a nearby bush. The orc stepped in closer to examine where the tiny critter had gone, hoping to catch it and bring it home as a new plaything.

Tana observed the orc pulling away leaves and branches from the nearby bush, apparently searching for the odd bug-like entity. But as she saw him bending low to peer beneath the leaves of an adjacent fern, she heard a sudden rustling sound. Out of the bushes directly behind him was a huge beast. It leapt through the air and pounced heavily on the orc's back, sending him to the ground with a bone-crushing thump.

She froze with fear as the powerful shape loomed over the orc's stunned body only a few paces in front of her. She wrapped both hands tightly over her mouth to hold back her screams as she observed the scene.

The creature plunged its maw down at the orc, gripping him firmly around the head and making a sharp twisting action. She could hear the firm snapping of bone within the orc's neck. The animal pulled back to study its prey, which now lay motionless on the ground. It promptly crouched low on its haunches and glanced back towards the camp, but no other orcs appeared to have noticed the sounds, it was so quick and deadly.

The beast then grabbed the body by one arm and dragged it around to the side, further away from the camp and behind a row of thick bushes. Tana could only see the shuddering of leaves as the beast stopped a short distance away.

Kaliya, now in tiger form, pulled the orc's body into a secluded cover of underbrush where she could then study his appearance. Her objective was to refresh her personal memory of orcish anatomy, as well as to study the body of a known orc from the camp, so she could take his place. The orc was currently lying face down, so she began with that, moving over the length of the body to absorb every detail.

Tana struggled to remain perfectly still so as not to make any sounds. She could still see the movement of leaves and bushes where the beast took its prey. She assumed it was feeding now. She wanted to run, but she was too close. She couldn't get up for fear she would attract it by the sounds of her own movements. She could only sit and wait, hoping it would feast, become sated, and finally to move off elsewhere.

Kaliya was satisfied by her study of the orc's back, so she gripped it in her claw and pulled it over to examine the other side. Tana took notice of the continued movement in the bushes, and so she waited for it to settle down. It was the only thing she could do, hoping to find her opportunity once the creature was relaxed into its meal. She briefly glanced back at the camp, but the activities inside were nowhere as imperative as the events transpiring only a short distance away from her.

Kaliya had taken full note of every detail she could handle at one time. She felt ready to try out her new shape. She laid herself next to the body and drew an image in her mind of her new form, changing herself into a likeness of the orc, with the only exception being the injuries she inflicted. She sat up to examine her work, confirming the details to ensure a convincing display. When she was happy with her appearance, she stood up.

Tana continued to wait, feeling only slightly more at ease now that the creature seemed to be settling. The scene had gone quiet, but she still felt it was not yet safe to move, at least not for a few more moments when the creature would be thoroughly content with its meal, and thus allowing her to sneak away. Then she saw movement again.

A wave of shrill terror rippled through her as she watched what seemed like the orc standing up from the ground and casually strolling back to the camp. She found herself gripping her mouth even tighter to hold back the sheer panic rushing through her at the impossible sight. It showed no signs of injury, and no indication of having been mauled by a huge vicious predator. It simply walked back home as if it was making a pleasant return from the local relief hole.

Kaliya reached the edge of the camp. She looked around at the two sides with their independent campfires and respective gatherings of orcs. She takes a few innocent steps forward in the direction of the set of buildings that formed the channel leading up to the conveyor apparatus. She made one more careful survey, and then ducks down into the hollow between the structures, making a quick march toward the equipment.

She understood implicitly that once she arrived back in view, someone will take notice and move to intercept…most likely a camp leader. Time is of the essence here. She arrives near the equipment, still hidden between the buildings, and peeks around the corner to see who might be the most likely to cause her trouble. On her left, there was another building obstructing the immediate view of the eastern campsite, but the western side was open, and she could see several prospective candidates to be aware of. She plans her act, and pops up to examine the first objective, this being the cooling system.

She glances around quickly, taking notice of a panel on one side. She brings up a finger and reshapes it into a five-pointed key to fit the screw head. But her presence is soon noticed by a camp shaman. He moves around to question her.

"You! Get out!" he calls. "You do not touch that. Only the Horn-tails may touch that."

"I do not touch," Kaliya pleads innocently in orcish. "No, I do not touch this, only look. I look for fun things."

Kaliya pops open the panel and studies the controls inside, locating the power switch.

"You will break it!" the shaman continues. "You do not touch! Get away."

"No touch… No touch… Everyone says no touch. Look, I touch, but no break, see?"

She flips the switch, and the fan shuts down.

"Oops…" she mutters, quickly closing the panel and locking it again.

The shaman closes to intervene, now shouting louder and drawing the attention of others within the campsite.

"You broke it! You bonehead! You broke it! The Horn-tails will be angry! Get out! Go away!"

"No, not broke! It sleeps…very tired. Long day, now it sleeps."

"Sleeps? It does not need sleep!" he argues.

Kaliya snaps over to the reactor, having noticed a similar panel already. She presses her finger into the screwhead to unlock the panel door and pulls it open. She glances over the control assembly inside, taking almost immediate notice of the large red button.

The shaman is now moving around to the side of the conveyor, still shouting, and appearing as if to stop her.

She hits the button before he can come into view, then closes the panel and locks it.

From inside, the shutdown sequence emits the traditional beeping, with the other sounds of the valve and control rods to follow. Kaliya gets up and leaps out of the arrangement of equipment, now walking away into the camp while the shaman rages at her.

"What did you do?" he screams. "You broke another one? What is that sound?"

"Sound? What sound? I do not hear a sound. Oh wait, yes! Bugs! I see big bugs under there. Not good, I think they bite."

"Bugs?! Bonehead, that sound is not bugs!"

"Yes, bugs! You should not go there. Maybe they eat you!"

Kaliya plays her role like a person losing their mind. She giggles wildly as she begins prancing around the camp.

"This is fun…I look for fun things. Maybe we play a game. Yes! Nothing to do here, so we play a game now."

As she makes her rounds, the rift generator finally shuts down when the reactor power supply halts. And now the shaman flies into a new rage.

"Bonehead!" he shrieks.

Kaliya now begins rushing through the camp, peeking through the tent flaps of various huts. The other orcs in the camp look on, bewildered by the idiotic display.

"I look for fun things. Where are fun things? Are there fun things in here?" she peeks inside a hut. "No, no fun things. Oh, wait! I know…" she turns to a nearby orc. "Where is great shaman's hut? Great shaman always has fun things."

The orcish warrior reflexively looks across the campsite to a large hut on the other side. But before he can speak, Kaliya is already dashing over to it and ducks inside the flap.

"Fun things!" she yips. "Ooh, I like fun things."

The shaman stalls in his footsteps, astounded at the sight of this errant orc diving into his hut, an action that's considered taboo in orcish culture. Incensed by the violation, he chases after her.

"Bonehead! You get out of my hut!"

Kaliya realizes time is now very short. She makes a quick scan of the interior furnishings. She sees pottery, baskets, a sleeping mat, and piles of local herbs and bones for his shamanic practice. She moves further inside the hut towards the rear and finally sees something unusual.

In the corner against the rear wall she spies a long staff-like object. It was decorated with feathers circling one end, and with tassels and more feathers hanging off the other end. She grabs it just as the shaman enters the room.

"You put that down. Do not touch!"

"I do not touch, I only look."

"This is my hut, hut for shaman, not you. You get out now!"

Kaliya ignores the demand and studies the object. It was clearly made of metal. She looks at the feather-covered end to see it is hollow, and the tassel end shows something like a trigger and a bolt latch. She slides open the bolt to reveal a cartridge chamber.

"I like fun things! What is this?"

"You put that down. That is not for you, Bonehead!"

The shaman is now infuriated with the impudence of this lesser orc. He starts moving forward to take back his personal belonging, but as he gets within range, Kaliya alters her stance and deploys a hard side kick into his chest, knocking him backward onto the floor.

"Great shaman, what is this?" she repeats in her moronic innocence.

"You kicked me!" the shaman shouts as he catches his breath.

"Oh no, I did not kick you. You fell down. Great shaman, it is not good to fall down. What is this? Did the Horn-tails give this to our great shaman?"

"Fell down?!" he bellows. "I…you…argh! That is a bang-stick. The Horn-tails gave it to us to hurt the blue-skins. Now put it down and get out!"

"Ooh, I like. Great shaman has fun things. What goes inside? It looks empty. Does something go inside?"

Kaliya looks around the corner again, noticing a pouch that appears to be of a finer craftsmanship than what you might normally expect to find in orcish possession. She picks it up to examine it.

"Ooh! What is this?" she asks as she opens it up.

"Bonehead!" the shaman rages, once again advancing on her.

Kaliya thrusts a firm elbow jab into his chest, followed by a karate chop to the temple, again knocking him backward and dazing him.

"What is this? More fun things for great shaman?"

She peeks inside the pouch and finds a collection of silvery missile-like projectiles. They appeared to have short wing-like stubs towards the rear, and something resembling a rocket nozzle embedded in the back.

"Oh great shaman, tell me, what is this? Did the Horn-tails give this to you? Why?"

The shaman struggles to pull himself back into focus after the latest assault.

"You hit me!" he yells.

"No, no," she begs innocently. "I did not hit you. You bumped your head on the wood pole. You did not see it?"

"That was not a wood pole!"

"Oh, great shaman is confused now. But tell me, what is this inside here?"

"Agh! Scream-bugs! They hide inside the bang-stick and wait to fly out to sting the blue-skins."

"That is all I needed to know. Thank you, great shaman. But now I need to take this back with me."

"What?!" the shaman screeches.

The shaman was ready to lunge at her for this latest offence to steal his possessions. But before he could make his next move, Kaliya spins a roundhouse kick, slamming him in the head. He twists and falls to the side. She quickly glances at the tent flap, but no other orcs were coming inside yet. Instead, they seemed to be waiting for the shaman to correct the situation. She waits as he tries to pull himself off the ground again.

"Great shaman, you should know..." she states calmly. "The Horn-tails no longer help you, and the blue-skins are not happy with you. You lie to them, play like friends, and then kill them. You call yourselves proud warriors? You bring shame to that word. You listen to the Horn-tails, but what do they tell you. Do they tell you to go to battle somewhere?”

“Bonehead, you are crazy. Yes, the Horn-tails tell us to jump into the spinning eye to fight a great battle. You do not know this?”

“Spinning eye? Is this what you call that thing? Whatever… You will not find battle there now. I am here to stop you. You are alone here, all of you. How many do you have now? The Horn-tails tell you to go to battle, but do you know what is on the other side? Death…”

The shaman halts and frowns at the suggestion.

“Bonehead, I will tell you one more time. Put down my bang-stick and get out of my hut!”

“No, great shaman… Those Horn-tails gave you toys you should not have. Now, I will tell YOU one more time. I am here to stop you, and you do not tell ME what to do.”

Kaliya now transfers her loot to one hand, and then enlarges her fist to super proportions. The shaman gazes at it disbelievingly as she draws it back and slams it fiercely into his body, lifting him off the ground and sending him flying through the roof.

The orcs outside had been holding back during the heated exchange inside the shaman’s hut. They were not allowed to enter without the shaman’s permission. But when they saw him rocket through the roof of the hut, they craned their heads around to follow his motion until he made impact behind them. Then, one of the larger orcs decided he needed to take action against the offender. He raised his spear and roared, leading a charge of others into the hut…only to find it empty.

✦✦✦

Kaliya had returned to the tactical office, and was now setting the captured items on the table, displaying a proud grin for her achievement.

“And how many did you have to kill for this?” Thaelyn asks apprehensively.

"I wouldn't be so quick to say he's dead, but you can be sure he won't be running any marathons for a while. This was inside the shaman's hut."

"Only the one? What about the rest of the camp?"

"They were all outside during this time. I made quite a show of a very loose-horned orc…assuming orcs actually had horns, but to say someone running through the camp like he'd lost his mind. This defrayed any immediate and direct action, I think."

"How interesting, and quite clever."

She now directs their attention to the strange objects as she makes her presentation.

"This is what he called a bang-stick, which seems appropriate enough for a rifle. This pouch holds what he described as scream-bugs, and they hide inside the bang-stick so they can fly out to sting the blue-skins. Now, if you interpret all of that, I believe we have our weapon."

"Kaliya, you are turning out to be a fine agent. Med-tech, what do you think of these items?"

The Med-tech picks up the pouch and pulls out one of the missiles while Kailen takes the rifle. He studies the elongated barrel, which shows distinct grooves etched inside as rifling guides for the missiles to follow during launch. He then examined the bolt latch and trigger.

"Cu'Nar's grace," he moans. "This looks like something out of an ancient history lecture, at least by our standards. But, all things considered, it does actually look very efficient."

Ankhia made a close study of the missile to make a preliminary assessment.

"This looks like a guided projectile, rocket propelled by either a compressed gas or maybe a super-cooled liquid. Knowing how the Suuden-Aryku use nanotechnology, almost anything could be inside here, so I'll want to take this back to my lab and…very carefully study it."

"I wish you the best of luck, Med-tech," Thaelyn asserts. "And do be careful. If it does contain a biotech seed, I would not wish to see you become infected through some unfortunate mishap."

"Oh, absolutely. The interesting part would be to see if it's still viable. This unit is completely sealed, which means the contents could be in some form of stasis. Wouldn't that be nice. I could have some fun with that, and it'll give me the best specimen to study if I can extract it safely."

"The next item on our list would be to find a solution for it, if such a thing is possible."

"Once I have it in my lab, I'll take it apart molecule by molecule if I have to in order to find a cure. You can be sure of that. I owe it to our people, especially Tyanna, as she was a good friend of mine."

"One last thing," Kaliya notes. "Before I left, I tried sharing a few parting words with that shaman…carefully, of course."

"What kind?" Thaelyn wonders.

"As you can probably guess, he was steaming mad by the time I was finished. He tried advancing on me several times to take this away, so I had to use a few of my new combat moves to stall him."

"You're able to attack someone in that form?" Ankhia shudders.

"It seems to have worked on this occasion. I was able to strike him and knock him back. And that orc I took down for my disguise, well, it was necessary to kill him in order to remove him from the equation."

"That sounds scarier than anything else."

"Anyway, I tried to impress on that shaman that the Horn-tails, as he calls them…which I'm going to assume to be the Suuden-Aryku, in this case…are telling him and what's left of his people to jump through that so-called spinning eye of theirs for nothing more than a quick death. And his actions where our people are concerned are shameful for a proper warrior."

"How so, in this case," Thaelyn asks.

"To lie to someone, pretending to be a friend, then to turn around and kill them. If orcs regard themselves to be proud warriors, this would be a very shameful manner of conduct."

"Indeed, Kaliya," he smiles. "You are learning your lessons well. Nicely done. But was he impressed by these words?"

"Not especially, probably because he was too angry for it. He just demanded I give him back his toys. So, I created a huge, oversized fist, and launched him out of the hut," she smirks.

The other officers shared a guarded chuckle.

"A spinning eye…" Kailen muses. "This is their name for a conveyor, I suppose."

"Yeah, it seems that way," she relents. "They have instructions from the Suuden-Aryku to jump through it to some great battle."

"Well, that great battle isn't as great for them anymore."

Thaelyn listened to the statements and suddenly had an idea flash into his mind.

"Spinning eye…?"

He turns to face the others, checking each of them for any reaction.

"My Lord?" the General ushers cautiously.

"A spinning eye!" he announces boldly. "What was that prophecy again? Vulgar manners…a question answered…"

"A question answered…" Kaliya ponders. "And a, um…no, wait… it was a swirling eye to teach."

"Swirling or spinning, I think it could be the same, and it could also give us our answer."

"A conveyor," Kailen concludes.

"According to Priestess Sehnisavain, the orcs were once used to invade the dwarven home world of Morndindor. Later, her own people were used, and our dwarven mining troupe explained to us a history of these invaders arriving through a portal. This could just as easily be a conveyor, and it could also provide us with the answer to how they maintained this knowledge over the course of generations, if we consider it to be programmed into the addressing matrix of the unit."

"So, all you need to do in that case is simply reconfigure it for another destination index, assuming it still holds the programming."

"My impression is it must. But now we need to ask which one, as there are three to choose from."

"With two of them having gone offline by now."

"True, so if we are to suggest the others are down simply for equipment failure, perhaps this can be repaired. Otherwise, we may be limited to just this one."

"Then we need to hope nothing bad happens to it."

✦✦✦

It was early afternoon on Ruuki uy'Daan when a beleaguered scout came stumbling into the hideout. Her face was pale, she was weary, and out of breath. Her neatly applied body paint was smeared from her hurried retreat, and her foliage apparel was tattered and falling apart after a mad run to escape from her former post. She trudges into the gathering room and nearly falls into one of the chairs.

Sulíma and Túfula were both in the room, having just finished a lunchtime snack. They were engaged in conversation over the work outside when they took note of the arrival.

Captain Lapäli was sitting at his strategy table. He also perked up at the sound of the young woman as she came in, and eyed her carefully as she plodded along, similarly noticing her ragged condition. He jumps to his feet to meet her as she settles into the chair.

"Cadet!" he shouts. "What happened to you? You're a wreck!"

The disturbance spread to a few others who were also gathered in the room, including a mature but youthful male. He springs out of his chair and rushes over, then takes up a position next to her and wraps his arm around to comfort her.

"Tana!" he urges. "Are you alright?"

The young woman looks up into his eyes, and glances around at the rest of them as the attention draws more people in.

"Father," she wheezes. "I'm fine, I think…physically. But I'm asking myself if I ever want to go back out there again. I think this might have cured me of all my wanderlust for nature."

"What do you mean? What happened out there? You look like something was chasing you."

"No, not chasing, but it sure caused my horns to go flying off.

I'll be searching for a month trying to find them again," she strains a weak chuckle.

"Cadet," the Captain begins. "What actually happened out there? Did the orcs do something?"

"Oh, yeah, they did something all right," she emits sarcastically. "And I think they're still doing it, although I don't know what their result will be."

"You're not making a lot of sense. What is it they're doing?"

"Well, right now, probably looking for someone. But Captain, may the cu'Nar help any of us if they find him…it…whatever it was, that started all this."

"Cadet, you need to try to calm yourself and just tell me what you saw."

"Captain," she begins to wail. "You wouldn't believe me even if I had pictures to prove it!"

The Captain leaned back and studied the others in the group. He glances at the girl's father, who also seemed very concerned for her. He then looked into Sulíma's eyes as she sat next to the girl to support her.

"All right," he continues. "I need a report, so just give it to me as best you can. First of all, why are you in this condition?"

"I ran all the way back. Once I was able to move my legs again, I just couldn't stop."

"Able to move your legs?"

"Captain, I was paralyzed with fear! I saw something out there that seemed right out of a vid-com horror show. I was hiding in my usual spot, just north of the camp and watching the orcs. Everything was normal. Then I saw one of the orcs start moving to the edge of the camp. I figured he was just going to find a convenient bush, like they always do. The next thing that happens is he's distracted by something flying in the air. I could see something that looked like a bug, but I have no idea what kind. It seemed to be playing with him, and he followed it out of the camp and into the jungle, then it dove into a bush…and I don't know where it went after that."

"So, he follows a bug into the jungle. So far, this doesn't sound very horrifying. How does this relate to the rest of it?"

"He was poking around inside that bush when suddenly a huge beast jumps out of another bush right behind him and kills him."

"A huge beast..." he muses quietly.

The Captain recoils at the statement, glancing briskly at Sulíma and Túfula for their impression.

"That could be horrifying," Sulíma relents. "Especially if it's right in front of her..."

"How far away was this from you?" he asks.

"Just like she said," Tana responds as she glances at Sulíma. "It was so close that I could almost reach out and touch it. I don't know what it was, but it was big...bigger than me, and pure muscle, teeth, and claws. I've run around out there enough times in my life to know a few things, but this was new."

"I see," the Captain relents. "This sounds like an ambush predator. We shouldn't have any of those in this region, especially with all the orcs around. Can you describe it?"

"Well, it was big, like I said, four-legged with a tail, sharp claws and teeth, and fur-covered in a kind of yellow-orange with lots of vertical black stripes. It looked like it might be made for taking down big prey...and it was silent, too. It didn't make any noise when it hit."

"That would be horrifying even without the ambush part," Túfula admits.

"The orc had his face in that other bush, and I heard just a quick rustling behind him when this thing jumped out, landed on his back, and then took his head in its mouth and jerked hard on it. And I'm sure I heard bone snapping."

"Breaking its neck..." the Captain considers. "That sounds like a very efficient kill, but your description doesn't sound familiar to me. I'm trying to recall our early surveys of this world, and I don't recall anything like that coming up, at least not on his continent. Not on the others, either, from what I can remember."

"Captain," Sulíma offers. "That sounds almost as scary as the thing itself. If it's not native to this continent, how did it get here?"

"And if it's aggressive enough to attack orcs," Túfula adds. "That puts us all in danger."

"Not simply aggressive enough, but successful enough."

"And it was big," Tana offers. "I would think, if it's so big and fierce, it would probably stand out, not be so unknown to all our fourteen hundred years of surveys of the place."

"That's a good point, actually," he affirms. "All right, let's not get our tails tangled just yet. So far, it's on the other side of the city, and if it likes to hunt orcs, that's fine by me. It knows where they are, so we'll need to keep a special watch for it if it comes this way. But it needs to go through the city for that, and I doubt it would find anything of interest in there."

"What about the mutants?" Sulíma asks.

"Well, all right, other than that, but you still need incentive to look for them, and those orcs are out in the open."

"Of course, you're right."

"Cadet," he resumes. "So, this animal attacks the orc. Let's count our blessings it got him and not you."

"Yeah, but, um, Captain, that's not really everything so far."

"No? All right, let's hear it. What else happened? You said something about orcs going out looking for something...this animal, perhaps?"

"I doubt they know about it yet...or if they ever will. This is why I'm so scared right now. I can deal with an animal jumping out and killing an orc, so long as it doesn't see me in the process. But what happened after that..." she shudders visibly and clutches at herself.

The Captain, along with the rest, could see her clear nervousness. He reached over to pat her on the shoulder to help her refocus.

"I really have no idea where this thing came from," she relates. "I was there most of the morning and didn't see anything, and this creature looked hungry. It dragged the body off into the bushes a short distance away, but still so close that I was afraid to move. I couldn't actually see it, but I could see the rustling of the leaves where it was...um..."

"Feeding?" he concludes tenderly.

"Captain," she whines with tears welling up now. "I don't know what it did, because a few moments later, I saw the orc stand up and walk back to the camp like nothing happened."

The Captain gazes at her in disbelief. He leans back, and then stands up, once again glancing around the group and trying to judge their reactions.

"And then," Tana continues. "I saw him duck between those two rows of buildings. He ran through that alley up to the conveyor and I think he started playing with it. A shaman saw him and started shouting. I could only hear a few words out of it, but he was calling him names and telling him to stop touching things. One thing is for sure, he was very angry."

"Why?" Sulíma asks. "What was this other orc doing? Other than playing with something he probably shouldn't be playing with."

"I couldn't be sure at first, so I thought about moving closer. I didn't see any more movement out of that animal, so I tried moving forward for a better view. I heard what I think was the fan shutting off, then more shouting by the shaman, and then I saw that orc duck behind the water tank. I don't know what went on after that, it was out of view, but I think I heard a faint beeping and some popping sounds."

"The reactor..." Sulíma suggests.

"Next thing you know, he's jumping and running around the camp like he's lost his mind."

"It sounds like he did," the Captain muses.

"The shaman was yelling even louder now, and I saw the orc run into what I think was the shaman's hut. I know this is bad, because I know a few things about orcs, and going into that one is a definite no-no."

"Oops!" Sulíma mutters cutely.

"Yeah, oops is right. The shaman went berserk and chased after him. I could hear more yelling...lots of it, but I can't be sure of what actually happened in there. And now, here's the final part. If you thought this sounded crazy before, try this one for size. I saw the shaman flying…and I mean FLYING through the roof of the hut into the middle of the camp. He looked like he was hit by a truck."

"Was he dead?" the Captain inquires.

"No, I don't think so, he was still moving…hurt, but moving. Then a bunch of warriors took the initiative and charged into the hut. But I think this other orc was gone, because they came out almost immediately and started scouring the place looking for him. That's when I left. The whole camp was going crazy by this time."

She sighs tenuously and looks into her father's eyes, then leans her head into his chest.

The Captain gazes at the poor girl, and then her father.

"Jarel, I'm going to have you take her to her room and put her to bed for a while. Túfu, maybe you can fix up some of your tea for her."

"Sure," she affirms. "But Captain, what about that orc? It sounds like he just shut down the conveyor."

"Not just that, Túfu," Sulíma winces. "But an animal that suddenly appears, and then disappears, and a dead orc that gets up to go play with something he's not supposed to touch?"

"And goes into the shaman's hut," Tana adds. "That's forbidden in orcish custom. And then his behavior…it's like he was intentionally trying to make trouble."

The girl gets up and totters off toward the tunnel leading to the bedrooms. Her father helps her along, and the rest simply watch.

"There's something wrong here," Sulíma mumbles cautiously.

"I think I'd have to agree," the Captain admits. "That animal doesn't sound like anything that should otherwise be here."

"Captain," Túfula begins. "Are we saying it shouldn't be here because it's not native to this region, this continent, or even this world."

"This world?"

"You said you don't recognize it from any studies, on this continent or any other. And Tana, her comment about how long we've been here to actually study things."

"That's right," Sulíma affirms. "Also, you don't just go around snapping someone's neck and they get back up again like nothing happened."

"No, you don't," he accedes. "Unless she's actually mistaken about that, but this still doesn't answer why the animal would attack in the first place. If it's hunting, it wouldn't simply bring down a kill and drag it off into the bushes to allow it to recover and walk away."

"And the conveyor…" Túfula wonders. "Do these orcs actually know enough about them to turn one off? And then…why?"

"An uprising?" Sulíma whispers privately.

"A what?"

"Túfu. First, you need tools to access those controls. And by the sound of it, he went around really fast to open those control panels."

"Which suggests he either had one with him, or those panels might be open to begin with…maybe?"

"Maybe, but in my opinion, unlikely…none of the others were. And according to her, he was just wandering around before this."

"You know," the Captain admits. "This might actually stand out. If that equipment was delivered by the Suuden-Aryku, maybe also to say it associates with their…god, I would think no average orc would have tools for it just hanging off their belt. If they had anything at all, it would probably be in the possession of a camp leader, like that shaman."

"You're right," Sulíma nods. "So, we have an orc with nothing else to do. Then bam! He's hit by a large animal, and all of a sudden, he wants to turn off the conveyor? With tools suddenly in his hand to do the work? Sure! A vid-com horror show? No doubt! And all this after he's distracted by some kind of alien bug. Not from this world? What if we got someone's attention with Petrith's little display at Camp Two? Because someone out there wanted Camp One shut down now that the others are gone."

"Yeah, something smells here, and it's not natural."

Chapter 3

THE LOST ONES

"**Y**ou have two objectives ahead of you now, Kaliya," Thaelyn declares. "There are two other conveyors, but inactive as far as we can tell. We need to confirm this at the source. Either they are the result of equipment failure, or something external brought them down."

"And this is why you're suggesting the idea of a possible orcish uprising, and if maybe a renegade group destroyed them?"

"Yes."

A week has passed after Kaliya's successful espionage mission on the orcish camp to disable the conveyor for Portal One. The portal is still down, and based on her debriefing review, the orcs likely do not have the technical savvy to re-enable it. Still, Thaelyn and his officers agreed to keep the garrison up, just in case. Now, they are turning their attention to the other portals to find out what happened. It is a new weekend, giving Kaliya most of the day for her mission.

"We are mostly guessing at their placement," Thaelyn continues. "So, your mission will not be easy. If we are correct in assuming a triangular formation, with the city in the northwest, and the previous orcish camp in the northeast, then this leaves us to look southward in both the western and eastern domains."

"So, by triangular, you're talking about three of the four corners," she observes as she studies the map.

"Correct, unless there are orcs to the west of the city. But the Commander says your city displaced any local habitation, so unless they reestablished during this time, it might still be vacant. We need verification of this, by the way."

"To verify if orcs retook the northwest? Why is that?"

"If we consider Portal Three was in a plains region, which the Commander suggests is more likely to the eastern side, while Portal Two was near hills, more likely west, and if we assume both were attacked, rather than Portal Three simply failing, then the attackers had to come from somewhere. Yet, for the timing, with Portal Three going first, the most likely direction is north at Portal One, which is still active with orcs supporting Sargeras."

"And that's not likely to be a source for renegades."

"Further, if we reverse these locations, then Portal Three is west and Portal Two is east, where the most convenient source is closer to the city. However, your interaction with your mother suggests the orcs do not live within the city bounds, so it must be outside to the west. Either way, the northwest is the only open location we can think of, within logical constraints, for a stray war party to come out and attack anything. Portal Three seems to have cleared out its local area, and Portal Two was nearly at that point, leaving nowhere else for orcs to emerge except Portal One, or some unaffiliated location."

"Got it."

Kaliya sighs heavily at the complexity of the analysis, and then continues.

"So, the end result seems to be, I'm going to have a lot of flying to do. Which side do you want me to start with?"

"If you make a sweep west from the city, you can help by confirming if there are any obvious orcish settlements in the region. From there, move south and see about any camps near hills. The conveyor assembly appears to use a water source, so keep this in mind for your assessment. And if the equipment is painted a bold white, it should stand out nicely against the terrain."

"Being a bird, in this case, will also help with my field of view. Well, here I go."

Kaliya flashes a farewell wave and disappears from sight.

✦

"Have we been able to repair any of those rechargers yet?" Sulíma asks a crew of workers in one of the shops.

"We were able to clean the coils, but the big problem isn't the recharger, it's the power cells having lost their capacity to such extreme that they don't respond to the recharging input. We could try rebuilding them, but it's going to require a cleanroom and maybe some industrial equipment to repack them since the materials are often so very reactive."

"Wonderful. I guess we'll have to pick up on that later. Where did we used to make these, anyway?"

"There was a facility in town. Of course, what condition it's in, I have no idea. For now, we're doing well enough using the power lines and adapters to run things on cords. We just have to watch ourselves, so we don't get all tied up in knots."

"And be careful you don't cut any of those lines. I don't want to come out here smelling a barbeque in the workshop."

Sulíma was checking the work in the shops outside the mine. The buildings and sheds in the work yard had been reorganized to store the equipment they salvaged from the city, and many of the students were taking lessons from their former instructors and others on how to repair things. None of the survivors was an engineer or a technician, but many of them knew at least a little bit, and shared this with each other to fill in the gaps, hoping it was enough to get them started.

The fusion reactors had both been installed in an area across the river and beyond the waterfall pool. A long power line was stretched from there along the bridge once used to roll out the vehicles on their cross-country trek, and it continued into the work yard, connecting into a refurbished conditioning station.

The solar arrays were installed just long enough to power up the cooling systems and electrolysis separators to provide some initial fuel for the reactors, and also to deliver the initial boot-up charge to power on the reactor containment field. Once the reactors were running, they were able to maintain themselves as a dynamic interaction, so long as fuel was supplied.

Much to the intrigue and surprise of Sulíma and the Captain, they seemed to defy many of their expectations for the laws of physics and the rule of Conservation of Energy, where the output was greater than the input. This resulted in enough power to relieve the solar arrays of service, allowing the work crew to pack up the arrays and store them, hiding them from open view in case anyone came looking.

The rift generators were also hidden inside the storage warehouse, since the people couldn't be sure where they led, and didn't want to use them only to find themselves in the Suuden-Aryku's backyard.

To further hide the stark white equipment from open view, the Captain ordered up a special production of paint using whatever methods Túfula could muster, which typically involved mixing crushed minerals with plant oils, to disguise them with colorations resembling the local landscape. In addition, shrubs were installed to act as a screen.

The vehicles had been parked alongside one of the buildings in the rear of the yard, away from the mine. Initially, they were pulled out on a few occasions to pick up something big from the city, but they quickly proved to be cumbersome and impractical. So Sulíma commissioned some of the workers to make a series of smaller wagons that just one or two people could haul, depending on the load.

* * *

Kaliya arrived in the downtown section of the city again. She had a lot of work to do, and was eager to get to it. She changed herself into a hawk and lifted off the ground to fly west into the fields that used to be the farmlands where they grew much of their food.

She passed over the outer residential areas of the city into the grassy fields, taking note that the farms had reverted to wilderness. In the distance, she could see the river crossing to the north and away to the seashore.

She was flying mostly centered to the fields, not along the hillside, to afford her a wider view of the area. From where she was, she could look south and see the old mining camp where she observed the various buildings and sheds that once processed the minerals into refined materials for their industry. It seemed as dead as the rest of the city, with no outside movement, and the buildings looked mostly worn and decayed.

She saw a row of old trucks lined up along one building, apparently lifted onto some sort of wheeled platforms, and interpreted them to be remnants of a forgotten cargo transport system to move the raw materials from the mine to the refinery. The scene was a symbol of a lost civilization, a remnant of what once was. It was typical of what she expected.

As she continued across the river, she looked to the north at the distant shoreline and recalled her youth when her mother would take her to the beach. She remembered the soothing sounds of the waves splashing against the shore, and the salt air blowing in on the wind. Those were the memories of a time before the pressures of war.

She turned to look forward again, scanning ahead at the open fields extending out into the distance. She decided to gain more altitude for a broader view. She climbed higher, looking around at the foothills, the undergrowth of shrubs, a few odd structures dotting the land from a forgotten society, and a range of trees in the distance marking the line of a forest. She continued onwards until she passed over the valley at the end of the row of hills leading down from the mountain range. Beyond this would be another coastline, and she could see no orcish settlements in the area, so she turned south.

"Northwest..." she muses. "Well, there's nothing up here, so I wonder if there's anything on the other side of these hills."

She travelled along the valley. The mountains that marked the boundary of her home moved past her, and now she was crossing into another section of jungle on the opposite side. It seemed dense, but again, there were no signs of habitation. She continued along, contemplating how long this might take, but realizing it must be done. Scouting work was never her favorite, but the need for it couldn't be denied, and she was the only one who could do it. She had to admit, she at least felt useful in this regard, more so than anyone else could be at the moment.

She made a series of zigzag patterns across the jungle terrain, but it all looked the same. No orcs and no big white things…just trees and ferns.

"I need to find a way to do this a little faster," she considers. "At least before my body starves or something," she chuckles.

From this location, her objective could be several hundred miles away, and she couldn't be sure how long that might take. And this didn't take into consideration if it was anywhere along her projected path. She recalled it was grasslands and hills, so she was sure it had to be considerably more distant from where she was. Then she began asking herself if there could be a way to accelerate her movements.

"I'm in control here, so I suppose there's no real reason for me to move simply at your average bird speed. In this space I have will… so, what if I could 'will' myself to move faster?"

She ponders the thought and feels a giddy sensation come over her.

"That would be wonderful…to move around at, say, sonic speeds, like Thaelyn and his gryphons. Perfect!"

She briefly reflected on her ability to fold herself from one location to another within line-of-sight. But this example must be to accelerate her current motion freeform. Therefore, she must imagine herself travelling faster.

She applies her mind to her perceived movement in relation to the ground. This would be like a junior version of folding her image. After all, she might be a bird, but who said she needed to actually flap her wings. So, she tucked them in just enough to maintain lift and pressured herself to rocket forward.

The application was slow to realize initially, but as she gained a feel for it, she took notice of the land passing by faster and faster beneath her. Her speed was now being governed directly by her mind, and the concept of flying no longer seemed to apply in the traditional sense. Now she zipped along, weaving left and right as if flying a jet aircraft.

"Woohoo!" she squeals. "I like this! This'll take the monotony out of things for sure!"

She dived and climbed over the landforms, circling around groves of trees, and darting forward from one region to another. If she had lips, she would be smiling right now. With speed no longer an issue, she was able to cover a much larger area in less time, and a high enough altitude would afford her a broad view of the terrain below. Soon, the hills of her destination were coming up just below her.

She made a quick circle, newly inspired by her ingenuity, and chose to sweep the local area before moving on. There were still no indications of life down there, but she did see the occasional remnants of old camps. She pressed forward, flying over the hills and into the lands beyond.

The further south she went, the thinner the jungle became. She followed a line of mountains paralleling the western coastline, zipping forward to a new location, then slowing to make a careful survey before moving on. All she could see were more remnants of old orcish camps.

"Cleaned out, for sure!" she muses quietly. "They must all be up at Portal One by now. Those who are still on this world. The rest...well, dead and buried on Therinë."

Finally, she saw some grassland and hills in the distance. She figured she must've travelled at least a few hundred miles by now. As she entered the region, she observed outcroppings of rocky hills, patches of trees, and grassland stretching out to the horizon.

"Here we are," she notes privately. "These are the southern ranges of hills. We have trees, grassy fields, and occasional rivers and streams. Now to make some assumptions..."

She recalls the briefing with Thaelyn and the details of the camp at Portal Two.

"A hillside and grass, but we need a nearby water source. They would build it on flat land, so I need to find flat stretches of land in grassy areas, but next to a hill and a river."

She scans the local area, but it's too hilly, so she moves to the east. The area there shows too many trees, even though she found an abandoned camp in the area, but no conveyor. She turns more to the south and tries flying higher for an even wider view above the elevated landforms.

She continues making more zigzags, mentally crossing off locations and the occasional campsite with no obvious white objects. Time seems to be moving slowly for her, but she presses on. She tries moving more to the east where there are fewer hills and more open terrain, but sees no camps in the area, so she turns south again, following a new line of hills along the edge of a grassy plain.

She crosses a small forest and sees a camp at the bottom of a hillside ahead of her. It was set near a small river that came out of a maze of hills across from it and angled away to the south, but there were no white objects. She scans for other camps nearby, but there was nothing else in view.

She is just about to leave the area when something catches her eye. Near one of the huts was a dark stain on the ground. It seemed unusual as compared to the rest of the dirt. She circled a few times staring at it. It was irregular in shape and not situated anywhere near the fire pit, so it couldn't be ash spilling out. And then there was the color. She came in lower, and finally settled on the ground, where she reshaped to her normal image so she could study it.

"This looks like…something…"

She bends down to touch it. It was crusty by now, and only on the surface caked with the loose dirt.

"This looks like blood. Something bad happened here."

She begins inspecting the huts. The scene appeared as if suddenly abandoned, but she could also see additional blood stains on some of the mats.

"This place was attacked by someone. Could it be another victim of that uprising? There's no conveyor, so it's not the one for Portal Two."

She continues wandering around the camp, and finally to the campfire.

"This is partially covered with dirt. Someone came in, threw dirt on this to douse the fire, and then attacked the people living here. But where are the bodies? Did they haul them away somewhere?"

With nothing else to see, she could only shrug and continue on her way. She morphed into her bird shape and lifted off again. She persists in this pattern determinedly until she finally moves out of the hills to the far south. By this time, she couldn't be sure how long it had been, but it seemed to be getting late, so she decides to call it quits for now.

She was secretly hoping to be able to return home with good news again, but it didn't look as promising this time. Although she felt frustrated, she didn't allow herself to feel as if it was a total loss. There was still plenty more space out there to cover, and lots of time to do it.

✦✦✦✦✦

"Captain," announces a scout just returned from his late-night patrol. "We were able to approach Camp One again, and still no sign of that animal."

"That's good, but also bad. I want to know where it disappeared to. But if it's not in the area, maybe it left due to too many orcs…or maybe the orcs took care of it. What did you find?"

"We were able to send in Tana one more time, same as before. She was reluctant to go back out there, but after we saw it was clear of anything, she gave it a try. The rest of us stayed back as cover in case anything was lurking in the bushes. She got in and made a quick inspection of the conveyor. It is indeed shut down. We have been watching the camp all day, and the orcs don't seem very happy about it, either. They were moping around like they were bored and angry."

"Yeah, what do you expect when their favorite toy is broken? The problem now is what are they going to do next? Before this, they put all their attention into using the conveyor to go wherever it was the Suuden-Aryku told them to go. Now, they're stuck here, so I'll bet they'll start stomping around the city again, or maybe go back to their original camps. They might even start making trouble for us."

"We should probably start making more surveillance of the city, as we did before."

"You're right. I'll have Cadet Girhani start making his old rounds again at the school. That'll give us a heads up on whether they start moving into the city again. I wish we could feel confident about using some of the rooftops, but those mutants live inside there. Maybe up on the hillside. That would give us a good view. But we also need protection, so we need to keep a strong defense on-call here."

✦✦✦✦✦

"Do not worry, Kaliya," Thaelyn reassures. "Even the best scouts return empty-handed on occasion. It is unfortunate that even though it seems you covered such a large area, there were no clear signs of the conveyor. Even if it were destroyed, there should be something left behind."

"At least I learned a new trick along the way."

"Indeed! This is surely a step forward for you. To invoke your projection to move under an imposed will, rather than a perceived movement by more conventional means. You should share this discovery with Aelwyn. I am sure she would be pleased."

"And then we have that one camp, which looked like the result of an attack."

"If these renegades are attacking other camps, it could be you found another example. And if this was in the west, we may be right that they are assaulting locations in that region. But with no obvious points of origin, such as in the northwest, as we were suggesting, this leaves us with a few paradoxes."

"Maybe they came from a central location, further east?"

"This is a good suggestion, and one we can investigate next time."

"All right, I'll try again tomorrow, this time to follow some of those rivers. A camp on a prairie next to a river shouldn't be quite as hard, I think. More open space and fewer things in my way."

"Yes, an open plain is an easier terrain to scout than hills," Thaelyn accedes.

"Then there is the problem of it being so empty out there. Not one orc and lots of abandoned camps."

"This is a cause of concern for us. We have assumed previously that these portals were clearing out the local regions, so this falls into perspective. The fact of it seeming so empty means they may have already used a greater portion of their population in this affair, and this could put a serious crimp on their survival as a race. Shutting down the conveyor at Portal One may have saved a few lives."

"It almost sounds like a contradiction, after our war for so many centuries, but I have to agree. I remember how I felt before you arrived. I wanted every last one of them dead. But now, I actually feel sorry for them at the hands of Darumon and what he's doing."

"Indeed, I must also admit to this, even from our first declaration of war against those we had on Tae'Eladar. And yet, I cannot stop our campaign if any of those who remain carry the knowledge of portal magic. The simple fact that they have seen it in use as a conveyor might be enough for them to attempt to discover it by magical means, and then we cannot be sure where it will lead them, including back to us."

"That's a problem."

"For now, we will continue our course. Somewhere out there ought to be a conveyor where that region emptied into. As for these renegades, if they truly are such, perhaps they may be a roaming band, since you did not find any obvious encampments in the northwest. This may also follow if they cannot feel secure to stay in one place for long."

"Good point. Anyway, it's getting late, and I apparently spent most of the day out there."

"We have studied the passage of day and night through the portals and gained a fairly sound idea of the timing. If you return around midafternoon Ruuki uy'Daan time, you will arrive here in the evening in time for a late meal and bed."

"All right, thanks."

"Now, try to get some sleep and return here tomorrow for another run."

Kaliya makes her salute and returns to the guildhall for a meal, and finally to bed.

The next day, she wakes up and attends to her morning routine. It is the second day of the weekend, giving her most of the day to make another attempt. She returns back to the tactical office to check in and see if there are any new issues.

"We will have you make a run along this river here," Thaelyn directs at the map. "This is roughly central to our interests in the eastern plains. If nothing comes up, try again with the next one. They seem to begin in this range of mountains just to the north and descend into the valley leading to this series of large freshwater lakes in the south."

"I should be able to zip along those fairly quickly using that new trick I learned. With nothing obscuring my view, I can see a lot farther."

"Most excellent. Let us see about this, and then go from there."

Kaliya smiles brightly as she draws in her focus and transports herself back to her hometown again.

She arrives in her usual spot and immediately changes into a hawk, taking off and flying high in the air. She would need to travel far to the east this time, following a series of landmarks to locate herself on her way to her final goal. She begins taking note of the terrain around her and in the distance ahead, to gain her bearings. Then, using her new skill, she zips away at high speed until she finds her first landmark.

She crossed a lake far to the east of the orcish camp. This was her first waypoint. Next, she needed to locate a wide river snaking its way through the jungle from a region of mountains in the distant south. The mountains were a high range that marked a boundary between the jungle and the plains on the other side.

She continued until she found the big river, then turning to follow it south. She pushed herself to move along quickly in order to expedite the process, as this was mostly just crossing terrain to reach a goal. She didn't need to pay as much attention to what was underneath her.

She eventually found the mountains, and crossed over them to the other side. At this moment, she expected it to be two rivers away, so she turned east again and counted them as she passed by. The second river was her mark.

When she arrived, she returned to the north slightly to check the region at the base of the mountains, but nothing came up. She then turned south, looking out over the broad plains. She could see ahead of her a lot of distance to cover. She jumps from location to location, examining the local terrain, but finding no signs of current habitation or conveyors.

Just like before, she sped along at what seemed like sonic speed or better, then slowing once in a new area to make a more precise survey. She studied the landscape in all directions just in case the camp was not immediately on the river. Along the way, she passes over a small grove of trees and sees another empty camp ahead on the river's edge.

"Isn't that cute," she remarks. "They built a little bridge next to it. I don't remember seeing anything like that before. They must have made a lot of trips across for hunting or something."

The camp was typical of all others except for this one feature, and unimportant to her needs as it had no conveyor parts on display, so she moved on.

She continued along the river across the wide-open expanse, catching sight of several more camps interspaced along the way, but still no conveyors. She made steady progress at high and low altitudes until she finally came upon the great lake in the south.

"Well, that's all for this one. Next..."

She turns west and goes in search of the next river to repeat the process, this time following it to the north to its starting point in the mountains. The day wears on into afternoon and she stubbornly continued along, determined to find the upper end.

Somewhere in the northern area of the plains she crosses a point with another bridge. She scans the local area, but there are no camps nearby.

"Another bridge?" she muses. "But it's out in the middle of nowhere! Is this part of some kind of roadway? Well, maybe. Orcs do travel, I guess, and I sure wouldn't want to wade up to my chest in icy cold water all the time."

After studying the curious anomaly for a moment, she returns to her travels until she finds the high point. At this time, the day was getting late, and she recalled the time offset from Tae'Eladar, so she gave up and returned back home. She will try again next weekend.

✦✦✦✦✦

"Captain, I'm back," Petrith announces as he returns from his daily patrol.

"Good to see you, Cadet, do we have anything interesting going on out there today?"

"Yes Sir. I saw an orcish patrol come into the city today. They circled around through the streets a few times, as if looking for something, but I didn't actually see them do anything specific. Eventually they went back home. All was calm from then on."

"I wonder what they're looking for. Is it another raid for trophies? They took enough of those in the first years after the attack, there's nothing left of the city from it."

"No idea, Sir, but this is the second time in a few days, which seems too often for comfort. They're up to something."

"I would agree. But, so long as it stays in the city, I don't think we have too much to worry about. Keep up your patrols and stay alert."

"Captain," Sulíma infers. "We still have some stuff in the city I want to bring out here. If the orcs are making raids, I want to grab it before they break anything…well, that is break it more than it's already broken."

"Suli, it's becoming dangerous out there. I don't want you to get hurt. It was one thing for you to go out there while the orcs were busy with their conveyor. At least, at that time, they were distracted, and the only thing for you to worry about was the mutants. Now we have orcs making a return and it seems to be getting worse."

"Then I simply need to time my visits between theirs, that's easy enough. But we need that equipment, one way or another. What's more, I was hoping to pay a visit to the old foundry to see if we could refurbish any of the machines in there."

"I think we should give up on the idea of retaking any of the old factories for now. Those orcs will see it, and then it's all over for us."

"Petrith, how many orcs are in these raiding parties?" she asks.

"Not many at one time, maybe half a dozen at most."

"If we bring some of our own people with bows, we could pick off a few, setting up ambushes to take them out."

"Fine, Suli, but then what?" the Captain continues. "In time, they'll get wise to something going on and start sending in bigger war parties."

"Not simply that," Petrith adds. "But we also have that old idea of trying to convince them to stop following Sargeras. If we start… picking them off…we might finish them before we can turn them around."

"Yes," Sulíma considers. "But we've already decided most of their heavier warriors were probably sent away, so maybe that puts us in a position to make a few moves. We can't just keep hiding like this. In the time it'll take for us to rebuild to where we might have pulse weapons and shield generators again, they'll repopulate the whole planet! We need to draw a line here. It's supposed to be OUR city, not theirs."

"But this whole world is theirs, Suli," the Captain suggests.

"Captain, didn't we make a deal to be given that space for OUR use? And then what? They betrayed us with the attack. Shouldn't that be considered a crime?"

"Well…"

The Captain paused to think. He knew the girl was right, but his tendency was to err on the side of caution. It was a habit he had taken ever since the day of the attack.

"I would tend to agree with you, but 'crime', in this case, may be a very subjective topic for us."

"Maybe so..." Sulíma admits. "But at least allow me to go in and check on things. It couldn't be any worse than the old days when I made my visits, and I know my way around the alleys well enough to find good hiding places if I see trouble. I can go in and make a quick inspection of some of the machines to get an idea of what we need for it."

"Suli, I guess I can't argue with you, especially if we hope to rebuild to a point where we can take control of our lives again in the face of those orcs. If they made a tour through the city today, then they might not be back for another couple of days."

"Great! And I'll bring my new wagon in case I find anything useful."

✦ ✦ ✦ ✦ ✦ ✦ ✦

It was the week following Kaliya's most recent scouting venture. Thaelyn and the others were once again convened in the tactical office. On this occasion, Ankhia was included as a follow up to her investigation of the biotech seeds.

"As we all know," Thaelyn begins. "Kaliya's most recent expedition to Ruuki uy'Daan turned up negative again. But this will not deter us, as there is still a lot of ground to cover. Those conveyors must be out there, and we still have two rivers to study. I was also thinking of having her make another pass through those hills just in case the view might be obscured somehow by the local foliage."

"These next two rivers would run through the central part of those plains," Kailen notes. "This locates them outside our original interpretation of their placement, assuming a triangular formation. Could it be our earlier assumptions were wrong about them?"

"This is essentially unknown territory, so just about anything is possible. Until we can gain a better perspective of what is out there, we should not take anything for granted. We will continue in a methodical pattern, investigating the most likely locations and moving to the second and third choices until we find something. For now, I believe time is on our side, for as long as those orcs do not try tampering with the conveyor at Portal One to re-enable it."

"Do you think they could actually do that?" Ankhia wonders.

"All I can say with certainty is Kaliya's mischief probably stirred up an angry nest, and they might try anything to restore themselves to full operation. As I once said to her, I will also say to you. Darumon delivered the seed of advanced knowledge to a lesser-developed society. The Estelar hold their belief in the Measure of Balance, and such a practice as this is forbidden, instead to allow that younger society to grow at its own pace, maybe with only a minor form of guidance. But with this level of exposure to such as a conveyor, it is enough to tip this balance, therefore possibly causing them to seek other secrets they might not otherwise be ready for."

"Including how to operate such equipment as this," she relents. "That sounds dangerous, at least up to the point of being able to turn it on and off, to say nothing of making any errors along the way and causing the whole thing to simply blow up."

"And so we must keep our watch on this side just in case we see the reappearance of the exit point. If they are successful, we will need to send Kaliya back there and try something new, although what she might try next is so far a mystery, as I doubt they will allow anyone to come too close to it a second time."

Thaelyn glances at the map one more time before putting it aside to attend the next order of business.

"Now, Med-tech," he resumes. "You mentioned something you wanted to share with us?"

"Yes!" she affirms eagerly. "I was successful in extracting the components from one of those missiles, and I'm truly amazed…as well as revolted…but from the scientific side, it's a marvel of engineering."

"Indeed," he replies intriguingly. "And what did you find?"

"First, I think I should inform you that our society is well-known for its nanotech engineering, and this projectile certainly shows it.

It uses a super-cooled hydrogen rich propellant that also doubles as a cryogenic refrigerant to keep the seed in stasis until used. As I'm sure you probably know, hydrogen, if mixed with oxygen, will combust, so it makes a very good form of rocket fuel."

"Yes, it does, but it is also a rather dangerous substance if not carefully governed."

"That's right, but the Suuden-Aryku are using a nanotech flow regulator and mixer with the native atmosphere to afford a smooth ignition and propulsion system. It also appears to contain an image-recognition circuit, so it can home in on its target even if the user is a terrible aim. And I would imagine orcs aren't very good at firing rifles."

"Indeed, and they are not especially talented with bows either," he chuckles.

"Once deployed," she continues. "The action of firing triggers the seed to recover from stasis. It is packed in a type of gel that protects it from the extreme cold…a type of antifreeze…and I believe the heat from the propulsion would trigger a rapid recovery inside the capsule. Then, based on the design of the projectile, it seems like it's made to inject the seed into the body upon impact, embedding it into the native tissues where it begins to grow. I hate to imagine what happens after that, but those photos Kaliya took show the end result."

Thaelyn and the others in the room grimace at the gruesome depiction.

"This would likely account as one of Darumon's worst offences, if he is the one to authorize this particular study."

"I think I should probably remind you," Ankhia informs. "My early medical studies from my old university once told me this is some kind of old tech from our early days of space exploration, with the idea it could be used to augment our bodies to survive in hostile environments."

"Yes, and that High Commander Geilv also mentioned this same principle. But given that Darumon has had his fingers in your society for so long, we must ask whose original idea it was to develop this, especially as we see it being used today for so many current applications."

"Oh dear cu'Nar, I wish you didn't just mention that. All right, so our next objective is to try to find a way to kill it. I need to do a lot more testing of the genetic coding, but after examining the photos, as well as those Suuden'kai bodies we had once, I think the seed acts as a nerve core for the organism. On the surface, it appears parasitic in nature, so what we need is a way to essentially kill it without killing the host. Unfortunately, my records in the medical lab lack some of the historical data on this precise tech. It wasn't something we used or studied, so we didn't keep it in our main database."

"This may slow us down, but if you have enough equipment to study it, perhaps you could rebuild some of that."

"Maybe, but I actually know of a better way. Although the medical database in the Naarg uy'Sodrad didn't carry as much detail, I know we brought along a large volume of holo-disks from Azgarén with a lot of our historical and scientific data. In the beginning, we kept these inside the ship for the convenience of it. But then, as the Suuden-Aryku started hunting us, it became more of a safety precaution. Once we arrived on Ruuki uy'Daan, and after a while to enjoy our peace, we felt relaxed enough to build real libraries and research centers, where we offloaded these into vaults for our people to access for general study."

"Ah! And these vaults might still be over there…and still intact?"

"They were built very securely, so I doubt the orcs could do a lot of damage to them. If Kaliya could gain access to this, for instance the vaults in our old research center, she could bring this back to us, and I would be able to bring our people up to full speed on everything."

"This is a fine suggestion. Then, we will have her attend to this beginning with her next sojourn. Perhaps we should make this a priority, if for no other reason than to reunite you with your old wisdom. We could have her make a number of trips to locate and return these libraries to you. Then we could build new libraries here for your people."

"That would be wonderful, Your Lordship," she smiles. "I'm

sure our people would thank you for it. I'll brief her on where to go, but I recall the room was secured behind a door with a key-code panel. I'm sure it doesn't work by now, so she might have to find a way around it, or else break through somehow. I'm not sure how she can do that, but she seems to be discovering new ways to use this skill, so let's see what we can do."

+ +✦+ +

"Suli, are you going back to the city today?" the Captain asks.

"Yeah, I found some stuff yesterday, but it didn't all fit, so I'm going back for another load."

"Do you remember that little discussion we had about the orcs making more frequent visits?"

"Captain, you don't need to remind me. Yes, I remember, so I'm going to be extra careful today in case they make another trip through."

"You're going to cause me a lot of premature aging, Suli, but go ahead and good luck."

Sulíma steps over and gives him a gentle hug, then leaves the hideout to pick up her wagon. She starts towing it behind her as she travels into the fields towards the city. It was morning, and turning out to be a cool day with only a few clouds in the sky.

Kaliya was visiting Firstfall in a briefing with Thaelyn and the others. Ankhia was present to give her instructions relating to the medical center and the archive vault. Thaelyn also provided some large bags to collect the holo-disks. They put off her other objectives for now so she could attend to this uninterrupted. As the meeting wraps up, she makes her exit.

She arrives in the downtown area again and pauses briefly to orient herself on the landmarks and road signs. The streets are clear in all directions from where she stands, so she makes a brisk trot along the avenue in search of the cross street that will take her into a section of tech industry and research centers. This is where she would find the medical archives building.

Sulíma was arriving on the edge of town. The trip across the fields was a little rougher than usual as she was trying to drag the wagon behind her. On this occasion, she was hurrying to get in and out, hoping to beat the timing of any orcish patrol that might happen by. She slithered her way through the streets, peeking around corners to ensure the coast was clear before coming out in the open to jog down the lane. Her objective was the south-central district, the one where the research and industry was conducted.

Kaliya turned the corner and made her way further along the block to find the archives building. The structure bore the same neglected condition as all the others. Vines grew wildly on the walls, chipping and pulling the exterior masonry away. Sections of the roof had collapsed, and there were signs of charring from fires.

She walks up to it and searches for a convenient way inside. The windows in front were broken, so she peered through to see the interior office space. It was dusty, and the furniture was smashed and scattered across the floor.

Rather than trouble herself to enter through a door, she simply folds herself to a location inside the room, and from there she tries climbing over and around the debris to a door in the rear. She wends her way through musty halls, passing offices and laboratories, and finally to a door along one side at the end that led to the vault. It was closed and showed no obvious signs of damage.

"Well," she surmises. "I guess they didn't get this far inside to break anything."

She examines the keypad, but it appears dead. She then looks through an adjacent window into the room. The room seemed to be in good condition, at least as compared to the rest of the building. She examined the window itself, which was also still intact.

"Thank goodness for solid construction. Reinforced tempered glass and concrete masonry, stuff that doesn't burn or break as easily."

She studied the space inside the room. There was a convenient location on the other side of the window. She considered how the folding process isn't necessarily restricted by physical matter, as made evident by her ability to travel to far locations simply by thinking about it. The process pinched the folds of space together, bypassing anything in-between, and allowing her body to simply pass across. So, she focused her attention on that point in space and translocated herself through the window without interaction. She then turns to examine her result.

"A girl could get used to this," she mumbles to herself. "But now, I have no idea how they organized their filing system, so when in doubt, take everything," she grins impishly. "After all, if I'm going to be a proper cat burglar, I need to be thorough."

She looks around the room. It was dimly lit from a window at the end, and contained many racks of holo-disks. Not knowing specifically where to begin, she tried judging how many might fit into the bag and started shoveling them in. She could always return home for another bag to finish the job.

Sulíma had arrived at her destination. It was a machine shop where she found several pieces of equipment she desired to recover. There were some precision tools, circuit tracers and breadboards, plus boxes of replacement electronic components, many of which were still intact, although buried under the rubble of the scattered furniture. She also found a vacuum pump and a pressure-sealed glove box for handling reactive materials.

She continued to search around the shop for anything else she could fit into the wagon, but as with so many other buildings around the city, there was so much disarray that she had to dig through mounds of rubble and loose junk.

Kaliya had filled a couple of bags by now and returned with one more. She was nearly finished collecting the full library, having invented a new image along the way with an additional pair of arms to expedite the process. The lower set would hold the bag while an upper set gathered up the disks and dropped them inside.

"If only Aelwyn could see me now," she snickers. "I think she might have another of those empathic outbursts of hers."

She continued filling up the bag until the last of them was collected.

"Ankhia and her team will be busy for months trying to sort through all this. But at least she'll be happy."

She closed up the bag and made one final survey of the room. Then a thought came to her. She recalled there was only one functioning holo-disk reader in the research lab at the Naarg uy'Sodrad. She considered looking for any others that might be in an operable condition to take home. She folded herself back out into the hallway and worked her way to one of the laboratories.

She entered through an open door to find the room was just as much a mess as everything else. There were overturned tables and chairs, lab equipment tossed around the room, and some of the research consoles appeared to be smashed by clubs. She checked another laboratory to find similar disarray, so she tried one of the offices.

In one office, she found shelving pulled off the walls, and decorations strewn about the floor. A computer terminal had been knocked over on the desk, but under it was a reader peripheral. She grabbed it and stuck it in the bag. She then tried other offices to see about finding more.

She moved along the hallway from room to room until she found another one with a reader still in fair visible shape. She took it and put it in the bag, considering by now these might be the only items she might find in a salvageable condition here.

Sulíma was pulling up some overturned furniture to peek underneath when she heard noises from outside. It sounded like shouting. The voices were rough and angry.

"Uh oh...orcs!" she mutters to herself.

She creeps along the wall to peer out the window and sees a patrol just up the block from her, having apparently diverted from the main avenue onto the cross-street near the intersection. It appeared as though they found something in the corner building across the way, and they were trying to haul it out.

Kaliya was coming out of the hallway into the front office, still wondering if there could be any more salvage to be found, when she heard a ruckus echoing through the street. She knew instantly the sound of orcish howls and shouts. She rushed up to the front window to take a look. The disturbance was apparently coming from further up the block on her side. She peeked outside to see the orcish patrol pulling out a man from the corner building. He was one of the Daanen'kai mutation victims.

"Dammit," she scolds. "Orcs… They're coming into the city again and harassing our people, no doubt because they're bored and looking for some fun."

She was incensed by the atrocity, despite the fact that she earlier admitted to feeling pity for their survival as a race due to Darumon sending them to their death.

"I could go out there and attack," she considers. "I should be able to take them down easily enough."

She pauses to contemplate the idea.

"No, that's not the answer. Shameful behavior or otherwise, at the very least, if some go missing, others will come looking for the reason. I need them to stop coming in altogether."

She continues pondering the situation.

"A threat… Something big and nasty to chase them away…yes! And KEEP them away. But it has to be very…hmm…"

Then an ingenious thought came to her.

"Ooh…" she croons. "But I'll need to improvise on a big scale here, and do it fast."

She sets the bag down and begins drawing up a new image in her mind, then folds herself out onto the street.

Sulíma was holding back against the wall. The orcs had pulled one of the mutants out of hiding and seemed to be harassing him by kicking and poking at him.

"What are they doing out there?" she wonders. "That's a mutant, and they're abusing it!"

She gapes at the scene, aghast at the flagrant display of brutality. Then a new sound interrupts the spectacle. A big sound. A very, very big sound!

She freezes in her thoughts as an immensely heavy crashing of thunder comes booming down the road from behind her. It vibrated the ground and shook the buildings. It was a sound equivalent to explosions, and repeating like footsteps. She turns stiffly to look down the other direction, catching a glimpse of something huge pounding its way along the road surface, but it was only the feet.

She tries angling up through the window, observing knees, then further to see thighs. At this moment, however, the upper limit of the window, compounded by the eaves overhead, obstructed her view, so she dragged herself over to the door to poke her head outside. She saw the hips, a torso, gigantic arms hanging down, and finally a head so high in the sky above, she almost lost her balance looking up at it.

The orcs halted instantly, now petrified with fear. The male victim lies on the ground staring up at the massive figure, unable to comprehend what he's looking at, to say nothing of what to do about it.

Sulíma was crouching behind the door, just barely peeking outside to observe a figure that resembled a stone colossus standing almost five stories tall. She nearly forgets how to breathe, and her muscles go limp from her panic. She falls against the door frame just as the figure passes by on its approach to the orcs. It then comes to a halt, towering over the group, and bends over, angling unnaturally at a right angle with the hips and glaring downward.

Kaliya looks down into the paralyzed faces of her opponents. The orcs had stepped away from their victim, bewildered and unsure how to react to the stone giant. She begins to speak, forming her voice into an appropriately giant-sized bellow.

"You! Bad orcs!" she yells. "You are not welcome here. I rule this place now. You offend the blue-skins, and now you come back to hurt them more? Run away from here! And maybe I will let you live. Tell the others…do not come back here, or you will make me ANGRY!!"

The titanic booming of her voice rattled the windows of the surrounding buildings, to say nothing of the nerves of all those in attendance. The orcs screamed and struggled to their feet, then scurried away shrieking in terror.

Kaliya looks at the man lying on the ground, his eyes bulging with a terrified stare. She knew she needed to do something to relieve him. She speaks again, but softer, this time in the Daanen'kai tongue.

"Do not fear me. I will not hurt you. Go home."

Sulíma watched the display with sheer panic running through her. The words were mostly lost to her as she didn't speak orcish, and the native words simply didn't register at this point. When she saw the monster beginning to turn back down the road, she pulled herself up and darted around the corner of the building into an alley. From there, she simply ran, leaving her wagon behind, and too frightened to look over her shoulder at what the giant was doing next, or where it was going.

Kaliya transformed herself and folded back into the building where she retrieved her bag. She checked the scene outside one last time, but it seemed clear now. She grips the bag firmly and returns home.

When she arrived at the tactical office, she placed the bag on the floor next to the others she had delivered earlier.

"My Lord," she announces. "We may have a problem on Ruuki uy'Daan, but I hope I found at least a temporary solution to it."

"Oh? What is that, Kaliya?"

"I suppose this should be expected now that the portal is down. The orcs are making incursions back into the city. I saw one such occasion just up the road from where I was. They pulled one of the mutation victims out of a building and were assaulting him."

"This is not good. If they continue this practice, we may see more victims of their abuse. What was this solution you applied?"

"Well, um…" she rolls her eyes around the room innocently. "It would surely impress Aelwyn, I think…as one of my new inventions."

"Indeed, are you now improvising a new talent here?"

"Simply a variation on a theme, only larger in scale, and…" she coughs subtly, "…maybe a little bit scary…you know, to give the orcs a reason not to come back."

"I see…" he eyes her suspiciously. "And how would this new, larger, and scarier improvisation find definition, in this case?" he raises his brow.

"Um…as a giant stone god figure who's now taking over the city on behalf of the blue-skins?"

Thaelyn glared at the girl, then turned to the General, and finally to Kailen and Ankhia. He then feels an uncontrollable surge of laughter bursting out, followed by the rest.

"General, do we have this young lady on our list yet?"

"I don't think so," he admits. "She's only recently come into our service."

"Then we will need to add her to it, but how we define this is as yet unknown."

"Indeed, my Lord! We might need to create a whole new category just for her."

"A list?" Kailen wonders cautiously.

"I heard about that," Kaliya winces. "Relissa and Marelle got on it once."

"Indeed," Thaelyn resumes jovially. "Every so often, I place a special note on those who portray some unique quality or talent, and your delightful sister just found herself a special mention. But now, Kaliya, what sort of result did you find?"

"Well, at first, I thought about simply going out there and fighting them. But this didn't work for me because I figured they'd just send more hoping to find a little excitement. I decided we needed a way to keep them in their own corner, not ours, and this required a guardian figure. So, I pulled together a few images from my classes about stone golems and giants, mixed in a little sculpture from my old art class, and created something really big and scary…a giant stone goliath. Then I roared a warning in orcish at them that they're no longer welcome to come here, that I rule this place, and I'm angry with them for what they did to the blue-skins."

"This sounds as if you are playing a continuing role after that part with the shaman."

"Yeah, so it fits a little. Maybe they'll start putting a few things together after this. As for the result…well, if screaming all the way out of the city is any clue, I think that's a result."

Thaelyn stretches a broad grin across his face as he listens to the description. Kailen and Ankhia also give their nods of approval.

"Congratulations, Kaliya," Thaelyn accedes. "You brought about a bloodless solution that could afford us a lasting effect. This is to be admired. Not only can this provide protection for the people in the city, but it can also perhaps help to contain the orcs themselves. But what about the victim in all this…surely, he would also be a witness, and just as likely frightened by it."

"Right. Just after the orcs were gone, I tried speaking to him to tell him not to be afraid and I wasn't going to hurt him, so he should go home. Although admittedly, I can't be sure how he might interpret this in his condition."

"Very well, it is as good as we can hope for, under the circumstances. But now, this brings us to a new problem, and that being to monitor this situation. Your solution may very well invoke enough fear in them to keep away, but it would be a great help to have eyes in the area to confirm this, maybe even to reinforce the idea of confidence in this new god image protecting the city."

"You mean to make repeated visits just to stomp around and shout a few times, to remind them I'm still there?"

"While this might serve our purpose, I would not wish to distract you from so many other objectives here at home. And we cannot have you parading around full-time."

"Well…wait. What about the mutation victims? Could we recruit any of them to help? They live there, and surely, they have eyes to watch things for us. It might not be perfect, but something is better than nothing."

"This is an interesting suggestion, and I know I have used this same expression many times. But considering their disabled condition, do you think we could properly organize them to serve as spies for us? I would not wish to place them at any unnecessary risk."

"Unnecessary risk…as compared to being used as toys for the orcs? If we have a god figure behind them, at least in concept, I think the risk factor just changed."

"You may have a point. Very clever, indeed."

"And what about this…" she asserts enthusiastically. "What if I coordinate through my mother? We could use her as a local commander, where she could collect the details and relay them to me on future visits."

Thaelyn gazes at her endearingly, once again passing his glance around the table.

"Young lady, I think some of your former Sentinels training is beginning to shine through. Perhaps that, combined with a bit of our own, and you are turning out as a fine young officer."

"Well…I…" she blushes. "Thank you, my Lord. That means a lot to me."

"Let us speak a moment about your mother. What does she actually know about us over here?"

"I haven't told her a lot, at least in part because I don't want to confuse her with a lot of details she can't handle right now. I told her we have friends, and that those friends are helping me learn these new tricks. She's actually very excited to hear about this as she was once trying to understand it from her own studies."

"This is before the attack, right?"

"Yeah, when she worked at the university…she was a professor in psychology. I did tell her we have this need to press our advantage against Sargeras and Darumon, if only because they represent a danger to a lot more than our own."

"And how did she respond to that?"

"She's not militia, and she doesn't like warfare in the least. She's not happy I'm signed up in a military, but she's accepting it, if only for the reason I explained about Darumon and what he's done…at least somewhat. Like many of our people, I suppose, she's generally afraid of Sargeras for his presumed capabilities as a highly proficient being of what is essentially alien origin. Along the way, she, like most others, became afraid of the Suuden-Aryku for their hostile behavior against us, but I recall mentioning that Darumon did something to hurt them in similar ways to our own. She seemed concerned about this, as this was new to her."

"Very well, so as a professional who is also very pacifist in nature, much like your father, I suppose, she does at least recognize the dangers presented before us and the offences played on others."

"I told her I was in training to learn this Prodigy skill, and also magic…and she's very interested to meet the people who are able to teach me all these fantastic skills. But she tells me she wants me to finish training before I actually do go off to war somewhere. I think she's just trying to stall for time, hoping I'll turn my horns around again and reconsider the idea," she chuckles.

"Yes, I suppose I can understand this," he smiles. "You are her child, and she wants you to live a long and happy life, safe and secure from any harm. Unfortunately, war is not always a choice for us."

"I actually mentioned this to her, that its bigger than all of us, and we need to do this."

"But now I must ask you this, and I feel this is necessary when you consider our situation of security, and potentially that spy we spoke of once. How well can she be trusted with any of this information we are speaking of?"

"Perhaps I could answer that," Kailen responds. "Our mother is a very responsible woman, and she's strong, even for one who doesn't like war. She suffered right along with our father through all the attacks we had, and all the lives lost. Neither of them really has the fighting spirit to turn this around, but they also realize a greater need, and will rise to serve it to the best of their ability if it holds a demonstrable merit."

"A demonstrable merit…" Thaelyn muses. "Spoken like someone from a society of scholars and scientists. Very well, then we should provide one for her to analyze, but I would advise moving slowly to build her up, rather than dropping too much on her at any given moment. Although SHE might know who you are and what you are capable of, let us not confuse the issue too greatly with a lot of unnecessary minds sharing these details. For the moment, I will have you instruct her to say that…a friend…is helping her to help the others against the orcs, and they should not be afraid of this friend. In this way, if the others see you in this gigantic form again, you will not panic the entire city."

"Sounds good to me..." Kaliya notes. "Very few people knew about this gift, anyway. According to my father, they mostly kept it secret amongst the Council and some of the higher-ranking members in the Sentinels. It was classified in much the same way as the Elders did the study of telepathy."

"Ah, and here we have that mention of telepathy again. I recall this from our early meetings. Who was it...your Elder Vankkar who holds such aversion to it?"

"The reason it was classified, Your Lordship," Kailen responds, "is mostly because it was considered a security risk. First, if the common citizen knew how to use it, it could cause any number of personal violations of privacy, and security issues in government affairs."

"I will admit it can hold this potential, but if we reflect upon our application of magic, our people are simultaneously trained to respect this ability and show the proper discipline. What applies in one direction can also apply in reverse, so restraint is paramount on all sides. Why not in your case, especially when your people are so advanced in so many other ways? Is this only amongst you here, or is this commonplace for the Suuden-Aryku as well?"

"I don't know if I can speak for the Suuden-Aryku, but I do know only my father is trained in this, and he tells us he learned this as part of his early training with his scientific faction on Azgarén. Personally, when I listen to this, I feel this might have been a coveted secret amongst the higher-ranking officials hoping to keep the knowledge to themselves."

"Ah," Thaelyn chuckles. "This now rings home with some of our early wizards and mages from times long past. The application of magic in those days held a similar value, and they kept it very close to them. They might hire apprentices to aid them in their work, in exchange to share one or another of these secrets, but they often jealousy kept their relations very distant."

"Probably the same idea here then..." Kailen proposes.

"I think this may also apply as part of our factional ideals," Kaliya adds. "The riddle of metaphysics, which no one else in our society cared much about since it was all mysticism," she flutters her fingers.

"Indeed, and this is a good point," Thaelyn nods. "And so, none of you in the present day understands this, at least as much for fear of the potential security implications as maybe also the mystery behind it. But I must wonder as to the prospect of having this gift at all. If we reflect on our previous meetings about the Prodigy Gift, and how we believe it came about, could the gift of telepathy stem from a similar root? Can this be another latent quality within your species, and can we apply it to our combined benefit?"

"Oh dear cu'Nar," Kailen moans. "Are you now going to start teaching us this?"

"Commander, as one who comes from a society where telepathy is as commonplace as any other form of interaction, I must reflect upon my own experience and the remarkable utility of the skill. If your people are able to perform this at all, I would wish to at least investigate its potential application, perhaps as a component to our greater needs. We do not need to teach every citizen, but at least those who are educated in the proper discipline and responsibility to join our cause. Therefore, I think I would desire to have Aelwyn expand her teachings, perhaps beginning with Kaliya as our pioneer in the field, and see where it takes us."

"Well, all I can say is, she's your soldier. If you think she's up for it, I won't stand in the way."

"Just keep in mind we need to maintain our secrets from those who might be spying on us. Perhaps this skill can assist us in rooting them out."

"Now that's an interesting idea! If Darumon is still watching us, he probably wouldn't be happy about us learning telepathy. And if he's actually vulnerable to it, it might be the incentive to finally leave us alone."

"This reminds me of young Leesa from the city," the General recalls. "We had her spying on Darumon as he played the Governor, and taught her ways to defeat the skill if he should try using it on her. She was apparently successful, and she is not even telepathic on her own. This is a good indication of how one can learn responsibility over their own thoughts."

"Indeed it is, General," Thaelyn nods. "And no different from our people back home. Then Kaliya, since you are still in projected form, I will have you make a brief return to inform your mother that we can use her help. Tell her she must speak to the other survivors and try to organize them to make regular meetings to gather information."

"Absolutely," she affirms. "I'm sure she'll be happy to have something to do again."

Kaliya steps back from the table and pulls her thoughts into focus, then vanishes from the room.

Thaelyn and the others sit in quiet contemplation for a moment until he begins to speak again.

"Commander," he begins. "I need to discuss a very important matter with you, and I hope you can see it from the intended perspective."

"Certainly, what is it?"

"Irrespective of these other issues of security and a spy, I must ask myself about one ultimate concern…Sargeras…and for that matter Darumon, if he should ever have a reason to visit us to check on things."

"You mean, even if he's not currently spying on us?"

"If we suggest he has no more interest in our affairs, retreating back home to plan his other advances on the Estelar, we might be a simple matter of 'out of sight, out of mind.' Regardless of this, at some moment, we might find ourselves on Azgarén again and right in his backyard."

"And this places us within notice at some moment, spy or no spy. All right, got it…"

"We may suggest to ourselves that we need to keep our security, and this might include all or most of your population, as I am fairly sure he ought to know you quite well by now, if he has been following you for so long. You are a closely knit society in that ship of yours."

"This much is true."

"But it would seem to me, your governing officials might be our weakest link. Surely, either or both of Sargeras and Darumon ought to hold such powers as telepathy. And if they should use this at any moment on those who might be in the higher positions of knowledge, we could lose some of our advantage."

"All right, I think I see where this is going. Just like I was saying a moment ago about security leaks, this would be a nasty one."

"Wait a moment," Ankhia interjects. "Are we trying to suggest here that we stop feeding them any kind of information for fear Sargeras might try to steal it?"

"Ankhia," Kailen reflects. "He does hold a very important point, and this is likely our worst weakness. The Council virtually demands to be made aware of every little detail out there. And by the way, this goes all the way back to Azgarén and how THEY behave."

"Oh wonderful!"

"With apologies," Thaelyn relents. "From my interactions with your people thus far, this does seem to be the case. And surely, Darumon, for all his spying, likely found this to be very useful as a shortcut to keep aware of your activities. If we should find ourselves arriving on Azgarén, he may try this again, and for this point, I feel we should starve him of any opportunity to learn what we have done together."

"Meaning to say, we stop feeding them any new information. I swear! I see your point, but I don't like it."

"I would tend to agree, but spy or no spy, it becomes apparent that we need to limit our liabilities. Therefore, Commander, it becomes necessary for me to ask you this question. How well do you trust me…as a leader, as a war commander, and as a friend?"

"I've come to trust you very well, Your Lordship. You've done a great deal for us, and I don't think there's any doubt in my mind that you would do us wrong. We've experienced a lot of strange and shocking revelations together, and I'm asking myself what the greater meaning is to all of it. But it would seem we were destined to find you and ask for your help."

"But in relation to your Elder Council…?" he asks tenderly.

Kailen sighs deeply and gazes into Ankhia's eyes before replying.

"The Council has never led us wrong in the past that I know of, and I have no objections to their authority. But if we're suggesting them to be a potential information feed to Sargeras…not necessarily a willing one, but from this telepathic theft, and then to suggest this can happen even just once at some critical moment…" he shakes his head. "From the military perspective, this is an unacceptable risk, if we should have any hope of succeeding in our objectives."

"But isn't there some way to protect ourselves from this?" Ankhia objects. "The General here just now mentioned something about training to guard against it, right?"

"For those of us who are better accustomed to telepathic interactions," Thaelyn advises. "We know of a variety of ways to block or otherwise interfere with such attempts. It is here where I offer lessons to our cadets in the academy for this purpose. However, we must then reflect on your people for a moment. You do not train this at all, and I think it should be apparent that Darumon would know this. We could train you, but then if he should make his attempt, he would notice something new in that place, and this might cause him to become even more suspicious."

"And this could make him try even harder, maybe?"

"I would say more than that, actually," the General offers. "If he should become sufficiently suspicious, he could also become desperate, thinking our secrets could hold such critical details he cannot take any chances against, especially if we went so far as to safeguard the Elder Council from his prying eyes."

"Cu'Nar's grace, I see it now. So, on top of everything else, he would suspect we're suspecting HIM of using HIS telepathy to steal from THEM…and so we took this extra precaution…ugh!" she moans. "This is enough to make me pull my horns out!"

Kailen reaches over to wrap his arm around her and squeezes gently.

"And therefore," he concludes. "It's better to simply not open us up to all this intrigue. Let him have his fun if he thinks he can get anything out of it."

"Precisely," Thaelyn affirms. "There is a philosophy sometimes mentioned that ignorance is bliss. If they never trained in telepathy, they would not know how to defend against it. Therefore, what they do not know cannot harm the rest of us. If Darumon or Sargeras should try to peel this away, all they will find is emptiness."

"And when we are speaking of such remarkable gifts as these," the General offers. "This is surely a most extraordinary sensation as to turn the tides of any engagement. We would certainly not wish them to know any part of it."

"I understand, and I have to agree," Kailen accedes. "I don't like the idea of keeping this away from them...they're good people with our best interests at heart...but their ignorance could be a tool in our defense."

"Very well, Commander," Thaelyn concludes. "Then we should limit their involvement for anything critical relating to our conjoined military advances."

<hr>

An irregular clopping of feminine hoof steps echoes through the tunnel leading into the mine hideout. Through the opening of the passage that leads into the large gathering hall stumbles a distraught and exhausted young lady. Her breathing is raspy. She appears faint and barely able to stand upright. She draws the attention of the people in the room as she staggers through, toppling chairs and collapsing into tables. Her motion is stubborn and motivated by an unseen compulsion that pushes her to tread forward.

Túfula was sitting at one of the tables taking a rest as Sulíma entered the room. She calls out to the girl, but gets no response. The Captain also saw her as she entered, realizing immediately that something was seriously wrong. He jumps up and runs over to catch her. She continued pushing forward, unable to stop, even though he was holding her.

"Suli!" he shouts. "What happened?"

She doesn't respond, not even glancing up to meet his gaze. He pulls her in, embracing her tightly, and whispers softly to settle her down. Her motions slow until she finally collapses. Túfula and several others rush to their side.

"Suli, what happened out there?" he asks softly.

Her breathing is still ragged. She can no longer hold herself on her own feet, so the Captain brings her to a chair and sets her down, kneeling next to her and supporting her.

"Suli? Can you hear me?"

"Big..." she wheezes.

"What was big? Did you see something?"

"Big... Big-big..."

"Suli, I need to know what happened out there. Please try to tell me."

"Biiig... Rock...feet...boom-boom..."

The Captain gazes at Túfula, then continues around at the others now hovering over the table where Sulíma was sitting.

"Were you in the city?" he asks, trying to keep his voice low and calm.

"...Orcs...talking...big... Mutant... Run..."

With these last gasping words, she faints from exhaustion.

"Captain," Túfula notes. "That sounds a lot worse than that animal report, especially as it resulted in her fainting. She must've run all the way back in a panic."

"Not just a panic, Túfu, but traumatized. I want to know what did this to her, and if I have to go out there myself and kill it, I swear I will."

"Captain, normally I wouldn't argue with you, but under the circumstances, it might prove wiser to refrain from carrying out any vendettas. I've never seen Suli like this before, and I don't know what it would take to send her into this condition, but whatever it was, it had to be serious."

"Fine..." he sighs tensely. "Maybe one of our scouts saw something. If it was so big, it might be visible from our other positions. Let's put her to bed and wait. I'll sit next to her to make sure she's alright. Túfu, if anyone else comes in, send them over."

The girl nods as he lifts Sulíma in his arms and carries her to bed. He lays her down and pulls the covers up, and then sits on the floor next to her with his hand holding hers to maintain physical contact.

A short while later, more pounding is heard stomping through the entrance of the mine. Several scouts all arrive at once, puffing from a hard run. Among them is Petrith leading the charge. He searches urgently around the room.

"Túfu, where's the Captain at?" he shouts. "We need to see him, now!"

"Petrith, did you see it? Suli came through a little while ago from the city and collapsed in a heap. The Captain brought her to bed, and he's sitting next to her."

"Oh no... Is she alright?"

"I can't say. She barely spoke a few words, and then fainted."

They strolled across to the tunnel leading to the sleep chambers. As they arrived in the room where Sulíma slept, they found the Captain still sitting there holding her hand. Petrith and the other scouts took up seating on the floor next to him.

"Captain," Petrith calls quietly. "How is she?"

"Sleeping, hopefully just shock-induced... The bigger question is how badly she got hurt by whatever happened out there. I'm going to guess you're all in here for the same reason, so it had better be good."

"Yeah. Captain, we all saw it, whatever it was. It stood well above most of the local buildings, so it was kind of hard to miss."

"It stood...above...the buildings?" he winces. "In the name of the cu'Nar, what are we talking about here?"

"I have no idea how to describe it other than to say it looked like a gigantic stone statue, and it was animated, walking along the street."

"How do you animate a stone statue?!" he whispers urgently, trying to keep his voice low.

"Sir, I don't know. It breaks every rule I ever grew up with. And then, we have the next part. It just appeared out of nowhere near the industry buildings. And when I say appeared, it was poof, there it is, and then poof again, and it's gone."

The Captain glared at Petrith and turned again to Sulíma on the bed.

"Poof..." he murmurs. "She said something about orcs and a mutant before she fainted. Did any of you see anything?"

Tana was among the scouts travelling with Petrith, and now she speaks up.

"Captain, I don't think any of us could actually see the street level from our position, but I've been around enough times to know this thing can't be natural. I've studied the orcs many times in my life to see them fashion effigies and idols, but nothing of this sort. So unless someone created something monstrous using this magic of theirs, I can't believe this thing could be native around here."

"Then what is it you're actually saying, Tana? It came from some other world?"

"At this moment, I may have to. And this reminds me of that animal now. I can only think of two reasonable possibilities right now, and I think one of those is out the window from the start. Petrith, you heard it talking, right? The voice was booming all across the city. I can't imagine anyone could miss it."

"Yeah, I heard it," he admits. "But my orcish is really bad these days."

"Well, mine is a little better…not great, but I know a few things. When I was little, I had an interest in learning from them…what little they actually tried to show us. Like I said, I've spent most of my life trying to study them, hiding in the bushes, watching from afar, and hoping to understand some of their tribal culture and methods of using the natural resources. This is where I learned a lot of my tricks for using herbs and such."

"And you shared some of that with me in my lab," Túfula affirms.

"Right. Now, I know this magic of theirs is real because I've seen them use it on occasion…mostly the shamans, as they're the ones who study it. So, if we simply say it was someone who let it get out of hand, it could be they created a monster of some kind."

"Tana," the Captain emits cautiously. "When you say, to get out of hand and creating a monster, I'm getting some nasty visions, some of which reflect on their original attack on the city. How do you mean this?"

"Let's say they're bored or angry about the conveyor being down. If they have nothing else to do, maybe they're experimenting with something, and using their magic in ways that might be, oh… Unconventional."

"That sounds dangerous, even though I can't really imagine how, since I can't imagine the possibilities of what it can do if let loose on a large scale."

"But maybe that's what we need to be afraid of the most, is what the imagination can do. It doesn't fit with our technological perspective at all. So, I think we can't allow ourselves to use our science with it. It just doesn't work."

"You're not going to throw that old riddle of metaphysics at us now, are you?" Túfula smiles delicately.

"Well, maybe not specifically, but this might actually be where it comes in."

"All right," the Captain considers. "But then, do you have any other ideas?"

"I've watched the orcs, and tried dreaming up all kinds of ideas, including this concept of spirits doing the work from behind some hidden veil. But it still doesn't work for me."

"Are you saying you've actually tried it?" Túfula wonders.

"Yes, I have, secretly," she sighs. "I was hoping to bring this to our people one day. But so far, it's still a mystery. Anyway, if we say there were orcs present at the time, maybe we can say they were experimenting with something, using our city as a test bed, rather than their jungle. But here we have a problem, and that is what I heard this thing say to…someone…in orcish."

"I see," the Captain resumes. "And what did it say?"

"First, it was angry. It was apparently speaking to orcs, by the words it was using. So, if Suli mentioned orcs, maybe she saw something in the area. I heard it call them bad orcs, and telling them to go away."

"Go away?" Túfula muses distantly. "Then, are we saying it's at odds with the orcs?"

"Not just that, but I think I also heard it say something about hurting someone, and I heard words like blue-skins."

"Blue-skins?" the Captain wonders. "Are we speaking of the mutants, or us?"

"Or maybe Suli," Petrith notes. "If she was present, did they find her?"

"Maybe, and this thing intervened."

"This is where I think it cannot be native," Tana considers. "If the orcs created something, it probably wouldn't reference blue-skins at all. Here is where I'm reminded of that animal. It literally appeared out of nowhere, killed that orc, and then I saw that same orc stand up and walk away. But what if it wasn't actually the ORC standing up, but a creature that can create any odd shape it desires?"

The Captain peers over his shoulder and glares at the girl.

"A shapeshifter of some kind?" he mumbles.

"Cu'Nar's grace!" Túfula shudders. "That's even scarier than the rest."

"But think about it," Tana submits. "An alien bug, then an alien animal, then an orc who so conveniently knows how to shut down the conveyor, using tools he shouldn't otherwise have in his possession."

"Oh dear. So, when Suli mentioned Petrith's actions at Camp Two, what did we stir up?"

"I heard it say it how it…something…this place, I couldn't get that one word, and demanding them to run away and not come back…and to tell others not to come here. It was giving a warning."

"It…something…this place…" the Captain muddles. "It guards, it owns, it controls… Is it setting itself up as taking possession of the city?"

"I don't know, but if it's hostile to orcs, and if it shouted at a group to leave the city and not come back, I doubt ANY of them will come back."

"Then how does this relate to us?" Petrith asks. "Blue-skins? Well, all right, we have blue skin. But is this to say it doesn't want us in there, or what?"

"And what about Suli's mention of a mutant?" Túfula offers. "Even with the mutation, they still have, um…well, sort of blue skin, if you don't count the splotchy gray and all the muck on them."

"The orcs sometimes referred to us as blue-skins," the Captain recalls. "If this thing is speaking orcish, it's using their native terms."

"That's right," Tana affirms. "Which means it must be familiar with them to understand the language. Captain, that animal, or orc, or whatever it was, wanted that conveyor shut down. If these orcs are travelling off somewhere, and if we're right in saying they're being spent on something, and the other side is a death trap, then whoever is on the other side may have found us and wanted to put a stop to it on this side."

"This might reflect on our earlier discussion about their migration," Petrith muses. "They had orders to move to one point and file across for some reason."

"But is it now taking control of our city?" the Captain wonders. "Why? Does it see vacant land on OUR side and wants to fill in to occupy it?"

"I don't think that makes sense, Captain," Túfula considers. "The city is a wreck, so there's not much value to it. If we're talking about a blue-skin, and Suli saw a mutant, either we're speaking of it, or else her, whichever comes first. Tana, you said something about hurting something?"

"Yes, but I couldn't get some of the words. Um, wait, let me think... Something about blue-skins, and they come back...and hurt more. Yeah, that's what it was."

"Hurt more?!" Túfula surges. "Hurting more of what? Who are they hurting this time?"

"All right, everyone," the Captain announces. "I think before we go any further on this, we should wait for Suli to wake up and hope she can give us a little more information. She might hold an important clue to all this."

"Fine, Captain, but if this thing isn't from around here, I want to know what it is, where it came from, why it might actually be here, and why in our city...not that it really bothers me that much if it wants to take control of that pile of junk...but still, why would it try drawing a line in front of them. And then, if it can change shape, as well as go poof... Cu'Nar's pity, where is it right now?"

✦ ✦ ◆ ✦ ✦

"Túfu," Petrith whispers. "Has she said anything else?"

"Not much...not since the Captain got those first few words out of her after she woke up. Since then, she's just been sitting there nursing that cup of tea I made earlier."

"I see Tana over there. Has she made any progress?"

"I'm not sure. From what I've seen, she's mostly just babysitting and waiting for her to say something. Petrith, I'm worried for her. She's not usually this quiet. Maybe we should try talking to her?"

"We should, but I didn't want to disturb her with anything complex."

"Same here, but we can't just ignore her, either. Let's go sit next to her and try starting some light conversation."

It was the next morning after the giant stone creature was seen in the city. Sulíma woke up early, but still visibly drained from her ordeal. The mood among the people in the mine was slow and uncertain. The Captain was sitting at his strategy table in muffled conversation with one of his officers, trying to assess the situation and decide what possible course of action to take. So far, the usual scouting patrols had been put off until they could gain a better understanding of this latest episode. As for the rest, they were just finishing up breakfast and waiting.

Petrith and Túfula ambled over and gently sat at the table near their traumatized friend. She didn't make any outward indication of their arrival, instead just staring off in the distance, as if lost in thought. Tana sat on the other side of the table, occasionally glancing at Sulíma, and trying to invoke a few words here and there.

"Suli?" Petrith mutters softly. "How do you feel?"

She takes another sip from her cup and slowly swallows it, still staring into space. Petrith leans over to look at her face. She timidly turns to look back at him.

"I lost my wagon," she responds with mournful eyes.

"Suli…cu'Nar's grace, don't worry about that, we'll get you a new one."

"But I liked that one, it was special…and it was my first. Besides, I had some good stuff in it."

"Suli, seriously, I really doubt anyone is going to bother it. And it's not actually lost. We know exactly where it is, so we can go back and get it. We're just waiting to get a grip on the situation."

"Will you go get my lost wagon?" she curls up a hopeful smile.

Now Petrith has an idea to ease the tension by attempting a humorous gesture. He pulls himself up into a confident pose with a proud air of bravado.

"I will storm through the streets in the face of a hundred orcs to get your wagon back," he proclaims with his exaggerated display. "But not until the Captain gives the go-ahead," he whispers, casting a glance at the Captain's table.

"Wow, Petrith!" she perks up unexpectedly. "Maybe you really do like me after all! Would you cut down that monster with a butter knife, too?"

Petrith pulls back at the surprising alteration. He glares at Túfula, and then at Tana, then back to Sulíma, who was now showing a warm grin.

"I don't believe this!" he wheezes. "You're faking it! Túfu, do you believe this?"

"Actually yes, knowing her like I do."

"She was showing signs of recovery from some time ago," Tana admits. "But she told me not to say anything. She was waiting for her Big Strong Man to come over here first," she grins.

"Oh, great!" he shakes his head. "Is this another attempt at swinging her tail around? As if I haven't seen enough of those…"

"Hey!" Sulíma argues. "I have a reputation to uphold. And I think I'm entitled after what happened out there."

"All right, fine, I'll give you this one. But are you actually feeling better, or just finally lost your mind?"

"I can't be sure right now. Tana was telling me a few things about what you said last night, so I'm sitting here thinking a lot."

"Did you remember anything more about the incident? You didn't give us much when you first woke up."

"I think I was still in shock. My mind went numb after a while. The sheer size of that thing was enough to send my horns flying off in every direction."

"I'd have to agree. I could see it from my post, and that was several blocks away."

"I was perched on the hillside," Tana offers. "So, I had a great view of the city. Then that thing shows up towering over most of it."

"Tana," Sulíma resumes. "You said it was shouting at those orcs to run away and not come back. Well, they certainly did, screaming all the way…as far as I can remember in my delirium. I don't know any orcish, so I have no idea what was actually said, but it hit them hard. And then we have that mutant."

"Right, you mentioned you saw it, and they apparently pulled it out from one of the buildings."

"And then this…thing…shows up at just the right moment."

Sulíma holds her statement and peers around the room to find the Captain.

"Captain?" she calls. "Can you come here for a moment?"

The Captain turns expectantly at the call and lurches out of his chair to join the group. He had taken a special interest in the girl's health, and was particularly interested to hear if she had anything else to say. He takes up a chair across the table from her.

"Yes Suli?" he asks gently. "Do you need anything?"

"Do I need anything, hmm…" she mulls privately. "Well, some new anklets would be nice. I like gold chains with little blue and green crystals. Something delicate, to make me look nice for the boys."

The Captain hesitates and raises his brow before looking to the others at the table for an explanation.

"She's feeling much better, Captain," Petrith relents. "This little tail-yanker is back to her usual tricks, which she's apparently milking for all their worth at the moment."

"Oh, she is, is she?" he kids. "All right, so do you want a belt to go along with that?"

"Ooh, would you?" she beams brightly. "But now for the serious stuff… I'm really thankful I have so many good friends…it makes the healing part of things so much nicer."

"I'm glad to hear it, Suli. But do you have anything else for us?"

"Maybe. I was talking to Tana a little, and trying to remember things better. Now I'm wondering about what I actually saw out there. That thing, whatever you might call it…a stone giant? It appeared right when those orcs were attacking that mutant, like it was a response of some kind, and it seemed to be as a way to help the mutant."

"Attacking?"

"Yeah, I remember now. They pulled it out and were starting to abuse it. I couldn't actually believe they would be so brutal against something they once created to attack us. Now I'm asking myself why. Tana said something about blue-skins, hurting something, and coming back to hurt more. Are we actually talking about the orcs versus the mutants?"

"So, is this to say, they were hurting the mutants before, and are coming back to do it again?"

"This might make sense to me," Tana suggests. "At least a little bit. For a long time, the orcs entered the city, but did any of us pay attention to what they were actually doing there, or simply if they were passing through to find us on the other side? The mutants hide in those buildings, many of which are out of view from our usual vantage points. And we never really paid any attention to the relationship before this, as we regarded ALL of them as enemies to us. All we ever cared about was whether they were moving in our direction."

"Right, and so we didn't really care what the orcs were doing with the mutants, or what the mutants did with the orcs…only what they MIGHT do to us. This sounds like a failure on our part."

"Then, the orcs made this change where we saw them moving to Camp One and that conveyor. So, we need to return to the idea of something dramatic happening on the other side of that conveyor that refocused their attention. Now, the conveyor is closed, and their attention is redirecting to their old habits."

"Good, this makes sense now."

"It also seems to confirm our ideas about the battle scene on the other side," Sulíma adds. "Something big happened, and they were given instructions to send everything into one spot, but probably as a suicide march."

"A suicide march," Tana muses. "But voluntary or unknowing, that's the real question."

"Well, let's ask the obvious. Would you willingly walk into a death trap? I don't think you can see where you're going through that swirling vortex, so it falls to whatever someone told them to do."

"Granted."

"Therefore, whatever the reason, if something found its way back here to stop it, the battle must be over by now. And now they... whoever or whatever 'they' are in this case, are advancing on this world to finish the orcs."

"But this still doesn't answer the part of its relationship to us," the Captain offers.

"No, it doesn't," Tana admits. "But it sure doesn't seem to like orcs. And again, it used the term blue-skin, which must mean us. So, maybe it encountered our people on the other side and fought back alongside them. Now, here it is cutting off the flow through that conveyor, and then here in the city, which does actually benefit us to some degree."

"For as long as they don't try circling around these mountains and up the other side."

"Captain," Túfula interjects. "Once again, I think I would need to ask why. At this moment, they have a lot of other directions to go that are a lot more convenient to them than to circle all the way around these mountains to this valley over here, which they never really showed any interest in prior to this. Not with those conveyors in operation. And right now, for what's left of them, east and south are much shorter walks."

"You have a point, Túfu. You definitely have a little of your father in you. All right, so we can suggest the orcs may be cut off from us, and might not have as much reason to circle around, especially with so much other free territory closer at hand. And then we have a huge godlike thing guarding the city."

"Godlike!" Sulíma yips. "Yes, that's the reason! Captain, if we're speaking of something that can change its shape, and if you wanted to teach a bunch of rock-headed orcs to do or not do something, how would you do it? With something unimaginably big that you might think to be a god."

"And possibly overriding their existing god worship," Petrith muses.

"All right," the Captain nods. "So, it creates a god image and yells at that group to leave, and that it…something…this place. I'll bet it's saying it owns or maybe rules this place. This is its territory now and to stay out."

"That makes perfect sense to me," Túfula agrees. "But we still come down to the rest of it where those mutants are concerned, and also the rest of us."

"Somebody knows something about all this," Petrith considers. "And it's not us. If they don't know WE exist, it's instead protecting THEM."

"I can tell you one thing," Tana submits. "We definitely don't want to make an enemy of it, whatever we do. If it can appear out of nowhere and kill that orc, I don't want to be on its bad side, to say nothing of whatever else it can do."

"But Tana," Sulíma wonders. "If we're also saying it knows the word blue-skin, and if it knows what a blue-skin actually is, could we be saying it's working with our people? Maybe the people from the Naarg uy'Sodrad found new friends…big ones."

"While that's a fine suggestion, Suli," the Captain relents. "It's a question I don't think we can afford to get wrong. It might only know this word from a previous encounter with the orcs here in this world and felt sympathy for that one mutant."

"Sympathy…" Sulíma muses distantly. "Wait, I remember now. It said something else, but softer. I think I had already lost most of my marbles by that time, and my horns had crawled off to hide under a rock. But now I remember the words. It was saying it won't hurt him and not to be afraid, then to go home."

"All right," Túfula accedes. "That's a clear sign of compassion for the mutant, so it's taking sides with them. Whatever relation it, or they, might have with anything else, it holds something special with them."

"But this also means it can speak OUR language," Petrith admits. "And this suggests an encounter with us at some moment."

"Us who, Petrith?" Túfula shudders. "Us here, or from the Naarg uy'Sodrad? We still can't be absolutely sure where it came from, or how it got here. For all we know, it just doesn't like orcs and how they treat things. Maybe it's been here for much longer, studied us for the language bit, or maybe the mutants, and then went to war with the orcs just out of spite."

"If it knows about us," Sulíma notes. "And it hasn't done anything with us, I think either it doesn't care about us, or doesn't WANT to do anything with us. Maybe it thinks we don't need help if we're all the way over here and the orcs don't travel this far."

"And therefore the mutants, who are vulnerable inside the city, with orcs who make habitual raids, but not for trophies. Instead to abuse things."

"You're right," Tana considers. "The only real evidence we have is it defended a mutant from a bunch of orcs who were clearly behaving badly. This might bring its own answer, regardless of a relationship to anything else. Whether or not it's at odds with orcs to begin with, it doesn't really matter who or what they attack, it's still offensive."

"But this still doesn't answer the question completely," Sulíma interjects. "If we're saying it's at war with the orcs, why did it ONLY shut down the conveyor? If this thing can create a godlike stone monster, it should be able to just stomp around that camp to smash everything else."

"It wanted them to stop going through," Túfula reasons. "That's all. Just to get them to stop. And those in the city, you said it simply yelled at them, it didn't kill them outright. So, it may or may not be truly at war, but it's not trying to destroy them…"

"…As a race," Petrith concludes. "Now I'm thinking of Camp Two again. It must know they're down to their last. So, the compassion bit might work both ways. It wants the fighting to stop, to protect lives on both sides. The orcs WERE jumping through that hole in space, and probably being cut in half by something, and these others finally got tired of it, since the Suuden-Aryku probably gave orders for this to continue forever. So, they sent someone here to stop it."

"But what does this say for the Suuden-Aryku on the other side?"

"What Suuden-Aryku? Túfu, if they were splashing their hooves in the wrong puddle over there, they might not be an issue by now. Maybe they pulled out and left the orcs to suffer in their absence."

"To be thrown away… But then…um, wait a moment. That change in behavior. If we say those conveyors were in place for a much longer period of time, it must mean someone was laying siege to that other world…for a long period of time. THEN, something happens, like maybe what? New people joining the fight?"

"New people…" the Captain muses.

"If they can somehow arrive here and do this…" she considers. "I think, if they were previously on that same world, they might have done it a long time ago. This has to relate to that change in behavior."

"All right, you have a point. Someone new who knows how to fight. And before Tana over here chews my tail again, THESE people actually DO fight."

Tana let out a soft giggle at the suggestion, followed by the rest.

"And then," Túfula resumes. "If we say the orcs are being spent on something, like we thought once upon a time, and if they made someone angry, could it be they did something to invoke this, and THAT is why they're being sent to their death…by that creature that doesn't like little things who don't behave according to plan?"

"Cu'Nar's pity, Túfu," the Captain winces. "That's a clever thought, if also cruel."

"No worse than what that same creature ever did to us," Petrith affirms.

"But here we have this other society that doesn't like things being thrown away," Túfula continues. "Not even orcs. So, it comes here to stop them, then discovers that mutant and offers to help. And now it draws a line in the city to keep what's left of the orcs in their place."

"But for how long?" Tana asks. "How long do you think it'll keep this line? Will it stay here forever, just to watch them? Are more coming to finish them? Is it holding this space for something to occur later? What if those orcs should somehow reactivate that conveyor? Or what if they should make a desperate surge into the city to fight this thing? Can it hold ALL of them back?"

"Do you have to ask so many questions?" Sulíma urges sternly. "Just when I was starting to relax a little."

"One thing is for sure," Petrith suggests. "We need to be extra careful in the city from now on. We don't want to make any offensive movements towards anything. If it's been studying us at all, maybe it knows we're here, but it's been ignoring us because all we ever do is hide inside this mine."

"Petrith," Sulíma wonders. "What about that little…" she coughs subtly, "…episode down at Camp Two?" she smiles innocently.

"Yeah, but again, I'll point out my reasoning. And if THEY are on the other side, they would probably know how to interpret it, even if one of them was spying on us out there doing it."

"All right, I suppose I can go with that."

"And even if not, I don't see how we could offend anything that shouldn't already be offended by the conveyor sending orcs across. Maybe we did them a favor."

"Uh huh…a favor. The next time I see that stone giant, I'll ask it how it appreciated the thought."

"This just leaves one last thought on my mind," Tana reflects. "Why was it running through the orcish huts, and what did it do to that shaman?"

"It was probably looking for something," Petrith suggests. "And the shaman got in the way. That display you spoke of might have been to defray attention, an excuse to give it time, maybe also to keep the masses away, as you said the others didn't go in until AFTER the shaman went flying through the roof. Then, poof again."

"Well, I suppose. But, in all the nether-space, Petrith. It can come in, do whatever, and poof, it's gone without a trace. That's dangerous! But Petrith, what could an orcish shaman have that might be of interest to a shapeshifter that can change into…well, maybe anything. And if it came from another world, it must also have access to some impressive technology as well. So, what could a shaman have that it might find so interesting that it would behave like an idiot looking for trouble?"

"Whatever it was, it must've been important."

◆◆◆◆◆

"Captain, I'm back."

Petrith announces, in his usual manner, his return from the daily patrol. He and the other scouts were returning to their usual watch points, albeit very cautiously, to scan the city for anything out of the ordinary, which at this moment could be anything at all.

"Cadet Girhani," the Captain responds. "Do we have anything out there today?"

"No orcs, but the mutants seem to be active, much more than usual. Lots of them."

"What are they doing?"

"They're moving around the streets, like they're on patrols. Some are moving along the main avenues, almost up to the edge of the city, while others were moving to and from the estates on the north side."

"Why would they go up there? The orcs generally come in from the east and mostly along the avenues. Have you ever seen orcs go up through the estates before?"

"I don't recall any, but then some of those areas are partially obscured from my vantage. I've seen them in the downtown region, the industrial section, but not too far to the north, so maybe there's something else happening up there."

"These mutants normally keep to themselves in hiding, but these last two days since that giant, they're starting to move around, and I want to know why. Is it related? And should we be worried about it?"

"Captain," Sulíma interjects. "This may be related if we consider that entity. Since that giant came in and apparently helped that one mutant, maybe there's an arrangement of some kind, and maybe we should check on it, but carefully."

"How do you mean check on it? I hope you're not thinking of going up to one of those mutants and asking it."

"Well, it's an idea. Maybe we should. If it's helping them, it might also help us. If it speaks our language, it had to learn from somewhere, right? So, is it working with the people from the Naarg uy'Sodrad, or was it studying us? If it had anything against us, and it knew we were here, I think we'd know about it by now."

"All right, let's say it knows we're here. If it wanted to make contact with us about a mutual defense agreement against the orcs, why didn't it do this a long time ago?"

"Um, all right, then let's think about some of our other statements. Maybe it only arrived just recently…like we were saying about shutting down that conveyor. If this is the case, it had to learn from the people on the ship. Maybe it does NOT know about us yet, especially since we never go outside or do anything like normal people."

"All right, point made. But I might also wish to counter by factoring in the Suuden-Aryku. We all speak the same language, you know. Maybe it had some sort of contact with them, and maybe that contact turned sour."

"Oh great, Captain, there go my last few hopes. So, you're saying it may have had an agreement with them like we had with the orcs, and this went bad, so they turned on them, and for that matter anything that sided with them?"

"It's just a thought, Suli. I have to think about these things as a precaution."

"Fine, a precaution. But at the same time, I think there's a problem with that. One, we're not Suuden-Aryku. We don't look like them, don't behave like them… And if the deal went bad…for THEM, why would they help a mutant, who might be a RESULT of them? At least indirectly."

"Indirectly?"

"Well, sort of… If we say the orcs made the mutants, and they're siding with the Suuden-Aryku, maybe we can say, very indirectly, the mutants are the result of this alliance…whatever influence it created. And those mutants aren't Suuden-Aryku either. This has to represent a dividing line somewhere."

"Possibly. And we might also need to involve Sargeras in this. Yes, you may have a point. This might also reflect on Petrith suggesting some hidden knowledge that isn't ours."

"Right. Therefore, I might also say, if they knew of us in any way, this dividing line, which seems to favor whatever those beasts did to our people, should also favor us. If they don't like things hurting other things, we are certainly victims for our part."

"This is very true."

"But regardless, we're never going to know anything unless we go out there and start asking questions."

"I don't wish to argue this, Suli, but do you remember anything of the attack? You were a child at the time and hidden away inside those shelters at your school because someone got the evacuation orders backwards. I was out on the front lines and saw our people turned into those things, and then sent out to harass the rest."

"Harass? That's all? Captain, I remember the stories, but this was three and a half centuries ago, and since then they haven't hardly come out in the sunlight except to scrounge for food. This one I saw appeared more like a disabled person than a monster who could kill anything. If the orcs were abusing him just for fun, what really happened on the day of the attack? People were running in all directions, everyone was in a panic, it was mass hysteria. If all you saw was something 'harass' the rest, can we even be sure what the orcs were doing with the mutants, or were we too busy watching our horns go flying off everywhere…as usual?"

"As usual… I detect a subtle hint in that statement, Suli. Between you, Petrith, Tana, and others…"

"We're getting tired of this, Captain. It's all we ever do. To the nether-realms with the lower rungs of the tech ladder! We're supposed to be intellectuals trying to solve problems, not run away like frightened animals. And then we had the attack where so many people apparently just stood around waiting for the end to hit. One might even say, if those mutants were supposed to frighten us back to the ship, they didn't do it well enough, for all the bodies you found lying around."

"Granted."

The Captain taps his fingers on the table mulling over the suggestion. The recent sequence of events demanded investigation, and so far, the only ones who might know anything were the ones he held the most aversion for this side of the orcs.

"All right, but we do this very carefully. Petrith, I want you to take a couple of scouts with you…females, fast runners in case things get nasty. If these mutants are out roaming in circles again, see about sending someone to follow a few, but keep out of sight."

"Do we try to interrogate any?"

"First, follow their patrols. The ones on the avenue make sense if they're watching for orcs, but maybe the ones going into the estates might be more informative. Maybe something is using a house up there as a base."

"Those on the avenue might make sense," Sulíma muses. "If we consider that godlike thing making a deal, and this is a kind of display…a show to reinforce the idea."

"Good point. So, the orcs would see them outside and realize they're not hiding anymore, because they have a big friend behind them. But this just makes it that much more delicate on our side if they don't know about us or hold any other feelings."

"Maybe so. But on the other side of it, if we could make our own deal, maybe we could also take benefit."

"And the mutants?"

"Well, so we have a few questions to answer. That's what it's

all about, right? That hidden detail. We need to know what it is…
finally."

"Right, so Petrith, watch where they go, and use caution. Approach only if the situation affords a safe opportunity."

The next day, Petrith takes Tana and one other with him to his perch on the fields outside the school overlooking the city. They settle in and watch for signs of activity on the streets. It doesn't take long before they see a patrol on the main avenue heading eastward. They watched the mutant as he slowly walked along the road, pausing intermittently to look around, and then continuing.

"That's definitely a patrol for orcs, Petrith," Tana remarks.

"A patrol for orcs, yes…" the other scout notes. "But why is he simply looking into every window? Do we have orcs running the local shops now?" she giggles.

"All right, but I'm going to make a guess and say…if anyone is watching him, like orcs out there in the bushes, it suggests he's actively patrolling and keeping a close eye for anything."

"I agree," Petrith nods. "This tells of confidence to go outside and get busy. So, I think we'll wait for one to go up north again, then have one of you go out and follow it."

"Petrith, these are mutants, and I'd be lying if I said I'm not afraid of what they're capable of based on the stories."

"Tana, those stories only tell of something harassing something, and only on the condition you weren't losing your horns so badly that you might actually turn around to see it."

"Well, all right, fine."

"Therefore, we may be wrong with some of those stories. I mean, after all, we have stories of then running around, but do we have any stories of anyone actually taking injury from them?"

"Actually, no. We had people with their horns flying off simply to see them standing there. Look, I'm not against trying, but wouldn't two be better than one? It'll provide backup in case something goes wrong."

"That's true. But just remember, we're not here to fight, especially if that entity is watching somehow. We don't want to provoke anything out of it. If you go in, you do it quietly to observe, and only interact if you feel an advantage for safety. And keep an open path behind you in case you need to run, then head straight home, not here. You'll find better support there."

"Got it. So let's see what comes up out there."

The morning progresses and more mutants show up on the streets, some travelling through the avenues to the east, and others in the industrial areas in the southern district. Then a few start making trips up north.

"There, see that one?" Petrith directs to a new sighting.

"Right, we're on it."

Tana leads as the two scouts dash off down the hill behind a row of commercial buildings lining the avenue. They peek out onto the road to check for any patrols and hurry across into an alley on the other side. They continue moving through the alley to the next street, checking for more patrols and rushing across, passing several streets in this fashion until they come up parallel to the mutant they were sent to spy on.

He was strolling along the road northward, moving sluggishly due to his deformation. He made steady progress until he came to the northern residential district of estate homes. He turned and proceeded down the cross-street to another intersection, rounding the corner and ambling along to one more intersection, where the road terminated at a T with another. He crossed the street to a large home on the other side.

The two scouts followed behind, keeping low behind walls and fences, and peering through bushes, until they saw him enter the house. They rushed around to look through a side window to see him enter the family room in the main portion of the home, then to meet with another mutant, a female.

"Boy meets girl?" the second scout whispers humorously.

"I doubt it," Tana mutters softly. "Not unless that girl has found a new profession, with so many customers making visits."

"You should talk, Tana, the way you show off to all the boys back home."

"I'm not showing off. You know as well as the rest that my clothes gave out centuries ago, and this is all I can find these days."

"All you can find? Are you even looking?" she chides playfully.

Tana smiles and nudges the girl on the shoulder as they continue to study the situation.

They move to another window further around the side, hoping to catch some of the conversation. The sounds were muffled by the glass and the language was terse. The meeting overall seemed very short, more like a briefing than a casual exchange, and then the male departs, while the female returns through the hallway to another room.

"So, now what?" the second scout asks. "That didn't give us much."

"Personally, I didn't expect it to. Barely a report to say, nothing to see. But this looks like a central operations post. I hate to say it, but I think we might need to go in and start asking questions."

"What do we say? How do you think she'll react to us?"

"Surprised, maybe," Tana considers. "I doubt she would know of us any more than anyone else around here. We just go in, keep our horns aligned, and we watch her. There are two of us, so maybe that'll keep things in our favor. Let's check the front in case there are any more out there before we go in."

They cautiously creep around the house, peeking around corners to ensure no one else is coming up the street, then move up to the front door. The door was open at this time to allow visitors to come in. They make one more quick survey before entering, and step inside slowly and quietly.

Although the term 'tiptoe' may not apply correctly with hoofed creatures, they were attempting it, nonetheless, hoping to keep the traditional clopping sounds of their hooves to a minimum. They passed through a foyer and into the family room. They noticed the typical disarray of debris, which was so commonly found everywhere in the city, but one feature stood out, a table in the far corner of the room. They carefully walked over to it.

On the table, they found a collection of small statues, some of which appeared damaged by time. They looked to be the work of a child, and took the form of various animals and people. They also saw a set of old photographs in their dusty frames. The two women turned to each other with confused glares. Tana carefully picked up a photo while the other one crouched down to examine the delicate sculptures.

On the photo, Tana saw an image of a young girl in a birthday dress, a celebration of a moment neither of them has enjoyed for centuries in this fashion. She puts it back and picks up another to see that same young girl, a young man wearing the uniform of a Sentinels officer, and accompanied by an older woman.

"Do you know these people?" she whispers.

The other scout shakes her head.

"What do we do now? Call her out, or just leave? I'm getting chills in here looking at this. It's like a shrine of some kind."

"Maybe it's a clue," Tana submits. "Old memories, and they still remember and mourn for it."

"Fine, so they mourn, are you saying they feel lonely?"

"Well, I suppose anything is possible. Maybe Suli is right. Maybe we're missing something. If this were family, and you were left behind, how would you feel?"

"I was left behind, and so were you. But yes, you're right. When we saw the ship flash out of sight, I was crying for weeks that my family was gone. But what about the mutation, and all this going on outside?"

"There's only one way to find out," Tana asserts. "And it's why we're in here."

She puts down the photo and they move into the center of the room, making sure they have a straight run to the front door if they need it.

"Who wants to call her," the scout asks. "You or me."

"Does it matter?"

"I suppose not. I'm just nervous. Maybe I'm trying to stall for time hoping we'll come to our senses."

After the prolonged discussion, which was kept at whisper level, Tana attempts to collect her nerves enough to make a call into the hall.

"Hello?"

A thump is heard from a back room, followed by heavy hoof steps into the hall. They see a shape lumbering towards them, and shivers run down their backs. They hold up their spears defensively as the large, disfigured body of the female emerges into the room.

Tyanna enters the room with a curious stare. She sees the two young women standing there, nervously holding spears and looking very frightened. She feels a cold spike of her own run through her, worrying over who these people were and why they entered her home with weapons. The three of them gazed at each other for a pensive moment.

The two young women glanced at each other tensely while staring at the disfigured female, wondering who would speak first. Finally, Tyanna initiated the conversation.

"Who are you? Why you come here?"

The scouts gaze at each other, until Tana decides to speak up, as she was the one to make the initial call.

"We don't want any trouble. We just want to talk. Can we do that?"

"Talk? Yes, we talk, but why you come here with pointy things."

"It's a dangerous world out there. We've been fighting for our lives, and we don't know who we can trust."

"You afraid..." she nods subtly.

Tyanna studies the girls up and down, examining their perfect uninjured forms, as well as their lack of proper attire.

"No clothes?"

Tana glances at herself, along with the other girl.

"It's been a long time. Our original clothes fell apart long ago. This is all we have now."

Tyanna shakes her head disapprovingly, but realizes this is likely to happen.

"You not hurt. You make home here? Orcs not hurt you?"

"Hurt? No, we hide from them."

"Good. You hide, orcs not hurt."

"Wait, I'm not sure I understand. You're actually happy the orcs didn't hurt us?"

"Yes! Why you ask? Orcs come, orcs hurt people...hurt me. You look..."

She turns slightly and points at the impact point of the seed entity on her back. The two scouts wince at the sight.

"Yes, I see you look. Me ugly. Orcs come, hurt people, hurt me."

"The mutation," Tana mumbles softly. "Right, they did this to you. But there are a lot of things we don't understand."

"What you not understand? You come here, you talk, you want understand?"

"Yes. Can you help us understand?"

"Me try. What you ask? And why you here? Why you not go to ship?"

"The ship? It was gone. We were left behind."

"Oh no..." Tyanna hangs her head and mourns. "People still here...not good. You look young. How old?"

"Me?" Tana wonders disbelievingly. "Cu'Nar's grace, I'm getting lost now. First, you're upset we didn't get to the ship, and you don't look especially happy that we're walking around naked...not that I can actually blame you for that part, and now you're asking me how old I am."

"You talk strange. What you think...me happy you here with orcs?"

"Um, well...what I mean is, um..." she vacillates.

By this time, both women were deeply muddled in the contradicting statements and interpretations. They gazed at each other while Tana tried to reconcile what was taking place.

"Just a moment... What actually happened here? We were children when the orcs attacked. We have stories from others that they did this to you, and then you started chasing others trying to hurt them. What was that about?"

Tyanna stared at the girl, trying to interpret the statement through her inhibited faculties.

"Other people?" she asks. "What other people? More people not hurt?"

"Yes, there are others like us."

"Where? You make home here?"

"Um, no, not in the city... Outside..."

"Not here. You hide from orcs. How many?"

"Um," Tana glances at her companion, unsure if she wanted to answer completely. "Well, there are a lot of us, and we all hide together."

"Many. But wait. Why not go to ship? Other people lost here same?"

"Yeah, a lot of people. Some were chased out of the city and couldn't get to the ship. And then there's us, we were in shelters hiding."

"Wait, me try understand. You hide and not go to ship. People run, and you hide? Why? All people go to ship."

"Yeah, well, we got the wrong instructions. Like I said, we were children. We were in school, and the administrators told us to hide in the shelters, not go to the ship."

"No, this not right... Elder people say, go to ship."

Tyanna was clearly disturbed by this suggestion. She glanced around the room as she tried to collect her thoughts.

"What other you ask. People go make hurt?"

"People make..." she closes her eyes and shakes her head as she tries to interpret the broken words. "The mutants... Um, yes, the orcs came, they did this mutation thing," she wags a finger at Tyanna's injury, "and those people were seen running around trying to hurt others. Why?"

"Oh...yes, me understand now. You not understand what they do. You hide, other people run, people afraid, not see what orcs do."

"That sounds like Suli now," Tana muses softly. "People losing their horns, rather than thinking rationally."

"Yes," the other girl shrugs. "And this coming from one of those we were supposed to be thinking rationally about. Now there's a rub."

Tyanna continues, "Orcs come, orcs fight, you remember?"

"Yes, well at least for the stories," Tana nods. "We didn't actually see it."

"Yes, people talk, you listen, but you not understand. Orcs come, hurt people, hurt me. Orcs make more hurt, make people run, yell, make big scare…scare other people."

"Cu'Nar's pity!" the second scout shouts. "I get it now. Terrorist tactics! The orcs were abusing them and forcing them to attack the others, or at least to make it look that way."

"The word is…harassing," Tana scorns virulently.

"Right. And all of us, running scared to begin with, now forced to run harder and faster, and even MORE scared."

Tana glared at her companion, and then at Tyanna. Her revulsion was clearly showing by now as she tried to envision the scene.

"I swear to the cu'Nar!" she screams and throws down her spear, then stomps around in circles. "And I thought I hated those orcs before. Now it's even worse! And not just for the orcs, but us as well. It's just like Suli said! We're behaving like animals now."

"Worse, Tana. Even animals learn to fight after a while. Suli was right. We were missing something big in all this."

"Missing something big?" she growls. "We're supposed to be scientists, but all we ever do is run at the first big noise with our tails between our legs. Some scientists! And for three and a half centuries! Hiding in a hole in the ground, not even TRYING to figure it out. Suli, and also the Captain, when he said we made a big fail. Cu'Nar's pity is right! He'll lose his horns completely after this."

"Now you understand," Tyanna continues. "Hurt-people not bad. You hide from orcs? Hurt-people hide from orcs. Orcs come, try hurt more, people hide."

"Yes. All right. I'm sorry," she sighs tensely. "We have stories, and a lot of people are afraid. Nobody knows what happened. Everyone was screaming and running in all directions. And this just makes things worse, for all the times we were hunted by the Suuden-Aryku. We're so conditioned to just pick up and run at the first sign of trouble, never to ask questions or try to fight back. I'm ashamed to be part of this society."

Tana pauses in her tirade as she takes a deep breath. She studies Tyanna and her deformity. This would count as her first time getting up close and personal with a mutant, so now she wanted to see what it actually was.

"What exactly is this thing?" she points. "This is from the orcs, right? Do you know what it is? I, uh..." she leans in for a better look. "It doesn't look right to me."

"Me not know name," Tyanna admits. "Me head not good. Me think maybe know, but thinking not good."

"I understand. Will you let me look at it closer?"

"Me ugly. Not good to look."

"I'm a grown woman, in case you couldn't tell for all the foliage," she attempts a soft smile. "I can handle it."

"Hmm..."

Tyanna glances at herself, feeling self-conscious about her appearance. But simply standing here was already exposing herself to view, so it hardly mattered at this point. She turned slightly for Tana and her cohort to step in closer.

Tana found herself trying to hold back her trepidation as she made a close examination of the seed entity on Tyanna's back. She referred to her companion as she made her observation.

"Look at this thing. This isn't a normal mutation. See here..." she points to a divide between surface layers. "This is her native skin, but this thing...it's a whole other thing...some kind of growth."

"Like a parasite entity," the other girl winces. "Something attached to her. Can you do that with magic?"

"I don't know. This looks like something climbed on her back and started feeding off her. Look here at her side. It's piercing through to the inside!"

"Ugh! How can a person survive something like that? I see multiple of those punching through, and on both sides..." she observes as she glances around the woman's body.

They pull back to ponder their thoughts.

"Do we have anything around here like parasites that can do this?" the girl asks.

"Not that I've ever seen," Tana shakes her head. "And certainly not on this scale for the size of it. It looks like it covers her whole back, and then some."

"Can you tell us what you think it is," she inquires of Tyanna. "What did the orcs do to make this?"

"Orcs come," Tyanna recalls. "Orcs fight, make big noise, people run. Orcs have…erm…" she searches for an appropriate word to use. "Gun. Yes, gun. Suuden'kai give gun to orcs."

"A gun!" the two scouts shout.

"In all the nether-space!" Tana shrieks. "Those tail-yanking Suuden-Aryku are going to drive me insane! A gun? To do what! Shoot something at you?"

"Tana," the other girl wonders. "This thing is biological. And we do know our science is able to engineer stuff."

"Oh! Wonderful! So they engineer something as a terrorist weapon! And for what? Simply to make sure we don't have any horns left over?"

"Well, it would certainly make us run that much harder, but this one is simply nasty."

"All right. Next. Um…" she flusters. "Mutants…outside. Yes. What about recently? As if we actually need to ask this by now. We see them outside walking around. What are they doing?"

"Yes, people go look for orcs," Tyanna explains. "Orcs not come, but we look. Orcs stay out. No more come hurt people."

"And they come here and talk to you?"

"Yes, they go out, look for orcs, come here, tell me what they see."

"And also that big thing," the second scout offers. "What was that? Do you know?"

"Big thing?" Tyanna wonders.

"Yeah, we saw something big…really big. We think it was yelling at some orcs. One of us saw it up close and was really frightened. She told us she saw a mutant out there and the orcs were hurting it, and this thing showed up and scared them away."

"Yes, big thing…"

Tyanna now reflected on Kaliya's new god image and the

instructions relating to how she was supposed to describe this to the others.

"Big thing… You see this? Hmm, yes, me say we have friend. Friend helps keep orcs away."

"Where did this friend come from?" Tana asks. "We think we saw it over in Camp One…um, the orc camp outside the city. Do you remember that one?"

"Orc home…yes, me remember. You go there?"

"Yes, we're trying to spy on them, to watch them. I was out there one time and saw something scary. I don't know what it was, but I think it might be this same friend."

"What you see?"

"I saw a big animal kill one orc and then…um…" she coughs gently and turns to glance at her friend, "…well, I was scared really bad. I saw that same orc, which I thought was dead, get up and walk into the camp, then shut down the conveyor they have in there."

"Agh," Tyanna winces. "That not good to see. Friend tells me orcs have conv-yer in home. They go fight people from ship."

"The Naarg uy'Sodrad? Cu'Nar's grace, so is this friend working with them?"

"Friend helps, yes, but friend says not tell much. Hurt-people heads not good. Keep words small."

"Right, I get it. But what about us? I mean, can this friend be our friend too?"

"Yes! All our people. Friend fights Suuden'kai and Sarg-us."

"Oh! So we finally found someone to fight Sargeras? It's about time!"

"Yes. Me not like fight. But me understand must fight. Me not happy, maybe people get hurt."

"Better to fight and TRY to live, than run and get hurt for sure."

"Maybe. Many times, people hurt. Me not like. Me sad. But me think friend want to talk, ask who are you, where are you, how many…ask many things."

"Well, yes, I suppose that makes sense. How do we meet this friend?"

"Friend not here now, but comes to talk. Me tell friend, we all talk."

"All right, so should we come back here, or will your friend come looking for us?"

"Does your friend know about us, maybe?" the other scout asks.

"Me think friend not know. Me not know. You come here, now me know."

"So, this friend didn't know about us before."

"All right," Tana affirms. "This might suggest it's new here, and maybe like we said, in relation to this change in the orcs' behavior. Someone gave instructions to jump through that hole in space as a harassment tactic, but it's a death trap on the other side. Now it's here to stop this. But I think before we can go too far with this, we need to report in. The Captain needs to know what's going on out here."

"Not just that, Tana, but we need to better organize ourselves. I mean, cu'Nar's pity, we've been hiding from these people all our lives when we should've been trying to help them."

"I know," she moans. "But how could we know about all this? Most of us were kids at the time and too young to do anything."

"And the rest were simply too scared of what those orcs did to our people with this crazy magic thing no one understands."

"Yes! And this is the most ironic of all. Isn't it the purpose of our science faction to study these things? But is anyone actually doing it?" she huffs. "And now we have this thing…whatever it is… running around as a five-story tall monster. We'd better make a good effort to become friends, and fast."

"Yeah, so let's get back there. This will unravel a lot of people's horns."

"Oh yes! And I'm ducking under a table when this many goes flying. Um, by the way," Tana redirects at the woman. "What's your name? I think the Captain might want to know."

The elder woman takes a deep breath before answering.

"Me name is Tyanna."

"Tyanna what?"

Tyanna now tries to voice the remainder of her name, which she has not used for centuries. And even though she was conscientious of her deformity, and her inhibitions to expose herself, she realized she needed to reveal her full identity.

"Tyanna…Nazég."

Now shivers run through both girls as they associate the name. It was famous, and not just for her personal merit.

"Cu'Nar's pity," the second scout whines. "Not that one. Velen's wife?"

"Those horrible little creatures," Tana scorns with her face flushing now. "If this doesn't finish it for me…"

"Which horrible creatures, Tana? The orcs, or the Suuden-Aryku and their terrorist toys."

"Yes, them as well! Especially them! We need to tell the others, and fast."

"Yeah, tell them, and then listen as they scream every curse word they can conjure up?"

"Well…" she shrugs timidly.

"All right, Madam Nazég, we need to go now, but I promise you we'll do whatever we can to help from now on."

"Good," she assents. "You help people here, we try help you. We all work now."

The two girls rush outside with their heads in a tizzy. They dash away through the streets, no longer concerned about remaining hidden from the mutants, as everything they thought they knew about them was apparently wrong. They arrive on the main avenue in plain sight of everything, including Petrith at his post, and Tana begins shouting at the top of her lungs.

"Petrith, get your tail down here! We've got work to do!"

Petrith saw them running along the street, then halting at the intersection, even though he could also see several mutants shambling along not far away. He stands up and peers down at them, amazed that they would be standing out in the open and shouting.

"What are you doing out there? What about them?" he points at a couple of mutants just down the road.

"I said get down here, Mister Petrith Girhani!" she roars. "We're up to our tail-pits in trouble. We need to report this in, now! They were never the problem, but WE sure were enough times!"

"They... We..." he flusters.

"Yes! Our limp-horned attitudes to run at the first sign of trouble, and never to ask questions about it, may have cost the lives of people who were just as much victims as we ever were. And our droop-tailed manners to never stand up for ourselves is once again preventing us from simply surviving!"

Tana and her team returned hurriedly to the hideout with their report. The astonishing revelations shocked everyone in the room about the wrongful tales and long-standing abusive behavior of the orcs on their former citizens. These people had been victimized more than what the refugees in the hideout were considered to be. But the news hit hardest with two people in particular.

Sulíma had gone into an uncontrolled wailing after hearing of her best friend's mother being turned into a mutant. Worse, she now couldn't help but to think Kaliya was killed at the same time, since Tyanna was cut down in the streets before reaching the Naarg uy'Sodrad. Petrith sat next to her, no better for the wear, but trying to comfort his dear friend. Tana cradled the girl while Túfula hovered nearby trying to console the rest.

Captain Lapäli sat on the edge of his desk with his head in his hands, feeling his own failure for not investigating some part of this much earlier. Now he was contemplating what to do about this latest disaster of misinterpretation.

"We need to get control of ourselves here," he begins gently. "Suli, Petrith, just because Madam Nazég was hit doesn't mean anything where the girl is concerned. Maybe she got away after her mother went down."

"Captain," Túfula suggests. "I've heard she was a star athlete on the track, so I think she should've gotten away. She was smart, fast, and well, I don't know what else after that. I never knew her personally, but I wish I did."

"I remember her in my gym class," Tana reflects. "We didn't do anything together, we were in different sports classes, but we shared space. I remember she was talented, and popular with a lot of people."

"I remember when we were little," Sulíma tries to recall through her blubbering. "Back then, I used to visit her house. We'd go out for walks, go shopping, and her mother would sometimes take us to the beach. We did everything. And Petrith too, we were a team together."

"But none of this means she's dead," the Captain reaffirms. "Only that this poor woman got hit, and apparently even that didn't stop her. Just look at her; she's organizing the others into a city patrol, something we should've done years ago once you kids were old enough. She's actually outperformed me, and I'm a Captain of the Sentinels!" he attempts a mote of humor.

"Captain," Tana asserts. "With respect, we didn't have a god image to back us up in those days. But speaking of organizing, this simply reminds me of something, and I feel a need to speak up on it now."

"Oh no, not you again. All right, what is it, Tana?"

"I'm sorry, Captain, but I'm angry enough to pull out a decade's worth of horns, and not simply at the orcs, or even the Suuden-Aryku, but us as well."

"Us? How do you mean? As if I actually need to ask this by now."

"Yes, that too. We're supposed to be intellectuals, but we're so conditioned from all our suffering due to the Suuden-Aryku that we behave more like animals that pick up and run at the first big noise. We don't ask questions, we don't try to understand anything, and most importantly, we don't FIGHT! Granted, the Suuden-Aryku have a big nasty military now, but is it any better that we became their favorite victims? We probably should've turned this around several millennia ago when it became so obvious how they WERE hunting us like animals. Sir, we need to grow a few teeth and claws if we're going to survive like this. To all the nether-realms with whatever tools we have, as it doesn't matter if we don't learn how to use them."

"Tana, I would tend to agree, at least in principle. But I'm not the one who makes those decisions, and unfortunately, our people don't like warfare."

"Precisely! WE don't like warfare, but THEY apparently do, and we became their targets for it. If the ship was found so quickly after this last jump, or maybe followed and attacked as soon as it set down, that's just one more example of how they treat us. How many people have we lost among all the worlds we crossed in this time? We don't like warfare…but do we like dying so much better?"

"All right, I get the message. It's a bad situation that never improved, even though we hoped it would. But it was a vain and empty hope by people who simply didn't want to believe in anything else."

"You know," Túfula interjects. "I'm reminded of my father and his stories of our old history. The Eracyodines…what they were before they became us. But it seems we're still more THEM than US, at this point…prey animals."

"Anyway," Tana asserts. "We need to get together with these people and form up teams. If they're out there watching for orcs, we need to back them up. We're better equipped, even if it is just sharpened sticks, and if we can reclaim any part of the city along the way, that gives us the chance to rebuild something. And this time, it had better involve weapons that go boom!"

"And what about this friend of hers," Túfula offers. "If it really is working with the people from the Naarg uy'Sodrad, that answers several important questions for us, not the least of which has to do with the orcs, their conveyors, this migration, and what's happening on the other side of it."

"You're right, Túfu," the Captain admits. "I suppose there's no more arguing the point. They met someone, and that someone must have some remarkable talent. It's about time…"

"That's what I said in that house!" Tana chuckles ironically. "And this remarkable talent might actually be living proof of that riddle of metaphysics," she glares at Túfula briefly. "Maybe THEY know the answer."

"I still say it had to be recent, though," Sulíma accedes. "That change in behavior had to be triggered by something."

"They found new friends. Those Suuden-Aryku must've splashed in something that backfired on them."

"And they could be allies," Túfula adds. "And maybe good ones. I think we need to make a strong impression to become friends with this thing. In the cu'Nar's name, like Tana said, it could help us retake the whole city!"

Tana nods, "Tyanna said they apparently have in mind to fight this all the way back to Sargeras. THAT might be a good indication of how determined they are. It may simply be this friend and whatever attitude it has for him, but it might also be the rest of our people finally learning their lesson. Cu'Nar be blessed for that."

"Incredible," the Captain muses. "But I still feel a need to take this slow. We might have a big friend on our side, but there are a lot of orcs over there, and we can't trust them to simply stay on their side of this line it drew. Like we said earlier; what if they try making a large-scale charge at us, or at this thing, hoping to take it down? So far, all we've seen is a god image to frighten them, but can it wage war with them?"

"Well, all right," Túfula admits. "You have a point, but maybe the god image is all we need for now."

"I don't think I want to take that chance until we're ready with a few contingencies."

"Fine, but we still need to make contact somehow."

"I agree, but how, that's the question."

✦ ✦ ◆ ✦ ✦

Kaliya had just finished another day of scouting. It was the first day of a new weekend, and she made another run to Ruuki uy'Daan in her continued effort to locate the conveyors relating to Portals Two and Three. On this occasion, she made runs along two more rivers further west from her previous run.

"I'm sorry, my Lord," she admits. "I feel like I'm failing you in all this."

"Again, do not despair," he comforts. "It could simply be we are mistaken in our earlier conjectures, but we will persevere. Like I said, scouting is a patient game. We know it must be out there. Perhaps this conveyor is found on a smaller tributary, not the main river. Our view through those windows was very narrow, so we are making a lot of assumptions here. But we will study the maps and begin anew tomorrow. Go find yourself a good meal and some rest."

Kaliya makes her salute and leaves the room. She returns to the guildhall cafeteria for dinner, and then back to her dorm room to sleep.

The next morning, after she finishes her breakfast and freshens up, she heads over to Firstfall to meet with Thaelyn and his officers. Once again, Kailen was present to assist in studying the map. He greets her as she arrives inside.

"Good morning, Kaliya," he announces. "Did you sleep well?"

"Reasonably. I had a lot of thoughts going around inside my head, so it was hard to get settled."

"Well, try to pull yourself together. We have a few items for you to check on today, but we're waiting for sunrise over there before we begin."

"How much longer?"

Thaelyn pauses to pull out his timepiece and check the time.

"I would suggest another two hours until it is light enough to begin."

He turns to the map to continue.

"Look here and follow along with me. We will return to the east again. This first river you crossed seems like a fairly substantial one, according to this diagram. Due to the region being so flat, there are very few opportunities for tributaries to develop, except for a spotting of hills here and there further to the east and central to the plains. These hills do not present a very good potential for creating a respectable source of runoff, but at the moment, it is all we have. I was examining this earlier to see if there were any lakes or other bodies that could support rivers draining out of them, but I do not see too many of those, either. Therefore, we will have you make your first run out there to see how it appears. You will then return back, and we will continue from there."

"Sounds good. I'd also like to make a quick run to check on my mother to see if anything new has developed in the city, in case we need to take some kind of action."

"Very well, that should not take long. Once we have a bit of daylight, we can attend to that. Meanwhile, we should reexamine these hills in the west to see where we can go next."

"My Lord, one thing that bothers me, at least as much as the missing conveyors, is that I didn't see those solar arrays, either. Even if the conveyors are hidden in the underbrush, those solar panels would need to be out in the open to catch the sunlight, and that would be an obvious sight from the air."

"Indeed, this is true. And in those hills, where the other equipment might be hidden, those arrays would need to be positioned such to make efficient use during the day, likely on top of a hill or along a side that would catch most of the daylight sun."

"And I didn't see anything, just trees and grass."

"I wonder if the conveyors may have been removed from the area," Kailen offers. "Or maybe the Suuden-Aryku actually did come back to reclaim some old equipment."

"We could possibly suggest this for Portal Three," Thaelyn responds. "But how do we explain Portal Two with the severed head coming through to our side? I somehow do not believe the Suuden-Aryku would stoop so low as to throw a head into the conveyor. It seems much too primitive an action for them."

"Yes, of course," he relents. "And why would they do it as a demonstration to other orcs or if they believe us to be in control on this side. It holds no meaning in that case."

"What about this," the General considers. "If the assembly came under attack, could it simply be removed from sight, maybe hidden or buried in the underbrush?"

"This is a good suggestion," Thaelyn accedes. "And it could answer part of our mystery. But if it is, our work to discover the truth may be even more difficult without perhaps some very close inspections."

Kaliya listened to the statements and tried to recall the images of her patrols, along with the thoughts that had been disturbing her all night. Then, an idea suddenly flashed in her mind.

"Removed from the area," she muses. "Or perhaps buried or something. What about the orcs? What if they moved them somewhere, maybe to carry away as trophies or collector's items?"

"Given enough manpower," Thaelyn suggests. "I suppose the orcs might have the capacity to transport such equipment, but there are a few obvious flaws opposing this theory. First, this equipment would require a significant level of technical understanding to disassemble it. Second, where would they transport it to, and why?"

"Technical understanding…yeah, unless you simply try hacking it to pieces, which is much more likely of them. As for where… this is a big question, as I couldn't find any active camps, not even nomadic ones, although I did see a few bridges on those rivers…"

"Bridges?" Kailen asks.

"Bridges!" Thaelyn exclaims. "What manner of bridges?"

Kaliya jumps at the sudden response, darting her eyes between the two men.

"Oops, I guess I still need a few lessons on orcish culture," she admits timidly. "Do orcs build bridges? I thought they looked a little unusual, but I wasn't sure what the orcs were doing over there, so I just skipped over them thinking they were trying to build a roadway of some kind."

"While I can certainly understand your confusion, and we cannot know precisely what they might be attempting over there, or what the Suuden-Aryku or even Darumon may have shared with them, but my experience with orcs tells me they are not very good at bridge building. What I recall of it from our own experience is most often very crude designs using felled timbers across smaller streams.”

“I think I might concur from our side,” Kailen nods. “At least, during the time we were there.”

Kaliya now perks up with a renewed sense of contribution again.

“Well then, maybe I do have something after all. Yes, I recall seeing several bridges, one on each of those rivers. They were all towards the northern end of the region, some of them in the middle of nowhere. But they didn’t look like simple logs felled across the water, and these rivers were more than just small streams. And further, one of these was right next to a camp.”

Thaelyn had been leaning over the table while he examined the map. As he listened to this new report, he stood up and considered the suggestion.

“Did you get a close look at them?”

“No, I was passing well overhead at the time, but they looked like well-built bridges, maybe a bit crude in design, but definitely made by someone who put some time into it.”

“Can you recall any of these locations specifically, well enough to revisit them briefly for a close inspection?”

“I think I can try for that camp, and work my way across. If I’m right, these things may have been part of a road of some kind, so they might travel in a straight line, or generally so.”

Thaelyn returns to the map for another review.

“Where was this camp?”

“On the first river, the one more to the east,” she replies as she studies the map. “I’m going to guess about here,” she points at a location. “It was just below a bunch of trees on the open plain. The camp was on my left, so to the east side of the river.”

“Meaning someone had to cross the river if they were travelling to or from the west. This still supports our theory of someone in the northwest quadrant, even without any obvious signs of habitation. But then we must ask ourselves who. I find it hard to believe orcs would desire to disassemble a complex set of technological gear, unless they wanted trophies of some kind and, as you say, simply hacked them to bits to cart away in fragments."

"Personally," Kailen admits. "I can think of better items to make trophies out of than broken pieces of a conveyor assembly."

"I as well, but for the moment, we may need to consider a number of possibilities."

✦ ✦ ✦ ✦ ✦ ✦ ✦

"Good morning, Petrith," Sulíma yawns as she rises from bed.

Sulíma, Túfula, and Petrith, among others who shared the communal bedroom quarters, were just waking up to a bell being rung through the tunnels by a watchman who made it his duty to sleep outside and catch the first rays of sunlight so he could wake up the rest. Life inside the mine had no proper sunrise or sunset. And with no clocks to tell time, a system had to be created to help the people measure the beginning and ending of each day.

Petrith was lying on his bed, staring at the ceiling. He grunted a response to Sulíma's welcome, but did not speak.

"Petrith? Are you alright?" she asks softly.

The shock from the scouting report a couple of days earlier was still unsettled. Most of the people felt a sense of relief at the situation with the mutants, feeling free to pass in and out of the city more regularly. But there was also a muted sense of rage at the orcs for their disrespectful behavior, and furthermore, frustration for their own lack of attentiveness. However, between Sulíma and Petrith, they were still in depression.

"I'm fine, just laying here thinking," he responds quietly.

"About what?"

"Nothing special... I woke up some time ago and couldn't get back to sleep."

"Yeah, I think I know what you mean. I'm having trouble sleeping too. I keep having a lot of old memories pop up."

"I have that too sometimes, but this is different. I had another of those stupid dreams. Last night and also yesterday during my nap."

"Uh oh, more? Petrith, this isn't healthy."

"You're telling me? At least she wasn't in the shower this time."

"All right, so what was she doing this time?"

"What are you two talking about?" Túfula pipes up as she eavesdrops on the conversation.

"Túfu," Sulíma explains. "Petrith has been having some strange dreams off and on for…well, a few centuries, it seems. He sees Kali in them, doing various things."

"What was this about a shower?" she smirks. "Is our little Petrith getting urges lately?"

"You may be right, Túfu, so what should we do about it?" Sulíma grins.

"Will the two of you quit fighting over me?" he declares buoyantly. "I'm virile enough to take both of you on!"

The two girls giggle spontaneously.

"Anyway," he continues. "These were actually kind of boring by comparison. I had one last night where I simply saw her sleeping in bed."

"Oh wow, Petrith. That sounds exciting!"

"Yeah, I know, although it looked like a comfortable bed. And the one yesterday was almost as bad. She was sitting in a chair, and again looked like she was sleeping."

"Sleeping in a chair?" Sulíma yips. "How dull! No wild adventures across the open plains fighting great beasts and bringing home trophies? Petrith, you need to sparkle up those dreams of yours a bit more."

"What's so special about these dreams to begin with?" Túfula asks.

"First, he says he saw her in a militia uniform doing patrols, or something. More recently, he told me about how she was in a different uniform and apparently in some kind of training academy."

"Isn't that backwards? Shouldn't she be in training before she goes out on patrols?"

"Well, you know Petrith," Sulíma chuckles. "The weirdest one was this shower scene."

"I'm not sure if I want to know about this one."

"Oh Túfu, poor little Petrith, he didn't get any action, he just watched…and studied how she was washing herself. Not the important parts, but rather the soap she was using. You know…the one thing a young guy like him should NOT be paying attention to."

"You're kidding me!" she huffs. "And here I was thinking we might have a vigorous young stud on the loose, ready to satisfy our wildest fantasies. So, what was so special about this soap that it took his eyes away from her body? I'm assuming she was naked?"

"Oh yes, and then there's that. We were talking about this once, and it's actually a little strange."

"Why is it so strange, as if he's never seen a naked girl before. You do remember those bushes near the pond, right?" she smirks.

"Yes, Túfu, and you know, we once had a serious conversation about this. He admits that he and a few of the boys did take a peek on occasion. But this was way back, I think."

"Oh! So, at least a few of those hoof prints might be real? And who were they peeking at, any of us?"

"Túfu," Petrith mentions. "That's not really the point Suli is trying to make. And at this time, I don't know if I could answer…it was so long ago. All I actually remember is a bunch of girls taking a bath, and some of us got curious to see how the other half looks."

"All right, I get it. Youthful curiosity, we all get that at some moment. But why is it strange for Kali."

"Because the last time I saw her was as a young girl in school, not a full-grown woman taking a shower in all her mature feminine glory."

Túfula stared at him in amusement, trying to envision the scene.

"Well, all right, but I still think it shouldn't be so strange. If you know what a fully grown woman looks like…after all, we all took those adult lessons with the instructors at our first centennial, right? And, generally speaking, we all look very closely similar to one another. So, I think it's just the role of the imagination. And I think the imagination doesn't need much. Just look at Suli here, or Tana, for what little clothing…if you can call it that…she actually wears."

"Yeah, her example is a good one," Sulíma admits. "I think the only bit of leather she uses is a...what do they call it?"

"A loincloth," Túfula offers. "In her case, a very small one just barely wrapping around. She claims she loves the feel of nature, and doesn't need or desire anything else."

"Especially in this jungle heat..."

"Well, yeah, we have that too. And then she has a thin strip hung around her shoulders and draping down in front. The rest is just leaves and ferns she weaves together as a kind of grass skirt and top."

"But she still has a lot of open skin."

"But not the really important areas, Suli," Petrith admits. "So, for as much as the two of you might complain about her swinging her tail and showing off, I don't see it this way. She's clearly very comfortable with herself, so I respect her choice. She says she leaves what little leather we actually do collect for others who don't spend as much time out there putting as much wear and tear on things."

"It's still a little strange for someone of our society," Túfula muses.

"She was always like that," Sulíma recalls. "Even when she was little, she liked running around out there. Her normal clothes didn't last long after that, for all the tears and shredding they took in the underbrush."

"All right, Petrith," Túfula asserts. "So, you see Kali naked, and you apparently didn't show an interest in that, maybe because you have so many real-world examples to stare at. Then, what was it you were looking at, in this case?"

"Her soap..."

"Oh great..." she rolls her eyes. "Yeah, Suli, I think you may be right. How do you suggest we correct this?"

"This will take some work," she considers. "Probably both of us combined to remind him what girls are good for."

"All right, so do we take turns, or attack him in a joint effort?"

The two of them let out a round of bold giggles.

"Cu'Nar's grace," Petrith relents. "The Captain is right about one thing. We're all hitting that age where things are going to get steamy soon."

"We have nine hundred young people," Túfula accedes. "All coming of age and getting anxious. And so far, most of us, as far as I know, have been holding back on it, if only because of our close quarters in this mine and no real privacy."

"That's an explosive situation."

"So…why soap? What was so special about her using soap that got your attention?"

"It was a solid bar, not a liquid or anything we might be familiar with from our own experience."

Túfula halts as she stares blankly at him for his mention.

"A solid bar of soap…" she emits slowly. "Petrith, where did you get this idea of a solid form of soap? I'm no expert on the matter, but from what I understand of dreams, you need at least a little something in real life to give you the ideas that become your dreams. And we don't even KNOW of solid soap, let alone dream of it."

"I know. Suli and I talked about this once. She mentioned something you were talking about at one time, and this just didn't make sense."

"Was that before or after the dream?"

"Um, we talked about this after the dream."

"So the dream came first. Interesting. Well, maybe you heard of something somewhere. I suppose that isn't too difficult to suggest."

"How about the indoor waterfall shower?"

"An indoor waterfall shower?" she raises her brow. "Now THAT is interesting. You must have some really nice dreams inside there. Was she in some sort of luxury resort?"

"No, I think this was that training academy again, and likely after some kind of Phys. Ed. class, with a bunch of others going off to a shower room."

"And they were all aliens," Sulíma smirks cutely.

Now Túfula lurches forward on the edge of her bed and glares at the two of them.

"Just a moment here!" she shouts. "Petrith, what is it you're actually saying? Is this related to that other training you mentioned earlier?"

"I think so. I've seen her in several dreams so far...recently that is, and apparently in this same training academy, but in different areas, I think."

"What?!" she screeches. "Tell me more. What did you see?"

"Túfu," Sulíma contends. "What is this? Why are you so interested suddenly?"

"Suli, I don't know yet, give me a moment. Petrith, can you tell me about these other dreams?"

"Well, like Suli said, they've been going on for a long time now. I recall once seeing her in what I think might be a classroom. But not young, like we were in those early days. This was easily at or beyond the first centennial."

"Really!"

"Later, I saw her in a militia uniform, often wandering around outdoors in different settings, but I couldn't really tell the details of it."

"Why not?"

"Everything was blurry. I could see Kali clearly, but everything around her was very blurry. I could only pick up a few impressions, like the ground under her hooves being grass or dirt, or a floor."

"But nothing else? Strange... What about other objects, or people?"

"I could sometimes see movement, like other people, but again very indistinct. I could also hear sounds, but just like the image, it was also indistinct, or maybe to say muffled."

"Let me think a moment. You could see her clearly, but everything around her, both sight and sound, was hazy. Could you tell if these locations were familiar to you?"

"Not in the least."

"Well, like to say a jungle, like what we have outside?"

"No jungles. Grass sometimes, barren dirt, maybe rocky hills or outcroppings."

"That doesn't necessarily sound like anything nearby, but then again, the imagination can do weird things on occasion."

"Túfu," Sulíma urges. "Can you tell me what you're driving at?"

"I'm trying to analyze these dreams, Suli."

"So, are you now trying to play the paranormal scientist on us?" she grins. "He's having visions of strange places and strange people."

"Well, Tana did say once how this is supposed to be our science faction."

"Oh, right. I forgot!" she giggles.

"Suli, I'm actually trying to be serious here. I have an idea in mind, but I need to study it. Petrith, what about these people? Aliens? What do you mean?"

"Well, again, it was blurry," he reflects. "But most of them appeared shorter, and one in particular I would see often seemed to have gray skin. And they apparently spoke a different language from ours."

"Cu'Nar's grace!" she wheezes. "How close would you say you were to Kali in the old days?"

"We were very close, I think. Suli was also close, of course, and I think the two were trying to compete for my attention."

"You may be right, Petrith," Sulíma sighs. "And it seems I still am."

"Let's not get our horns locked here," Túfula advises. "I don't know of any rules that say we can't all be good friends and share our affections. It's better than fighting."

"All right, Túfu," she smiles gently. "But you definitely need to get your tail in motion if you want to keep up with me."

"Oh, cu'Nar help me. Petrith, what else can you tell me? What about this academy?"

"These are more recent dreams, the last couple of years, I think."

"Couple of years..." she muses distantly. "That almost sounds like the timing of this change in the orcs' behavior."

"Uh oh. That mysterious...thing...that happened? But then, um..."

"Just go on with your dreams for now."

"All right. I sometimes see her in what I think is a classroom. She's sitting at a desk and seems focused on something ahead of her."

"But she's an adult now?"

"Yeah...just like us, actually."

"Incredible…" she gasps. "Can you hear anything?"

"Well, again, it's not clear, but I think there are other people around her, and I hear talking…a lot of talking, nonstop."

"Nonstop talking? Cu'Nar's grace, what kind of class just throws stuff at you nonstop?"

"Not the kind I want to attend," Sulíma winces.

"Then there was some kind of combat practice," he continues.

"Combat…so this might relate to that militia thing?"

"I have no idea, Túfu, she wasn't holding a gun of any kind."

"What was she using?"

"Sometimes I saw her with a long stick."

"A long stick?!" she yips urgently. "Like a spear?"

"No, not a spear, more like a staff…and other times using just bare hands and hooves; punching and kicking, spinning, dodging… like she was working out on a target of some kind."

"Petrith!" she yelps. "What kind of military practice does that? Not ours! That sounds like some kind of martial arts. My father would sometimes tell me stories of the old days. He was a historian if you recall."

"Right, I remember."

"And so he liked to share stories about things. He used to love the classic era of our history, but even THAT doesn't accurately match what you're describing. How is she dressed on this occasion?"

"Some kind of cloth uniform…"

"Every time?"

"Yeah, even after that shower scene. She finished, picked up a towel, went to what I think was a locker room, and got dressed in that same uniform."

"Grace of the cu'Nar, Petrith!" she screeches and grabs her horns. "And you can actually SEE her like this?"

"Túfu!" Sulíma shouts. "What are you yelling at?"

"Suli, I don't think these are simple dreams. He's showing up something like a kind of Sight. She's actually doing this!"

"Sight? Like he's actually seeing her? But Túfu, if we're saying she's taking lessons, who is she taking lessons with, if this sort of training is so alien…" her voice cuts off abruptly.

"Suli, I think you just answered your own question. Petrith, did you see anything else?"

"Well, yeah, I did. I didn't want to mention this to anyone, especially her," he thumbs at Sulíma. "Knowing how she probably wouldn't let up on me for a month, thinking I'm crazy or something."

"Well, all right, but what was it?"

"This was when I came home from a really boring patrol and took a nap. I was feeling a little nostalgic, so I pulled out my old class photo for another look, recalling old times, and then I felt tired, so I went to sleep. In this dream, or whatever it was, I saw her doing practice again…I think."

"You only think?"

"I'm not sure what it was. I think she was outside, and focused on something in the distance. I could see a strange glow surrounding her. Then I saw her extend her hand, and I could swear I saw something fly out of it."

"Did she have anything in her hand?"

"No, it was empty. It reminded me of some of the stories I heard from the others about the orcs and their magic, but that's ridiculous, isn't it?"

"In all the nether-space!" Túfula whispers. "She's learning magic, on top of everything else."

"All right, Túfu," Sulíma ushers sternly. "Now, if you're finished, will you please explain to the rest of us what you're talking about? What kind of Sight? Like a prophetic vision or something?"

"No, I don't think this would fit a prophetic vision. This sounds more like it might be real-time. My father once told me the Elder Council kept a lot of secrets, one of them being telepathy, saying it's a big security risk. It was against the rules, but he told me a little bit about it just to give me something to think about once. He explained to me how our research faction once studied a number of interesting mental abilities. Some of these, like telepathy, we were able to train in a few people."

"Like Velen, right? I remember people saying he could use telepathy."

"Right, that's one example. A few of these others were theory, and still under investigation, at least until Sargeras showed up and spoiled things for us."

"Yeah, he spoiled a lot of things for everybody, it seems."

"But Petrith here is showing what I think my father once described as clairvoyance."

"Clairvoyance? What's that?"

"Basically, it's the ability of the mind to see other places, or people, especially if you're familiar with them so you can focus in on it. He knows Kali very well. The location may be blurry, but she's apparently very clear to him. If he could allow himself to gain better control of it, maybe he could learn to focus on it better. But Petrith, you need to admit to yourself, you're not just dreaming. You might be projecting your mind outside your body when you do this."

"Cu'Nar's pity, Túfu," he relents. "So, I'm not just seeing weird visions of her naked in a shower, I'm actually seeing HER naked in the shower? I need to go back there for another look..." he muses mischievously.

"Hey!" Sulíma gripes. "What about me in all that?"

"Well, the next time you and Túfu go out to the pond, let me know so I can take a quick nap. Then I can watch you from behind those bushes without leaving any hoof prints."

"Um, Túfu," she mutters nervously. "I think you're giving him some bad ideas now."

"Well," she concedes. "At least this time, his focus will be on something other than soap," she giggles. "But so long as it's only his vision projecting outside, not his consciousness, like my father once said about this Prodigy Child thing."

"The what?"

"Yeah, this was the latest and greatest secret the Council was talking about not long before the attack. Apparently, someone found a Prodigy Child, and was trying to research it."

"Túfu," Sulíma urges cautiously. "For those of us not on the Council, what is a Prodigy Child?"

"The biggest secret of all they were keeping to themselves. The story goes that long ago on Azgarén, there were these children who could project themselves outside their bodies. The body was lying in bed asleep, but an image projection was outside talking to people. It was a very rare thing, and no one could really understand what it was."

"That sounds creepy just listening to it, to say nothing of being there watching it."

"Then, someone here found one, so my father said there was a research project going on at the old university to try to understand what it was. Of course, it didn't get very far before the orcs decided to attack."

"Wonderful. Do we know who it was?"

"No, no names were mentioned that I know of. And since we don't see it here, I have to assume whoever it was either left on the ship or, um…well…"

"Right, I get it. So, what we're trying to say is Petrith is losing his mind, you're helping him lose his mind, you're also causing ME to lose MY mind, and Kali is training with a bunch of aliens using some weird combat art and magic. Yeah. Well, it's back to work for me," she chirps. "I wonder what machines I can try fixing today that'll break tomorrow."

✦✦✦

"Are you ready, Kaliya?"

"Yes, my Lord, my first stop is that camp to check the bridge, then travel west to find the others for comparison. I'll return back as soon as I can."

Kaliya is preparing for her new scouting run, having already projected herself and now making a quick review with Thaelyn before leaving. She fades from view and transports herself to the region of the camp she once found in the prairie by the river. When she arrives, she finds herself in the sky above, as recalled from her memories, however she forgot to change into a bird, and now she begins plummeting to the ground.

"Oops! I guess I should've thought about this a little bit better," she chuckles. "I could change, but what's the point, I can see where I want to go anyway."

She gazes at the ground below near the camp and folds herself to that location, reappearing in a standing position on the edge of the camp. It is early sunrise, and the sky is showing the initial hues of daytime.

She looks around the area briefly, checking for tracks or impressions in the soil left behind by objects that might have been sitting there. But in the many months since the close of the portal, she figures the imprints have probably all been obscured by the elements. So she strolls over to examine the bridge.

She studies it for the style and quality of the craftsmanship. It was hewn out of cut logs and lashed together by rope, not the sort of construction Thaelyn was suggesting of orcish design.

"This thing looks strong enough to haul a wagon over," she observes.

She steps out onto it and strolls midway across, studying the support pilings and rails, and the crossbeams forming the deck.

"This takes engineering skill. And this wood looks fairly recent, too. Not old, like from years or decades past. And I doubt it would still be here if it were centuries old. Not sitting in water like it is. It's not preserved in any way."

She surveys the local region for any forested areas that could supply the wood, and sees something to the north. She changes to a bird and zips across for a quick review, settling on the ground nearby several stumps. She examines them up close.

"This looks recent. I can see marks of chopping them down, and the cuts might be from metal tools rather than stone. That leaves out orcs, unless we say they scavenged something. And the quantity might be enough for that thing down there," she glances at the bridge again.

When she feels confident that she has studied the scene long enough, she changes into a bird again and heads west, using her ability to accelerate across long distances to shorten her travel time. She finds the next river and stops to examine the local bridge. It was not necessarily in a straight line from the first, not that she had an accurate way to measure it, but it certainly was near enough to represent an association.

"This looks generally the same," she muses. "The same construction style, and the wood looks the same age. This has to be something like a road, and fairly recent. I wonder…"

There were no camps nearby, so she begins surveying the local terrain to see about any kind of leveling or packing of the soil to form a roadbed. Eventually, some distance away, she noticed what appeared to be a ditch that had been filled in, along with some debris that had been moved to one side. She could also see ruts in the soft soil.

"This was made by wheels."

She studied the markings carefully, taking notice of multiple layers overlapping each other.

"Something heavy came through here, and more than one, along with a lot of foot traffic."

She picks herself up and continues this way across the plains for the remaining two rivers, but as she arrived at the last of the major rivers, she had one additional idea.

"I wonder about that camp I saw once."

She now tries to recall the camp with the blood stains on the ground. She struggles to focus on the image, although it had faded somewhat by now, but she manages to recall it well enough to fold directly over to it.

She arrived in the empty orcish camp where she could again see the remnants of the stain on the ground and on mats inside the huts. She begins a careful survey of the surrounding area, again looking for markings in the soil. Some distance off to one side, she finds her mark, with a series of ruts in the grassy landscape, seemingly pressed into it by something heavy, and close to the water's edge where the moisture was higher.

"Was this before or after…" she wonders. "Probably after if Portal

Three is over there and this is Portal Two. So, they hit Portal Three because it was empty, swing around to this one, take out the orcs, steal their goods, and run off with it. But wheels?"

She stands up again and folds her image back to Firstfall to report her findings.

"My Lord," she announces on her arrival. "This is weird. I made a quick review of these four rivers," she points to the map. "Each of them has a bridge over it in very close alignment and of the same design. They appeared to be cut logs, bound to support rails and pilings sunk into the riverbed. This is clearly the work of a more advanced form of engineering, and it looks fresh, by the condition of the wood. I also found a source of tree stumps near that one camp that looked like they were cut using metal tools."

"Metal, is it?"

"I can also see where ditches were filled in, and signs of wheeled vehicles moving through the region, probably pulled by people on foot…lots of them."

"How interesting," he muses. "Then unless we are to assume these orcs have made a rapid advance in bridge-building techniques, as well as fashioning vehicles to go along with it, then someone else did this."

"Furthermore, I visited that one camp with those blood stains again. I saw more ruts from wheels, so I have to assume it to be Portal Two on their side."

"Indeed!"

"But this leaves us asking who, and maybe also why, to say nothing of using wheeled vehicles along the way, which is a lot more elaborate than a rogue orcish raiding party."

"Yes, it is. This now bears a resemblance to a collection effort if that equipment is missing. I wonder. Do you think any of the mutation victims might be capable of this?"

"I doubt it. My mother told me they mostly hide in the buildings around the city. These were at distance…a LONG distance, and you would need outdoor survival skills to make that journey."

"Naturally," he nods. "Then perhaps we should ask this, although it may be moot, but are there any other advanced races on that world? Possibly on another continent if orcs dominate this one?"

"I don't know. Kailen?" she asks.

"I'm not aware of any," he responds.

"Then unless someone else has arrived on that world," Thaelyn resumes. "We might be speaking of refugees who opportunistically scavenge whatever they can find. They might have found these two conveyors, realizing one was abandoned and the other one poorly guarded, and took advantage of both."

"How do we explain the severed head in this case?" Kaliya wonders.

"It must still be a statement, and probably intended for orcs, if they believe there to be any on the other side of the conveyor. They attack at night and by stealth, douse the campfire to further cover themselves, and then quickly killed the orcs in that camp."

"This matches that one camp," Kaliya nods. "The campfire did have dirt in it to kill the fire. I saw blood stains on the mats inside the huts, so it was likely a nighttime hit. And a big stain outside, where maybe that head came from…as unpleasant as it sounds," she shudders. "But there were no bodies, so maybe the bodies were removed."

"Perhaps, and with the clear absence of the conveyors, it left you confused for the result."

Thaelyn leaned back in his chair and began chuckling softly.

"This reminds me now of our early tactics with the orcs here. Hit them fast and remove the evidence."

"So, someone did this to us now?" she smiles. "Cu'Nar's pity, now that's a cute turn."

"Yes, someone might be playing with us. Although, it is unlikely they know of it. Let us consider… The timing would indicate a planned assault, possibly taking advantage of the low population in that camp, which might represent an opportunity to claim a valuable prize, followed by this statement and the shutdown of the conveyor. Now it makes sense, if only we are correct on this notion of refugees."

"If that's the case," Kailen concedes. "We need to know where they're hiding. Kaliya, did Mother say anything about anyone else living in the city?"

"No, only the mutation victims."

"Are there any natural caves in the region?" Thaelyn asks.

"Not that I'm personally aware of," Kailen offers.

"I wonder, how would they move these articles?" Thaelyn muses. "You said you found tracks from wheels. Do any of your vehicles move on land?"

"No, everything is hover-enabled. We don't technically have a need for roads, even though we still keep them for vestigial reasons to delineate city blocks. But after so long, and with the city in so much disrepair, there's probably no power, so the hover-trucks' power cells would've died a long time ago."

"Therefore, you would need to revert to an earlier form of transport," he grins bemusedly. "Relissa once jested on the notion of reinventing the wheel. It would appear someone may have done exactly that."

The others give off a gentle round of laughter.

"But these conveyors used fusion reactors," Thaelyn continues. "This would be an excellent source of power for an advanced race like yours."

"Yes, it would be a very tempting target, especially if you're a survivor of a civilization brought into ruin like ours was."

"And for this reason, where would be the best place to return these items, but back to the source of that civilization."

"The city… But then, where could they be hiding if our mother doesn't know about it?"

"We clearly need more information. In the meantime, speaking of her, Kaliya, you should take a moment to go visit. While you are there, make a casual pass around the city and look for any wheeled vehicles. If you should happen to find anything, also keep a lookout for the conveyors."

"And if I should find any refugees?"

"Indeed, this is a good question. We will surely need to make contact at some moment, but we cannot be sure how they will react to it. Our primary objective is to verify the condition of the conveyors for Portals Two and Three. This will allow us to relieve our people from duty at those garrisons. Beyond that, I can only suggest using your best judgment in this matter, but in your bird form, it might prove difficult for them to interpret. First, let us see who is there, and only interact if the situation provides a fair opportunity for us."

"Got it. Wish me luck."

Kaliya departs from the local space and once again returns to Ruuki uy'Daan, arriving inside her old home. She steps through the family room and surveys the surroundings. It is late morning, and all is quiet.

"Mother?" she calls. "I'm back."

A thud ushers from the rear room and a quickened pace comes down the hall.

"Kali? You come back again?" Tyanna replies as she trudges into the room smiling at her daughter's return.

"Mother, how are things here?"

"Kali, me happy to see you. People go look for orcs, but no orcs come walk in new days."

"Mother? Is your language improving? Maybe all this interaction is helping you recover a little bit."

"Me not know, me feel better, little bit. You help me talk more and make me work again. Me happy."

"I'm happy too, Mother."

"Kali, me have something big to say. Me see new people. They come here, talk long time."

"New people?" she yips. "Mother, I was out there looking for those other conveyors, but they're missing. We think someone took them, maybe to use them. But it can't be orcs, and it's probably not the people here, so maybe there is someone else out there. We're thinking there may be people still here after the attack."

"Yes," she nods. "People come, two girls, young like you. Bad clothes..." she frowns and chuckles softly. "We talk, say ship go, but people stay here. Say people hide, but not here. Me not know where, but me think not in houses."

"Oh great, someone missed the boat? Wonderful. But not in the houses, so we're talking maybe outside the city. Who are they, do we know?"

"Me not know names… Erm, wait. One name. Tana. Has plant clothes," she chuckles.

"Uh oh, a little nature girl?" Kaliya smiles.

"They say they hide from orcs. And they say they hide from hurt-people."

"Hide from you? Why?"

"They tell old stories. Tell how hurt-people go fight, make trouble."

"Oh no, so these people…right, I think I understand. I remember those days. I remember seeing and hearing a few things about this as we were running to the ship. Others saw this too. Did you say something to correct this?"

"Yes, me tell them, hurt-people hide from orcs. Orcs come and make more hurt. Hurt-people need help. But oh! Girls angry…" she rolls her eyes. "Tana angry, yell at orcs and Suuden'kai."

"She sounds a lot like me. All right, I'll keep this in mind."

"But they say they talk to other people, try to help."

"Good. I need to find them and talk to them. We all need to come together. Maybe we can make a deal of some kind."

"Yes, you go talk. They angry many things, not understand many things. I try to help. Now they want to talk."

"Good. Anything else?"

"This…" Tyanna points at her seed entity. "They ask to see. Want to understand. Ask me how. I say orcs have gun. Suuden'kai give them."

"Uh huh. And how many horns went flying with that one?"

"Many!" she chuckles.

"Yeah," she smiles. "Did you tell them about me?"

"They say they see big thing. Ask, what is it. Me say big thing is friend."

"Hmm…this should be interesting."

"They say they see big animal kill orc, girl was scared."

"Oops! Yeah, I'll bet. I'll need to excuse myself for that. And then, how do I approach this. I'm already getting ideas of where this might go," she sighs heavily. "And then what to say to Thaelyn when I get back. Cu'Nar's pity, this will cause a bit of a stir, I think."

"Kali, you go back, you learn more?"

"They have me on a very full schedule over there. I think most of my study for this Prodigy Gift is done, and it's just a matter of practice and learning new stuff as I go. But now, they're going to start teaching me telepathy. Can you believe it?" she smiles.

"What teach?"

"Do you remember telepathy, to think and talk to people," she points at her head. "Like Father, what he learned once back on Azgarén."

Tyanna pauses to interpret the notion.

"Oh!" she intones boldly. "Yes! Me remember. You learn think-talk? Oh, what say Elder people this?"

"Elder people?" she giggles. "You mean the Elder Council. They don't know. We're not telling them."

"What? Why? Elder people need to know all things."

"Yes, Mother, but listen. We need to keep this quiet because of Sargeras and Darumon. They can probably do this also, and listen to the Elder Council if they think everything. It's all a big problem with security. If you want to steal something, who do you steal it from...but those people who know everything."

Tyanna contemplates the statement, and reluctantly comes to terms with it.

"Yes, me understand. Elder people not be happy, but me think Elder people not happy Sarg-us listen and learn things. Me remember Elder Vankkar. He talk much on this."

"Yeah, it's a bit ironic."

"You think you fight Sarg-us with think-talk?"

"It can be a tool for us, this is certain. Using this can give us some very clever tricks to play. So, we're thinking of teaching many people to do this."

"Ooh...this me want to see."

"We're not sure how all this will work for us yet, but we have to start somewhere and learn new ways to use it. This, and also the Prodigy Gift, we're testing more people to see if they can do that."

"More people learn dream-walk? But... How? Me remember children learn this. You find more children?"

"Not children, Mother...adults. We think it doesn't matter. If we can do this at all, it might not matter how old you are. It's a hidden talent we may all have."

Tyanna glared at Kaliya for the statement, trying to reflect on what little she could compose of her thoughts on the matter.

"More people learn..." she muses distantly. "Me want to learn more. Me sad, me head not good."

"Ankhia is still working on that, so let's keep our spirits up. But now I have work to do."

"Kali, you learn much. Learn good. You remember me not like fight. Me understand Sarg-us bad, people need fight. Me not like, but me help."

"Thank you, Mother. I need to go now. I have to go look for those people."

"Me love you, Kali."

Kaliya steps over and gives a pleasant kiss on her mother's cheek, and then leaves the house. She changes into a hawk again and starts flying around the city, trying to decide where the best place may be to go look for those people.

"So, the game is they're probably not inside the city, and this makes sense if the orcs were known to come around so often, but where else?"

She circles around, flying towards the downtown area and around through the industrial section, then back out west.

"Not inside the city," she muses. "Probably not east...that's where all the orcs are, so it has to be west. A natural cave? Wait a minute! Kali, you idiot! Sometimes I think you have your horns turned backwards. The mine!"

She angles out towards the western fields and the mining camp.

"And I remember seeing something out there with wheels on it!"

She makes a brief jump to arrive in the area just north of the mine's work yard. The area looks abandoned with no visible activity outside. She makes a circle at high altitude scanning for anything white, but everything on the ground looks dirty and old.

"Dammit, where are those reactors!"

She sees a set of wheeled vehicles and dives down to land on one. It was an old hover-truck, apparently a former utility transport from the civic service department.

"This doesn't belong here, and especially not with wooden wheels under it. Not wood, of all things!"

She drops to the ground for a closer inspection of the undercarriage, passing her glance between the two vehicles on either side of her. She notices caked-on mud stuck to the metal treading and rims.

"But they were used to go somewhere dirty."

She walks out in front of the vehicle to study a long towbar with crossbar grips suitable for a team of laborers to haul it.

"Well now, isn't this quaint," she jests. "I wonder if they had a whip and a taskmaster."

She continues into the work yard. She can hear noises from one of the buildings. She runs up to find the door slightly ajar and peeks through. Inside she finds several Daanen'kai workers sitting at tables, apparently trying to repair some old equipment. She pulls out quickly and ducks around the corner.

"People!" she whispers. "I can barely believe it. What in the cu'Nar's name are they doing here? How could they possibly miss getting onto the ship. I thought everyone got in, and those who didn't were killed…or at least should've been, for all the orcs!"

She briskly surveys the work yard and the other buildings, wondering what might be inside each. She walks back into the yard trying to decide which way to go, then recalling her mission to find the conveyor parts. She sees something that looks like a warehouse at one end, and makes her way over to it.

"So…" Tana grins. "Petrith is having visions of Kali naked in the shower?"

"Yeah, apparently," Túfula asserts. "I think he's showing signs of a skill my father once described as clairvoyance, where you can see people and places normally outside your view."

"That could be useful if he can refine it. He could scout those orcs in Camp One without ever leaving home."

"Can you tell us more about this Prodigy Gift?" Sulíma asks. "Like, for instance, how does it work?"

The three girls were sitting at a table in the gathering room inside the mine for their lunch break. Tana was taking time off from her scouting to visit home, while Sulíma and Túfula were relaxing from their work outside.

"My father only told me a little bit," Túfula responds. "They didn't know much about it, and it's so rare that it's almost a myth. Apparently, the person goes into a kind of dreamlike state and their consciousness comes out into physical space."

"That sounds creepy," Tana winces. "What do they do after that?"

"It's said they can interact with people and objects, but there's a lot we still don't know about it. This is why it was being researched, and why it was so hush-hush. He told me the study of telepathy was the same way, along with all the rest."

"Telepathy? Like what they say Master Velen has? But why don't people ever tell us these things? Is it so bad? This is supposed to be our science faction, after all!"

"According to my father, the top officials were afraid because it can be used for a lot of bad things. I guess they were trying to study this too for the same reason, maybe to try to understand it well enough to control it."

"But couldn't it be used for something good?" Sulíma wonders. "I mean, just think of being able to go to sleep and dream yourself outside playing with your friends. It would be nonstop fun, day and night."

"Or what about dreaming yourself going to meet with a secret lover," Túfula giggles.

"Ooh, I like that one. And if you and he could both do this, no one would ever know."

"Learning to control it is one thing," Tana suggests. "But this also sounds like controlling it for private use, or out of prejudice. And I still say, this is supposed to be our science faction. Who, of all people, would be more qualified to understand how to use it responsibly than those who are trying to learn these things to begin with? Prejudice? Maybe with all those other science factions who didn't like ours. But WE are the ones trying to understand it, not them."

"You're right, Tana," Túfula nods. "Unfortunately, it seems we're just as edgy as all the rest. My father didn't think we were responsible enough to handle it, even if we ARE the ones researching it."

"But one thing I can see already," Tana smiles. "If Petrith has this clairvoyance thing, no one is safe out by the pond anymore."

"Yeah…" Sulíma grins. "We would often joke about hoof prints behind those bushes, but using this doesn't even leave any."

"Well, I won't complain about it. If he wants to watch me taking a bath, he can study me all he likes. I'll even flaunt myself a little if it helps give me some attention."

"Now just a minute, are you trying to steal him away from us?"

"Oh, Suli, I'm sure he has his eyes on you enough times. But for all the tail swinging you do; I need a little of my own."

"Yeah, you're right. But you don't need too much of it. Every time I see you walk by; half the boys are following your tail."

"Following and chasing are two different things."

"But Tana," Túfula considers. "Are you sure you're not sneaking off to some quiet little nook out there with a few of them?"

"Túfu, even though I know of this wonderful little nook I'd like to sneak off to, I haven't actually done anything like that, despite how I dress and how many boys are watching my tail. Just like the rest, I don't feel comfortable with our situation here to play around like that."

"Yeah, the same for all of us."

"Anyway," Sulíma relents. "It's time to get back to work. Are you finished with lunch? I could use a hand in the warehouse. Petrith finally brought my wagon back yesterday, so I need to go look at all my new toys."

"Right behind you," Túfula admits. "Tana, what are you doing next?"

"I'll be heading back out to my post in a moment. I'm just going to freshen up my paint a little."

"Freshen up? Is that what you call it?"

"It helps cover my skin, so I blend in better. I need to keep it up, especially in this jungle heat where it tends to come off as I'm moving around out there."

"Maybe you need a permanent paint job?" she giggles.

"I wouldn't actually mind having a way to apply something like a tattoo, but I don't really know how, nor would I feel completely comfortable using what we have. Maybe one day I'll figure it out, but not now."

The three of them get up from the table and head off to their respective duties. Tana moved away to her room where she had a collection of oils and mineral powders she would use as her body paint, while Sulíma and Túfula went outside to examine some of the new equipment they had recently gathered.

The two of them walked outside and down the ramp into the work yard, making their way up to the warehouse on the other end. But as they approached, they noticed an odd bird standing next to the solar panels and rift generators at the rear wall.

"Hey, Túfu," Sulíma mentions softly. "You like to go bird watching. What kind is that?"

Túfula stares at the proud creature, taking note of its brown and tan coloring, yellow eyes, sharp beak, and strong talons.

"I have no idea. It doesn't look native to the area. That looks like a hunting bird, Suli. I've never seen anything like that in this region."

"Why is it inside here? Should we be afraid of it?"

"Well, it's a bird, so I don't think it'll bother us. Maybe it's just looking for something it saw run inside here."

Kaliya had been studying the solar panels and rift generators at the rear of the warehouse, counting parts, and scanning the remainder of the room for the other pieces. When the two girls came in and started speaking, it caught her attention, drawing her gaze towards the door.

"So, um," Sulíma mumbles. "Should we get out of the way? It looks like it wants to leave, and we're standing here."

"Yeah, it might be a good idea to give it a clear path. We don't want to frighten it."

They step out of the way, leaving the path to the door free of any interference.

Kaliya realizes she should be going now. The only things she found here were the solar panels and rift generators, no fusion reactors. Without them, the conveyor wouldn't work anyway, but she was still curious. She wanted to know where they were. If these people had taken them, they had to be installed and running in order for them to conduct any work.

She calmly walked towards the door, her mind deeply immersed in her thoughts while she once again reviewed the shelving, along with the equipment she had examined on her way in. The two girls watched as the solitary bird casually passed by, apparently browsing the equipment racks as a shopper at a hardware store.

"Túfu, you said it might be looking for something," Sulíma whispers as the bird passes by. "So, why is it looking at all of our equipment?"

"Well, it's obviously hunting for something…" she considers.

"Hunting for what, the daily sale special?"

"Oh, I'm sure there's a reason. It's just curious."

"Well, follow it, just in case," Sulíma hushes.

Kaliya exits the building into the yard and begins another visual scan around the scene. From her angle, she could only see the workshops and the random placement of crates and used equipment. She felt confident in her disguise that the two girls regarded her as just a common animal, so she took her time as a way to demonstrate a relaxed posture.

Sulíma and Túfula watched the bird as it lingered on the ground in the open yard.

"Túfu," Sulíma asks quietly. "Do you know of any bird, or animal for that matter, which walks this close to people into an open space and just stops to study the place?"

"No I don't, so unless this species is very bold, I can't imagine why it would, or what it's looking for, and especially why it's not paying any attention to the two of us standing almost next to it."

"It's a spy."

Túfula looks into Sulíma's face to check if the last bit of sanity has finally left her.

"It's a bird, Suli."

"Is it? Like that stone giant was just a garden statue, or that animal out at Camp One was someone's stray pet? You said you didn't recognize the species. It doesn't belong here."

"Well, um…"

"And Tana said she met with Tyanna and talked about that friend of hers. Maybe this is it, and it's checking up on us."

"Suli, I…well…"

"It's a shapeshifter. It can alter its form. Think for a moment of our school studies on metaphysics. Nothing unknown exists. It only exists after it is known."

"Yeah, and I never understood that part."

"All right, but think about the orcs and their magic for a moment. Somehow, they create something out of nothing. They imagine it, and boom, there it is. It's all about the mind. It defines its own perception of reality and alters what's around it to match. Remember what Tana said. Maybe this thing is another example, and it can apply this to its own body."

"Cu'Nar's Grace, Suli," she winces. "You're simply scary when you talk like that."

Kaliya decides to take off into the air and make a circle around the work yard, thinking the reactors must be hidden behind one of the buildings. The two girls breathe a sigh of relief to see the bird appearing to leave, but then gulp a new one as it only circles around the camp, now very distinctly weaving in and out around each building.

"Túfu!" Sulíma shouts. "Get the Captain. It's spying on us!"

"Yeah, right, he's going to love this one," she relents tensely.

Túfula stalls for an instant as she watches the bird loop around one of the buildings on the side of the yard, then sprints off towards the hideout. Sulíma rushes out into the yard to follow the bird.

Kaliya notices one of the girls running up to the mine entrance and the other one into the yard staring at her. She glances between the two of them as she glides along the side of the yard, trying to think of what to do.

"Oh great…" she mumbles to herself. "Now you've done it. They must be really nervous around here…not that I can blame them, I suppose."

She continued sweeping across the camp, but felt the pressure of time on her now, to say nothing of drawing a lot of unwanted attention. So she decides to try a new approach.

"I don't see anything white, so they must be hidden in, under, or behind something. Wait…the power cords. When in doubt, follow them up to the source."

She looks around on the ground to see a tangle of power cords coursing between the buildings, many of them leading around one workshop near the front. She follows them to find a power conditioner unit alongside one of the buildings and dives in for a better look, landing on the ground while watching the one girl rushing in behind her.

"Who are you!" Sulíma shouts. "Are you spying on us? Or maybe you came here because we were speaking to the people in the city?"

Kaliya took a brief moment to study the unit and the variety of cables coming and going. But when Sulíma made her announcement, she turned and looked up at her curiously, cocking her head at the strange form of interaction.

"You do realize you're talking to a bird, right?" she squawks.

Sulíma felt an instant sensation of awkwardness, coupled with a bit of alarm over the talking creature. She placed her hands on her hips and turned away timidly while she composed her answer.

"Um, well, yeah, I think so."

"Do you often go around talking to strange animals?"

"Not usually, but you're new around here, so I thought it might be nice to make an introduction."

"Uh huh, right. And here I am thinking you might have lost your mind."

"I'm asking the same thing, actually."

"Well, don't worry about it too much. We all have our delicate moments," she cackles.

"Oh, thank you," she smirks. "But what are you doing? What are you looking for?"

"I'm on a rather important mission, and right now I'm being a bit stubborn to get it done."

"Oh, a stubborn bird, on top of everything else. Is this normal for your species?"

"Oh, you don't know the half of it. Once we set our mind to something, it's hard to let go."

"All right, so is there something I can help you with?

By this time, Túfula was just emerging outside and leading a parade of others. The disturbance caught the attention of both Sulíma and Kaliya.

"Yeah, maybe so," Kaliya responds briskly. "Before I get involved in any of that…" she points with a wing, "…are you people responsible for the…ahem…disappearance of two conveyor assemblies?"

"Um, maybe…" she responds innocently.

"Well…maybe you can tell me where the rest of the equipment is. I need to confirm its condition for our people on the other side."

"Oh, well, all right. But is there any particular reason for this?"

"We have garrisons over there that we would like to relieve of duty, rather than simply standing around in an open space."

"Oh! Yeah. That makes sense. Well, I guess you saw those pieces in the warehouse, and the reactors are over there…" she points across the river.

Kaliya turns to find where the girl is pointing, and soon notices a power cable stretching across the bridge and into a grouping of bushes.

"Just a moment…" she ushers and takes off to make a close inspection.

The Captain and the others were now arriving at the base of the ramp into the work yard.

"Suli, what's going on out here?" he asks urgently. "What are you doing with that bird?"

"Showing it where the reactors are. It needs to check serial numbers and ID tags, just to make sure everything is legitimate."

The Captain glared at her, along with Túfula who joined beside him. Tana followed up close behind and studied the scene.

"Suli," the Captain emits cautiously. "Did I just hear you correctly? You're talking to a bird about stock inventories?"

"It's a very stubborn species. They need to be sure the invoices are correct."

"I think this is a clear indication she's lost her mind now," Túfula relents.

"It must be a leftover from that incident in town with the stone giant," Tana adds.

Kaliya arrived at the reactor assemblies and settled down on one of the units to study it. The full array had been painted in a smooth camouflage motif to conceal it from view.

"Clever sharp-horned people," she mumbles. "No wonder I couldn't find it. And no doubt I passed right over it on my first run. But then, how could I know?"

"So, Suli," the Captain continues. "What are we actually doing out here?"

"Captain, I think that bird is that friend Tyanna was speaking about."

"You think so. And why is it looking for the reactors?"

"It says it needs to confirm the situation for their people on the other side. They apparently have garrisons over there, which means those orcs WERE on a death march, and probably all thanks to the Suuden-Aryku throwing them away for some reason."

"All right, but I would still like to know more about what's going on and what motivations it has here."

"All I can say is to give it a moment. Like I said, it's a stubborn species and wanted to get this out of the way."

"Suli, are you actually feeling alright?"

"Well, I think so…as much as one can be when talking to birds."

The Captain closes his eyes and shakes his head.

Now that she had found the conveyors, Kaliya's primary objective was complete. But she had a new problem to solve, and naturally, she was unsure how to proceed, given her unusual presentation. She looked back across the river at the work camp and the large gathering of people accumulating outside.

"Cu'Nar's grace," she mutters softly. "How many do we have over there?" she shakes her head. "Improvise… Yeah, Aelwyn will have a field day when I report THIS one back."

She lifts off again and flies back across to the camp. The people usher up a series of oohs and ahs as she glides in to settle on the rooftop of one of the workshops.

Sulíma and Túfula move to one side of the building, while the Captain centers himself along another side. Tana takes up at roughly midpoint, and the rest gather loosely around the area. Sulíma stepped forward to interact with their visitor again.

"So, um…" she considers her wording. "Do we pass your inspection? Do we get to keep our operating permits for another year?" she grins bashfully.

Kaliya stared at her, realizing this presented an opportunity to ease the tensions somewhat. She found herself recalling a little of Relissa's quirky manners and decided to apply some of her own.

"Well, before I can grant you an extension, I'll need to check with Central to see if that paint is up to code."

The gathering all gasped at the words spoken by a bird, but followed with a cautious round of laughter.

"Do you people know how long I've been looking for that stuff?" she asks while pointing a wing at the reactor assemblies. "I've been all over the southern half of this continent searching for big white things sticking out of the ground."

"Oh, well, sorry, but we saw it out there and didn't want it to simply go to waste."

"Yes, I can certainly appreciate that, but we had no idea you people were out here. Technically speaking, where the ship is concerned, you aren't supposed to be here. And by all reasonable expectations, when you consider the orcs, you shouldn't STILL be here," she shakes her head.

"Yes, well, we had a few problems with that, to say the least."

"Then, I took notice of all those bridges you left behind and we're asking ourselves, do orcs actually build bridges as nice as these? Then I found ruts from wheels everywhere. Wow…how did THAT happen?" she chuckles as she glances at the vehicles behind her.

"Yeah. We saw the first one was clearly abandoned, and we needed the boost here. Then, we saw the second one, and, um…"

"Uh huh, so you decided, why not take both, I suppose. I'm trying to imagine people hauling those things around. If I had a camera, I'd love a keepsake. Maybe we could arrange a publicity photo. Welcome to Ruuki uy'Daan," she waves her wings theatrically. "Here is the local tour train."

The group let out another burst of laughter at the obvious play. The gesture was clearly relaxing the tension.

Kaliya continues, "We were trying to plot what we thought to be their approximate locations on a map, but the lack of any evidence had us a little confused. The first one went down several months ago, and we thought it might be from equipment failure, because the camp was interpreted to be empty. Then we had that little display of yours at the second one."

"Yeah, um…" Sulíma submits tenderly. "We saw there weren't very many orcs left behind, and we were passing through from the first one, so we took the initiative. Is that alright? We didn't mean anything offensive, at least not to you."

"I suppose it's moot," she shrugs. "They would've likely jumped through to our side soon after, so the outcome would probably be the same. But that delivery you made had a few of us scratching our heads.”

“Better yours than his,” she chuckles. “It’s just that we thought there were orcs on the other side, that’s all.”

“Right, we figured as much. It gave the impression of some sort of uprising on this side. But this only added to the confusion of who they were, where they came from, and if they could also be responsible for the first one. But without any debris, and then bridges and wheel ruts…um…”

“Uh huh, I suppose that might stand out.”

“It might stand out if you know what to look for. It’s highly unlikely for orcs to do the deed…why would they? Trophies? Probably not. A rebellion against Sargeras? Maybe. But then, why remove the remains? It’s not your average orcish mindset to clean up so nicely.”

“Really! So, I guess you must know a few things about them. Um, but does this mean you were at war with them on your side? You spoke of garrisons, but…”

“War…ugh!” she tosses her wings up. “Don’t even get me started on that one,” she waves one at the girl. “Three and a half centuries of them parading around our backyard as if they owned the place.”

“Ouch! That’s not nice!”

“But this does tell us it started way back in the beginning,” Túfula notes.

“Yes, so this might serve as confirmation for the timing.”

“Yeah,” Kaliya affirms. “The whole thing was staged. We had them on one side, the Suuden-Aryku on another side, and a third group that was corrupted to serve Sargeras on yet another…would you like to be in the middle of all that?”

“No thank you!” she shouts boldly.

“Exactly. We were pinned down badly for a long while. We couldn’t even go outside to smell the charred flowers. Fortunately, we had some new help arrive recently, and this turned things around for us. As the result, we finished all of it just a bit more than a year ago.”

“Finished?!” Sulíma blurts abruptly. “But wait. We saw what we considered to be a change in behavior over here of the orcs all moving to this one point. And that happened, um…a couple years ago, maybe?"

"If you saw a change in behavior, it would've been the result of this new help arriving and turning things around for the rest of us. That world was under siege and blasted down to almost nothing by that time."

"Ouch! Again!"

"And if I may add one more thing to make your horns fly off, it is BECAUSE of them that this new help arrived…very unwelcomed by those who were oppressing the rest."

"Oh no!" she screams.

"And it finished just recently, with the last of the orcs, a rather large population by this time, cleaned out."

"And another ouch! So this means, the group we see over here could be the last of their kind by now?"

"Yeah, and not a good thing to see, if you hold any value in preserving life."

"Oh!" Tana huffs. "Preserving life…of THEM? After everything they did to us?"

Kaliya turns to study the girl, taking special note of her leafy apparel.

"Let me guess, you're Tana, the nature girl with plants for clothes."

"Um, do you know me?"

"My contact over there recalled you, as well as your temper," she chuckles softly.

"Oh dear. Sorry. But yes, I do have a few opinions about things, and the people around here know this."

"All right, fair enough. But I'll ask you to tone it down a little, because there are details you aren't aware of on this side of Creation which could change a few perspectives for you."

"Uh oh. All right, I'll try to hold onto my horns a bit longer."

"You also mentioned the Suuden-Aryku," Sulíma continues. "What about them?"

"Yeah, they turned and ran all the way back home with their tails between their legs," she cackles. "We also learned a few important things along the way, and this demands we continue this all the way behind them."

"Oops! What does that mean?"

"These new people know who Sargeras is. And he's not even supposed to be alive, much less making trouble for people."

"What?" she gasps.

"That's right. If the cu'Nar told us he comes from a dead race, it's because the people we met recently are the reason for it!"

This announcement caused a sudden eruption of gasps and moans amongst the crowd.

"Grace of the cu'Nar!" Túfula yelps. "Just who are you people? I'm assuming you know our people from the Naarg uy'Sodrad, right?"

"Know the people… Yes, I think we can safely say that. Um…" Kaliya emits cautiously as she examines a wing. "We can also say I'm one of them."

"One of them!" she screeches. "How can you be from the Naarg uy'Sodrad? Do we now have talking birds as part of the crew?"

"Well, it's a strange world," she shrugs. "In reality, this is just a disguise. Trying to fly by flapping my arms doesn't work as well. You might say I'm in training with some really nether-wild skills."

"Nether-wild is right! Would this have anything to do with that old riddle of metaphysics?"

"It would, in a certain manner of speaking. There are a lot of possibilities out there, if only you can imagine them. And that is the key…not numbers or empirical calculations. It's the mind imposing itself on Reality. You don't measure this with precision instruments. You use your head, literally. Unfortunately, we're so heavily conditioned to think by the numbers, we don't have any imagination anymore."

"Oh, wow, thank you."

"Also, it helps to have tutoring from people higher than we to show us how it's done."

"Higher than we…" she murmurs timidly. "So, um, does that mean, um…"

"Yeah. It's a little ironic, actually. You travel up the ladder, and generally away from everything you think of as mystical. Then, one day you arrive at a point where you're conducting this as your primary study topic. How do you like that?"

"Oh, cu'Nar help us. So this is where it leads. Wonderful!"

"Yeah. For instance, the people I'm working for now. If you thought those orcs with their magic were bad, they were amateurs compared to this next group."

"By the way," Tana wonders. "Were you that animal out at Camp One?"

"Camp One? You mean the one over there?" Kaliya points a wing off to the east.

"Yeah, I saw what I guess was you dressed like a big orange and black striped animal that killed an orc and then took its body, then walked back into the camp to shut down the conveyor."

"Yikes, you actually saw all that? I heard about you from my, um, contact in the city."

"Yeah, I saw it!" she snaps. "If it was any closer, you would've been climbing on my back. I was hiding in a bush right behind you."

Kaliya studies the girl for her strange manner of dress.

"Well, in your case, I'm not actually surprised I didn't see you. You look like a bush, even now."

"Yes, well…" she glances at herself. "This is what happens when you spend most of your life running through the jungle."

"Yeah! It grows on you!" she bellows a hardy laugh, followed by the rest.

"Oh! Yes! Thank you very much," Tana retorts playfully and throws up her hands. "Very good, another one getting on my tail about it…"

"What about that stone giant in the city?" Sulíma adds.

"Yeah, that too," Kaliya nods. "I was in town on an errand and heard the noise from those orcs coming in. Then I saw them harassing one of the mutation victims. So I decided to try a cute little trick to scare them off."

"A cute…little…trick?" she yips. "Sure! About that! Would

you mind watching where you step? I was right under you when you did that."

"Oops, sorry… I didn't see you down there. Where were you?"

"I was in one of the industry buildings looking for some salvage to bring back."

"Ah, but then those orcs came along."

"Yeah, and then YOU came along…stomping along the roadway trying to set off an earthquake."

"No, I wasn't really trying to set off any earthquakes. I'm not that advanced yet," she cackles again.

"Oh, excuse me," she giggles. "But you scared my horns off so badly, they went ricocheting around the room. Then, I ran back here in such a panic, I apparently fainted once I arrived."

"Ouch! I'm sorry about that. I was simply responding to a crisis."

"Um, about that…" Tana huffs and crosses her arms. "Why not just kill them, for all they did to us during this time."

Once again, Kaliya studied the girl for her posture. It seemed so familiar to her from her own history.

"The thought crossed my mind, but if any went missing, or ran off with stories of a fight, it wouldn't help matters. And it's not my function to exterminate people."

"Not exterminate?" Tana retorts brashly. "After what they did to us? We heard about that gun thing they used on our people."

"Yes, the famous gift of our old technology. I hear you, and I felt the same for a long while. I wanted every last one of them dead. But then I met with these new people and learned a few very important lessons on life…that it's not something you simply go out and destroy for its simple existence. Those orcs behaved badly; this is true. But they're also victims, even if they don't know it yet. They're down to the last of their kind, all because of some fiend who told them to jump through a hole in space to be slaughtered as worthless examples of flesh. Now, what do you think I should do with that?"

"Um, all right," she relents timidly. "I think I see your point. But…"

"But… Yes, I can already guess what you want to say. I was there myself. Life is a precious thing, Tana, and it needs to be respected no matter who or what it belongs to. We may fight the evil it creates, but we still need to honor the essence of life as an element in and of itself. Those orcs are following a beast of a god image. THAT is our enemy here. I think, if the orcs knew who Sargeras really was and what he was doing to them as a species, they would probably agree. The problem is, they're a primitive form of life that worships strength as a prestige of leadership. Therefore, as I'm already working on this, I'm trying to break them of this image to realize what he has already done, and where they stand as a result."

"In all the nether-space, you're worse than my father!" she mutters as she glances at the man standing in the background. "Is this what these new people teach over there?"

"It is, and I got my tail chewed badly for my own errors once. Then I had to go into a form of rehab to calm my rage and realize a bigger picture. So, I don't blame you for yours. Like I said, I had my own issues for everything they did…and not only them, but also the Suuden-Aryku, when in fact it's Sargeras who is the one at fault here…he and Darumon, no one else."

"Wait a minute," the Captain interjects. "Who is this Darumon?"

"Darumon…you know, the Marshal… Oh wait!" she slaps her head. "That's right, you DON'T know! We've been talking about him for so long, it's common speech by now. But for you, we have to go back to the beginning. Wonderful!" she tosses her wings up again. "All right, here we go. These are some of those lessons we've been learning since we kicked their tails off this next world, which we call Therinë. First, we crashed there due to sabotage inside the ship."

"Sabotage! In all the nether-space, who was responsible for that?"

"This third race they corrupted recently. They're also practiced in magic, much more advanced than these orcs, and can use it to create an invisibility cloak. Using this, they were able to simply walk in, do the deed, and no one could stop them. They tampered with our nav systems, the engines, and many of our computers were wiped. Our navigation was scrambled, and the engineering section blew out inside the slipstream. So we're buried under a hill now."

"That's not at all good to hear. What about casualties?"

"Lots, nearly half of the surviving population, plus more in the siege we had to endure since then. It was a trap. They were waiting for us on the other side. As for..." she coughs emphatically, "... Marshal Darumon, as he's known to all his followers, he's Sargeras's right-hand man, and someone we apparently don't remember arriving on Azgarén along with Sargeras himself."

"Really! So Sargeras wasn't alone? How nice."

"We suspect his name was intentionally omitted, or maybe downplayed, because he likes to hide in the background so he can sneak around and stab people in the back. The Suuden-Aryku apparently describe him and Sargeras as, get this, benefactors, for this tail-yanking promise of great wisdom they apparently made once, while he leads them on some glorious crusade to recover stolen goods, or some such nonsense."

"Stolen goods? And how do we explain us in all this?"

"First, Darumon lies about virtually everything. He controls people at least as much with falsehoods and misinformation, fabrications of detail, and so on. Worse is he might also control them with devices and even mind-altering drugs if they don't otherwise behave as he wants them to."

"I don't believe this!" Sulíma gasps. "He must be some kind of monster!"

"To put it lightly, yes..." she shrugs. "As were all of their kind. They played with little things like us as toys. Either we serve a utility function, like the Suuden-Aryku for their military capacity, or entertainment, maybe like us. But either way, we're all simply slaves to their interests. As for us, well, we didn't play the game like he wanted, so we became expendable."

"Expendable?" Tana moans. "Just because we have minds to think, we become expendable?!" she shouts.

"Easy now, and listen up," Kaliya soothes. "In answer to you, yes. Little things like us aren't privileged enough to think of what WE want. These are gods, and with a god complex to go with it, a bad one. So, we're all inferior creatures by comparison. Does this give you an idea of things?"

"Wow, and yes. But you said someone is responsible for killing them off finally?"

"Yes…more of the same, a newer generation that replaced the older one. But here it runs a bit deeper. We're simply a side show in a much bigger game. On Therinë, we found Darumon impersonating a local governor. He can apparently change his form, so he can impersonate anyone. And as a nearly godlike being, he has an innate ability to fold space, meaning to transport himself place-to-place, no conveyors necessary. Therefore, he can come and go anywhere, and no one can stop HIM, either."

"I don't like the sound of that," the Captain groans.

"We believe he was with us on the ship, and THIS is the reason we were found each time. We jump, and he calls it in. He was spying on us."

"And I certainly do not like that!" he growls.

"Then we have that wild jump, which was likely him at the nav station programming the coordinates to this world. We were brought here intentionally."

"So that's it!" the Captain shouts angrily. "I never could accept that we were simply so lucky to hit a valid target."

"Yeah, you and a lot of others."

"But what's so special about here?" Túfula asks.

"For one thing, he owned these orcs for many millennia, long before we ever arrived. He used them previously to invade other worlds. They were simply babysitting us until he grew tired of carrying us along for his fun time. He came to this universe for a reason, to find some special materials to make a kind of weapon to use on his old enemies."

"I'm not so sure I want to ask this, but who are these enemies?"

"And also," the Captain wonders. "Why would he program OUR jump drive, if he has his own method?"

"The reason why," Kaliya responds, "is to claim we had this tracking device that so conveniently attached itself to our ship as we jumped away. And this is to give justification for those dull-horns back home to follow us. How do you like that one?"

"I don't, and on multiple levels."

"As for who these others are… Here is where our kind needs a history lesson. Like I said, these are gods. So, religion or not, you need to realize WE are just children. THEY are the ones who own the place. And they are billions of years old by now. So, godhood, in whatever context you would like to define it, is real. It just takes several eternities to achieve it."

"Oops!" Túfula yips.

"They call themselves the Estelar. They are a conglomeration of anything that managed to evolve so high, they don't even live in a three-dimensional universe anymore, and neither do they possess corporeal bodies."

"OOPS!"

"And they are the successors to Sargeras and his kind after a series of wars to wipe out the former and replace it."

"And Super-Oops!"

"Sargeras and Darumon are believed to be the last survivors of a precursor god society. The Estelar call them Primordials. They were an overseer society that literally held a god complex of authority, dictating life and death based on whatever conditions they felt were appropriate to the need, but never to allow anything to evolve up to a point where it could compete with them. They loved their position of power too much."

"Oh wow, that doesn't sound good,"

"This would then explain Tana's statement of having minds for any reason, thinking or otherwise. No, you're not allowed this, not unless they tell you to perform a juggling act in a circus. Beyond that, you don't even qualify as fertilizer."

"In all the nether-space, it's that bad?" Tana whines.

"Then, one day, after probably an eternity and a half, their society begins to decline, leaving gaps in their authority for some other race to finally push its way up. Here come the Estelar, who probably discovered the Primordials at some point, learned who they were and what they were doing, and took an instant loathing to it. Thus we have what we call the Celestial Wars to destroy them. Unfortunately, and we think perhaps during the final battle, Sargeras and Darumon ran off and hid. But this was yet another eternity ago, and so no one remembers them by this time. Due to this, they're now coming out hoping to take revenge. And this is the glorious crusade those dull-horned galoots are actually taking under the guise of returning stolen goods. They don't even know what they're doing or why they're doing it. And our lovely Elder Council probably bowed down to them as soon as they heard the words 'great wisdom' come out."

This statement sent another wave of shock through the assembly, and they all wheezed and gasped again.

"And this is what he wanted from us," Kaliya continues. "Dull-horns, who coincidently have no idea of the history behind it, to do his dirty work. And unfortunately, they're not smart enough to actually ask what it is he's telling them to do. How do you like that for a society of scientists? It kind of makes you wish you were some other species…like maybe a talking bird," she glares at Túfula.

"Lovely," Túfula smirks. "So, how much do nest apartments cost back home, and do they come with built-in appliances?"

The group now ushers up a round of laughs and giggles.

"But surely," the Captain offers. "They ought to know the difference between us and these old enemies. Can't they at least see we don't have a military to fight with down here? They just come in and blast things. Falsehoods or otherwise, I would think some of them at least still have eyes."

"You have a point," Kaliya affirms. "I don't personally know what story he gives them about us, other than to say we apparently joined the other side, and this paints a target circle on us. But this next world was filled with a technologically inferior society, and they blasted nearly the whole world just because Darumon told them they were associated with his old enemies, whoever he describes his enemies to actually be. It was a form of containment…blasting them down to a handful of cities just to contain them. As if they might pose any kind of threat to such as we to begin with. So, whatever story he's telling them about us, I guess it's moot. Especially as they just follow orders with chips in their brains to enforce compliance if they can't do it right any other way."

"What?" Túfula shrieks. "They have chips in their brains?"

"Yeah, described as military grade control chips to enforce compliance. This is apparently how you get people who would normally hide under a rock at the first big noise they hear to instead go out and do any real work. That, in addition to that old biotech garbage on their backs. We still haven't figured out why he wanted that."

"Biotech garbage? The mutation?"

"And therefore, those guns," Tana huffs.

"Yeah," Kaliya nods. "Something we think Darumon pulled out of an old closet. It's part of some ancient study to create an artificial lifeform as an augmentation for colonizing hostile environments. This, I suppose, as compared to simply putting a breather mask on your face," she giggles ironically. "But no one liked it, so it was tossed out. But it seems he brought it into production again. All their military seems to be using this. And apparently the same as what the orcs did to our people, although in our case a different formulation, and no thanks to that gun you mentioned...a rifle I found in that shaman's hut over there."

"Oh!" Tana blasts. "So THAT'S the reason you went running around the camp like a loose-horned goon. I saw you go in there. But what did you do to that poor shaman to make him literally fly through the roof?"

"I hit him with an oversized fist," Kaliya smirks. "It wasn't intended to kill, but simply to apply enough force to lift him up and out, therefore allowing me to escape sight-unseen."

"And the rifle?" Túfula resumes. "What does it actually shoot?"

"It's a launcher to fire a remarkably advanced mini missile projectile, with an image recognition circuit, hydrogen fuel mixer, and a cryostasis compartment with the seed core inside. The design could win an award for the technological achievement, if only it was used for something sane."

"Sane is right!" she shouts.

"The original design is supposed to enhance the host body, but ours was made to debilitate the target. It's a pure terrorist weapon to frighten whatever remaining horns we might still have as we're panicking through the streets."

"Unbelievable!" Sulíma moans. "Nothing is sacred to that guy."

"And so we have the attack..." Túfula muses. "Just to entertain someone in the most villainous manner possible."

"Very good," Kaliya asserts. "But there's more we learned back home, which I think I should leave for later. I don't want to unload too much on you at once. We're a little concerned over Darumon continuing to spy on us. Although, I find it unlikely he would know of you here. More likely, he would think you should be dead."

"Probably, and at this moment, I would be thankful for that."

"I would instead say I'm absolutely amazed to see you still alive, especially under these conditions. How is it you managed to survive out here?"

"The orcs never knew we were here," the Captain responds. "They apparently turned back once they were finished in the city. They never came out this far. And now that we know of those conveyors, we understand why. Although we didn't know of them until recently."

"Then what were you doing all this time if not running from them?"

"Just trying to live, mostly by hunting and gathering."

"And moping a lot," Sulíma adds.

"Moping?" Kaliya considers. "Yeah, I suppose that might make sense. You were probably surrounded on all sides, at least initially. We were doing it too...that is, until Thaelyn showed up."

"Who is that?" the Captain asks.

"He's the one who chased Darumon away, along with his Suuden'kai loyalists. He's the king of yet another world, one that Darumon was trying to encroach upon, but got his tail spanked for it. He's a being called a Celestial, and he's directly related to these Estelar. Oh, and you might want to know this. We were expected to arrive."

"Um, expected to arrive? How do you mean?"

"For this, we need to go back to the cu'Nar again. They're spies working for someone, a member of the Estelar who knew of Sargeras and was watching him. They were sent to evacuate us with a ship donated by that same individual explicitly because she knew Darumon would chase us up to Thaelyn's front door, and carrying a message from the cu'Nar on who and what Sargeras actually was…a Titan."

"All right, in order to keep what's left of my horns, help me to understand the reference here. Does that word hold special meaning to these people?"

"It does, to those with such ancient background that they might remember the Primordials. No one else would likely recall it by now, except for such as the Estelar themselves, or beings like the cu'Nar who are probably also ancient. We think this person couldn't take direct action at the time, so we had to come to them and bring with us this message. That other world, one we call Tae'Eladar, is a garden world that was apparently built and cultured for this reason. They are the counterforce to chase HIM now."

"But they couldn't do this earlier?"

"I could answer that in two ways, both of them no. First, they're in yet another universe and with no way out. And they're not space capable. But they do have a form of magical device similar to our conveyors. So, spaceships or not, they CAN travel to other worlds, so long as they have an index."

"Oh wow," Sulíma croons. "That would be interesting to see."

"And second, they didn't know anything until they bumped into us on Therinë as the result of the ORCS using such a method, thank you Darumon for the thought, and using this to escape from them after starting a war over there."

"Oops!"

"Aside from that, the Estelar are a little strange in how they do things. They like to teach and test younger societies like ours as part of a growth and learning exercise. This one individual, known as Maker Kuroku, seems to be laying low and directing others, like Thaelyn, to do the work. Sargeras might not pay as much attention to one such as he or his people to sneak up on him, as he might with an Estelar proper."

"Oh, I see," the Captain accedes. "Let me guess, to make a surprise hit on him this time."

"Right!" she nods.

"But then, how about this new society. How advanced are they to compare with such like the Suuden-Aryku? They must be very advanced to chase them away."

"Uh…" she coughs. "Yes and no, and not the way we would define advanced. Here is where we need another lesson. We need to put this into context. WE are the unfortunate runts here. We come from a universe, probably one of the very few, that does NOT have the good stuff in it. The orcs and their magic? It's powered by an energy layer we are completely unfamiliar with because we weren't born into it. It allows for a uniquely different tech tree, and it does NOT follow like ours did. These people were able to use portals, which are similar to conveyors, long before they understood how to use electricity. And primarily, as I understand it, simply because someone got tired of walking the distance."

"Oh, well…" Sulíma huffs sarcastically. "Isn't that just tragic!"

"But how is that even possible?" the Captain urges.

"They don't need science," Kaliya responds. "They don't need machines. They don't need empirical study. All they need is the imagination, and the sky is the limit after that. Right now, by tech terms WE would understand, we might see them as Early Industrial. But by magical terms, they beat us in several areas already, even WITH all our tech."

"In all the nether-space, that'll twist a few horns."

"Yeah, and most of us have lost several years' worth just trying to interpret the possibilities. Even the riddle of metaphysics, as we thought we understood it, seems a little amateurish by now."

"Um, but wait," Tana interjects. "So, this Thaelyn guy is hoping to chase after Sargeras and the Suuden-Aryku, but just how does he hope to cross over to Azgarén if the ship is dead and he's…" she coughs for emphasis, "…only Early Industrial, and without space tech? You mentioned conveyors, but you also mentioned a need for an index, which I'm sure we CAN understand."

"Yeah, this will surely cause your horns to drop off. One, like I said, I'm in training, and studying their magic. Once done, I will hopefully be able to lead them to this world using one of these portals. Two, we hope to find access to another world after this, and we currently suspect one of these conveyors of holding the link to where we believe Darumon has a mining operation. These orcs were once used to assault that world. From there, we ought to be able to steal some of their own tech, like a conveyor or something, and boom, Azgarén. Does that answer your question?"

"Which one, finding your way to Azgarén, or me looking for my horns?" she slumps. "But you say they're actually teaching you magic over there? Oh, I wish I could learn a few things. Can you teach me something?"

"Well, this isn't something to take lightly. It's actually a very potent force and needs a lot of respect. I could maybe give you a little lesson, but let's wait until later for that."

"All right, but please-please," she begs. "I want to learn how this works. I've tried so many times to figure it out, watching the orcs from my hiding places, but I could never get it to work."

"The orcs wouldn't be good teachers, I'll bet. But these people have structured education courses, and it's also a licensed art."

"Licensed? They actually place a kind of government authority over it? Wow."

"They study it like we study science. It's very integral to their culture. But it's also a power with a lot of potential for misuse. Therefore, discipline is paramount, and you need to declare your responsibility over it as you learn."

"Amazing."

"But now, I need to ask about you people," Kaliya directs. "This is taking longer than expected, and I was only supposed to be making a quick survey before reporting back."

"Where is your home base?" the Captain wonders.

"I work for Thaelyn, and right now, he's on Therinë, but I'm also still in training, and that's on Tae'Eladar."

"I see, but…wait. If he doesn't have space tech, and you need a portal to arrive here, but you don't have one yet…I think I'm getting lost."

"Yeah, I suppose you might. One thing at a time, because to answer that question will probably do more than just make your horns fall off. First and foremost, how in all the nether-space did you get stuck here in the first place. You look like, um…"

Kaliya glares at the Captain intensely, trying to judge his identity by his tattered uniform.

"You look like Sentinels, or what's left of one. I guess three and a half centuries, and no clothing stores…" she chuckles as she glances around the group.

The Captain examines the rags that were once his uniform, then around to some of the others who were in a similar or worse state.

"Yeah, the centuries took their toll on us."

"Especially this girl over here," she points a wing at Tana. "Do you have any actual clothes on underneath those weeds of yours?"

"I have a loincloth, is that good enough?" she smirks.

Kaliya covers her eyes with a wing as she shakes her head.

"And besides," Tana continues proudly. "I'll have you know these aren't weeds. They are a carefully woven mat of fern leaves and native grasses to create the latest fashion in jungle apparel. Just the sort of thing every young girl craves around here."

"Oh, I see, and do you have any formal designs? We talking birds like to go out on the town every so often."

"I suppose I could make something up, but I'll need measurements first."

"Uh huh, and the body paint?"

"My own design…" she issues confidently. "Only loosely copied from the orcs. I was thinking of marketing it one day. For the girl on the go who wants to stand out…or maybe to blend in…to the local scene."

Kaliya glared at her, then broke out with outrageous laughter at the bold assertion. But as she studied the girl and her presentation, she couldn't help but appreciate how well-played it actually was.

"That was very good. But you know, you would make a good druid."

"A what? What's a druid?"

"A druid is a priest of nature that holds a religious reverence for the natural world and all living things. They dress a lot like you, too. They can only wear garments created of natural materials, they learn how to live with the natural elements, use herbs and organic ingredients to create healing agents and other remedies, and they teach others about living in harmony with nature, that we are all a part of the natural world and need to respect it. I know some people back home you might want to talk to."

"Are you actually serious? These people you met hold a religious practice and speak to nature in some way?"

"Yes, they do…well, some of them. These people pay special honor and a form of piety to the Estelar as a god society that teaches them a variety of principles of life, which is where I got mine. I'll bet you picked up a little of this from the orcish shamans, right? Well, the Estelar teach younger societies like ours as a means to help guide us. Where druids are concerned, they revere a goddess named Mielikki, also known as the Forest Queen."

"A goddess…" she muses. "But if I understand correctly, this isn't some kind of mysticism like a shaman and how he might do it. It sounds more like we're taking up a form of study under these beings, right?"

"In a manner of speaking, yes. And we should be careful of the word mysticism. I used that a few times and got my tail chewed for it. It's only due to our empirical-minded conditioning that if it isn't measured in numbers, it isn't real. But the relationship these people share is rather unique. You might say they work as a kind of extension of their philosophical principles where they go out and solve other people's problems."

"Even if those problems are found on other worlds and in other universes?" Sulíma smirks.

"Especially that kind," Kaliya counters. "Thaelyn loves challenges."

"Oh dear. I was actually joking, but that's scary."

"Not as scary as to see him when I laid that Titan message on him that day. Ugh! Anyway, back to you..." she redirects to the Captain. "What's your name? Your badge, what's left of it, isn't legible anymore."

"I'm Captain Tudorin Lapäli."

Kaliya was stunned at the mention of that name. She gaped at the virtual phantom standing in front of her, and began stumbling back, letting out of bold wail as her voice kicked in.

"Captain Lapäli?!" she screeches. "Grace of the cu'Nar, it's you? In all the nether-space! How...how..."

Kaliya fell backward, and although she wasn't physical, her mind simulated the emotion of shock and a panting effect.

"I don't believe this," she wheezes. "You're a hero back home. They even commemorated you..." she reflects briefly. "Although it was posthumously...but still..."

"Well, I suppose I should be thankful for that," he sighs.

Kaliya raises herself up again and starts pacing around nervously as she tries to collect her thoughts.

"Padriyl is going to lose his horns after he hears this. And Tanjhira! Oh dear cu'Nar, I hope they don't make ME do this!"

The Captain perks up at hearing the names.

"They're still alive over there?" he asks tenderly.

"Yeah, they were lucky. But oh, this is going to hit hard. Do you know how many of them argued over you being out there to begin with? Some were saying it was a completely futile and wasted effort. Why did you do it?"

"Well, I recall Velen came to me once, privately, and suggested I needed to do this."

"Velen!" she shrieks. "Oh wait! Was this that thing with the cu'Nar I heard about?"

"Yeah, he got a visit from the cu'Nar shortly before, suggesting I had a purpose for myself."

Kaliya pauses as she connects the meaning. And as it snapped into place, she quickly lost control. She screams and runs in circles waving her wings.

"In all the nether-space! Maker Kuroku, just what are you doing out there! Argh!"

The Captain and the others glared at the abnormal behavior, glancing around their group to observe each other's reactions.

"I wonder," Tana muses. "Do they have bird psychologists over there?"

"Maybe we should call for the birds in white jackets?" Sulíma wonders.

"Where do you put something like this," Túfula adds. "A padded nest?"

After several moments of Kaliya screeching a series of exclamatory remarks in multiple languages, she finally ran out of steam enough to find her focus again for the conversation.

"Old lizard, indeed!" she grumbles coarsely. "If Aerlie ever wanted a talk, I'm going to have a few of my own words. Captain, the cu'Nar told you to stay behind? Did they give a reason?"

"I can't be sure," he replies. "You know how they are for their messages."

"Oh! Yes! I know of a few things where THAT goes! And where it comes from, too! All right, let's examine what we have here. I see a lot of people. How many are we counting out here?"

"We have around fourteen hundred survivors here," the Captain responds.

Kaliya froze in her tracks as she gawked at the man. Her body seemed petrified with another jolt of shock. She then let out a soft whine as she slowly toppled sideways and stiffly rolled onto her back with her feet sticking up.

"Well, you killed it, Captain," Túfula announces perkily. "So much for our partnership."

The Captain set his hands on his hips as he turned to raise his brow at her.

Kaliya gazed ahead blankly, seeing the world upside-down from her stricken posture.

"I'm…not…going to…survive…this…" she mutters flatly.

"Let me guess," the Captain begins. "You probably weren't expecting that number, am I right?" he smiles tenderly.

"Not expecting?!" she yelps as she tries to reorient herself. "Cu'Nar help us, now I think you're deliberately trying to torment me. There are societies out there with laws against abusing animals, did you know that?"

The group lets out another bold laugh at the mention.

"How did this happen?" Kaliya asks urgently. "Did we actually have so many people missing the boat?"

"Yeah, it seems a large number were cut off by the orcs and chased out of the city. But the rest were hiding in shelters at the junior school."

This time, Kaliya felt faint, being completely dumbfounded by those words. She tried shaking her head in disbelief as she feebly passed her glance around all the young faces. She began awkwardly stumbling back. Her voice failed her, and all she could do was make subtle whines as the notion settled in. Finally, she collapsed.

"The…school…?" she wheezes faintly.

She continued studying the assembly, most of whom were arranged in front of the building, with several lined up near the workshops.

"THE SCHOOL?!" she screams boisterously, this time reverberating her voice.

The shockingly loud booming of her voice rattled the assembly. It echoed off the hillside and resounded amongst the buildings, causing the mass of people to cringe under the pressure of it.

"In all the nether-space…" Sulíma murmurs.

"Yeah!" Kaliya shouts. "In all the nether-space, indeed! Do you have any idea what this'll do back home? Grace of the cu'Nar! How in all the nether-space did THAT happen?!"

Now, a wave of emotion takes over, and she begins to break down. She collapsed fully to the rooftop and tried covering her face with her wings. And again, although she was unable to feel the physical sensation of weeping, nevertheless, her mind felt the intense pain, and she began to sob.

"Cu'Nar's pity, Captain," Sulíma whispers. "What was all that about?"

"Just try to imagine it from their side, Suli," he emits gently. "All you kids being lost over here, and they probably thought we were all dead."

"Well, yeah, I suppose, and for all we went through here, we also had our share of it."

"And all because of that monster," Túfula scorns. "I wouldn't be a bit surprised if he was the one responsible for those orders."

Kaliya continued to whimper as she reflected on her past miseries.

"And I thought I was the only one..." she moans. "All alone. So many memories torn away. My entire life...I was simply too young for it."

The gathering waited several more moments as she tried once again to pull herself together. Kaliya stands up again, but feeling weak for all the stress.

"How..." she asserts firmly. "That's what I want to know. In the name of the cu'Nar, how? There simply has to be a reason, right?"

"Normally," the Captain admits. "I would have to agree with you. But we had a few of our own problems along the way, at least one of which relates to someone getting the evac order backwards."

"Backwards!" Kaliya shouts. "Captain, how do you get an evac order backwards?"

"We don't really know how it happened. Whoever it was that got it wrong isn't here with us."

"Oh wonderful, and I'm sure the Council would love to hear about this. But to be honest, I don't think I want to be in the same room when that happens," she waves it off.

"Yeah, I think I can appreciate that much. All we know is someone in the admin office delivered instructions for the full body to go into the shelters. From my perspective, this essentially countermanded the Council's orders."

"Countermanded!" she screeches. "You don't countermand the

Council! Not during an evacuation, with sirens going off and people screaming in the streets!"

Kaliya began pacing around the rooftop again.

"Yes," the Captain concedes. "Although those alarms cut off very early after they got started."

"Yes, I recall that, I think. Worse is that so few people actually got to the ship on this occasion."

"Yeah, we saw large pileups of bodies in the streets, many of them cornered in alleys."

"I don't like the sound of that, Captain. And I doubt anyone else will either."

"And we didn't like the sight of it. We found it this way as we were trying to sneak back in so we could bury the dead."

Kaliya stopped in her tracks and glared at him.

"They just left them there?"

"Yeah, it seemed that way. Then they went home, and I'm going to guess they were playing with their shiny new conveyor, since they didn't seem to have any further interest in the city, except for the occasional raid for trophies."

"Oh, this is going to sting a few tails. Now I understand nature girl over here and her tantrum. Dear cu'Nar, just wait till they hear about this one. Forget the rest, this will send them climbing the walls, and then some."

Suddenly, she halted as her mind began to ponder the implications. She perked up and began scanning the audience.

"Who do we have here? How many got out, Captain?"

"As far as we can tell, except for that one administrator, we seem to have the full assembly. Roughly nine hundred kids, all the teachers, and the rest of the staff."

"Nine hundred…and the teachers…" she drifts off. "Where were they when you found them?"

"Just coming out onto the playfields as the ship flashed out of sight."

"Oh, such marvelous timing! Come on out, kids, and watch your life flash before your eyes. Then run for whatever is left of it!"

"Yeah, that's just about how it happened," he huffs ironically. "I think we got lucky. The orcs had diverted through the northern part of town to the ship, while my team was circling around to the south. This allowed us to evade them, and it also placed us in close proximity to the school at the time."

Kaliya halted abruptly at the statement and jerked around to glare at him.

"So, you just happened to be by the school at the time they came out? And naturally, you meet, and the only thing left to do is run out here, I suppose."

"Yeah. Fortunately, the crop fields were tall enough to conceal us behind them."

"Captain, are you listening to yourself right now? You meet them at just the right moment as they were coming out, then run out here with such convenience as to have sufficiently tall crops to cover you. And the orcs had no further interest in anything after the ship was gone. And all this thanks to the cu'Nar telling you to stay behind."

Now it was the Captain's turn to be stunned, along with Sulíma, Túfula and the rest. They gazed at each other, and further to study the full assembly, as they all began to realize the association.

"Cu'Nar's pity," Sulíma moans. "And maybe literally so. It was planned. They knew about it."

"More likely Maker Kuroku knew about it," Kaliya asserts. "She's the driving force behind their so-called prophecies. She has an agent we call Adalon. SHE is the prophetess, and likely through her, they are driving a lot of things."

"So, is this to say we owe them our lives? Well, um, naturally, I would thank them, I suppose. But it's a very strange way of doing things."

"These people have a very appropriate saying to go along with that. The gods work in strange ways, and I swear, does that ever hold up. But, all things considered, for what you had to work with, let's not argue the point."

"Absolutely!"

Kaliya circled around on the rooftop again as she tried to collect her thoughts. Her mind was swimming in a swarm of details and portrayals, and she was dreading the effort of reporting any of this back. Furthermore, she was growing increasingly nervous for the extended time she was spending, and what Thaelyn might be thinking right now. She pauses to glance at the myriad of faces staring up at her.

"I don't recognize anyone here. But then, three and a half centuries does things to a person."

"Yeah, it turns some of us into talking birds," Sulíma jibes.

"You know, I could bring back that stone giant, if you were so impressed by it."

"Impressed?" she retorts. "Like, into the ground? No, thank you."

"You're quick on the rebound," Kaliya muses affectionately. "You remind me of someone I once knew."

Kaliya pauses to scan the attendance again, trying to pick out faces.

"All adults now…" she whispers. "I wonder what sort of relations… You there, nature girl," she directs. "Tana, is it? Tana what?"

"Me? I'm Tana Lar'akan."

"Lar'akan…" Kaliya muddles. "Wait, would you happen to be related to Navina?"

At the mention of the name, Tana instantly began to feel tears welling up.

"My mother?" she murmurs softly. "Is she alright?"

A man from the crowd hurriedly rushed out to her side.

"I'm Tana's father, Jarel. What about Navina?"

"Well, for one thing," Kaliya notes. "She'll probably explode after hearing about you two. She once told me how she was nearly meteoric over this attack and losing you."

"Yeah, that sounds like her. She always was a very passionate young lady."

"It seems a lot of us are like that. Aside from that, she's fine. She's in training alongside me back home. She just recently signed up, in fact, and I'll probably end up sharing a few of my lessons with her soon. We're assembling a team, as it turns out."

"A team? What kind, and what kind of training?"

"Military, with a few interesting twists, and certainly NOT Sentinels, with all due respect, Captain. Ours is going to be special, designed to fight wars…and win."

"Um," Túfula speaks up anxiously. "What about my father? Elder Vankkar, is he alright?"

Kaliya stared at the girl as she came to the realization of her identity.

"Are you Túfula?" she wheezes. "Oh wow… I don't want to hear him react to this one. Of all things, I do NOT want to be present to give this to him. Yeah, he's fine. He still screams out his contentions on the Council, and a lot of them at me for one thing or another. Although, I'll admit, he was in terrible shape after the attack."

She then turns to the nearest face, the one she got started with on her first arrival.

"And then we have you," she points and asks. "Why do you seem so familiar?"

"Um, well," Sulíma emits. "Maybe because I'm just so darned likeable?" she smiles innocently.

"Yeah, you…that attitude…that face…um, you… Oh dear cu'Nar, please…"

As Kaliya gazed into the girl's eyes, she began to make a connection. Despite the long duration of time, the features were starting to stand out.

"Suli?" she mumbles.

Kaliya instinctively starts backing away as she tries to reconcile her interpretation of the girl's face.

"Suli, is that you?"

Sulíma glanced at Túfula and Tana before returning to the bird on the rooftop.

"Yeah, my name is Sulíma Tad'vaal."

Kaliya jerks back and wails boisterously as she falls down again, then kicking to back away further from this seemingly ghostlike presence.

"Well, Suli," Túfula declares cutely. "You just succeeded in scaring the life out of a talking bird. Congratulations, I think this makes up for your incident with the stone giant."

"Well, at least I didn't kill it, like the Captain. See, it's still twitching!" she playfully jabs a finger at it.

"Maybe so, but it's seriously going to need therapy before this is over."

"Túfu," Tana submits. "I think most of us will need therapy. We're talking to a bird. I think Tyanna is going to have her hands full soon. If she wasn't busy enough with her city patrol, now she'll need to make time for counseling sessions."

"All right, fine," Sulíma relents. "But why is it behaving like this? Do we know each other or something?"

"Suli," Túfula asserts. "When was the last time you had a friend who was a talking bird?"

"Well, I'll admit, a few of them had some flighty attitudes, but at least they kept their feet on the ground."

Kaliya had suffered yet another breakdown and was sobbing again, laying on the rooftop and covering her face. But as she listened to their conversation, she managed to pull together what few remaining fragments of courage she had left and hoisted herself upright again.

"I swear, Suli," she whimpers. "You haven't changed a bit. How did you do it? Three and a half centuries…here! Moping, you say? And yet, look at you. You're doing better than I was during this same time."

"Um, why do you say that? What happened to you?"

"Oh! Let's see now…" she tries to sit up. "Shock, trauma, rage, frustration, and a vicious tail itch for vendettas. And I got into a lot of trouble with the Council for going out and nearly getting myself killed on multiple occasions. All because of what those…" her voice trails off as she glances in the direction of the city and the orcish camp. "I had nightmares of the attack. I was running down the street, everything was burning, people were screaming. I would wake up with cold sweats. My general attitude to life was dismal.

And I stopped talking to my father for three and a half centuries, all because I couldn't..." she ducks away.

"That sounds bad," Tana muses. "You must've got hit hard by it. But you know, a lot of us got hit too. When we saw the ship flash away, many of us were crying for weeks just for this alone, not to mention the carnage we found in the city and so many dead family members. Suli lost both parents, we found Túfu's mother, Petrith's father..."

Kaliya instantly perked up at the mention of the name.

"Petrith? Is he here too? Oh great, one more thing on top of all the rest."

Kaliya scans the area for the young man, but he doesn't seem to be present.

"Where is he?"

"He's on patrol right now in the city. He works for the Captain. So do I, for that matter. We're scouts to watch the city and the orcs."

"I see. And you must hold some talent, for your disguise."

"Yes, and I'm kind of proud of it, too."

Kaliya nodded as she examined the girl's outfit.

"I'll admit, although our culture might disagree, it's not bad."

"So, what's the deal with you falling apart up there?" Sulíma asks gently.

"Three and a half centuries, Suli," Kaliya sighs. "And I never thought I'd see you again."

"All right, but does this mean we know each other? That is, other than this bird costume you're wearing."

"Yeah, other than for this..." she glances at herself as she extends a wing. "This is the hard part."

Kaliya shakes her head and turns away. She steps off to the side where she hopes to find a little peace to collect herself.

"The whole junior school," she mumbles to herself. "Still alive..." she glances at the assembly again. "How am I going to bring this home. And worse, now I need to try explaining this next part. Maybe I should've stayed at home today."

She closes her eyes as she reflects on the conversation.

"No, it had to be done, and I'm the only one who can do it. No one else has learned this thing yet. And we needed the information."

Kaliya knew this was going to come out eventually. But it was made more difficult by having so many faces, some of them familiar, now watching her. She stepped forward again to rejoin the group. If she were corporeal, she would be breathing a heavy sigh, but as a projection, she didn't actually breathe air. Still, she felt an urge to simulate it as best she could.

"Um…" she glances uncertainly at herself. "All right, this may be a little awkward…"

"Awkward?" Túfula retorts. "We're talking to a bird, and YOU think it's awkward?"

"Hey, we all have our issues. After all, I was preening myself all morning before going out today, and now look at me."

Sulíma couldn't help but explode with a spontaneous round of laughter, followed by Túfula and the rest, while Kaliya steps over to the edge of the rooftop to peer at the ground below. She turns once more to look at Sulíma before making her transition.

"So, you panicked and ran all the way home after that stone god image, right?"

"Yeah, and then collapsed from exhaustion once I got there."

"Well, at least this time you don't have as far to run."

She returns her focus to the ground and folds herself down to it, transforming herself along the way into her natural form. She materialized in front of the crowd, much to their amazement, and looked directly into Sulíma's eyes.

"Hello, Suli. It's me, Kali."

Sulíma's eyes bulged, at first from the transformation, then further after seeing who it was. She gasped briskly, and attempted to squeak out a scream while raising a finger to shake nervously at the unexpected apparition, then wheezed and fainted, with her limp body crashing to the ground.

Kaliya stood there and set her hands on her hips, shaking her head.

"Poor girl, I was afraid of this."

She stepped forward to see if she could offer assistance, kneeling down next to the girl.

"Túfu, Tana, the three of you seem like close friends these days. Help me with her. My interactions with people are still a little shaky."

"Huh? Me?" Túfula blurts. "I mean, yeah."

"Interactions?" Tana ushers uncertainly. "Anything like with those orcs? That seemed solid enough."

"Yes, well…" Kaliya shrugs.

They all converge on the fallen young lady, lifting her up and trying to revive her.

The Captain, and most of the others in the group, gawked at the scene, trying to find their collective voices.

"Kali?" he mutters disbelievingly. "As in, Velen's daughter?"

"Yeah, that one. My…contact…in the city is my mother. We're using her as a local commander to organize a series of patrol displays to keep up an image for the orcs out there. At least until something better comes along."

"Yeah. We found her, and shortly after that, we fell apart from it. Poor Suli was a mess when she heard what happened. And then I had to listen to Tana and one of her tirades about us not holding up our tails as we should."

"Really. So…" she redirects. "Are you a little scrapper like me?" she grins tenderly.

"I have my moments," Tana smiles.

"Then we should get along great. But I do have a few standards for the dress code," she eyes the girl for her scanty apparel.

"Well, if you can direct me to a clothing store with my size in stock, I might take a look."

"But Kali," the Captain begins. "What did we just see? How are you able to do that?"

"Yeah. Um, Captain, we have a little security issue here that needs to be understood before we go into that."

"All right, what kind?"

"It reflects on Darumon again. This could be the turning point for us to do away with that beast. And I'm something of a pioneer."

Túfula had been patting Sulíma on the shoulder and face, trying to get the girl to wake up. Finally, Sulíma begins to groan as she regains consciousness. She looked up into Kaliya's eyes, a sight she never expected to see again, and returns a delicate smile.

"Kali…" she ushers softly.

"Yeah…" she returns pleasantly.

"Yeah?!" Sulíma snaps brashly. "Is that all you can say? The least you could've done was warn me before popping into existence like that. I didn't ever expect to see you again. And when we found your mother…cu'Nar's grace, I was a complete wreck."

"Well, there's not much I could've done except to show myself. I don't think giving my name would help much if you were simply talking to a bird. I could try for that tiger image again, but then it might be Tana who would faint. And I'm not fully trained on reviving plant people," she flashes a grin at Tana.

"Um, you could try throwing water in her face. Plants like that!"

"Excuse me," Tana protests. "I just finished reapplying my paint. That stuff doesn't grow on trees, you know."

The group all glared at her, and then erupted in a brisk laugh.

"You people…" Kaliya smiles and shakes her head. "Anyway, Captain, we have a number of military secrets we're keeping to ourselves, and this also means away from the Council. My father isn't the only one out there with telepathy. Beings like Darumon and Sargeras should have this as a standard feature, and the Council is likely a prime choice to steal stuff."

"Uh oh," he moans. "So, Elder Vankkar might have a point with all his rambling about security threats?"

"Yes, but it could actually be worse if Darumon was spying on us and could simply go up to one of them and start a conversation. The Council, and this could reflect all the way back to Azgarén, tends to place itself with an absolute need to know everything about everything, and this makes them THE most vulnerable information leak if you simply know how to approach it."

"Oh great!"

"But at the same time, I'm working with Celestials right now.

Telepathy is a common feature in them too, and they might use it as often as common speech. It's all a matter of discipline to use it right. Elder Vankkar is simply concerned we're not ready. Regardless of that, I'll be training it soon from a professional. By comparison, we might say my father is an amateur with whatever he has."

"Wow. That puts it into a new perspective."

"And yet, it doesn't stop there. We're discovering we might have a few hidden qualities in us as a race. What you saw here was one of them, and probably THE most important thing we could ever hope to discover in our lives. It's called the Prodigy Gift."

Suddenly, Túfula screeches and falls away from the group. She glares at Kaliya with her eyes bulging as she tries to study the girl for her mystical presentation.

Kaliya and the others jerk back at the unexpected display.

"Are you the one?" Túfula utters tenuously.

"The one what?"

"The one they found once. My father said something about finding a Prodigy Child and they were trying to study it."

"He actually told you this? I thought it was a secret."

"Well, yes, it was…um, is…or was. And then we had the attack."

"Yeah, and then that, which traumatized me so badly, I lost it for a few centuries, along with most of my marbles. But yeah, my mother was trying to research it, although she didn't actually tell me anything about what I was doing, so I had no idea until I rediscovered it with Thaelyn's help. You need something like a Celestial to help you figure it out. It's literally a godlike skill we, as a species, shouldn't have. But it seems we do. And you can thank Darumon for that, as well."

"Uh oh…I don't know if I like that. Why?"

"Let's just say for now, our history isn't what we thought it was. I'll fill you in with the details later. Anyway, it's probably our biggest secret to keep away from him, as he surely wouldn't want us to learn about it. Not with his attitudes on little things."

"So, you actually learned what it is, finally? Can you tell us a little?"

"It's the ability to project your spirit consciousness outside your physical body into physical space, and then to make it tangible enough to interact with things. You can also change shape to whatever you can imagine, assuming you can put enough visual detail into it, and you can move by thought from place to place."

"Wow! And so, you can create these shapes, and even sounds, like that shout you did earlier."

"Yeah, so it seems. I can also invoke my image to move at unnatural speeds, like during my scouting runs south of here, travelling at perhaps sonic speeds or better to cover more ground."

"Amazing! Is there anything you can NOT do with it?"

"I don't know yet. I'm still learning what I CAN do. My mother once coined a phrase while she was researching this. In this space I have will, and my will can alter this space. This reflects on our studies on metaphysics, but she didn't know just how close she was to a revelation, because I'm doing it now."

"But it's still a little scary," Tana reflects. "You can appear out of nowhere and attack something, and even kill it."

"That orc was caught off-guard, I think. I used one shape to draw it out, and then the tiger to take it down. I'm not entirely sure how it might play out in a fair fight, although I did well enough with that shaman inside his hut…well, reasonably so. He didn't actually expect me to hit him…multiple times," she grins.

"Uh huh… I was out in those bushes and could hear the shouting. He wasn't at all happy."

"No, he wasn't. But then, neither was I."

"But wait," Túfula interjects. "My father also said something about children on Azgarén. This is supposed to be a really rare thing, isn't it?"

"The original Prodigy Children…" she nods. "It's actually a latent ability only now showing up. So the term 'rare' is subjective if you leave it ONLY to a random child randomly discovering it… as opposed to taking structured lessons in a classroom."

"Oops!"

"I suppose we can also say subjective for a bunch of dull-horns who need to measure everything in numbers, and who do NOT believe in anything supernatural, even if they're trying to study such a fantastic concept as metaphysics."

"OOPS! That doesn't sound good for any of us."

"Yeah, and we're the best qualified to actually study it. You can blame it on our origins and what we're generally lacking to do it with. But a society like the Celestials live and die by this stuff."

"Really. But what about everything else we think is so important?"

"Obsolete by that time," she shakes her head. "It might still come into play, but only if you live in those spaces where it actually applies."

"Wow. Like a three-dimensional universe, as you said earlier?"

"Yeah, and yet another of our failures. We use the term 'netherspace' to mean a mythical place you don't believe in, and wouldn't want to find yourself lost in. But it actually relates to those places OUTSIDE a three-dimensional universe. The sort of places you need to evolve into if you ever want to continue up the ladder."

"Oh great!"

"Right now, we're testing people, including Tana's mother, to start using this as part of our new military team. It'll be quite a spectacle, I'm sure. We can barely even imagine how we might apply it, but those examples you saw here are just a taste."

"I'm not so sure I want to see where it goes, however."

"Yeah, but if it holds the potential to turn things around on Darumon, I'm all for it. He killed those first Prodigy Children simply because he didn't like the idea of us with something like this."

"Cu'Nar's pity!" Sulíma shrieks. "Doesn't he hold any respect for anything? These were children, you say?"

"That's right."

"But still, it's simply incredible," the Captain mumbles breathlessly. "So, this isn't actually a real body we're looking at?"

"It's described as a metaphysical manifestation of my spirit essence, then translocated by my will to whatever location, and whatever form I choose. My real body is sitting in a nice comfortable chair in a quiet room in the guildhall where I'm training on Tae'Eladar."

"A chair…" Sulíma muses. "Does it appear to be sleeping or something?"

"This is generally how we would describe it."

"But you know, Kali," Túfula admits. "The more you talk about this, the angrier I get over everything he did to us. And I'm not so sure I can forgive the Suuden-Aryku either. Someone needs to take a little responsibility here."

"I would agree with you, and I recall hearing Navina say something similar. But they're still a world, and also a universe away from us. However, if it makes you feel any better, I can tell you this much. After beating them on Therinë, and they were now in retreat, Thaelyn used a lost trans-com we found once to contact their base HQ. He spoke to their HC, someone named Geilv. According to the recording he made, Geilv was apparently also under a control effect."

"Their HC is under a control effect? But shouldn't he be the top guy in charge?"

"Not with Darumon in there. HE is the top guy, and the rest are puppets under him. But Geilv also seemed to be fighting or resisting it somehow. He was having a kind of feedback reaction to some of the statements relating to his errors in attacking inferior societies, and even us who never fought back. So, it might seem the control effect isn't perfect. He even apologized for himself once he understood how he wrecked someone's home without justifiable cause."

Túfula gaped at Kaliya for the statement. It contradicted so many millennia of their experiences relating to those she and the others had so often regarded as monsters during the long chase.

"So…" Tana ponders quietly. "They're still people, after all. Although they're also dull-horns to the extreme, and I'm still ashamed to be a part of the same species."

"Yes, many of us feel this way, actually," Kaliya finishes. "Nevertheless, they need our help."

"Kali," the Captain wonders. "If they had already blasted that whole world, and then this Thaelyn shows up, how did he actually manage to push them back?"

"Darumon made the mistake of thinking he was just another

plaything to toy with. Thaelyn is a clever guy, who spends just as much time concealing his origins as Darumon might his. Initially, he reinforced our position, along with the others, and slowly began to investigate and dismantle all of Darumon's games on that world. Meanwhile, they have a magical shield that's sturdy enough to repel the Suuden'kai pulse rifles. It's probably invincible to just about anything you can imagine, even an antimatter device."

"And they're only Early Industrial?" he grimaces.

"Yeah. It hurts a little to think of it. And I know, as I was under one of these shields when he blasted the place once. His people don't bother with guns, they still use swords, shields, and bows, although magically enchanted to offer increased potential. Between this and direct magic attacks, we were winning consistent victories against their soldiers, which is where we had a chance to study their bodies in autopsies. We found these chips, those seeds, and also learned how they're extremely vulnerable to physical injury. Scratch that seed the wrong way and boom, it kills the host underneath it. How do you like that for a puppet master and his toys?"

"Not at all."

"Cu'Nar's Pity!" Tana gasps. "So, in all this time, if we only had a simple bow and arrow, we could've fought back…assuming we had the horns to actually do it."

"Yeah," Kaliya nods. "Especially the part about the horns… We don't know the first thing about how to fight a proper war. We don't have the predator instinct in us to do it with. It's no wonder he put chips in his people, to actually make them fight."

"Uh huh…and here we are with so many of my…tirades," she glares at the Captain.

"But Kali," the Captain resumes. "Just who is this Thaelyn of yours? Because he sounds like a miracle worker. He slams the Suuden'kai HC with his own mistakes and draws out an apology. He chases something away that is described as nearly godlike, and he's willing to travel impossible distances to fight another one?"

"He's a soldier, a warrior, a messiah for his people, and a scholar and father figure to one and all…and race doesn't matter. And as a Celestial, they don't take no for an answer. It's that simple. Dimensional bounds don't stop them."

The Captain wheezes as he pulls back to consider this portrayal.

"And we only just now found him," Túfula moans.

"It probably couldn't be helped," Kaliya affirms. "Adalon wrote a set of books with a series of very peculiar prophecies describing Thaelyn, his wife Aerlie, and the history of Tae'Eladar once they arrived, leading us up to where we are now with a final chapter talking about us, our history, the chase, and Sargeras and Darumon. It apparently goes on with more we're still studying that we think leads us up to their downfall."

Now Túfula gaped at her for this new depiction.

"Kali, you mentioned something about a big game out there…"

"Yeah, and it's apparently been going on for a LONG time. Like I said, Tae'Eladar is a kind of garden world the Maker was culturing. It started out as a dead planet in an ice age, then she came along with some help to refurbish it, seed new life on it, and after a while, she installed Thaelyn to take over the place. He united the various nations into one world body under his rule, and now here we are."

"Wow!" she croons. "Now you're talking my language. You know, my father is a historian. He used to tell me stories when I was little of knights on crusades, riding on noble beasts, with chivalry and honor, and bringing the world together under one rule."

"Well, you should take a look at Tae'Eladar. They have a rich history with all that and probably a lot more. But in their case, they have flying mounts called gryphons, and using their magic, they can send those things at supersonic speed."

"You're kidding me! They don't even need something like aircraft?"

"Not specifically. They use portals as a kind of mass transit system for virtually everything. So, unless you have a need for such as scouting patrols, or maybe combat, air travel is moot."

"Oh! Really! So trucks, cargo vessels, and such, are yesterday's news? Instead, you have an industry make something, and zap! It's pops directly into a store?"

"Almost. They're entering a mechanized era now, so ground vehicles are used locally, like maybe for coaches and deliveries, and then portals for longer distance cargo runs. Many other things might be foot traffic, as they engineered the place to be very efficient for pedestrian travel. And oh! A new development where Therinë goes. They're redesigning the portal transit to use a vehicle, much like a ground vehicle, since it's so convenient, to carry passengers between worlds. How do you like that?"

"Uh huh, I think I was born on the wrong world. Do you live there now?"

"Yeah, I joined his military, so I'm an official citizen there."

"And you're in training. Hmm, this reminds me. At least now we know what Petrith was staring at all this time," she smirks naughtily.

"Huh?" Kaliya frowns. "What do you mean?"

"Oh, yeah," she rolls her eyes innocently. "He watches you while you're out on patrols, while you conduct your training, while you're in the shower..."

"Wait a minute! When you say he's watching me in the shower..."

"Yeah, he has these funny dreams where he thinks he sees you doing stuff, like this one where you were in this really luxurious waterfall shower, probably after your Phys. Ed. class, or whatever you call it over there. He took special note of your bar of soap, as I recall, and then the towel you used to dry off, just before going off to the locker room to get dressed in that uniform you wear."

Kaliya was stunned as she listened to this. She passed her glance around the group as she tried to find her voice again.

"And just how is he able to...dream...all of this? Because you're describing the guildhall shower room...and likely after my combat practice."

"We were talking about this just recently. I think he's showing signs of something my father once called clairvoyance."

"Oh, really! That's...well, that's actually very interesting. That's another Celestial power. I wonder if I can do that. I'll need to ask Aelwyn about that when I get back. Where is he? I think I need to share a few words with him about peeking in on me in the shower."

"Just remember, he was more interested in your soap than your body, apparently."

"Is that so?" she huffs. "You know, I happen to be quite proud of my body. I wash and maintain it regularly. So, next time, tell him to pay closer attention. That soap is scented!"

The group shared a bold laugh together.

"This is another one?" Tana wonders. "This clairvoyance thing?"

"There are many different kinds of Celestial powers a person might possess, depending on who they are and what special talents they're born with. So far, we're working on the Prodigy Gift and telepathy. But if Petrith is showing this one, we certainly need to investigate the idea. And this makes me wonder what else is out there. But I'll tell you, it's scary to think of what else we might have."

"Yes, I think I would agree."

"But anyway," Túfula sighs. "Now that you're back, I guess my chances at him are out now."

"You and he were trying for something?" Kaliya asks.

"Only if Suli gives me enough time for it..." she smiles gently.

"Oh, well, yes. I know about her. Is she still doing it?"

"Almost every day..."

"I see. Well, to be honest, I've been gone for a few centuries. So I can't, and probably shouldn't try making any claims on anything. No doubt, I would think many of you have paired up by this time."

"Technically, no," Tana admits. "Our situation in the mine, the lack of privacy, the orcs... We couldn't settle ourselves for anything. Not even a quiet romp in the woods."

"Um, excuse me, young lady," Kaliya raises her brow. "How do you explain the running-around-tail-naked aspect of things? What do the boys say about that?"

"Oh, well, for those who can find their voices, I sometimes hear a few whispers."

"Whispers..." Kaliya studies the girl's figure. "I would actually expect more than just whispers. But I guess you must feel very comfortable running around like that."

"You get used to it after a while. Petrith once mentioned how he respects me for my choice, and doesn't see me as a sex object. So, we all came to an understanding together, especially as most of us are naked to some degree or another. Just look at Suli, with or without her tail-swinging. Besides, in this jungle heat, clothes just get in the way."

"Yeah, I suppose they might. Although I'm sure my mother would have something to say about it."

"She did once, when we met her that day."

"Uh huh… But you know, you would fit in nicely with the philosophies they have on Tae'Eladar. Of course, they don't walk around naked, but they do have a rather relaxed perspective on nudity. They regard the body as a beautiful natural creation. In the right context, it's an acceptable form of expression."

"Really! All right, I'll keep it in mind. Just don't tell my dad," she glances over her shoulder. "Oh, wait, here he is. Oops!" she smiles innocently.

Kaliya raises her brow and glares at the two of them.

"I can only imagine the trouble she caused you during this time."

"You have no idea," he relents.

"But just so you know," Túfula resumes. "Petrith still thinks about you often. So, don't feel too left out."

"Really," Kaliya smiles. "All right, that makes me feel a little better."

"So, where does all this leave us?" the Captain asks.

"It leaves me with a horn-puller of a report to turn in," Kaliya accedes. "And I'm not looking forward to it. But I would imagine the first thing on the list is to offer some kind of aid. Maybe also a few new sets of clothes…" she glares at Tana, "…or at least some underwear."

"Hey," she retorts. "I told you I have a loincloth. But all right, I won't argue if you can bring something new. Just keep it light. I tend to move around a lot."

"And can you send any soap this way?" Túfula asks. "No one here knows how to make the stuff."

"Once I report in," Kaliya continues. "I would imagine Thaelyn will have me make a lot of trips to deliver stuff. So, just make up a list and we'll see what we can do. Oh, and Captain, I think Kailen will want to know who's over here. I'm sure he'll be asking you for a full assessment, so you should probably put together some kind of census, as well as a report of what happened."

"All right, this is reasonable," he nods. "But why Kailen? Is he in charge of security over there?"

"He's the High Commander now."

"Him? Is he old enough for it?"

"Old enough isn't the question; it's more like who is available to take the job, since we lost the last one in the crash."

"Cu'Nar's pity, what has that monster done to us."

"It's not just us, but now it's time to take it back to him. We've been coming into a lot of new information as part of these prophecies and some other research. The result is twisting a lot of horns, and it dates back even as far as the REAL origins of our species. But I'll have to leave this for later. For now, let me get back to work before they start poking my body trying to wake me up."

"Can they actually do that?" Túfula winces.

"I don't know, I'm not at home for it," she grins.

Chapter 4

FORWARD MOMENTUM

Kaliya was just returning to Firstfall after her meeting on Ruuki uy'Daan. She was mentally exhausted from her ordeal, but her work wasn't finished yet. She arrived through the gateway into the village square and strolled over to the tactical office for her review.

"Knock, knock…" she sighs as she enters. "My Lord, I'm sorry for the delay, but I got involved in some discussion over there."

"Kaliya," Thaelyn responds enthusiastically. "We were becoming concerned over what happened. You were gone for an extended period, and the Commander and I were speculating on what you might be doing. Do you have something special for us?"

"Special?" she emits uncertainly, with a faint chuckle. "Do you mind if I sit for this? I had to stop by to pick up my body so I could have a justifiable reason for a headache."

Thaelyn and Kailen examine each other as she plops down into a nearby chair.

"First of all," she begins. "I just went through a grueling interview, so go gently on me, please. This is going to send horns flying on an epic scale. Kailen, once we get into it, you're going to start screaming, so all I ask is for you to turn the other way for it. Padriyl, you'll probably have a meltdown. And then we have such as, oh…Ankhia, who will probably explode all over the med-lab. And then there's the Elder Council… Dear cu'Nar, Kailen, I'm glad you're the HC and not me. I don't want to be present when Elder Vankkar goes ballistic."

"Kaliya," Kailen ushers. "Slow down a moment. What actually happened over there?"

"We have survivors living in the old mining complex outside of town."

"What?" he shouts.

Thaelyn pulls up the map they were using before to pinpoint locations in the area.

"Where is this located?" he asks.

"It was just west of the city," Kailen recalls. "Near a river and a small lake with a waterfall…" he peers down at the paper. "Here…" he points.

"Very well, this confirms our theory about the northwest. But survivors? How many, Kaliya?"

"Here's where the pain begins," Kaliya asserts. "Can I ask to run through the smaller bits before I hit you with the apocalyptic parts?"

"Very well, Kaliya. I can feel your stress levels from here. How do you wish to proceed?"

"Well, in answer to your question, I'm told there are perhaps fourteen hundred."

"Fourteen hundred!" Kailen blasts.

"Yeah, and like I said, you're going to start screaming."

"How is that possible? I thought everyone made it to the ship… well, except for that one last squad," he issues tenderly as he glances at Padriyl.

"Yeah, I suppose that's reasonable. But in the chaos…" she shrugs.

"Right, and this one was bad."

"It was probably engineered that way, if you consider those rifles."

"Oh, yes! And then we have those."

"And as Captain Lapäli said, many were just running off into the woods, cut off from the ship entirely."

Kailen's voice quickly left him as that bombshell made landfall. He simply glared at his younger sister's smug expression. But before he could react further, Padriyl suddenly stiffened and drew in a sharp gasp, as he covered his mouth in shock. Soon after, a wave of emotion ripples through him and he covers his eyes with his other hand, then leans over the table resting on his elbows.

Kailen turned to find Padriyl burying his face and whimpering on the table. He reaches over to place his hands on the young officer's shoulders to offer support.

As for Thaelyn, he simply raised his brow as he observed the cleverly disguised play. He then glanced at the General for his impression.

"Should I prepare the list, my Lord?" he whispers.

"Make it ready."

Kaliya continues, "Yeah, it would seem not only did he survive, along with his team, from what I saw, but he's still kicking tails. Of course, then he had to round them all up. Fortunately, the orcs were going home by that time."

"Great," Kailen moans. "This makes me wonder how many times this ever occurred on any of the other worlds."

"I don't know, Kailen, but it's a little bit scary to think of. Although, at the same time, I might also say the severity of this one made things worse. The others simply made people run, not flee in all directions."

"Maybe."

"He also says the orcs were mostly directing themselves north at the ship, and his team evaded to the south. So, we can say he got away clean."

"How lucky for him!" he muses optimistically.

"Oh, absolutely! Especially as it put him right in front of the junior school just as those kids were coming out of their shelters. Who would've thought!" she grins.

This new bombshell quickly caused Kailen to lose control.

He gapes at her and wheezes, then pulls back, grabs his horns, and screams. His voice bellowed through the room, and drew the attention of several people from outside, bringing them rushing up to the door to investigate.

Thaelyn and the General both glared at the seemingly innocent delivery, studying the cute smirk on Kaliya's face and Kailen's uncontrolled reaction.

Captain Hagmaert peeked inside to see what the commotion was about.

"My Lord, is everything alright in here?"

Kaliya turned around to respond.

"It's alright, Captain. I just came back to see how badly I can twist my brother's horns."

"Oh, is that how you people treat your family?" he chuckles. "Gracious, I'm glad I don't have a sister like you."

"Yeah, well, I've been so busy at the academy, I haven't seen him as much lately," she smiles. "But in actuality, I just came back with a very disturbing report. We apparently have survivors on Ruuki uy'Daan, and this hits very close to home for us."

"Great gods, how is that possible? Aye then, if you need anything, I'm right outside here."

Thaelyn studied the interaction and leaned forward in his chair to inquire on the strange sequencing of events.

"Eh, young lady," he begins. "Did I not hear you suggest a moment ago to refrain from any apocalyptic statements?"

"Yeah, well, technically, I only asked for it. I didn't say I was actually going to do it," she smiles innocently.

"Oh! Powers help us, how could I have missed that part," he closes his eyes and shakes his head. "General…" he thumps a finger on the table in front of them. "This will likely require a special category."

"Indeed!" he intones boldly.

"My Lord," she offers. "I don't think there's an easy way to do this. I went through my own out there, multiple times, and I guess it just worked out that I needed to release a little of my own stress. Sorry, Kailen," she reaches out to pat him on the arm.

Kailen was panting as he spent his breath on his startling outburst. He glares at her for her perky response.

"Yeah, right," he responds wearily. "Do you want to try for a follow-up, or will you allow me time to find my horns first?"

"Commander," Thaelyn wonders. "Does she have a history of this sort of behavior?"

"Oh, I've been through a few moments here and there, especially when she was young. I had to play the role of surrogate father while she was in that rebellious mood of hers once."

"I am sorry to hear that, but at least we can say she has come out of that now. My only fear at this time is what she might be capable of with her newly coordinated thoughts."

Kaliya giggles as she prepares to continue.

"All right, so here's how it goes. The Captain evaded to the south, basically escaping from the orcs, who seemed focused on the ship. In doing so, this brought him conveniently into proximity of the junior school just as the kids were emerging out of the shelters. It would seem some administrator told them to hide, not escape. According to the Captain, this may have countermanded the evac order, and since the sirens cut off so early, we might say there was no other incentive to correct this before it was too late. By the time the school figured it out, the ship was going bye-bye. So, the Captain grabbed the kids, ran behind the southern crop fields, which were also very conveniently tall enough to hide them from view, until they arrived at the mines. And the orcs, with nothing else to attract them in the city, simply went home to their shiny new conveyor someone probably delivered behind our backs."

Thaelyn, Kailen, and the rest glared at her for the lengthy report, each turning to the other for their impression before returning to the conversation.

"Kaliya," Thaelyn wonders. "I am detecting a series of words in that statement that I feel are necessary to comment on."

"I'll bet you are! The cu'Nar are said to have delivered a message to my Father telling Captain Lapäli to stay behind, that he had a purpose waiting for him, although with no clear indication of what it was. And we both know who owns the cu'Nar, so you can guess where the message came from."

"Indeed! So, it was premeditated."

"This has always been a focus of debate and argument for us," Kailen admits. "The loss of such a good man. And I know I'm not the only one. Padriyl here, his mother, and I don't know how many others, all criticized the decision."

"Well, here we are on the other side of it," Kaliya notes. "The Captain didn't fully realize this until I heard his statements and put it together. If to consider the school was countermanded to go into shelters, it stands to reason they're going to be lost once they come back out. The Captain might be lucky the orcs were so focused on the ship that he could get away, but to the south where the school is found? And so conveniently at THAT moment when the kids are coming out? Convenience, maybe. And then the crop fields… maybe another convenience."

"That is indeed a lot of conveniences," Thaelyn nods. "At least some of which might simply be Fated to occur."

"But to assemble all this to rescue people that probably would've perished somewhere along the way, had to be a rather well-timed masterpiece of intrigue. So, I think we all owe Maker Kuroku a big thanks for her help."

"Absolutely! I would certainly agree to this."

"Now, there's more. They ARE responsible for the conveyors at Portals Two and Three. They apparently hit the first one because it was abandoned and the second for being poorly manned. They commandeered a series of old hover-trucks from a utility station and put wheels under them, then hauled them using manual labor. I wish I had a photo of that, so maybe one day I can take a camera back there for a reenactment shot," she giggles.

"That would be a rather interesting collector's item," he smiles.

"Also, they have the reactors plugged in and painted in colors to mask them from easy view. It's no wonder I couldn't find them."

"This would surely make sense, and clever thinking on their part."

"The Captain also reported on a few other things. Some of this

I don't think we can do anything about, other than groan for the atrocities played on our people. The orcs apparently slaughtered our people in groups during the attack, and maybe due to the sirens cutting out early, where they couldn't figure out what to do afterwards. He said there were pileups of bodies in alleys and such, where they must've been cornered by the orcs and simply butchered. So, the only way I can see people getting caught like this is if they're simply standing around like dull-horns."

"I may have to agree with you, as unfortunate as it may seem. Perhaps your long duration of freedom on that world left many of you with the impression of respite after the chase."

"And very disconcerting, as well. The idea of that wild jump made many of us feel the Suuden-Aryku should NOT be able to find us," she sighs mournfully. "Worse is the orcs didn't even bother with disposing of the bodies, as they might with their own. They just left the bodies to rot in the streets, leaving it to the Captain and his people to do the work in secret."

"Unbelievable!" the General shudders. "Even for the worst of orcish behavior. Their dedication to Sargeras must be so vile that nothing else matters."

"One girl, Tana Lar'akan, Navina's daughter, had her tail nearly as crinkled as mine was in those early days. She saw my tiger act at the east camp, which sent her horns flying, and several of them apparently saw my stone giant. Poor little Suli laid it on me that I almost stepped on her," she giggles.

"Suli?" Kailen frowns. "You mean…"

"Yeah, Ankhia's little sister. Good luck in bringing this to her. We also have Túfula Vankkar and Petrith Girhani. Kailen, I want you to know, I love you. It was fun knowing you during this time," she takes his hand and shakes it vigorously. "But I'm not sure if I'll see you again after you finish in there."

"Thank you, my little sister," he chuckles sarcastically.

"Anyway, Tana was huffing that I only used a scare tactic in the city. So I had to lay a little of your famous Measure of Balance on her that this is not the way."

"Indeed!" Thaelyn muses. "Are you now taking up the role of a priest on us?"

"Well, on this one occasion, I had to. She needed to calm down. And it fell to me to do the deed. Although, it might seem a little weird to be preached to by a talking bird."

Thaelyn glared at her uncertainly, then quickly glanced at the General.

"Uh huh, you were still in your bird persona during this time. General, we may need to apply another mark."

"Oh dear," he relents.

"Hey, we were doing great," Kaliya retorts energetically. "They must've put something together on their own after witnessing those other apparitions, so they figured I was just another of the same. Suli came up to me when I was inspecting some of the power equipment, trying to locate the reactors. She started asking if I was the one doing the other stuff. Of course, here I am as a bird, and asking her if this was a normal practice for her to go up and talk to strange animals."

"Powers help us…" Thaelyn moans and covers his eyes. "This must be a gender thing with their kind."

"After that, and then taking a close look at the reactors, I flew up to one of the rooftops and started giving my lectures. My roleplaying was actually working out as a great way to carry this weird conversation. At least up to the moment when I had to reveal who I really was."

"And how did they respond to that?"

"Well, Suli fainted, the poor girl. The rest were awestruck. Then I had to explain a few things about myself, but also to stress our situation of security along the way."

"Good, this is important."

"And this generally brings us current. I have Captain Lapäli working on a census for us, as well as a report of some kind. I imagine we'll be sending supplies over there to help them. Most of them are running around nearly naked by now, especially Tana. She's a perfect example of a nature girl. I think she might also be a good candidate for a druid. She's already halfway there."

"Seriously?" Kailen frowns.

"Yeah. She dresses up in natural foliage and body paint, and works for the Captain as a scout. She feels entirely comfortable in herself, and our conversation tells me she studies the shamans a lot to learn from them."

"Incredible. Well, if this is her calling, why not."

"One thing that comes to my mind immediately," Thaelyn considers. "Is how to bring this to the rest of your people. Surely, they should know, but I feel we still have a few issues that need resolving. One of these being our concern for the spy."

"Oh dear cu'Nar, I wish you didn't just mention that, but you're right. Then, how do you suggest we do this? Because we can't just hold this back."

"Of immediate concern is those people are outside our view and support, and could be vulnerable if he should decide to perform some devious act."

"I personally don't believe he would know of them," Kaliya mentions. "Not so far, at least. Like the rest of us, he should think they're all dead. Of course, this could change, but for now, they seem safe."

"Perhaps, so we should maintain this as best we can until we can find a way to deter any future interest by Darumon. And it must be a complete solution. This threat potential is becoming very bothersome. Let me think a moment."

He stands up and begins pacing around the room as he considers his options.

"We need to apply some form of incentive to keep him away," he muses. "Even though he might no longer hold any interest, I still feel we should not take this for granted."

"This can really yank a person's tail," Kaliya scorns. "Assuming they had one," she smiles gently. "The worst of it being he can come and go at will and impersonate anyone he desires. How do you fight that?"

"If we reflect on him as the old Governor, we were able to drive him away with the threat of the Estelar arriving and investigating his actions in this world. And we know he is hiding from them. Therefore, he would not want to be discovered. The elves held their religion, and the humans were beginning to reassociate with theirs, and in so doing, this might bring their focus on this place. Any interaction with that might expose himself in their eyes. But your society is not religious, so we cannot necessarily... Um...hmm... Or can we? Wait a moment."

He pauses and taps a finger to his chin as he formulates a plan.

"This is an interesting thought, and a rather peculiar one, but it could serve us nicely. Commander, may I offer a suggestion to you. Although I realize your society is not religious, I think we have made enough progress here that your people can begin to understand and recognize the existence of the Estelar, correct?"

"Well, I suppose," he accedes. "Word has certainly spread about them after your activities in Rolsklinde, and also this news of Darumon and Sargeras being refugees from some ancient battle. So, what do you suggest, that we take up a new religion now?" he smirks.

"Perhaps! You do not necessarily have to take up a full religion, but if you could join us in a form of association, it might bring your people under their supervision just enough to keep Darumon away. Let me see...who would be appropriate for you... You are a society of scholars... Ah! Yes!" he snaps his fingers. "This is perfect! Lord Oghma, Sage of Wisdom and Adherent of Inspiration. He presides over the domain of intellectual advance and scholarly pursuits. He would be perfect for your society...and maybe your people could even learn a few things from him if you should go so far as to try communing."

"That sounds interesting, and I might even be willing to take a look at this myself. But how do we do this?"

"General, send a note to Aerlie and have her send some of her people out to the Naarg uy'Sodrad to begin teaching them about Lord Oghma. We should also assemble some manner of shrine for them to visit. And we should further have each member of their society make at least one visitation of the shrine, and then perhaps occasional returns to maintain the association. If Darumon should see any part of this, he would surely wish to keep away from it."

"Excellent, my Lord!" he affirms. "Perhaps we could also entice one or another of them to take up lessons to supplement this association in a sort of quasi-religious dedication, to further cement the relationship."

"Indeed, this would provide a very good service. Then we would not need to concern ourselves as much for a spy, although I would still caution the need for security in case of a telepathic intrusion."

"So, we take up a new religion to cover our tails from Darumon," Kailen shakes his head. "I never thought I would see the day, but if it gives us the peace we need, I'll take it. Kaliya, do you have anything else?"

"Yeah," she affirms. "I'm sure we have lots of work ahead of us. For one thing, they seem to be holding their own, although just barely by the appearance of it. The orcs apparently don't know about them, and they've been able to send out spies and scouts to watch them. Between them and their scouting, and me with mine, I think we can safely say all the orcs are in that one camp by the city. This represents the last of their kind. And that's not a good thing...for them, at least."

"No, it is not," Thaelyn advises.

"They mentioned a wish list of things they'd like to have. They're apparently trying to repair some old equipment from the city, but I think we can do better if we can provide something ready-made."

"I would certainly agree. I can call for some donations of goods, including tools, perhaps blankets...clothing, if they are so badly lacking..." he grins gently.

"And Kailen, for all this time spent in that mine and trying to keep them alive, I think we need to do something special for Captain Lapäli. What do you think?"

Kailen sighed and retracted into his thoughts, along with the rest of them as they reflected on the report and its clear implications.

"He's alive..." Padriyl whispers to himself as a tear gently rolls down his cheek. "But how do I tell my mother about this. She'll lose it completely."

"This is simply unbelievable," Kailen mumbles. "Three and a half centuries trying to survive in a world of hostiles, and at the same time babysitting all those kids."

"Commander," Thaelyn remarks softly. "If there could ever be one so deserving, this man is most certainly the highest form of it to receive our finest accolades."

"Your Lordship," he sighs. "I won't argue this, but at this moment, I can't even think of what I could offer him as a commendation for what this represents, and especially over this length of time."

"If you need help with that, I could suggest a number of medals from our own collection, but this might also require something new. As for me, although he may not be a citizen of my domain, this man is most certainly worthy of the most noble of bestowments. I would wish to offer him an honorary blessing of knighthood for his extraordinary deeds."

"I'm not sure how to respond to that. I heard about this from the Lieutenant here telling me of what you did with Captain Kholgard. I can't even recall any historical moment where we had such a thing, so an honor like this would be a first for us."

"But now," Thaelyn declares. "It becomes obvious that we need to make a series of careful decisions."

"That we do. Kaliya, you mentioned having him write up a report, right?"

"Yeah, as well as a census," she smiles. "I know you, dear Brother."

"All right, good thinking…" he nods.

"Kaliya," Thaelyn notes. "How many do we have from that school, and what are their approximate ages by now? They surely cannot be children any longer; not after all this time."

"No, they're not," she affirms. "They would all be around my age, give or take a few decades."

"Good gracious," the General chuckles. "When you put it into such terms as those, it seems just a tad unusual to still be speaking of children in a school."

"Yeah, but we don't fully mature into adulthood until two centuries. Anyway, it seems we have the full assembly, about nine hundred kids, plus teachers and staff members. Like I said, I met with Suli, Ankhia's little sister, and Túfula Vankkar, among others."

"Right," Kailen relents. "And here is where I need to go to Elder Vankkar and somehow withstand his screeching about his daughter. I don't know what Elder Girhani will do. She's not quite as, um, well... And then there's Ankhia. She'll probably fly into hysterics over this. She was in hysterics once already after the attack. Um, what do we know about her parents?"

"According to the Captain, they're both dead, along with Petrith's father and Túfu's mother."

"And this will simply aggravate things. Although, we were assuming they were all dead to begin with. But it's like reopening an old wound."

"Yeah..."

"Kaliya," Thaelyn begins again. "You mentioned this countermanding order to go into shelters. Do we know anything more about the reasoning? Or could it simply be an error."

"Your Lordship," Kailen interjects. "I can't see how it could be an error. The school would be a priority to give the evac order."

"Perhaps so, but for some reason, they did not receive it."

"According to the Captain," Kaliya replies. "What they know of it is someone in admin got the order backwards and sent everyone into shelters. But we don't know who it was, since the one who did it is apparently MIA."

"Great," Kailen relents. "So, is this to say he managed to escape after figuring it out, but forgot to tell the rest? Or maybe he was simply lost. And I still don't understand how ANYONE could get those orders backwards!"

"Commander," Thaelyn muses. "If we assume this person is with you presently, do you know who it might be that you could locate him for interrogation?"

"I don't actually recall anyone from the school...not the junior school...who survived with us. I would need to confer with Ankhia, as she maintains the death records for those who died in the crash. Maybe he was among them. In fact, Lieutenant, call her up and see if she can locate anything."

"Yes Sir," Padriyl nods and pulls out his trans-com.

"And yet," Thaelyn continues. "I must ask myself this same question. You might have a situation where a few stragglers are left behind, which is unfortunate enough, but a full school assembly sent into shelters during a citywide emergency…this is unacceptable."

"I was arguing this same point with the Captain," Kaliya notes. "This is where he believes it to be countermanding the Council's orders. Can you imagine anyone doing that?"

"Not in our society," Kailen mutters sternly. "Not with the Suuden-Aryku hounding us as they were, and our people being so heavily conditioned to pick up and run when those sirens go off."

"But Kailen, like we said earlier, our long stay there may have softened us. We were so sure that wild jump had to be our salvation. How could anyone possibly track us into a new universe?"

"Yes, you have a point. So the simple disbelief might confuse people."

"And this is where I'm also thinking the sirens cutting off so early may have complicated matters. It left too many people standing around scratching their tails."

"And just waiting for the orcs to come at them, but all too late."

"And yet, Commander," Thaelyn asserts. "We DO know they found you, or rather the wild jump was not so wild. If we now suggest Darumon took advantage of your lull, and further to involve Maker Kuroku and the cu'Nar, this almost seems like a planned countermeasure to a conspiracy."

"In all the nether-space, do you think so? Oh wonderful."

"And therefore, the missing link," Kaliya muses. "That one admin gone MIA. It was him."

"But this simply begs the reason why. Would he actually be so callous as to send a school full of children into shelters rather than evacuate?"

"Let us approach it this way," Thaelyn suggests. "With regrets that I must use these words, you are a hunted society. Why would you have shelters to begin with if your enemies are just as likely to hit you with bombardment weapons and your first reaction is to evacuate off-planet?"

"This sounds a bit like Tana's argument," Kaliya mumbles. "The Captain says she complains about not holding our tails up like we should."

"Eh…" the General emits curiously. "How do we interpret that statement?"

"This is a delicate delineation of terms. It means to show pride in ourselves and stand our ground…essentially to fight back, as opposed to tucking our tails, representing a fear reaction, and running away every time we hear a big noise. We can also have drooping tails, which describes a shameful LACK of response to a situation."

"I see, and how curious. And this also sounds much like an instinctive reaction."

"Maybe so," she shrugs. "And so unfortunately for us being prey animals rather than predators."

"Now, now… Let us not mock ourselves too greatly. We simply need to bolster your resolve."

"And here we have the positive side of the Measure of Balance again," she smiles tenderly.

"But you know, Kaliya," Kailen reflects. "She sounds a little like a certain young girl I once knew," he smiles. "As for the shelters, they were installed in case we had trouble with the natives, and our children needed protection, regardless of what the Suuden-Aryku might do. We were really hoping that wild jump gave us the escape we so desperately wanted, and the only thing to worry about now was the local concern."

"Very well, this is reasonable," Thaelyn nods. "But then, let us ask ourselves how this might play out. We are already aware of Darumon spying on you during your full journey, and likely directing you to Ruuki uy'Daan intentionally to place you under the supervision of his orcish minions. Virtually anything and everything that comes after this is now suspect in my mind. Therefore, you receive some manner of notice of an attack, and so you issue an alert of some kind, correct?"

"Are we doing the inquisitor bit now?" Kaliya grins. "I've heard about that."

"Indeed, and it does provide some valuable direction for us."

"And it seems I'm in the chair now," Kailen observes. "Yes, I was working in the Security Division at the time when we had a report come in from an outer watch post that a large number of orcs were moving in our direction. We had been taking notice of a buildup, but when we asked them about it, they said it was just a ceremonial tribute to their god, which called for a large number of them to come into worship and make offerings."

"And when we consider who their god might be in this case, this is already suspicious."

"Yes, I suppose it is, at that, although we didn't have the name Sargeras associated with it. They called it the Great Horned God."

"Interesting. And I think I recall a description of Darumon as having horns."

"The next thing you know, there's a large mass of bodies charging at us."

"And so your security office issues an alert, which goes out as a citywide evacuation order."

"Right, and under the circumstances, the Council made the decision this was incentive enough that our time on that world was at an end. So, yes, it came out as a full evac alert."

"This must be where we have the cu'Nar's orders for Captain Lapäli," Kaliya considers. "Father knew ahead of time. Therefore, it becomes an evac order. If not for that, I wonder what would've happened. Could we actually fight them back?"

"I think their numbers would've overwhelmed us, regardless."

"Maybe. But at the same time, simply calling an evac, and then the alarms suddenly going out, rather than militia troops charging through the streets fighting something, overwhelming numbers or otherwise, would make a bigger showing for the people to actually do something, either to run away, or to pick up any loose stick or rock and join the fight."

"I suppose you have a point. A bigger showing to drive the people one way or the other, but not simply to stand still."

"More of that escapist mentality. The orcs should not have represented that much of a threat to us. Not with our better weapons, or at least higher intellect to think of ways to fight back."

"Should I remind you of their magic?"

"Kailen, the shamans are the ones using magic. Take them out as a priority and you'll have fewer fireballs coming at you. After that, it's clubs and stone knives. Do you think we could fight back against that?"

"All right. Got it. But I might also mention us being here to find them," he points at Thaelyn.

"Yeah, part of that Master Plan."

"And indeed," Thaelyn reasons, "this does seem like a smaller part to a larger game. Something prompted this. An intentional play followed by an intentional counterplay. And if Darumon is responsible, he would need to hold a position of authority, I should think. He would need access to critical information, as well as control authority to make decisions. What happened next, precisely?"

"Control authority…cu'Nar's pity," Kailen moans. "Well, let's see. There was a lot of panic as the orcs overran portions of the city. People were running in all directions trying to escape, but those orcs were quick, and used their magic to set fires and caused a lot of death and destruction. We sent out the alarm, but it was only a short time later when those signals seemed to cut out."

"Are we speaking of the orcs disabling those systems?"

"We generally suspect this is the case, although the Suuden-Aryku may have also had a hand in it, so we can't be sure. No one among us here recalls seeing them on the ground."

"So, unless we suggest the destruction brought by the orcs was enough to damage one or more of these systems, we might say there could have been additional saboteurs on the loose, perhaps more like what you had within your ship."

"That's a good point. Someone may have simply turned it off."

"And here we have the loss of your alarms, followed by, as Kaliya suggested, your people, um, scratching their tails…" he smirks. "And waiting until the last moment before seeing the orcs rampaging towards them."

"You know," she smiles. "I think you're having too much fun with our language."

"Well, my dear young lady, you are contributing a fair portion of it yourself."

"So I am."

"And this now follows with taking advantage of your lull and your sense of security after that wild jump, which should have preserved you from further discovery."

"That's simply nasty," Kailen grimaces.

"This would also give them time to use those rifles of theirs," Kaliya offers. "A lot of stationary targets to aim at."

"Indeed," Thaelyn nods. "And then, we have the school, where you say your Captain described it as a countermanding order to go into shelters rather than to evacuate at all. Now, if we were to bring this full circle, we should also involve this change of manner in Darumon. He was no longer interested in carrying you as his playthings. Therefore, the sabotage to maroon you here. And this naturally brings us to Adalon's prophecy."

He turns to the table behind him to find a notebook that was lying nearby. He brings it around for a quick review, flipping through several pages until he finds his mark.

"Upon a shore, they come to rest, the Forgotten One's entice… If we are correct in assuming this is your arrival on Ruuki uy'Daan, with you being Darumon's playthings, then we may be speaking of this occasion. Then this next part… Until a tender moment lends, a Child and its device… A child, Commander, perhaps in a literal sense of the word, and one who was attending that school sent into shelters rather than to evacuate, as the rest of the city was ordered to do."

"Darumon trying to confound something," Kaliya murmurs indignantly.

"I think I'm starting to hate these prophecies," Kailen groans. "If only for what they suggest that monster is doing to us. But who, in this case, and what is this device?"

"I think I could give you a highly probable suggestion..." he turns to gaze at Kaliya.

Kaliya feels a sudden cold spike run down her back.

"What are you staring at me for?" she protests.

"We must now reflect on several points in collection, beginning with those original Prodigy Children. If Darumon is responsible for their deaths, this is a clear indication he does not want your people to know about or learn to use this Gift. And if I recall correctly, your mother was conducting research on yours, and you were surely a student at this same school, correct?"

"Oh great!" she barks. "So, he tries sacrificing the whole school just to kill me?"

"He made a change to his designs at this moment where your people are concerned, sending saboteurs into your ship to disable it, so you could no longer move around. He was now discarding you as his playthings, maybe to take one final bit of pleasure out of you after arriving here on Therinë, as this would be his final staging post for his plans against the Estelar. After this, he would likely have no further interest in anything other than his primary minion society. And then you come along with your Gift...a tender moment, and one he would not allow to proceed to any point of fruition."

"All right, fine, but why not just kill me outright, like all the rest?"

"One possible reason could be he did not know your name. Was it not said by the Med-tech that it would be unprofessional to reveal the patient's name?"

"Yeah..."

"It may also seem suspicious for you to die of precisely the same cause as those original children. If memory serves, those news sensations were claiming it to be possibly an infection or some such of alien origin. And here we are located on a different world in a different universe. Although, at the same time, one might also ask if he would care as much, for all his other manners."

"That's for sure," Kailen nods.

"Commander?" Padriyl interjects. "The Med-tech just called back with her report. She says she checked the records for anyone from the school, admin or otherwise, and nothing came up. She's also asking why it's important at this time. So I simply said you'll brief her later."

"Oh, thank you, Lieutenant. You're so considerate."

"Just doing my job, Sir," he smiles politely. "It's the burden of command."

Kailen glares at the young officer, then raises his brow as he turns away.

"Well, at least it makes logical sense, as we're too far away from it by now. So instead, he orders an attack by the orcs, tampers with our alarms, tells the school it's just an uprising and not to worry so much, instead to hide in the shelters and wait. Then bam…the rest of us flash out of sight. How nice…"

"But Commander," Thaelyn adds. "This also tells me he had to be someone in a high position of authority to know about it in the first place. If this were indeed a secret project, who would hold the authority to have access to this sort of information?"

"This was considered a top-level concern, so it would probably involve the Elder Council, as most things do, also the High Commander, and the head of the Security Division. Not even I knew of it, and she's my sister."

"I am sorry to hear that. But now, let us see if we can narrow it down to who he may have been impersonating. It was likely a familiar face, and likely from the beginning, although with the ability to change shape, I suppose he could represent multiple people."

"That doesn't help matters."

"No it does not, but let us see if there is a common denominator in all this. We will start with the High Commander. I suspect you did not hold this position at that time, as you said you were working in the security office."

"Right, he was killed in the crash, so I was bumped because I was essentially all we had left after he and several others died."

"That is not a pleasant way to earn your rank, Commander. I am sorry for your loss, though I will admit you have proven to be a fine example of one."

"Thanks, but it hasn't been easy. I had a steep learning curve to climb when they pinned the clusters on my sleeve. But anyway, the head of security didn't make it. I think someone said he was cut down in the street."

"This leaves us with your Elder Council, which makes good sense if you want a position of status and authority, but it is also disturbing for the implications."

"It is, but personally, I'm reluctant to point fingers because each of them has proven to hold their full share of responsibility for our people since arriving here."

"Since arriving here… Very well, then let us approach it from the other side. What about on Ruuki uy'Daan. How did they behave over there?"

"Elder Vankkar has been with us for a long time. He began as a history teacher in one of our old universities. I don't know much about his personal history, as most of it came well before me, but he was born somewhere along the way on one of the first few worlds we crossed. Of course, we have my father, but I would hate to imagine he might be an imposter."

"I think if the cu'Nar are interacting with him, he must be true to himself. I doubt they would relay such details to anyone else."

"All right, but then we have Elder Drescuul, who came before Girhani. Elder Girhani was originally an undersecretary to him on Ruuki uy'Daan, but she got bumped after we arrived here when Drescuul was lost along the way."

"Therefore, she is new to her position. But how long have you known this other one?"

"Since Azgarén, actually…"

"And he was lost along the way…" he muses. "How was he lost?"

"This was when the sabotage took control of our ship. A few

moments later, we lost containment of our engines and there was an explosion in the engineering section. We lost a lot of good people down there when the bulkheads blew. He was presumably down there investigating the damage at the time."

"He was investigating it? Did he hold a specialty in engineering that he might be able to repair it? Forgive me, but this does not seem like the most opportune moment to go into an engineering segment to repair damage when you are currently flying out of control and this damage is likely to blow out the entire segment."

"Well, maybe not, but we didn't have much choice except to launch when we did. The orcs were pounding on the hull at the time, and we couldn't take any chances of them causing damage to it that might prevent us from launching at all."

"I see, and this could offer us the motivation. So then, this Elder Drescuul goes down there to investigate, doing whatever he can to find and reverse the damage. Unfortunately, it would seem he did not succeed. What sort of damage are we speaking of here? Was it something physical, or perhaps a configuration anomaly?"

"According to what I can recall of it, we launched from Ruuki uy'Daan, and it was not until after we entered the slipstream when the navigator called out a corruption in the conduit. It was altering spontaneously to a new coordinate. An override, that's what it was."

"An override...from the tampering, perhaps? This might apply for the navigation console, I suppose. Although I might also suggest that to alter a destination index while inside a conduit is a rather risky procedure."

"Yes, I would agree."

"Could the Flame Elves have done this?" Kaliya muses. "They were found inside, but can you say THEY actually did it? This is a very technical thing, simply to input the numbers."

"What do you mean, Kaliya?" Thaelyn asks. "If one were to teach such a thing..."

"Yeah, to teach something...to a bunch of people who don't even understand electricity. Also, to a bunch of people used as decoys to divert attention, like on Morndindor."

"Dear Powers, yes!"

"Oh dear cu'Nar, Kaliya," Kailen moans.

"We see them wandering around," she continues. "And boom, we kill them. But Darumon! Oh yes! He ought to know how to reprogram a nav console with an override. Then maybe to lock it so no one can fix it. And surely, if he owns the place, he will know the numbers."

"Absolutely, Kaliya, I would have to agree. And then I recall the ship shuddering as we were losing guidance control. We were experiencing inertial fluctuations, and people were tumbling across the floors. But I also recall shouts and screams as the engines were suddenly overloading and there was a containment collapse."

"A collapse..." Thaelyn muses. "Commander, just out of curiosity, if we reflect on Kaliya's statement of Darumon tampering with things, he may be present to reprogram your navigation, and this could divert you to this world. But if you were ONLY diverting from a controlled heading up until this moment, then 'suddenly' to lose containment of your engines, can these two be related? An override... By the nature of this ship, and who we may suspect is behind it, it might be sturdy enough to take the forces from the unexpected diversion. Then, what is actually necessary to blow it up? Could it be from some other form of tampering, or could someone invoke this manually?"

Kailen studied him for a long moment as he pondered the issue.

"Manually, like with a shutdown override? He was in engineering at the time, and I know there was a control console down there that could invoke an emergency shutdown of the envelope containment. But we have safety procedures to prevent this from being used while inside a slipstream. So unless he, or this sabotage, disabled the safety protocols..."

"And if it was?"

"The feedback would probably overload the nacelles and blow up the engineering segment," he hangs his head. "But then, if this was Darumon..."

"He could simply pull the switch, and then fold out of the local space to find his own exit, leaving you and the others to take the damage."

Kailen sighs heavily and leans back in his chair.

"That monster…for all the lives he cost us, just because he wants to play with toys."

"We will see to him, Commander. Be sure of it. Although at this moment, I must admit, nothing we can do to him would be enough to pay back for all he has done to others. But if he was once impersonating a now defunct Elder, unless he took a new form later, he may actually be gone from our sight. Let us see about covering our tails, as you say, and install this new plan for your people, and then work on the rest as time permits."

"All right, I agree."

"In the meantime, we need to offer support to those people on Ruuki uy'Daan. I will put out a call for supplies to be assembled, and Kaliya, I think it goes without saying you will have more work waiting for you."

"Yeah," she sighs. "I figured that one a long time ago."

"Are we going to bring them home at any time?" Kailen asks.

"At some moment, yes…" Thaelyn affirms. "But for now, and perhaps for multiple reasons, I think it would serve us nicely to keep them at their current post. First, they are unknown to the orcs. Second, with Kaliya's god image, even if the orcs should discover them, they must first overcome this illusion of that big friend behind them. Also, we could use them as a local watch, to ensure the orcs do not go off causing more trouble without supervision. And we will provide supplies, as well as weapons, to embellish their position and strength."

"What about their living conditions? They might be surviving inside that old mine, but I can think of better places to call home."

"I as well, so if we are able to stabilize the security in some portion of the city, perhaps they could reclaim some of their former homes, maybe on the outward side away from the orcs. Kaliya can use her fear tactics to keep the orcs at bay, at least for now, while they refurbish some of the housing. We could also offer seed to help reestablish some of their farming."

"Almost like the old days," Kaliya remarks. "But in this case, more by remote control. What about the mutation victims? If Ankhia is able to find a cure, how do we deal with that?"

"Let us cross that bridge when we come to it. For now, we will encourage them to work together to their mutual benefit."

"We should also establish some form of reliable communication," Kailen offers. "I'm sure there are a lot of people who would like to reconnect with friends and family…what's left of it."

"Perhaps we could employ something like a mail service, where we could have Kaliya serve as a delivery agent on a scheduled basis."

"Vid-mail, this is what we usually use. But for this, you need a vid-com terminal, and we could relay the data on holo-chips. I'm sure we could put something together, and then have Kaliya deliver it."

"Do these use some form of internal power source? If those reactors are located outside, as I would normally expect, they would need to run some rather long cables into that mine."

"Well, yes, that's true…"

"What if we could provide some of our own fuel cells, like those we were using outside here during our initial engagement? Kaliya, you recall those, right? You spent enough time studying them." he smiles.

"Yes, I remember those," she affirms. "But how would we do this? What sort of power output do they have? Would we need some kind of converter?"

"I can answer that," Padriyl responds. "My mother has already worked on this at the Bahlaie testing center. She and Professor Cogswoggle were using a number of those units for some field testing of some early equipment, and had to assemble a power conditioner unit for our equipment to work. I'll just relay word to have her put something together for us and have it ready for delivery."

"Padriyl, you'd better make the assembly easy enough for someone like me, or those people on the other side to figure out. They won't know how to use equipment like this."

"I'm sure we can figure something out."

"And I'd like to recommend one more thing," Kaliya notes. "I'd like to suggest we hook up one of those conveyors over there to act as an emergency escape, just in case something bad happens."

"Yes," Kailen nods. "I would need to agree on this. We can keep them there as our advance watch post, but having a backup is always desirable. It could also serve as an emergency message chute in case something happens on the other side, and we need Kaliya to jump over there to assist."

"Very well, Commander," Thaelyn affirms. "This is a fair offer."

Kailen was returning home to the Naarg uy'Sodrad for a rest and to visit his wife, Ankhia, in the medical center. He had just finished his meeting with Thaelyn and Kaliya, and now he had several new plans circling in his mind.

"Ankhia?" he calls into the room.

"Yes... Kailen?" she calls out from an office on the side.

She emerges into the room and rushes up to him for a hug.

Her assistant also entered the room to see what the commotion was, not having any other important business to attend.

"Commander," she smiles. "You've been away at that new station of yours a lot lately. Do we have anything special happening out there?"

"Likha," he responds cautiously. "It's turning out to be mostly business as usual, trying to tidy up loose ends and settle our most important needs."

"In other words, you're still not telling me," she sighs. "Well, that's the life of an underling, I suppose."

"Likha," Ankhia submits. "It's not like that. His work is just very tedious, that's all."

"Ankhia, I know the deal where the higher authority goes, and it usually involves details that lesser stations like mine don't get access to. It's alright, but it is a little frustrating when we have so many possibilities ahead of us, and so little information coming in on what we're doing with them."

"I know you want to learn what's happening out there, but you're right, there are some delicate security issues we need to maintain until we can move forward with the larger projects."

"Delicate security issues and larger projects... I'm a medical intern, so I might not qualify for anything military, but all I'm hearing about is a new shopping center being built outside. Is that large enough?"

Ankhia gazes wistfully at Kailen as she knew the concerns of Darumon and his spying, and the rest of the Daanen'kai population had to be kept in the dark about virtually everything until this could be resolved.

"Likha," he assures. "We have a new plan we're working on right now that could possibly answer some of this."

"Oh? What's that?"

He glances briefly at Ankhia as he continues, but choosing his words very carefully to feel out the situation. Likha was a well-known face in the medical lab, so he felt she was probably reliable, but the uncertainty factor was annoying, to say the least.

"His Lordship is offering us a rather remarkable opportunity for a new form of interaction. He's calling on Lady Aerlie...you remember her, right?"

"Yes!" Likha affirms. "She was that lovely, winged priestess we were working with when we were helping remove those implants from the people of Rolsklinde."

"Good! Anyway, she is going to start sending a few of her people over here to help us understand these Estelar a little better. What do you think about that?"

"The Estelar? Those are the beings I think it was said Darumon was afraid of, right? The whole reason he picked up and left. Is she going to try teaching us about them now? But Kailen, we're not a religious society, and as I understand it, they're treated like gods of some kind."

"While this is true, they're still a society of beings, not mystical images, and they have a lot they can offer to the younger races. They behave a bit like teachers, maybe even parental figures."

"Really! So, what are we supposed to be learning from them?"

"He's recommending one called Oghma, who is supposed to preside over such things as scholarly pursuits and intellectual development. He thinks this would make a good example for us. They're going to build a little shrine outside to get things started, and then each of us will make a kind of association with him to become familiar with who he is and what he teaches. And in this way, we can bring some part of the Estelar into our society to watch over us, maybe to give us a new sense of direction, much like the others did that sent Darumon running in the first place."

As Kailen finished his statement, he studied her for her reaction. Ankhia also watched and listened, but the statement, in and of itself, seemed very suspicious. She turned and glared at him. Kailen took notice of her reaction, so he simply shrugged.

Likha studied both of them, darting her eyes between them, and began to suspect there was an ulterior motive at play.

"Kailen," she wonders. "When you say we're all going to make an association with these Estelar, how do you mean this as far as those big things happening that someone like me might not normally qualify for due to the security issues?"

"Because we think he might try spying on us."

"Oh! So THAT'S the problem we have now. Well, hey, if you doubt my integrity, I'll just prove it...somehow...um...but how?"

"Likha," Ankhia asserts. "It's not that we specifically doubt you. I've known you for a long time and I feel very comfortable..."

"Ankhia," she interjects. "If the High Commander is in doubt over something relating to security, you don't argue with it. And I know Kailen. He wouldn't suggest something like this unless he's trying to find an answer to it. I'm not offended. I just need a way to prove I am who I appear to be. That Darumon was impersonating a human over there, right? This means he can alter his form. I get it. But how do we solve this... Oh! I know. I'll run a genetic scan on myself to show I'm real. Darumon is basically an alien lifeform, right?"

She now steps over to the station where they conduct their medical analysis. She takes a hypo-spray extractor and prepares to draw a blood sample from her arm. She presses it to her skin and the micro-needle array inside pulls out a clean specimen into a small vial.

"Now, we'll just run this through the scanner and let the computer do the work."

She loads the vial into a slotted tray that slides into the automated analyzer. She then programs a sequencing operation, and orders up a comparison analysis to common Daanen'kai genetic coding.

Kailen and Ankhia exchanged glances while they waited. Likha studies the readouts as they scroll along the monitors. After several long moments, the computer is able to provide a superficial scan of her coding pattern.

"Here we are," she reports. "With a 0.06% variance to the average individual..."

"Hmm..." Kailen muses. "I'm not so sure I would trust that number. Maybe if it was 0.04%, but that extra two in there..." he smiles.

"Kailen!" Ankhia slaps his arm. "All right, so what are we talking about here? What is His Lordship doing to us this time? And by the way, what was that bit with the school administrator?"

"Yeah, you're absolutely going to love that one," he remarks ironically. "Um, Ankhia, you're going to want to sit down for this."

She gazes at him for the suggestion, and then glances at Likha.

"And Likha," he continues. "Until we can resolve the issue of Darumon poking underneath our tails, this information is classified. His Lordship and I have decided the ONLY way to ensure Darumon leaves us alone is to associate ourselves on some level or another with the Estelar. He won't want to be anywhere near us after that, for fear of his own safety."

"So, we need to take up a religion now?" Ankhia asks.

"Not so much to take up a full religion, although we can do this if we like, but simply to call their attention to us so we have a little insurance. Besides, this one they call Lord Oghma might not be such a bad choice if he can actually teach us something along the way."

"All of us?"

"We need complete coverage, Ankhia. Everyone needs to make at least one visit, and preferably more to ensure we maintain it."

"All right, if this secures us from him, I won't argue. How about you, Likha. Does your 0.06% allow you to join a cult?"

"Well," she considers distantly. "I may have to adjust it by a few fractions, but maybe. So long as it doesn't involve hugging trees or painting tattoos on my body, like those druids. Now, what is it we need to sit down for?"

"We found survivors on Ruuki uy'Daan," Kailen informs. "One of them, by the way, may actually become a druid one day."

"You must be joking!" she yelps. "On both of those points... Survivors?! What do you mean; there are still people on Ruuki uy'Daan...even with all those orcs and everything else going on?"

"Yeah, Kaliya encountered them earlier today and made contact. Ankhia, do you think you want to sit down now? If not, we'll probably find ourselves mopping the floor after you blow up."

Ankhia was still glaring at him for his original statement, but finally relented and found a nearby chair. Likha took up another one and sat next to her, while Kailen pulled around a third.

"First," he relates. "We were looking for evidence of those conveyors the orcs were using to arrive here. We found them. These people must've seen them sitting out there and scavenged them for the reactors. Kaliya found tracks and other evidence of wheeled vehicles being pulled by manual labor making rounds to visit a couple of sites where we think the two conveyors were located."

"Unbelievable!" Likha whispers. "People hauling around wheeled vehicles on their bare hooves?"

"Without power, this is where it brings you," Kailen shrugs. "They're living in the old mining complex outside of town, and the orcs apparently don't know about them. They were probably too busy with their conveyors to bother."

"So, our people were able to hide in the mine," Ankhia considers. "But how are they able to survive over there?"

"They were apparently living off the land as best they could, and scavenging whatever they could find in the city. They were also watching the orcs, using spies and scouts to follow their movement, and recently noticed them accumulating around Portal One, which on their side is that camp just east of the city."

"Are we doing anything to help them? I mean, I'm sure we must be, but what are we doing?"

"We're making plans to send supplies over there once we collect everything. We'll take care of them, Ankhia, don't worry. But now, get this... Captain Lapäli is still alive and leading them."

Ankhia gasped and slapped her hands on her cheeks. Likha followed suit, and the two of them turned to each other.

"The Captain is alive?" Likha emits disbelievingly. "In all the nether-space, how did he manage that? Everything I heard of the attack said the city was being overrun!"

"Oh, I'm sure it was, at least up to the northern side with the ship. This seemed to be their main focus. According to him, they did overrun most of the city, and we did lose a huge number of people. Between those of us in Firstfall, we think the sirens cutting out may have led to a lot of confusion and disarray as the people simply stopped running, not sure what to do until the very last moment when they saw orcs charging at them. But by that time, it was too late."

"But Kailen!" Ankhia urges. "For all the previous times..."

"Yes, but THIS time we had an extended lull after what we were so sure had to be safety with that wild jump into a new universe. How can you expect someone to follow you across THAT if it defied all our science for the pure existence of it?"

"Yeah..." she sighs.

"So, the sirens cutting out early made it seem like either an error, or something that was quickly corrected. The Captain said his people were able to sneak back into the city afterwards and found groupings of bodies left to rot in the street by those horrible beasts, and it appeared as though they were cornered in alleys and then slaughtered."

"Oh, cu'Nar help us."

"Actually, they did, at least partially. But that Darumon, he's the real trouble behind so much of this."

"Yeah. That wild jump, the orcs, and everything here on this world…"

"…And then the administrator at the junior school countermanding the evac order and sending them into shelters."

Ankhia froze at the abrupt disclosure. She glared into Kailen's eyes as he displayed a quirky little smile. Kailen then pulled back, hoping to avoid the blast effect of her reaction.

"What do you mean, countermanding the evac?!" she screeches.

"They're still alive," he relates calmly.

Now he braces himself for impact.

Ankhia wheezed and grabbed her horns. Her eyes grew wide, and she screamed fiercely. She stomped her hooves as she released her boisterous bellowing. Then she took to pounding on his shoulders for the favor.

"You did that on purpose!" she shrieks.

Now she begins to break down. Kailen took her in his arms to embrace her, holding her tightly. Likha was stunned, and tried to wrap her arms around the stricken woman. Together they waited a long moment for her to settle down enough to continue the conversation.

"Kailen," she whines. "When I find my horns again, I'm beating you with them."

"I already got mine from Kaliya. She pulled the same trick on me at the office."

"Oh! So you need to pass it along now?"

"Well, I suppose there's no other way but to share the pain. But now, do you think you can take the rest?"

"You have more? I hope you're not going to unload another bombshell like that on me."

"No, one per day is good," he smirks.

"Oh, you!" she slaps his shoulder again.

"Kailen," Likha submits. "I'm glad I'm not married to you. I don't know if I could take it."

"It's alright, Likha," Ankhia soothes. "He means well. And fortunately for me, he's very patient. I've shown as much for him in the past, so it's mutual. But now, Kailen, how many survived?"

"We have the full school assembly, nine hundred kids, including Suli, plus we have Túfu Vankkar and Petrith Girhani. So we need to bring this up to the Council sometime and somehow endure THEM now."

"Oh, please. Yeah, I don't envy you on that one."

"But not until we finalize this new procedure to scare off Darumon. Those people are outside our protection."

"Right, I get it. But Kailen, just how did this happen?"

"This is nasty, Ankhia, so hang on to your horns a bit longer. The first thing to realize are those controversial orders by the cu'Nar for Captain Lapäli to stay behind, remember?"

"Yes, I recall this, as well as everyone arguing it."

"Well, this is apparently the reason. To rescue the school once they actually did come out. Father got a visit shortly before, so we're suggesting the attack was no secret to him, and therefore, perhaps, additional incentive to order a full withdrawal, rather than simply stand our ground and fight, as Kaliya and a few others might suggest."

"She says that?"

"It's a thought, and she tells us a few of the kids, one in particular, are known for their complaints about not holding our tails up," he smiles.

"Oh! Really! So Kaliya isn't the only one who likes to make noise."

"Maybe, but I think she does hold a valid point here."

"Yes, I suppose you're right. By now, you might think we would learn something."

"Kaliya says it's the difference between the prey animal and the predator, so we need to grow some teeth. Anyway, the cu'Nar gave word, and probably again from Maker Kuroku, to tell the Captain he has a purpose of some kind, and to stay behind. And as it turned out, the orcs largely ignored him as he circled to the south while they went north to the ship. So he got away."

"Lucky for him."

"Maybe so. But it also put him in proximity of the school just as the kids were coming out. So here we have a meeting, right when the ship flashes away."

"Oops! I wouldn't want to be any of them at that moment."

"Yeah. Then, he led them around the southern field, where the crops were apparently just tall enough to provide cover. So we have a series of coincidences, but it all fits together as a plan of intrigue to counter another plan of conspiracy to trap those kids intentionally."

"Intentionally! In all the nether-space, why?"

"In a word, Kaliya. One administrator is missing, and he's probably the one who gave the order to go into shelters. The sirens cut out, likely due to more saboteurs simply hitting a switch. This left the people in a state of confusion, and the school with no more reason to think of a full evac, instead allowing someone to tell them it's probably a simple little thing and to go hide in the shelters. If Darumon was ordering the attack, he must've had a reason…that change of motivation that would ultimately mean discarding us as his toys. That prophecy, a tender moment, and a child and its device. Kaliya and her Prodigy Gift, which the Elder Council would know of, and the perfect place for a spy to steal information from. And he who wouldn't care for it."

"Grace of the cu'Nar! So he's making another attempt to kill it."

"And in the absence of knowing who this new Prodigy Child was, he probably opted for a blanket effect."

Ankhia reels back and screams again, pounding her fists on her knees.

"We think he could've been Drescuul," Kailen asserts. "He was with us from the start, and so conveniently down in the engineering section when it blew. If it was him, he might have pulled a switch down there to intentionally collapse the containment fields and blow up the engines. Then he would fold away to preserve himself."

Ankhia gaped at him and shook her head disbelievingly.

"He might also be the one sabotaging things," he continues. "Like reprogramming the nav station, maybe also locking it so we couldn't undo the damage, and those elves were simply a distraction to turn our eyes away from anything local...as usual."

"Oh, how nice! I swear, Kailen! To think of any creature playing games such as these."

"Meanwhile, we have a total of fourteen hundred people left behind, between the school and a few stragglers who missed the boat."

"Incredible!" she wheezes. "That...creature...and I use the term loosely. I don't even know if we have a word in our language strong enough to describe such a thing. So now what? What can we do about any of this?"

"I want you to help me coordinate our people. You're the chief medical officer, so you can assist in processing everyone. We need each member of our population to pay their respects at this new shrine as a means of checking for imposters. Everyone...no exceptions..."

"What if we did a genetic study?" Likha offers. "Like I did just now? Couldn't that be of some value?"

"If you want to do that, maybe it can serve as a supplemental aid. But you'll need an excuse for it, I think. Nevertheless, we still need this association with the Estelar as a permanent cover to dissuade him from trying anything new."

"So we take up a religion," Ankhia chuckles ironically.

"And then we make plans to take this back home."

✦✦✦✦✦

During the following week, Kaliya was delivering a series of crates to Ruuki uy'Daan to begin supplying the refugees with fresh goods. She had previously delivered their instructions from Kailen on a set of data-pads for Captain Lapäli to disseminate, and he was now assigning new work teams.

The people were reorganizing themselves into new group projects, some of which were assigned as clean-up teams to begin reclaiming certain portions of the city, while others were ordered to clear and prepare the fields for new farming activities. The concern over raising dust, which might draw the attention of the orcs, was being partially dismissed, if the orcs could be kept at bay on the far side of the city and largely out of view.

"Here we go with another load," Kaliya announces.

"What do we have this time?" Sulíma wonders.

"We're setting you up with a supply of weapons, just in case. We have some combat knives, and my next delivery will be staffs for the girls."

"Staffs? You actually use a staff as a weapon? How do we use that, hit them over the head?"

"No, not quite… I've been in training with one for a while now. It's a simple but efficient weapon if you know how to use it right. I'm going to be giving you some lessons once we get things ready over here. We also have some new clothes being made for you, and I have a box of soap, so you should be happy for that, finally."

"Well, that sounds just wonderful. Maybe I can finally draw Petrith's attention by showing off a new bathing technique," she smirks. "But now, can you show us where we can find a nice hot bath, so we don't freeze our tails off trying to use it?"

"Um, well, the hot water might take a little longer," she chuckles.

"All right, maybe once we can get some of the city utilities working again, we can restore power to our homes and start living like normal people."

"We were using the fusion plant before this," Kaliya considers. "But to get that to work, you'll need the hydro-processor and the solar collection plant up on the coastline. That's a lot of work still. And last I heard; the solar field was badly damaged."

"Yeah, we had some people run up there to inspect it, but it looks like it'll require a lot of new parts. We were hoping that the people in the Naarg uy'Sodrad could manufacture some replacements, but this might take some time."

"Patience, Suli… The city wasn't built in a day, and it won't be rebuilt in one either. We're doing all we can. But maybe I can pass a few ideas back to Chief Tech Lapäli for some interim solutions."

"All right, we'll just keep working with what we have for now."

"Speaking of which, do we have that conveyor ready for testing?"

"The guys were pulling one out of storage and setting it up across the river. The cable from the reactor to the rift generator is kind of short, and we don't have any of the same style we can use to reach into the camp."

"It could be designed that way intentionally if the power flow is sensitive to the length of the cabling and the resistance values along the way. But in the end, it probably doesn't matter too much, so long as we get it running."

"Yeah, that's what I was thinking, so let's go out there and check on it. They should be ready by now."

The two of them were in the work yard as Kaliya had been delivering her loads. There were a large number of others moving between the workshops and the mine, sorting their new equipment, and arranging their new tasks. Sulíma led the two of them across the bridge and over to the row of bushes that concealed the reactor assemblies. There, they found Petrith and several others putting the final touches on the hardware connections.

"Are we ready to turn that thing on yet?" Sulíma asks.

"Just about," Petrith responds. "I was just testing the electrolysis unit to make sure it was working. We're setting up those solar cells again to supplement our power out here, and I was checking the plumbing for the water pump to make sure there are no leaks."

"Which unit is this?" Kaliya wonders.

"As far as I can recall, this one should be from Camp Three, although don't quote me on that. I'm trying to remember the order in which they were loaded up on the trucks, and then offloaded into the warehouse. But for all the packing and repacking we've done since then..." he shrugs.

"All right, fair enough. It's just that each of them opened up to different regions on the other side, so we need to know where to look, assuming these things are still pointing the right direction."

"You think something may have changed?"

"It mostly depends on how they're designed. We're thinking

the best way is to use a satellite positioning system to locate their coordinates, as well as the exit points on our side. If this is the case, they could be located virtually anywhere and still work."

"And if not?" Sulíma asks.

"If not, it could be a hardcoded algorithm, but this doesn't make as much sense as it would need a lot of custom configuring per each unit."

"Oh, right. So, if they made these in batches, it would serve better to use a common configuration method."

"We also suspect one of these units may have been used at one time for the orcs to launch an attack on another world where Darumon had an interest in resource harvesting."

"Resource harvesting? What kind of resource, and why use orcs?"

"The resource is a special kind of metal he needs to make a weapon. The orcs were probably an early attempt to see what sort of result he might have in taking that world, but it seems to have failed miserably. We found a group of slaves in a mine who told us a story of another invasion only about four centuries ago using some people we know to come from Therinë. As far as they understood, this was still an ongoing effort, but those other people, who are known as elves, tell us it ended only a short time after it began, and used a large part of their population along the way."

"Oh great. So, we're not the only ones he likes to use up to the last."

"Not in the least. These slaves are a race called dwarves, and they say their leader, known as a thane, tells stories of large-scale warfare occurring outside their city, which in their case is located underground. But if there's no real fighting going on, at least not with these elves, we have to wonder what really is happening, because the dwarves were working this mine while under a drug influence to put them into a mindless state of servitude. This tells us the Suuden-Aryku must be present and secretly controlling the whole thing."

"I just can't believe some of these stories, Kali! This Darumon must be THE most sinister creature in existence. So, you think one of these conveyors points to that world?"

"The dwarves tell us the elves were supposedly emerging out of a portal. To them, we might be speaking of a magical version of a conveyor, at least in their eyes. And generally speaking, orcs aren't supposed to be good enough at magic to do this. Thaelyn tells us he saw a group doing this on Tae'Eladar once, but that might be a special case. Therefore, we're hoping one of these gives us the answer."

"But I suppose we don't know which one. Well, there's only one way to find out. Petrith, do you think we can give it a try?"

"All the connections look good," he admits. "I'm just waiting for you girls to finish your little chitchat so we can get back to work," he grins.

"Just remember, Petrith," Kaliya smirks. "You're on my list for that shower thing. And here I thought you had a genuine interest in me," she huffs playfully.

"And I was hoping he would peek over those bushes by the pond at least once," Sulíma frowns. "Instead, he travels off to some faraway world to study a shower room in some resort education center."

"Well, if it's any consolation," he offers. "I did pay attention to the lavish accommodations. I wonder, how much does an apartment cost over there?"

The group enjoys a moment of laughter as they gather around the conveyor. Petrith kneels down to examine the status display on the reactor. The readouts all showed nominal operating conditions.

"Everything here looks good," he relates.

He moves across to the rift generator and peers inside the control panel. He hits the activation switch and waits.

Kaliya studies the unit for its compact design and curious layout.

"We were speculating if Darumon may have applied a little of his own brand of proprietary tech into this thing. That, and the fusion reactor, for standard tech like ours, might not work. It's too tiny. But if to apply a little arcanic tech…"

"Arcanic tech?" Sulíma wonders. "You mean, to use magic as technology?"

"Yeah, you can do that if you know how. Thaelyn's people use this, and it's enough to blow your horns off."

The unit powers up and runs through a diagnostic procedure, followed by an indicator where it was apparently attempting to link to a remote data source. A moment later, the handshaking signal is replaced with a data download, and the unit began an auto-configuration process.

"Well, isn't that just typical!" Sulíma yips. "They put satellites over our heads, and we didn't even know about it."

"At this moment," Kaliya muses. "It doesn't surprise me. They had time, opportunity, and we apparently weren't watching, nor could we do anything about it if we did."

As the configuration display comes to a standby condition, an iconic menu pops up. Kaliya leans down to examine the icons.

"It looks like we have a variety of options here," she considers. "Activate the conduit, run diagnostics, recalibrate the satellite positioning, and so on, and finally to shut down."

"All right, here we go," Sulíma declares.

She reaches down to touch the screen, selecting the option to activate the conduit. The display alters to show a new menu selection list. In this case, it displayed two entries.

"Hmm," Kaliya ponders. "That's interesting."

"Two of them?" Petrith mutters. "So, are we talking about two destination points here?"

"It would certainly look that way, from what Kailen once tried to explain to me about conveyor operation. And if this is the case, we may have just gotten lucky. But we need to be sure of what we're looking at. Hit the first one and let's see what it does."

Sulíma touches the first index option, and the display begins scrolling a data list for the index calculation. After a moment, the rift generator comes to life. A flash erupts within the aperture, followed by a funnel-like vortex streaming out briefly, and then settling into a flat swirl. The sudden eruption of energies caused each of them to pull back reflexively until it stabilized.

"All right, I'm going back to check on things," Kaliya states. "Don't get any funny ideas about jumping through while I'm gone. I'd hate to have to go chasing you down on some other world."

"Don't worry, Kali," Sulíma notes. "I'm happy to stay here and play with all our new toys."

Kaliya steps back and brings her attention to the tactical office in Firstfall. Sulíma and Petrith watched as she faded from view in a puff.

"And to think," Petrith mumbles. "I saw her once sitting in a chair, and she was actually over here flying around as a bird."

"My Lord," Kaliya reports as she enters the office. "We have one of the conveyors up, and we think it might be Portal Three, but we need to confirm this still. Do we have anything coming in yet?"

"Nothing as of yet," he reflects. "General, send out a note to each of the garrisons. See if they have anything to report."

"In the meantime," she continues. "We also see this unit has two index coordinates listed. So, we're asking ourselves if this could be that one linking to Morndindor."

"It would be a most convenient turn of events for us. But let us first see if we have a valid result before we begin celebrating."

They waited several long moments while messages were sent out via rune transport to each of the garrisons at Portals Two and Three. After a while, the replies came in.

"My Lord," the General informs. "Neither of them is reporting any activity."

"Very well, we will try that second choice and see if it brings our result. And let us hope it works, otherwise we may have a new concern if these units are not functioning as desired."

Kaliya offers a quick nod and flashes back to Ruuki uy'Daan to rejoin with her friends.

"So, what's the verdict?" Sulíma asks. "Go, or no go?"

"Neither of the two exits is showing anything, so we're hoping this next one works. Otherwise, we might have a problem."

Sulíma nods as she touches a cancellation icon in the bottom corner of the display and returns to the list of indexes. She then selects the second item on the list. The rift opens again and stabilizes, and Kaliya makes another return to check in. She arrives in Firstfall at roughly the same moment as a messenger with a note received through the portal arrival zone. They convene inside the office.

"Very good," the General nods. "We have Portal Three up again."

"Excellent..." Thaelyn decrees. "And this further suggests we may have fulfilled that line of Adalon's prophecy. This could be our answer to the question of finding our next step. We must pay close attention to that conveyor in order to secure it from any loss."

"My Lord, I must now ask myself if Adalon gave any new instructions for the next part. Perhaps we should inform Archivist Windsong about this success so she can review the forthcoming quatrains for any clues."

"This would be a good suggestion. Send a note to her and let her know of our findings, and what we expect might be on the other side. Perhaps she can give us some idea of what to expect once we move forward. And Kaliya, I will have you return with this news and inform them to take good care of that unit."

"Yes, my Lord!" she salutes and leaves the office.

"Your Lordship," Kailen begins. "If we refer back on this topic, the Suuden-Aryku ought to have a functioning base of some kind on that world. If this mining operation has been in effect for as much as four centuries, I would imagine they should have a full command base somewhere over there."

"A full base," he considers. "Such as what they had here at one time? Yes, this would make sense."

"And including a conveyor unit. Under these circumstances, this could provide us with a means to reach Azgarén."

"I agree, but I will want to take this one intact, not allow them to destroy it like the last one."

"Naturally, so we will need to make our plans very carefully."

"I would also imagine there should be a facility of some kind to process the metal into Darumon's weapon. And if this material is so volatile, I hesitate to think of where that might be."

"I wouldn't even know where to begin with that," Kailen sighs. "But I would suggest it's likely to be found as another destination on the conveyor, to make things efficient. They might use their base as a collection point, both for the mine here and whatever they have on that world, and then forward it to a processor."

"I would further suggest there ought to be a storage site. If it were me, I certainly would not wish to have my entire stockpile go up if there should be any small accidents along the way inside that processor. A remote storage depot would be preferable. Somewhere isolated and calm."

"Dear cu'Nar, when you put it into such terms, it sends shivers down my tail. But you're right, so either another destination on the conveyor, or maybe a chain of them."

"And then we need a way to dispose of it, and this leaves me with my own shivers, Commander."

"My Lord," the General offers. "We should also consider the dwarves in this, and that Thane of theirs. We certainly would not want him to know anything before we can contend with him."

"And also to discover who and what he is. If he is an agent impersonating a dwarf, can it be Darumon in disguise, or perhaps someone else. Darumon once claimed to be the last of his kind, so how is he managing this operation. We will need to study this carefully."

✦

Kaliya had returned to Ruuki uy'Daan to check in with Sulíma and Petrith after their work on the conveyors was finished. They were now reconvening in the work camp.

"By the way, Kali," Sulíma poses. "I seem to recall you once promising to teach us a little something about this magic."

"Yes, I did. We seem to have a little time on our hands, so do you want to try this now?"

Sulíma smiles and nods energetically.

"All right," Kaliya accedes. "Gather up a few people and let's give this a go. Where's Tana, she seemed really interested in this."

Sulíma rushed back inside the mine to find Túfula and Tana.

A few moments later, the three of them emerged outside to rejoin with Kaliya.

"First, we need some kindling wood," she announces. "Any kind of dry stick will do. Bring several of them so we have something to practice with."

Tana rushed off to a materials store where they kept some surplus firewood, and brought back several thin pieces of kindling.

"Good," Kaliya continues. "Now, let's sit down in a little circle and settle ourselves for some serious work. Remember what I said, this is a powerful force we're dealing with, and the first lesson they teach is discipline to control it."

Sulíma and the others position themselves in a close circle on the ground. The scene was starting to draw attention by some of the other workers, and now an audience was forming.

Kaliya stood over the circle ready to give her instruction.

"Now, listen carefully," she begins. "Keeping in mind I'm still in training, so I'm not a professional teacher, but here's what I can say about it. Magic, as we so often call it, is a force driven by an energy source called the dynamistic flows. The Estelar use this term a lot, but we might also call it arcanic energy. In this universe, this energy is an ambient flow that seems to be generated dynamically…therefore the name, I suppose," she chuckles. "It's apparently a byproduct of a form of life on another dimensional level outside of ours. This is the result of a kind of symbiosis with corporeal life, like ours, and the natural life energies we produce and how we interact with them."

"A symbiosis with another form of life on a different dimensional level?" Sulíma winces. "No wonder none of us could ever figure anything out! This is an extradimensional product!"

"Yes, it is! Maybe one of these days, we'll find time to learn more about it. But using this, we can control the elements around us, impose certain effects on things, and even create imagery as a type of illusionary display. It's used on Tae'Eladar in industry, art, entertainment, military combat…many things, including basic home applications."

Her audience ushered up a series of oohs and soft murmuring at the suggestion.

"But the Art, as they call it, is delicate. They have structured learning programs for their citizens, and each grade mark, which they call a Circle, carries its own demands for respect, responsibility, and needs to be recorded and licensed to demonstrate your skill level."

"This sounds very advanced," Tana muses. "A lot more so than what these orcs seem to know."

"Oh yes. These orcs are very primitive in how they approach it, and I'm sure they tend to covet the knowledge from one shaman to another. On Tae'Eladar, I'm told there was a time when they had powerful wizards and mages who did the same, until Thaelyn came along and began to change how things worked, including providing lessons to common citizens on how to use it. This changed their entire way of life, and essentially began a new era for them."

"Wow..." Túfula croons. "I can't wait to get over there and read up on some of that history."

"I've been studying some of this in my classes, and it's really interesting to see how their society grew up. But now, here is your first lesson. I don't want to carry you too far without proper controls, so we're going to keep it simple. These sticks you have in your hands..." she directs. "We're going to ignite them to create a simple fire that you can use almost anywhere, like to start campfires, light ovens, and so on. From here, we can have you practice on occasion to build your skills, but let's not go too far with it. I don't want to come back here and see a bunch of barbequed people."

The group ushers up a cautious laugh.

"This energy is worked by the mind," she continues. "Mental focus and control, you direct it, you govern it, and you invoke it to your will. The way Thaelyn first convinced me of it was by helping me realize what it is and how to apply it. I didn't believe in it at first, but after several failed attempts, I nearly exploded my stick all over the camp."

"Oops!" Sulíma yips. "Did anyone get hurt?"

"No, and it was a very fulfilling moment to realize I could actually do it. Like all the rest, I just figured this was some kind of mysticism and mostly shrugged it off. But as I began making success, I could actually feel it swirling around inside of me. I felt a strange sensation, like a tingle, gathering up inside. Then, as I caused it to flow along my arm and into my stick, I could almost see it. This was the evidence I needed to accept it as real. And in so doing, I finally managed to prove, at least in concept, that old riddle of metaphysics."

"That's been a problem for a lot of us," Tana reflects. "How did you actually manage to prove it?"

"In this universe, and likely using these energies, it becomes possible to do this. My father was probably ahead of his time back home on Azgarén, maybe also outside his element to do it with. I've been asking myself recently what caused him to pursue such an unorthodox study as metaphysics. One of these days, I might need to ask him, because in a society that outright rejects the idea, I can only guess he had something turn his horns around for it. Maybe a personal experience to open his eyes."

"You know," Tana recalls. "I was once asking why we, as a faction, aren't actually studying this magic from the orcs as our faction should be doing."

"Yeah, it seems a little backwards. But I'll say again, our tendency to think in terms of numbers doesn't allow it. Maybe, if given enough time and opportunity, one of us might have been successful, but these energies are like a shortcut to a lot of things. I've been able to create objects out of nothingness simply by thinking them into existence."

"In all the nether-space, just by thinking of it?"

"This is what the riddle was telling us. You first need to define it in your mind, where your perceptions provide the recognition of what you want. This involves a clear definition of the existence of the thing, and from there, your will can very literally alter the reality of the space around you to create the substance."

The audience murmurs another round of whispers on the subject.

Kaliya continues, "But these are skills for people who are probably much higher than we are. The simple fact I was able to do this, even in a controlled environment during my own training, is simply amazing. And it says something about what we might think ourselves to be, if not the simple beings we always thought we were. The Prodigy Gift, for instance, is described as a godlike power, and we should not be in possession of it. This is a power for beings on the scale of what they call Celestials, which are much closer to godhood than where we stand now."

"But then…" Túfula wonders. "Why is it we have it?"

"Unfortunately, this is where Darumon comes in and those statements by Adalon. If we are his children, so to speak, for what he did to the Eracyodines, we inherited some truly remarkable Gifts from him. Telepathy, for instance, like what my father was studying, and who knows what else he might have had on the books, and therefore his ideas of us evolving into something great. The thing is we're not evolving into it, we're already there. According to Aelwyn, my trainer, we hold qualities, like our lifespans, and a few other things that should already place us in the realm of Celestials."

"Oh wow."

"But as a species, we're still much too young even to know what this means, to say nothing of how to use it."

"Yeah, and so we have people like my father who runs and hides from it."

"Exactly. Thaelyn and his kind are known to have these features commonly, and they don't run from it. They use them almost every day. So, if you were to ask me, we need to learn those same lessons, if only to demonstrate our responsibility for what we have. But anyway, here we go. Take your stick in one hand and hold it out."

She watches as the three girls hold out their sticks at length.

"Hold it like a little torch you would light by any other means. Then, you need to convince yourself there is this invisible layer of energy around you. This may be the hardest part, because we don't have any convenient way to measure it, and it might seem a little strange to think of something invisible that doesn't react to any other form of science we know of. But it's out there, trust me. And if you can wrap your horns around it, you can make it flow into you, using your body as a vessel to contain it. Just be careful of how much you pull in. We only want the stick to burn, not the whole work camp," she chuckles.

She watches as each of them seems to descend into a quiet concentration, attempting to reach out with their minds to the invisible and otherwise untouchable force around them.

"Envision this layer gathering around you, even penetrating into you, as if you're charging yourself like a living battery. We only want enough to light a small fire on the end of the stick, nothing more. So we'll start small and work our way up the scale until we have a satisfactory result. It may take a few tries, so don't be afraid of missing the target."

She pauses to allow them a moment to feel their way through this step.

"Then, you want to channel it, which means to send it, by the sheer power of your will, along your arm and into the stick. Your mind controls this, but you work it like an extension of your body… not a physical one, but mental. And you need to maintain your focus all the way through. You can't allow yourself to become distracted. That's where accidents happen."

Again, she waits and watches. Sulíma seemed deeply immersed watching her arm and following the length of it out to the stick. Túfula was reaching a hand to her temple as she was trying to focus her mind on it, while Tana was attempting to coax the energies using her other hand as a guide to direct her attention.

"As you push these energies along, try to envision your objective in your mind of what you ultimately want, which is the eruption of fire on the end of the stick. You want to accumulate a cluster of this energy at the tip, and Thaelyn taught me to use my free hand with a pair of fingers extended to direct the flow into a little ring, circling twice to enrich it, then to bring it alongside and snap my fingers. This serves like an actuator, to disrupt the image and collapse the ring into the stick to invoke combustion."

Sulíma tried it first, struggling to draw the energies out to the end of her stick, then drawing a ring and attempting to snap, but nothing happened. Túfula followed along with hers, but had similar results.

Tana was feeling a slightly stronger sensation, for all her previous times studying the orcs and making her own private attempts. She could feel the slight tingling sensation inside, and drove herself to direct it along her arm and into the stick. She could just barely envision a faint glowing stream, then circling her fingers. But as she snapped, it was clear that it wasn't enough. She created a small spray of sparks, which in itself was progress, but not a full result.

The other two girls jerked back at her partial success and smiled. The remainder of the audience gushed with soft whispers at seeing the mysterious display.

"That's actually a good start, Tana," Kaliya admits. "I had the same once…just before I blew the place up."

The gathering erupted in laughter as she directs them to try again.

"Give it another go, but keep your focus. Go until you can feel it, continue until you can see it, and try again. Pull in a little more and keep it up until you get a result. We're not finished here. It took me several tries to get this far, so don't feel bad."

They try again. This time feeling a little more inspired.

Sulíma made her attempt, this time feeling more of a welling inside her. She brought it into sharper refinement and sent it along her arm into the stick. She could see the faint stream, but felt a little unsure of the intensity. So she decided to limit herself on this occasion before snapping her fingers. This time, like Tana, she got the sparks, and she could see the tip of the wood appeared slightly burnt.

"Not bad…" Kaliya mutters supportively.

Túfula followed with better precision on this attempt, but not quite enough for sparks. She only barely felt the surging, and it resulted in just a brief glow among a few stray splinters sticking out along one edge.

Tana felt a little more confident on this attempt. Her previous experience gave her an idea of how to proceed on this try. She forced a stronger flow along the stick, this time exerting more pressure on the accumulation in the ring at the end. And when she snapped her fingers, she was able to create a tiny blue flame just barely surrounding the tip. She studied it and smiled.

"Well, it's small, but it's burning," she admits. "Probably not for long, though. A slight breeze could put this out. Can I try again?"

"Absolutely! Do it until you get a solid flame you can use to start a campfire."

Tana blows out her previous attempt and once again they each try to ignite their sticks.

Sulíma feels the pressure to get it right this time, so she motivates herself to dig deeper into her thoughts, calling up the energies into a fuller sensation of cycling within her. As before, she directs this into the stick, but as she runs the circle with her fingers, she places more care into confirming there is actually something present to make a ring. She continues pulling from the surrounding environment and imagining a flow like a small river running through her arm and into the stick. When she is ready, she positions her hand on the side and makes a solid snap of the fingers.

On this occasion, the stick bursts into flame, engulfing the upper third of its length and sending burning splinters flying out in all directions. The other two girls jerk back, broken out of their concentration as they try to dust themselves off.

"Yeah, Suli," Kaliya sighs. "You and I are so much alike on some things. But congratulations, anyway. Just try not to burn the city down...again."

Túfula redirected herself for her next attempt. She tried judging herself based on the other two for their results, hoping to aim for a middle ground. Her previous attempt managed to scorch a few embers, but this time she needed a proper flame. On this occasion, when she snapped her fingers, she was able to invoke a smallish eruption on the very tip, which was just enough to carry it forward as a burning matchstick.

Tana felt better for this next try. She needed just a little more to make it work. She applied herself the same as before, but embellishing it slightly higher. When she snapped her fingers, she was able to create a hearty flame at the end, which would surely suffice for any utility need.

"Here we go," she smiles. "I could work with this."

"Nicely done, people," Kaliya applauds. "Of course, another handy lesson is how to put OUT fires, so we can keep Suli in check," she grins.

"Now just a minute," Sulíma gripes. "It wasn't THAT bad!"

"How do you do that?" Tana wonders.

"It works a little in reverse," Kaliya offers. "You need three basic conditions to make fire. A fuel, oxygen, like from the air, and heat. Just remove one of these and there you go. Generally, we learn to remove the heat aspect. I do it with a squiggle raining down on it, then a little circle to bullseye the flame, and wave it away, imagining a burst of extreme cold permeating the stick to douse the fire."

Tana studies her stick, which was still burning vigorously. But putting out a fire shouldn't be anywhere near as dangerous as starting one, so she tried her example. She first imagined the effect in her mind, and then drew a squiggle in the air with her fingers descending onto the stick. From there, she formed a circle to concentrate the energies gathering around the flame. Now, she needed to imagine a sudden shift of cold permeating the stick. She then waved her hand across it, as if shooing the fire away.

The flame on her stick instantly sputtered out. The result was so complete, it didn't even leave any residual smoking effect. She tried touching it to see how it felt.

"It's cold to the touch…abnormally cold. Wow."

"That's precisely how they teach it," Kaliya notes. "You're good. I guess studying those orcs for so long gave you a few ideas. With some proper instruction, you could go places."

With the day's lesson complete, the group went back to work. Kaliya gave her goodbyes, and then flashed out of sight.

Chapter 5

OF GODS AND ORCS

An orcish scout was returning to their camp on the east side of the city. He had been assigned to observe the recent happenings from the jungle's edge.

"Chief? I am here now."

"What do you see?" he asks. "Do you see the stone god again?"

"Not this time. I think maybe he sleeps, or maybe he hides."

"Hides? Hmm, yes, hides and waits for us to go back. He comes out, yells, stomps his feet, and tells our warriors to run away. Now he hides and waits for us to go back. What about the ugly blue-skins?"

"I see them walking, many of them. They walk around and look for something."

"Look for something? Look for what, a big animal? I think there are no big animals in the blue-skin village."

"No, I do not see any animals. I think they look for us. Maybe they look for us and tell the stone god."

"This is bad. Something is different here."

The Chief glances around the camp, which was unsettled and disturbed over the recent events.

"All my life," the Chief reflects. "The ugly blue-skins hide in the broken stone huts. They do not come out. Maybe to find food, but no more. They are weak and do not fight. Now we see the stone god, and the ugly blue-skins come out. They walk like scouts, looking for danger, looking for us. They did not do this before."

"Could it be…" the scout begins, but his voice trails off before he could finish.

"What…" the Chief asserts.

"No, maybe nothing. Maybe it is not good to speak of."

"Speak, and I will listen. I will not think bad of it."

"If you say so. I was thinking of that bonehead and the spinning eye. He makes it sleep, and we cannot go to battle again. But this was many days ago…many, many days. Then we go back to the blue-skin village. We find an ugly blue-skin and pull him out. Then the stone god comes and chases us away. Now the ugly blue-skins walk around. You say something is different. Can this be the reason? Is the stone god here because the spinning eye sleeps now?"

"Hmm, this is a good thought. The bonehead made the spinning eye sleep many days ago, but our warriors did not go back to the blue-skin village until now. And it is now when we see the stone god, but only after we find the ugly blue-skin. I will need to speak with the great shaman about this. Maybe he can help us understand this. But I still say, something is different now."

✦✦✦✦✦

Aelwyn was reporting to the tactical office on her recent efforts at processing a number of Daanen-Aryku in her new evaluation program for future training. Over the course of these past several weeks, a large number of Daanen'kai volunteers had been making visits to Tae'Eladar in small batches for testing.

"Our initial results were difficult," she relates. "But I felt the need to press forward, despite the initial failures, as I had a suspicion based on our previous discussions. Eventually, we began to find our success, and I believe the original difficulties were largely based on the subjects' inhibitions and inherent skepticism interfering with their capacity to perform."

"What was the final result?" Kailen asks. "Did you find anything?"

"Indeed I did. Each and every one was able to project themselves."

"All of them?" he yelps. "Cu'Nar's pity, then what are we saying here? This was always said to be an extremely rare occurrence."

"Perhaps it was stated this way as the result of only those few rare cases of children accidentally discovering it. But if we reflect upon Adalon's prophecy, it mentioned Children of Breed with a slumbering gift. This suggests to me a latent ability that is only now becoming apparent in your full species, with those initial children being the forerunners now discovering it."

"Then my father may have been right, at least to some degree. This could be the beginning of a new stage of development for us."

"But as with all things, it must be treated very carefully. This new Gift of yours could hold immense potential, and in multiple forms, not all of which may be beneficial. Kaliya has already demonstrated a number of capacities during her training and exercise, and although I am confident that she is qualified to use it properly, others may not hold such discipline or restraint. Therefore, if we are to train them to serve our cause, we must be as precise to imbue the same manner of esteem and responsibility as what she holds. She could even serve as a role model for others to follow."

"I wonder what she would have to say about that. She always did desire to offer something special to our people, but I doubt she would ever have expected anything like this."

"This may be forced upon her, despite any other ambitions. These people will need a standard to follow, and so far, she is all we have."

"This can also provide us with a rather remarkable opportunity," Thaelyn asserts. "Using this as a foundation element, we could create a team of specialized operatives, capable of performing in ways we can only imagine thus far, not the least of which would be for scouting and reconnaissance. This skill might even rival that of what Darumon was using during his efforts in this world, and maybe more beyond that."

"That makes them at least as dangerous as he was," Kailen winces.

"But if we're using this as a counteragent, just what kind of war are we looking at when we finally arrive on Azgarén?"

"I would imagine we might try playing his own game back on him," he smiles.

◆◆◆

The orcish shaman is sitting just outside his hut in the village east of the city. He was deep in thought over the recent events affecting his people, beginning with Kaliya's orc image shutting down the local conveyor, and then more recently the stone giant image in the city that seemed to be protecting the mutation victims.

"How much longer," he muses privately. "We sit here, and we wait…wait for the Horn-tails to return and wake the spinning eye. Why do they not see it? And the Great Horned God. Surely, he must see it. Maybe he does not look? Maybe he turns the other way? And then we see that stone god. He comes and chases us out of the blue-skin village. Why is he here? Where did he come from? He is new here. New…" he mulls quietly.

The Chieftain observes him sitting by himself, so he carefully strolls over to see if he can engage the shaman in conversation.

"Great shaman?" he calls softly. "You are very quiet over here. Do you want to talk, or do I disturb you now?"

The shaman gazes up into the chief's eyes, but his focus seems to drift away. He quickly diverts to a spot next to him and pats the ground for the chief to sit down.

"I sit here, and I ask myself how long we must wait. What do the scouts say about the blue-skin village today?"

"We still see the ugly blue-skins walking around. They do not hide anymore."

"But they only walk around inside the village? They do not come here?"

"Yes, only inside."

"And the stone god?"

"We do not see him today."

"Yes, I think we will only see him if we go inside their village. That one time, he yells and tells us to run away. He wants us to stay out."

"Do you think this is because the spinning eye sleeps? Maybe he comes here now because we cannot go to battle inside the spinning eye."

"Hmm, maybe. But I ask why the Horn-tails do not come to wake the spinning eye. Does he chase them away as well?"

"He is only inside the blue-skin village. The Horn-tails come from the sky, right? I think the sky is big. They could go around, come from the other side, where the stone god cannot see them. Maybe from the direction of the rising sun."

"Yes, this is good. We have many trees to hide them. But they do not come. Maybe they do not look. Maybe they do not know. But this is not right. The Great Horned God should know, and tell them to come wake the spinning eye. Something is wrong here."

The two of them sit in front of the hut, contemplating these and other thoughts as they watch the others in the camp attending to their duties. In their long history, they had become accustomed to the Suuden-Aryku making routine visits to maintain the conveyor equipment. It was a familiar sight, much like a scheduled ritual. To break this for any reason was out of context for them, as their god was believed to be ever-present and watching. He would surely see to their needs.

◆◆◆◆◆

"Santari," Ankhia urges. "I'm making this an official demand for all our people, regardless of duty, station, authority, or anything else. And this includes you. And as the chief medical officer, I actually hold this level of authority."

"But Ankhia, you're asking us to go out and…I can't believe I'm saying this…pray to an idol?"

"Oh come now. I'm not saying for you to go out, get down on your hands and knees, and bow down to a hunk of plaster and stone.

This is a symbol to the one they call Oghma, who is a member of the Estelar and offers guidance to younger races…like ours, by the way…relating to intellectual advance and scholarly pursuits. He, along with the others, occasionally give out small bits of wisdom to the younger races to help encourage them to grow and develop along certain lines that are ultimately intended to lead us towards a more enlightened future. And besides…" she turns and looks away innocently. "Darumon doesn't get along well with them, so it makes good sense to become close friends."

Elder Vankkar was in his quarters in discussion with Ankhia over the new move to their religious association. But as a diehard scholar, he was reluctant to participate. He studied her posture and reflected on her final words, and a thought began to emerge.

"Um, wait… Am I to interpret we are making this conversion for our own benefit that we might learn from this higher form of life, or are we making it as a form of shelter from that creature that took possession of our people on Azgarén?"

She glances at him nonchalantly, and then turns away again.

"Yes."

"Yes to which one?"

She now turns back to him and smiles.

"Elder Vankkar, you may choose whichever you desire, but I'm ordering you to get your tail out there and participate, or else I'll drag you by those sagging horns and sit you down myself. Either way, it'll keep Darumon away from us, so that those of us who constantly bark out their contentions over security issues can finally find some peace."

She turns and marches away on her return to the medical lab, leaving the Elder staring at her retreat. He stood there, mulling over the idea, then to realize her direction. So he curls a tiny smile and turns to leave the room, casually meandering through the many halls and corridors of the Naarg uy'Sodrad until he found an exit leading to the new village square that was developing outside.

He stood there surveying the area and sniffing the fresh air, which was a pleasure he hadn't experienced since his life on Ruuki uy'Daan. He strolled through the square towards the new shrine that had opened up recently with the priests from Tae'Eladar giving their lessons. And as he arrived, he found a convenient spot and sat down.

The open-air shrine was only a temporary arrangement until a proper temple could be built, and involved a lean-to shelter for the icon and several rows of outdoor pews. There were a number of other people currently in attendance, all of whom had been 'encouraged' by Ankhia to join in. The priests giving their service were the same ones that once served as spies and agents infiltrating Rolsklinde and Kynesoth during the struggle to uncover Darumon's intrigues. They were chosen for this duty as they were among the few who could speak the local language.

Ankhia returned to her lab, where she found Likha in the process of reviewing several reports on their studies of the biotech seed.

"Likha, where is that diagnosis of the Suuden'kai specimen again?"

"Oh, right here, Ankhia."

The younger intern passed a data-pad with the report for Ankhia to review the details. Ankhia sat down at one of the analysis stations and referenced the report on the data-pad as she reviewed another one she pulled up on the computer.

"This sequencing seems different from the other specimens," she notes. "Did you see this?"

"Yes, the one from Ruuki uy'Daan seems designed to debilitate certain body functions while the other one seems to augment a few. And I see a lot of unrecognized coding patterns in there, so I'm not sure how to catalog those yet."

"Do we have anything in the archives?"

"What I'm able to pull out only gives a few early design schematics, but this is dated as old tech. So, they must've reopened it sometime recently and modified it."

"Why doesn't that surprise me?" she huffs. "Well, old or new, we need to understand how it works so we can figure out how to kill it."

"One concern I have is the computer is having a hard time deciphering the chains. It's like something really, um, well, alien got inside there."

"Alien? Yeah, and if Darumon is involved, I'm not so sure I want to know what sort of alien coding he put in there to make them look and act like they do."

"Right…" she sighs. "Do you have any suggestions on how to begin? Personally, I shudder at the thought of what might be needed to test this."

"Me too. When I look at those photos of Tyanna, and compare to the Suuden'kai cadavers we brought in, one thing I can say right off is I need to know how it gets inside there."

"Ankhia, I hope you're not thinking of calling a volunteer to take one of these."

"No, never that, but we do need a control of some kind. And at this point, we might need to clone something."

"A clone…" she muses. "But from what I recall of those autopsies, this thing permeated most of the upper body."

"Right, so we'll need to create something to act as a replicant. It has to include as many of the features of a living host as we can fit into it in order for this thing to think it's found a new home."

Likha grimaced at the depiction, but she knew it was better than nothing.

"This means we would need to clone virtually every internal organ and somehow hook it up to a functioning circulatory system. It would also have to be supported within some kind of artificial skeletal frame. We don't have those kinds of facilities here."

"Then we'd better start designing a few. We have plenty of details in these records, so let's call the engineers and put something together."

"But where will we put it? We'd have to convert half the lab to support a cloning tank, an organ replicator, some sort of artificial life support frame, bio monitors…cu'Nar's pity!"

"That's right, and this is only the first step. After we infect it, we'll need to learn how to kill the thing."

✦✦✦✦✦

Several days have passed, and tensions are rising within the orcish camp. The long wait for corrective action, either by their god or the Suuden-Aryku, was wearing on their nerves. And Kaliya's repeated visits to reinforce the stone god image was also grinding on them now.

"Great shaman," the orcish chieftain argues. "Why do the Horn-tails not return to wake the spinning eye? It has been a long time now."

"I do not know," he ponders distantly. "I remember they come here many times. We could count how many suns each time. But no more. They stopped coming long ago. Maybe they fight too hard. Maybe they go far away and do not see it."

"But the Great Horned God should know it is sleeping. Why does he not help us?"

"He has been silent a long time. Maybe he also sleeps. Maybe he is angry with us that we do not fight well. Maybe he thinks we are unworthy."

"Do not fight well? The eye sleeps! How can we fight if the eye sleeps."

"Yes! You are right," he chuckles feebly.

"And then we see the stone god in the blue-skin village," the chief pauses to consider his words. "When was the last time you saw the Horn-tails?"

"Hmm…" he rubs his chin. "Many seasons ago, I think. Yes. I remember now. This is the time we see other tribes come to us and go into our spinning eye. They speak of going into this one spinning eye more than any other. The battle is stronger here."

"I remember this," the chief nods. "And we see many others come here…"

The chief passes his gaze across the assembly of the village, with so many family units that had accumulated during the mass migration to this one point.

He continues, "…And then we have that bonehead who made the eye sleep. Great shaman, maybe that bonehead offended the Great Horned God."

"Yes, that bonehead was crazy. We all saw it. Maybe now the Great Horned God thinks we are unworthy."

"This is bad. Great shaman, we must prove we are worthy! We must find a way to wake the spinning eye."

"Only the Horn-tails know how to keep the eye awake. They did not teach us the way."

"But they do not return, so what can we do? If the Great Horned God does not hear us, and the Horn-tails do not return to help, we are alone. Can this be a test?"

The shaman glances at the chieftain for his statement. He then peers over his shoulder at the conveyor assembly, which was still dormant after Kaliya shut it down weeks before.

"We also see the stone god in the blue-skin village," the chief adds.

"I have not seen it," the shaman responds. "But sometimes I can hear it. Its voice roars through the trees. The warriors who go look at the village say it is big and angry. I think there is a new god here, and he has taken the blue-skin village."

"What about the ugly blue-skins who live there? Is this their god?"

"It came to chase our warriors away when they pulled one of them out. Let me think… It was long ago when the blue-skins came to this land. The old stories tell how they came from the sky. Our ancestors made talk and gave them that land where they built their village. They built their huts of stone and shiny things, and they made strange sounds and talked to the air. But we do not see a god come to them."

"But the stories also tell us about the Great Horned God…the old carvings on the stones in the mountains."

"Yes!" he nods affirmatively. "I know this. My father took me there many times when I was young. He taught me how to read the stories from our ancestors. It is said the Great Horned God came to our people once long, long ago. He tells them he will give them great strength if we worship him. It is said he carried some of our people to another land, where they would grow and be strong. We would stay here, and remember our brothers."

"And then we see the blue-skins come down from the sky."

"Yes, the Great Horned God told us to give them this land, that we will let them live there. But my father told me a secret. It was a secret held by his father and his father's father. All the shamans were told to keep this secret. The blue-skins were enemies of the Great Horned God."

"Why would he let them come here if they are his enemies?"

"He was watching them. He needed them to come here. We did not know why. He only told our people he was fighting a great battle, and the blue-skins were cowards who ran from this battle. We were told to be friends when we talk to them, but we would make ourselves ready for battle when he called us. We were not ready yet."

"Yes, I understand. And so we made ourselves ready for battle and the Great Horned God tells us to attack the blue-skins."

"And they run again. They climb inside the flying village, and it leaves this land. Now the Great Horned God tells us we are ready to follow, and he sends the Horn-tails to bring their gifts, that we may go fight in the great battle."

"The spinning eye…" the chieftain glances at the dormant conveyor unit. "But now the spinning eye sleeps."

"Yes, and this worries me. That bonehead made the eye sleep. How could he do this? Only the Horn-tails hold this knowledge."

"I think he broke it."

"Maybe…he was not behaving right. Maybe he ate something bad, I do not know. He said things in my hut, but I think he was crazy."

"What did he say?"

"Pah!" he huffs. "He was a crazy bonehead…that is all."

The shaman looked away as he pondered his own words. Deep down, he wasn't so sure of his feelings, as he reflected on Kaliya's orc image and the interaction they shared inside his hut, including the conversation and the final eviction she delivered that sent him flying outside.

The chieftain also recalled this, as did most of the orcs around the camp. Many of them witnessed the event of the shaman being hurled through the air, and word spread quickly about the rogue orc making trouble. But it was generally taboo to discuss anything that cast doubt on the shaman, so they didn't talk about it openly.

"Great shaman," the chieftain continues. "I must ask this. What do we say about the words spoken by the stone god?"

"I have heard of these words. The warriors came back and told me what it says. It is angry at us, this I know. It is angry that we attack the blue-skins. It tells us to keep away from their village. We are told they were cowards who run from battle, but this new god tells me something has changed."

"But we do not see any blue-skins in the village, only the ugly ones, and they are no good at fighting."

"You are right. I remember the Horn-tails gave us the bang-sticks to hunt them. This was in the old days when the Great Horned God told us to attack the blue-skins in their village. The bang-sticks send out the scream-bugs, and this hurt the blue-skins. Now they cannot fight."

"Great shaman, forgive me, but now I must ask this. Why attack the blue-skins with the bang-sticks only to hurt them? This does not make sense to me. They do not fight, maybe they do not want to fight. And so we use the bank-sticks to hurt them so that they are even weaker?"

"Yes, I hear these words. I do not know the answer to this."

"Then, the stories say the Great Horned God tells us to attack and kill them, and we did. I remember my father tell his stories of how we killed many of them with spears and fire magic. Why did we need the bang-sticks when they did not kill the blue-skins, only hurt them?"

The shaman gazed pensively at the chieftain. The statement made sense, but it was a suggestion he had not considered before.

"The stone god is angry that we go into their village to hunt the ugly blue-skins. They do not fight...cannot fight, and we hunt them. This I can understand. The stone god now protects them. It is angry that we hurt them, and now we hunt them when they cannot fight…" he pauses in his words as another memory surfaces. "Proud warriors…" his voice trails off.

"Great shaman? What do you mean?"

"That bonehead…"

"The bonehead?"

"Yes, I hear the words of that bonehead again. He comes and makes the spinning eye sleep. Did he break it? The Horn-tails do not come to wake it again, and now the stone god protects the blue-skin village. You said you found that bonehead in the bush over there," he points to the northern jungle area outside the camp. "You said he was dead, and you think it was by a big animal. What big animal? We do not see any here."

"I do not know" he sighs mournfully. "We sent warriors out to hunt for it, but they cannot find it."

"Yes, cannot find a big animal that is strong enough to kill one of our warriors. No one heard the attack. There was no battle cry, no screams…it was quick and silent. Now we must ask, if he was killed by a big animal you cannot find, was he killed before or after he made the spinning eye sleep?"

Now the chieftain appeared puzzled. He studies the shaman as he tried to reconcile the meaning, to say nothing of the timing.

"Great shaman, how could he come here if he was killed by the animal before this?"

"Maybe what we saw was not the bonehead. He was fast. He understood how to make the spinning eye sleep. Not even I know this secret. And then the words he spoke in my hut…" he drifts away again. "Now we see the stone god, and he is angry that we hunt weak and ugly blue-skins in their village. Do proud warriors hunt weak and ugly things that cannot fight?" he shouts.

The chieftain listened and quickly realized the error. He perks up and glances around the camp at the other warriors who were watching and listening.

"Great shaman, you are right. But again, I must ask, we tell stories of hunting the ugly blue-skins a long time. Why only now does the stone god come to stop this?"

"I think something happened inside the spinning eye. That bonehead came to stop something. He said…" he halts and frowns as he contemplates whether to repeat Kaliya's earlier message.

The chieftain watched and waited for the shaman to continue. He glanced again at the others sitting in the circle around the campfire. There were many eyes watching, and ears listening.

"…He came to stop the spinning eye," the shaman continues as he turns to examine the conveyor apparatus behind him. "He was angry, like the stone god. Maybe he was a spirit sent to stop the spinning eye."

"Do you think he serves the stone god?"

"Maybe. He kills the warrior, changes to look like him, runs into the village, makes the spinning eye sleep, and then runs into my hut to take my bang-stick. He asked what it was. I think he was searching for it, maybe to understand what the Horn-tails gave us to hurt the blue-skins."

"He must be a friend of the blue-skins."

"He said the battle is finished, and now only death waits for us."

"Death…" the chieftain muses. "I think he only tries to frighten us. We see the stone god in the blue-skin village, but does he come here to kill us? We see that bonehead run around like he was crazy. Does he try to kill us? He kills one warrior, yes. But this is only to take his shape. After that, he only makes the spinning eye sleep and takes your bang-stick. If he is so angry that we hurt the blue-skins, he should do more than take a bang-stick."

"Yes, maybe. He told me we do not have many warriors now. This makes us weak."

"Yes! And if we look weak, now they want to hunt us."

"Maybe you are right. He said the blue-skins are angry that we make a face of peace but talk war in secret. This also makes me think of their village. Our ancestors gave that land to them, and then we go to attack them. He says we lie to them."

"But you said the Great Horned God and the blue-skins are enemies. What does this bonehead want? Does he want us to make friends with the enemies of our God? Pah!"

"Again, you are right. But I think a lie is still a lie. To give something and then take it away, and more, to kill them after we talk peace. This is still a lie. If the Great Horned God is an enemy to them, let HIM tell these stories. It shames us, as proud warriors, to do this."

"Hmm... Maybe."

"And then he said the Horn-tails will no longer help us. Maybe they did not fight well, or maybe he is trying to fool us. Maybe THIS is why we do not see then come back."

"I say this is a test," the chieftain affirms. "Lie or no lie about their village, the Great Horned God tells our people we will be strong if we worship him. I do not care if a stone god takes the blue-skin village. It is burnt, let him have it. We were told to fight inside the spinning eye, not the blue-skin village. Now they try to fool us. Maybe they are the ones who lose the fight and try to make us think we lose it instead."

The shaman stares at the chieftain as he boasts his bravado. He ponders the suggestion, and a part of it holds merit. In his mind, his god was all-powerful, and the stone god only limited itself to the city.

"The stone god does not come here to hunt us. Maybe he is here only to find the ugly blue-skins. He keeps us away, but we are proud warriors who should not hunt weak things!"

The camp ushers up a loud roar of approval.

"What should we do, great shaman?" the chieftain asks urgently. "The spinning eye sleeps. Do we sit here and do nothing? Maybe we go fight the stone god?"

"I think I will not send our warriors to fight that. It is in the blue-skin village. Like you said, let it stay there. That is not our fight. It protects the weak and ugly blue-skins. No, we must learn the secret to wake the spinning eye. If the Horn-tails do not come, we must learn to do this ourselves. Then we will show the Great Horned God we are worthy. We are strong, like he wants us to be."

Again, the camp sounds out in cheer and applause as the shaman gets up and steps over to the conveyor arrangement.

"Great shaman," the chieftain wonders as he tags along. "Do you remember how the Horn-tails did it before?"

"The spinning eye has always been awake, as long as I have been shaman here, but I remember when the Horn-tails come to look at it. They looked at the wind box and the spike ball, but they did not speak of what they do."

He turns and walks around the conveyor to examine the various devices that are part of the assembly. He recalled Kaliya's orc persona playing with the box unit first, so he moves around behind it.

"He was fast, this much I remember. I saw him, but before I could walk over here, he made this one sleep."

The unit was essentially featureless except for the panel door on one side. When Kaliya was finished toggling the power switch inside, she quickly closed and locked the panel again. Now the shaman studied the box and saw the panel.

"This here," he points. "I remember now. This pulls away."

He examined it closely, but the seams were too tight to wedge anything between them, and the panel was hard, so he couldn't push or pry it open. Furthermore, there was no obvious damage from Kaliya's orc tampering with it. And so he surmised the small round screwhead must be important.

At first, he tried pressing on it, but it made no movement. He tried pushing it sideways, but also no success. It appeared to be thoroughly stuck and immobile.

"I think this is the secret, but how do we move it."

He studied it closely, looking for any kind of track it might make in the white paint, but there was none. He finally took note of a tiny scrape mark just under the edge of it following the curve, and an idea comes to mind.

"I need something..." he mutters as he struggles to think. "It must be hard...and pointy."

He begins browsing around the camp, peeking inside huts and the various bags where they kept many of their tools.

"We need one of the tools we found in the blue-skin village. This might work for us. Something with a point and little carvings..."

Now the camp comes to life as several others begin pulling out bags and pouches to search for any of the items they had been scavenging over the years from the city. Finally, one of them locates a slot-head screwdriver.

The shaman takes the tool and gives it a try. He inserts it into the screw head and gently tries twisting it. It wasn't a perfect fit, but his efforts were able to nudge the screw just enough to confirm his suspicion. He continues turning it until the latch pops open and the panel becomes loose.

"Here, do you see?" he chortles. "Now it opens, and we can see inside."

The camp shouts out a new cheer and encourages him forward.

He looks inside the control panel. He sees the status display, but it was clear. There were no easily identifiable features, at least not to his mind, so he starts poking his fingers inside with the idea that he might tickle it somehow to wake it up. As he moves his fingers through the innards of the panel, he hits a red switch tab. It pops from a downward position upward. The fan comes to life and the unit begins humming again.

The camp lets out a roar of praise as the cooling unit seems to wake up. The shaman beams a proud smile at his achievement. He peers inside to study the arrangement.

"Do you see this?" he points at the red switch. "I think I understand this one."

He tests his theory by flipping the switch again, and the fan cuts out. He then flips it the other way and it turns on again.

"This moves. Push it this way, it comes to life. Push it the other way, it sleeps."

"Yes!" the chieftain exalts. "The great shaman is wise. Now we understand this secret. We shall remember this."

The shaman closes the panel door and turns the screw to lock it.

"The bonehead played with this one, and then the spike ball. We will look there next."

As before, he found a panel and tried using the screwdriver on the latch. With a little effort, he was once again able to open the door. He peered inside, but this configuration was clearly different.

"Hmm," he muses deeply. "I think they play tricks on us. I do not see the same here as over there. Let me think."

Inside he saw another display monitor. The display in this case was more advanced, with iconic choices and status details. There were no simple red toggle switches. He studies it, thinking the other unit came to life when he touched something red, so he tries the red shutdown button, but nothing happens. The only other thing to touch was the broad display monitor. He presses his finger on the display near one of the icons, and the monitor changes to paint a new image with data details in a language unknown to him. But it was at least a change in activity, and it gave him an idea.

"I think these small pictures hold meaning, like our stone carvings on the mountain. But I do not understand what they say."

"It must be the words of the Horn-tails."

"Yes, I think you are right. They are the only ones to look inside here, so it must be their words. I will need to guess what this is."

He tried pressing several other icons until he came to one that had a flashing, colored background to it. As he touched that one, the unit made a whirring sound and a series of pops. The sounds continued with a soft rising whine, like a power charge building up, followed soon after by a sudden rush as the fusion reaction came to life. The display changed its image to show something new. He pulled his hand out and studied it a moment. The device had now settled into a familiar humming.

"Great shaman," the chieftain whispers. "Is it awake? Why is the spinning eye not open?"

"I think this one is awake. I remember that bonehead played with this, and I heard those sounds. Now the sound is the same as before. But you are right, the eye still sleeps. I must think. The Horn-tails are strange in their ways. Maybe this is a test to learn why the eye sleeps."

The shaman leans over to examine the reactor from different sides. He takes notice of the power cable running out the back and into the control box on the rift generator, where he sees another panel door. He gets a new idea.

"Yes, I think I understand now. I must remember what my father once told me. The wind box feeds the spike ball, and this goes into the hard pouch," he points at the high-pressure tank. "See here, this hard-vine, it comes out of there and goes in here. And we have another that comes out and goes into the spike ball. This tells me one feeds another, and that feeds another. But now, look here," he points at the power cable. "I think the eye needs many things to wake up. It needs the roar of the wind box and the popping of the spike ball. Now I think we need to look inside the eye to find the last secret."

He quickly closes the reactor's panel to secure it and moves over to the rift generator's panel. Again, he uses the screwdriver to work it open, revealing the conveyor's control monitor touch screen.

The display showed a series of icons for the various operational modes. As before, he tries selecting one to test it. The display clears to list a single line choice, along with another icon on the bottom corner. Uncertain as to what to do here, he interprets the line as something to touch. He presses his finger on it and the rift generator erupts to life with a flash and the funnel vortex, which then stabilizes into a flat swirl. The sudden disturbance causes him to jump, along with the other orcs around him. Then the camp rises up in a loud roar, raising their spears in celebration of the shaman's clever discovery.

"Great shaman," the chieftain shouts. "The eye is awake! Now we can go fight again!"

"Warriors! Make your spears sharp and give your praise to the Great Horned God. We will feast this night, and go fight when the sun rises."

"General, a message has arrived from the garrison at Portal One."

Thaelyn and the others were taking a break in the officer's lounge in Firstfall when a messenger rushed in with a note just received at the inbound portal receiving zone. He hands it over to the General.

"Blast..." the General mutters. "My Lord, we have a problem."

"What is it?" he responds.

"The garrison at Portal One is reporting the portal is active again."

"And here we have our answer," he nods. "Are we getting any new arrivals?"

"The report doesn't say anything new is coming through yet, so they could be in a preparatory condition."

"Perhaps this gives us a small amount of time on our side," he pulls out his timepiece. "We may need Kaliya again, but let us first try to examine the portal window to gauge their activities, and then we will see about our response. I think simply shutting the conveyor down will not be an option this time, so we will need to think of something more drastic. Find a page and send word to Kaliya to meet with us once she finishes her classes."

"Yes, my Lord."

A page is called in and a quick note is rushed off to the guildhall. They continued to monitor the situation, now returning to the tactical office for another review, and waiting for further news to come in. It was not long before another delivery was received from the garrison post.

"My Lord," the General offers. "We have something here. According to our observations at the garrison, the orcs seem to be in a state of celebration, as far as we can tell. So my guess is they might engage in one of their feasts before going to battle. We might not see anything until morning their time."

"That may give us some time to prepare, but it does not solve our greater problem. If they have meddled with the conveyor long enough to figure out how to enable it, simply shutting it down again will not serve us. It must be disabled in a way that cannot be repaired."

"Your Lordship," Kailen suggests. "Even if we should try something that might involve disabling those devices, I seriously doubt the orcs would allow us to go anywhere near it before they rush to interfere with our efforts."

"Indeed, and I cannot be certain how Kaliya might respond to that in her projected state. She will certainly need time and opportunity to enact any sort of espionage, and it would have to be largely out of their view. Furthermore, it must result in a lasting effect."

"Out-of-view leaves the camp off limits this time, so it might need to involve those solar panels. If she could damage or disrupt them in some way, it might not provide an immediate solution, but once the existing fuel supply runs out, the reactor should default to a fail-safe scram mode."

"Yes, this may be our only solution," he muses. "But now we must imagine what method we will use. If we go in and simply unplug them, the orcs will surely try to reattach them. If we try destroying the units, they will desire to seek out the ones responsible, and this could cause them to go in search of any new perpetrators, which could potentially leave our friends exposed."

"What if they are simply removed from the area?" the General offers.

"That would certainly create a happy little mystery for them," Kailen smiles. "Kaliya can unplug the solar panels and remove them, perhaps to our people on the other side. They could probably use the extra power, anyway."

"But we still need an excuse," Thaelyn cautions. "The orcs will want to know who stole their possessions and where they travelled off to. And this could cause them to go in search of them. Although it might buy us a little time, depending on where they go, it could eventually lead them around to that work camp, even if they need to take the long way around to avoid her stone god image."

"This could be a problem, so we'll need to be ready with a contingency plan."

"The only viable plan we might have at hand would be the removal of those people. But we should also remove some or all of these devices to prevent them from being reclaimed by the orcs and reassembled into another functioning conveyor."

"That will take some time, and probably a lot of manpower."

"That group you sent for special training could possibly be rushed into service, but I hesitate to push them so hard when they are still a little shaky with these skills."

Thaelyn leans back in his chair as he ponders the situation.

"Once we have Kaliya back, perhaps we can analyze this better from her perspective after surveying the camp. She has certainly invented some clever applications so far. But this also makes me think of our future direction."

"A future direction…beyond this one camp?"

"Yes, this now reminds me of that prophecy."

"In relation to what, in this case."

"We have that one conveyor we suspect points at Morndindor, and I would not wish to lose that potential. Evacuating those people, or otherwise displacing the equipment out of sight could disrupt our efforts. But when speaking of manpower, we should also consider our ultimate direction. If we reflect on the statement regarding the Hooves of Storm, this sounds like it could be a significant fighting force. We should therefore think of our longer-term goals, meaning to say where it might ultimately take us. If this skill can be found in so many of your people, I might wish to exploit it on a larger scale than a simple team with a small handful of people. Do you think you could offer a few more into the equation?"

"I think I can dig up some more volunteers. How many do you need?"

"If we reflect on that prophecy, it speaks in terms of something substantial. We may be speaking of enough to fill a small army. Further, we should revisit my offer of a combined military service. One way or another, this will take time to train and prepare."

"I remember this offer, and I know the Council deliberated on it for a long time, but ultimately, I think it comes down to individual choice. We've had a lot of people expressing an interest in studying your magic, and there has been some initial feedback since that first group started taking lessons. But if this is going to involve the projection skill, it will need to take on a whole new perspective. Then we have the Council. After a while, they'll probably begin to notice our population thinning out if they're all signing up for your military training, and this also leaves a lot of vacancies in our local workforce."

"We could possibly solve the issue of the workforce if yours and ours combine in a cooperative effort to supplement the vacancies. As for your people signing up for our military courses, perhaps we could arrange a compromise, at least until we can see ourselves through this war. What happens after that, well…" he shrugs. "I cannot be sure how this might play out, so we may need to take it one step at a time. But if you can donate enough to make up a sufficient command, Aerlie and I have already developed some rather intriguing thoughts on how best to use them. We are envisioning this as a kind of Special Ops unit given their unusual traits. And as Aelwyn suggested, we will need someone who is especially inspirational to lead them. But for this, she will need a small promotion to get her started," he smiles.

"I always hoped one day she could earn a command rank," he grins. "And if this becomes her chance, it'll be one for the books."

✦✦✦✦✦

"Suli," Kaliya announces. "Are you ready?"

"Yeah, we're ready here. We can tie them into the existing grid, so if you just drop them out there in the field, we can move them from there."

"Maybe not just drop them, Suli," Petrith suggests. "Set them down gently. After all, they're solar panels, and a little on the delicate side."

"Petrith, are you trying to make trouble for me?"

"No more than you usually make for me," he grins.

"You two never change!" Kaliya jibes. "I still remember when we were kids together. Anyway, here's the plan. It's getting late, so they should be settling down about now. I'll go in, unplug everything, and bring it back here. The problem is, we can't be sure how long it'll be before they figure out the array is missing. And once the fuel runs out, which could be anytime in the next few days, they'll start getting restless again."

"We once thought about unplugging the array and decided not to touch it," Sulíma recalls. "So, if they start looking around for their missing arrays, that puts us in trouble if they come around this way."

"We've already thought about this. I don't think they'll try coming through the city. None of you have seen them approach the outer limits on this side, right?"

"Not so far. And with that god figure of yours, if they try it, they'd have to go the long way around…through the river valley, behind these mountains, and up the other side to the west, which is bad because it comes up behind us."

"Yeah, and here we have this again. So, we'll need to keep a close eye on them to see what they do afterwards. If we're lucky, they might try looking to the east or south, instead. Although this doesn't sound very reasonable if they think there's no one else around here to steal them."

"Yeah, the stone god figure would make a tempting culprit for it."

"Unless…" Kaliya perks up with a mischievous grin.

"Uh oh," Sulíma mumbles. "Petrith, she's got that look, do you remember it?"

"So long as it doesn't stomp around downtown frightening the wits out of a certain impressionable young girl I know."

"I'm not impressionable! I was just a little bit surprised, that's all."

"A little bit?" he balks. "That surprise sent you home in such a panic, you couldn't stop moving once you got there. Then you passed out."

"I'm really sorry about that, Suli," Kaliya pleads.

"It's alright, Kali," she relents softly. "I was feeling better the next morning. Besides, I'm glad it was you and not some horrible monster."

"Well, you might want to hold that thought until tomorrow morning," she grins.

"Um, what exactly do you mean by that?"

"Darumon used deception for most of his tricks, so we're going to do the same. I'm going to create a new god for the orcs to blame, and it's going to move off in the other direction."

"Kali," Petrith asks. "Do you think maybe this god thing is going to your head just a little?"

"Would you rather have the orcs come knocking at your back door?"

"Actually no, go ahead, play god as much as you like!" he chuckles.

Kaliya gets up from the evening conversation and changes into her hawk form, then lifts off to find the solar panels. She soars high above the ground past the city and into the jungle. She observes the orcish camp settling for the night, but the orcs seemed a little more active to watch for intruders than previously. She continues to the southeast and into the hills.

The units had built-in battery packs to store the daily charge, and this kept the equipment down below running until sunrise the next day. She would need to be quick in disassembling everything. Once the last panel was disconnected, the fan on the electrolysis unit would stop, and that would be their first indication of a failure. From there, she would need to transport the pieces before the orcs get any ideas of coming to check on it.

She lands next to the array and reshapes herself back to normal, bending down to examine the connections. Sulíma gave her advice on how to disconnect the cabling and fold up the flaps. She unplugged the first unit to make it ready, but the device was too large for her to grip easily in her arms, so she enlarged herself for a longer reach until she could fully lift it. She picked it up and folded herself back to Sulíma and Petrith, repeating for each unit until the final piece had been unplugged and delivered.

"Now, my dear little corporeal friends," she tantalizes. "It's show time. I just need to think of a good one. By now, I would imagine that camp is going crazy trying to figure out why the cooling unit has turned off."

She folds herself back to the hills and takes a look around to make sure the area is clear of any orcs, and puts her imagination to work again. She searches for a convenient flat area and folds herself over to it, transforming her shape into another behemoth.

She takes the form of an enormous bird-man apparition, with a body like a person, plus wings and a bird-like head. It stood easily as tall as her stone giant image. She moves in small circles, making sure to stomp heavily to attract attention, sounding out a series of boisterous shrieks. She turns back to where the solar arrays were positioned and spreads her wings, in part for a larger show, as well as to obscure her actions, then begins shouting in orcish.

"Ooh! Shiny things! I like shiny things! I take shiny things! I go home now and make a new nest high in mountains!"

At the end of her overly conspicuous display, she cackles loudly and turns away from the orcish camp, spreading her wings to fly away to the east.

The activity in the orcish camp from the failure of the cooling fan had disturbed most of the residents by now. But the presentation of a gigantic bird-like god figure visible over the treetops sent waves of panic through them. Now they had two gods to cower from, one on each side.

Kaliya flew far to the east, realizing her image could probably be seen for miles. When she felt she had travelled enough, she canceled her image and returned home.

⬩⬩◆⬩⬩

"A giant bird god stole their solar panels for its new nest?" Thaelyn laughs vigorously. "This is one we should record for our history books. Good work, Kaliya. This buys us time on both sides, and solves a troubling issue. The orcs, if they should ever develop enough courage to go looking for them, will search high and low, and this will distract them from the city and our friends."

"And besides that," Kailen adds. "If they should try looking for the other conveyors, they won't find those, either."

"But in either case," Kaliya submits. "They'll be looking in places that'll take them away from the city."

"Nicely done," Thaelyn concludes. "Now, it is late, and you need to find some sleep before your class in the morning."

"Technically, I'm already sleeping."

"This is true, actually," he shrugs. "And such a curious premise, but nevertheless you should return home."

Kaliya makes her salute and returns to her body on Tae'Eladar, where she awakens from her meditation and trots off to her room.

"My Lord," the General notes. "I must wonder now. What might we expect from the orcs as far as the portal is concerned? Will they try to make an incursion on this side, or might they actually be more worried about the safety of their own camp and possibly the recovery of these items. Could we suggest they might be ignorant of their value?"

"At this moment, General, I think I would not suggest they are as ignorant as we once hoped. If they understand this equipment well enough to follow a power-up sequence, I think they might realize the need for those arrays. Even if it was accidental, they will still figure it out."

"Then I foresee two possibilities. Either they will divert to recovering these items, or they will make a mad rush while the portal is still open."

"If they divert themselves, we have time. If they rush through, we must make a decision as to our response. Destroy, or attempt to capture."

"We have a large enough garrison out there, so either is within reason."

"Then send word that we will attempt to capture, and only kill if it becomes necessary."

⟡

"Great shaman!" cries the chieftain. "What was that? Another god? It looked like a bird god, but what was it doing?"

"It was looking at the small mountain and talked about shiny things. Send warriors up there...now! See if the sun shells are still there."

The chieftain calls up a group of warriors and sends them into the hills to inspect the solar array. When they arrive, they find the array missing, with the power cables lying loosely on the ground. They grumble at the obvious theft and return back to report.

"What did you see?" the shaman demands as he notices the scowls on their faces. "Did the bird god take the sun shells?"

"Great shaman, the sun shells are gone. The hard-vines were cut, and the sun shells taken away."

"This is bad. The wind box is dead, and I think soon the spike ball will die too. Then the spinning eye."

"You said the wind box feeds the spike ball," the chieftain reflects. "But what about the sun shells?"

"They feed the wind box. They bring water from the lake, and the wind box uses this. But without the sun shells, all this will die now."

"The spinning eye is still awake. Maybe we should go to the battle before it dies."

"We could, but the Horn-tails once told us only the warriors can go to the battle. The women cannot go fight, and the little ones are too young to fight. And we need some warriors here to hunt food for them. But now the sun shells are gone, and when the eye dies, we cannot go fight for the Great Horned God again."

"Great shaman, the bird god offends us by taking the sun shells. If we cannot go fight inside the eye, we must go fight the bird god and take back the sun shells."

"We will need many warriors for that," he concedes, looking around the camp at what's left of their population. "I will think on this and give my answer when the sun rises again. It is dark, and we can do nothing now."

The other orcs in the camp listen to the conversation, mumbling about what the shaman will decide. With nothing else to do, they slowly try to settle themselves for the night.

Morning comes and the camp sluggishly stirs to life, still in shock over the events of the previous evening. The shaman comes out of his hut to join the others by the campfire for a morning meal.

"Great shaman," the chieftain asks. "Did you think of what to do about the sun shells and the bird god?"

"Yes..." he sighs. "Long into the night was I thinking of this. I did not sleep well. I tried to remember the stories of my father and his father. I tried to remember the stories in the carvings on the mountain. We talked about the stone god in the blue-skin village. Now we have this other one. We wake the spinning eye, but before the sun goes down, this new god takes the sun shells. What does this mean? Did he see us wake the spinning eye? I think the Great Horned God will not be happy with this."

"We want to show him we are strong," the chieftain admits. "But do we go into the spinning eye, or search for the bird god?"

"Like we said before, only the warriors are allowed inside the spinning eye. The women and little ones must stay here. But if we send all our warriors into the spinning eye, there will be no more here to hunt food, and we need food. Soon, I think the eye will die and we cannot go fight. There is only one way. We must find the bird god and take back the sun shells, and then I will try to bring the spinning eye back to life."

"But if we send all the warriors to find the bird god, again there will be no more here to hunt food."

"Yes, I know, I was thinking of this. We will need all our warriors to find the bird god, but we cannot leave the women and little ones here alone. I think the bird god has offended the Great Horned God. Now we must all go find it. The Great Horned God will see us, and he will be pleased with us again."

"The great shaman is wise. Yes! We will all go and make the Great Horned God happy with us that we take back his gifts and bring the spinning eye to life again."

The settlement erupts in a cheer as warriors raise their spears and cry shouts of battle against the bird god. The camp comes alive as some of them begin packing up pouches with food and other supplies, while others tear down hides and wooden poles from the huts to serve as temporary shelters for their camps along the way. But even though the tribe is preparing for this momentous journey, the shaman is not so sure. He sits and watches them collecting their belongings, but privately, he reflects on the sequencing of events and quietly asks himself what it all means. The answer must be out there, but they will not know of it until they find the bird god...or not.

Chapter 6

CONTAINMENT PROCEDURES

Thaelyn was making a return to Firstfall after a visit home to attend some administrative duties at the guildhall. On his arrival, the General was waiting with an update from the garrison at Portal One.

"My Lord, we have what I must assume to be our answer to this morning's meeting over there."

"I hope we do not have anything especially unpleasant on this occasion. What is it?"

"Indeed, my Lord, this is interesting, and it may also be promising, at least for our side of it. If you recall, earlier in the day, our guards reported what appeared to be a camp meeting with what we believe to be the local shaman. Since then, we have been receiving a number of updates during the day, and now we see some curious activity."

"This is still on their side of the portal?"

"Yes. When the meeting ended, there was a flurry of activity, and the reports said there was a lot of material being gathered up and carried away. Now they're saying the camp seems to be emptying out completely."

"Then we might suggest to ourselves they are either relocating to other camps, or perhaps they actually are brazen enough to pursue Kaliya's bird god image."

"Personally, unless there is something wrong with their existing location, moving to the others doesn't make sense. Their population count is too small to make it viable."

"Good point, General."

"Therefore, if they are going after the bird god, they must be taking the full camp. My thoughts on the matter tell me they would need the majority of their warriors, and therefore do not wish to leave the family units behind without support."

"This is reasonable, and it could buy us a considerable amount of time, depending on how long they take on this quest to return the stolen goods. They could journey halfway around the continent before they give up. The only question then is what they might do afterwards."

"This could also give our people an opportunity to claim that last reactor," Padriyl notes. "Once the orcs are outside the area, we could ask Kaliya to go in and tell our people to take that final conveyor. If the orcs ever do return, it might offer further confusion and perhaps demoralize them, making them easier to contain later."

"Yes, it would, and I am sure your people could use the additional power. But we should still consider the repercussions. The orcs may be demoralized, but I think we cannot guarantee this condition. If they were inspired enough to play with the equipment until they discovered a way to reactivate it, we must then consider how they might feel if they cannot find the missing solar panels. This reflects once again on Darumon giving them an opportunity to see how a higher form of knowledge works, and it appears to have already corrupted their natural development."

"So, they might look for an alternate way to solve their problem? That doesn't sound good…not for us or those people over there."

"At the very least, they could go in search of the other conveyors.

Surely, they still remember them. This could buy yet more time on our side, but you are right that we should ultimately bring this into our favor. At some moment, we will need to bring our armies to that world in order to secure it. It would be much easier for us if they were all in one place and already largely subdued."

"Which means we need to convince them not to bother with it…" he muses. "Essentially to say this battle of theirs is over."

"Precisely. Therefore, if the orcs should return to find yet more of their equipment missing, we must consider what condition they may be in at that moment, being unable to find the solar cells, and then what new condition they might dive into as a result of this latest offence. For this, perhaps we could have Kaliya massage the situation somewhat to tenderize the result. I cannot be certain how, but she has been demonstrating some clever plays thus far, so if we should happen to see a fair opportunity here and there, we must be ready for it."

"That girl is growing up fast."

"She has many fine qualities in her. She simply needed a proper outlet to focus them. Unfortunately, your dilemma with Darumon did not provide a very fertile environment for it."

"That much I can certainly agree on."

"Then for now I would suggest we allow these orcs to vacate the area fully before sending anyone in. We will send Kaliya on a few short runs to observe their movements before giving the word. Afterwards, once we have this last conveyor in our possession, your people can make use of the reactor, and perhaps we could also examine the unit to see if it holds any additional secrets for us."

"You mean like more index coordinates? Maybe."

"We should begin our observations this eve and continue for the next few days until we can feel confident of the situation. After that, maybe to follow them to see where they go and to monitor the timing of their travels."

✦ ✦ ✦ ✦ ✦

"Great shaman... Where do you think we should look for the bird god's nest?"

"I heard it talk about high mountains. It flew away in the path of the rising sun, and we must follow. But I think we must look on all the mountains. The Great Horned God will watch, and he will not be pleased if we pass the mountains and do not look. We will start here. Take your warriors and look in the mountains above us," the shaman points at the set directly to their south. "Look high and follow them to the end. We will keep walking in the path of the rising sun."

"How far will we walk? There are many mountains along this path."

"I remember tales from my father about a great river, with high mountains where it comes down. I think we must go there to search for it. But we must be careful to search all the mountains, if the bird god made its nest near to us."

"The great river is far from here, but if the Great Horned God will be pleased with us, we will show him we are worthy."

The orcs have begun their travels eastward, vacating their settlement with as many supplies as they can carry. Hunters and scouts moved ahead to survey the territory and procure food for the nomadic congregation as they marched forward. Their journey was expected to take many months, first crossing the jungle floor until they came upon the large river that cuts through the land, and then turning to follow it south to a range of tall mountains, the tallest range known to them.

In the sky above flew a majestic bird of otherworldly grace. Kaliya, in her hawk form, circled overhead to study the motion of the large gathering moving away from the camp. She was sent to follow them, for the moment to ensure they were indeed travelling outward, leaving room for the survivors to move in from behind and claim the last conveyor set. This was only the first day, however. She would follow them for a couple more days before giving the go-ahead on the plan.

This change of behavior was a welcome sight, as it would allow

Thaelyn to finally disband that last garrison outpost and relieve the remainder of his troops. It may not be the final end of the war, but it was a welcome relief.

In the days that followed, Kaliya made two more trips to oversee the orcs and their progress. They continued to move further away to the east, sending scouting parties into the neighboring mountains to check for any nesting activities on a scale larger than the traditional birdlife. Finally, the order was given to Sulíma and her team to go in and take the conveyor.

During this time, the engineers at the Naarg uy'Sodrad had been working to provide replacement parts for some of the more critical equipment on Ruuki uy'Daan, including the vehicles. Replacement power cells had been fashioned, and Sulíma's teams were completing some much-needed repair work, removing the trucks from their primitive wheeled platforms, and returning them back to their normal mode of operation. So, when the word was finally given to pick up the conveyor, they were able to simply drive to the location.

✦✦◆✦✦

"What do you mean, the school was hiding in the shelters?!" screeches Elder Vankkar. "The order was to evacuate! How could they misinterpret that simple instruction?"

Kailen and Ankhia were making a much anticipated, as well as dreaded, visit to the Council chamber with Velen and the Elder Council. As expected, the emotions were running very high.

Elder Vankkar was flying through the roof at the ludicrous notion of the failure of the evacuation order to circulate fully, especially to such a high-priority facility as the school. Elder Girhani was doubled over on the desk at the news, covering her face and weeping. Velen tried to caress her shoulder while at the same time gaining control of the situation.

"Santari, please," he soothes. "This is a very sudden and troubling turn of events for all of us."

"Velen, to say it's troubling just doesn't cover it! This is completely absurd!"

Elder Vankkar sits back and takes a deep breath hoping to collect himself. He glances at Elder Girhani, who is still whimpering, so he rises from his chair and steps around to offer a comforting embrace and soft whispering in her ear.

"Elder Vankkar, Elder Girhani," Kailen submits. "We have more we need to report, and it goes well beyond the fact that we have survivors on Ruuki uy'Daan from the school."

"Commander," Elder Vankkar emits tenuously. "I'm not so sure I want to hear what else you have to say, although I realize I must. But can you first explain what we're doing about this situation?"

"I can explain many things, but I would also ask for you and the others to try to contain yourselves. The rest of this report isn't very pleasant."

"How much more unpleasant can it be, Commander? All right..." he returns to his seat. "What is the rest of your report?"

"First, I would like to preface this with a delicate statement. I have no objections to the Council and its efforts to preserve and maintain our people. I'm sure you have all worked hard and under some deplorable conditions. But if you recall that issue of a security risk relating to a potential spy, we are still concerned about it. And it carries a specific direction, which is why it took so long for us to bring anything new to you."

"And what is this direction you speak of Commander?"

"The Council's history of demanding to know about every tail-yanking thing we do out there. If you were a spy and wanted to steal information, where would you go for it?"

"Blast!" he scorns. "So WE become the security risk! Wonderful!"

"Yes, unfortunately, and I think we can say it likely dates back all the way to Azgarén and the Council there, which I suspect behaved the same way."

"I suppose you have a point. It has always been the tradition for them to know everything."

"Therefore, we essentially created a situation for ourselves to centralize all the critical information, and make it easy for an espionage attempt to take it away. As such, with respect to all of you, I must take action by requesting the Council to retract itself from the military aspect of these affairs, effective immediately, so we can take out the threat before it takes us out."

"I understand, Commander. I'm not happy about it, but I would be even less happy about another surprise hit. But can you explain how this spy can actually get in here and where it comes from? And is there anything we can do to protect ourselves from it?"

"Technically, we're already doing it, by taking up a religion. Darumon is the spy, and the Estelar are his enemy. So, by siding with his enemy, we can deter him from coming anywhere near us again. But it doesn't end there."

"Uh huh, and what else is there?"

"Such beings as he and Sargeras would be the personification of metaphysics. Telepathy, among other things, would be a commonplace feature in them, and unlike some of us who cower in fear of it, they would probably use it often. This now becomes the secondary threat."

"Oh! So, my long-standing aversion to it might actually hold merit?"

"It does, within a certain context. But there's also a small stipulation. If our society is able to do this at all, it might mean that we, as a society, should embrace it more eagerly. If we did, we might not be so easily taken advantage of in this way. But our aversion to it makes us vulnerable to something we refuse to acknowledge openly."

"And this is where it once again bites me in the tail," he sighs.

"Probably not just you. Our entire society regards such things as mysticism, all the way back to Azgarén, so it's out the window before we even have a chance to recognize what it can do. Father, you once said how the Council rejected so many of your ideas for our faction, and when the cu'Nar came, they simply threw you out the door with your warnings. That's how our people think of such things that aren't measured in numbers."

Ankhia now steps forward with her contribution.

"Elder Vankkar, Elder Girhani, and Master Velen," she begins.

"We've been learning a number of things in this time of who Sargeras and Darumon really are, where they come from, why they are here, and our role in all of this, and it runs deep. It was shocking for us, and now I regret we must lay it on your horns so you can appreciate why we are where we stand right now."

She pauses to collect her thoughts before continuing.

"Sargeras and Darumon are remnants of a dead society. So, if the cu'Nar once told us this, it is because the Estelar are the reason behind it."

The two Elders gasped and drew back in their chairs as they listened, quickly glancing at each other as Ankhia continued.

"We are speaking of god societies here, beings of such a high evolutionary scale that they can be said to have achieved true godhood by now. Metaphysics is probably more of a way of life for them than the more common laws of physics we so often use. The Estelar would describe beings like ourselves as the Child Races, because we are so young in comparison to them. And then we have the Celestial races, like Thaelyn and Aerlie, who are halfway to godhood, either as the result of their extreme evolutionary advance, or being hybridized with the Estelar themselves."

"Amazing..." Elder Girhani croons. "Just to think of something like that."

"Sargeras once belonged to a society the Estelar call Primordials, a precursor god society that came before them. But this group was not at all pleasant. They held a firm dictatorial grip on everything out there, literally decreeing life and death based on whatever values they saw fit to apply to all the rest. Life, to them, was much like a game for their amusement. They were once found to be creating life, like a full species, and using them as expendable entertainment in a gladiatorial contest to the death."

"Oh, how nice of them!"

"The loser out of the two sides would then be wiped from existence, and a replacement made in their stead for the next game. So, to give you an idea of why someone would want them dead, you need go no further than to realize their crimes against everything out there."

"This may apply to Sargeras, but what about Darumon?" Elder Vankkar asks.

"He would be a servant creature under him, likely to perform some part of the physical labor on behalf of his master. And again, presumably the last of his kind, much like Sargeras."

"All right, but I need to ask this now. How do you know this?"

"We have a combination of things here. During the war, one of Thaelyn's spies recorded a conversation at the Governor's office in Rolsklinde where he was overheard admitting to some of this with one of his assigns. He also said his kind were overseers, not underlings to someone else, like the Estelar. So it becomes clear they held pride in their position, and truly hate the Estelar for theirs."

"That doesn't sound very nice for the rest of us, given their manners."

"We also have some information passed along to us by agents working for the Estelar themselves, and this tells of a much longer history than any of us would know about."

"While this is fascinating, it seems very strange to think of gods, simply for the concept of it, passing any kind of detail to people like us. All right, please continue."

"I suppose it becomes necessary, as here we are with one of them out there. The Primordials once ruled everything, at least until the Estelar rose up. It is likely the Primordials, being such an ancient race by this time, began to fade, and their grip on power weakened, thus allowing another race to rise up and take over."

"The Estelar, in this case."

"Right, and so we begin to see a series of battles, which they often refer to as the Celestial Wars, to literally extinguish the Primordials from existence. We think Sargeras and Darumon, during what was likely the final battle, ran away and went into hiding. This would probably have been an eternity ago by our measurements. There, they would wait until the dust settled, and everyone forgot about them, then to sneak out and see about taking revenge."

"Oh, revenge, is it? And what about us in all this?"

"Unfortunately, their desires for pleasure turned us into a circus sideshow. And likely because we didn't choose to bow down like all the rest."

"Oh, well excuse me!" he blasts sarcastically.

"Yes, well…" she shrugs. "The cu'Nar, as it turns out, are spies working for one member of the Estelar called Maker Kuroku. She apparently knew of them and sent the cu'Nar to follow and observe. Now, I need to apply a little speculation here, based on our informational background, and say that since the two of them were in a dormant state, they were a nonthreatening target at the time. It wasn't until after they went active when they posed any new threat potential."

"Yes, I suppose this might follow."

"Now, we need to branch in a couple of different directions here for our details. We can say their arrival was expected, eventually, as they went active. Our ship was planned, and donated to us by the Maker. The cu'Nar delivered it to us to evacuate us in front of Darumon, who was expected to follow a path leading him back to the starting point of that last battle for his revenge. And it had to cross Tae'Eladar, as that universe is where it occurred."

"Uh oh…"

"This world, as it turns out, was being used as a staging post. We were simply a little entertainment while Darumon oversaw his troops massing outside our view. They were apparently swarming across most of the eastern plains south of us."

"Really!"

"And we were arranged to join the show to draw all his toys into one basket."

"Yeah, and this is starting to twist my horns a bit. And here we have that sabotage."

"Right. Then he made his advance on Tae'Eladar as part of this plan, but this is where Thaelyn comes in. He is Maker Kuroku's answer to Darumon and Sargeras."

"Um, all right, one moment. I recall the prophecy about the

Divine One, but can you explain this in better detail for how it plays out?"

"Tae'Eladar is a special project the Maker began some time ago. Thaelyn was installed to bring it into fruition. This probably began when she first saw Darumon go active with some part of his plans, as he seems to be the one doing most of the work. There is an individual called Adalon the Silver, a prophetess. She seems to be an agent for the Maker, and wrote a set of books with a life history of Thaelyn and Aerlie, and how they would bring Tae'Eladar into the modern day, but these came out long before they arrived."

"Wow! But that might also sound planned."

"It can, if the Maker was directing some portion of it, and perhaps allowing other portions to simply follow a natural flow. Then Darumon arrives, along with us, here on this world, and with our impromptu meeting, where poor young Kaliya tries relating the story of the cu'Nar about a Titan, and BAM!" she slaps her hands together. "Association. Because Thaelyn, who was previously unaware of us, or Sargeras, or anything else, would make the connection. It would seem the Maker gave us a message to give to him about them. That word, Titan, is a keyword for a Primordial."

"I, uh, see. But now I simply must ask THIS question. If she was expecting him, why not tell Thaelyn beforehand?"

"The Estelar do not simply give away detail. The younger races, including the Celestials, are expected to grow and learn, and solve their own problems. It's a simple rule of life and growing up, even if you're halfway to godhood."

"In all the nether-space, now there's a concept," he chuckles ironically.

"So far, this is one direction for the story of Sargeras and Darumon, but there's another one. And this one bites. The people of this world, the humans and elves, are essentially stolen from Tae'Eladar. And also, a society of orcs were deposited there about ten millennia ago. This is when Darumon seemed to go active on an official level for his plans, and it also coincides with his arrival back home."

"Oh no..."

"This means he owned Ruuki uy'Daan long before we ever arrived, and he owned this world, as he seeded it once in preparation for where we are now."

"But…"

"One moment, please. I can already guess what you want to say. Our wild jump wasn't wild. HE programmed it."

"But wait, how could he do this? Is this to say he was on our ship?"

"Ever since Azgarén. He was spying on us from the beginning. HE is the reason we were found every time."

"Argh!" he screams and grabs his horns.

"He can apparently fold space," Ankhia continues. "Which is essentially to translocate himself from place to place by the sheer will of his mind. So, if the riddle of metaphysics says anything, look no further than his example. And as a being with THIS level of capacity, we aren't safe no matter where we go."

"So, we never had a chance…ever!" Elder Girhani moans.

"No, but ours was a chase with a purpose, even if we did lose a lot along the way. All of Creation, as Thaelyn might say, is in danger from him. Our losses would be small by comparison. The cu'Nar gave us a ship and a message to sneak away from him to Thaelyn's side, there to pass it along so he can sneak back and take action on our behalf. Neither Darumon nor Sargeras would likely take notice of him, as they would the Estelar themselves, if he makes an advance. Their bigoted attitudes wouldn't regard anything less than other gods to be a bother."

"How lovely."

Ankhia glances up at Kailen to pass it back to him. He straightens himself up to speak again.

"There is a hidden purpose here," he begins. "Which none of us would be aware of, and likely for good reason…if you were Darumon or Sargeras. First, Darumon seems to like to remain hidden. Only you, Father," he directs at Velen, "can recall his name by now, which might suggest the rest of us either didn't pay as much attention, or his presence amongst us downplayed the name to conceal himself. He likes to use misinformation, propaganda, and other falsehoods to conceal his actions. This might suggest how we like to point fingers at so many OTHER people to place our blame, when in fact HE is the only one to point a finger at."

"And the Suuden-Aryku?" Elder Vankkar mentions.

"Unfortunate pawns, just like the orcs, the Flame Elves, and anything else he ever touched. And worse, in their case, so thoroughly misled that they have no idea what they're doing, apparently…other than crusading on some grand campaign for the benefit of a gloriously benign creature who came to us with a most unfortunate problem."

"You must be kidding me!" he shrieks.

"Yeah," Ankhia offers. "Those final battles outside here allowed me to finally examine a few bodies. I found their mutation is actually some old biotech garbage our ancestors once toyed with as a possible way to colonize hostile environments. It's a kind of parasitic implant to augment certain features of the body. Why he would want this, I don't know. But I do know it was nearly tossed out the window, once it was researched, because no one wanted to try it."

"That's really nice to hear," Elder Vankkar huffs.

"Next is a set of neural implant chips. These seem to control certain aspects of their behavior. So, what this essentially means is whoever controls the on/off switch, controls the military. With the push of a button, you can order them to kill something without care or concern of who or what it is they're killing."

This caused the full Council to reel back again with gasps and wheezes.

"And this is probably the result of that promise of great wisdom," Ankhia retorts brashly. "Thank you, Council of Elders on Azgarén, for your kind consideration of our people."

"Indeed!"

"Furthermore, I think, in fairness for some of our people, I would like to offer up a small side note, which, by this time, should be painfully obvious for where we stand now."

"Uh oh…and what is that?"

"With respect to all of us as a species, we're a bunch of pacifistic prey animals who don't know how, or have the will to actually fight.

How do you correct that? Apparently, with devices in the brain to force the issue. But on the other side of it, WE became the victims who refused to fight back…at ANY moment…to preserve ourselves… assuming it might actually matter for the tech they created in this time. And a lot of us are very tired of it."

"All right, point taken, and I might have to agree as part of that. Although, like you said, I have no idea how we could fight back, for the war machine they built."

"Granted. But now, there might be a small promise of hope here. The orcs used a rifle weapon on our people on Ruuki uy'Daan with a variation of this biotech seed. I'm currently working on a solution to counter it, but it's a delicate procedure. We also found out those chips might have a weakness of a sort. Just as Darumon was pulling out, Thaelyn found a lost trans-com which linked to their command base. He spoke to their native HC, one named Geilv. He was also under this control effect, which tells us Darumon is in charge of their military, not the HC."

"I don't like the sound of that. It sounds like he completely took over the planet."

"Probably so. But even with this effect, Geilv demonstrated a subtle level of wherewithal as Thaelyn began chastising him for his actions on this world."

"Chastising?" he chuckles. "That must've been fun to watch."

"And believe it or not, the HC actually apologized for his actions, once he put it together that he was told to do something that didn't hold any logical purpose. This world was presumably associated with Darumon's enemies, whoever he claims them to be, and needed containment…which resulted in blasting this world to bits. That's how Darumon likes to 'contain' an inferior society that holds no true threat potential to people like us."

"Cu'Nar help us all," he hangs his head.

"It seems Darumon told them to go on some great crusade to recover something stolen. Along the way, it would also seem he's telling them to blast anything that might make good target practice. And unfortunately, either due to these chips, or his policy of lies, our glorious society of scientists and scholars forgot how to analyze the situation."

"I'm very sorry to hear that, and also sorry to be a part of it, whether as part of that glorious society, or the target practice."

"But it would also seem one of these chips has a feedback reaction to it. This seems to be the weakness if it needs to zap them to make them behave."

"Ouch! All right, I get it. Can we do something about this?"

"We have to find our way there first, but it's something to think about. Meanwhile, he also has a special interest in us as a species," she again glances at Kailen.

"You're going to make me do this one?" he protests.

"Consider it payback for that little trick you played on me in the med-lab," she smiles.

"Uh oh… All right," he chuckles. "It would seem our history isn't as we recorded it. One of the things we learned from Adalon, and likely passed down from Maker Kuroku, is we didn't evolve as we thought we did. She and her spies were watching Darumon, probably since that final battle, and this includes his REAL discovery of our world, somewhere around two million years ago in the time of the Eracyodines. HE is the reason they made that miraculous leap from grass-eaters to world-conquerors. We're his creation."

This latest revelation blasted the Council with another hit of shock and awe. Each of them recoiled in their seats, letting out moans and whines.

"According to Adalon in this one book of hers," Kailen continues. "She has a full chapter dedicated to us and our history, up to the moment where we are here, and presumably our journey home to take him down. She describes us as a nascent breed that was suddenly uplifted with sentient minds. That's our history, and everything else is Darumon culturing us to be his minions from the very beginning."

"I don't believe this!" Elder Girhani shrieks. "We were MADE to be his playthings?"

"We were more likely made to be his instruments of revenge against the Estelar. Our people here became playthings when we ran away. But we ran away at the demand of the Maker to bring this to her side and those he wouldn't otherwise pay attention to, so they could take it back. It's like a big game, and again we might need to use the word pawns, but pawns with a purpose to catch a god that might run if he sees the bigger players entering into it."

Kailen pauses to observe the Council's reactions, none of which were good, as they all huffed and panted for the outrage.

"But this might also answer a number of really interesting things about us," he continues optimistically. "So, let's not get our tails in such a tangle that we can't offer a little 'thanks' to our father."

"Thanks to our father…" she wheezes. "How do you mean? As if I wanted to know."

"First, our outrageously long lifespans, which seem to come out very soon after the uplifting. Most of our history records us with this extreme longevity, so this is not an evolutionary thing. We didn't earn it, and neither did we augment ourselves. It went poof, and here it is. Since then, we barely evolved anything at all, as our reproduction and generational turnover is much too slow for it."

"Um, not being a medical or biology expert, I'll simply take your word for it."

"Good enough, but this isn't all. Telepathy, for one thing. This is most often described as a Celestial skill. You need to evolve something like this, and as Father has said before, having this might be an indication of a form of advancement. And then, we have the Prodigy Gift. This is truly…godlike…such that people like us shouldn't have it at all. According to Celestials, who are already halfway to godhood, you would need some extreme evolution to earn this one. And who are we with our extreme SLOW rate of advance that mostly went poof in the beginning, and then crawled after that. This makes us a hybridized species. We are half Eracyodine, and half Darumon. This is how he apparently did it, and why we have these qualities now."

"Ugh…" she grimaces and turns away.

"Our inbreeding as half-siblings is probably the most prominent form of evolution for us at this point. We are slowly refining ourselves with his nearly godlike intrusion of genetic material. This would probably be the advance Father took notice of once. And we're only now discovering it. But Darumon would also know of this, and if he had no other way to uplift something, he might expect this, but he wouldn't want US to know of it. Therefore, a falsified history to cover it up. And worse would be the Prodigy Gift. Those early children died of something…alien. It was him, murdering them to keep it hidden."

"What?!" she screams.

"And then he shows up to take…official…possession of us, as a race, to direct his larger plan of revenge. Maybe also as a result of us discovering things, and now requiring more direct management. And by this time, we had the technology he desired to carry him forward, and so here we are."

"I swear, Commander!" she blasts. "What are we, his pets? I suppose we are," she relents and turns away.

"And this is where we come back to Ruuki uy'Daan, the orcs, and the junior school."

He clears his throat to prepare himself for the remainder of his official report.

"First, to bring you up-to-date on a few things. During this time, the orcs were using a series of conveyor devices donated by the Suuden-Aryku to relocate them here as part of their siege, and later a harassment tactic on our positions."

"A harassment tactic?" Elder Vankkar muses.

"In relation to any of us, they wouldn't represent a true threat, except maybe for their numbers. And they were all under orders not to make any direct attacks on anyone. So, yeah, a harassment tactic to keep everyone pinned down. That's all it was. Darumon was playing with his toys."

"Wonderful. Are they still doing this with His Lordship out there?"

"Were, would be a better term. There were three portals they were using. One was inactive, as it had apparently cleaned out the local region on the other side. A second was almost cleaned out, and the third was serving as a collection point for whatever remained."

"That sounds like a very complete relocation effort so far."

"Yes, their full population, other than family units, was relocated to this side simply for the purpose of fighting what they think to be a glorious battle in the name of their god."

"Uh oh…that doesn't sound good, suddenly. Not that I care much for orcs, but still…"

"Right, I understand. The third unit seemed very active, giving the impression of a consolidation effort on their side to our nearest exit point…more harassment with proximity to make it convenient."

"Uh huh, right."

"We had Kaliya over there scouting for these conveyors, hoping to locate them and shut them down. But two of them went dead on us, those two that were already depleted. Kaliya learned it was actually Captain Lapäli, who also discovered them in this condition, and he scavenged them for his own use."

"How very clever. Good for him."

"But at the same time, those who remain are very few in number by now. We might be speaking in terms of thousands, out of what was once their full nation. As a species, they might be described as endangered by now. And all thanks to Darumon throwing them at us as a disposal technique for his displeasure of them drawing Thaelyn here and spoiling his plans."

"Oh great! Now I suppose I need to feel sorry for them."

"Thaelyn has an idea to try to preserve them as a race, and relocating them somewhere away from here to give them a new chance at life."

"Really! How does he hope to do that?"

"Likely with a little…divine aid," he grins and flutters his fingers.

"Oh dear," Elder Vankkar moans. "You know, Commander, you're starting to worry me a little."

"Now, in the process of locating these conveyors, Kaliya found the survivors living inside the old mining complex. She made contact and gathered up as much information as she could, and then brought it back to us. Right now, Thaelyn and I have been collecting and delivering supplies and equipment to bolster their position, and giving instructions to reclaim some portion of the city, at least temporarily until we can arrive there personally."

"How do you plan on arriving there personally? The ship is dead and very literally buried. Our navigation records are lost, and my understanding of his kingdom is it's not sophisticated enough to engage in space travel, to say nothing of interstellar transit."

"This is true, but he has hopes she might be able to use her Gift to bring some specialized equipment there that could enable them to create one of their Gateways to that world."

"Really! This I'd like to see. So we're delivering supplies to them. What about the orcs? What are they doing?"

"Right now, they're going in search of some missing pieces to their local conveyor. Kaliya essentially stole a few vital parts as a means of disabling it, and left clues that it was taken by something travelling away from the city, to give our people some relief."

"Hmm, very clever. Maybe that young lady has finally overcome some of her earlier ambitions and found a new direction for herself. I just hope she doesn't get any ideas about stealing anything from us," he chuckles. "Did I hear you mention some other issues among these that you wished to report? And I am still waiting to hear if there is an explanation for why they were in shelters and not evacuating."

"Yes, and we have a few things to say about that. Let's first speak of Captain Lapäli. One thing I would like to bring to the attention of the Council, to which my dear beloved Father might hold some responsibility, is the actual reason why the Captain was told to stay behind," he smirks.

Both Elder Vankkar and Elder Girhani glare at Kailen and his seemingly smug expression, then turn to Velen to see his reaction. The elder statesman leaned forward uncertainly, and quickly took notice of the two others staring at him.

"I thought this was already common knowledge," he offers. "The cu'Nar came to me once and gave a message for him to stay behind due to some purpose he held. And I recall so many who argued with it."

"Yes, but the cu'Nar always appeared to hold some form of higher wisdom which seemed prophetic to us, and we learned to trust their opinions of things."

"Yes, although this one was so very difficult to accept, and I also felt awful for the deed afterwards."

"Father," Kailen soothes. "You did exactly as you were supposed to do, as we NOW know the reason. Here we are on the other side of it, with HIM rescuing the junior school."

"What?" he wheezes.

"Thaelyn's people love to use this expression…the gods work in strange ways. This falls to Maker Kuroku again, as the messages you've been receiving are most likely from her and passed along through the cu'Nar. So, higher wisdom? Yeah, on the scale of a goddess. She must've seen that little incident with the school, and this is her answer to save those kids."

"Our children were saved by a goddess?" Elder Girhani gasps. "Oh wow, this is enough to make me go back outside and start praying to something."

"Maybe so," he chuckles. "This is clearly a piece of intrigue to solve a problem. Captain Lapäli tells us the orcs mostly directed themselves north at the ship, while he evaded to the south, coincidentally near the school. He found them just as they were emerging outside, so he grabbed them, and with nowhere else to run, he took them west through the crop fields. The crops were high enough to offer cover until they arrived at the mine, and there you go."

"That's a rather incredible series of events."

"Incredible, perhaps," Ankhia submits. "Some of it might simply be good timing, but there was clearly a hidden design to it, and it also relates to them being in those shelters to begin with. This is the part you're not going to like. Maker Kuroku is fighting against Darumon, at the very least. Some of those prophecies by Adalon speak of actions to counter other actions. This might suggest Darumon doing one thing and the Maker is doing something to oppose it. And here we are with the school. It was sent into shelters intentionally. It was not an accident. And we believe HE is the one responsible."

Elder Girhani gasped and jerked back. Elder Vankkar similarly wheezed and recoiled from the desk.

"One prophecy in particular reads like this…" she continues. "It starts with us arriving on Ruuki uy'Daan, described as arriving on a distant shore. She uses a lot of metaphors in these things. Darumon is described as the Forgotten One, and we are his entice, meaning his toys. Then a tender moment occurs with a child and its device. This means something happens to change Darumon's opinion of things, and it seems based on a child doing something. We already knew he changed his attitude with us during this last jump, as he was probably close to his final launch, and now he's tossing away his toys. The sabotage, for instance. He doesn't want to chase us anymore, and instead nails us down to finish us while he takes his revenge on the Estelar. But something apparently invoked this on Ruuki uy'Daan, and it was in that school. Kaliya, and her Prodigy Gift. Another of the same as on Azgarén."

"Oh grand!" Elder Vankkar rages. "So he wants to do away with more of his evidence of tampering with us as a species?"

"But in the absence of knowing precisely who it was, he probably chose to apply a blanket effect."

Velen covered his eyes and leaned over on the table as he mourned the suffering of the school, all because of his daughter discovering this most precious of gifts. Elder Girhani took notice of him and set a hand on his shoulder to comfort him. Elder Vankkar soon followed on his side.

Ankhia continues, "It was a play of intrigue to counter a play of conspiracy, as Kailen said to me. And very cleverly done if I may say so. A lot of people may have been hurt by the prospect of the school being lost, but at least we can rest easy knowing that someone was watching over us on this occasion. A critical piece of a larger puzzle was preserved, and we are using it now as our weapon."

"Then I think we all owe her a deep thanks," Elder Vankkar emits softly.

"But overall, this last attack was simply nasty. The alarms may have been cut off intentionally, maybe by simply turning off a switch.

This left a large part of our population just standing around with no true understanding of why the alarms were on to begin with. Our disbelief that we could ever be found after that wild jump, and the long duration of peace on that world softening our stance, then the abrupt nature of the sirens cutting off, followed by the sudden rush of orcs, who were playing nice with us for so long, left most of our people simply waiting to be butchered in the streets. And once again, as Kailen and Kaliya have said, along with the Captain and several of those kids all tangling their tails over it, we are acting no different from our prey animal ancestors, waiting for the slaughter. Our pacifist nature is killing us…literally."

"All right, Med-tech, but what do you suggest we do about it? Go to war with everything we see?"

"Going full and indiscriminate military is not what I'm talking about. Wisdom still plays a role, but wisdom to realize a survival instinct. If it's pointing a gun at our heads, I think we might have no choice in it. But we don't even do this much. They come, we run, they come again, we run again. Now, we had Darumon driving us during this time, so this might affect the outcome. But overall, and as one of those kids said, we need to learn to hold our tails up. If we're hybridized with something that is nearly a god, we shouldn't be running so often. It has been suggested we could qualify for our own Celestial position, and this means we hold a uniquely high station of responsibility and direction. Therefore, rather than running from that predator, we should probably be chasing it instead."

"Speaking of Darumon again, do we have any idea who he was impersonating during this time."

"We've come to the conclusion he had to be in a position of authority as well as central to the information loop. Now, what does that sound like to you, Elder?" she smirks.

Elder Vankkar glares at her for the bold assertion, then turns to face Elder Girhani, who returned a concerned stare back at him.

"Um, Med-tech," Elder Girhani asserts. "I hope you're not speaking of one of us."

"In the present day, no. But who was in your position before you took over? And he was original all the way back to Azgarén. Drescuul."

"Oh wonderful! There goes my lifetime career prestige. But didn't he die in the crash?"

"Our thoughts are circling around the tragedy. We had the navigation console scramble on us. We were redirecting to a new heading, using an override, of all things. And no doubt, this is bad enough for the stability of the conduit. But it might not be so bad as to destroy the engines. However, here is where Kailen and His Lordship, along with Kaliya, all had a potential realization. Those Flame Elves may have only been a distraction, once again to point a finger the wrong way. An override would require advanced programming techniques to make it work, and maybe also to lock the configuration so the helm couldn't reverse it. I doubt Flame Elves could do that."

"Oh dear…him again?"

"Probably, and especially if he knows the right coordinates for it. Furthermore, if someone was down in Engineering turning off the containment field with a shutdown override, this could create a feedback effect to blow the whole section. But you once again need programming skills to override the safety protocols. And why would Drescuul, or anyone else for that matter, choose THIS moment to try repairing something when we're already in motion. If Darumon ordered the whole thing, he was probably down there to finish it. Then he simply folds away while we crash."

"This is unbelievable!" Elder Vankkar shouts. "Where does a creature like this come from?"

"No doubt, this is the same question the Estelar asked in those early days," Ankhia accedes. "But Elder Vankkar, this hits close to home for many of us. My little sister was in there, no different from your daughter or Elder Girhani's son, among so many others. We each hold our own pain, but we aren't getting any closer to a solution simply by shouting. Darumon is a monster, by any definition of the word, and then some. Such a thing as he truly shouldn't be allowed to live, but somehow, he has hidden himself away from his proper judgment."

"And is this what that Maker Kuroku hopes to accomplish once she meets up with him? I sure hope someone does."

"I'm sure she must have a plan, but it seems very complex. We believe we are also intended to rescue the full population of Azgarén along the way. But so far, these plans are being laid down very carefully. These prophecies are being revealed to us only in that time frame when it becomes relevant."

"I see, as aggravating as it might seem."

"So, our suggestion is for the Council to refocus themselves on the non-military activities of rebuilding and supporting our people, and leave the military issues to those of us who are more directly involved. Perhaps a day will come when our people will grow a little more, and we can better safeguard ourselves from this type of intrigue and conspiratorial guile. But I am going to suggest it'll likely require us to accept some of our 'higher' qualities much more intimately," she smiles.

"Uh huh. Thank you, Med-tech. All right, I understand. I just hope that one day, when all is said and done, someone provides me with a summary of what actually happened. This would make excellent reading material."

"I'm sure it would. In the meantime, it would seem a portion of our society will be taking up new studies for, um…new cultural and artistic applications of these magical services, since we have such a wonderful opportunity to learn what this is now," she grins.

"Really!" he intones intriguingly. "Cultural studies…and as for our local workforce?"

"His Lordship has made a very generous offer to assist us with some of his own people in exchange until we can resolve our population count."

"How nice of him. But does this mean we now have to get jobs that earn actual money? We haven't used that since sometime after leaving Azgarén."

"Yes, I know. On Azgarén, it's said our economy was fully

electronic, but since we had to leave, life was simply too difficult to allow ourselves to bother with one, as it hindered our ability to get anything done before being chased away. But now that we have a real chance to establish ourselves again, we'll need to blend in with the rest, and they use actual coinage here."

"Well, I just hope someone will explain to me which one is which for the next time I go out for tea and a pastry."

✦ ✦ ✦ ✦ ✦

"My Lord, I'm ready," Kaliya offers as she arrives in the guildhall tailoring center.

"Good, we are making ready to design your armor, and as you know, we need to take a series of measurements in order to fit it properly to your form."

"What kind of armor do you have in mind for me? Aerlie was suggesting something like plate, but wouldn't that make things too bulky for the kind of training you're giving me?"

"Under the circumstances, we are creating something new for you. You will need flexibility in the joints, but protection in the critical areas. It will need to be lightweight, but still sturdy enough to offer durable protection. We are hoping you will not go up against anything critically dangerous, but Darumon's creation represents a dire example in and of itself."

"Do you think we'll actually go to war with them?"

"I would like to follow a more clandestine method, but we cannot allow ourselves to become lax. We may still need to engage in a few actions here and there, if only to capture targets."

"Of course."

"So, we will hope for the best, but prepare ourselves for the worst. We will not cover you with so much that you cannot move, but you must still represent a formidable target."

"All right, I'll do my best."

"This will not be simple armor either, not like our usual designs, as we will be incorporating a few ideas not previously conceived."

"New ideas? Are we speaking of something that borrows from our old Sentinels design?"

"In some ways, perhaps, but more to a militaristic appeal. We will base it on our adamantium plate for the durability, but involve some technological components for additional benefits. Either way, the first step is to take your measurements for the base model, and then build on that. Then we will pass this to our researchers at the Bahlaie center for study and some preliminary design work."

"This should be fun. When do you think they'll have something ready for testing?"

"It might be a few years, so do not hold your breath for it. But we must begin the process so that it will be ready when you are."

"Right, and I still have a long way to go on my side of it, too."

"Speaking of which, the most serious of your studies is becoming more of an issue when we consider these orcs on Ruuki uy'Daan. At some moment, I would expect them to return from their quest for their missing solar panels, and they might not be very complacent to simply remain in their camp. We must consider what to do with them, and do so with haste. That goes for both of us."

"How do you mean?"

"On your side of it, I am thinking of accelerating your mage studies."

"Accelerate? Cu'Nar's grace, my Lord, I'm already pushing so many topics. How do you mean accelerate?"

"Traditionally, we train one Circle during any given academic year. But your instructors have been giving me reports as to your proficiency in your practice, and I am wondering if we could double-up your classes. We normally break the classroom studies and the field training on an even-odd interval. But if we give you consecutive classroom sessions and devote a separate time period during the day for your field training, we could deliver two Circles each year, halving your total time for that and allowing us to reach Ruuki uy'Daan sooner than previously thought."

"What about the part of developing discipline and responsibility for the craft?"

"I believe you are wise enough to understand the need for this, even with your accelerated schedule. If you should wish to devote extra time in training, I would suggest the mage craft rather than combat, as you are already doing quite well in there."

"How many Circles are you thinking of giving me? I know seven was the need to mark a rune, and I'm in the third one now."

"There are still some aspects of your training that I am trying to sort out, just to see how far you should go and what might be the best use for you. But at present, I am thinking of eight Circles."

"Wow…that sounds like a lot. I know I got the violet, but just what is it you're trying to make of me? This sounds like I'll be a lot more than just a soldier."

"Yes, you will be something of a one-woman army, no matter how we train you. Your skills, combined with your weapons and armor, must give you the power to stand against Darumon and whatever he might have in mind for us. To see this through, it is my duty to ensure that you have the best I can offer."

"All right, so when do I begin my new schedule?"

"We shall reorganize your classes beginning this next academic year."

"That sounds good, I suppose. It gives me time to finish what I've got and try to make myself ready for the next set. But now, what did you mean about your side of things with the orcs?"

"By their nature, I cannot trust them to behave themselves, even without Darumon supplying them with conveyors or anything else. They have proven to be learning new ideas, and this can be dangerous. Recall what I once said in the beginning of a higher form of intelligence delivering knowledge to a lesser one, thereby corrupting their natural progression and perhaps their character. This has clearly been demonstrated with the orcs. Whether or not they still possess the knowledge of portal magic, in time they may discover it on their own, and then who knows what might happen. Either way, I will not stand for it, so I must find a solution."

"I see. And have you made any new decisions on this, and how does this reflect on Ruuki uy'Daan?"

"There is a fork in our path…to destroy or to preserve. There was a time when I once vowed to wipe them from existence as a race. But this was here on Tae'Eladar and before I knew of you on Therinë. Since then, I have come to understand a much larger picture, and I would wish to rescind my earlier pledge. I have effectively accomplished this here, but I would not wish to spread this to other worlds. Therefore, I would instead desire to relocate them to a place away from us, away from Darumon, and hopefully away from anything else they might have easy access to. This will give them privacy and opportunity to grow, and maybe to evolve away some of their more aggressive tendencies."

"That's a very noble perspective," she smiles. "And one very becoming of a Celestial."

"Thank you, Kaliya. But in order for me to do this, I must find assistance. This new home should be one outside an arcanic cloud, to deny them the ability to use magic. We will allow them to grow in a more conventional manner, so if one day they should still desire to launch out against other worlds, they will need to find the technological means, and this will take time."

"What sort of assistance do you need for this, someone amongst the Estelar?"

"Technically yes…" he considers. "There is a race amongst the Outer Planes that is well known for their meticulous examination of all things in Creation. They are a race of living machines, and make their home in Mechanus, the realm of Ordered Neutrality."

"Living machines!" she winces. "Great cu'Nar! Where did they come from?"

"Their history runs deep, I should think. Although I am not personally familiar with it, I might speculate one of two possibilities. Either they were once created by a corporeal society as mechanized automatons that outgrew their original design, then to evolve and join the Estelar, or perhaps they were created by the Estelar, or some early Celestial race, as a form of artificial sentience, to be used to catalog and record all their knowledge as they progressed across the Seas of Creation."

"Wow," she croons. "Either of those would make for a fascinating history."

"It would. In the modern day, they are called Modrons, and their leader, if one were to use such a word in this case, is one called Primus. This would represent a sentient supercomputer the size of a small universe."

"Cu'Nar's pity!" she shouts. "How do you power something like that, to say nothing of maintain or even to find anything within its memory systems!"

"This is a good question!" he chuckles. "Fortunately for us, there is a platform one can stand on to gain its attention and make inquiries. But one must be careful to phrase these statements very cleverly, so you do not overwhelm yourself with the results."

"No kidding!" she laughs.

✦✦✦✦✦✦

Sulíma was sitting in the large gathering room inside the mine. She had taken up a seat in front of their new vid-com terminals, which were recently delivered and installed to provide a mail service with the people from the Naarg uy'Sodrad. But she wasn't studying the computer terminals. This much she understood well enough from her previous experience in better times. Instead, she was studying the peculiar devices sitting on the floor that powered the rest.

Túfula was walking by as she was coming up from her lab deeper inside. She paused to examine the bewildered girl who seemed mesmerized by the mysterious apparatus.

"Suli? Are you still staring at this thing?"

"Túfu, it doesn't make any sense. I was talking to Professor Lar'akan to see if he could offer me any ideas on what we're looking at, and both of us are pulling our horns out."

"It's supposed to be a fuel cell, from what Kali told us, right? She said this box over here converts hydrogen plus oxygen from the air into power with the byproduct of water."

"Right, and Professor Lar'akan says this much is reasonable, as it fits with our science. But this thing…" she points at what appears to be a pressurized tank with some strange rods and plates mounted inside. "This pipe coming out passes through this glass cylinder with this little ball floating inside. He says this looks like a primitive flow indicator, to show the flow of a gas passing through the pipe. It might also serve as a type of ball valve to stop the back flow if you turn the thing off."

"All right, this sounds good to me. So, this tank is filled with gas, and it's being regulated as it comes out to the fuel cell."

"Right, so far, so good. But according to Kali, it's not simply filled with pressurized gas. This thing inside here MAKES the stuff dynamically. Túfu, this DEFIES our science. We're talking about a device that could theoretically just keep on going, and the only thing it might need is occasional maintenance to replace worn parts…although nothing seems to be moving in there to wear out. So, how do you make hydrogen out of thin air inside a sealed tank that doesn't have access to the thin air?"

"Um, right…" she hesitates. "Well, she also said something about them creating some kind of technology out of their magic."

"Yeah, she says those plates in there conjure the hydrogen. It's a process kind of like how we were learning to make fire just by thinking of it, only this applies it as a device. But Túfu, according to Professor Lar'akan, who's currently in his room trying to turn his horns back around, this thing represents something like a perpetual motion machine. And according to our science, that's supposed to be impossible!"

"Well, Suli, I don't know how to answer that. Maybe that's why it's called magic."

"Oh, thank you! And this brings me to something else she was talking about as she was helping us install everything. She was describing some power generation facilities they've been developing over there. Now get this. You know hydroelectric, right?"

"Hydroelectric, yeah," she reflects. "You have something like a river, build a dam on it, and let the water flow through a series of turbines to make energy."

"Good, but now try to picture this. You take a body of water, in this case maybe a lake or just a large reservoir, and also probably a closed container to prevent evaporation. You send it through your turbines, and you make energy. Are you with me so far?"

"Yes, but we have a little problem if this is only a reservoir with no input from the outside. Once the water runs through the turbines, it drains away somewhere, and your reservoir is now empty."

"Right, and we're talking about a mostly gravity-fed system here. But rather than simply draining away, it falls through these portals of theirs to recycle the spent water coming out the bottom back up to the top to refill the reservoir."

"Huh?" she shouts. "But Suli, that really IS a perpetual motion thing. If all you need is a big box filled with water, and use something like a conveyor to recycle it, then let gravity do most of your work… cu'Nar's Grace, I wonder if we could do something like that here."

"Better yet, just take one of these," she points at the fuel tank again, "and ramp it up big enough to support a fusion reactor. What else do you need after that? You could throw away the rest of that stuff outside…the electrolysis unit, the solar cells…and just plug in something like this. All that stuff up there on the coast, the solar plant, the hydro-processor. We don't need it, not if we can build a series of these fuel cell things large enough to power up the old fusion plant directly."

"We would still need a startup charge for it, but if something like that could actually be done, it would be fantastic."

"We just need to be sure all the power lines and the rest of the infrastructure is in an operable condition. We don't want to short out what's left of the city. This might also allow us to reclaim some of the old industry."

"Yes, but Suli, can we actually do this here? We need engineers to do this sort of work. Also, how long would it take, and will we be staying here that long? Once Kali brings those people here, I'm hoping to join the rest at the Naarg uy'Sodrad."

"You're right, but it's something to think about, and I would certainly want to investigate it, if not for us here, then for the people over there. It could apply for them also."

✦

"Chief Technician Lapäli," ushers a squeaky voice from somewhere below. "I've just received some new instructions from the Lord and Lady. Do you have a moment?"

The graceful form of the Chief Technician had been reviewing some recent reports relating to the research of some captured Suuden-Aryku equipment and native Daanen-Aryku technologies. She was the lead Daanen'kai representative working in conjunction with the gnomish team at the Bahlaie Research Center on Tae'Eladar.

Among other things, she was one of the lead researchers decoding the holo-disk data brought back by Kaliya from Ruuki uy'Daan, as well as trying to integrate their technology with Tae'Eladaran arcanic forms, which was proving to be challenging, to say the least. Outside on the field were the spoils of their wartime victories, including the large cargo transport once piloted by Marelle from the dwarven enclave north of Rolsklinde. The ultimate result of this research would be a new hybrid form to be used in their later engagements.

She turns to find the small voice echoing up from around her knees. It was Professor Cogswoggle, the Tae'Eladaran chief scientist. During the time they had been working together, she found interacting with him to be an inspirational challenge, in part due to his perky character, as well as the fact that she had to kneel down just to speak with him.

"Yes, Professor," she responds politely as she repositions herself. "What do we have?"

"His Lordship has requested we begin work on designing a set of armor for our Daanen'kai specialists. It will be based partially on our adamantium plate designs, but apparently, due to the nature of the enemies we face, in addition to the special training and service potential of these operatives, he has requested us to involve a number of ring-dingally fantabulous technological features. He's asking us to start researching this to have it ready as a prototype by the time the team is ready.”

“How long is he giving us, and what sort of features?”

“The team is being selected right now to go into training, so it might be a few years before they’re finished in the academy. But what he’s asking for is going to make this a hootilly-do piece of work! There will be both male and female models. The female design will involve plate segments for protection of the critical areas, but needs flexible joints that are free enough for their martial arts combat moves, while the males will be juggernauts of indestructible devastation!” he intones mightily.

“He doesn’t ask for much, does he,” she smirks. “Let’s take the female first. Which joints would need to be flexible?”

“All of them, I think. They’ll need the shoulders and elbows, and the hips and knees. These are the most important for their combat moves. But I think we should also offer something in the torso for ducking and dodging maneuvers.”

“We could design the joints with a fibrous carbon-polymer composite, but this may make them vulnerable to piercing weapons. Maybe we could overlay a mithril studded mesh?”

“Ooh, I like that, and it will bend nicely into the creases when they start jabbing and kicking their foes halfway across the playing field,” he states as he comically animates the movements.

“That’s right, Professor,” she grins. “As for the torso, the chest piece can be solid for the protection, but it should probably be hinged or disjointed from the abdomen panel to allow some movement.”

“Maybe we can use overlaid leaves…” he considers. “That could serve us on both accounts.”

“You know more about these designs than I do, Professor. Our people were never a very militarily proficient race. Next, I think the back will need to be ribbed to offer flexibility for bending and twisting, while the pelvic segment can be solid, and then hinge to the other sections.”

“Wonderful! I can’t wait to see the concept drawings.”

“What else?”

"He also wants a technological variant of our Infinity Shield. Personally, my thoughts are to apply an emitter on their shield arm that can be activated on demand. We could have it project a tower shield design for best coverage. We might also want to consider some kind of umbrella projector where they can duck down inside of it in case they see something really nasty coming down from above."

"If I'm interpreting this shield of yours correctly, like from those times you used it outside the Naarg uy'Sodrad, this would make them virtually invulnerable to just about anything. Cu'Nar's grace, Professor, they'll be unstoppable."

"He would also like to see some kind of armor reinforcement, so they can take a few hits without causing critical damage."

"This would represent a form of ablative armoring, and we actually use this on our own designs, so this should be easy to implement here. But we need to be careful not to bulk it up so much that they can't move...maybe a layer over the critical areas and the rigid portions of the extremities."

"Marvelous! And finally, he wants it sealed to survive in a variety of unfavorable environments, just in case they try throwing something new at us, or if we have to go places otherwise not very pleasant."

"I think we can do that. It sounds like we'll be encasing the occupant inside this monstrosity anyway, so why not finish it with an internally regulated environment. And for the men?"

"From what I understand, they aren't built the same way as the feminine gender..." he halts and begins giggling at his mindless absurdity. "What I mean is, the females are very sleek and graceful while the males are simply brutes...no offence."

"Are you trying to flatter me, Professor?" she grins. "But yes, I understand your meaning. This has always been an issue with us, by the way," she peeks at his notebook. "It looks like we'll be aiming for heavier armoring and maybe some exoskeletal augmentations. In all the nether-space, they'll be a walking bunker! And equipping heavy arms as well..."

"I believe that's the plan. Now to get down to the nitty-gritty and figure out how to make everything in time for the party."

"I'll get our design teams working on the models. We have a lot of segments to piece together, plus internal components. If we're enclosing the occupant, the helmet will need to provide internal communications, and maybe we could include a heads-up display for them to see what they're doing."

"That sounds like so much fun!"

"It will be for the one in the pilot seat!"

Thaelyn and Aelwyn were meeting in the guildhall courtyard for a quick review of the details of her new class project.

"Aelwyn," he asks. "Have you made any new progress with your students?"

"We are moving forward. During this past month, we have stabilized their ability to project themselves consistently, and we are finished with the incense. From here, I hope to follow the same training practice as I did with Kaliya, perhaps with a few small changes to optimize the process for the sake of efficiency, now that we have so many results from her original exercises."

"This is good. If we continue like this, we will need to standardize some form of official academic procedure."

"Do you anticipate more of them joining up?"

"I do, and as soon as we are finished here, I will need to speak with the training sergeant about some expanded class studies."

"How many are we suggesting?"

"A small army, Aelwyn," he grins. "And our efforts here may even evolve into something more prolific in later generations. As such, I might ask you to refrain from any curious ideas of returning home anytime soon. As of now, I am placing you on our official pay wagon."

"Why do I have this feeling that you are trying to keep me here as your newest academic specialist?"

"Because you are such a fine example of one...and I need you. The demands of our situation require these people, and you are our best hope in this regard. We will soon find ourselves with thousands more in need of instruction in this and other areas, including telepathy, and I may need to employ myself and probably Aerlie to assist with this."

"Thousands!" she winces. "Powers behold, I wonder if I should call Nemelle down here, perhaps even Aristan."

"Are you still parading about with that curious fellow?" he grins.

"He makes me feel good, and he carries a considerable amount of charm."

"Indeed he does. As for calling for assistance, they are all welcome to join us, as we are creating a rather unique society down here."

"But this war of yours is becoming ever more complex. Is this the typical manner in which you conduct yourself here in the Primes?"

"Aelwyn, it goes without saying we have never faced such a foe as a Primordial before. I find myself calling upon every spark of wisdom and strategic principle I have ever studied to see it through. Our enemies are unique, our circumstances are complex, and so must be our approach to engage them."

"As one who is unaccustomed to warfare, I am uncertain how to interpret my role here. I never trained as a soldier. I do not have this mindset. As a Celestial, I know my place in the Measure of Balance, but I always took a background role. Perhaps this would make a good study for me to understand the diverse experiences involved. In my free time, would you permit me to observe some of your other classes as a way to understand these principles?"

"But of course, Aelwyn, you know as well as I that one should never go slack in their studies. Learn our methods and the teachings I give to others, and you will gain a deeper understanding of how we operate, therein to know better your own role in our affairs."

"But can I trust my dear spirit-brother to offer me so many free moments during my day to find these studies?" she smirks. "Or does he hold such imperativeness that he would inundate me with all his new students?"

"Aelwyn," he smiles. "While we do have many pressures upon us, I am not so oppressive that I would deny my dearest spirit-sister a moment or two to catch her breath. Perhaps we can work a solution to this. Speak with Master Sagrid and coordinate with him in the administration office about refining the scheduling, as it would seem we will need to begin organizing ourselves on a proper time clock. And now, I should pass these instructions along to the combat hall. They must also make a few allowances."

"Very well, Thaelyn, I will see to my duties as you see to yours," she rises from the courtyard bench, but pauses in contemplation. "Would it not be a most fascinating sensation to find myself standing with you on the same battlefield," she smiles as she turns and moves away.

"It most certainly would, spirit-sister," he mumbles to himself as he watches her depart. "One I would never have expected."

Thaelyn gets up and walks through a side door and down to the training hall. There, he searches for the Sergeant to give a few new instructions. As the Sergeant observes him walk into the room, he brings the class to attention.

"As you were, students," Thaelyn calls out to the class. "Sergeant, do you have a moment?"

"Yes, my Lord, what do you have for me?" he announces eagerly.

"What I have for you is a rather difficult task, as it will involve a large influx of new trainees. These are not full cadets, mind you, but rather a cooperative effort with the Daanen-Aryku to combine our two forces into a coordinated unit."

"I see. I think I heard of something like this once, at least as a proposal. And what sort of training do you have in mind for this occasion?"

"We will follow with the established plan used by Cadet Nazég for the female combatants, but the males are not as nimble. Therefore, we should train them for the standard fare, but specialized both in heavy plate as well as arms. My personal choice is a two-handed dire mace. They will need strength training, along with endurance to hold up against a wall of opponents."

"Sounds like a nasty enough beast to come upon."

"In addition to this, each of them, both male and female, may be wielding some manner of ranged energy weapon, which is traditional to their race."

"Will we be adding this to the list for Cadet Nazég?"

"I suppose it is reasonable, although in her case, she may already have a fair amount of prior experience. But this is not a bow we are speaking of. This is more of a rifle weapon. Therefore, we will need to requisition some practice weapons for them to use out on the field."

"Right to that, so long as there's still a field left after their practice for the next group," he chuckles. "How many are we speaking of, my Lord? You mentioned something of a large number?"

"According to Commander Nazég, he will be recruiting upwards of four thousand from their workforce for this combined training."

"Dear gods," he exclaims as he glances around the training hall. "We don't have the capacity for that here. We'll need to send many of them to the other cities to accommodate their numbers."

"Clearly so, and at some moment, depending on how these events carry us, we may need to open a few additional military camps if we should hope to expand ourselves into our new territories. But for now, I will ask you to begin spreading the word and assist in coordinating these efforts. Can you do this?"

"Most certainly, my Lord!" he asserts strongly with a firm salute.

"You are a good man, Sergeant. You honor us with your service."

Thaelyn turns to leave the room. As he makes his exit, the Sergeant surveys the cadets in their training and whistles softly in wonder of these new demands.

✦✦◆✦✦

"Great shaman, it has been a moon and many days, and we have found the great river, but our warriors have found no nests in the mountains we have passed."

"Yes, it is as I thought. But I know we must be careful and look in all places. Now we must go look for the high mountains. They rise up and touch the sky at the place where the river begins. We may see another moon pass before we come to them, and then we will search for the bird god and his nest."

"Has the Great Horned God spoken to you on this journey? It has been a long time, and some of the others are worried that he may not be watching."

The orcish shaman looks around at the faces of the weary travelers. They had just arrived at the edge of the wide river in the eastern portion of the jungle, and would now follow it south to the range of tall peaks where it had its source. He tried peering through the trees hoping he could see his destination, but it would be a few more weeks before they reached it.

"He has not spoken to me yet," he replies concernedly. "I have not heard him speak to me for a long time. Maybe he waits for us to find the mountains and the nest. We will then make our camp and rest while the warriors search for the sun shells. Maybe he waits until we show ourselves to be worthy."

"You are wise, as always. We will show him we are worthy. Another moon, and we will find the bird god's nest."

The chieftain returns to assist in preparing the camp for the night while the shaman moves off to view the rolling current of the river. The hunters had been sent out to find food for the evening while other workers cut wood from the local trees for their fire.

The shaman watched the sky dim in the evening twilight. He examined the setting sun in the west and considered the journey ahead to find the mountains. All the while, he couldn't help but to reflect on the sequencing of events back in their old settlement near the Daanen-Aryku city. He begins recalling those words again.

"The Horn-tails no longer help us, and the blue-skins are angry," he mutters privately. "Angry that we lie to them, talk peace, but plan for war. Then the stone god comes to the blue-skin village and tells us to keep away. After that, we discover the secret to wake the spinning eye, and before the sun sets, the bird god takes the sun shells, and this will kill the spinning eye. Is there a meaning to this? It is too much, too fast. I think something bad happened inside the spinning eye."

Once again, in the sky overhead, flew a lone brown and tan bird spying on the activities on the ground. Kaliya had made it a practice to revisit the nomadic band of orcs since they left their camp. She has been following them across the continent, checking their progress and reporting back on their movements to keep Thaelyn and his officers informed of their actions.

The shaman surveys the establishment of their most recent camp, overseeing the building of a campfire and setting up several large lean-to shelters. He glances upwards and sees the strange bird in the sky above.

"It comes again," he muses distantly. "It comes and it watches us. Is it another spirit, like the bonehead? Will we find the bird god? I think we will not."

In the morning, they pick up again. They follow the river upstream, continuing their trek for another three weeks. The mountains come into sight along the way, and the group feels a renewed sense of inspiration that their goal is near. As they arrive at the foot of the mountains, they send out warrior scouts to search the area, following the range to the west and upwards. The search takes time, and while they wait, another group is sent to find a passable way across the river at its narrow points in the hills, then to extend the search more to the east while the remainder of the camp settles on the valley floor.

A month passes, but the scouts are unable to find any god-sized nests. With each new scouting report, their morale diminishes. During this time, the shaman stayed in the camp, along with the chieftain to keep the camp safe and organize the hunting parties. Another day comes to a close, and the shaman watches the encroaching dusk and a familiar sight appears in the sky above.

"Look there," he points to the sky. "It comes again. Many times, I see that bird fly across the sky. It watches us."

"What does it mean, great shaman? Is it a sign from the Great Horned God who watches us search for the sun shells?"

"I think no, it is not. I see it many times now, from the time we started this journey. It follows us, and watches us, but I think it does not watch us for the Great Horned God. I think it is a spirit, maybe from the bird god."

"The bird god waits for us. He watches and he waits."

"Chief, I must speak to you, but away from the others. I do not want them to hear."

The shaman leads the chieftain away from the camp to a quiet location so they can talk in private.

"Chief, this journey has been long, and our people are tired. They are not pleased that our warriors cannot find the bird god's nest, and I think we will not find it."

"Because the spirit watches us? What if we try to kill the spirit?"

"Chief, how do you kill a spirit? I do not know. And it is too high for us to use bows. I see it only at night when we stop and make camp. It does not come in the daytime. It watches us to see where we go, and I think it waits for us to understand we will not find the bird god's nest."

"Waits for us to understand? What do you mean? We saw the bird god take the sun shells, and he said he takes them to his nest in the high mountains."

"Yes, and this came before the sun is down after we wake the spinning eye. Did the bird god see us wake the spinning eye? We asked this before, but we said to ourselves the bird god offends the Great Horned God by taking the sun shells. But I must remember that bonehead. I think he was a spirit, and this is another spirit," he glances at the bird again. "They come to stop us from going inside the spinning eye."

"You still think something bad happened in there?"

"I think the bird god may be here for a reason. Think about it. The bonehead makes the spinning eye sleep, and our warriors hunt the blue-skins again in their village. A long time passes, and we do not hunt them. Instead, we are told to go into the spinning eye to fight the great battle."

"Yes, and we tell our warriors we will not go into the blue-skin village. But with the spinning eye sleeping, they go back."

"And then we have the stone god come and chase them away. It does not kill them, only chases them away."

"We said before it may know we do not have many warriors. This makes us look weak."

"Yes, we do not have many, but if it wants to hunt us, and we look weak, this is the best time to hunt us. And the bonehead said the blue-skins are angry. If the stone god protects them in their village, and they are so angry, it would come and kill us, but it does not. Then we learn to wake the spinning eye and the bird god takes the sun shells. It understood we learned the secret of the Horn-tails. This makes me remember more of the bonehead's words."

"What words were those?"

"The Horn-tails no longer help us. They do not come to look at the spinning eye for a long time. How long ago did they stop helping us and we do not know this?"

"I think I do not know."

"I think I can say. It changed when we were told to send more of our warriors into the spinning eye. All other things are forgotten, only the spinning eye is important. And then we see many other tribes come to our camp, and they go into our spinning eye. And we hear stories of other camps and other spinning eyes, but those tribes leave their camp and come to ours. Why? Why come to our spinning eye when they have their own?"

"We have stories of a stronger battle inside ours..."

"A stronger battle? That bonehead called it death."

The chieftain was clearly perplexed by this statement, as it now suggested a change of some kind where this one element was suddenly more important than anything else. He reflexively glanced back at the camp and what remained of their population. The shaman followed his motion.

"This is all we have left of our people," the shaman waves at the assembly. "There may be no others in all the land now. Now I ask you. We sent all our warriors into the spinning eye...our tribe and all the others. Do you know of any stories when they came back to us? I do not."

"No, I do not know of any stories of our warriors coming back from the great battle. They go in, but do not come back out."

"Then the Great Horned God tells us to send more, and more, do not go to the blue-skin village to hunt the ugly blue-skins, only to go inside the spinning eye. Then we see the bonehead make the spinning eye sleep and he takes my bang-stick. You say you did not find my bang-stick with him when you found him in the tall bush."

"No, we did not."

"This means he did not take it, but if a spirit came and took his shape, it might take my bang-stick to understand the work of the Horn-tails."

"The Horn-tails again…" the chieftain ponders. "They give this to us, and now the bonehead and these new gods try to take it away."

"My father told me the old stories of how the blue-skins went inside their flying village. It goes to the sky, and they are gone from our land. Then we were told by the Great Horned God to follow them inside the spinning eye. He says we and the Horn-tails fight together, but I think the Horn-tails lost the battle."

"And if they lost the battle, we also lost the battle."

"And now the blue-skins come back to help the others. They are angry for their brothers and sisters."

"And they send their gods to stop us from going into the spinning eye?"

"If the battle is lost, we only lose our warriors now, and they see we do not have many here."

"But great shaman, do we say they stop the spinning eye that we stop losing our warriors, or to hunt us here on our land?"

"This is a good question, but I think you and I do not have the answer," he looks up one more time at the bird flying overhead. "But the spirit might know the answer. It waits for us to understand something. It does not attack us. If it watches us, it knows where we are. If it knows where we are, others could come and hunt us, but they do not. Why? I must know the answer."

The chieftain pauses to glance at the bird making circles in the sky.

"Will you try talking to it? Do you think it wants to talk?"

"I do not know, and I will not know unless I try."

The shaman now returns to the camp, with the chieftain following close behind. Many of the others watched as the two of them made a brisk stroll over to the shaman's hut, where the shaman began collecting several pouches of herbs and other ceremonial trinkets. The sudden rush of activity drew the people's attention to what he was doing, and a hushed mumbling began to circulate as to his intentions.

Kaliya was making circles in the sky above, and although it was a fairly mundane activity, she was hoping to find an opportunity to follow Thaelyn's last suggestion of looking for openings to massage the scenario into better favor for the orcs and their perspectives of the overall situation. She would watch the shaman in particular, as she figured he was the most important figure. She reflected on her encounter inside his hut when she portrayed the orc taking his rifle. And from her vantage, she could see him and the chieftain speaking and staring up at her.

She was secretly hoping she could incite a reaction in the shaman, at the very least, that he might get curious. If the camp morale was sufficiently low, he might get desperate and want answers, so she kept herself visible for extended periods just to give him an opportunity. Now she observed as he made his hurried march back to his hut. She continued to watch as he seemed to be collecting something.

"What's he doing down there?" she mutters silently. "Just grabbing a few items for himself, or does he have an actual purpose. They were talking privately long enough."

The shaman collected his items and pulled out of his hut again. He stopped to glance around the camp at all the faces looking up at him.

"Chief," he begins. "I must take this away from here. I will go into the small hills and make my call to the spirit. I will come back when I am done."

"What if it attacks you?"

"I...eh..." he hesitates. "I think it only waits for us to understand something. I think it will not attack...I hope it will not. But listen to me. We cannot go to battle again…we have no more warriors for it. We must grow and live. If I do not come back, you must not return to the blue-skin village. Keep away from it. Find a good home for our people and grow, become strong again, but you should not attack the blue-skins again. Their gods may take revenge on us. They want to stop the spinning eye and take my bang-stick, but these were gifts of the Horn-tails, and the Horn-tails served the same God."

"But what does this say about the Great Horned God now?"

"I do not know, but if the great battle is lost, I think he lost also. This may be why the other gods are here now. I will ask the spirit and try to understand."

The shaman now makes his way out of the camp and begins a long hike through the jungle toward a series of foothills.

Kaliya was watching, and becoming more curious as to the shaman's behavior. She saw him now leaving the camp alone and going off into the jungle.

"Bold little guy," she muses. "Where does he think he's going?"

She followed him as she continued to circle high above, altering her course just slightly to follow his motions.

The shaman trekked for almost an hour until he came to a series of stepped rocky outcroppings leading up a hillside. He collected a bundle of firewood along the way and then began climbing the rocks. He was aiming for a small plateau on top of one ridge.

"I'll bet I know what he's doing," Kaliya surmises. "Those recent lessons I've been taking on orcish culture might be paying off a little. He's looking for a place to make a spirit call. This could be interesting, but it also means I need to invent a new act."

She waited for him to find his perch and observed the shaman begin making a small campfire. He hovered over his new camp and opened his pouches, periodically glancing up at the bird to make sure it was still there.

Kaliya had moved closer to the hillside for a better view, as well as to assure him that she was paying attention to his activities. When she saw him begin pulling out a collection of herbs from his pouches and taking a ceremonial rod in hand, she knew he was getting ready.

Timing might be important here to be sure he was well into his ritual before she descended for a meeting.

The shaman threw his herbs into the fire, and they created a small cloud of pungent smoke, he then started dancing with his rod and calling out to the spirit. This was Kaliya's cue. By this time, she had lowered herself enough to hear his voice, and when she heard him calling out to her, she gently glided in, making a couple of sweeps to appear as though she was still deciding her action, until she finally settled on a nearby rock overlooking his camp.

The shaman watched the bird descend and land nearby. He eyed it carefully, and when it came to a rest, he halted his dancing. He kept his posture low as a sign of deference to the spirit creature, and he crept forward to begin speaking.

"Spirit of the air, I come to understand your ways. I see and hear many things, and these bring questions I cannot answer. My people are tired, and we must know what is expected of us. Will you help me to understand?"

Kaliya studied him for his manners. This was a significant change from his attitude inside his hut that day. And in her bird form, she knew this would fit very nicely with their native mysticism. She began to speak in her traditional bird voice.

"What questions do you seek to answer?"

"Long ago, we listened to the Great Horned God tell us to fight a great battle inside the spinning eye. It is said the blue-skins are his enemies, and they run from him."

"Does he tell you why they run from him?"

"My father and his father tell stories of the old days, and we have carvings in the stones on the mountains. We are told the Great Horned God wanted them to come here, that he was watching them. But he did not say why he wanted them to come here, only that he was fighting a great battle, and they ran from this battle."

"And he wanted you to fight this same great battle?"

"Yes, but in the beginning, he tells us we are not ready to fight. He says we must grow and become strong. This was his promise to us. Our ancestors tell us he came to us and promised he will make us strong. Then he comes and tells us to attack the blue-skins in their village. This is the time when the Horn-tails come to us with their gifts. One of these gifts was the spinning eye, the other was the bang-sticks. They said we must use this to hunt the blue-skins and hurt them. After this, the blue-skins run to their flying village and leave our land, and we must follow inside the spinning eye."

"You are told to hunt and kill the blue-skins in their village. You are told to go into the spinning eye to continue hunting and killing them. But they also give you the bang-sticks. These do not kill, they only hurt, and you know this?"

"Yes," he sighs. "They make the blue-skins ugly. They are weak and cannot fight like this. My people..." he pauses and turns away shamefully. "My people are proud warriors. We tell stories of the hunt, of strong warriors that fight big animals and bring home meat and hides to show how brave they are. There was a bonehead...I think he was another spirit. He ran through our village and made the spinning eye sleep. Then he ran into my hut and took my bang-stick. He spoke words to me. I still hear those words."

"What words do you still hear?"

"He said the Horn-tails do not help us now, the blue-skins are angry, and we are not proud warriors. We lie to the blue-skins, and we hunt the ugly blue-skins. Do proud warriors do this? I think they do not."

"You understand this now, but there is more to understand."

"Yes, and I have more to ask. I was speaking to my chieftain, and we ask why the Horn-tails tell us to use bang-sticks to hurt the blue-skins when the Great Horned God wants us to hunt and kill them."

"They did not tell you why to use them, only to use them to hurt the blue-skins?"

"This is what they say. We see the bang-sticks do not kill, only hurt them."

"The bang-sticks are not made to kill. They are made to insult. They are made to hurt people that do not like battle. They are made to frighten others to run. These are not for proud warriors. These are for those who like to hurt weak things and play with them. That is all."

The shaman glared at the bird spirit on the rock. He was stunned that someone or something would create such a weapon only to play with another. He retracted momentarily and glanced around his campfire.

"Why would the Horn-tails tell us to use this if the Great Horned God tells us to hunt and kill them?"

"There can be many reasons. Not all people see the strength of body as a great pursuit. Some might choose great wisdom instead. But if they choose great wisdom, they may not choose to fight battles, as this wisdom may teach other ways to live. Your people choose the ways of battle and strong bodies. This may be good for your people, but it is not the way of all people."

"I see, and the blue-skins may choose to seek wisdom, not battle?"

"Yes. But the Great Horned God may wish to choose battle. He may be offended by those who do not like to fight. He may also be offended by other things. But to understand this, you must understand why the Great Horned God said they are his enemies. You must also understand what this great battle is inside the spinning eye."

"Yes, these are questions I must ask. I want to learn, spirit of the air. Will you help me? Tell me what is inside the spinning eye and why our warriors do not come back. That bonehead in our village said there is death inside. We are told to send our warriors, more and more. Other tribes come to us and go inside the spinning eye. We hear stories of other spinning eyes, but all is forgotten, and they come to us to go inside ours. Why?"

"Let me ask this first. Do they tell you why they come to your spinning eye?"

"They tell the battle is stronger in ours."

"Stronger? Maybe. But stronger for you? Or is it stronger for someone else, not you."

"Oh no..."

"Yes, all your people are told to come to your village and go inside your spinning eye. I have travelled across this land, and I see there are no others of your people here. Look there in your camp. Do you see your people? This is all there are now. There are no more. You say the Great Horned God promised your people he would make you strong. I think he lied. Look at your people, great shaman. Are you strong now?"

The shaman shuddered and paused to glance back in the direction of the camp. Although the view was mostly obscured by the jungle foliage, he knew what the bird spirit meant by its words.

"Why would he do this to us? Does he play with us now?"

"He plays with all things. The spinning eye takes you to a far land. This land belonged to other people. It was their land, their home. He played with them the same as all the others. The Great Horned God says he fights his enemies, but his enemies are not blue-skins, and not the people in this far land. They are other gods."

"Other gods!" he winces. "But why would he say the blue-skins are his enemies? And why would he call us to go inside the spinning eye to fight people in another land?"

Kaliya pondered how she wanted to respond to this, realizing she didn't want to give out too many of the larger details all at once. Then an idea comes to mind.

"Remember when I said he can be offended by other things. He likes to use such as blue-skins and others to do his work. The blue-skins refused, and these others were many in number, and not those who would follow him. They might follow other gods, but not him."

The shaman felt another wave of shock hit him. He stumbled back a step as he started to put it together.

"Follow other gods... Do we say these gods he fights in his great battle?"

"Yes."

"And these blue-skins, and those who live in this other land... Ugh! He wants to kill people who follow those gods, but it is the gods he must fight, not people who follow them! More who are weak, maybe? More who choose another way to live?"

"Yes. And much like with the hurt blue-skins, these others are hurt in other ways."

"Argh!" he growls. "Use things... Play with things... Lie to things... How can a God do this? What do we say about the Horn-tails? They also follow him, yes?"

"They do, but also from lies. He promised you great strength. To your people, this is the strength of a warrior. The Horn-tails and the blue-skins are the same people. He promised them great wisdom. The blue-skins ran from this when they understood the truth. The Horn-tails did not. Have you seen the Horn-tails? They are ugly like the blue-skins in their village after you use your bang-stick on them. This is what he gave to them, not wisdom."

The shaman cringed at the thought as he began to recall the last time he saw the Suuden-Aryku arriving to check on the conveyor unit. They were nearly as ugly as the mutation victims in the city. And as he reflected on this, he began emitting a soft wail.

"But now, if you want to know more," Kaliya asserts. "You must go and listen to the story of the blue-skins."

"The blue-skins...in their village?" he wonders.

"Yes, they come back now. The Great Horned God is running from us. Now we chase him. You came here looking for the bird god, yes?"

"Yes, we saw him take the sun shells."

"We did this to keep you away from the spinning eye. All your warriors are dead now. This battle is not for you. We do not want to see the last of you die. Not for the Great Horned God. He is not worth it."

"Then you are trying to help us?"

"Think of this a moment. Your people did many bad things to the blue-skins. We saw how you attacked them, killed many who could not run, they who could not fight, and then you leave their bodies in the sun. Your people hold a tradition to lay your dead to an honorable rest in the ground, do you not?"

"Yes, that, and sometimes to burn on a fire."

"But you did not do this for the blue-skins, to give them their rest?"

"We did not?" he wonders. "I do not hold stories of this, it was long before my time, and my father did not tell me stories of it."

"Then we must ask if the Great Horned God told your ancestors to kill them and walk away, or did they not care to give them a burial. Because of this, the blue-skins are very offended. There were many bodies left out there…many."

The shaman ducked his head and moaned in grief.

"But great shaman," Kaliya continues. "We hold our own honor. A warrior might hold honor if he is strong, but a wise man can also hold honor. We may not choose to kill if we can understand a greater truth. Life is a precious thing. Evil may need to be punished, but life is a thing to respect. But to him, he plays with life. The blue-skins chose not to follow him, and they became his enemies for choosing to be honorable. This other land, inside the spinning eye, and the people who lived there, might not wish to follow him, and so he killed many of them simply to clean the land of they who would not follow."

"Ugh!" he grimaces. "You are right, this is not honorable. We may fight to prove ourselves strong against a big animal, but to kill something only because it lives out there…"

"Yes. And now we come to you. You are no different from the others. He tricked you, and now you are down to the last of your people. Maybe he gave you this promise, and maybe he said to follow him to a great battle. But it was a battle to kill things who want to live. Then, when there were no more to kill, and he wanted to move to new lands, the other gods found him, found what he was doing, and they began to chase him. But here is where your people begin to fall, as they killed many who should not die. This was evil, and now they are dead."

"I understand. This would not be a fight for proud warriors."

"And here is where we found you and your spinning eye. We are not killers of weak things, and we are not killers of the last of a people. We try to help them become strong. We do this by teaching them greater wisdom, but only when they are ready to learn. All things must come at the time they are ready. But HE is an enemy of all life. We have seen this. We have seen him lie and trick people. And many people die because he sees play in it."

"He is a very evil god. But you say I must speak to the blue-skins. We see the stone god in their village. He tells us to stay away."

"It is true the blue-skins do not trust you now. They are not happy that you lied to them. The Great Horned God told you to do this, but when they came here, they believed they were safe from him. They did not know he followed them. He hid from their eyes as he tricked them to come here. And they trusted you to be their friend. If you want to know their story, you will need to appease them now."

"How do I appease them...and what about the stone god?"

"If you go alone, and bring an offering, the stone god may stay away and only watch. He will not attack unless you attack the blue-skins. Bring an offering of shiny things the blue-skins like, and speak to the spirit of the blue-skins. She will tell you the story of her people. This is all I can say for now."

Kaliya stepped back from the conversation and offered a courteous bow. To finish the presentation, she chose to vanish in a puff, rather than simply fly away. Her work was done now, and she wanted to maintain the mystical appearance of a spirit entity. Her final words would be enough to spur a new dialog at a later time.

The shaman gazed at the strange disappearance of the apparition. He returned to sit by his campfire and pondered the conversation, feeling a multitude of sensations ranging from fascination over the informative nature of the meeting, all the way to deep resentment and pain for the tricks played on his people. After a long while in contemplation, he dowsed the fire and made his way back down the hillside to the camp.

✦✦✦✦✦

"General," Thaelyn confers. "This last report given to us by Kaliya has revealed an extraordinary level of work on her part, and in areas

I would not otherwise expect of her…not for her existing training or for her age and past experience."

"Indeed, my Lord, I was actually thinking the same, although the aspect of age is a curious one," he grins. "Four centuries, and she is still described as young and inexperienced, at least in a relative way."

"Yes, this is an odd one, even for me," he smiles.

"And here she is, demonstrating not only a curious sort of talent with this projection gift of hers, which inherently demands a sizeable amount of improvisation and acting skill, but this last meeting she made with that orcish shaman is nothing short of a carefully played role of diplomacy laced with discretion and tact."

"I also took notice, by her wording here, she apparently played a lesson of the Measure of Balance on that poor fellow," he chuckles.

"Yes!" the General nods. "She certainly has taken well to that principle."

"I should think that one meeting alone may have turned the tides significantly, not simply for the wording, but also the way she appealed to their native beliefs and mysticism. If we were to try it any other way, it might result in a military action simply to get them to listen to us."

"It almost seems like cheating, in a way," he shakes his head amusedly. "But it probably did more, and with less effort, than days or weeks of formal diplomatic talks. I would say this skill of hers could work wonders on many levels."

"Indeed, it could. But as with all things, it must be respected."

"According to her last report, they were packing up to return home. She has in mind to continue this play once they arrive and the shaman makes his offering to…appease…the blue-skins," he grins. "Here is where she will go back to finish her role. My Lord, I would like to recommend her for a special commendation for all her efforts. This could very well put an end to this component of our war."

"Yes, and in a rather unique manner, but I think we do not have anything appropriate for this occasion. I am also reminded of her stone god act within the city to rescue that mutation victim. This saved lives on all sides. And when we reflect on her manners on that first day we met, this is a remarkable progression."

"This would be worthy of the White Sister award, do you think?"

"Yes, it would, but as for the rest of it, I think we may need to create something new in her honor. I will speak to our guild artisans about this and see if we can put something together."

"Most excellent, my Lord. In the meantime, she is collecting a few of her fellows who have progressed partway through their training and together they are taking a number of coaching lessons to develop their teaching skills. She wants to give a few of her friends on Ruuki uy'Daan some tutoring in orcish to prepare them for the inevitable."

"We do not have a great amount of time, so she will need to hurry. Will she be using the Elixir on this occasion? It would certainly help."

"Yes, we are preparing a batch for her to take along, as well as a series of tutorials to distribute."

"Very good, this will allow our people to interact in a meaningful way once the orcs arrive. We will need this for those occasions when she is otherwise unavailable."

✦

"Tana Lar'akan! Is this how you parade yourself around in front of all these young men? Cu'Nar's Grace, I'm gone for a few centuries and just look at you!"

"Oh great, here goes another one," the girl sighs deeply. "Mother, my original clothes were only useful for as long as I was half a century old and could actually fit inside of them. Since that time, I grew up, and the only things left for me were a few pelts and a lot of foliage."

Navina, Tana's mother, was accompanying Kaliya, along with one other assistant, as part of a tutoring team. They were all in projected mode and visiting Ruuki uy'Daan, delivering a number of books and other supplies, and selecting a group of locals, including Tana, Sulíma, and Túfula, for a lesson in orcish. Tana and her mother had been in contact through the vid-mail service on the video terminals,

385

but the view only included the head and shoulders. Now, Navina was looking at her half-naked daughter in full form.

"All right everyone," Kaliya asserts. "Let's try to pull ourselves together. We need our full concentration on this, and none of us up here is a professional teacher, so this is going to be rough. You will notice these vials here," she points to a series of bottles on a nearby table. "This is what we call the Elixir of Visions. Each of these is calibrated for our general body weight, and runs for four hours of duration. During this time, we are going to hit you hard and fast with the lessons in these books, just like they do back home. And believe it or not, you're going to remember every word of it."

"How do these things work?" Túfula asks. "I remember Petrith saying something about a classroom study you were in from his dreams."

"Oh, so he took notice of something other than me in the shower?" she chuckles. "This is a special formula they use on Tae'Eladar which accelerates memory function. It's made from a strange berry plant that grows in a permafrost region, and from the stories I've heard, it's not native to Tae'Eladar. So, where it came from and how it got there is anyone's guess, but we generally think it wasn't by accident."

"Meaning someone put it there intentionally?"

"Yeah, AND they gave instructions to someone on how to use it, which only surfaced later when the time was right for it."

"Sounds like someone is doing a little backroom dealing there," Sulíma giggles. "And the three of you are all going to talk at once?"

"We'll use what they call a round robin method, where we pass it around in sequence. But yeah, it does go fast, and it's just as hard on us as it is on the students."

The group settles into place and Kaliya oversees each of them take an elixir. They wait several minutes to ensure it has time to go into effect, and then Kaliya and the others begin the rapid sequencing of their lessons, reading a program script from their tutoring books. They would continue this every day after Kaliya's normal class schedule until the new students were proficient. The timing would hopefully allow them to be ready before the orcs returned home.

+‧+♦+‧+

The next two months proceed uneventfully as the orcish tribe makes its way back across the jungle. Kaliya chose not to follow them in her bird form, which gave the impression they were no longer being scrutinized as closely by their alleged enemies. This presented a more relaxed posture, allowing the orcs to contemplate the message of the bird spirit and what it meant for their god.

During their five-month reprieve, Captain Lapäli and the others were able to reclaim many of their former homes, along with several workshops. A series of temporary repeater stations were erected around the city to provide a communications relay service. It wasn't pretty, but it was functional enough to provide for their trans-coms in the critical areas. Work had been started on cleaning up and inspecting the city's main power station, although it would be a while before they could bring it back online.

Although it was expected the orcs may be in a state of low morale for the deceit played upon them by their god, and Kaliya's message to the shaman seemed to have left its mark, the Captain wasn't taking any chances where the safety of his people were concerned. Kaliya was given the additional task of training the young female cadets on the proper use of a staff weapon. It was a hurried lesson, but it was enough to give them experience to stand on their own.

As the orcs made their final drive into the settlement, one of the first things they noticed was the absence of the conveyor.

"Great shaman!" the chieftain shouts. "Look! The spinning eye is gone!"

"This does not surprise me. Look there..." he points at a set of obvious hoof prints in the soft soil. "The bird spirit told me the blue-skins are coming back. They now chase the Great Horned God. These other gods, the stone god, and the bird god, they must be here to watch them as they return to our lands. Now they take away the gifts of the Horn-tails."

The shaman looks at the jungle foliage extending towards the city. He sees where trees have been cut and a wide space cleared where the Daanen-Aryku vehicles pushed their way in to claim the conveyor.

"See there," he states. "They cut the trees and tall bushes to come in here. The path goes to their village. They must be there now."

"Will you go talk to them? You said the bird spirit told you to speak to the spirit of their people."

"Yes, and I think I must. The spirit has a story to tell, and I want to know this story. It can teach us who the blue-skins are, who the Horn-tails are, and who the Great Horned God is. I think they know."

"I still cannot believe all you told us about what the spirit said to you. All my life, I believe what the shamans of our people say about the Great Horned God. Now to hear a spirit tell us it was all a lie…"

"Chieftain, I am no different. Even you can see what he has done to our people. This is all we have now. The spirit said we have no more in all the land, and I believe this. Our people tell the same story. We see the stone god and the bird god protecting and serving the blue-skins, and taking away the gifts of the Horn-tails. This tells me the Horn-tails lost the battle, and if they lost the battle, the Great Horned God must have also lost the battle. And then to say the Great Horned God is an enemy to so many things…" he shakes his head. "Now they come here to chase him."

"Yes, I cannot argue this. When will you go to the blue-skin village to speak with their spirit?"

The shaman glanced around the remains of their village and the people who were just starting to put things back together again.

"Our people are tired and hungry. I am hungry. The day will end soon, and we need sleep. I will wait to see our people get food and sleep. I must also prepare myself. I will go when the sun rises again."

The orcs make their camp and rebuild some of their huts with the hides and wooden poles they took during their departure. The

hunters bring in the latest catch of the day, and they try to relax for the evening.

Morning comes and the shaman works to prepare a necklace of charms in the hope that it will offer some protection from the Daanen-Aryku spirits. He also prepares several offerings composed of items once stolen from the city, including some holo-disks, a data pad, and an assortment of jewelry and other personal effects. He wraps the bundle in a large hide and prepares to set off. It is late morning when he makes his way out of the camp.

Inside the city, Captain Lapäli is reviewing a rough map of the ruins with some of his officers.

"Lieutenant," he directs. "I want our archers on alert and ready, but stay out of sight. If any of those orcs decide to come into the city, I want them watched carefully, but our orders are to attack only if we feel threatened."

"This is a significant turn of events for us in this regard," the officer responds. "For three and a half centuries, we hide in the mines hoping they don't even take notice of us, and now here we are essentially revealing ourselves to them, at least philosophically, and trying to defend our former homes."

"I know, but according to Kaliya and her people, she's been making a few diplomatic moves to soften the situation. Cu'Nar's grace, if she can actually settle the situation into a manageable condition, we might finally find ourselves able to rebuild in peace, at least until official help comes to our side."

"Official help that leads us to join the rest in true freedom from all this harassment. Why did it have to take so long and with so many dead?"

"I don't know, Lieutenant," he sighs deeply. "I recall it being said that we were out of reach until just recently. I just hope the death toll wasn't in vain. That Sargeras is going to have a heavy tail-yanker of a bill coming due when these others finally catch up to him."

"In the meantime, as I understand it, Lord Thaelyn and Commander Nazég are working up a plan to relocate them somewhere, right? Where are they hoping to move them to?"

"All I'm getting out of it so far is out of sight and out of mind for the rest of us. Apparently, these orcs used up their full population in this war because that damnable creature spent them like water under a bridge. Regardless of whatever else they might be, you have to feel at least a small amount of pity for them."

The Captain and his officers had relocated back inside their old headquarters inside the city. It was still a wreck, but enough debris had been cleared to afford them space to set up a few desks. Having a base inside the city offered better response times for their scouting patrols and city defense, along with quicker returns on their communications, now that they had the network up and running again. Scouts could now patrol the streets and relay their reports by trans-com, rather than having to run all the way back to a home base.

Petrith was stationed at his usual perch on the school field overlooking the downtown section and the main avenue where the orcs often made their way into town. Several archers had been assigned to sniper locations on rooftops in the eastern section of town, even though it was hoped they would not be necessary. From here, they could watch for any orcs entering from their jungle camp. A ground team of both male and female cadets stood ready for defensive purposes, in case the orcs didn't take to Kaliya's messages, and everyone was equipped with trans-coms ready to report their sightings.

Tana led the scouting team, a group of females for their agility and fast movement rates. They waited with the Captain inside the office, ready to respond to any sightings so they could run out and investigate.

The orcish shaman treaded his way through the jungle foliage until the outer limits of the city came into clear view. He was visibly nervous and unsure of what to expect, but he recalled the bird spirit's words that if he brought an offering, he could appease the blue-skins and their gods. He had no other choice but to trust these words if he held any hope of learning their story.

He stopped momentarily at a clearing to examine the area, checking for any kind of movement. The city's edge and outer neighborhoods seemed empty, so he continued forward, cautiously passing through a broken entryway that marked the boundary between the city and the jungle. He followed an old path that once connected the two and was used as the avenue of trade and social interaction between the Daanen-Aryku and the orcs in days long past.

He enters a former park area that served as a small bazaar for trade interactions. The area was now thoroughly overrun by weeds and other jungle foliage trying to reclaim the site. He pushes through to a cross street on the other side and turns to walk towards the main avenue that leads into the downtown section. This was the route the other orcs had traditionally used to enter the city on their raids for hunting and scavenging. He crept along the road slowly, trying to present an image of penitence and humility.

Several sets of eyes followed his movements while he progressed along the main avenue, watching from the rooftops, and concealed behind veils of foliage placed as blinds to cover their hidden positions. One set moves away behind the false cover to make a call.

In the command base, the Captain was in conversation with some of the cadets when a harmonic beeping emits from the trans-com on his desk. He picks it up to answer.

"Captain Lapäli here…"

"Captain, this is Sniper Point Alpha, we have a sighting. A lone orc shaman is coming into the city."

"Is that so. We were expecting him, but to actually see it is another thing. Do you see anyone else out there, maybe approaching from some other direction?"

"No Sir, he's the only one out there. He's moving along Darkleaf Avenue, just coming in from the bazaar park. He's moving very slowly, like he's expecting something to jump out at him."

"Really," he chuckles. "Maybe this is a good sign. It means they're afraid and not willing to try anything reckless. Keep a close watch and report if you see anything else. I'll send a team out there to investigate. Hopefully, he's here because of young Kali's invitation for a chat, and nothing more."

"Yes Sir."

The Captain ends the link and turns to his cadets in the base, considering carefully how to respond to this.

"Tana, we have that shaman coming into town over on Darkleaf. He's moving slow and cautious. If Kali and her strange Gift are doing their job, he's probably here to talk, but I'm going by-the-book on this one, so go out there and check it out. For now, keep under cover and report back when you have a sighting. We'll take it from there."

Tana nods and gathers up her team. They sprint out the door and take a number of shortcuts through the alleys, keeping to the shadows for now until they come within view of their quarry. When they arrived in the eastern district, they found a convenient vantage where they could peek around the local buildings with a clear view of the road. Here they could see the shaman as he continued walking slowly along the avenue. They followed him as he progressed forward.

The shaman slowly plodded along the road, hoping to find some sign of life, and not some fierce predator or angry god looking for a quick meal. He felt as if he was being watched, but couldn't see anyone, or anything, peeking out at him. He stopped in his tracks and looked around at the surrounding buildings. All seemed eerily quiet, but not the same as during any of the visits he ever made in his early years.

Petrith noticed the shaman on the road, along with the movement of scouts from their base in the west. He watched as the scouts moved in from behind the local buildings into the alleys. He relocated himself to another position on the school field for a better vantage and more cover.

Tana pulled out her trans-com to report in.

"Captain, this is Tana. I see him."

"Good. Do you see anything else out there? And what exactly is he doing?"

"He's the only one I see out on the road, and so far, he's just walking along as if he's giving himself up for a sacrifice. I actually feel for him a little."

"Understood, and maybe this could work in our favor as we might hold the advantage in this case."

"He's also carrying something wrapped in a bundle of hides. It looks like an offering of some kind."

The shaman felt as if he could almost hear the whispers of the ghosts of the Daanen-Aryku who once lived in the city. The echoes of the conversation just barely touched his ears. He thought he could hear their footsteps, but there was no obvious movement out in the open. He was sure it was their spirits he was listening to, so he tried calling out to them.

"I am the shaman of the Ur'nuk tribe. I call to the spirits of the blue-skins. I come to talk, not fight. I bring offerings. Come and see. The bird spirit tells me to speak with the spirit of the blue-skins. I wish to listen and learn their story."

Tana could hear his shouts, and her new lessons in orcish allowed her to actually understand his words. She relayed this into the trans-com.

"Captain, he's calling out now to the, um…" she coughs subtly, "…the spirit of the blue-skins, and wants to talk."

"Right. This coincides with Kali's instructions. So we need to send word to her and hope we can get her over here quick enough to deal with it. Follow him a few moments longer while I call this in."

"Got it."

She ends the link and continues leading her troupe through the alleys and behind the local buildings as they followed him along the road.

The Captain dials up another link to a service desk at the mine's work yard. This office was being maintained in part due to their continued efforts in the workshops, as well as a connection to the conveyor in case they needed to toss any emergency notes through the hole. Sulíma was stationed at this office as part of her employment to oversee the repair projects.

"City Mining Agency," she chirps. "Our mine is your mine, even though it's not my mine. Suli speaking…"

"Huh? Suli, are you sure you're not letting this new job of yours go to your head?"

"Oh, Captain, you know me. It gets a little dull around here, so I need something to keep me occupied. What's happening on your side?"

"We have a lone orcish shaman coming into the city. He's apparently carrying something that looks like an offering and calling out for someone to talk to."

"Talk? As with words? Cu'Nar's grace, is this from Kali's work?"

"We think so, and I need you to send a quick note to the other side asking her to join us as soon as possible. Have her meet with me at my office and we'll go from there."

"All right, I'm on it."

Sulíma puts down her trans-com and writes up a quick note, rolling it up and tying it with a small string. She then runs outside to the conveyor and tosses it in, hoping the time delay for Kaliya to receive the message doesn't take too long.

The garrison at Portal Three maintained a careful vigilance over the portal exit, waiting and watching for any notes or other important deliveries. When they see the arrival of the small rolled-up note, they realize it must be forwarded to Thaelyn and his officers in Firstfall. A mage takes up a rune and enchants the portal energies while another guardsman drops the item onto the stone, causing it to disappear to its next routing step.

It was late afternoon, and Thaelyn and the others were relaxing in the lounge when the messenger came running through with the note. He passes it along to Thaelyn who unrolls it and begins reading silently, forming a curious expression as he finishes.

"My Lord," inquires the General. "Do we have something important?"

"Indeed, we may have here the result of a most inspiring form of diplomatic action. Page, go find Cadet Nazég at once and inform her to report here immediately in her projected form."

The page makes a quick bow and runs off through the portal gate to the guildhall.

The General leans forward in his chair as Thaelyn continues.

"General, that orcish shaman has made his arrival in the city apparently carrying an offering and asking to speak to someone. We must assume at this point he is seeking Kaliya's spirit image."

"Yes, I would agree. And this would surely be one for the books if we can maintain control of it."

"Let us hope she can arrive in time before he gives up, but I feel as though Captain Lapäli will apply his own efforts to delay for time, if necessary."

"Very good."

The page runs into the guildhall courtyard and makes a quick inquiry with the Watch Captain to see if he knows of Kaliya's current whereabouts. The officer was on notice to keep tabs on her in case of emergencies, and directs him to the mage training field.

Kaliya was working on her practice after school. It was late in the day, and she was putting in some extra time on the field when the page ran up to her.

"Cadet Nazég," he puffs from his quick run. "His Lordship requires you immediately in your projected form. He is in Firstfall in the officer's lounge."

"Did he say what for?" she asks anxiously. "Is this relating to Ruuki uy'Daan?"

"We received a note just a moment ago. I'm not sure of the content, but he's asking for you straight away."

"Great, now is the time to see just how fast I can project myself. And stress doesn't help matters."

She makes a quick trot back through the academy to a conference room she had used before that was usually empty and quiet. When she arrives, she takes up a seat and struggles to relax enough to make her projection.

Tana and her team had repositioned themselves as the shaman continued moving forward. Captain Lapäli made another call to check on their status. A muted beeping sounds out from her trans-

com. The volume was set low so as not to make a prominent display.
She answers the call.

"This is Tracker One, Tana here."

"I swear, between you and Suli and her antics. Where did that
name come from?"

"Well, I'm a scout, and I'm tracking something, and I'm the first
one on the scene, so it simply fits."

"All right, I suppose I can't argue with that logic. What's he
doing now?"

"He's still moving along slowly and approaching Meridian Street."

"Good. I'm going to have you convert from Tracker One to
Interaction One. We sent away a note for Kali to arrive, but I
suspect it might be a few moments before she gets here, depending
on how long it actually takes her to get into this spirit form of hers.
Meanwhile, we want to keep him occupied until then. I'll have
you go out there and stall for time. Talk to him, carry some kind
of conversation, see what's inside that offering of his…I don't care
what, but just try to hold his attention. We want to encourage him
to stay and talk."

"All right, Captain. Kali gave me a few ideas a while back, so
I'll give that a try."

They end the link and Tana brings her team into a comfortable
position ahead of the shaman as they prepare to emerge from hiding.

"Listen close," she emits softly. "I'll do the talking, since I'm
trained in the language, and I've studied these people, at least from
hiding, for most of my life, so I know a few things about them.
We'll go out there and wait to see what sort of reaction he has,
and take this slowly until we can settle ourselves into some kind of
conversational interaction."

The others nod as she leads them out in the open and onto the
street. They take up positions in a line crossing the road in front
of him.

The shaman halts in his tracks as he sees the three tall Daanen'kai
females step out from behind one of the buildings. They didn't look
like spirits, but he couldn't imagine them to be anything else, since

their kind had not been seen in the city for as long as the orcs could remember. He tries calling out to them.

"I come to talk. I bring offerings," he declares, holding up the hide bundle. "No fight. I come to speak with the spirit of your people. I am told by another spirit to listen to your story, to learn why you come here, and this fight you make."

"I know of this," Tana replies as she steps forward. "The spirit of our people is aware of you, and she will come and talk. We will wait for her. What is this offering you bring to us?"

"Here, I will show you…"

He kneels to the ground and sets the hide bundle in front of him. He waves them over to examine it as he unrolls the hide to reveal his offering.

Tana and the others move in closer and kneel to meet at his level to study his offering. They see several familiar items, such as the holo-disks and a data pad, and they guess the rest is from someone's home.

"These were once ours, taken from us long ago," she mentions.

"Yes, but it was not I who took them. These were given to me by my father and his father. They have been with us for many seasons."

"Since the time your people attacked us?"

"I think yes."

"I will not argue this, except to say we are not happy your people attacked and killed so many of ours, and we did nothing to hurt your people. Some of us were children at that time. We had mothers and fathers, and now they are gone. We only asked for a small piece of land to make our home. We had been running for a long time and were tired."

"I am sorry my people offended you. We were told by the one we call the Great Horned God that you are his enemies. He tells us we must wait and grow strong before we can fight. My people are warriors. We show ourselves to be worthy by fighting great battles and bringing back meat, hides, teeth and bones, and other things. We believe these carry the spirits of the beasts we kill, and these spirits can then guide us. But your people are strange to us. You come here in your flying village, you talk to the air, and you build your homes of stone that does not come from the ground."

"Yes, but we can do this because we have learned many things, and this knowledge teaches us to do more than what your people have learned so far. One day, maybe your people will learn these secrets, and you can do the same."

"My people are not many now. We have many women and little ones, but not as many warriors to hunt food."

"Maybe we can help, but we should speak to the spirit first and see what she has to say."

Kaliya worked to constrain her anxiety so she could project herself. She had developed the practice well enough by now to make the process quick, but it still felt like an eternity. When she sensed herself letting go of her physical form, she stepped out into the room and turned to look back at the chair to verify her success. When she was satisfied, she transported herself to the officer's lounge in Firstfall.

"My Lord," she declares as she arrives. "I hope I didn't take too long with that. What do you need?"

"Your orcish shaman is in the city making some manner of offering. We think he might be asking for a truce, but until we can speak to him formally, we are uncertain of his full intentions. Your first objective is to meet with Captain Lapäli in his new office to see what he has for you. As for my own instructions, see to it you are able to understand the shaman's intentions. If this is the final result of your previous work, you must ensure we come to a definitive conclusion, in order for us to finally resolve this element of our wartime struggles."

"I've been waiting for this, and trying to think of how it'll play out. This has to be as a follow-up to my conversation on that hillside."

"Likely so. Nevertheless, make sure he understands we will not permit any renewed aggressions, and that his people have been made as much a victim as the rest. Along the way, perhaps you could also make a subtle offer of mutual aid, as I would imagine his people are likely in a distressed condition after all this. A positive suggestion like this could demonstrate our desire for peace and an interest in mutual support while we fight a common foe."

"What about the idea of relocating them?"

"Yes, then there is that. I would still feel much more content if we could eliminate some of these variables, and I think a good motivating factor is the aspect of their corruption to use magic improperly, and also perhaps to remove them from Darumon's eyes if he should ever return. In their condition, they would make an easy target if he should ever desire to finish them personally."

"That sounds bad. All right, I'm on my way."

Kaliya gives a quick salute and vanishes. She travels to Ruuki uy'Daan and appears in front of the Captain's office. The door was open, so she steps inside.

"Captain, I'm here. What do we have so far?"

"Kali, good to see you," he states. "I have Tana and her team out there in a meeting with the shaman. Right now, she's stalling for time until you arrive. I need you to go out to Darkleaf and Meridian. That's where the meeting is occurring."

"Do you have any special instructions along the way?"

"Just try not to start any new wars. After that, whatever your own CO tells you is probably higher than me, since this is more his war than mine at the moment."

"Right."

She offers another quick salute and changes to her hawk form to fly out onto the street in search of the meeting site. She rises in the air for a better perspective until she notices a gathering near an intersection on the main avenue. She takes a brief moment to reimagine her new form, and then folds herself to that location.

Tana and her team were expecting her to arrive, but nevertheless they flinched slightly when she suddenly appeared next to them. The shaman, on the other hand, yelped and lurched back onto his hindquarters at the mysterious appearance of the strange specter.

Kaliya stood placidly over the group as the shaman gazed in

bewilderment at her stoic image. She appeared different than the other three women, who were dressed at this time in leather jerkins and leggings. Kaliya chose to display a flowing gown to symbolize a surreal apparition.

"You are the spirit of the blue-skins?" the shaman asks hesitantly.

Kaliya had been planning her responses for this occasion, realizing she would need to tell a new story. She now goes into her new act.

"I am the spirit of the blue-skins. I speak for those who lived here long ago, and I speak for those who live here now."

"I was told I must speak to you, to learn your story. The spirit of the air, a bird spirit, told me to find you and call to you."

"I know this, and I have waited for you. The spirits have watched, and many are not pleased for what the orcs have done to my people. But we are also aware of the one you call the Great Horned God, and the tricks he has played."

"Yes, the bird spirit spoke of this. My people are now angry. Many cannot believe these stories. They cannot believe the Great Horned God would play games like these. How can a god do this?"

"He is no god. Not a god we would wish to follow. If you want to know my story, you must listen carefully and understand. Are you ready?"

"Yes, great spirit. Tell me your story and I will listen."

"Good."

Tana and the others listened, although Tana was the most proficient with orcish, while the others were less studied. She watched Kaliya play out her act, realizing this must require forethought and some improvisational skills. She gazed at her strange apparition while Kaliya continued.

"We must now travel back to the beginning," Kaliya reflects. "There was once a great battle between the gods; good gods like those we would choose to worship, and evil ones like the Great Horned God, who played with people like us for their games. He and his kind lost the battle. Many were killed, others taken away, where they would never be seen again. But this one…he ran."

"Ran?" the shaman wonders. "Did these other gods see him run?"

"We think he was very clever to hide from them, and he hid for a long time. The others may not have known about this, but one of them did. She watched him. But the Great Horned God was not alone. He travelled with another. They have names, and we know these names."

"Names! Can you tell me these names, or is it forbidden to know?"

"I can tell you these names, and it will help with my story. One is a powerful god named Sargeras. The other is his servant, named Darumon. Darumon is not a full god, but to people like us, he may look this way, as he is still powerful, but not as powerful as Sargeras. He serves Sargeras, helps him, cares for him, and they travel together."

"This is strange, but I think I understand. Is this to say the Great Horned God is the one called Sargeras? Or is it Darumon?"

"We think Sargeras mostly sleeps. He stays hidden, but Darumon is known to move around and work to help his Master. And together, they once came to our home. My people live in a land very far from here...far into the sky and away."

"We have stories of your people given to us by our ancestors. They speak of a flying village. It came from the sky, and then returned to it and is gone."

"Yes, my people are old, and we have learned much in this time. We understand ways to travel to the sky. But you are young, and we cannot share this with you until you are ready for it. We believe that all people must grow only when they are ready. We had our time, and now you have yours."

"You are very wise."

"Yes, but even they who are very wise can make mistakes. When Sargeras and Darumon came to our land, they asked us for help. They told us stories of a battle, but it was a different battle. They told us Sargeras was a great leader, but he was chased away. They told us something precious was taken from him, and now he was hunted by his enemies and needed help, a place to hide. We did not know the old stories, they were much too long ago, before our time, and from lands too far for us to see. All we could do was to believe what they told us and give our help."

"You gave him help, and a place to hide in your land?"

"Yes, and he made a promise that he will share his great knowledge with my people if we help him fight his old enemies. But remember what I said just now about giving such high wisdom to younger people. My people might be old, but to him we are still young, and this offends that same wisdom, that we must learn when we are ready. But we made a mistake, and accepted his offer."

"You made this mistake, but can we also say he made a mistake to offer this to you?"

"We can say this, but we must also remember how he likes to play his games. It was a lie, and my people desired this, even though it offended our better wisdom. Our leaders took his offer and gave themselves to him. But there was one that did not, and he tried to warn the others, but they did not listen. So he gathered up as many as he could find, and ran away to find peace, knowing Sargeras would bring harm to the rest of our people."

"This is bad, I think. I remember the Horn-tails. They come to us and look at the spinning eye. They look ugly. The bird spirit tells me your people are the same, but you look different...a little different. The spirit told me about the bang-sticks and what they do. They are made to hurt the blue-skins, but not kill. Did Sargeras do the same to the people of your old land?"

"We think yes and maybe more. He continues to lie to them, saying he will give them gifts if they keep following him. But all he gives is more lies to make them think they will receive his gifts."

"How long can people follow this before they understand the truth? How long has he been telling these lies?"

"This is shameful to answer, but they have been following this for a very long time. I cannot be sure how or why they still do this, but he understands our people very deeply. He knows how to lie to them, to keep them in his favor. My people ran, hoping to find peace, but we did not know he was following us. He brought his new warriors to hunt us, but never to kill us."

"Playing more games, I think. Yes?"

"Yes, now you can see our pain. Then we come here to this place.

We made a long run to this place, what we call a wild jump in our flying village. It is like jumping off a tall rock with your eyes closed, not knowing where you might land. This is dangerous for us, but we had no other choice. And still, they came to hunt us again. He followed us to many lands, hitting us to make us move again. Then, one day, he made us come here, to turn our flying village this way, without our knowing, that it brings us to this place."

"Why here?"

"Because of you…"

This statement stunned the shaman, and he drew back from the discussion for a moment, as he tried to fathom what possible connection his people might have to be involved in any of this. Then he began to reflect on his earlier stories with the chieftain and the history passed down from his ancestors.

"Great Spirit, my father told me secrets, and we have stones in the mountains where we tell our old stories, stories from our ancestors. We know the Great Horned God came to our people once long ago and told us we would become strong if we worship him. Our ancestors agreed. We also have stories of how some of our people were carried away from here to another land, and we were told to remember our brothers and sisters. What do we say to this when we talk about the Great Horned God bringing your people here to us? Why to us?"

"It is because you offered yourselves to worship him, that he would now use you to watch us while he prepared to attack his old enemies. We were a game to him, but now he had other work to do, and you would watch us while he worked."

"Huh? But…but…" he slaps his hands against his temples. "He said you were his enemies, but he brings you here to play games, and then makes this new work to attack his real enemies, these other gods. Then he tells us to attack your people. You go back to the sky in your flying village, and we are told to go into the spinning eye to follow you."

"Yes. When you attacked us, we believed we were found again by our old enemies, and tried one more time to run from him. But it did not work. We travelled to another land after this, and the spinning eye goes to that same land. But he had a surprise for us inside our flying village. There were strangers in there that broke something and made us fall to this new land. Our flying village is now broken."

"Broken!" he gasps.

"Many people died in this. Then he calls you to hunt us, and he calls the Horn-tails to hunt us, and he sits in that land watching all his new fun. But they do not try to kill us. They come only to hit us quickly and then run back to their camp. And they did this again and again, keeping us from going out to build new homes and make new lives."

"More play!" he shouts. "Not to kill, but only to play!"

"And now, you speak of people once carried away, yes?"

"Yes, this was long ago."

"More of his games, I think. I know of people like you who were carried to a far distant land, very far. They made their homes there, but they never made peace with the other people who lived there. It was their land, their home, made by another god. And he put your people there to make trouble for those who lived there."

"And more of it…" he sighs. "What happened to our people?"

"The stories are long, but not good. There were many battles. In the end, a very strong leader came to the land and brought all the people together, but not the orcs. They would not join the others. They hated the others too much, probably because Darumon told them to follow him and no one else."

"Yes, he says this to us here."

"Then, one day, a new battle comes. The orcs turn evil. This is after your people go into the spinning eye to this new land, and he sends some of you to that same old land, where your ancestors were taken. They are told to find something for him. We think he tells them to be cruel, to gather up your brothers in that land and start new battles. But these are not battles for warriors to carry pride for their bravery. They did something even you would think to be very bad. They attacked and killed these other people…and ate them."

The shaman grimaces at the thought and retracts back.

"Ew!" Tana blurts as she listens in. "You didn't tell us that part before."

"It's not something you would want to hear about, I think. Cannibalism, even to orcs, should be taboo and offensive, but this example Thaelyn found over there was enough to finish it for him."

The shaman listened to the exchange, but this dialog was actually in the Daanen-Aryku native tongue, so he perked up to add his own.

"Great Spirit, you say our people would eat other people? No, this cannot be true. Orcs would not do this. It would offend our fathers and their spirits."

"Yes, I know this. Your people hold more pride than that. But these others…" she shakes her head. "Something must have changed with your people over there, great shaman. They were seen killing people, taking others alive, making them work until they were too weak to stand up, then killed and put with the rest, all to be eaten. This new leader of the land, and all of his people, were so deeply offended with this that they made war with the orcs of that land… all of them…to the last."

"Yes, I think I understand. My people would feel the same, I think. We would be offended by this, maybe to make war and kill those who offended us. This is not a battle to make proud warriors. What happened after this? They are all dead now?"

"Yes, but not before he learned where they came from…this new land you travel to inside the spinning eye. He learned they were given strange magic to open a spinning eye in the air. This is powerful magic, but also bad if you use it wrong…and they used it wrong."

"I do not know of this kind of magic. The Great Horned God gave this to our people?"

"Yes, in this land beyond the spinning eye, but we worry if he gave it to you here."

"No! He did not share this secret with me. And I am the last of our shamans in this land. All the others went inside the spinning eye. If he gave them this secret, it was in this new land, not here."

"I understand, but he gave you the other spinning eye, and this is also bad, because it can teach your people things you are not ready to know. Do you remember that orc you call bonehead who made the spinning eye sleep? Then you worked to wake it up again. While I can say you were very clever to do this, it is also a sign of you learning something you are not ready for, and it can be bad for your people. Remember what I said about growing only when you are ready. Darumon broke this wisdom for you."

"Yes, I remember these words. It was I who did this. Will you punish me?"

"I will not punish you for this. But you must learn the wisdom behind these words, and not do it again. You may show great wisdom, and learn many things, but you should use this to help your people when they are ready to grow. Many seasons may pass, and you may learn more. And as your people grow, so too will be the wisdom they all share together."

"Yes! These are good words. I will learn, Great Spirit, and you will be happy."

"Now, these people from this far land came to this other one. They followed the orcs Darumon sent, and now they learn of what he is doing. They speak to my people and learn of Sargeras coming to our old home with his stories and many lies. Now we make a new war to chase him."

"These other gods will chase him?"

"We all will, but we must be quiet. He ran from us once, and we think, if we make too much noise, he might run and hide again. We must catch him before he can do this."

"This is very wise. You hunt him, but quietly from the bush. But what about the Horn-tails? What will you do with them?"

"They are our brothers and sisters, and we want to help them. It is the same as you would do for yours. But he tells them lies, and we cannot tell them the truth until we can return to our old home. This is a problem for us, because to return there is to be seen by Sargeras and Darumon. We must take this slow and be very clever."

"Yes, I see this now. But now, what about my people? What will you do with us? We offended your people and now you are angry. I came here with an offering, and I ask for peace with the blue-skins. I came to listen to your story. It is long and not easy to tell. My people are angry and offended by the Great Horned God, but we have no more warriors to fight. We only have enough to hunt food, and this is bad for us."

"You must understand these next words, great shaman. We do not want to hurt people who are not our enemies, and we do not think of you as our enemies. The Great Horned God, Darumon, plays his games with all of us, but your people are now very few, and you will have trouble with food and other things. The first thing you must understand is we will not take any more fighting from you. We have bigger enemies to fight, and we want you out of this battle. It is not for you now."

"I understand, and we do not have warriors to fight now. I will tell my people we will not make any more trouble with the blue-skins. Your gods are very strong, and your story tells me you have other friends helping you now."

"We do, and even though they were very angry with the orcs in their land eating their people, they will not bring the same to you here."

"Good, this makes me happy. I would agree that this offends us. My people would feel the same."

"Next, our war will carry us to other distant lands, but we must travel carefully. And yet, we worry that Darumon might try to look in on what we do behind our backs. He is a clever one, and not to be trusted. This makes us think of you here. You are small in number, and he might be angry when he sees us here or if he thinks you are not doing as he wants you to do."

"Uh oh…" he mumbles cautiously. "What does this mean for my people? Will he come back and make trouble for us?"

"He is known to make trouble for many people, and for many reasons. We have seen this before, and we do not want to see this again. For this, we have an idea. We want to help you, but this help must carry you away to a new land where he cannot find you."

"A new land… You would take us away from our home?"

"He knows you are here, and his kind does not like small things like us who do not follow him. Just look at my people. We did not follow him, and he hunted us like tiny animals to play with. Do you want this?"

"No! No, I do not. Great Spirit, where would you take us, and how do we live in this new land?"

"This new leader now calls us to follow him, and he is very wise. He will search for a new home and call on his friends to help bring you there. But this new land will not have the same magic as we have here, so you will not be able to make the same bad magic as the others did. Still, you can learn many secrets and become very wise, like my people. It takes time, so you must be patient. Tell your children these stories that they might learn and remember. Tell them about us, and tell them about what you have learned here."

"Yes! These are wise words. My father told me many times to remember the stories of our ancestors. I believe in this."

"Good. Now, our leader tells us we should try to help your people. You have very few warriors to hunt food, so maybe we can help you with this. You will need help in this new land, and we must decide what we can do. Maybe your people and our people can work to help each other. We will then share what we make until we can find your new home."

The shaman paused to consider this suggestion, and it certainly did hold value, especially considering the dire straits his people were in right now. It would also help to heal some of the old wounds left behind.

"This is good. I should tell this to my people. But how do we help each other? The ways of the blue-skins are very strange to us. Can you teach us something that we may offer this new help to you?"

"I must first speak to my people and tell them what was said here. We will decide what is best for us, for your people and ours. We must remember our beliefs, that all people must grow and learn when they are ready. Maybe we can find something to offer you to help you here and in this new land, and I will return to you with our answer."

The shaman nods reflexively as he ponders the conversation. Once again, he finds himself astonished at the level of detail and new information he was given between this and the bird spirit. He begins to rise to his feet and makes himself ready to return home.

"I will tell my people, and I will wait for you. I thank you, spirit of the blue-skins. Your wisdom is much greater than mine."

The shaman slowly turned to walk home. His sluggish pace indicated his deep contemplation of their discussion, the unpleasant revelations of what his god has done to them, and the unexpected turn of goodwill by those the orcs once considered to be their most hated enemies. It was enough to make him wonder how wrong he and the others were in their actions, and how they were deceived by the one they used to call their god.

With the shaman on his way and out of earshot, Kaliya turned to look at the three scouts still standing next to her. Tana returned the stare, gazing at the ethereal image in awe.

"Kali, what is it they teach you over there?"

"Nothing quite like this..." she admits. "If you could've seen me a few years ago for my opinions of orcs, it would seem as though I was a completely different person. Since then, I've been studying their philosophies, their religious and cultural beliefs, and of course we have all the military briefings of our discoveries along the way, so it's a very different image now. But as for this..." she waves at the orc as he moves off in the distance. "I'm mostly making this up as I go along."

"You're kidding me!"

"Tana, I'm very literally writing the book on how to do this, and believe me, it's not an easy book to write. Let's go report in, and I need to take this back to Thaelyn."

Chapter 7

RUMINATIONS OF GUILE

"Kaliya, it is becoming quite obvious that you are developing skills well outside the soldier profession. I am tempted to enroll you in some diplomacy and politics courses."

"My Lord," she giggles. "I never actually saw myself as a politician, even though my father is the head of the Elder Council."

"Perhaps, but before the attack on Ruuki uy'Daan, I doubt you ever saw yourself as a soldier, either. Am I correct? Your primary interest at the time was athletics."

"Yes, this is true. I guess times change, and so do many other things. I'm just glad I was able to serve a useful role in this regard."

"And now it would appear that I must also serve a role. I should make my visit to Mechanus soon to conduct my research. The sooner we can divest ourselves of these orcs, the sooner we can relax from the immediate war efforts and concentrate on the next. In the meantime, you should return home and find some rest."

Kaliya's return to Firstfall brought a sigh of relief for many. The agreement of a truce with the orcs was a welcome sign, though it would be treated cautiously by those closest to the front. Her skills at brokering the arrangement had earned her a new level of esteem amongst her peers on Ruuki uy'Daan, which compounded with her occasional help in training their combat skills. When combined with the stories of her time in the academy, the people and lifestyle of Tae'Eladar, and the lessons she had learned about their culture and philosophy, it fascinated her former classmates, and many of them were developing an interest in seeing it for themselves, perhaps even to sign up for their own lessons.

"One last thing, before I go," she asserts. "Let's say we move them to a new world. It'll be hard for them in the beginning to get settled and find food, and the shaman told me they already spend a lot of time hunting for their people. We spoke about trying to find ways to help each other in these times, maybe to join together in a mutual effort and share the results. Our people are also trying to solve our food issues with new farming, and this would certainly provide a good boost to them, both now and later on another world. What do you think?"

"You are right," Thaelyn nods, "as this will be a serious issue during those initial moments when they are trying to build their homes in a new land. The concept of farming, maintaining animal pens, and even to preserve food for the fallow seasons would be a great boon to their survival. It can provide them with security, and it might also tame some of their wilder ambitions that come from hunting and other such warlike tendencies to conquer their environment. Perhaps we should donate a few lessons as a gift to help them succeed once they arrive at their new home."

"I think that would be a much better gift from a higher intelligence to a lower one than portal magic, and it doesn't hold the same potential of corruption. It would be much more like a natural step up from where they are now, maybe even inspirational to lead them to start learning on their own."

"It would, and if we are to be responsible for taking them out of their natural habitat, this would be a worthy contribution to their cause."

Kaliya makes her final salute and a pleasant smile at her contribution before returning home. From this moment, she could relax from her frequent scouting missions to follow the orcs, instead leaving it to the locals to watch over them. Now, she must refocus herself on her lessons, which would soon be condensing and becoming more vigorous with the coming seasonal change. Another two years, she estimated, to reach the Seventh Circle. Enough to mark a rune and lead their forces to Ruuki uy'Daan for a proper occupation. From there, she hoped they would find their way to the next world.

◆

Several days have passed since the meeting with the orcish shaman. New supplies have been delivered to Ruuki uy'Daan, along with instructions to the survivors to assist in helping the orcs learn the fundamentals of agriculture, and further touching on the domestication of animals, although they didn't have any ready examples to work with on Ruuki uy'Daan.

Thaelyn and his officers could finally find some time to relax from the drudgery of war, with the only real issue being that of the emergency evac portal the survivors were still operating on Ruuki uy'Daan opening up to Portal Three on Thaelyn's side. This became much more of a backup in case of some local disaster or medical emergency rather than a wartime event.

In the Naarg uy'Sodrad, an impromptu meeting had been called of the Elder Council to receive a royal messenger from Tae'Eladar. Velen and the two Elders assembled at the table as the announcer waited at attention. Kailen and Ankhia had also gathered in the room to participate in the event.

"This is interesting," Elder Vankkar mutters softly to the Council. "Why is he here?"

"I don't know, Santari," Elder Girhani responds. "But he looks important."

The man was ornately attired in a stylish steel blue livery coat with silver buttons down the front and lace stitching along the lapel and cuffs, accompanied by white pants, shoes and gloves. He also wore a matching blue and white tricorn hat. And he carried in his hands a festive scroll neatly rolled up as he waited to give his announcement.

Elder Vankkar studied him for the ornamental vestments and began to recall some of his old history lessons. The sight reminisced of his old romance with ancient Suuden-Aryku culture.

Kailen and Ankhia each took up positions near the table with bright smiles on their faces. When they were ready, Kailen nodded to the man to begin. The royal crier stepped forward and held up his scroll, unrolling it to give his announcement.

"Hear ye, hear ye! Be it known that forthcoming will pursue an event within the royal ceremonial chamber of the Order of Tyr, in the city of Bya'an Tamoranth, a special occasion to which you and yours are hereby invited to attend. On this occasion, a special commendation shall be presented to one of our memberships, of which this member is also a citizen of your own, come to us to become a Sister of our most noble Order, and during this time, in the due course of her activities, has earned for herself a most honorable mention. By commandment of our Lord and King, Thaelyn, this ceremony shall commence on the first day of this following month, by the calendar of Tae'Eladar, promptly at midday. Come one, come all, and participate in this most joyous of occasions."

Elder Vankkar was speechless at the pomp and circumstance of the announcement. If the simple presentation of this man's dress wasn't enough, his boisterous declaration finished it. Velen and Elder Girhani each reflected similar surprise at the unusual display as the man finished and rolled up his scroll.

"Um, excuse me," Elder Vankkar emits tenderly. "But who is it we're talking about here."

"He's talking about Kaliya," Kailen interjects. "Her recent duties on Ruuki uy'Daan have earned her a special merit."

"Kaliya? Great cu'Nar above, she must've made a significant turnaround since the last time I saw her. How long until this special event? I'm not familiar with the Tae'Eladaran calendar."

"This special event will occur in five days, local time," the announcer responds politely.

"Commander, you're more connected with this than I am, so

perhaps you can assist us in the preparations. Do we need to do anything special to participate in this event?"

"There is no special requirement on your behalf, good Sir," the crier affirms. "Simply to present yourself forward in fine fashion and appeal. This will be a formal occasion where we will call upon a gathering of witnesses from our own membership, as well as close relations and friends."

"I'm actually a little surprised to receive this, as young Kaliya and I have something of a history behind us that didn't always turn out so favorably. But I would be greatly honored to be a part of it."

"Most excellent!" he grins and bows energetically. "Then I shall return to my Lord and inform him to expect your attendance."

The man makes ready to turn and depart when Elder Vankkar calls his attention one last time.

"Um, excuse me quickly, but do you people often go around with so much bounce and exuberance?"

"Ah, but my good Sir, the people of Tae'Eladar are a fine folk with much to celebrate in our time. Even though we find ourselves in this unfortunate time of war with a most unexpected adversary, we must still afford ourselves the occasion to bring together that which demonstrates our finest virtues, and from this, renew our dedication to our gods and the inspired teachings they bestow upon us."

"Of course, and I think I'm starting to see how this applies recently. Forgive me, but this is still a little new to me."

"All in good time, dear Sir. Perhaps, if you were to visit Tae'Eladar on an occasion or two, even to partake of our culture and festivities, you might find a release to your own woes along the way."

"Thank you. I've considered this on several occasions, and I'm becoming even more curious the more I see from you people."

The man smiles and turns to depart from the room. The Elder Council glares at one another, and finally over to Kailen and Ankhia.

"Just what are you two doing in that military office over there?" Elder Vankkar intones suspiciously.

"Fighting a war, Elder," Kailen offers. "The only way we can."

"Jiggers, girl! Will you hold still while I button this up?!"

"Relissa, I've never been given anything like an award before. Well, at least not outside my old athletic practice. Can you blame me for being so nervous?"

"Aye, and when I think of all the hullabaloo you've been into, just in the time I've known you, to say nothing of before that..."

Relissa was visiting Kaliya's dorm room helping the young Daanen'kai hopeful prepare her formal cadet uniform. Just like with any young recruit, she wanted it to be perfect, and she wasn't making it any easier on the flustered dark elf to help straighten the wrinkles and fold the collar and cuffs just right.

"What about the tail?" Kaliya asks as she peers over her shoulder. "Does my jacket cover it enough? I don't want too much showing. It's not considered proper etiquette."

"By who's figuring, mine or yours?"

Relissa examines the girl's tail as it protrudes out from beneath the jacket's hemline.

"How much are we talking about here?" she asks.

"There's a short sleeve for it. The jacket should extend by a comfortable margin below the sleeve."

"You peeps are a puckish lot. These tails are a sensitive bit for you. Right, I don't think you need to worry about that. You have more than enough covered, even if you need to bend or kneel down."

"Good, and how about my pants, the hemlines at my ankles. They need to be just below the joint."

"Jiggers, girl, you have a lot of parts to watch over."

Now Relissa bends down to check the hemlines on the pant legs to ensure their proper length.

"Aye, you look good. Whoever did your tailoring knew what he was up to."

"All right, so what do you think?"

Kaliya now presents herself for a final review, turning full circle for Relissa to give her opinion.

"Prim and proper, like a good officer wannabe... Can we go now? If we pester over it any longer, they'll call the guards on us for holding up the whole affair."

The two of them now leave the room and meet up with Marelle who was just coming up the hall to check on them.

"What's keeping you?" she wonders. "They're nearly assembled out there."

"Oh, Marelle," Relissa retorts. "You know this girl, or maybe you don't, but I sure do. She's a picker if ever I saw one."

They hurried downstairs from the dorm facility towards the main courtyard, and through to the ceremonial room where they most often held such occasions as graduation and award ceremonies. It was an ornate hall, lined with pillars and statues, and with a long runway carpet leading from the front doors up to a throne.

On their arrival, Relissa and Marelle took up positions with the other witnesses, including Haran and Tristeen, Aelwyn, and many other classmates. Further along, Kaliya took notice of several exceptionally tall members standing out amongst the crowd.

She expected to see her brother, Kailen, and Ankhia, but then she saw her father and the other Council Elders standing with them. She gawked at them for a long moment, and found herself silently mouthing the word, 'You?' as she pointed at the group. Elder Vankkar saw her reaction, and he simply smiled and nodded.

Kaliya's training sergeant stepped up alongside to check on her and give a little pep talk.

"You look like a nervous rat in a box full of cheese, Cadet."

"Yes, Sergeant, and I feel like it, too. The last time I had something like this was in my old Sentinels' service, but it led to such a horrid experience later on that I felt I would never see anything like it again."

"Well, that's old business now. Pull yourself up straight and put on your best face. This is the Order, and we take care of our own."

"Yes, Sergeant, and I'm so glad to be a part of it."

Thaelyn and Aerlie were now arriving on the dais with the throne. They took their seats and allowed for the mumbling of the audience to settle down. A series of attendants lined up at their side and stood just behind, where they each held a small box.

"Now," the Sergeant whispers. "When he calls, you will approach the throne in a formal parade march, then kneel just below the steps as he makes his presentation. He will direct you from there."

"Thank you, Sergeant."

Kailen and the others in his group watched expectantly. Padriyl also had a video camera ready to record the occasion.

"Lieutenant," Kailen mumbles softly. "Do you really need to do this every time they hold some special event?"

"Sir, I figure this is an important moment, and I find it fascinating to watch, and want to keep a record of it."

"I think you spend too much time with Father and his stories, and Elder Vankkar and his history lessons. You're turning into a military journalist on us," he smiles.

"Personally," Elder Vankkar offers. "I think it's a fine idea. We could record this for our history, and look back on it one day. Having a journalist function is actually very useful."

Thaelyn waits another moment for the room to settle, and then nods to a set of drummers to provide a small ceremonial overture.

"Cadet Kaliya Nazég," he announces. "Approach and be recognized."

She responds to the summons with a formal march. The drummers provide a rhythmic beat for her to follow as she makes her way along the carpet to the dais, then to stop at the base of the steps and present herself with a salute, followed by kneeling before him.

Between Kailen and Ankhia, they attempt to offer quick translations of the dialog to the Elder Council, as they had not yet found time to study the local language.

"It has been many years," Thaelyn begins, "since we brought cadets into the field in the course of our service. The times of our world have changed, and so too have many of our practices. From time to time, there have been those who have demonstrated exemplary chivalry and valor, and for this we did honor them. But on this day, we have a special merit to award for a cause heretofore never experienced, and by an individual who did come to us by means most unexpected."

He pauses to observe the faces of the attendees, and also to give a slight break for the Daanen'kai interpreters to catch up.

"This individual is a rather unusual example on a number of levels. For one, she is the first person ever to receive the violet grade since Aerlie once attended these halls, and hers was the first one ever to be given out. We cannot know what future may be in store for this newest amongst us, but if her examples thus far are any indication, I will look forward most heartily to see it."

He glances briefly at Aerlie before returning to Kaliya in front of him.

"We also find ourselves in the midst of a time of hardship, and this hardship now causes us to exert ourselves in ways we have never seen before in our history. War is not unknown to us, at least from a historical perspective. But a war that carries us across entire worlds to frontiers previously unknown, and in pursuit of a creature that we could not have known to exist before this…one that should not exist…but in the name of those Powers we adore, we must pursue with all due diligence, and see to it he does not continue to cause any more harm as his kind once did in times now forgotten."

The crowd rises up in cheers and applause.

"And remarkably, amongst those we have met along the way, is this one who now comes before us, who has demonstrated her gifts in such ways that we cannot allow them to pass without our special mention. She alone, in this unique manner of hers, has provided us a solution to a problem unlike any we could ever expect…even myself as a Celestial. And this, by itself, is a most noteworthy mention!" he chuckles boldly.

The rest of the room offers up another cheer and some laughter.

"Under most circumstances, our cadets may rise through the ranks of our military Order during the course of their lifetimes, as time and opportunity permits, and in due course of their service and sacrifice. But ours is a pressing moment in history, and this young lady must feel the brunt of it, if for no less reason than due to her special talents and the value they represent to us at this juncture. Therefore, we must break with certain of our traditions, and provide unto her this first, of what we might hope to be many awards, to be earned over the course of her career."

He now turns to the first of the attendants, who steps forward with his box.

"Kaliya," Thaelyn continues. "I cannot recall a time when we awarded a service rank to one who had not yet finished their academy courses. But your prior service within your Sentinels has clearly left a mark on you, and therefore I feel this is warranted, based on the recent events we have seen of your active service during your free time in the course of this war that has thus carried us to the former home of your people, the world we call Ruuki uy'Daan."

He now motions for the attendant to approach. He moves alongside her and opens his box. Inside is a silver chevron insignia with a bar over it. He removes the badge and pins it to the left side of her vest under her name badge. He then steps away back behind the throne.

Kaliya felt a strong rise of emotion welling up inside. With everything else she had endured during this war, and in recent times between her studies in the academy and her work on Ruuki uy'Daan, she had difficulty keeping her composure.

"War is an abominable moment in our lives," Thaelyn continues again. "Our soldiers are sometimes made to conduct themselves in ways that may wrench the soul from its moorings. And we did most certainly see our share of this as we conducted our efforts in this world, and on Therinë, in the course of purging they who might represent such dire threats to our people, and then to you and yours. I once made a vow to my people to purge all orcs from existence for their crimes against us. But this pledge was in the space of our home, this world, and all the lands associated with it. When we discovered Therinë, we began to realize our woes were only a small part of a greater despair, and these orcs were under the subjugation of a being thought to be extinct."

He pauses to contemplate the recent memories of the war leading from Tae'Eladar to Therinë, and next to Ruuki uy'Daan.

"The orcs once invaded our world long ago. No one knew from whence they came or how they arrived. But now we know Ruuki uy'Daan is apparently their home, and from this place, a creature of ancient tidings brought misery and vice to yours and ours the same. And yet, within this chaos, a singular spark arose, one that was unexpected. This spark would evolve into a premonition of hope. It was the spark of Charity, and it came from one who held the greatest reason NOT to display it, as her people had suffered such violent discord and demise that she held all due and justifiable cause to resent they who were responsible. It could be counted no less than those orcs who were once found amongst us violating our own most sacred rites. And yet, she overcame this."

He studies her as Kaliya looked up at him from her kneeling position with tender eyes.

"In a peculiar moment, and using this most unusual Gift of hers, she found a solution to an issue of intrigue that not only preserved the lives of the victims of these creatures, but also of the perpetrators themselves. And this proved to be only the beginning. The nature of this display would offer future potential for the protection of other innocent lives, at least until a more secure solution could be brought at a later moment. For this demonstration, we must offer a special merit, one that I must admit is not as often given out, not because we do not have such people amongst us, but because it is often reserved for those truly exceptional occasions of service and solutions."

He now motions for the next attendant to come out.

"Kaliya, this symbol is granted to you by the prestige of our temple priesthood and the Powers we adore most for their teachings and the examples they set. It is called the Bar of the White Sister, the symbol of Charity and Compassion. Wear it with pride."

He directs the man to approach Kaliya and open his box, revealing a white bar with a thin silver cross running through it, which he pulls out and pins in the upper right quadrant of her vest. When the medal is affixed, he steps back to his former position.

By this time, Kaliya was struggling to contain herself. Tears were rolling down her cheeks as she discreetly tried to wipe them away.

"Finally," Thaelyn begins again. "As if this was not enough, we have one more item to deliver on this day, which in this case is truly unique. We have seen our share of individuals pass before us with their skills in presentation and diplomacy, but most often this was their profession. It has been a few centuries since we saw the last of the nations in this world hold independent ground. Some were friendly to our cause and joined with us in the harmony of a greater good. Others required a little, shall we say, convincing."

Thaelyn raises his brow and grins as the crowd ushers up a round of subtle laughter.

"Orcs, on the other hand, as we know from our long history, do not tend to negotiate using anything less than a heavy club. As we struggled to cope with our miseries on Ruuki uy'Daan, trying to decide upon ways to preserve lives while at the same time hoping not to be ultimately responsible for the destruction of a full race, another spark arose. It would seem this young lady carries a little of her father in her..." he pauses to glance at Velen and his group. "But I doubt even she fully realized this at first. She simply followed her instincts and did what was most becoming of her people. They are a society of scholars and wizened minds, and this would lead us to where we are now."

He makes another pass around the assembly before continuing.

"She began to build up an image of their wrongdoings by planting a few curiously worded ideas into their minds, just enough to cause them to pause and scratch their heads as to the meanings. The orcs are not well-known for any manner of high-level social skills, but this invoked the native shaman to pursue these notions by submitting to his cultural mannerisms, and thereby to conduct a meeting with what he believed to be a spirit entity."

He pauses as the gathering emits a series of oohs and soft mumbling at the mention.

"Now, even though this might seem to incur an element of falsehood in our eyes, the inherent manners of orcs might not otherwise allow a straightforward approach. However, on the other side of it, we do have a curious application of the Measure of Balance in how she presented it. And this did indeed preserve lives and set a new direction for their interpretations of their alleged god and his antics. She followed up on this with another meeting, now as a new entity representing her people to tell the tale of this creature that should not even exist."

The room responds with another low rumbling of murmurs and whispers.

Thaelyn continues, "The ultimate result was a full surrender by the orcs and a peace accord that technically joins us in the understanding of who the real enemy is."

Elder Vankkar and the others stared at the presentation as they listened. It seemed almost unreal in his mind, given her past record in the Sentinels, that she might have grown so much in this short period of time.

"This act would indeed demand some form of representation," Thaelyn concludes. "But never before have we seen someone perform such a feat as this in such a manner as a metaphysical projection, taking on whatever form might be required for the occasion, and then providing the associated acting performance to go along with it. This requires something new, and so we commissioned our guild artisans to craft a new merit award specifically for this occasion."

"Oh no..." Kaliya whimpers. "You didn't..."

Thaelyn peers down at her and smiles.

"Oh yes, we did."

He now calls up the last of the attendants, who steps forward with his box. This man makes his approach and opens his box to reveal a neatly crafted oblong bar with the image of a figure sitting on a hillside, and the silhouette of a bird offset in the sky. Kaliya gazes at it in awe.

"Oh, it's beautiful," she coos. "And so appropriate."

"We shall call this one, the Badge of the Inspired Diplomat, and it has been made especially in your honor, Kaliya. We shall keep this design in the event of any others such as you who should ever come our way, so that they will know whose footsteps…or perhaps we should say hoof steps…they will be following. Congratulations, Kaliya, you have just earned your lifelong wish. You have become a legend."

"No, I can't," she emits with a tremor. "You said it yourself, I'm just doing a job, a small wheel in a big machine. I'm too young and often too impetuous…"

"Kaliya, I once said heroes are not born, they simply happen along at those times when they are most called for. And this was your time."

Now she breaks down and sobs. She struggles to contain herself as the attendant pins the medal alongside the first one, and then steps away.

Thaelyn turns to Aerlie as she prepares to discreetly pass a kerchief to the distraught young woman. He now readies himself to bring the ceremony to its close.

"Although you are still a student in our academy, and have far to go in your studies, you have already set a proud example for others to follow. Rise and present yourself, Corporal Kaliya Nazég."

A rousing applause comes from the assembled audience as she climbs to her feet, barely maintaining her posture, and offers a salute.

"Thank you, my Lord," she mutters delicately. "I just hope I can live up to the new pressures you just piled on top of my horns."

"You will do fine, Kaliya, and we will support you."

Thaelyn and Aerlie both stand up, with Aerlie passing along the kerchief, and Thaelyn giving a subtle gesture for Kaliya to turn around to present herself. She makes an about-face to show off her awards to the crowd. He then signals for them to come forward and congratulate her, and they all move in with handshakes and pats on her back. As Relissa and her friends come up, they offer hugs and kisses, finally passing to Kailen, Ankhia, and most importantly, Velen, for a strong embrace.

◆◆◆

Another several days passed by, and Ankhia was back in her lab with her assistant studying the biotech seed specimens they collected from the rifles, and preparing their test subject.

"Ankhia," Likha begins. "When I first signed up for my internship, I never thought I'd be playing mad scientist by creating an artificial lifeform in a specimen tank. It's a little creepy."

"You and me both, but we really don't have any other choice if we want to understand how these seeds work. Our test platform is finally ready, so all we need to do now is try out a seed on it and study the reaction. I simply hope our efforts give us something worth studying."

"That's probably the worst part about this project, is that now we have to watch this horrid parasite invade our precious little Banni here."

"Banni?"

"Yeah, that's the name I gave him. It just doesn't seem right to go through all this work and not give him a name."

"You know, we didn't actually give our platform a gender."

"Well, a girl can dream, can't she? After all, I don't have a mate of my own, and there aren't any males available for me, so Banni is the closest thing I may ever have to one."

"Likha," Ankhia consoles. "From what I've heard, we have at least a few good males waiting for us on Ruuki uy'Daan. Plus there are a few hundred younger males from the school which we will have to consider at some point."

"Younger males… I had always envisioned mine to be a little bit older. Besides, they also have females over there to take up the numbers."

"That may be true, but we are so short on population, and with such an imbalance," she sighs. "Likha, some of us have had to consider our future as a race due to these discrepancies. We may not have a choice but to consider some very unorthodox practices if we want to ensure the survival of our people."

"As a race? But what about His Lordship and what he says about Azgarén?"

"Yes, but so far this isn't a guarantee. And like so many times before, we have to make do with what we have and try to repopulate our workforce. The biggest difference this time is the heavy loss we suffered on Ruuki uy'Daan and what it means for us in the longer term."

"Such as?"

"It involves this severe imbalance of our female-to-male ratio. Even with those survivors on Ruuki uy'Daan, we still outnumber males almost two-to-one. This means half of us may never mate and produce children. Not only does this leave many of us without a partner, but it also denies us to contribute to the genetic pool to increase the diversity of our offspring, pushing us through a genetic bottleneck, which is never a good thing for any species."

"No, it isn't. But what sort of alternative is there?"

"Our cultural tradition is to match one male to one female, but this might need to change for a generation, matching up multiple males to each female in order to grant enough diversity to our gene pool, and give each of us a chance to procreate."

"I see. From the scientific perspective, this makes sense, although I'm not sure how I would feel about being used mostly as a baby factory with multiple males."

"You're not alone, and it doesn't necessarily stop at one baby each. We may need to run this twice, at least, and in close succession to produce enough new offspring for the next generation to replenish our numbers after that horrible massacre on Ruuki uy'Daan. Even those who have mates already would have to take on a role here, but mostly only for the next wave or two of babies, and then maybe we can return to something more natural as they mature, and we can find new mates amongst them."

"So, I need to wait for my mate to be born and grow up before becoming ready for me? Ankhia, that almost sounds improper."

"It may seem that way from our standpoint at the present time. But you have to ask yourself, in a millennium or two, what does it matter? So what if there is an age difference of a few centuries, or half a millennium, even a full millennium. With our lifespans, after a while, the numbers don't seem that great."

"You're right, I suppose. But it tends to spoil a person's dream of finding that special someone from their own generation. In the meantime, those younger males won't be ready for me for several centuries. Not unless I want to engage in a little crib-hopping," she smirks.

"True. Sometimes, however, people do match up that are from different generations, even if they are successive by a millennium or two. And besides, younger males have more energy," Ankhia grins impishly.

"Yeah, but I hear they finish faster, too."

"But they also recover faster!"

"Just how many times do you think I need this?" she chuckles.

"Enough to settle that twitchy tail of yours that's almost ready to take on a replicant, if nothing else."

The two women let off giggles as they return to their experiment and their specimen tank.

"Likha," Ankhia begins. "I've prepared one of those seeds in the applicator. Bring it into position, will you?"

The intern operates a mechanized arm with an injector nozzle fitted on the end. Inside the injector was a biotech seed the team had removed from its projectile casing and made ready for the laboratory application to their test subject. It was still in its dormant state. The application process would simulate the firing from the rifle and impact to the target, but on a smaller scale and under controlled conditions. It was expected this would awaken the seed and cause it to go active on contact.

The arm extended down from above into the tank, lining up with the lower quarter of the simulated torso they had created out of cloned tissue. The body was an assembly of internal organs attached to a framework representing an artificial ribcage and spinal column, then wrapped in a layer of cloned dermal and muscle tissue to create an outer covering.

Although it would never pass for a properly cloned body, particularly since it had no head or extremities, it was sufficient enough to see how the organism might invade the tissues and interact with the various organs. It was technically alive, where the heart was beating with the aid of a stimulator, the lungs drew air with the help of a respirator tube, and blood flowed through synthetic veins to the other organs to keep them active. As Likha had mentioned, it was an unsettling sight, but necessary for the experiment to give results.

The body also included a number of sensors attached to monitoring readouts on the workstation where Ankhia was sitting. She waited patiently for the arm to come into position and studied the bio data displays to ensure the body was functioning normally.

"Ready here," Likha declares.

Ankhia makes one last review of the data displays, and runs a quick diagnostic on the sensor matrix.

"All right, let's do this," she announces. "Fire the seed and hold your breath. This won't be pretty."

"Poor little Banni," the young intern moans quietly as she presses a button on her console.

Inside the liquid-filled tank, they heard a dull thud at the launch of the seed projectile, immediately followed by another thud from the impact. Ankhia watched her screens as the monitors revealed the shock reaction of the tissues to the injury while Likha divided her attention between that and the tank itself to observe the action.

The seed made impact in the lower portion of the back, much the same as how it occurred with Tyanna, and likely many others, as they were most often hit from behind while they tried to escape from the orcs on that fateful day. The impact itself was not overly disturbing, but what followed after sent shivers through the two ladies.

The seed came to life with a frighteningly rapid growth phase, sending tendrils into the body, creeping under the skin, and writhing through the tissues as it sought out recognizable components to infect.

Likha watched the display through the transparent tank as the body almost came to life, a life that was never meant to be in such a poor example of a cloning simulation. The organism spread out over the surface of the body, puncturing the skin in new locations as it searched for more elements to take over. She covered her face trying to contain her fear and revulsion, stepping back away from the tank further with each passing moment. Her gut instincts gnawed at her to take off in a dash, to find a safe cubby to crawl into, but she knew she had to stand her ground to see this experiment through.

Ankhia watched her displays, occasionally looking over her shoulder to observe the action. The readings had gone off the scale. The physiological reactions of the native tissues by the initial invasion and the subsequent perforation, as well as the entanglement of the tendrils around organs, shot many of the monitors into the red zones for their tolerance levels.

Eventually the readings began to stabilize, and she could see a clear alteration in the functioning of the organs, with various chemical and hormone levels changing their composition and intensity. The heart and lungs, which were operating at normal levels typical to any living Daanen-Aryku, altered their rhythm due to the entity superimposing itself on them, and the other organs took on new properties, as if now governed by an alien influence.

"Cu'Nar's pity, Ankhia!" the intern gasps. "That's more horrible than I could've ever imagined."

"From where I'm sitting, it's even worse than that. These readings tell me the victim would be in agony for most of that. How they could manage to live through it is anyone's guess, but by the way their heart, lungs, and other organs seem to be taken over, I don't think they have much choice in the matter."

"How could someone do this to a person! What sorts of demons are these people!"

"I'm sure these are the questions our ancestors once asked when they first studied this technology, and probably the reason why they abandoned it so long ago. I can't imagine anyone ever volunteering to use this for any reason."

"But Ankhia! We saw this on the Suuden-Aryku, as well!"

"Yes, we did. But was it voluntary; that's the question. His Lordship already confirmed from that conversation he had with Commander Geilv that these neural implants control various aspects of their behavior, and those are apparently something they did to themselves willingly. Furthermore, this here is supposed to provide them with some form of unnatural capacity for those times if and when they find themselves in an inhospitable environment, which correlates with our historical reports. So, if we say they took this for a reason, and if their only true direction is to attack these Estelar, what are they expecting to find once they get there?"

"I would also ask why they ALL seem to have it. That is, unless we're saying ALL of them intend on going to war with these gods. Aren't there any who might stay at home?"

"None of our sightings in the past showed anything different, so unless we say all of their military is equipped with these things…"

"But wait, what if we say it was not voluntary. What purpose would it serve if someone forced it on them?"

"One answer that comes to my mind immediately is this death syndrome it invokes with even the slightest injury."

"And that tells me it couldn't be entirely voluntary. This sounds like a control mechanism."

"Maybe you're right," Ankhia considers. "And this augmentation effect might only be corollary…a superficial form of excuse to apply it at all."

"Great. 'Here, try this on for size…it won't hurt, and it's actually good for you.' Uh huh… And who do you think would be ultimately responsible? Do we say Sargeras, or perhaps Darumon? How does a society allow itself to be physically manipulated like this to such a point as to have such awful things stuck inside their bodies?"

"Likha, I would like to know the answer to this as well, but we won't find it here."

"So, everything we ever were as a race, all that we learned in our exploration of science and the stars around us, our discovery of other worlds, other forms of life, all our passions and moral values, can simply be erased at the touch of a button when they receive these implants. And then this thing, maybe as a last resort to convince them to do as they're told."

"I don't know, Likha, but if this is what Darumon is accustomed to having for a pet race, I wouldn't doubt it. I only hope we can discover a way to help them."

"Maybe. But after watching this thing attack poor little Banni, I don't think I want to go anywhere near that tank."

"My understanding is this thing isn't contagious to other people. Once it establishes itself in the host, it goes into a kind of support role to maintain its function."

"I don't actually care, Ankhia! I don't want to touch that thing!"

"That's what the remote manipulators are for. We'll be fine. Go pop the top and we'll pull it out onto the examination tray."

"Are you sure it won't jump out at me?" she asks as she cautiously steps back up to her console.

Likha returns to her workstation and begins operating the controls to unseal the tank. The tank was inside a closed bio-containment chamber, so there was actually no real danger of it jumping out and attacking anyone. But the close proximity, and the repugnant nature of the organism inside the tank, was enough to send chills through Likha's body.

She first ordered the injector arm out of the way, then operated a mechanical release to lift the lid of the tank and move it aside. Next, she brought in another arm from above to latch onto the artificial skeletal frame by means of a docking port at the top and lift it out of the tank, sliding it along a track, and laying it carefully on a flat tray under a set of surgical manipulators, which were also remotely controlled from her station.

"All right, I'm ready," she states.

"Very good," Ankhia confirms. "Now, we'll take this one theory at a time and hope we don't kill…Banni…along the way. After all, whatever procedure we finally settle on must not kill the host. We already know it has a death syndrome reaction to it, at least on the Suuden'kai design, so I think we should check to see if this one has the same. We'll try a small surgical procedure to remove a strand. Open the right sternal flap and let's see inside."

Likha directs a grasping tool to grip the edge of the right half of the torso at the sternum. Both halves were sectioned as hinged door flaps that can be opened to reveal the internal arrangement. As she pulls it open, she can see the penetration of the organism through the outer layers of skin and wrapping itself around the various internal organs. She shudders at the sight, still struggling to contain her emotions in order to focus on her work.

"And to think," she remarks softly. "There are people out there with this thing inside of them, actually in contact with their bodies in this manner."

"Try not to think about that. Let's just do our job. We'll test ourselves with the right kidney. That should make a good enough example for now."

Ankhia moves to work the remote operator grips for the surgical tools. She brings down a clamp to secure a small segment of alien tissue attaching itself to the kidney, and a scalpel to make an incision to cut away a portion of it. She glances quickly at a monitor listing the details of the kidney biorhythm function. The wave signs were stable, though abnormal for the foreign influence. She turns back and tries making a simple cut into the tendril.

An alert signal sounds off at her bio-monitor, followed by a sudden flash of activity and a distortion of the waveform. She turns her attention to the display, impulsively pulling the blade away from the entity. The kidney biorhythm spiked, revealing a surge of electrical impulses overloading the organ's tolerance and damaging the tissue, causing a partial necrosis and shutdown of the organ.

"That's not good," Likha notes.

"That resembled a kind of reflexive response," Ankhia muses. "And it correlates with our other observations. Open the other side, I'll try another one."

Likha brings her gripper around to open the other side of the sternal flap. Ankhia elects to try the liver next. She moves her clamp and scalpel to a new location, takes a gentle grip of another tendril and tries a new incision.

Another flash shoots across her monitor, now for the liver. As before, the waveforms deviate, and the readings show a similar surge of impulses causing damage to the liver. She is forced to pull out.

"Dammit," she mutters. "All right, clearly this thing has a self-defense reaction to it. If you try cutting it off, it kills you for the effort."

"That would certainly discourage anyone from trying to remove it," Likha surmises. "Once you're infected, you stay that way."

"Yeah, you might say it's a lifetime commitment to ensure loyalty to your master. I wonder who it was who actually invented this thing."

"Darumon?"

"Yes, I'm sure he probably had a hand in it, but this would require a medical lab and some form of industry to produce it. So, who else is involved, and do they know what they're doing, or are they just more machines with implants following instructions?"

"This reminds me of that package Padriyl found with that pharmaceutical inside. You remember, for those students in Rolsklinde."

"Right! I have that in cold storage. I think it said something like ARC on the label. So, if that's a medical industry, he must use them to make some of his toys."

"Great. So, not only does he control their military, but also their research and industry, and who knows what else."

"This still brings me back to the issue of whether this is voluntary or not. After a while, I think someone would take notice that if you so much as scratch this thing, it kills you. Why would you intentionally infect yourself with something like that?"

"There must be some kind of strong incentive, or else a strong control effect going on."

"Yeah..." she sighs. "All right, let's think for a moment. It's not your typical biotic agent, so I doubt your traditional antibiotics would work. I wonder if there is any sort of toxin we could try on it."

"I think they would've thought of that, and probably whatever it might take to kill the organism would also kill the host."

"You're probably right, Likha. This doesn't leave us with a lot of options, does it."

"And I think even our best medical recovery might not be adequate to help."

"What do you mean?"

"I'm just thinking, if we were able to remove any portion of it, it would cause so much damage along the way, our tissue restoration methods wouldn't be able to reverse the damage fast enough to save the patient."

"Yes, good point. Even if I were to rip this thing out with my bare hands, I couldn't do it quick enough to stop it from killing half the organs in the process."

"Ankhia, I'm worried… This thing wasn't designed to be removed. It's made to be a permanent feature for the life of the host. If we look at the Suuden-Aryku, and assume this was designed in a similar fashion, they never intended it to be temporary."

"I'm not ready to give up on it yet, though. I'm just thinking of what sort of agents we can try next. If we could weaken it, or perhaps infect it with something. Hmm, I wonder if it's susceptible to any form of infection or disease."

"Infecting a parasite with another parasite? That's a new one!" Likha chuckles weakly.

"It would be," she considers openly. "So, the trick is to weaken it, preferably to kill it, and in a way where we don't trigger that reflex action. We can't attack it from the outside, so it might have to be more subversive…from the inside."

"The only problem I can see with that is whatever might hurt the organism might also be dangerous to the host. If we're talking about a parasite, or an infection, it would have to be very specific to this organism's tissues and not infectious to us."

"Agreed, and conveniently this organism has a rather unique tissue structure as compared to our own. Remember those scans we made of all the alien coding?"

"Right…" Likha nods. "Then, what if we could custom engineer something? I just hate the idea of playing God by creating a new virus or some other creepy little thing custom made to eat away at this entity's tissues."

"We wouldn't be the first, Likha. Those Suuden-Aryku have made worse…"

Ankhia's words trail off sharply as a memory lurches forward. She stiffens her posture, bringing the recollection into focus.

"Cu'Nar's wisdom! Likha, you just gave me an idea."

"I did?" the intern mumbles as she follows Ankhia to another research station on the other side of the lab.

Ankhia sat at the console and started calling up some old notes on one of the monitors. She pulled up a file and displayed several medical scans detailing a body image of a humanoid form, then a close-up of the cranium.

"Ankhia, is that what I think it is?" the intern asks. "That's the scan of that human woman from Rolsklinde!"

"Yes, and if you recall, she had that peculiar virus that was eating away at her brain tissue. It had a very specific design, apparently noninfectious and custom-made for human genetic coding."

"But that's human coding, not this thing. Do you think we could alter it?"

"Let's take a look. Maybe we can get a few ideas."

"That would be an ironic twist…to turn one of their creations against another."

"Let's not get ahead of ourselves. We don't even know if we can do it yet."

The two of them studied the old scans taken of Marelle's mother when they had her in the lab during the time they were learning of the strange implants used by Darumon and his cronies on the humans in the city.

"I recall when we were studying this," Ankhia reflects. "Trying to sequence it, but then we had that glitch pop up."

"Did we ever figure out what it was? All I remember was shelving it after a while. Too many other problems to deal with…"

"Yeah, and then it fell into the background. But look here," she points at the monitor.

"I see it," she nods. "The scans came up with something that looked like a contamination in the filter."

"I'd like to get a fresh scan. Bring out one of those implants we have in storage and let's take another look."

The intern walks around to a door on the side of the room leading into a specimen storage closet. She enters and approaches a drawer in one wall where they were keeping the Rolsklinde implants. She taps on a button to unseal the refrigerated compartment, opens the drawer, and pulls out a tray containing an assortment of implants.

These represented the implants found in possession of the temple priests in the city, the ones who were ultimately arrested by Marelle and her team as they commandeered the building. The drawers also held the rest of the implants removed from the population after the attack. Ankhia's packrat-like tendencies to save everything drove her to find space for all of it.

Likha retrieved one sample and stowed the rest, bringing it out on a petri dish for transport.

"Personally," she mentions. "I wouldn't recommend we open this thing anywhere outside the bio-box."

"Yeah, and then draw a small sample and put it inside a specimen tray. We'll get a better reading with that, rather than trying to scan through that shell."

Likha places the implant on a tray that leads inside a safety sealed chamber used for examining hazardous elements, and again uses a control stick to manipulate an arm. She carefully pulls open the implant's tiny hatch to reveal the contents and uses a swab attachment to sample a small amount. She dabs this onto the lower half of a plastic slide with a hollow specimen compartment, then attaches the upper half to seal it up. This is then moved to a tray that draws it inside an automated analyzer.

With the sample in place, Ankhia programs a genetic sequencing scan of the specimen. The scan progressed normally, detailing the genetic triggering for the detection of a human neural cellular design, along with coding for a cytoplasmic digestive agent. The results they saw on the screen looked promising at first, and then it happened again. The display began showing anomalous readings ending in an error code representing an incomplete genetic pattern.

"Dammit, there it is again!" the Med-tech growls. "Likha, why can't we get a decent scan on this bug?"

"I have no idea, Ankhia. This was a fresh sample. Could it be another contamination?"

"This looks like the same result we had before. So, unless all these samples are contaminated in the same way, we have something in there that doesn't resemble a complete virus...or bacteria...or whatever it is. And certainly not one of natural design."

"If it was custom engineered, then maybe they did something strange to it in order to get it to function as they desired."

"Likely so, but what? That's the question. If they engineered a bug, it has to be able to find its target in the host and attack. We know it looks for brain tissue, in this case. Human brain tissue, so it shouldn't be a bother to anyone else. We know it was decomposing that tissue, and the computer identifies this agent here," she points to the sequencing for the digestive agent. "So, this is recognizable. But then we get this glitch before it gives us anything that might make it an autonomous organism, as a proper entity should be."

"Meaning, for it to reproduce and spread, as other bodies might. Ankhia, could they have made it neuter?"

"That would certainly be a fun trick, but where on a virus do you snip off the bits?" she giggles. "All right, let's try it this way. So far, we've been trying to get a genetic coding sequence, but this anomaly keeps biting us in the tail. Let's make a scan for the general chemical composition of the body and see where this glitch is coming up. Maybe it's some form of contamination that we need to recalibrate to filter out."

They reprogramed the analyzer for a detailed chemical scan, narrowing their focus to a small point in the sample. A brief moment later, the screen fills with a graph showing a lengthy list of substances and a 3D plotting image of their relative locations within the zone of focus. The two women studied the image as it formed on the monitor.

"Ankhia, what in all the nether-space are we looking at? All I can see in this is a jumbled mess of data."

"Right, we need to clean it up a bit. This isn't the normal way we study something new. Let's split this data up. You take one station, I'll take another, and we'll see if we can filter out portions of it."

"Sounds good…"

Likha sits down at the console next to Ankhia and logs in. Together they share the data set and try applying a series of filters to thin out the result. As they refine the image, Ankhia glares at her monitor.

"This doesn't look like any kind of virus I ever learned about from the lectures at my old university."

"Well, this is the Suuden-Aryku…and Darumon…and we already know they're playing games over there."

"You're right, of course, so they must've developed something new. But these readings seem to indicate this is no simple contamination. It's too uniform, like something combined with the virus itself."

"Could it be a micro-suspension matrix? Maybe it's not actually a virus, but some kind of amorphous goo composed of synthetic nano-droids with organic trigger cells."

"Likha!" she winces. "Although I appreciate the suggestions, they're turning my stomach."

"Sorry," she grins sheepishly.

"All right, let's try this. We think this should be some kind of living cell, based on the genetic scan, so let's look for the elements found in a normal living cell and identify them first. We'll then try to filter those out and see what's left."

"Good idea. We should see mostly cytoplasm, plus a few other things, right?"

"Right, so here we go…"

Both women begin reordering their lists. Ankhia conducts a review of the obvious components of a normal cell while Likha applies a new filter to remove those elements and see what's left.

"On my side…" Ankhia reflects. "I'm reading proteins, salts, water, cytoskeletal fibers… This all looks like part of a living cell. What about you?"

Likha's display was cleaning up from all the new filters she applied, removing the clear components of organic life to see what remained. When the list settled itself, it showed a comparatively short itemization, and none of it looked organic.

"Well, it's nothing like yours," she retorts. "And this surely must be that contamination. I'm showing up stuff like a polymerized silicon substrate, noble metals, synthetic carbon fibers… It almost looks like a circuit board in there."

"What?!" she shrieks and jumps out of her chair for a close inspection. "Cu'Nar help us, I hope you weren't actually right with that nanotech goo idea of yours."

The two of them were now staring at Likha's monitor reading the data.

"This looks very neat," Ankhia notes. "Like a logic chip, but so small?" her voice drifts off. "Wait, can this be…oh no… No, no, no!" she shouts. "Nanotech…microcellular… Likha, get another slab and put a sample on it for the microscope. I need to see this physically."

"Yes ma'am!"

Likha jumps up and darts over to the bio-box again, where she pulls out another specimen slide, this time a simple glass plate, and draws another sample from the implant. She dabs it onto the slide and places it on a new tray that runs along a belt and into an electron microscope. She closes up the chamber and evacuates the air for the beam analyzer.

The two of them return to their seats and wait for the image to form. They observe as the image reveals the shape of the strange viral entities in the specimen. Ankhia programs the console to rotate and zoom the image for a better view, selecting a single cell for study. She begins shaking her head morosely.

"Those Heretical Bastards!" she scolds.

"Um, yeah, I think we already established that once. So, what have they done this time?"

"Likha, they took a perfectly innocent wonder drug and turned it into a vicious weapon."

"A wonder drug? A virus with its own personal computer? Are you saying that contamination isn't actually a contamination? Then what is it?"

"We touched on this once in my university course for microbiological engineering. Have you ever heard of a science called nano-biocybernetics?"

"I'm sorry, Ankhia, I must've missed that lecture. But are you talking about cybernetics on a cellular level?"

"Yeah, and don't be sorry, we haven't studied it officially for a long time, not since Azgarén. We never had the facilities to fabricate it, so it was barely even academic for us. In fact, now that I think of it, I briefly recall passing over a mention of it in one of those holo-disks Kaliya brought back. I should go find it again for reference. I hope it holds enough information for us to study this thing. Likha, this baby is a beautiful piece of work. Too bad it got into the hands of those fiends."

"If you say so, but can you tell me what it is?"

"I'll teach you what I know, but more importantly is can it be reprogrammed."

"Reprogram? A virus? Just what is this thing?"

Thaelyn was emerging from his office at the guildhall into the courtyard, preparing to make his departure to Mechanus for his research on a possible new home for the orcs. Aerlie was waiting for him to wish him success and a speedy return. It was midmorning of a pleasant autumn day on Tae'Eladar.

"Thaelyn," she calls to him. "Do hurry back. And try not to get lost this time," she giggles.

"My dear, have you ever been to Mechanus?"

"No, and based on your descriptions, I think I wouldn't care much for it."

"Indeed. The modrons are forever reworking the clockwork labyrinth. My first time, which coincidentally was also my last time visiting that place had me wandering hither and yon just trying to find a simple portal out again. And Powers pay pity, those modrons are not the most supportive to those in need to ask directions."

"Yes, you told me once. Most are only aware of the strict hierarchy of order directly above their own position, as well as their peers. And those who hold authority ranks are similarly limited in their awareness of those in subordinate positions directly under them. If you want to find anything, you have to step through the ladder one rung at a time. It's enough to drive a person mad."

"And what is worse, I must speak with Primus directly for my inquiry. Depending on where I find myself as I enter, I may have countless steps to take to reach his position."

"Good gracious, Thaelyn," she smirks. "Will you be able to return back to me before I'm old and gray?"

"Fortunately, my dear, you shall never be old and gray, but I understand your meaning. My only saving grace in this regard is the fact that I can at least fold space while in that realm, which should cut my travel time down to a minimum."

"All right then, I guess there is nothing else for you to do but to begin your journey. But before you go, have you forgotten anything?"

Thaelyn checks his pockets and the surrounding area for any missing pieces, not that he was carrying anything important, but Aerlie's mention, and his distraction to his forthcoming work, had him second-guessing himself. When he was content that all was in its proper place, he looked back up at her, only to notice she was staring at him expectantly while gently tapping a finger to her pursed lips.

"Oh, goodness, but of course my dear," he chuckles thoughtlessly. "How could I leave without that?"

The couple engaged in a tender embrace and a firm kiss before he gave his final parting. He stepped away into the courtyard and engaged his Celestial recall, transporting him home to his place of origin, then to use the local portal networks of the Outer Planes to make his way to Mechanus.

Upon stepping through to his final destination, he found himself confronted with a maddening array of clockwork gears ticking and grinding in a rhythmic harmony of unfathomable complexity. The gears were massive; some of them hundreds of miles across, and others well over a thousand. They meshed with each other in all directions and angles, perpetually turning due to their inherent magnetic or gravimetric forces. The full volume of space was in motion, along with the ticking and clanking of hammers and switches, and the subtle droning of electrical energy. It extended as far as the eye could see, assuming the eye could see around all the obstructions.

The Modrons, the native denizens of this realm, were busy at work, tirelessly maintaining this incredible machine, manufacturing and remanufacturing the components, upgrading and refurbishing worn parts, and scurrying to-and-fro according to their assigned duties.

The curious creatures, though not organic in nature, were nonetheless regarded as a form of life in this strange cosmic menagerie. They generally took the form of polyhedral shapes, such as tetrahedrons, hexahedrons, octahedrons, and so on, counting the scale and multiplying by two, depending on their position along the order of hierarchical rank. The greater their number of sides, the higher their rank of authority. But in each case, they would only be personally aware of those either directly above or directly below their own position. You could not ask one about a rank more than a single step away.

Thaelyn walked up to a nearby candidate, taking a deep breath and preparing himself for what he expected to be a testing experience. The unit was hard at work and paid no attention to the unusual visitor. He recalled the manners of this local population, where emotional output was generally unknown and undesirable.

"Modron unit," he announces in a relatively flat tone. "I desire to make an inquiry."

The unit turns to meet its interrogator. It makes a brief scan of the visitor before responding.

"Organic unit," it replies in an artificially monotonal voice. "Celestial entity, non-inhabitant, state your inquiry."

"I seek your superior. Which unit is it?"

"My director is Unit 6A4R, Node M54X, Cluster 56K8, Domain 8UW4, Cloud…"

"Stop!" Thaelyn interrupts, realizing this could take the remainder of his immortal lifetime. "Perhaps you can specify where that unit is currently located? Is it nearby?"

"Affirmative, it is located on wheel 6D78BR51 at coordinate 34712.84 by 55836.52 by 684…"

"Stop!" he orders again, already regretting having made this effort. "I am not as familiar with your coordinate system. Perhaps you can simply point to the unit in question?"

The modron complies by orienting itself in the direction of its next-in-line and pointing its mechanical finger at the specified unit.

"That unit," it declares.

The unit it pointed to was towards the center of the current wheel, barely perceptible in the distance, and it appeared to be directing the flow of the local traffic.

"Thank you," Thaelyn proclaims with a sigh of relief.

He made his way to the next modron by folding the local space to hasten his travel time over the distance. He carefully presented himself to this new unit and asked, once again, for directions to the next higher in the chain of authority. This process would be repeated many times, until he could eventually find his final mark. Somewhere, probably far in the distance from his current location, was Primus.

✦ ✦ ◆ ✦ ✦

Petrith was in his usual perch overseeing the downtown section of the Daanen-Aryku city. Things were calm in the recent weeks since the truce was brokered with the orcs. There were no unexpected incursions, and the scouting reports showed they were mostly keeping to themselves, hunting local game, and maintaining their camp.

A group of them would venture into the city on a regular basis, in accordance with an agreement by the Daanen'kai refugees, to learn the basics of farming and animal husbandry in preparation for the time when they would eventually be relocated to a new home. The Daanen-Aryku didn't have any livestock of their own to practice with, but they knew of a suitable form of bovine native to Ruuki uy'Daan that would suffice.

They made a deal with the orcs that they would share the proceeds of the harvest with them as a form of trade for their assistance in the fields, and as further education of how to manage the agricultural development of the land, including the use of fertilizers, irrigation, and how to deal with the changes of growing seasons and fallow land. Surprisingly, the orcs were learning the trade quite well, which offered encouragement that they would survive well on their own in the new world.

As Petrith relaxed on the school fields with little else to do, he let his mind drift to the affairs of the rebuilding effort, and what future role he might have when they were finally reunited with their people.

"The Sentinels..." he muses silently. "It's not made for this sort of thing. I don't want to just sit around playing security guard...no offence to the Captain, but if Kali will be out there chasing after Sargeras and that Darumon character, I want a piece of it, even if it's just to get a little payback for all they did to us."

He glanced out over the remains of the city.

"They'll try rebuilding this, at least a little bit to hold us until we're pulled out to join the others. But then what? Do I sign up for military training? How long will that take, and do I actually have time for it. I don't know, but Kali sure seems to like that new job of hers."

He found himself sitting there pondering these issues for a long while, only occasionally interrupted by the beeping of his chronometer reminding him to report his status to the Captain. It was midday when a pleasant female voice startled him out of his musings.

"Petrith, don't tell me you're falling asleep on the job!"

He pulled himself out of his trance to see the image of Kaliya standing just behind him as she appeared on the field for a visit.

"Kali! What are you doing out here?"

"It's mail day. One of those few days they let me rest from the hectic drilling they're giving me at the academy. I just finished delivering this week's vid-mail chips and picked up the return bundle. But before I go back, I wanted to spend a little time with my friends."

"Have you spoken to Suli yet? I hear she's been anxious to tell you about our work with those orcs out in the fields."

"Yeah, it seems things are coming along smoothly on that. Once we get a decent harvest, we need to be sure to teach them how to preserve food for the cold season. Not that we actually get any of that in this region, but we don't really know yet what this new world of theirs will look like."

"I'm still amazed at how you handled that situation. Three and a half centuries of hiding in that old mine wondering if they're ever going to attack, struggling to hunt food for ourselves, barely surviving, dodging them and the mutants every time we entered the city, and then you come along and change everything almost overnight."

"Well, Petrith, we didn't have it any better on our side. At least you had peace inside that mine of yours. We were involved in open field warfare the whole time."

"It makes me wish I could've been there with you to offer support."

"I'm glad you weren't. My life there was a living hell, especially after the traumas I suffered from the attack here, our crash, the loss of so many people, and my extreme hatred for the orcs driving me to behave in ways that probably would've turned you and Suli away from me. It's best you didn't see that."

"How do you feel now?"

"I'm a different person now, back to my usual self in most ways, a little wiser for the wear, and full of hope for the future."

"It sounds like you've grown up, as we all have, I guess."

"You're right. Gone are the days of our innocence, not that we probably ever had any to begin with. This war, or at least the fear of attacks, has always been with us, for most of our people, ever since Azgarén. Only my father really knows what it was like before HE came along."

"Do you honestly think we can ever get rid of him? I mean, we've been running from him mostly because we never had the power to fight back. Even with these Tae'Eladaran friends of yours, will it be enough?"

"We were running because someone told us to run…right into their arms. Now, we and they are going back to finish it. I don't know how it'll actually play out, but it sounds like we'll have some special talent on our side, and that talent is apparently going to make a demonstration of some kind."

"But we don't know what."

"Adalon is keeping her secrets very carefully, but if she sees it coming, I think we need to pay attention."

"All right, then I'll just keep my horns curled and wait for it."

"My biggest concern is the approach. If he sees us coming, he could run and hide again, and that could be the end of it for half an eternity. Whoever he finds after that won't have any idea who he is or what he's done. So, we need to finish this now."

"And meanwhile, we have time to rebuild. Kali, there's something we probably need to talk about. I'm not sure how we all feel about it, but I'm sure it'll come up eventually."

"What's that?"

"When we were all together here in the city…you, me, Suli…we were the best of friends. I'm sure most people expected the two of us to join together, but then this attack came, and you were separated from us."

"Yeah, I know. It hurt me too, being away from my two best friends. I expected you both to be dead, actually."

"I suppose that's reasonable, and if it weren't for Captain Lapäli, we probably would be. And neither of us could be sure what happened to you, but we thought maybe you got away on the ship, which really didn't help matters, because we were still apart."

"So, what is this we're getting at, Petrith? Are we talking about you and Suli here?"

"Not precisely, Kali. I still had dreams of the two of us, and then there were those crazy visions I would get on occasion."

"Yeah, I'm still trying to get over that shower scene," she teases. "Here I am, showing myself off to the world, and the one guy I always hoped would be mine is paying more attention to my soap than he is to my body."

"Well, we didn't have any soap here," he smiles. "So, it's a simple case of longing for a few basic amenities."

"Uh huh… And now, where does Suli come in, or does she?"

"Suli tried her best, the little flirt," he grins. "You know how she is."

"Oh yes, she hasn't changed a bit in all this time. I'm really very impressed that she was able to hold herself up under these conditions."

"She had her ups and downs, as we all did. The Captain had it hard too, and Túfu ended up spending at least half her time with morale pep talks."

"Really! And I see she's part of the gang now. I think I'm a little jealous. I feel like I've been replaced."

"No, Kali," he chuckles. "You haven't been replaced, but she did come into our group after we found ourselves pushed into that hole. I guess I should probably bring her into this discussion, while we're at it, since we've all become so close during this time, and this only adds to our problem."

"Competition, right? What about Tana. She seems to be active in a few areas, not the least of which involves running around nearly naked."

"She always loved to run around, and the naked part simply happened after her clothes fell apart for the final time. You should've heard her father complain about it. But eventually he had to relent that she had this wanderlust in her and a pure joy of nature."

"I still say she should sign up for lessons as a druid," she giggles.

"As for the competition…well, yes. Suli and Túfu seem to be competing for me, at least quietly, and I've spent just as much time trying to keep them from locking horns over it."

"Uh oh, that doesn't sound good."

"It's probably not as bad as that. They're good friends, and we tend to laugh over it as much as we can, but..."

"Yeah, eventually it comes down to making a decision. Right, I get it."

"And then you show up again. Suli hasn't said anything specifically, and neither has Túfu, but I suspect they're holding some feelings on the issue."

"Well, Petrith, if we found ourselves in any other situation, I probably wouldn't know how to answer that. I love Suli like a sister. I never met Túfu before coming here, although I know of her by name. I would love to have her as part of our team. As for Tana, assuming she's even a player in this..."

"I'm sure she's got plenty of choices out there. Don't worry about her."

"Yeah, after all this time, I guess there's no secret in what she has to offer," she chuckles.

"Not much by now, and I know a lot of guys have talked about it."

"But I'm surprised none of you have actually done anything with it."

"Our situation didn't give us much freedom to enjoy anything."

"Well, Petrith, speaking of freedom and enjoying things, we have a little issue on our side, as well."

"And what is that?"

"This last hit took too many people with it. Then we lost more during all the fighting we had back home. The end result is too many females and not enough males to go around."

"Oops! So, what does this mean for us?"

"It leaves a lot of our women without mates. There's been talk over what we can do about it, and most of it will sound a little strange, but it might be the only way for us in the foreseeable future to prevent inbreeding and other bad things. It comes down to using all our genetic resources to provide the best result for a new generation, and we need to make lots of them to rebuild our numbers."

"Wow, that sounds a little scary...but it could also be fun, I suppose," he grins.

"If you're a guy, maybe," she smirks. "But it's a matter of survival now, unless we can see a miracle occur on Azgarén, but who knows when or if that will happen."

"When or if, yeah... We need to get there first, and then see what condition it's in. So, what's this solution, or should I guess?"

"Petrith, my dear, it goes like this. We're all good friends, so if we can all agree to it, we'll just share, because it's just as likely you'll be serving all three of us in time, anyway," she snickers.

"Uh oh, that's what I was afraid of. Well, I guess my own words are coming back to me now."

"What words were those?"

"I recall once talking to Suli and Túfu when they were teasing about who goes first, and I said I'm virile enough to take on both."

"Really! Well, Big Boy, if you think you're tough enough for that...make room for one more. And make sure you eat all your vegetables. You'll need it because we're not going to make it easy on you. Now, I need to get back home. Until next time..."

Kaliya gives a mischievous wink and a frisky wag of her tail at the bewildered young male before disappearing in a puff, leaving him pondering the implications of that last statement.

"Guy, what have you gotten yourself into," he mutters.

✦ ✦ ✦ ✦ ✦

"Kaliya! Are you back already?"

"Yes, Kailen, I'm just returning with those vid-mail chips. Do we have anything interesting going on here in the city?"

"Other than relocating our operations from Firstfall, all is well. The new barracks and training hall are in full operation with new recruits training for the local law enforcement service, and the academy is currently signing up for its next semester of classes."

"I'm glad to hear it. Considering what this city looked like after the dwarves were finished, it's finally starting to look like a decent place to live. What about Tristeen and her family? How are they getting along in their new political positions?"

"Last I heard, her father and a few of the others were coordinating the development of a viceroy's office and a new parliament, and Tristeen seems to be settling nicely into her position as a High Council member. She's visited the city on several occasions that I'm aware of to help direct the rebuilding process, including this office," he gestures at the room around them, "and a new government center."

"That girl is a busy one. I hope she can find time for Haran in all that. Between the two of them, with him burying himself in his studies in the academy, and her bouncing from one government office to another, I wonder if they'll ever get time for themselves."

"They're both young, and I think once this rebuilding effort settles, they'll have time to catch their breath."

"So, we have a local viceroy and a parliament…hmm…" she muses. "It's not the sort of government we're accustomed to back home, but it doesn't sound too bad."

"Most importantly is that this governs all the cities in the region, not just here in Rolsklinde, but the Night Elf and High Elf cities as well."

"Don't they get some kind of localized council?"

"Yes, they do, on a city level, since each one technically represents a kind of city-state authority. But ultimately, they'll all answer to the regional parliament."

"Amazing, as if to say they're building a type of nation here together…or wait… No, maybe it's better to say a province, if this is actually part of the kingdom on Tae'Eladar."

"A province…on another world… That's a new one," he chuckles. "And for a society that's not even capable of space travel."

"Yeah, that one is the strangest of all. So, does this mean we're making Rolsklinde a capital city here?"

"That's a very good question, one you should probably ask His Lordship when you get the chance. But so far, it does look that way. Since this world is probably going to be largely owned by the Tae'Eladaran government, I would imagine this new capital might be planetary in scale, rather than regional or district."

"Planetary...wow. Moving on up, aren't we! A planetary authority for a provincial body within a society still in their Early Industrial era."

The two of them shared a brief laugh before continuing.

"Kaliya, I've never had the occasion to observe the first steps of a younger society branching out to new worlds, and certainly not in this fashion, but it's something of an honor and a privilege to witness these initial moments."

"Yeah, but now, what about us? Where do we fit with all this? We have the Naarg uy'Sodrad stuck in the mud over there, while we build even more stuff around it, and yet if Tae'Eladar is expected to claim their territory, do we take anything? And then...what about Ruuki uy'Daan?"

"These are all very good questions, Kaliya. I'm sure His Lordship will work with us to allocate a little space here, and to my knowledge, other than for the situation of war, he seems to be treating Ruuki uy'Daan as our turf, at least as far as the city goes. And it looks like we may inherit the rest of it from the orcs, though this is disturbing as I really hate the idea of stealing someone's home world out from under them."

"I don't think we have much choice if, as he says, they've been corrupted so much that their natural development is in jeopardy, and this is a corrective action to bring it back into alignment. We have this issue of them maybe one day trying to learn the secret of portal magic, and then who knows what they might do with it."

"Right, between that and Darumon trying to peek in on things and taking a little backhanded action. And we also need to remind ourselves that we have no true home of our own anymore, not unless we can somehow take back Azgarén. But that seems like a long way from where we are now."

"You know, he once mentioned having us join his kingdom. It's not such a bad idea. They might be considerably behind us in technology, but they do have a lot to offer, and you and I both know they'll grow and advance one day. These people seem to be moving very quickly."

"That's a little scary, but you're right. It also reminds me of that prophecy where we are said to be slowly grown, as if to say our slow rate of maturity was used to develop lethargic habits for our social and technological development."

"Maybe. Just look at me in his academy. Cu'Nar's grace, Kailen! Compared to my earlier education, I'm in hyperdrive mode over there!" she chuckles.

"And you're not the only one," he smiles. "But again, you're right. Kaliya, you were born on Ruuki uy'Daan, so all you really knew was what we had there. I was born on Ghabeel, which came just before that. I've seen our people get up and move to a new world once, and then struggle to survive, only to see it all torn away during the attack, and we crashed here in even worse condition."

"Yes, Kailen, I know. How many times have our people moved from one world to another looking for peace?"

"Too many, and most of them are tired. Our father is perhaps the worst among them. The travels have taken their toll on him more than any other, if only because he was original to Azgarén, where it all began."

"I'm very sorry for him."

"Thaelyn's kingdom, though it might be technologically primitive to ours, does hold a great deal of interest to me, largely because it's an established world filled with good people, plentiful resources, and a lifestyle that could actually seem fulfilling, even to someone from such a highly advanced race as ours. And I'm not the only one with this opinion. I've had a lot of our people come forward and tell me privately they might be interested in living on Tae'Eladar."

"Rather than amongst our own? Did they give a specific reason for this?"

"A few, actually… The most common is to find peace and to finally settle in one place where they might be able to live their lives without fear of Sargeras, Darumon, or anyone else."

"But how many of them know about these prophecies so far?" she grins timidly.

"Yeah, um…" he chuckles. "Most of that is still being held as a military secret, if only to keep them calm and largely out of the picture…that is, other than those new recruits we hired recently. Then there is the possibility of learning a new way of life. Many of them are very interested in studying this practice of magic and developing new ways of applying it. Also, we have those who are attending the academy over there and making new friends, and this is very good for morale."

"Yes, it is, and I know this from my own experience. How does the Council feel about things?"

"The Council hasn't commented on this for a long time. I'm sure they're listening to the local gossip, but they're trying to focus themselves on the rebuilding effort and not go too deeply into anything relating to our relations with His Lordship, if only to keep things under control in case Darumon should ever come back."

"This is good, I suppose, but if half our people are in training with Thaelyn's people for one thing or another, who's going to operate all our new industry?"

"We're creating something of a combined work crew with some of his people helping work the lines. You mentioned his people moving up the chain fast? Well, they're moving even faster than that, for all we've had to teach them."

"Cu'Nar's pity, they'll outclass us one of these days!" she chuckles. "But then I need to ask something. I was speaking to Petrith once about Ruuki uy'Daan. We were talking about our old city, and how between that and what we have here, we're spreading a bit thin."

"Yes, we are."

"And worse, with such low population numbers, we're not going to make much of a civilization on our own."

"Ankhia and I have spoken about that. We have this suggestion of a modified mating program to bolster our numbers, so we could tip the scales in our favor again. But the trouble here, which is unfortunately our lot in life, is that we have to wait a couple of centuries for the new generation to grow to maturity before they can join the mainstream workforce."

"It's not easy being who we are," she sighs.

"But with Thaelyn's help, and I strongly recommend we keep close to him, I think we could turn this completely around, which is yet another point I would like to consider for a union. If our people were to join his kingdom, as the other races have done, his people could help support ours until we felt a little more secure in our position."

"And after that?"

"Personally, I would desire to keep it that way, simply because it might prove to be more productive for all of us, and I think others would feel the same way."

"And again… What about the Council? Thaelyn is a King. His government is a monarchy, modified with an elected parliament. He has a privy council composed of representatives of the different races, so I guess we would get ours also, but…"

"…It excludes our own Elder Council. Yes, I know."

"Kailen! What are your thoughts right now?" she stresses. "You're not thinking of going against the Council, are you?"

"No, Kaliya, I could never do that. But at the same time, I need to consider where we are, who we are, and WHAT we are, and a nation we are not. We're barely even a refugee camp. First, we're too few in number, and we've lost too much. Second, we're running from our original society, and we're not a proper society on our own. Third, we were apparently driven here by Darumon, and also led by this Maker Kuroku, which means we were probably not intended to be a society of any kind, regardless…just messengers. So, it actually makes better sense to me to join with him than trying to create anything else of our own."

"Now there's a roundabout form of reasoning," she smiles. "But I suppose you do have a point. All right, then let me ask you this. Let's say we make it back to Azgarén and are able to reclaim our former home. What do we do then?"

"I don't know the answer to that, and I think it carries too many variables for me to offer anything."

"All right, good enough, I suppose. I don't actually have anything either. And technically, I'm already a citizen of Tae'Eladar."

Kaliya studies her brother as he appears torn between two worlds, realizing the bounty of a new life on one side, but strapped into the seat of a struggle for survival on the other.

"You look a little like I felt when all this began. I was out there listening to Thaelyn that first day, and how he described his people and his military Order. It represented a future outlook with a lot of potential, but you have to let go of a lot of other stuff first."

"Yes, maybe I do. Due to these confounding circumstances of Darumon and his intrigue, the Council is restricted to their chambers, so they can't see what's on the outside, as we do. They might listen to a few words here and there, but can we say they fully realize our situation as we see it here? The only answer I can give is no. I recall His Lordship once describing us as a nomadic society. This isn't good, as we can never set down roots long enough to build anything that lasts."

"Not with Darumon and his bullies jumping on our tails every few centuries to break everything we build."

"And so we need to associate ourselves with someone," he affirms. "And what better allies to have than those who are the direct opponents of that bully."

Kaliya smiled and stepped around the table to give her brother a big supportive hug.

✦ ✦ ✦◆✦ ✦ ✦

"Right then, let's go through it again..." Relissa recites. "We have the Loumara, the Obyriths, the Tanar'ri, and the Yugoloths. These are the main types of demons you'll find in the Abyssal Plane."

"Got it!" Marelle declares. "And coincidentally, we already know what some of those Tanar'ri look like up close and personal."

"Aye, that one we saw in Rolsklinde would send anyone skittering away quick as a bug."

"That one's obvious, but that…um…lady who was operating that curio shop up in Sigil…"

"Jiggers, don't even mention that one. When we first entered, it was bad enough how she came up so close, I could smell the sulfur fumes. But when Thaelyn walked in…" she whistles emphatically.

"Exactly! And she's described as a lesser tanar'ri. Now try to imagine the bigger ones."

"I'm really very glad I had other work to do that day," Haran states sarcastically. "That little adventure of yours sounds so delightfully frightful," he snickers.

"Oh, dear brother, I'm sure you would've found something of interest," Marelle grins. "For instance, that succubus who was operating the brothel seemed nice enough."

"Thank you, no. I like my soul exactly where it is."

The gang was convening in the guild courtyard on a pleasant sunny afternoon reviewing some of their week's lessons and enjoying a casual conversation. They had started a new year of classes, and as they progressed through their courses, the pressure of study was building.

Kaliya was returning from her visit to Rolsklinde and the new military intelligence center that was in the final stages of development in what would soon be the provincial capital of that world. She had delivered the vid-mail chips to the local command office for further forwarding to the Naarg uy'Sodrad. Now she was returning to Tae'Eladar, hoping to get a little extra practice in on her weekend break. Her schedule would be no less imperative this year than in previous ones, and in some ways even more burdensome than before. But she knew how important it was, and so she pressed on. As she enters the courtyard, she spies Relissa and the others in their group and pauses a moment to join for a few words.

"So, what is it we're doing out here today?" she asks. "I thought I was the only one with no free time on my hands."

"Aye, maybe so," Relissa responds. "But they have the rest of us working hard, too."

"It couldn't be anywhere near as bad as the schedule I'm on

this year. They're doubling up my mage courses to push me to the Seventh Circle in just a couple of years."

"Kaliya," Haran grimaces. "I struggled and slaved for years in the academy back home, and didn't make half of what you're accomplishing in a fraction of the time. I don't know if I should applaud you, or challenge you to a duel."

"Well, Haran, if you're going to challenge me, you'd better do it soon, otherwise I'll wipe the field with you," she laughs and pats him pleasantly on the shoulder.

"Not only that, but I've heard a few whispers in the halls of just how proficient you've become in the Circles you've already gone through as compared to the other students."

"I really don't know how to respond to that, other than to say once you get into the rhythm of it, the rest just seems to fall into place."

"I suppose it does at that, especially as it's all so neatly organized into these courses. If only they could've been so polite and efficient in our old academy."

"Not to worry, Haran. The new one opening up over there will be every bit as good as this one."

"Tristeen tells me she's anxiously waiting for her turn so she can take up a few courses and finish her own study."

"That would be great, and then you could throw fireballs at each other every time you get into a bedroom spat."

"I think I'll stay away from the house during those encounters," Marelle considers.

"Aye," Relissa affirms. "And maybe keep to the other side of the city."

Outside the guildhall, strolling along the avenue, an elder High Elf carrying a characteristically large bundle of books ambles up the hill to the front gates. As she passes through the gates, she smiles politely at the guards who stood vigil in their symbolic watch posts. She continues inside the courtyard and pauses briefly until she takes notice of a familiar shape. She then strides up to join the meeting of the young friends.

"Kaliya?" she calls.

Kaliya and the others turn to find Vonafel arriving behind them.

"Archivist Windsong!" Kaliya responds enthusiastically. "What brings you here?"

"A note telling me my presence was requested by someone."

"By someone? There was no name to it?"

"No, and this makes me wonder who it is I'm supposed to meet. Did you send anything, or maybe His Lordship?"

"As far as I know, Thaelyn is in Mechanus right now hoping to meet with Primus about finding a new home for the orcs. Maybe it was Lady Aerlie?"

"I think if it was her, I'd be going to the temple, not here."

"Do you know of anyone else here who might call you to visit? A relative, perhaps?"

"This is the question I'm asking myself, at the moment. My daughter works elsewhere, my granddaughter is with me in the Royal Archives, and most everyone else would at least give me their name, so I know who it is I'm supposed to meet. So, unless someone is playing a trick on me..." she smiles.

"Maybe they figure you spend too much time in that office of yours."

"Possibly. It could also be one of my spies, but even at that, I would instead expect them to come to me, not call me out here."

"Well, all I can say is it wasn't me."

"All right, then maybe I'll just give it a moment to see if anyone else shows...up...oh dear..."

Vonafel's eyes caught a glimpse of movement emerging from a corridor towards the rear of the courtyard. Strolling out from one of the halls leading deep into the guildhall was a strange figure. She was tall, more so than the average person, and remarkably slim. She moved gracefully in a fluid motion that seemed not even to disturb the surrounding air. She was dressed in a sleek long gown which appeared to be made of silver threads. Her skin was silver, her flowing hair was silver, and her eyes were silver...cat-like with vertical slits.

Everyone in the group turned to follow Vonafel's gaze. As the woman came into view in the courtyard, her appearance created a commotion with the other students wandering through the area. Hushed murmurs and calls between them brought their collected focus to her image. They all began to kneel low as she passed by.

"Jiggers," Relissa mumbles softly. "Who is that now?"

"It's her…" Vonafel whispers and then kneels.

Relissa took quick notice of the High Elf's reaction, and that of everyone else in the area.

"Aye, right," she mutters. "Whatever that means… Um, peeps, everybody's kneeling, so let's get down there."

The gang makes a quick effort to kneel respectfully as the tall woman arrives in front of them. They hold their position, waiting for some word as to what she desires them to do.

"Grand Dame Adalon," Vonafel ushers respectfully.

Relissa peeks over at the elder elf, and then timidly up at the silver figure.

"As in, Adalon the Silver?"

"Well," Marelle whispers. "She's got the silver part right."

The woman does not utter a word. Rather, she reaches down, with her open palm sliding benevolently past the dark elf's face, and Relissa feels the woman's fingers, with their exceedingly long nails, grip gently beneath her chin, then lifting her to a standing position.

Relissa crosses her eyes looking downward, uncertain as to how to react, but sheepishly obeying the gesture.

The woman simultaneously brings forward her free hand and curls her fingers in a come-hither gesture for the others to rise up. She gazes deeply into Relissa's eyes.

"You are Relissssa," she pronounces sedately with an extended hissing sound. "The dark elf… Who is not a Drow. I have known… Many of your kind… Dark One. But none of them… As promisssing as you…"

Relissa feels a strange sense of calm pass through her, not quite knowing if it's from the slow manner of speech, or the enduring hiss producing a hypnotic effect.

"Aye, and thanks. I hope I can make a good enough impression. Your name goes around a lot in these parts. Especially lately…"

"Yesss… I sssuppose it does. And as we get clossser… To the appointed time… It may become… Even more prominent…"

Relissa's eyes were feeling heavy at the elongated response, and she finds herself stumbling backward, catching herself just before she topples.

"Marelle," she inquires gently. "Can you stand here in front of me for a moment?"

"Why?"

"Because she's putting me to sleep with that voice of hers…"

"Better you than me," she chuckles.

Relissa flashes a glare at her friend before returning to the woman, who is smiling pleasantly.

"You fill me with hope… Dark One… That perhapsss one day… We might find… A sssolution… To our problem… With those… Who make their home… In the Underdark…"

"Me? You think maybe I can do something with it?"

"Your sssociety… Could afford usss… The potential… To break them… From their curssse… And return them… To the light. But thisss may need… To wait… Until later…"

"A curse?" Haran wonders.

"They turned away… From the ssSeldarine… And now languish… In the darknessss… Polluted by the thoughtsss… Of their new devotion…"

"Ah, I see now, and this poisons them in some fashion."

"Indeed it does…"

Adalon now turns to Marelle and studies her for a moment, laying a hand on the hesitant young woman's cheek.

"I foresssee… We shall share… A moment… Of anticipation… Together…"

"With respect," she smiles politely. "You have a little bit of a reputation. Can you be a bit more specific?"

"Indeed… Thisss is true… And for good reason. Then I will sssay thisss… To give you direction. You have a desire… To learn that… Which we do not teach here. From thisss… You will journey… To placesss… You never thought… You would sssee…"

"Well, I guess that's a little better. It went from moderately ambiguous to ridiculously ambiguous," she chuckles.

"Patience, young one. You will know of it… When it comesss to you…"

"That seems to be a common theme with you," Kaliya mentions. "And this Maker Kuroku of yours, as well as the rest of them."

"Yesss. It tendsss to be thisss way. The Essstelar… Do not make a habit… Of giving away detailsss… Freely. They mussst encourage othersss… To grow. And the Maker… Is no different… Than the ressst…."

Adalon now turns to Haran, who is observing with great interest this curious woman's interactions so far. She places her hand on his cheek next.

"I sssee greatnessss in you… Young mage. Sssuch that you… May ssstand againssst… Even the mightiessst… Of challengesss. Show no fear… And let not their wordsss… Dissssuade you…"

"Ay!" Relissa perks up. "Don't encourage the guy. His head is already big enough."

Adalon smiles brightly at the young elf's quirky comment.

"My thanks to you, Your Grace," Haran nods.

"Haran," Relissa teases. "Do you need to kiss up to every woman you meet?"

"Clearly, she's a very prominent figure, and her reputation tells that much, so one must show their proper form."

Adalon now turns to Kaliya. She angles up to gaze into the inquisitive young Daanen'kai's face.

"Few are the timesss… When I mussst… Gaze into eyes… Above my own…"

"My apologies, Your Grace, we're just made that way. But then, I suspect you know all about that, don't you…" she smirks cautiously.

"Indeed… I am aware… Of your effortsss… To undersssstand my writingsss… Tall One. I have sssseen… Many thingsss… And shared… Many of your woesss… Within my mind. I weep for you… As much as you… Weep for your people…"

"I thank you, but can you help us understand any part of it?"

"The anssswer to that… Is complex… And more than what… We can ssspeak about… At thisss time. But I will promissse you thisss. When thisss circle is closed… All will be revealed. There shall be no more sssecrets…"

"Great gods, Adalon…" Vonafel gushes. "I've spent all my life trying to understand you. Is this to say I might finally have the answer?"

"In due time… Yesss. But we are in… A delicate moment. And thisss requiresss… Precision… As well as tact…"

"Does this relate to any of those blank spots in your books? Thaelyn, Aerlie, and I all think there's some kind of hidden text in there."

"There is… And the keysss will occur… At certain momentsss… And upon certain eventsss. Be aware… And watch for it. Pay attention… And follow the wordsss… Carefully…"

Adalon reaches over and taps a finger on Vonafel's stack of books. The elder elf intuitively realizes she needs to pull out the prophecy book and open it up. She fumbles with her load, setting part of it down on a nearby bench, and opens Adalon's book to the final chapter, bringing up the first of several pages where she had previously been stifled by the blank areas. She stares at it in amazement. Some of them were no longer blank.

"Oh, wow…" she croons.

Adalon turns to Kaliya again.

"The cu'Nar once delivered… A messssage… To your father… Tall One. These were my wordsss to him. Your people had entered… Within our reach… And it was time… To lay the foundation… Of our work together. Archivissst… Please recite for usss… Those portionsss… That are available… On thisss occasion…"

"Absolutely…" she agrees eagerly.

Vonafel clears her throat as she studies the new entries.

"I have three new ones here. Number One… From out a shimmering door of light, the Divine One will emerge; where One is lent by Two divide, and to wickedness a dirge."

"Great cu'Nar!" Kaliya wheezes. "Those sound so much like my father's words. Is this how the original would've sounded?"

"The transsslation... Through the cu'Nar..." Adalon advises. "Leavesss much... To be consssidered. They cannot ssspeak... In verbal form... And therefore... They mussst interpret from me... And he mussst interpret from them..."

"I recall Thaelyn talking about this once, how some beings need to reinterpret themselves in order to speak to certain others."

Adalon nods and redirects at Vonafel to continue. The elder elf locates the next quatrain and prepares to speak again.

"Number two here. The Child who once upheld a gift, of mystery explore; lost it is, but found again, upon this lonely shore."

"Upon THIS lonely shore?" Kaliya wonders. "Which one are we talking about?"

Vonafel references the surrounding passages to gain her bearings.

"Let's see, we're playing even-odd here between sections. This one falls between the battered home of forlorn souls and where Thaelyn apparently had his conversation with Darumon."

"So, we're talking about Therinë, in this case. She must be speaking of me being found, along with my gift, and likely with all my other problems at that time," she grins at Adalon.

"Either that," Haran muses. "Or the Gift itself, like during your test, and here on Tae'Eladar, which is surely lonely in this space, being the only thing around here."

"Yeah, that works too, and perhaps even better."

"And now Number Three," Vonafel continues. "The weary wept and lost removed, their innocence defiled; until the Child with gift restored, unites the Ones Exiled."

"Unites? Oh dear cu'Nar, can we be speaking of those people still on Ruuki uy'Daan?"

"These are some fascinating clues," Haran muses. "But if they only reveal themselves after the fact, it makes things a little hard to predict what's coming next."

"From thisss moment..." Adalon submits. "You will sssee more... And they will offer... New direction. Sssome will occur...

Only after... A ssspecific moment. But here I mussst become... Generousss... To allow you time... To pursssue them. The final momentsss... Will require... Many piecesss... To fit within... A complex puzzle. You are wise enough... To dissscover your way... From there..."

Adalon turns as if ready to move away. She pauses briefly and returns to the group.

"Archivissst... You have your work. To the othersss... You mussst visit me... In my chamber. We mussst meet... In perssson... As we have more to dissscuss..."

She turns and begins sauntering off, disappearing through the corridor into the guildhall, and leaving Relissa and the gang gaping at her last statement.

"'Ere now," Relissa snaps. "Meet in person? What was this here then?"

"Well," Kaliya remarks. "From all the stories I've heard about her, I was actually expecting something a bit bigger. Maybe this was a projection?"

"Buggers! Don't even play that on me for fun! What about you?" she directs at Vonafel. "What do you think about it?"

"Well," she retorts affectionately. "If she didn't say it explicitly, and if you haven't heard of it anywhere else, then I'm guessing this is part of your learning experience."

"Ay! Buggers to you, Calaer!"

"Oh, come now, Morier, where's your sense of adventure?"

"It ran off when she hoisted me off the ground with those long nails of hers."

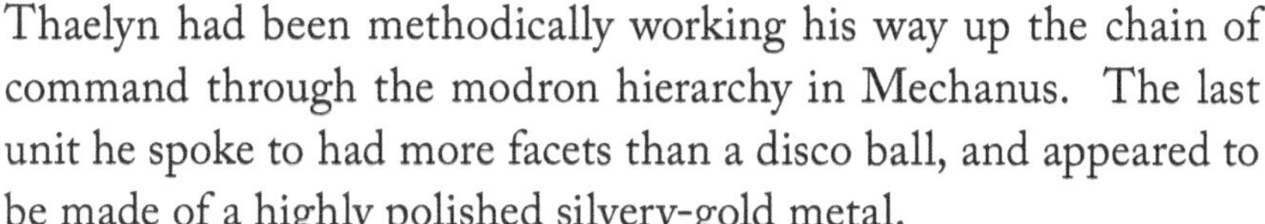

Thaelyn had been methodically working his way up the chain of command through the modron hierarchy in Mechanus. The last unit he spoke to had more facets than a disco ball, and appeared to be made of a highly polished silvery-gold metal.

By this time, he could see his final destination. He was weary, and his stomach grumbled from lack of food. He was unsure how long he had been in motion, but he felt it was surely a couple of days by now.

The endless array of gears penetrating throughout the local space churned and clinked. The thudding of hammers and ticking of switches reverberated through his battered mind, having been forced to endure the relentless clamor since his first arrival. And as he progressed to this point, it only became worse, as it all led up to Primus, the dominant godlike entity of this realm; a massive machine of such proportions that its full magnitude could not be wholly and completely imagined by any lesser creature.

He stepped forward onto a platform that edged its way up to the face of the entity. The apparition resembled a gigantic holographic visage of an anthropomorphic head belonging to an unknown racial origin. And the platform was a presentation dais for those who would wish to make personal inquiries of the sentient machine mind. Native residents of the Outer Planes might use a communications link, but Thaelyn left all that behind when he descended to Tae'Eladar.

As he takes up his position on a circular plate, it illuminates underneath him, and a column of light shines down from above. The visage opened its eyes and gazed down at him. He had the attention of Primus.

"Celestial Of Ordered Positivity," it announces in a resounding monotonal boom. "State Thy Purpose."

"I come to speak with the Great Primus and request an inquiry of pertinent need."

"Acknowledged. Propose Thine Inquiry."

"I seek knowledge to discover a median habitable body within a prime material fold, of particular characteristics for the purpose of relocating a local species deemed to have been corrupted by a higher sentience. The reason for this relocation is multifold. First, to prevent any further corruptive influence and to contain that which has already occurred. Second, to prevent the existing influence from imposing itself as an outward force where this species might use it destructively against others within its reach. Third, to protect this species from that same sentience, should this sentience wish to take offensive action that could harm or destroy the remainder of the species."

"Accepted. Doth This Sentient Influence Hold Malignant Directive?"

"It does, and we have already seen a considerable amount of harm conducted already. And I am currently engaged in pursuing this entity to bring reconciliation to this matter."

"Understood. Specify The Criteria For This Request."

Thaelyn pulled out a folded piece of paper from a pocket, as he knew he would need to be precise, and his prior experience in this place told him he should write it down.

"Our primary requirement: The result should exist in a natural fold that is absent of the dynamistic flows. It should be of rocky foundational composition, with local atmospheric and climatic conditions equivalent to that of the Prime world Tae'Eladar. It should contain flora and fauna species of a subordinate grade, non-sapient, non-pre-sapient, and of compatible genetic composition to serve as sustenance for the Prime species known as Orcs. I would request you to cross-reference this species for further details as to their preferred and tolerable habitat range and needs."

A series of whirs and clicks occur within the mammoth machine as it processes the request.

"Our secondary requirement: I would request the results be limited in number to a quantity of no more than ten most favorable choices. I would request the choices fall within the range of a galactic body, with a preferential distance of no less than one hundred parsecs from the next inhabited body of sapient or pre-sapient life."

Another sequence of whirring and ticking resounds from the machine as these limiting factors are added into the formula.

"And finally... My journey to this point was long and arduous, and my wits are strained. Can these results be delivered to me at my home on the Prime world Tae'Eladar?"

"Affirmative..."

"Further, I will also need the means of transport, to fully effect the relocation of this species, as my own arcanic portals are not likely to function in this regard to the specified location. Can you provide this means to me upon my final choice?"

"Affirmative..."

"Thank you, I am grateful."

Thaelyn pauses to consider if there is anything else he would wish to add, since it took so long to get here, and he didn't want to make the trip a second time.

"Before I depart, I would wish to make another input to be considered as a secondary inquiry to the previous one."

"Understood. Specify The Criteria For This Request."

"I am curious as to the nature and history of a member of the Estelar known as Maker Kuroku. Although I do not wish to violate any detail that might be of deeply personal interest, I would wish to learn of any publicly known details and activities, including her point of origin, relationships with any other prominent Estelar, involvement with any known Child Societies, and her known activities relating to Tae'Eladar. Also, if possible, her current whereabouts and duty objectives."

"Accepted... Be Aware That Maker Kuroku Maintains Many Classified Records. Only A Summary Review Of The Unclassified Material Can Be Provided."

"Very well, so be it. Please include this with the other report when it is available."

"Acknowledged..."

"I believe that is all. Now, if you would permit me, rather than to retrace my steps along this long path, I would instead wish to use an arcanic portal to take me directly home."

"Accepted..."

Thaelyn takes out a rune and struggles to focus his thoughts through the uproar of clockwork machinations around him, which now was further compounded by the clacking of Primus due to his inquiry. He manages to enchant the rune and eagerly claps his hand down on it.

Aerlie was in conference with Relissa and her usual gang about the previous day's excitement with Adalon. Word had been spreading, along with copies of the newly revealed passages, and notes by Vonafel on Adalon's statements during the meeting.

There was enthusiasm about what may lie ahead, but it was carefully tempered by the suggestion that they still need to work for it. Haran and Marelle each reflected on their individual forecasts, and together with Relissa and Aerlie, they wondered when the next quatrain might reveal itself and what it might hold.

Thaelyn emerged on a platform dais off to the side of the courtyard, which was typically used by the royal couple and their officers in the event they were ever away and needed a direct path to return home.

As he appeared in view, he showed visible signs of fatigue. His hands fell to his side, and he hunched forward to prop himself on his knees. He rubbed his brow gently while trying to take his bearings on the activity in the area. The sounds of his portal entrance caught the attention of those in the courtyard, and they all gave their traditional salutes and bows.

Aerlie sensed his distress immediately as he entered the local sphere. She rushed up to him at first thought. Relissa and the others followed closely behind, similarly realizing he was not in his best sorts.

Thaelyn was wobbling slightly and barely holding himself upright by the time Aerlie arrived at his side. Relissa approached and studied him just long enough to realize he needed additional support, so she moved around to his other side and squeezed under his arm. He looks down at her with a smile.

"Relissa, you are a very sweet Child," he states wearily. "I am honored to have so many good friends," he continues as he looks around at the group. "Now, if only I could remove this incessant banging from my head."

"Thaelyn," Aerlie laments. "My poor dear... Your head is throbbing. I can feel it from here. And you're starving! And you're dead on your feet!"

"Is there anything else you would wish to add to that, my dear?"

"That's good enough for the moment. Come, we'll get you some food, and along the way I will see about easing your headache. Then, you are going straight to bed!"

"Wow, and I thought my mom was bad," Marelle reminisces. "Can we suppose you at least got the work done, my Lord?"

"I did," he responds. "But the road to that end was as bad, or worse, as I could have expected."

"So, do you have some idea where we'll be sending the orcs?"

"Not at present. Primus will search and collect the results, and his servants will deliver them here."

"Ay, a delivery service!" Relissa yips. "That sounds ducky enough."

They ushered him across the courtyard, through the halls and into the cafeteria. It was evening, and he had been absent for two days. The dinner meal was coming out of the kitchen, and students were lining up for their plates. Like with everywhere else in the guildhall, when they entered the room, the assembly turned to offer their salutes.

It was not typical for him to visit the cafeteria for a meal, as he usually took his with Aerlie in their private banquet room. The cafeteria was mostly for the students, but it was convenient, and the food was ready.

They approached the food counters to see a long line standing ahead of them. The people in the line all turned to offer their salutes and bows.

"At ease everyone," he announces. "This is not a formal occasion. We are simply here to dine with our beloved students."

"My Lord," responds one of the students. "Are you just returning from your travels? You've been gone for a bit."

"Indeed, and it was a difficult one."

"Aye, and by the appearance of it, it took its toll on you. Here, you should move ahead..."

"I may be worn, but this does not give me right to cut in line."

"Right, as I might expect of our most beloved Lord. What say everyone?" he calls out. "Do we let him stand there drooping like that, or give him a special privilege?"

The line of students all looked at each other, and then made a substantial step backward, clearing the way for Thaelyn and his group to move ahead.

Thaelyn shakes his head modestly with a broad grin at the gesture of familial concern, as they all tended to look up at him as a father figure.

"Powers pay witness, for what we have created together. Very well, thank you, my Children."

He offers a gentle nod and steps forward to the counter.

"Greets, my Lord," announces the cook behind the counter. "What's your pleasure for today?"

"A plate piled high for two days' worth of hunger."

"Aye, sounds dandy enough. And what to drink?"

"A good half-yard of Dwarven Brown…"

"Whoo…" he whistles buoyantly.

The cook raises his brow at the drink order and rolls his eyes at Aerlie and the others holding the beleaguered nobleman upright.

"Right!" he replies. "Just one sec…"

The cook has his assistants fix up the plate while he runs in back for the brew. They present it together and Thaelyn selects a table. The group helps to settle him in and Relissa and the others go back for their own food. When they reconvene, they try to engage in a little conversation to lighten the occasion.

"Is it just my muddled focus," he observes, "or is there a distinctly lighter mood this eve?"

"My Lord?" Marelle offers. "What do you mean? Maybe it's because you're back home? I'm sure we're all happy to see you again."

"While I am quite certain of that, and it does warm me to feel it, this seems centered on something else that occurred recently."

Marelle looks around at the assembly and tries to interpret if there is anything of special note that might be causing him to sense this mood change. Then she surmises it must be the event of the previous day.

"Maybe it's because of Adalon. She came out yesterday, which apparently isn't something she does often these days. And she spoke to us."

"Indeed!" he perks up. "Dear Adalon, I keep telling her she should make her presentations more often. The people do love her so. Did she offer anything of special interest?"

"Aye," Relissa replies. "We had a good little talk out in the courtyard. Vonafel was there, too. She was apparently called by someone who didn't give a name, and then Adalon comes strutting out."

"Really..." he smiles. "So, is this to say Adalon sent an anonymous message simply to offer a little surprise? How charming of her," he chuckles ironically. "And what did she have to say on this occasion?"

"Dear," Aerlie asserts. "I have a copy of some notes Vonafel has been distributing. This is mostly a summary of what was said. Apparently, Adalon is allowing some of those hidden quatrains to be revealed now."

"She is!" he intones avidly. "We must be approaching a time of some importance then. What were these particular entries?"

"These represent a selection that occurs within some of the passages that have already come to pass, and they resemble Velen's message from the cu'Nar. Adalon admitted that she is responsible because his people had come into range for us to get involved."

Aerlie passes a paper across for him to review with Vonafel's notes. He takes a moment from his meal to study it.

"Very interesting..." he muses. "This is how it was supposed to appear, but likely due to the inherent difficulties of interpretation between each of these parties involved, including the cu'Nar, the result was rather distorted. I suppose this is to be expected, as the cu'Nar might be a difficult race to interpret if you are not fluent in a true telepathic language."

"Just for the sake of argument," Marelle wonders. "How does a true telepathic language appear?"

"Mostly as thoughts, images, sensations, and perhaps memories encapsulated to represent concepts. If the phrase, 'a picture is worth a thousand words,' holds any meaning, a properly formed telepathic delivery with just a simple series of images could hold enough context to fill many pages of written text."

"Wow, so with just a single thought, you can give complex instructions to someone with less effort than to actually pronounce it in words."

"Correct. And if the cu'Nar are a fully telepathic race, as I believe it was once said, they would use this. Velen, with all proper respect, might have trained himself to use telepathy, but I suspect he still uses words to compose his thoughts rather than images."

"She also said," Aerlie continues, "that the other quatrains will come forward with the arrival of certain events, and we need to pay attention to the details because it will give us direction for something we need to do. Also, the final moment is going to represent a complex puzzle of many pieces we need to assemble."

"Dear Powers, as if we did not have enough work ahead of us."

"And not just you," Marelle recalls. "She also gave me and Haran our own objectives to follow. Although, in her usual manner, the words didn't really tell us much other than to say something is going to happen and we'll know of it when it does."

"Oh, is she playing that game on you now?" he chuckles. "Very well, and can you tell me what it was? I think I should know of it in case the mischievous siblings should find their way into more trouble."

"My pardons," Haran interjects sarcastically. "But at last reckoning, my name was not on that famous list of yours. And further, I understand Marelle was the first one to be included for at least a century or two. This is surely a notable example."

"Yes, but perhaps I should consider being more generous in these times," he smiles. "So, what did Adalon say to you?"

"As for me, it seems fairly straightforward. She sees something great coming my way, and I'm going to guess it has to do with my ambitions to study the mage craft. But then there was some kind of mention of going up against big challenges and to show no fear in front of it."

"Indeed! Well, if you do choose to go all the way to the Ninth, you will certainly qualify for many intense challenges, and not all of them involve politics or academics."

"Yeah, so it seems, and this is all the more reason for me to pay close attention to my studies."

"On my side of things," Marelle explains. "She hit me with a double whammy. The first one was a simple phrase that we will share some kind of excitement together, but it was a little too vague. So, I asked about it, and she went to the luxurious extreme of giving me something so wickedly indecipherable that I doubt I'll know what it is until it actually hits me."

"Yes, good old Adalon," he chuckles. "She takes after the Estelar and the Celestial Races so much for this point."

"She said that I want to study something you don't have here, and that it will take me places I never thought I'd see."

"Well, one must admit, it does sound intriguing. Then, we will need to watch for some manner of opening and see what is necessary to fill it in."

"She even gave a little something to Relissa."

"Oh, she did? And what sort of trouble is she suggesting to the one who is well known for her own."

"Ay! I'm not THAT bad," Relissa snaps playfully.

"Oh? Allow me to recall a moment of a young duo who once piloted a large Suuden'kai transport when neither of them held any proper training."

"Aye, but you might also recall Marelle was in the pilot's chair and I simply got hoodwinked."

"You could have stayed on the ground…" he raises his brow.

"Um…" she flusters. "Aye, I suppose I could've…but…well, I had to keep a close eye on her to make sure she didn't flub up."

"Ah! Yes, but of course, the good friend attending to her sense of duty…" he grins. "And what did she say about you on this occasion."

"Mine I think is a message for something maybe later on. She said that my people might be able to help with the Drow, to bring them back into the light, or some such."

"Interesting. Yes, I suppose we do have a curious potential there. But I would first wish to see a conclusion to our current objectives, and perhaps also to see a few more of your people passing through the academies to give us more examples to work with."

"Aye, sounds good to me. But these objectives are piling up just a wee bit. It was bad enough when I thought the Suuden-Aryku was the whole of it. By the way, she also invited us to visit her in her chamber. She said something about meeting in person. So, um, if what we saw outside wasn't her...in person...what is?"

"How did she appear to you, a tall female in silver hues?"

"Aye, so I guess that's how she does it often?"

"Typically, if she wishes to walk amongst us. It is a form of avatar her kind may use from time to time."

"Right. So, are you going to tell us what she really looks like?"

"You do not already know?"

"Uh-uh... People don't talk much about it for some reason, and since she apparently doesn't come out to play much, we don't get a chance to see it."

"Yes, I suppose this tends to be the case. Those of us who are native here know of her from a historical perspective, so it does not necessarily play into common gossip. Also, I suppose, since she does spend so much of her time in her chambers, it plays a little like 'out of sight, out of mind' for many. And if she is requesting an audience, I suspect she has a reason for it, maybe as part of this continued education, or else to play some role in these plans of hers. I cannot be sure, so I think I do not wish to interfere with her games."

"Do I need to bring a change of britches with me?" Marelle asks timidly.

"If you desire," he smiles. "But let us hope it will not be necessary."

"Jiggers," Relissa moans. "All this hullabaloo is enough to drive me to another one of those ales."

"Another?" he asks curiously. "Do you drink beer, Relissa?"

"Not in the slightest, except for that one time when they filled me up on three of them."

"Three... Ah, I think I understand your meaning. You mean that quaint little initiation rite the students tend to perform," he grins.

"Aye, I barely ever had a sip of wine in my day before that one."

"And how did you fare?"

"I got through it, but just barely. If it weren't for Marelle and Haran holding me up, they'd be dragging me out by the heels."

Thaelyn lets out a soft laugh.

"Yes, the students have been running that tradition since the early days; a pint of each of the three most popular dwarven ales, White, Brown, and the infamous Black."

"The White wasn't so bad. The Brown had my head spinning. But that Black…and then that wacky dance they spun me through. I nearly painted the walls with my innards."

"The Black is not for the faint of heart, especially for an elf. You should have seen Aerlie when it came to be her turn."

"Aerlie? You did that too?"

"Oh yes," she admits. "I went through all the traditions and rites, the same as the rest. I was young, and the only Avariel in the academy, and I wanted to earn my place of respect amongst the others. I had never tried any alcohol before this, as my people never had the privilege to make it. And being Avariel, I was not even as sturdy as some of the other elven races. So, I decided to build myself up a little by sampling different brews over the first few months before taking my rite."

"And still, I had to carry her to her room," Thaelyn chuckles. "But she did finish before she passed out."

The group shares in the humorous memory and continues on to other topics while they finished their meals. Later, they split up to find sleep for the night, each going to their respective dorm rooms, while Thaelyn and Aerlie ventured home to their own beds.

"A moment of excitement," Thaelyn muses privately. "And learning that which we do not have here, and then travelling to places she might not otherwise see."

"What are you mumbling about this time?" Aerlie wonders.

"If Adalon is passing more messages, and if she is now suggesting that we must pay attention to these details in order to assemble a myriad of puzzle components, then perhaps we should start with this one. I am thinking of Marelle and her role."

"All right, and what do you think it could be?"

"If she is to learn of something not otherwise found here, and this leaves open a great many possibilities, and then to travel to places she might not otherwise see, I am tempted to suggest she will learn ways to perform this travel, and those places will be the natural destination where we wish to go."

"All right, and if we're travelling outside our own planar fold, this might mean to other worlds."

"And this might then reflect on that little mention of her joyride in that transport, where she would need to take these lessons from the Daanen-Aryku, not us."

"As we don't have any flying craft here," she surmises. "But Thaelyn, there is a bit of a difference in flying an aircraft as opposed to travelling to other worlds."

"Indeed there is, as would be the things one would see along the way…" he whistles energetically.

✦

Thaelyn was arriving at the new strategy room that was part of the military intelligence building in Rolsklinde. It was a new day, and he was feeling much better after his visit to Mechanus. The General and the other officers were already in attendance reviewing several reports concerning the new construction efforts in the city, as well as those around the Naarg uy'Sodrad, and some of the results of the joint research effort at the Bahlaie Research Center on Tae'Eladar.

"My Lord!" the General calls. "It's so good to see you up and about."

"Thank you, General. A good meal and a pleasant night's sleep, especially with the aid of a large ale to dull the pounding in my head, can work wonders on occasion. Do we have anything interesting occurring around us?"

"We have a number of progress reports here on the construction efforts. For all the work going on, we should have a very fine example of a city before long. The outlying farming communities, not only here at Rolsklinde but also around the other cities, have been pulling in a bountiful harvest this season, and I hear business is booming at the local shops."

"Food is very important General, and I am glad to see they have enough to supply them. But now, what about other resources? I am recalling our talks about the possibility of new adamantium, and perhaps mithril deposits on this world. Have we had any luck with our surveys?"

"Professor Cogswoggle and Chief Technician Lapäli have managed to devise a way to scan the terrain for the molecular signatures of these materials. This is a result of our combined technological development. Using samples we provided back home, the Chief Technician was able to adapt some technology they use for locating mineral deposits to now detect these special metals. Using this, we have sent out a few survey crews to several promising locations to test it. So far, we think they found a potential site, but they need to drill a few core samples to verify it."

"Excellent. I am of the mind that once we begin moving forward, we can use all we can get of this metal. Not simply for our armies, but I believe some of our equipment and new vehicles can benefit. Which brings me nicely to my next concern, Lieutenant?"

"Yes, Your Lordship," Padriyl responds.

"With all the research projects we seem to be juggling together, how is the work on the aircraft we acquired from the Suuden-Aryku? And for that matter, any other designs you may have been working on."

"Our teams have made a thorough review of the one found at the Dwarven enclave. It appears to be a fairly standard design, as compared to many of our own, except for its size. As you may recall, we didn't have much need for aircraft in any of our previous homes because we mostly kept to just one city using ground transport. We might use a few aircraft in the initial surveys of the new worlds we discovered, but we didn't keep them long since we always expected to be evicted by the Suuden-Aryku...or perhaps I should say by Darumon...and saw no point in wasting our resources on it."

"What about combat craft? It is one thing to build a survey or cargo vessel, but did you ever build anything for military use?"

"Never during our long journey, and I'm not actually sure if we ever had anything on Azgarén. Commander, can you recall anything?"

"All I recall of our old history," Kailen reflects, "was that we were never a militaristic society, so we didn't have a full and proper military. Our present-day Sentinels force is generally derived from what we once had back home, and it's largely a security force, at least in our case as we had to work so closely together that we didn't have much in the way of crime. If this is the way it was on Azgarén, I might expect security patrols, maybe with light arms, but not much else."

"This presents us with an interesting topic," Thaelyn ponders. "Commander, considering what Darumon may have been up to during this time, do you think you can speculate on how Azgarén might appear in the modern day?"

"That would be almost impossible for me to predict with any accuracy. But if to consider what we've seen whenever they attacked us, they clearly have a heavy military force now, with pulse plasma weapons, battleships capable of bombardment, and who knows what else."

"Very well, so if Darumon is building a sizable military as a forward advance on the Estelar, or whatever he hopes to use it on, it is likely to carry a fair amount of offensive power. But now, what about defensive? If all you had prior to this was a mere security force, you could not have been afraid of any external threats, correct?"

"I suppose you could have a point, although I'm not sure if my personal knowledge can confirm this."

"But let us consider for a moment. First, if we say there were no natural enemies to your people, or at least none who could potentially pose a threat to you, and this leading up to the moment of your departure. Then, if we suggest Darumon would not likely permit any potential…interference…to his plans, therefore causing him to choose your world if it were not in someone's immediate line of sight."

"That's an interesting perspective. He picks a world that is outside the range of anyone taking notice."

"Next is to say you were such a highly advanced society that you may have had enough opportunity to explore much of your local space, therefore you might feel very secure in your position."

"As if to say we knew there wasn't anything bad out there, so why bother with a strong defensive force. All right, I'm with you so far."

"I once recall a conversation suggesting you had comparatively little experience with anything external to your world, at least until this pursuit, where you apparently came into so much of it along the way."

"Yes, and I believe I've heard Ankhia mention this once or twice."

"Now, we have Darumon and Sargeras corrupting your people, and what we see coming out of this is your new military…an offensive military."

"An offensive military performing a lot of atrocities, from what we've seen down here."

"While this is true, did you ever see them use any form of aircraft on your positions?"

"I'm only twenty-one centuries, so I haven't seen that much. The invasion on my home world, which we called Ghabeel, was in the form of a brief land assault, and a few potshots they took at us from space. But from all the stories I've heard, I don't recall any mention of this before."

"Then, if we consider this prospect of your old security forces, and if we further suggest Darumon would wish to keep the local population under surveillance and control, it might be more of the same, but not necessarily a full military power keeping them oppressed."

"Not if he's using these chips and whatever else he puts inside their bodies. I don't know what the civilians might have, but if it's anything like their military, I shudder to think of what it looks like over there."

"I as well, but this could give us a potential clue. And here we come full circle. If any of this is correct, we might have a fairly weak underbelly. If a true military threat were to arrive on their doorstep, Darumon would find himself in a pinch to defend against it."

"Well, yes, but then I need to ask this. Are you planning an actual assault on Azgarén with a military air strike?"

"The answer to this is clearly subjective on what we find. But Commander, you and I both know that air superiority represents a key tactical advantage in any wartime situation. While I would not wish to bring any real harm to your people on Azgarén, I must also consider what Darumon will throw at me, and then compare that to the greater need, which at this point might be a full world population of innocent lives."

"Dammit," he curses under his breath. "Yes, I understand. This is one of those horrid little learning curves I had to take during my training as the HC. Acceptable losses for the greater good..."

"And further if you consider these chips," Padriyl adds. "Recall when Commander Geilv admitted they had one of military grade, and whatever it is that might place them under a control effect."

"And that just makes things worse. If Darumon uses these chips to create an army of forced compliance..."

"Indeed," Thaelyn admits. "I do not expect Darumon to go down without a fight of some kind, so we must be ready with our own, and this further brings me to any other defensive platforms, such as anti-aircraft weapons. If you are not expecting anything to come at you, would you even have such available?"

"That's a good question. Just how much is he expecting to come back at him for all he's done to everyone else?"

"He probably doesn't think anyone can or will," Padriyl suggests. "He's doing more damage to them, with nothing left TO come back."

"And so he leaves Azgarén virtually open. All right, Your Lordship, what do you have in mind? We've never built anything like this, and your people don't even have aircraft technology."

"Perhaps, but this must change," Thaelyn admits. "As we move forward, we must teach your people the proper conduct of war. As for ours, this will need to take the form of a careful military secret until our society is mature enough to accommodate it."

"Well, boys and girls. Are we ready?" Aerlie asks the group.

"There's actually only one boy," Marelle suggests, thumbing at Haran next to her.

"Aye," Relissa moans. "And I can't say I'm sure about this, but we're in it up to our backsides, so we may as well finish it."

"Oh, come now, Relissa," Aerlie reassures. "It won't be that bad."

"Right. And this coming from someone who keeps spinning wild tales and dangling half-eaten carrots in front of us."

"Have I ever led you wrong?"

"No, my Lady, it's just that whenever you or Thaelyn say such things as, 'it won't be that bad,' it means something wacky is coming our way," she chuckles.

"Dear Child," Aerlie begins as she places a hand on Relissa's shoulder. "We are teachers, and life doesn't always lay things out in the open for us to see them ahead of time. The lessons we give are to help you strengthen yourselves against the unknown."

"Aye, I know that. I'm just ribbing you. But from all the things we've seen so far out of this Adalon dame, I'm not too sure I want to go meet her…in person."

"Just remember, she's on our side, so don't worry that you'll become her next meal."

"I'll just hide behind Kaliya here. By the time she finishes choking down those horns of hers, I'll be halfway out of there."

"Hey!" Kaliya gripes. "I happen to take great pride in my horns. They're useful for hanging garlands of wolfsbane and garlic, and other stuff to scare away the bad things. You should be happy to have me around."

"Aye, and maybe I can hang my coat and bags on you, too?"

"Ah, well, I charge for that service," she grins.

"Very well, we should be on our way," Aerlie asserts. "I will accompany you through the passage that leads to her chamber since, if you recall, its sealed by a set of magical doors left behind from the old days when we were still concerned about the Drow coming up and making trouble for us."

"Did you actually expect them to try something?" Marelle asks. "I thought they mostly kept to themselves down in the Underdark."

"They do, but they're a devious bunch, so you can never be too sure. There were times when they would make incursions to harass our people."

"Is that in modern times? Or was this sometime long ago in history?"

"Mostly historical… Since then, we have been able to reveal to them, within reason, as they don't care to talk much, that trying to come up here won't result in anything productive. Although they don't seem to take the hint very precisely."

"Not precisely… In what way?" Haran muses.

"Over the course of time, we learned where they typically make their exits. There are a series of caves and passageways that lead down underground. And in each of those cases, we built garrison forts with large walls blocking their access. When they come up, we will simply shine a bright light in their faces, which is intolerable for them as they are very sensitive to light, living down there in the darkness for so long, and call for them to turn around and go home, since they don't seem to care for taking any other message. This leaves them with nothing else but to comply."

"And the very precisely part?"

"They keep coming back."

"Oh! And how often do you see this occurring?"

"Unfortunately, it seems to go a few or several times a month. They apparently NEVER learn, and we think it's due to their goddess simply telling them to make harassment moves without sharing the details of what they're banging their heads against once they arrive. She's nearly as bad as Darumon for her authoritative methods."

"Gods above…and below, for that matter," he chuckles. "That's not a promising sign."

"They are known to be an exceptionally paranoid society, especially about us, and don't even get along well with their own kind. Deceit, intrigue, even murder, if it serves a role to leverage you up a notch in their ruling hierarchy, is all fair game for them. The life expectancy of the average Drow is not nearly their full lifespan. It only lasts for as long as they keep their back to the wall and a knife in their hand waiting for the next person to round the corner."

"Ouch! How are they able to reproduce under those conditions?"

"Indeed! We had the good fortune once or twice to know of a few refugees who managed to escape to the surface. The stories they told were shocking. Their religion is ruled entirely by the females, who govern their society as a matriarchal oligarchy. Males are subservient to the females, and most often used for home defense as a personal security force to the ruling dynastic Matron Mother. Sometimes they are used as an offensive force to attack other dynastic houses in a bid to destroy the rank above their own, thus allowing them to level themselves up. The top eight houses apparently rule as a council for a city, so being one of those is a highly coveted position."

"One to kill for, by the sound of it."

"Yes, so it is. There is no love for your family members, as brother competes against brother for higher favor in their station of authority, sometimes also for the favor of one or another of the sisters."

"Incest?" he winces.

"It would seem that way. The houses are more in competition with each other, rather than friendly relations to intermingle. Further is sister against sister for the next-in-line to become the new Matron Mother. And SHE has to watch her back constantly, as her first daughter will plant a knife in it at the first sign of weakness. It's awful."

"Great gods…"

"As for reproduction, get this. While incest may be a factor, more often they hold special ceremonies at their temples. The priestesses will select from a group of males and engage in a group activity right there on the temple platform. And it's regarded as obligatory for the males. This is where most of their babies actually come from. But even at that, mothers don't hold much concern for their offspring. They are most often handed down to a caregiver to raise them, maybe a younger sister or a house servant, until they're old enough to go into an academy and learn to fight. They need to prove their strength constantly or perish, as per their religion that doesn't tolerate weakness in any form."

"Are we speaking of negative polarity here?" Kaliya wonders.

"The worst!" Aerlie nods. "And very chaotic, on top of things. That goddess of theirs is simply awful. Some might say she goes beyond reason for her polarity. And assuming they survive any of this, they join the rest and compete for their stations until one day someone bests them."

"That's not a nice place to live, if you ask me," Haran mourns.

"And those people worry about you up here?" Marelle grimaces. "By the sound of it, they'll kill each other off long before you get any ideas of it. But these are old stories, I guess. What's the situation with them now?"

"Largely unchanged, as far as we can tell," Aerlie reflects. "We've made attempts, mostly using stealth, to spy on them. But the complexity of the tunnels is a bother, as you have a number of native creatures that live down there that like to burrow and dig out new nests. This can change the geography of the place on occasion. Making maps is therefore problematic, as nothing is set in stone..." she pauses, and then giggles at her own pun.

"Uh huh... Like Relissa said a moment ago."

"How long do you think this will go on?" Kaliya asks.

"Obviously, this must change at some moment. Thaelyn and I are aware that the Maker is most displeased with their goddess, whom the Drow refer to affectionately as the Spider Queen. She does not hold right to be here, and neither at stealing away a part of the elven nation, even though the old Ssri did violate the ancient traditions and descend into chaos from it. She probably took advantage of this for her own ends. We have held back on doing anything with it, at least in part for trying to decipher those passageways to find anything, as well as simply to appear in their native holdings, as this might incite an instant reaction, and not a good one."

"Sounds like a tough obstacle."

"But this reminds me of our meeting," Haran offers. "It sounds like where Relissa and her people might be able to help somehow."

"Maybe," Aerlie considers. "If to use them, they might not stand out as much. But we might also need to use a number of tactics to soften things up. If they refuse to realize the futility of banging their heads against a wall, maybe they need to realize where that wall came from, and what is on the other side that they should probably keep away from to begin with."

"You know," Kaliya notes. "This actually sounds a little like our methods with the orcs and others during this campaign we're on now. To apply a little of our own propaganda. And then the Suuden-Aryku, with Sargeras and his promises that drove them to do things, and how we need to turn it around. So, do we simply push him out of the way, or go in undercover and turn things upside-down on him," she snickers.

"Indeed, maybe we could reuse a few of these techniques. I would surely wish to see the Estelar police themselves on this one. But if to replace her image with something else as a form of rehabilitation, this would be more to our level. But it would need to be carefully considered. Generally speaking, I foresee two possibilities: An all-out military strike to simply take over and erase their former culture, replacing it with our own until they finally convert, or maybe something more subversive that could invoke a movement of some sort."

"If you're thinking of using a subversive method, this will likely take time. That goddess of theirs sounds like an iron-horned example, especially if she's telling them to bang their heads on a wall that she doesn't let them acknowledge exists."

"Perhaps..." Aerlie agrees. "I am aware of Nemelle, up in Sigil, who has sometimes dreamed of ways to help her mother's people. But without any obvious method to conduct this, she has often felt stifled. So, if Adalon is suggesting Relissa's people could offer a solution, this might just be the advantage she is looking for. We should bring you together one day and see what we can do about it."

Aerlie pauses to survey the courtyard of the guildhall, and then turns her attention to a corridor leading off behind the group into the building.

"Anyway," she concludes. "We should be on with today's chores."

She directs the group through the corridors and into a rear section representing a much older part of the structure. She unlocks a hefty wooden door with a silver key, and they pass through, closing the door behind them.

"That didn't seem so magical to me," Marelle comments.

"That one is just a simple security measure to keep the students out. They wouldn't know how to defeat the traps, and we don't want them getting hurt."

They turn down a hall constructed of old stone blocks, and descend along a shallow stairway. The air seemed musty and stale from age, and there was a slight chill as there was no circulation with the warmer air above.

They approached the first vestibule. Opposite them was an ancient door set with runes and arcane glyphs. To either side of the door were a set of metallic sculptures resembling winged serpents, standing upright in a ready posture.

"Stop here behind the line," Aerlie instructs, holding out a hand in front of them.

The group nervously halts in their tracks. Relissa looks down at her feet, trying to locate the line Aerlie mentioned, but there were no clear markings to be seen.

"What line is that, my Lady?" she asks.

"The one you're very nearly stepping on," Aerlie grins. "If you cross it, you'll trigger the trap."

"Aye, I think I get that part, but...I..."

Relissa kneels down to take a closer look at the floor. She spies a hairline seam in the stone tiles crossing the hall.

"Buggers," she mumbles. "That's not much of a line."

"Of course, if it were obvious, it would defeat the purpose of the trap."

"Right then, so what happens if you cross it? Or maybe it's best I don't ask that."

"You can test it if you like. Just make sure the others step back to give it room, and you should duck down low."

The rest of the group automatically steps back at the mention. Relissa notices the movement behind her.

"'Ere now, peeps!" she argues. "Just what do you think you're doing?"

"We know you, Relissa," Haran offers. "So we're just letting you have your fun."

"Thanks, I'll let you know how it feels in the afterlife."

The young elf ducks down on her haunches, leans back on her hands, and extends one foot over the line. She carefully brings it down on the stone just on the other side of the crack.

The two serpent statues suddenly erupt to life, shooting out from the wall and taking a vicious swipe in the air over the girl's head. The group jumps back, and Relissa flinches, falling further to the ground. The statues then return to their resting position, becoming inert once more.

"Bloody jiggers!" she snaps. "If a flaming fool were standing there, he'd be ripped open by that."

"Now, Relissa," Aerlie announces soothingly. "You're the scout. You should be taking some classes in trap detection and disarming. Can you reveal this to us?"

"My Lady, I've only just started that by now. This one looks a mite trickier than anything I could figure."

"Give it a try. I'll help if you need it. Just be sure not to trigger it again."

Relissa pulls herself back up and studies the line in the floor tile, noticing it follows the outer edge of the tile fully around.

"This tile must be a pressure plate. If you step on it, you trigger the trap. To keep it from letting go, there must be a switch of some kind to hold back those nasty snakes."

"But where is the switch?" Marelle asks. "It should be somewhere within reach, right?"

"Aye, and probably hidden on one of these walls."

The girl begins a careful study of the wall on her left, then the right, but there do not appear to be any hidden switches or moveable blocks. The only things remaining are the torch sconces.

She takes a closer look at the sconce on her left. The mounting bracket seemed normal enough, but the sconce itself appeared as a round brazier emitting a magical fire, set onto a post that fits into the bracket. The other sconce appeared the same, and both had sets of runes inscribed on small plates stuck on the facing around the brazier, with another one on the forward side of the bracket. She had an idea.

"These runes here, I'm betting they play a role, right?" she asks, looking over at Aerlie.

Aerlie remained silent, offering only a gentle smile and an innocent look of uncertainty.

"Buggers to you on that," Relissa taunts.

She studies the runes on both sconces. Between them, they appeared similar, but the mark on each of the brackets was different. She surmised the sconces had to be turned to line up an appropriate rune, but there were none to match the one on the bracket. There must be a missing piece to this puzzle.

She made one more study of the runes, thinking it might be a two-part key on each side. Her studies had been teaching her to identify the runic language, and she tried different ideas on how to interpret the runes into a word or concept. Several possible combinations came to mind, but the question now was which one would do the job. There was still something missing.

"Criminy, you don't make it easy, do you."

"Our foes are Drow, in this case, Relissa," Aerlie admits. "And surely they are very clever warriors and mages, so we must be even more careful."

"Aye."

Relissa considers there might be a clue, and then she notices some runes on the wingtips of the serpents. She leans in as close as she can for a better look. The runes appeared unfamiliar to her at first, until she realizes they are inscribed upside-down, as if rotated a half-circle.

"Wait a sec," she muses softly. "That looks important."

She searches the nearest sconce and locates runes with a similar design, but inscribed in a normal orientation, and turns the brazier portion until the two lined up. Nothing outward happens, and she feels suspicious that the deed was incomplete.

She examines the runes on their individual plates, realizing they appeared to be separate tiles set onto the brazier, rather than molded into the casting. The rune on the bracket appeared similar. Furthermore, the plates were half-round, and between the two, they formed a circle. In their current alignment, they were in reverse order, from top to bottom, as compared to the order on the serpent moving left to right. A grin curls up on her face as she tries rotating the set. They slide along grooves inside the fitting, turning half a circle to match the runes on the wingtips.

The orange flame in the sconce flickers, now changing color to blue.

"Nicely done, Relissa," Haran remarks. "Assuming this is a good thing, of course."

The girl flashes a mischievous glare at him before moving to the other side and performing a similar study of the runes, comparing with the corresponding serpent for the key markings. As she makes her choice and arranges the set, that flame also changes to blue.

"There now," she declares. "So, who wants to be the first chump to try it out?"

The group examines each other briefly, and finally turns their gaze back to Relissa.

"Aye, that's what I thought. Hang back while I give it a run."

Once again, she ducks low to the ground and reaches over with a foot to tap the stone tile. Nothing happens; the serpents remain stoically at attention. She stomps again, harder, but still no reaction.

Then she puts both feet on the tile, still crouching on the floor. The scene remains the same.

"Congratulations, Relissa," Aerlie applauds. "I'm impressed. This is actually a much more difficult arrangement than where you should be in your courses so far."

"Aye, but maybe from all my dealings with you and the others, I got a few early lessons out of it."

Aerlie steps up to the door and lays a hand on it. It opens by itself at the mere touch.

"Now wait a minute," Marelle complains. "Do you mean it opens if you just touch it?"

"Not entirely. It unlocks at the same time as the trap is disarmed."

"Oh, well, all right, that makes more sense."

They continued through the hall and downwards, until they came upon another vestibule. Relissa is paying closer attention this time and holds the group back on the last step before arriving. She kneels down to inspect the flooring again, but doesn't see any cracks or seams in the tiling like the last time.

On this occasion, there are two statues in shallow semi-circular alcoves, one on each side, and a third carved into the door. The two in the alcoves appeared as knights standing sentry with their swords held upright in a salute. The carving in the door simply stood at attention. The eyes in the side statues were set with clear crystals, while those of the door carving appeared to be mirrored. Above the room was an odd arrangement of colored lenses circling around a brightly glowing enchanted light source hanging from the ceiling. She also noticed a set of levers on one wall.

"All right, peeps," she notes as she studies the situation. "This already looks nasty. If these knights behave in any way like those snakes, we're in trouble. The thing of it is, what's the trigger?"

Relissa glances at Aerlie, but knowing she'll get no help from her, she turns to carefully examine the room.

"Relissa," Kaliya observes. "I would be really careful of this."

"Oh? What do you think of it?"

"As we came in, I guess we disturbed a little bit of dust, and I happened to notice some of it passing through light beams reflecting off the sides here."

Kaliya points at a set of reflectors on the walls. Relissa looks around and tries collecting a small mound of dust from the floor. She cautiously blows it from a distance past the reflectors.

A beam of light was revealed apparently passing from the central source to a mirrored surface on one wall in the upper corner, then zigzagging across to the opposite side, down to a lower set, and repeating until it made a final course at the bottom where it terminated with a rune-covered disk. The arrangement created a web of light beams barring the path.

"Aye, I see it now. Jiggers, that goes a little beyond my experience. And I'd think probably more than your average Drow if they follow the same ways as the rest of us. So, if we pass through that, I'll bet those knights will have something to say about it."

"More than likely," Marelle mutters. "They won't bother with words."

"And I might further mention," Haran adds. "They don't actually look to be a part of that display. They're not carved out of the wall, and it looks more like they're just standing on top of that base, not attached to it."

"What do you mean by that, Haran?" Marelle asks.

"If they would go to so much effort to trap the majority of this hallway with this light, breaking it might cause those things to come to life. And right now I'm thinking of some manner of golem."

"Golems!" Kaliya interjects. "I remember those from our lessons on creature lore. You can't kill those things with anything less than highly enchanted weapons and a lot of work."

"Which makes them exceedingly dangerous," Haran concludes.

"Right," Relissa considers. "But for the moment they're sleeping, so how do we keep them that way? They're facing this light in the middle, generally so, and I'm going to bet these levers aren't here for the joy of it."

She tries pulling one lever. It turned a hinged armature operating the turntables above the array of lenses, causing them to rotate, bringing some of them inline to the light source and thereby casting colored beams into the eyes of each of the statues. The carving on the door, with its mirrored eyes, was reflecting its beams into one side of the golems, while another beam shines into the other side directly. The beams are of different colors.

"Interesting..." Kaliya notes. "So, are we supposed to match the beams?"

Relissa returns the first lever and tries pulling another one, resulting in a different set of lenses coming into play with a different color pattern.

"I'm going to guess you need to use a combination, Relissa."

"Aye, I think you're right. But then we need to ask, what are we actually aiming for here."

"All right, let's analyze for a moment. There must be a clue, right?"

Aerlie stands back as the group ponders the situation. The combination of wit and experience between them offered an amusing display to test their ability to solve problems together.

Relissa studied the two golem statues, looking for a clue as to the color she was supposed to match up. They were mostly made of stone, but the swords were clearly metal. There were no discernable markings, until she noticed the pommel in the hilt of the sword. It was set with a colored jewel.

"Ay, there we are," she points to the jewel. "I'll bet that might be something. And it's a different color on each side."

"Orange on the left, purple on the right," Marelle considers. "I see orange and purple lenses up there."

"Aye, let me see if any of these levers line them up."

She tests each lever individually, to see what sort of interaction it had with the turntables at the top of the lens array. There were four levers on the wall and two turntables of lenses. Hinges and gears seemed to interact to turn the inner set to shine one color into the eyes of the door carving, while an outer set turned with individual colors for the golems. Each lever seemed to cause a different amount of shifting of the wheels.

"Right then," Relissa mumbles. "So, we need to find a nice middle ground here. Trouble is, how many times do we have to move these levers to find it."

Kaliya studies the arrangement for a moment and comes to an easy conclusion.

"Sixteen."

Relissa huffs and glares up at her tall friend.

"Huh? Just how do you figure that? And worse, so bleedin' fast?"

"It goes with my training in computers back home. It's based on a numbering system we call Binary, or Base 2, where you only have two digits, zero and one, rather than ten as we normally use for counting on our fingers, which runs zero through to nine as the single digits."

"All right, and how does this add up to sixteen?"

"When you count, you normally start with one and go from there, then roll over to a two-digit number at ten and begin again with the lowest digit at zero. Technically, we can say the higher digits are present, only counted as zeros, and we don't usually include them until they bump up to one or more."

"Uh huh... And with this other one?"

"Same idea, but instead of ten digits, you only have the two, so it goes more like zero, one, ten, eleven, and so on. We can convert this to decimal with a little math, and get a number we're more familiar with. But a four-digit binary number gives a total of sixteen combinations. You simply multiply each switch with two possible positions, either on or off, four times over."

"Hmm, that's a clever one. Math wasn't one of my biggest thrills, but I guess I'm going to get hit by it one of these days, so I should make myself ready for it."

"We can also say to raise two to the fourth exponent, in case you should ever take something like algebra."

"Aye, fine, but for now, I just want to open a bleedin' door."

Kaliya looks over at Aerlie and sees a broad grin spreading across her face.

"Very good, Kaliya," she accedes. "Your skills in this area tend to stand out. But keep in mind, this is intended to be a tricky puzzle, and we should not be overconfident."

"Yeah, overconfident," she declares sarcastically. "Spoken by someone who trains people to sit still while you blast the place with an antimatter device, and they call it a little house cleaning," she chuckles. "All right, but at this point, I might suggest, if it's not too many combinations, we simply try it by brute force and see what we get out of it."

"All right, give it a try and see."

"Relissa… Here, follow me and I'll demonstrate what I mean. Let's put them all up, which equates to all zeroes for our purpose."

They arrange the levers and Kaliya helps the bewildered elf pull the switches in a binary progression. First, the one on the right, then returning it up and pulling the next one, followed by that plus the first one, then both up and the third one down, followed by the sequence of the previous two. Lastly was all up and continuing to the fourth one, followed by repeating the earlier sequencing.

All the while they were pulling the levers, they were taking note of the lenses and how they shined into the eyes of the statues, until one combination rotated a purple lens on one side and orange on the other side, which seemed to match the pommel gems.

"And there you have it," Marelle smiles. "Each golem has the right color pointed at it."

Haran studied the action and watched the turntables rotate to find the correct alignment of colors with the golems. But then an idea flashes into his mind.

"Wait a minute!" he urges. "I don't trust this."

"Uh oh… Why not?"

"It was too easy…too straightforward. If all it took was some number of systematic combinations, any halfwit could do that much. But if this path is guarded by a pair of stone golems that'll cut you in half, and then some, if you make one little mistake, I think this is a false positive to fool you."

He glances at Aerlie to check her opinion. She simply raised her brow inquisitively.

"Buggers to you, Haran," Relissa groans. "But aye, I might have to agree. Then, what do we do after this?"

He studies the levers, and the golems again, and then takes note of a series of symbols on the statue carved in the door. He notices two columns of four symbols. They appeared as a circle, a line, a chevron, and a triangle. In the first column, the chevron was overlaid with gold leaf. The second column showed the triangle the same way.

"Kaliya, do you see that?" he points at the door.

"Yeah, and it's about as much help as this lady leaning against the wall over here," she thumbs at their chaperone.

"Aye," Relissa grins. "Who wants to grab her and tickle the answer out of her, ay?"

They all share a round of laughter at the suggestion, including Aerlie.

"Now, now…this is a test," Aerlie reassures. "You've done well so far, but can you finish it? Haran, did you have an idea on something?"

"Yeah, we should be paying closer attention to these inscriptions," he chuckles. "But I'll tell you one thing, if you weren't supposed to be in here, you'd probably be in a lot of trouble on this door. Those symbols look like geometric enumerations to me. Kaliya, what do you think?"

"Yeah, you're right," she pauses to study the positions of the levers again. "And the values don't add up right for the way these levers are set."

"How do you mean?" Relissa asks.

"If you consider those symbols represent numbers for how many sides they have, a circle is often used to represent an empty set or a value of zero, the single line is obvious, the chevron is basically two lines, and a triangle has three sides."

"Great, so what is it we're talking about. The first one shows a two and the other one a three?"

Relissa studies the levers on the wall again. Haran also studies them, and begins counting privately on his fingers while mumbling to himself the binary values.

"Zero, one, ten, eleven," he examines his fingers. "Four digits, so zero to three…"

"Good, Haran," Kaliya affirms. "So, if we assume this is to mean we divide these levers into groups of two, we can fit the values into the groupings."

"But, like you said, this isn't right. We have down, down, down, up. If we're assuming up is zero and down is one, this is three and two. It's backwards as compared to the symbols."

"Those runes on the other door were upside-down," Marelle muses. "Could this be another reversal?"

"It could be, but I think not. Like I said, this seems too straightforward. Backwards or not, if this is a trap, they might make it seem this way as a convenience. I would suggest we try it according to those numbers, which show two and three. Let's change these levers and see how it looks."

"Just how bloody wicked do you have to make it for a bunch of Drow, anyway?" Relissa moans. "Do you think they would know how to count like this?"

"Probably not," Aerlie responds. "But the point was to make it so difficult for them that they would either give up at this moment and try leaving, or simply rush it."

"Um, my Lady," Marelle inquires nervously. "I noticed you used the words TRY leaving. That door back there closed behind us. Is there a way to open it from this side?"

"Yes, but it requires a magical key, which will allow it to open and disable the trap for as long as it stays ajar. As we came in, the sconces on the walls reset themselves, so the trap is set again. When leaving, one person needs to hold it open to keep the trap secure, while the rest pass through, and then hurry across before it closes again."

"Well, that's lovely. So, what is it you're actually saying if there were Drow in here?"

"The first trap could be fairly easily discovered by a clever Drow spy. So, for as much as Relissa can be proud of her efforts being a neophyte, a veteran could probably figure that one out quickly. But then we come to this door. Presumably, all the Drow would be inside here, and we certainly wouldn't want any of them leaving to tell our secrets to others. So, this entire hallway is essentially a death trap for them. Let's proceed and see if you can finish here, and then I'll explain the trick behind it."

"All right," Kaliya nods. "So, we need the first set as down and up, and the second set as down and down."

"And hope the down position is actually your value of one," Haran snickers.

"Well, let's try it and see what we get."

Relissa rearranges the levers, and the turntables rotate with a red light shining in the door carving's eyes while yellow shines at one eye in the left golem and blue at one eye on the right golem. As before, the door carving reflects the light to the opposing eyes in the golems.

"Interesting…" Marelle muses. "They're not the same anymore."

"Primary colors…" Kaliya mumbles softly.

"Huh?"

"Yeah! Primary colors!" she announces boldly. "I think Haran was right. The first one was a ruse to make you think you got it. But if this is a death trap, you certainly wouldn't want anyone to think they got it so easily. So, you use primary colors to combine into your target."

"'Ere now," Relissa yips. "Aye! I see it. So, you combine red and yellow to make orange, and with blue to make purple. Bloody tricky, I say!"

"I don't see any noteworthy changes, though," Marelle ushers tenderly.

"Part of the plan, I'll bet," Haran suggests. "If you have two possible scenarios, you don't want them to know which is correct. This might also explain those symbols. The last batch was upside-down, so you might think the most obvious solution here uses a backwards notation, therefore the coincidence of the numbering."

"Blast! I'm starting to feel sorry for those Drow. But wow! If this is what they teach around here, it would boggle anything we ever got back home!"

"I'm sure of it. But as for the real answer, while I feel confident we might have it, I'm not as eager to step out there without a little confirmation. My Lady, this is where you come in."

"All right," Aerlie responds. "At this moment, you have done as much as I could expect of you, and I will give you credit for it. There is a change, but it would not be outwardly apparent, and precisely for your reasoning, Haran. Remember what I said about this hallway serving as a kind of death trap for any potential Drow. Even if they got it by accident, they're not supposed to know about it. And it's not simply for the twisted nature of the puzzle. There's another reason we feel is important here."

"Would you like to help us understand that reason," Marelle asks. "Or is this only on the final exam?"

"First, recall that the Drow live underground, and so there is no sunlight. They live mostly in darkness with only fire, most often magical fire, and enchanted stones as illumination to see by. As such, they are very sensitive to light. Open sunlight would blind them. Even this light here would be painful in their eyes."

"I see, so they might not even want to tussle with it, I guess."

"This is one deterrent, and the use of light in this manner might be largely unknown to them, as there is so little in their native environment. They might choose to use mechanical traps, but not as likely to use light, as they tend not to care for it in the first place."

"If you're underground, you only have what's in your hand, I suppose. But now, what do we do? Is it safe to go through?"

"Yes, it is. Now, listen carefully and remember. This is only for guild members to know about. Relissa, try stepping through the light beams here."

Relissa gazes hesitantly into Aerlie's eyes. Aerlie simply nods and motions ahead. The girl takes a tenuous step forward, creeping up to the web of light. She tries to angle sideways to see if the light was still shining in the mirrors. It did appear so, and the disk at the bottom was still illuminated.

"Are you sure about this? I'd like to keep my head for at least a few more years."

"It's alright, go ahead."

Relissa takes a deep breath and makes a cautious leap of faith by stepping through the beams to the other side. She checks herself to see if she is still in one piece, then turns to look at the others.

"Right. Now what?"

"Here is how it works. The golems are only brought to life if someone breaks the light beams, but if the proper lights from above shine in their eyes, they are held back. However, they are held back only for as long as those lights shine in their eyes. And for this, you need to remember the door and the reflections coming out of it. Change that while someone is still stepping through the light beams, and you break the spell."

"Aye! I think I got it. So, everyone needs to come inside here first before we open the door, because once that swings open, the mirrors aren't shining at the golems anymore."

"Clever bunch of people!" Marelle muses softly.

"I have to admit," Haran considers. "I wouldn't want to be a Drow trying to navigate this hall."

"Indeed," Aerlie concludes. "And very well done. Now, everyone move forward, but be mindful of the light from above. Do not get in the way. That means you, Kaliya, as you are much taller than our usual visitor through here."

They step forward as a group, with Kaliya hunching low so as not to disturb the apparatus above her. When the last of them passes through the light beams, Aerlie reaches out to the carving and touches it. The door opens, and as described, the red light reflecting from its eyes is redirected elsewhere in the room as it moves.

"That's it, little guys," Relissa mumbles as she watches the door open. "You just stay nice and comfy there."

"Do those things respond to any verbal commands?" Haran wonders.

"They do, actually," Aerlie nods. "As a safety backup just in case the trap is triggered accidentally. But you need to be quick."

They move through the doorway as quickly as they can fit into it, coming into another segment of hallway that seems to lead around a curve. They follow it around, still descending a long flight of stairs that began at the top entrance.

"Just how deep are we going in here?" Haran wonders.

Aerlie directs them further without answering, only giving a pleasant smile.

"You pull her out of the Underdark only to bury her back in it again?" Relissa smirks.

"Not quite," Aerlie replies. "The Underdark is indeed very deep. We were simply trying to afford her substantial room in here. She likes big spaces."

"How big does she need?" Kaliya ponders. "The whole mountain?"

"Oh no, half of it will do," Aerlie giggles.

They come around to a small antechamber furnished with a bench and some pottery. A tapestry drapes down the back wall with the Order heraldry emblem on it depicting a shield fashioned of dragon wings with a dragon head bust on top, a set of weighing scales set above a hammer, and laurel vines held in the talons.

"Peeps," Relissa declares in a hushed voice as she studies the room. "I'm suddenly getting a crazy idea."

"Relissa," Haran offers. "At this moment, can I entice you to keep it to yourself? I'm already feeling claustrophobic, and I don't usually get that way."

They enter the room and Aerlie takes a seat on the bench, where she makes herself pleasingly comfortable.

"My Lady, are we resting here for a reason?" Haran inquires.

"I am. This is your visitation, not mine. I'm just the escort through the halls. You will continue through there and onto the ledge," she points at the archway on the other side of the room. "There you will find a gong. Use that to let her know you're here. She's probably in another chamber, so you'll need to announce yourselves."

Aerlie displays a flirtatious smile and pulls out a book from her handbag. The others exchange glances and hesitantly turn to face the archway leading out to the next room. One by one they pass through.

They enter a gigantic cavern and begin walking along a broad ledge that drops off sharply to the floor far below. Nearby is a ramp leading down to the floor, and on the far side of the ledge was a large ornate gong hanging within a wooden frame. Sitting next to it was a gilded hammer with a leather cushioned head resting on a stand.

They moved forward slowly, studying the size and dimensions of the massive space. It extended deep into the darkness and appeared to turn to the left. The roof of the cavern seemed sculpted, but it was so high, they could barely make out the details. The walls were carved with columns and buttresses, and set with small alcoves displaying statuaries and busts.

"Haran," Relissa whispers. "How's your claustrophobia working for you now?"

"I can't feel it anymore," he whimpers faintly. "My mind has gone numb trying to imagine what's around that corner."

They approached the gong. It was neatly polished and appeared made of gold, but more likely it was gold leaf over brass, as gongs most often are. It was suspended from a rosewood frame, also trimmed with gold.

"Who wants to do it?" Marelle asks tepidly.

"Um," Relissa pauses. "We all know I'm not the strongest amongst us, so…"

"Now there's an excuse if ever I heard one. All right, Haran, you're the man in the family."

"I just now recalled a little-known social tradition," he mumbles. "Within a family unit, it's considered bad form for second-born siblings to conduct announcements using such things as, oh, gongs and other instruments, when calling the attention of high-ranking officials."

Marelle turns an astonished glare at her younger brother as she tries to reconcile the abnormal revelation.

"Second-born? And just where did you hear that extraordinary verse?"

"Oh, it's an old tradition. I just happened to come across it once in our old library at the academy."

"Is that the same one so badly marred by the old Dean? I don't believe this. All right, Kaliya?"

"What about you, Marelle?" she replies. "That makes you the first-born, right?"

"Oh! That! Yeah, um, well, I'm not in uniform. So it's up to you, I guess," she smiles.

"Cu'Nar help us all… You people."

Kaliya steps up to the instrument and picks up the hammer in one hand. She then made a casual but firm swing at the large disk. Her strike causes it to let out a loud crashing sound.

"Jiggers, girl," Relissa yelps, but trying to keep her voice low. "Did you have to bang it so hard?"

"I didn't, I don't think. These things just tend to make a big noise."

The sound of the gong echoes off the walls from deeper within the cavern system. Kaliya turns to put the hammer back, and as she reaches to set it down, the group hears a low grumbling reverberate throughout the chamber. Their muscles freeze and their breath catches in their throats.

"Kaliya," Relissa whines. "Please tell me that was your stomach."

"Sorry, Relissa, it's too tied up in knots to do that right now."

"Haran?" Marelle moans.

"Yeah, Sis?"

"How good are you at fighting golems?"

"Not good enough, I'm afraid, but I wouldn't mind giving it a try."

They hear the clicking and scratching of something hard against stone, along with the heavy thumping of something exceedingly large moving through the chambers. The sound echoed out from the connecting corridor at the far end of the room.

"She really does need to trim those nails of hers," Marelle suggests coyly.

Relissa gingerly turns around to glare at the woman before turning back into the darkness ahead. She continued to listen as the thudding sounds approached.

At the far end of the great cavern, a massive head juts out from behind the corner, suspended high above the floor on a muscular neck. It pauses to angle around the corner and gazes directly at the visitors.

"Great cu'Nar above!" Kaliya gasps.

The head was adorned with rows of short spiky horns rimming the sides of the snout, and long twisted horns extending from roughly the temples upward and back along the crest. A set of prominent fangs could be seen, both upper and lower, at the forefront of the jaws, as well as rows of other teeth. The creature puffed a short blast from its nostrils and began to move again, emerging fully into view.

It plodded forward on four powerful legs, each equipped with long talon-like claws. On its back, just behind its shoulder blades and folded up neatly along its sides, were two enormous wings. And trailing behind was a long and equally impressive tail, studded with a row of spikes on the upper side. Most importantly, the entire creature was adorned with brightly shining silvery scales.

"Kaliya," Haran cries. "You were saying something about expecting her to be bigger. Is that big enough for you?"

"Yeah, that'll certainly do it."

The immense beast towered over them, filling the greater portion of the cavern with its bulk. It lumbered its way into the room and approached the ledge, looking down at the four petrified guests.

"Marelle," Relissa squeaks. "You got any more of those britches handy?"

"Sorry, no. They're all in the wash by now."

"Dear Gods," Haran screeches. "Now I know why she's addressed as The Silver."

"Oh, dear brother?" Marelle counters. "What was your first clue?"

"Well, yes, granted. But Sis, they identify themselves by the color of their scales. That's how they set themselves apart from the rest!"

"You mean there's a difference? That is, other than the simple color thing?"

"Yes, she's a Metallic. They're the good ones. Positive alignment, I believe. The others, the Chromatic, are the ones to watch out for."

"Haran," Kaliya yelps. "Is that what I think it is?"

"Yes, Kaliya, that's an actual, real live dragon! Perhaps the most powerful creature known to Man this side of the gods. And even the gods might take a second look if they ever saw one like this."

"And no doubt the reason for that heraldry symbol," Relissa adds. "The strength of the beast."

"Oh indeed! No wonder they're so unstoppable!"

Adalon stares down at her patrons from her fully upright posture, surveying them from well above the ledge. Her form fills most of the local space, from the floor below nearly to the roof, and further to extend almost as far as the corner passage behind her.

"Long ago and far away... Ssstolen Children led assstray... Found again by errant deedsss... And reunited with their ssseeds..."

"Oh look," Marelle whimpers. "She's making rhymes."

"Aye," Relissa replies. "Cute ones, too... And what's more, she's telling the story of us going to Therinë, I think."

"Yeah, was that one in her book, or did she hold it out special for us?"

"Ladies," Haran whispers. "Don't you think it might be a good idea for us to show our respect?"

"My knees are locked, Haran," Marelle notes nervously. "I can't move."

Haran reaches over to grab Marelle around the shoulders and help her down, gesturing imperatively at Relissa and Kaliya to do the same. They manage to come to a kneeling position and wait.

"You need not... Kneel here, Children," Adalon consoles. "You are my guesssts... Kindly relax yourssselves..."

"Our thanks, Grand Dame Adalon," Haran acquiesces.

"Haran," Relissa mutters. "Do you remember what I said about kissing up? Well, aye, kiss up all you like if it makes you happy."

"Yes, well, this is what Vonafel used, and some of my research in the libraries up there tells me this is the traditional way to address them."

"I'm just looking at her," Marelle remarks. "And I'm thinking we wouldn't even make a light snack. What does it take to feed something that big?"

"You could ask," Relissa offers. "But if it counts more than a small village, I don't want to hear about it."

"Actually..." Adalon replies. "I can enjoy... Many thingsss. But we Draconicsss... Tend to have... Our own food sssources... And we produce them... In a native realm... Outssside thisss plane..."

"Oh, um, well," Marelle falters. "Just for the sake of argument, what is it?"

"We tend to favor... Mossst of all... A sssort of bissscuit... That combinesss many elementsss... Both meat and vegetable... Into one easy package. It is ssso very... Convenient...."

"Really! Does it taste good?"

"Indeed it does... And there are... Many flavorsss..."

"But I'll bet those buggers have to be big to fill you up," Relissa adds.

"Naturally... Sssize is important... But we alssso have... Very ssslow digessstion... And an efficient metabolism... Ssso a little... Goes a long way..."

"Jiggers, the things you can learn around here."

"I have heard... Many thingsss... About you..." Adalon states. "They echo... Through the hallsss..."

"You can hear them all the way down here?" Marelle asks.

"Not ssspecifically... In thisss manner. Thaelyn and Aerlie... Share them with me..."

She glances in the direction of the alcove where Aerlie was peeking through the doorway.

"And I can alssso... Sssense the happeningsss... With a form of ssSight. For inssstance... Your passssage through the doorsss... Was very... Insssightful. You are good friendsss. Ssstay clossse... And you will find sssupport."

"Aye," Relissa answers. "We'll do that. From the looks of things, it works well for us. What about you? Do you ever come out to play?"

Adalon makes a rasping laugh that echoes through the cavern.

"Sssuch adorable little onesss. I am not as young... As I once wasss. And play for me... Is an ancient pleasure... That I can barely recall. Inssstead, I ssspend... Much of my time... Contemplating...

And perusing… The great mysssteries… Around me. There is much… On my mind…"

"That's a little like an understatement, isn't it?" Kaliya submits. "If you know we're all trying to decipher your prophecies, and that statement you made up there in the courtyard, you must be spending a lot of time watching this war, more than anything else."

"Very well… Thisss I mussst admit. It has been… A primary focusss… For a long while. But can you deny… It mussst draw… Ssso much… Of my attention?"

"I suppose not, but it does raise a lot of questions for your relationship with the Maker, the cu'Nar, and whatever else may be involved."

"Perhapsss it does… But these are quessstions… That mussst wait… Until later. Recall what I sssaid. The sssecrets will be revealed… When the circle closesss."

"All right, I guess that's just the way it has to be. Poor Vonafel, she tells us you must know a lot more than you're letting on, and I think that much becomes obvious by now, maybe even more than that."

"I am sure it does. And you would not be… The only onesss… To sssuggest thisss. But there is a reason… I mussst be… Ssso elusssive… As I mussst keep… To my own courssse…"

"How long does this date back?"

"Longer than… I would wish to remember…" she closes her eyes and turns away solemnly.

"Something bothers you," Marelle wonders. "Doesn't it. All these secrets of yours, you bottle them up, making all these prophecies as your only outlet, but you can't say anything until the very end."

"You are right. I have ssseen much… In my time. My visionsss show me… Many thingsss…. And not all of them… Are pleasant. I sssee the sssuffering… Of whole sssocieties… At the handsss… Of that creature. I hold… A deep loathing… For what he has done. But I alssso know… If we move too quickly… Thusss to reveal oursssselves… Along the way… He and his massster… May attempt… To flee again. And the circle we follow… Will ssstretch… For another eternity…"

"And that's clearly not an acceptable solution. Who among us might be around at that time to do anything about it? Except possibly the Estelar themselves."

"Thisss is correct... And who among... Any othersss... Might sssuffer in that time?"

"I don't even want to think about it."

"Nor do I..." she sighs. "But mine... Is the hardessst... And on multiple levelsss..."

Aerlie pulled herself around into view as she began to pass through the door. The others took notice, including Adalon, as the winged elf made a casual approach.

"And then we have you..." Adalon chuckles. "Did I not hear... The echoesss... Of your wordsss... Calling me... An old lizard?"

"Jiggers,'" Relissa yips. "Peeps, maybe we should move to the other side, just in case any fire comes out of her mouth."

"Actually," Aerlie notes teasingly. "In her case, as a Silver, it's ice, but I think I can handle it."

"And my paralyzing breath...?" Adalon jeers.

"That might be a little more difficult."

"Speaking of old lizards..." Kaliya blushes.

"And another jiggers!" Relissa moans. "I'm surrounded on both sides."

"Yeah, well..." she shrugs. "Adalon, I feel it's important I say this. On behalf of my people, I want to offer our most humble thanks for the junior school on Ruuki uy'Daan. That must've involved you and the Maker, I just know it."

"Thisss is true ..." she nods. "I will not allow... Darumon... To take any more from usss... If it is within... My power... To do ssso. His deviousss nature... Has already taken... Too much..."

"Grand Dame," Haran considers. "If I may, I am trying to associate with my teachings. Would you be considered a Wyrm by now?"

"You do not need... To addressss me... In sssuch formal repose. I tend to prefer... The casual appeal..."

"Aye, Haran," Relissa gripes. "I think maybe you can reel in the kissing up part. It's getting a bit too mushy."

Adalon lets out another laugh.

"Many might demand... Sssuch formalitiesss... But I alwaysss held... A different perssspective... With what I regard... As my Children. But in anssswer to you... By my yearsss... I would in fact be... A Great Wyrm! By thisss time... I am at... My finessst form..."

"Gracious, such magnificence, to be able to look upon you so closely."

"Haran," Relissa groans. "Did you get my bit on kissing up?"

"But seriously, Relissa, would you ever have expected to see a dragon, at any stage of their development, to say nothing of the highest level, and certainly at this close range."

"And not be inside of it? Aye, I guess I have to agree with you on that."

Adalon gazed down at the witty young dark elf and smiled, at least as much as a dragon could smile for all the stiff scales.

"I can sssee... Why Thaelyn... Has his eye on you... Young Morier. You are a charming companion..."

Relissa looked up at her and felt a warm snuggly sensation come over her. To make an impression on something this powerful was a sure accomplishment.

Kaliya gazed at the magnificent creature as they carried their conversation. She was fascinated by it, at least as much for the unimaginable size, as for the unfathomable power it must hold. And as she studied it, she felt a strange craving come into her.

"You're all probably going to think I'm crazy with this," she offers tenderly. "But Adalon... Would you allow me to...touch you?"

The group gawks at Kaliya, trying to gauge her sanity, but she can only shrug and look up at the huge creature.

"Well," she adds. "How many of you people ever placed a hand on something like this before?"

"Buggers to you even for thinking about it," Relissa moans.

"How amusing..." Adalon retorts curiously. "Do you now...

Feel ssso bold… Tall One?" she responds with resounding laughter. "I remember once… A conversssation… About jumping on the backsss… Of dragonsss…" she glances at Aerlie.

"Um…" Kaliya follows her direction. "Yeah…" she titters.

"Very well… But be aware… Of the ssspines. Though you are sssmall… They can ssstill be… Abrasssive…."

She turns her head and lowers it to the ledge within easy reach of the group. They step in close and reach out to her.

Aerlie held back to observe the exchange, allowing the young attendants to make their close contact. She smiled fondly at the affectionate moment.

"Now you understand," she mentions softly. "This is who we are in this world. This is what gives us our strength, and the reason we might even challenge the gods themselves if they should stand in the way of what is right."

"Even the Estelar?" Kaliya wonders.

"Fortunately, the Estelar are already generally well-behaved, although I suppose there might be a few here and there that need watching. But for any others out there who would pretend to be gods…" she shrugs.

Kaliya returns to Adalon, examining some of the spikes along her snout, and then the scales, laying her hand on the smooth surface. She slides her hand in a small circle. It feels solid and very hard. She tries tapping it with her fingers.

"Haran, check these scales. They're rock solid. I'll bet you could pound them with a hammer and not even make a scratch."

"Aye," Relissa agrees. "Why don't you try it and see how she feels about it, ay?"

"Yeah, thanks, but I think I may pass on that. Adalon, are all your scales like this?"

"Yesss… As we mature… They become… More resssilient. At my age… They are harder… Than mossst metalsss."

"That would make you an incredibly formidable opponent, against virtually anything."

"The Draconicsss are… A Guardian Race… Designed to

protect… Againssst many foesss… Of a sssimilarly durable… Or potent nature…"

"What is it you're protecting, and who are you protecting it from?"

"One of those was once this world," Haran notes.

"That's right."

"Ah…" Adalon responds. "Thisss is a mossst… Curiousss quessstion. Assside from that one… Example… The Draconicsss were created… By Maker Kuroku… And for reasonsss… She tendsss not to reveal. At leassst not… To the Child racesss… As thisss tendsss to run… Outsssside of their… Persssspective…"

Kaliya and the others now burst out laughing.

"Right. And I had to ask. We already know she's even worse than you for all the secrets."

"Indeed. And we cannot allow it… To passss ssso easily…" she chuckles.

"Well, whatever the reason, I can't imagine anything that could possibly stand up to something like you. In all the nether-space, even Sarg…" her voice abruptly halts as the thought ticks once over. "Oh dear cu'Nar…"

Kaliya suddenly gets a flash in her mind. A cold chill runs through her, and she gapes at the idea.

"What is it, Kaliya?" Haran asks warily.

"Silver wings…" she whispers quietly.

Kaliya steps back to take in the whole figure again, trying to judge size, mass, strength, and most importantly, color.

"Adalon…" she wheezes. "My father's prophecy, when Vengeance arrives on silver wings."

"Very good… Tall One. And for thisss… You should conssssult… With Thaelyn… In his new office…"

"Why, did something just change?"

"Thisss moment… Was another trigger. Now you musssst make… The asssociation… To your needsss…"

"Gods be blessed," Marelle moans. "You planned this, didn't you!" she huffs as she sets her hands on her hips.

Thaelyn and Kailen were still in their conference in their new office relating to the proposals of their future war plans.

"So, we'll need to design and build what sounds like a fairly substantial air force," Kailen considers. "But this won't be easy, first because we've never built combat aircraft, and second, we also need to consider the pilots. Some may be our people, while some may be yours, so the cockpit arrangement will need to be configurable to suit their needs."

"This may not be as bad as you suspect, Commander," Thaelyn suggests. "The seating can move to fit the leg space, and the consoles can be set on some manner of hinged bracket, motorized if need be, to make the entire assembly customizable for the pilot. The craft itself will likely be the most difficult to design, as it will need to be fast, maneuverable, and of course involve weapons."

"Are we speaking of weapons similar to what was used in the city, or more like our small pulse rifles?"

"Naturally, the size of the weapon will scale to the craft itself, in relation to the mounting points and power demands. And they will need to be potent enough to take down other aircraft, perhaps also ground vehicles and maybe some surface structures, for instance if we find ourselves up against strategic targets such as weapons platforms."

"This sounds like a serious operation, but considering we don't know what Darumon has been doing over there, I suppose I would have to agree."

"As for the type of weapons, I have a few ideas. We can borrow from the pulse plasma concept, but in our case, we will combine some of our arcanic technologies. In addition to this, I think I would make our weapons configurable to involve multiple modes of operation. Once upon a time, Aerlie and I developed a type of electromagnetic pulse we could use if Darumon and his Suuden-Aryku forces should ever try coming our way."

"I remember this," Padriyl interjects. "I recall my mother assisting in the testing of that technology out on the field at the research center."

"Correct, and it seemed effective enough on powered devices such as vehicles and other items. Now, if we use our arcanic technologies, we can combine this into one weapon, and the pilot would naturally need to be trained in mage studies to use it."

"That would be a sight to see," Kailen chuckles. "Combat pilot mages shooting pulse weapons and EMP bursts."

"Indeed, but I want to create something the Suuden-Aryku cannot so easily defend against. Our arcanic technologies would be perfect for this, since the Suuden'kai military demonstrated a severe lack of capacity to defend against us here during our engagements, and I want to maintain this image on Azgarén. We can then create a situation to disable some of their technology without causing any significant harm to the people. Perhaps we can convince them to back down sooner rather than later, regardless of those chips."

"That would be a very desirable outcome."

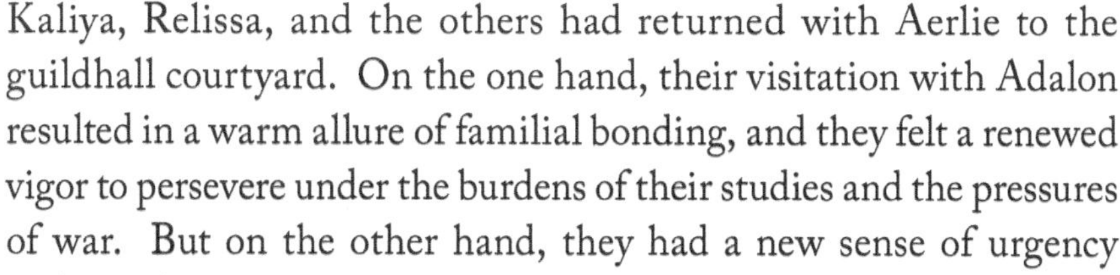

Kaliya, Relissa, and the others had returned with Aerlie to the guildhall courtyard. On the one hand, their visitation with Adalon resulted in a warm allure of familial bonding, and they felt a renewed vigor to persevere under the burdens of their studies and the pressures of war. But on the other hand, they had a new sense of urgency rushing through them.

"Watch Captain!" Aerlie shouts into the courtyard.

"Aye, my Lady!" he responds with a bow and struts over to meet her.

"Find a page and send him over to the Royal Archives to find Archivist Windsong. If she's present, send her to meet with us and Thaelyn in Rolsklinde."

"Is something amiss, my Lady?"

"We had a new prophecy event occur and we need to analyze it. I'm on my way there now."

"Right, then… I'll get on this promptly."

"And tell her to leave that mountain of books of hers behind," she smiles. "Only to bring Adalon's book…and maybe one notebook if she must."

Aerlie now leads her delegation out of the courtyard and down to the local Gateway link. They follow the network to the hub station first, and from there, they hired a VIP coach for the new custom transit to Therinë. On their arrival in the upper plaza district, they all step out and Kaliya turns to examine the neatly adorned transport.

"I swear! Riding a wheeled vehicle through a hyperdimensional conduit. What'll they think of next."

Thaelyn and his officers were just finishing up their earlier meeting.

"And therefore, Commander," he continues. "We should begin training our pilots as soon as possible, on your side as well as mine, and this means we need to devise our plans for the strike craft quickly. Lieutenant, I will have you pass the word along to the research team to begin some manner of design work. Not only do we need the final product, but we also need training facilities. And I have one particular young lady in mind that we should start with, to whom I once promised this opportunity."

"And I think I know which one," he smiles.

Aerlie and the others marched across the plaza and into the new military building, then through the doors and along the hallways to the meeting room.

"Thaelyn!" she calls. "We have something."

Thaelyn and the others all perked up at the sudden arrival of Aerlie's entourage. They each turned to see the arriving group of determined bodies entering the room.

"Aerlie, what is it? You look like something serious has occurred."

"Adalon…she's playing her games on us again. I've called for Vonafel to join us, so we should give her a moment to arrive, but we were meeting with Adalon in her chambers, and she mentioned the meeting invoked some kind of trigger event."

"Indeed!" he intones ardently. "That, in itself, is a curious statement. Are we again speaking of her books and those missing elements? Aerlie, this represents a form of craft I have only seen on a few rare occasions in such places as Sigil and other regions of the Outer Planes. It is not a simple encryption enchantment we speak of here."

"What do you mean?" Kailen wonders.

"Commander, when speaking of using an arcanic cypher on a body of text, like on a page, there are different methods one can choose from. The simplest, and therefore the most common, is to encrypt it based on a word, or perhaps a simple phrase…or maybe if to bring forward a special object which will allow it to be revealed. Another method is to expose it to some environmental condition, like a special form of light, such as moonlight during a seasonal event."

"I swear," he chuckles. "If ever the day should come when I can understand any part of this,"

"Yes, I know, and this does carry some peculiar elements. But to create a situation where such text is revealed by some external factor not otherwise under the direct control of the one handling it, requires a very complex and precise application of not only arcanic energies, but of a mental perception of the event, somehow encoded into the enchantment. Relissa, do you recall our visit to Sigil where I was explaining to you that statue in the museum of the fellow who was so well known for his curses, he cursed himself to stone, but could be released if someone were to speak his name?"

"Aye," she nods. "And jiggers, just to think of something like that, and how it might be applied. So, someone comes along, speaks his name, he comes to life, but according to you, he's not a nice guy to deal with, so the guy standing there might not be a happy bugger by the end of the day."

"Now, if to consider such an application, where the wording would need to involve such elements that it could be invoked into existence on the occasion of some event to occur, whether in or out of sight of the one who originally wrote it," he sighs and shakes his head. "Suddenly, my appreciation of Adalon's skills has risen considerably. I must ask myself where she learned of this and why she would go to so much effort."

"My Lord," the General considers. "If she went to such an effort as this, her involvement in these affairs must be regarded by someone to hold critical importance, and this simply brings me back to Maker Kuroku. Could she have been given special instruction at some moment?"

"This is very likely, I should think. And all the more reason for us to pay close attention to these upcoming quatrains as they reveal themselves."

Vonafel was just arriving outside through the local Gateway link. On this occasion, she was carrying only two books, one of which was rather hefty regardless, and the other a simple notebook. Once she gained her bearings on the local sights, she rushed across to the new military building and hurried inside.

"My Lord? Aerlie!" she announces as she arrives.

"Vonafel," Thaelyn waves for her to join the group. "I am going to make a small assumption here and suggest you have something new to share with us."

"Yes! When Aerlie's page came storming through the door of my office, I turned immediately to my copy of Adalon's book. I keep it open and propped up on a stand so I can watch in case anything happens. Then the page comes in and tells me I'm needed."

"Did you take notice of anything occurring?"

"Not at first, as I had the pages open to what should be the next in the present-day sequence, at least for how I'm interpreting them to be written. So, I decided to browse the rest of it...we only have another couple of pages by now. It was on that last page. You remember...the one I told you about that was empty."

"All right, now, before we delve into this, I would like to build a picture of how these are occurring. Adalon is using a most unusual form of encryption here that involves external events to invoke these reactions. Aerlie, you said she mentioned some sort of trigger. What was it?"

"It was Kaliya, I think," she responds.

"Do I need to put down another mark on my list for her?" he grins.

"Well, maybe a small one," she smirks. "After all, she wanted to make physical contact for the mere feel of it."

Thaelyn raised his brow at the unorthodox mention.

"Uh huh..." he moans uncertainly. "She wanted to touch her. How curious. Were her horns still attached at this moment?"

"Actually, I think I saw them running off as Adalon peeked around the corner into the audience chamber."

"Naturally..." he shakes his head.

"Oh, you people," Kaliya grins. "You're having too much fun with our terms."

Thaelyn and the General both share a laugh, which was quickly joined by Aerlie and her group, and followed by a cautious contribution by Kailen and Padriyl.

"Kaliya," Aerlie continues. "Tell him what happened."

"Right, put me in the spotlight here," she smiles and steps forward. "We went down there to meet with Adalon, and as we were talking, I came to a sudden realization. Kailen, I think I finally know what Vengeance is."

"Vengeance?" he wonders. "Kaliya, if we look back on some of your previous escapades in life..." he smiles tenderly.

"Oh you!" she snaps and gently palm-slaps him on the side of his head. "You dull-horned galoot, I'm talking about Father's vision."

Kailen smiles back at her as he recoils from the playful strike.

"His vision! Wait, um... Vengeance...on silver wings, right?"

"Gods above..." Vonafel gasps and peeks inside her book.

"Just what are we speaking of here?" Thaelyn asks. "I recall this from your earlier recital, but we were thinking this to be some kind of metaphor."

"Yeah," Kaliya responds. "But in this case, I think it's literal."

"Kaliya," Kailen inquires. "How do you mean this? What are these silver wings?"

"Adalon…"

"All right, you just lost me. Why her?"

"She's a Draconic."

"A…Draconic… Um, wait, I think I've heard that word pass by once or twice in our language studies, but help me to understand, what is a Draconic?"

"Imagine a creature that might resemble something reptilian, but my understanding is they're not true reptiles. I think we might better describe them as a saurian species of lukewarm-blooded egg-layers that form communities and actually nurture their young."

"As opposed to many reptiles that tend to be solitary, where they lay their eggs and then walk away from it?"

"Right. Anyway, this is a quadruped with huge wings and a long spiny tail, covered in scales so tough, you might need a plasma torch to get through them. Then with long sharp teeth and claws, pure muscle from head to toe, and finally, scaled up to the size of a five-story office building. That's a Draconic."

Both Kailen and Padriyl reeled back from the depiction. Their faces were aghast at the horrific imagery.

"Cu'Nar's eyes, Kaliya, and where were you at this time?"

"You mean, in relation to her? Well, under…looking up…and trembling…" she giggles. "Beyond that, we were inside that mountain behind the guildhall. She makes her home down there. They're a race said to live mostly in the Outer Planes, but apparently, from what I've heard, some of them have been known to take up residency on Tae'Eladar. She is a very notable example of this for these prophecies of hers. And she's silver in color, just like the metal."

"Suddenly, I'm a little unsure if I want to be present when that 'vengeance' actually arrives, silver wings or otherwise. All right, so what actually happened, and why do you think it's her, other than for the clearly imposing image she seems to represent."

"Kailen, I was so close, I actually touched her. I laid my hand right against her. Her body radiated with strength. To feel that kind of power is indescribable. I doubt there is any force in existence that could oppose one of those creatures. So, if the mention of silver wings holds any meaning, I think she's going to be involved. She told us their kind are guardians of some sort, and something like this might actually qualify, as she would certainly compare to whatever Sargeras might represent as a combatant. Then, when we were speaking, she also mentioned seeing so many things in her visions, and loathing Darumon for all he's done to so many, not simply us. And when I made this association, she told me to come here and speak to the rest of you to find what this association actually does."

"And so," Thaelyn considers. "This trigger event would represent your revelation. Such a fascinating method she is using. Very well, Vonafel, what do you have?"

"My Lord," she emits tenderly. "If you will indulge me for a moment. Kaliya, do you recall that meeting in the courtyard when she gave us those other quatrains, and this apparently reflected on your father's words."

"Yes, I do," she admits. "Only her words are much more elegant than what he got out of that vision of his."

"Well, all right, but aside from that, can you give me his words as a reference. I would like to compare what she passed through these cu'Nar versus what she's saying here."

"All right, let's see. What he actually wrote down went like this. From a circle of light, he shall come; the Divine Justice, One divided by Two."

"All right, one moment... This would fit nicely with this first quatrain revealed to us earlier. From out a shimmering door of light, the Divine One will emerge; where One is lent by Two divide, and to wickedness a dirge. Only his words didn't involve that last part, it would seem."

"Not directly, but his next words might offer something. He followed with: In his hands he carries, the Power of Infernal Destruction, and the Power of Blessed Life. Evil will crumble under the weight of his majesty. Do you think that holds any relevance?"

"I don't see any specific mention of these powers. But that last part, with evil crumbling, might associate with the wickedness, so this could anchor us to this section here between the tide of vulgar manners flowing, and the battered home of forlorn souls."

"So, in this case," Thaelyn interjects. "She added something into the cu'Nar's message that was not necessarily part of her original writings?"

"My Lord," Haran notes. "I recall that first day where you laid all the hells upon the land. And then where I was speaking to Kaliya about the sequencing of it. I might guess this was involved as a clue to her that you were the answer to THEIR prophecy come to save the day."

"Yes," Kaliya affirms. "A statement... I was there, I saw it. If I didn't know anything else about you or how you might associate to these visions, I wouldn't have any other way to know what I was looking at other than to see you wreck the place and then put it back together again."

"Ah! Very good," Thaelyn nods. "To witness the event... You are not a religious society, and neither do you understand magic. Therefore...of course! Empirical evidence, to demonstrate a point. You are a society of thinkers, and this would nail home the idea of who I am in association to Velen's visions, so you would know what relationship we might have together."

"I swear," Kailen relents. "This is enough to tangle one's tail after a while."

"I suppose it is. But now, what about the next part?"

"The next quatrain she offered must be Kaliya and her gift," Vonafel offers. "This is next in line after the battered homes. The Child who once upheld a gift, of mystery explore; lost it is, but found again, upon this lonely shore. We're suggesting this is the discovery of Kaliya and her gift during your meeting, possibly also as the result of her test."

"Very good, this follows nicely."

"As for this one..." Kaliya surmises. "All we have on our side is Velen's next line, and it was simply to say a Child would find its gift."

"That's all he said about it?" Vonafel asks.

"Yeah, by this time, his visions were fading too badly to recall anything clearly."

"Wow, that's not good. And what came after that?"

"Let's see. He continued with the Lost being found…"

"Lost being found…this must be the next one, which comes after the unwanted minds meeting. The weary wept and lost removed, their innocence defiled; until the Child with Gift restored, unites the Ones Exiled."

"The people on Ruuki uy'Daan…"

"I'm wondering about that innocence defiled," Marelle submits. "What sort of innocence are we talking about here?"

"Innocence…" Thaelyn muses. "Maybe of youth. Children, young and impressionable… Yes, perhaps. And living such a pleasant existence in that world, until the horror of battle robbed them of everything they once held dear."

"Yeah, that would surely defile something."

"Finally," Kaliya concludes. "His last words, which probably don't hold a lot of clear meaning at all, go like this: The Sundered will be restored, as Vengeance arrives on silver wings."

"And here we have the silver wings," Vonafel smiles. "All right, I can't say what that first part is, but this last part falls well after the present moment. We're on that last page, and I am going to guess it represents an event at or around the final moments, or as Adalon likes to call it, the closing of this circle."

Vonafel turns to the latest passage and prepares to read it.

"The Forgotten One, whose guile intrigued, so many brought to mind; shall meet his match on field of play, with Silver Wings aligned."

"Powers behold," Thaelyn wheezes. "She WILL be involved. It must be."

"Then she represents much more than a messenger," the General suggests. "She holds an active role in all this."

"Guile intrigued, many brought to mind, meeting his match…" Kaliya ponders. "You know, if we look at Velen's first part, this could relate to the sundered being restored, the undoing of all his intrigues on Azgarén. We're going to rescue them. But probably in a planned sequence relative to how he laid it down initially."

"This is a fine piece of deduction," Thaelyn nods. "And I suspect it might involve a fair amount of effort to see it through. But then, we have a field of play. This is an interesting depiction. Are we using a metaphor here, or is there a meaning to it, such as a battlefield of some sort? But if this is the case, she must join us there somehow."

"For this point," the General concedes. "I might suggest this is the reason we are given this passage at this moment in time. It could be one of those puzzle pieces we need to prepare and have ready."

"Indeed, General, and this would certainly require some planning."

"How do you bring something like that to another world?" Marelle wonders. "I seriously doubt you could just load her up in a buggy and wheel her around," she chuckles.

"No, hardly that, to be sure. And Azgarén, if this is our destination, is another world located in another universe. We will need a ship…" his mind suddenly drifts off and he sighs deeply and grins. "Oh… That old soft scale, she is indeed a clever one."

"My Lord?" the General smiles gently. "Do we have something?"

"General, if it could ever be said that we are being directed by a higher Power, whether it be a divine one or just an old lizard, this sequence of events just seems a little too convenient. We were only now speaking of designing a new array of military vessels. Granted, of combat design, but here we have Adalon provoking her meeting, and unleashing this event upon us that we now need to consider something new…a transport vessel."

"A transport," Kailen considers. "But to haul around something the size of a five-story office building?" he winces.

"Oh, surely, Commander, this will require something special. If we were to analyze this a moment, I know from my own experience that the Draconics do have an innate ability to transport themselves around the local planes, as well as to project avatars on occasion. But here we are speaking of a world in another dimensional fold, and a barren one at that. If we suggest this to be normally outside their convenient reach, and especially without the dynamistic flows to aid them with a return, then we need an external means."

"All right, so far, I'm following you. But how do we load up a five-story office building inside a cargo transport?"

"I doubt it would go inside, so we must improvise. I am currently developing a vision of a possible answer. Consider this…"

Thaelyn begins gesturing with his hands for the others to follow.

"We must build a vessel of an appropriately sufficient size, perhaps as much or greater than she is by lateral dimensions. This vessel would employ perhaps a type of armature along the sides as a grappling device to lift up an external object from ground level within a suspensor bubble. We actually have a mage spell we could borrow from which allows us to encapsulate a body within such a field, and this encloses it sufficiently enough that it is protected from any outside environment. This might do well for us if we employ any amount of space travel, as I am sure we must in this case."

"Dear cu'Nar," Padriyl moans. "And you people are only Early Industrial. My mother is going to lose her horns again."

"Does she still have any left?" Kailen adds amusedly.

"The bubble will encapsulate the body," Thaelyn resumes. "And the controlling beam emitters will lift it up inside this grappling cage, thereby locking it in place. From there, the ship may travel normally to its final destination, where you will simply release your cargo into the new environment."

"And um…" Kailen coughs emphatically. "Just how is this ship supposed to travel anywhere while carrying a five-story office building worth of mass under it?"

"Oh, but Commander," he smiles mischievously. "We should not worry about that, as the five-story office building, in this case, will have no mass at all inside that bubble."

"All right, come on you little stub-tail, do as you're told."

"Ankhia, with all due respect, do we actually know what we're doing here?"

"The cybernetic interface has a signaling scheme where an external controller can recode the patterns for the viral genome configuration. According to the last set of scans we made, the identification strands within the virus's nucleus matched up with the alien genetic structure, as opposed to the human pattern it had before. So, if I'm reading these instructions correctly, it ought to work."

"And how long do you think before we have a result?"

"I don't know, Likha, but I'm going to make a guess based on the progression of the virus on that human patient we had in here once. She was infected, and apparently within only a few weeks, she was dead. I'm actually amazed she survived even that long, for all the damage in there. Now, if we consider how much was in that implant, and make some calculations using the specimens we have in storage to multiply the effect, factoring in the size and volume of this entity as compared to a human brain... Well, I'm trying to be conservative here with Banni, so we'll aim for maybe a month."

"Meanwhile, we need to make daily scans and measurements to see how it progresses."

"Right, I want reports on all the bio-indicators to see if the organism is reacting to it, and once it does die, to see if it takes any of the body components with it."

"Yeah, that would be a little counterproductive to our cause."

Ankhia had been spending the last several weeks pouring over the holo-disks and working with engineers to design the new equipment needed to access the cybernetic attachment to the virus she was researching from the implant used on the humans of Rolsklinde. She had managed to recreate the technology interface, and isolate the signaling patterns to reprogram the device using the genetic coding of the alien organism in the biotech seed. Now she was ready to test it.

She had a sample of her altered viral entity loaded up in a hypo-spray vial ready to be applied to the simulant in their specimen tank. She lowered a manipulator arm into the tank with the hypo-spray attachment and applied the serum to the skin of the simulant, rather than directly into the organism, since it tends to react badly to direct interaction.

"This should find its way through the local blood stream," she states.

"Like it did with the human female," Likha responds.

"Right, and now it's just a matter of time. From here, we'll monitor the situation and hope nothing crazy happens."

Chapter 8

OUTPATIENT

"Cap-in, Ankhia talk today?"

"No word yet, Madam Nazég, but I'm hoping to receive an update soon on her progress."

"Wait…more wait… Kali say wait. Ankhia say wait. Cap-in say wait. Me try. Me not good wait long time."

"Is that thing bothering you today?"

Tyanna was visiting the Sentinels HQ on Ruuki uy'Daan. The building had been partially refurbished over the last several months since Kaliya brokered the deal with the orcs. Much of the debris had been cleared, and many of the computer consoles and other pieces of equipment had either been repaired or replaced, in part from the efforts of Sulíma and the other Daanen'kai students taking up engineering studies, and partly from the efforts of the new industry appearing near the Naarg uy'Sodrad on Therinë.

By this time, the mutation victims were a regular sight, coming and going with their assignments, as best they could for the debilitating effect of the biotech organism they were afflicted with. They mostly assisted with the recent farming activity, as it was the easiest for them to attend.

Along with the Daanen'kai field workers, groups of orcs also participated in the efforts as a continued study to learn the trade in preparation for when they would be relocated. The initial introduction to the craft was a difficult step for the orcish warriors who were much more prone to the hunt. But combined with many of the females, who were also put to work, they learned the values of a communal effort to provide for the tribe.

Tyanna stood there in the office. She studied herself briefly, glancing over her misshapen arm and the growth covering her back. She winced at the sight of it each time she turned around.

"Cap-in," she replies in her typical broken language. "Me no like this. Cap-in understand, me want this out. Me wait…" she sighs heavily, "…me try wait. Me head not good, me want better."

"I understand, Madam Nazég," the Captain relents. "It hurts me to see you like this, and I'm sure it hurts a lot of others. I can't imagine what kind of monster would do this sort of thing to people."

"Kali say, Dar-mon make play with people," she shakes her head. "Me not understand. How make play like this."

"You're not the only one. It shocks all of us, I'm sure. If there was any way for me to help make it go faster, I would. But these things can't be rushed. You either do it fast, or you do it right. Sometimes you can't have both."

"Yes… Me come talk. Orcs go home today. Food taking all done outside. Now go to big house to make new food. Good to eat new food, me happy."

"I sometimes wonder what you and the others were using for food all this time. We all need to eat, but it's hard to imagine what might have been out there for you."

"Cap-in no ask. Not good me say. Me not want think of old food."

She shuffles around the room as she tries to compose her thoughts through the muddling effect of the entity dulling her natural intellect.

"Me not want think of old food, not want think of old days, orc attack, many things. Not help, me still think. Bad thinking stays, me think all time."

"I fully understand. We all have our bad memories…you, me, all of us. But we're all working together now. We'll get through it."

"Me happy Cap-in and other people help hurt-people. Me happy Kali people help. Me think, not long time, wait, go see. Me not like Kali go fight Sarg-us. Me sit, me wait, ask cu'Nar help people."

"That's about as much as any of us can do right now. From what I hear, those people are working up some big plans."

✦✦✦

"Your Lordship," Kailen announces as Thaelyn arrives in the strategy room in Rolsklinde. "Some of our people have been submitting ideas for possible aircraft designs. Our researchers are currently reviewing these for design correctness and plausibility, but I thought maybe you'd like to take a quick look to offer your ideas."

"Very good, Commander. And what about the training simulators and light aircraft?"

"The simulators are in the development stage as we speak. They're actually not too difficult for us. We're just borrowing from some template designs we've used before. The aircraft, which in this case are a standard pattern we use for scouting new worlds, should work well as trainers for our new pilots. We just need to tailor the new industry to fabricate the parts, and for this we need the right materials. So, between our industry and yours, we're now trying to bolster the material supplies."

"Excellent. I might also suggest we consider land-based assault vehicles, as well. Even if the Suuden-Aryku do not make extensive use of air defenses, they ought to have ground capabilities. We saw some of those during our time here, where they used troop transports."

"I already thought about this and dropped a few ideas on the heads of our research teams. We can probably put together some mobile armored vehicles easily enough, and if we're able to use this adamantium as armor plating, that should give us some good defense."

"Indeed, as well as some of those other technologies currently in production. I hear they are close to perfecting a defensive layer based on our Infinity Shield. This should make our people very hard to kill."

"Those Suuden-Aryku won't know what they're up against," he chuckles.

"The only question on my mind now, and one to which I will need to find a proper solution, is our supply for the flows."

"Oh great, that's right, Azgarén is in this barren fold, as you call it. Would any of this actually work over there?"

"It would need to carry a charge of some sort, this much is certain. We must then consider how to approach this. There are ways to store an arcanic charge of energy into a body, and we have experimented with a few ideas in the past. But since we live in an environment where we have this ambient source, it is difficult to test any of these ideas. Therefore, we might actually have to wait on that until we can find an appropriate moment to play with it. This means to find our way there and perhaps with enough time on our hands to test some of these ideas."

"That's cutting it a bit close, if you ask me."

"We may not have a choice in this case," Thaelyn accedes.

"All right, so then we just need to get our people in under the fence quietly enough so we can make our final plans and catch them off-guard."

"If we suggest this Suuden-Aryku base on Morndindor should have a conveyor, this is one possibility, but I suspect it opens up to a military base on the other side."

"That's not a good thing."

"Indeed, so I am going to place my trust in Adalon that she will reveal to us a little secret to help us infiltrate their world sight-unseen. I doubt she would carry us all this way simply to stumble on the last step."

"Absolutely."

"Of course, we still need to reach Ruuki uy'Daan, and then to examine that one conveyor. I do hope it leads us to where we want to be."

"How much longer before Kaliya can finish up her mage lessons?"

"She is midway through the school year and now entering the Fifth Circle classes. Another year after that, if all goes well, and we may be ready. I am simply trying to consider how we might do this now."

"What do you mean? You said she needs the Seventh Circle to mark a rune, right?"

"Yes, but in her projected form, I do not believe she will be able to perform this directly. To properly conduct a magical incantation, you need to be physical, using your mind and body together to channel the arcanic energies."

"Right, I think I recall this once. So, what do we need to do?"

"It will need to be conducted by means of a scroll, or some other external method, which will imbue the necessary energies within its own body. We have a few options available to us in our recent history for the technology we use. So we will need to conduct some tests to refine our technique. She will likely need some special apparatus to act as a focus, since her own body will not be available."

✦✦◆✦✦

"Ankhia! It's dead! And the best news…Banni is still alive…well, sort of. You know what I mean."

"In all the nether-space, it's about time! What were the last results before it let go?"

"Here, I have the charts on this data pad."

Ankhia studies the final results on the data pad. They had been waiting almost a full month for the biotech seed entity to weaken to the point where it could no longer sustain itself. Over the course of these past weeks, they had observed a progressive diminishing effect in the organism's tissues and apparent life functions, representing a loss of tissue integrity and producing a sagging effect as observed in the external portions of its body. This corresponded with a disruption of its control of the simulant's organs and tissues to the point that they were growing concerned that the failure of the organism might also take down the host body's life processes.

The death knell, as described in the results, showed a simple failure of the regulating processes with no significant reflexive reaction on the host body. This, as compared to what they discovered when they tried attacking it directly with a scalpel. At this moment, the body's natural biorhythms seemed to have resumed, and now the entity appeared to be retracting away from the various internal organs and shriveling up.

"Ankhia," Likha submits. "As I look at this, not only do I get shivers when I think of what it's doing in there, but now I'm thinking of it pulling away from the host and leaving all those holes behind, to say nothing of what's inside."

"You're right, of course. Now we need to see about removing it physically. And this won't be easy. That thing is everywhere. And we'll need to carry this through until that little tyrant is completely gone from the body. Let's go see what it looks like and what needs to be done to free Banni from its dastardly clutches."

"Ankhia, are you sure you're not becoming a little too attached to this idea of the name? I mean, I know I'm the one who originally named it, but you're treating it more like a boyfriend than I was."

"Don't worry, Likha, you can have him back once I'm finished with him," Ankhia grins. "Besides, our platform represents an analogy, as it stands for every one of those victims on Ruuki uy'Daan, and maybe a lot more after that. We're pioneering a new technology, or maybe an old technology reimagined, but it's new to us, and we need to be sure it works. A lot of people could be saved by it. So, naming our experiment makes perfect sense to me. Come on, let's go see what we've got."

✦✦✦✦

"Well, Kaliya, it's official," Haran laments. "You've passed me up."

"I'm sorry, Haran, I didn't mean to. I know how long you've struggled to study the mage craft, but with the schedule they put me on this year, I'm running two Circles back-to-back."

"It's alright, I'll catch up in time. Remember, I hope to run the full distance, so if you only go to the Eighth Circle, I'll be ahead of you again regardless," he grins.

"Well," she retorts with a modest laugh. "I won't hold it against you. But for now, I need to pay extra attention to my practice. Speaking of which, I need to get out there. They gave me some new scrolls to copy into my book, and now I need to try them out, as well as refine those from the previous set."

The two friends part ways as Kaliya ventures out of the academy into the lower mage training field. The field was set in a reserved area behind the mage academy, one of two fields for student practice. The lower field was designed for the lower classmen, while the upper field was located in a secluded area higher in the mountain range behind the guildhall. It was a much larger area, and far removed from the other structures, which afforded greater safety for the upper classmen to invoke the more powerful spells.

Kaliya passes through a short wrought-iron gate that marks the training field. She sees one of the Masters from the academy supervising the cadets in their exercises. The field was arranged in stalls, where each cadet took up his or her own position. During busy days, students might need to double-up, but today it was much calmer with a smaller gathering.

She gives a wave to the Master, clocking in with him to record her practice time. She then chooses an open stall located between several others.

The stall represented a long alley, where she stood at one end by a small table, and focused herself on a set of target dummies along its length. The dummies were lined up at different distances, depending on which spell a person might choose and what range it offered. She set her mage tome on the table, freshly inscribed with her new spells from her class assignment.

During their class lessons, the students would occasionally receive one or more spell scrolls to scribe into their tome. It was a practice learned as part of their early lessons in mage craft at the First Circle. The tome was their personal book of spells, and would typically include all the spells from the standard course, plus whatever they might involve for their school specialization.

In Kaliya's case, since she hadn't been directed to any special focus, her tome only included the standard spell groupings. Thaelyn had been promising to recommend her into a specialization, but so far, they were still studying her capabilities and unsure which course would suit her best. Their thoughts had been leaning towards elemental spells since she was essentially being trained in the offensive arts. To test this, she had been given a new spell as part of her initiation into the Fifth Circle...the fireball.

Kaliya took her stand near the table and lined herself up with the alley. She had to maintain her focus only on her target, not become distracted by the other students and their activities. The demands of discipline were becoming more intense with the higher Circles, and especially as she was being rushed through them.

She runs through a few of the simpler exercises as a kind of warm-up before trying any of the heftier spells. She works her way into the Fourth Circle, selecting a few prominent choices from her tome, targeting one or another of the dummies and letting go. The dummies were specially designed to be highly resistant to magical attacks, to give them extended longevity to the wear imposed on them by the students.

Then she turns the page in her book to the new set.

"Fireball..." she muses as she begins to visualize the formula.

As she studies the runes, images begin to flash through her mind of the attack in her home city on Ruuki uy'Daan. The orcs were seen throwing fireballs into buildings and at clusters of people. She recalled how she was running through the alleys as a child, trying to escape the madness, fleeing ahead of the advancing wave of orcish shamans and hoping to find refuge in the Naarg uy'Sodrad.

Explosions rocked the buildings. There were screams echoing through the streets. She remembered dashing around the corner of a civic building towards a line of Sentinels, only to see part of the line blasted by a fiery impact. Homes and office buildings were ablaze. The streets were pitted with craters. Bodies lay everywhere.

"Kaliya… Cease!" shouts a stern voice through the mayhem.

Kaliya is shaken out of her visions. Her training in the academy had conditioned her to instinctively check herself for any magical energies still forming in her hands, dismissing them to make her safe.

"Huh? What happened?"

"What happened?" asks the supervising Master. "I would wish to ask the same of you, Kaliya. You seemed to have drifted off there, and look at what you did."

He directs her to look out onto the field. The entire row of training dummies in her alley lay uprooted and smoldering, along with the two adjacent alleys. The other students had ducked for cover and were only now peeking out from behind walls and shrubs to see the carnage on the field.

"Oh dear cu'Nar, I'm terribly sorry, Master. I think the pressure on me from all these lessons, and this one spell, caused me to recall memories of my youth on Ruuki uy'Daan. The orcs used this spell on us, killing many of our people and destroying half the city, and now here I am using it."

"Perhaps you should avoid this spell?"

"It would be better if I tried harder to put my past behind me and focus more on the present, don't you think?"

"Indeed, it would. A good choice, Kaliya. But now, as I look out there on the field, I must consider another choice. Is this the first time you have ever used this spell?"

"Yes, I just got it in my lesson today."

"And already you blasted away everything within range. Your proficiency with the Art, young lady, is extraordinary. So much so, that I think it best for you, and the rest of us, if you were to continue your training in the upper field."

"But isn't that reserved for the advanced students?"

"Based on what I see out there, you are already in a class by yourself. This field is clearly too small for you, but the one up there will provide you enough space to blast away the tops of the mountains. We will have you relocate up there. As always, be aware of your strength, and I hope to hear you are better able to control these unfortunate outbreaks."

"Thank you, Master," she concedes, and packs up her things to move on.

✦✦◆✦✦

"Is that all of it, Ankhia?"

"I believe so, but I need to remind you, this example was easy compared to a live subject."

"Of course, especially since it has such a conveniently hinged chest cavity," Likha grins.

"What do the bio-monitors show?"

Likha glances quickly at a set of monitors displaying the statistics of the tissues and organs in their simulant.

"All nominal… I see heart and lung function at the prescribed rate, and everything else is functioning within parameters. Although, I should remind you, much of this is artificially regulated to begin with."

"Well, yes, but at least we don't have that awful necrotizing effect. And this horrible little monster is dead and buried."

"Now what do we do, Ankhia? The next step would be to use this on a live subject, right? That scares me a little. The entity may die and leave the organs living, but we couldn't test the reaction on the brain."

"I know. There were certain limitations in our study that couldn't be avoided. But I can't think of any other course except to take it to the next level, and that means we need a volunteer."

"One of the mutation victims…"

"We'll need to present this to Kailen, and then get Kaliya to deliver one of the victims to us so we can try it. And then pray to the cu'Nar, or even that new one, Oghma, that it works as advertised. Otherwise, it's been a long struggle for nothing."

Likha began the process of cleaning up, while Ankhia packed up her notes and a data pad with the reports and diagrams they had recorded over the course of this experiment, and prepared to leave for Rolsklinde to meet with Kailen.

Thaelyn was visiting the new parliament building, standing on an observation balcony overlooking the debates on the floor. The representative members were busy reviewing and voting on several recent issues concerning the appointment of new land for farming, the development of a forestry service, and the allocation of space for mining and heavy industry.

The parliament members involved all the major races in the kingdom. Some of them were from the local cities of Rolsklinde, Solinaia, and Kynesoth, while others were statesmen imported from Tae'Eladar. They deliberated the proposals, some offering suggestions for assigning certain regions as natural buffers and wildlife preserves, while others argued the high demands of the burgeoning local culture.

A page walks up to Thaelyn on the balcony. He taps on his shoulder gently and speaks in a low voice so as not to disturb the delegation below.

"My Lord, your presence is requested in the strategy room."

Thaelyn nods in acknowledgement, his eyes still on the activities of the floor below.

"Look at them," he remarks proudly. "We come to this world and find it in chaos, under siege by machinations beyond their comprehension."

The page turns to examine the political leaders in their debate.

"Aye, my Lord," he agrees. "That we did."

"And now, we see them empowered enough to take back their lives, rebuild their cities, establish law and civility, and discover a future filled with hope for themselves and their children. This will keep them for a long time."

"Let us hope so, my Lord, and with you guiding us most of all," the page concludes merrily.

Thaelyn and the page turn to exit the balcony and proceed around to the entrance, leaving the building and crossing the plaza back towards the military intelligence building. A sign was being lifted into place above the front doors. Thaelyn pauses to examine it.

"Watchmen Intelligence Center," he announces. "Our newest branch of the Order, to serve and protect the people of this world, may they know law, justice, and freedom."

"Aye, my Lord!" the page concurs proudly. "And a fine one it is."

They enter the building and make their way to the strategy room. There they find the usual assortment of officers, including Kailen and Padriyl, the General, and now Ankhia.

"My Lord," the General begins. "I hope we didn't disturb your little outing too deeply."

"It was a pleasant interlude, but work has a habit of bringing me back prematurely. It is the unfortunate condition of my station. What do we have? Med-tech, should I assume your presence holds some relevance?"

"Yes, Your Lordship, I have news. I've been presenting my report to Kailen here, but I also wanted to review it with you."

She sets the data pad on the table and pulls up the charts and recordings of her experiment as she begins her lecture.

"As you know, we were conducting our study of that biotech seed. Along the way, we created a test platform which we shall call Banni."

"Banni?"

"Yes, my lab assistant is actually the one who gave it a name. She's a lonely girl and apparently pretending this to be her new boyfriend."

"Dear Powers, Med-tech, I would not wish to be a Daanen'kai male if this is how you treat them."

Ankhia grins as she continues with her review.

"Anyway, Banni is essentially an assembly of cloned body parts arranged in a pseudo-form frame and wrapped with cloned dermal tissue."

"Sounds delightful… If I should ever need any replacements, I will be careful to stay clear of your lab," he chuckles.

"Oh, come now, Your Lordship. We had everything connected and working until we infected it with the seed."

"Until… And what occurred after?"

"Well, if you'll look at these images here," she replays the recordings of the initial infection. "You can see what followed. It's a gruesome process, and I shudder to think of this actually happening to our people."

"Ugh…" he grimaces. "Indeed, and I fully sympathize. That sort of trauma will not fade easily. But now, were you able to find any manner of solution to it?"

"Essentially yes, but with some small considerations."

"And those considerations are?"

"First, we had to relearn some old technology. Fortunately, those holo-disks Kaliya brought back from Ruuki uy'Daan were very helpful in piecing things back together. Your Lordship, I can't be sure who to point my finger at the most, the Suuden-Aryku or Darumon, but whoever it is that invented this thing has violated almost every rule of ethics I can imagine where our old medical practice was involved."

"Oh? In what way? That is, above and beyond everything else we have discovered about them."

"True, they've broken a lot of rules. It has to do with this little guy here…"

She pulls up the electron scan image of the virus from the Rolsklinde implants.

"How adorable," Thaelyn joshes. "And I see you gave it a little hat. Are we celebrating some special occasion here?"

"Cute, Your Lordship. This is the virus from the implants found here in the city. You remember, the ones that were causing the humans to die at age fifty or so."

"Indeed, but this does not look like a typical virus. Not that I am especially skilled in the medical arts, mind you, although Aerlie might find this of some interest. So, what is this attachment here?"

"Remember when I said I was getting an odd anomaly during my initial scans? Well, this is the reason. I was trying to scan it as an autonomous entity, as any virus or bacterium should be. But the computer, which would normally expect a functioning set of genetic material inside the nucleus, was coming up with an error for an incomplete set. We tried other methods, and finally just put a sample under a microscope and this is what we found. Our data indicated this odd piece to be a cybernetic attachment to the cell."

"A cybernetic virus?" he emits intriguingly. "Incredible! Med-tech, your technological standing, in my eyes, has just been elevated a few steps."

"I wish I could take credit, but this technology has actually been around for a couple hundred millennia back on Azgarén. It's called a Belvik Spore. It was once an invention that most people heralded as a type of wonder drug. The virus only contains part of its normal genetic coding, enough to provide its function to the host, but not to reproduce and grow out of control, and the attachment controls the coding. It's programmable, so whatever you need it to do, you just give it the instructions and let it go."

"What sort of uses did it serve?"

"It could be used for hormone infusion, micro-vaccines, and to supply medicinal therapy without the need for the patient to spend time in a medical ward. It could also be used to destroy diseased tissue that might otherwise be located in places too risky for surgery."

"That last part resembles what we had here in the city, but not nearly to such benign ends."

"You're right. Somebody took it and modified it, essentially to weaponize it, and used it by means of those implants."

"I am tempted to place this on Darumon, since this might play into his joy of abusing lesser creatures, but at the same time, I must also ask where he got it. There must be some sort of industry to produce these things."

"If he uses the same industry often," Padriyl suggests. "I wonder if it relates to where he found that pharmaceutical they were hoping to use on the old academy."

"Perhaps, so we should keep this in mind as a strategic target, at least to investigate, if not also to interfere with it somehow. But now, Med-tech, how does this apply to our other problem?"

"Very simply, we turned it around on them," she smirks. "I pulled up some of our old records, and brought in a crew of engineers to help me design the equipment necessary to make a link with the control interface on the nanotech chip. We learned the coding sequence well enough to reprogram it for the tissue patterns of our little friend here, and guess what? We killed it! Banni lives!" she cheers.

"Med-tech," he smiles. "While I will certainly congratulate you on your victory, I think you and your assistant should spend more time out in the fresh air. Well done. But now, to the next part..."

"Yes, but we still have a little problem."

"Oh no, a complication?"

"Well, it might not be a complication, but we are concerned about something. Banni represented an incomplete simulation of a body; in other words, no head, and therefore no brain tissue to be infected. We can't be entirely sure how the death of the entity will affect that, even though everything else was able to recover. In a living host, obviously this is an issue. My suspicion, based on my results here, suggests it will simply release control back to the natural rhythms. But without any actual data, this is only theory."

"I see your point, so what would be your suggestion? Do you consider yourself to be at that moment where you must apply this to a live subject?"

"I can't see it any other way," she sighs. "I've discussed this with Kailen, and we would like to call on Kaliya to go find us a volunteer."

"Very well. General, find us a page and send the word. Let us attend to this and be on with it."

A page is called up and given word to retrieve Kaliya. He hurries out of the building, through the city hub gate in the plaza, and along the network to the guildhall. He checks with the Watch Captain, who is still trying to maintain tabs on Kaliya's activity schedule, and is sent to the lower mage training field. As he arrives, he checks with the supervising Master in charge of the field.

"Master, I was told Corporal Nazég could be found here. Has she departed?"

"From here, yes, but you may find her at the upper fields."

"The upper fields? Has she been bumped in her class?"

"In a manner of speaking. She is still Fifth Circle, but her skills have developed to such extreme that I felt it would be safer for all of us if she practiced on the larger range."

"Really! Very well, I will search for her there. Thank you, Master."

The page continues around a walkway to a circular platform that serves as a local teleportation pad to the upper training field.

The upper fields were located at a significant distance, as measured on foot, from the rest of the guild. The platform served as a convenient shortcut, rather than to make the long hike up the stairs to the top of the mountain. He steps up on the pad and is whisked away to a similar one at his destination.

On arrival, he scans the area, observing several students from the upper classes of mage study practicing their most powerful spells. Earthquakes, lightning, fiery hail, and meteoric impacts shook the fields and left the terrain appearing as a charred and ash-covered wasteland. The local supervising Master glances at him inquisitively.

"Can I help you, page?" he asks.

"Aye, Master. I'm here to fetch Corporal Nazég. I'm told she might be found here."

"Yes, she is. Go there, around the path to the left, and continue along the way. She tends to stand out, so you should have no trouble finding her."

"Thank you, Master," the page offers with a bow.

He scurries off around the walkway, which in this region wrapped around the local mounds and gullies of the terrain. He sees Kaliya in the distance and rushes up to her.

"Corporal Nazég," he calls. "Your presence is requested in the strategy room at the WIC."

"WIC?"

"Aye, the new sign is up, so it's official now. The Watchmen Intelligence Center."

"Oh, in Rolsklinde? All right, do they need me projected or physical?"

"As I understand it, you'll be going to Ruuki uy'Daan again, so I suppose it might be best to go prepared."

"All right, thank you, page."

They leave the training field, with the page returning to the city and Kaliya to her favorite location to practice her Gift, which was a quiet conference room inside the guildhall.

Thaelyn and the others wait patiently in the strategy room, realizing the time requirements to deliver the message, and then for Kaliya to arrive. They engage in some secondary discussions over matters of the new industry and the rebuilding efforts, until the conversation is interrupted by the arrival of their tall messenger.

Kaliya steps into the room and marches up to the conference table, offering a salute on her arrival.

"Yes, my Lord. You requested me?"

"At ease, Kaliya," Thaelyn directs. "Our time has come, though with a bit of reluctance it would seem, to find ourselves a volunteer amongst the mutation victims on Ruuki uy'Daan. Med-tech Tad'vaal has developed what she believes to be our best hope at giving aid, but there is a small concern."

"A small concern?"

"Kaliya," Ankhia begins. "We have what we think is a counteragent, based on the viral entity used on the human population here once, but now serving our cause. My tests show it works, in a controlled setting on a simulated body, but that body was not a complete and fully formed host. So, there is a small question still plaguing us as to the effect on those body components not involved in our test, specifically the brain."

"What do you think it might do in this case?"

"If it functions in a living host the same as it did in our test, I expect it to simply let go and the body returns to its own control. But I can't do anything more with it in my lab. I need a volunteer from Ruuki uy'Daan for the next step."

"I see, and you want me to go over there and select someone?"

"I'm not sure how you might select someone, Kaliya. More likely you'll tell the Captain, and he can ask around. And then we need that person to come here so I can administer the serum."

"Got it. This sounds tricky."

"Yes, it's likely to be that way for our first run. From there, we can refine our technique, if need be."

"All right, I'll be back shortly with my results."

Kaliya places the image of Ruuki uy'Daan in her mind and vanishes from the local scene. She arrives outside the Sentinels HQ building, which has become her usual practice so as to avoid bumping into anyone who might be moving around inside the offices. She steps in through the doors to find the Captain.

It was early afternoon on Ruuki uy'Daan. The Captain was busy at his desk, a feeling which was familiar, but at the same time nostalgic. He recalled the days of his early career in the force and the routine law enforcement duties he would prescribe to his junior officers.

Sulíma had stopped in briefly after a lunch break to check in on the latest news in the city before returning to her work out at the mining camp. Tyanna was also present, having been given her own desk on one side of the office. Though debilitated, she still held a firm grasp of her duties and the affairs of the others. Her daily interaction with the Captain and the other refugees helped her strengthen her resolve, subtly rehabilitating her and allowing her to force her own will over that of the entity infesting her body.

Kaliya enters the room. Her arrival is quickly noticed by those in attendance.

"Kali!" Sulíma shouts. "Have you been ignoring me?" she pouts mockingly.

"No, Suli," Kaliya grins. "And I think you already know that, you little tail-puller."

Kaliya looks over to see her mother rising from her chair to meet them. She moves to intercept and offers a hug.

"Kali come back?" Tyanna asks.

"I'm here with some news. Ankhia is done with her work and is now looking for someone to come try her new antidote. We need a volunteer."

"Does this mean she finally found a way to kill this thing?" Sulíma wonders.

"Yes, but there's a catch…"

"Oh great, there's always one of those, isn't there?" she huffs.

"Yeah, unfortunately, but we're hoping it won't be a problem. And so, I've been sent to have someone come across so she can test it."

"What kind of catch is it you're talking about?" the Captain asks.

"Her simulation tested many of the organs and they all came out fine, but her example didn't involve a way to test the reaction on the brain. So far, it looks like the entity simply dies and lets everything go back to normal. But without a way to actually see this in a real body, that one little question remains unanswered."

"Is that so, but the overall result looks good enough to try on a real person?"

"She's up to that point and there's no other way but to do it."

"All right then, so we need to find someone willing to go to your world for this second stage of the trial."

"That probably shouldn't be too hard," Sulíma suggests. "I'd personally love to jump through, if the Captain would let go of my tail long enough," she flashes a wink at him.

"Young lady, need I remind you that I'm a married man, and one of these days I'll be jumping through myself. I'm sure my wife will have a few things to say about that."

"I'm just playing with you, Captain. You know me."

"Tyanna, do you understand so far?" the Captain inquires. "You're the one who usually manages the mutants. We need someone to go across and try this new medicine."

"Me think now... New med-cine kill thing inside? Yes, me happy hear this. Ankhia work long time, say med-cine kill thing? Yes, me want."

"Mother," Kaliya hesitates. "There's still some question on how it will affect you..."

"Me want. Me wait long time. Me head not think good. Me want better. No more this thing. Ankhia make med-cine, me take. Not ask other people, me take."

"Mother! Didn't you hear what I just said? We don't know what it can do to your head. Ankhia thinks it will die and you go back to normal, but we're not sure."

"Me understand, Kali. Ankhia think med-cine work, not have

other med-cine. Long time, Kali... Me hurt, hide in house, eat bad things. No more, Kali. Me take. Tell Ankhia, me take."

"Captain, can't you do something?"

"Kali, your mother has shown herself to be well enough in control to make decisions. I can't argue with her, she's certainly suffered long enough. And unless Ankhia can come up with another solution without any mysteries attached, someone has to do this, and I guess Tyanna is putting herself up as our new test subject rather than send someone else."

"Suli?"

"Sorry, Kali," the girl responds tenderly. "I have to agree with the Captain, your mother's a very strong woman, and I also know she's a stubborn one. I doubt I could change her mind."

"Cu'Nar's pity, you people are going to make me pull my horns out!" Kaliya sighs heavily. "All right, Mother, fine! If this is how you want it... We need you to jump through the conveyor. We'll pick you up on the other side and bring you to Ankhia."

"Me go to Ankhia?"

"Yes, she needs to see you in her lab to do this right."

Tyanna makes a cursory review of her deformity, frowning at the notion of being seen by the others.

"Me not want go. Not let people see me."

"Mother! Do you want this or not?" Kaliya asks sternly, with her patience over her mother's stubbornness now growing thin.

"Kali, look, me ugly. Not let other people see. Not let Father see. Not let Elder people see," she sighs despondently. "Kali ask Ankhia, bring med-cine here. I stay."

"Oh please, Mother, are you saying you don't want them to see you like this?"

"Yes, me say. Kali bring med-cine. Me take."

"I don't believe this! Now she's worried about her self-image."

"Well, Kali," the Captain offers. "I suppose a woman in her position does hold this privilege."

"In her position?" she shrieks. "She's my mother!"

"Yes, Kali," Tyanna offers soothingly. "Me mother of you. Me wife of Velen. Me teacher of big school. Me high of people. Me not want people see me ugly. Kali understand?"

"Cu'Nar give me strength," she relents grudgingly. "All right, Mother, you win. Let me go talk to Ankhia and see what she can offer. You wait here, I'll be back soon."

Kaliya vanishes instantly after finishing her statement. She reappears near the conference table in the strategy room with a prominent scowl on her face.

"Ah, Kaliya..." Thaelyn begins, then taking notice of her expression. "Is there something wrong?"

"Yes! My mother!" she blasts.

"Do we have a problem?"

"She's as stubborn as a pond cow!"

Thaelyn raises his brow in amusement at the suggestion, looking up at Kailen for his reaction. The tall officer looks away grinning and silently chuckling.

"Excuse me, Kaliya," the General intrudes. "What do you mean by that, exactly?"

"Sorry, General. I only know of this as an old expression. Our language seems to have a lot of those. A pond cow is an animal native to Azgarén. It's a type of mammal that's supposed to make its home in ponds and small lakes. Four-legged, bare skin, a bit on the plump side, loves water...a little too much, and has a reputation of resisting all efforts to pull it out."

"I see, and how does this relate to your mother, in this case?"

"She wants to be our first test subject, rather than send someone else."

"Ah, and you are offended that it's your mother rather than another person?"

"I...well, wait a minute. Let's put this into context. I know that question is necessary, if also a little unfair. Of course I'm worried, and not simply for her, but whoever it is that takes this since it's still kind of experimental. And yes, it does hit home for me as she's my mother and this gets personal. But that's not all. She doesn't want to come here and let everybody see her in this awful condition. She wants this as a sort of outpatient treatment on Ruuki uy'Daan."

"That sounds like our mother," Kailen admits ironically.

"But Kaliya," Ankhia argues. "I need her in my lab to study the effects it has on her. Did you explain this?"

"Yes, fully, and she understands, but she's adamant to stay on Ruuki uy'Daan, claiming she doesn't want Father, the Council, or anyone else to see her like this, her image is so tail-yanking important."

"Well isn't that just typical! I know she can be stubborn, but this is the height of it."

"Med-tech," Thaelyn offers. "Do we have any solutions to this? Clearly, if she is choosing to take this upon herself, and from what I hear, she is of sound enough mind to do so, then we must honor her wishes. If the only condition is that she remains on Ruuki uy'Daan, sight unseen by her peers, and whereas you need to make reports of her progress, can we assign someone locally to do so?"

"I suppose we could. I can rig up some bio-monitors that we could send over there and have someone take occasional readings on her status, feeding it back to me here for review. But I think I would make another request, just in case."

"And what might that be?"

"To either move that conveyor, or hook up another one locally, in the event of a medical emergency. If something bad happens, having them drag her all the way to the mines would use up precious moments. I want a conveyor set up right next door to the Sentinels HQ, and keep her close by under constant watch. I want daily...no, twice daily reports on her. I'll show those people who's in charge of the medical ward!"

Ankhia pulls out her trans-com and dials up a number. A pleasant female voice answers.

"Medical Ward, Intern Vuurti here..."

"Likha, it's me. We have ourselves a volunteer."

"Great, I'll get the lab ready for them."

"Actually, we have a little problem with that. It's Tyanna, and she doesn't want to come across for it."

"What? That's crazy! We need her here to study her reaction."

"I know, but she's worried about people seeing her in this condition."

"Oh, wonderful! Of all the times to worry about appearances! Fine, so what are we going to do about it?"

"First, put together a hypo-spray with our serum and deliver it to me here. We can at least get that much running while we work on the rest. Then we'll need some bio-monitors to send across so we can have someone over there do our work for us. Maybe I can get the Captain or my sister to help."

"All right, that shouldn't be too difficult. But what if something goes wrong?"

"We're going to tell them to set up a conveyor close by for emergencies, and hope we can react fast enough to bring her here."

"That's a little risky, but if this is all we have…"

"Oh, and while we're at it, let's bring out a field kit with artificial cardiac and respiration stimulators. We can deliver that in case something happens before we can react."

"Good idea. I'll be over in just a bit with the hypo-spray."

Ankhia puts away the trans-com and looks back up at Kaliya. The girl was still pouting, but not as badly.

"Don't worry, Kaliya, we'll do everything we can."

"How long do you think this will take?"

"The example with Banni took nearly a month."

"Banni?" she raises her brow.

Ankhia sighs as she needs to explain this once again.

"Yeah, Likha's new boyfriend. Since we're running a little short on males, we had to build one in the lab."

"Does he talk much? I just hate it when they start rambling," Kaliya grins mildly.

✦✦✦✦✦

"Tyanna, are you sure about this?" Sulíma asks. "Maybe someone else can go this time?"

"Me ask Suli, why other people, not me? Why not me?"

"Well, we all love you very much. What I mean is we love everyone. But you, well we go back a long time, and it feels different."

"Maybe Suli say. Maybe Suli think other thing."

"Like what?"

"Suli tell me, what you think? Why not me? Me wife of Velen? Me teacher in big school?"

"In other words, Suli," the Captain infers. "I think she understands the risk, but the rest of us are treating her different than the others."

"Sure we are. With all due respect to the others, no one is expendable here, but Tyanna is a little more important to some of us. I don't want that to sound wrong, but she is. Maybe to say, she's a high-ranking official, and that carries value. Did that sound right?"

"Suli," Tyanna continues. "Me understand. Me want help hurt-people. Me not want hurt more. Me take med-cine. Me think long time this. Me head not good, me try think. Thing inside not make me sick. Med-cine for sick people not help me. Thing inside not make hurt, not same hurt like go outside, fall down. Med-cine for hurt not help me. Suli understand?"

"Yes, this is different from simply being sick or going outside and falling down. It's a living entity that needs to be removed, or killed, or something."

"Ankhia make med-cine kill thing. Me take. Med-cine work, other people take."

"But Tyanna," she sighs tenuously. "What if it doesn't work, or maybe it hurts you more or, um, if it kills you?"

"Suli," she closes her eyes and sighs. "Me understand. Me afraid. Me think Ankhia try make good work. Me take, me wait. Me afraid. No tell Kali."

"All right, I won't tell her."

Kaliya returns outside the Sentinels building and once again steps through the doors to find the group waiting patiently.

"Mother," she announces. "And everyone else. Here's the deal.

We'll do this, but Ankhia is going to hang a lot of work on your horns during this time. First, I'll be delivering some monitoring equipment for you to watch her and record her progress. Ankhia will give you instructions on what, where, when, how, and why. Suli, Captain, this means you."

"That doesn't sound so bad," Sulíma offers. "I'm sure we can do that."

"In addition, we'll be sending an emergency kit with a heart and lung stimulator, in case her heart fails, or if she has difficulty breathing."

"That's a little more disturbing, but I suppose it's to be expected."

"And finally, we want you to set up a conveyor just outside this building for emergency evac should something critical happen."

"That's even more disturbing, but workable."

"We're actually thinking of switching to the one we pulled out of Camp One over here, and taking down the other one. This would allow us to relieve that one garrison outpost, which is far to the south and getting into the colder season, and we can set up the other one which has better weather."

"What, you don't like snow?"

"Actually, I don't think they get snow this time of year, but it does get a lot of rain and the ground gets slushy."

"Aw, poor little soldier boys."

"Meanwhile..." Kaliya sets the hypo-spray on a nearby table. "Someone needs to do this. In my phased condition, we don't want to take the chance it could cause complications while re-phasing inside her body."

The Captain and Sulíma exchanged glances trying to decide who's going to do it.

"Oh, come on people," Kaliya groans. "One of you must know how to use a hypo-spray. Suli, you're the sister of a medical technician, this sort of thing runs in your family. Didn't you once tell me you and Ankhia played Little Med-tech when you were a kid?"

"But I..." she protests. "Oh, fine. Which side is it that goes against the skin?" she winks.

Sulíma picks up the hypo-spray and makes ready to use it on Tyanna.

"Do we have a preferred location for this?"

"Actually, yes. Not on the organism itself. It apparently reacts badly to direct interaction, or at least what it might regard as a kind of attack. Ankhia suggests on the skin in close proximity."

"What dosage?" she asks while examining the gradation settings. "Or is it already set?"

"It's already set, I think. For the quantity of the dosage, she suggests applying portions of it in two separate locations to distribute it better."

Sulíma nods as she brings the hypo-spray up to Tyanna's back, peering under her garment and selecting a set of locations near the entity. She presses the instrument against the skin and carefully injects the dosages. When she's done, she hands the device back to Kaliya.

"Thanks, Suli. Now, I have a special instruction for you, and maybe you can recruit some others as well."

"What's that?"

"Don't take your eyes off of her!"

"Will you at least allow me to get my beauty sleep on occasion? After all, I have to keep up my good looks so I can torment the boys."

"Only if you alternate with Túfu," Kaliya grins. "Maybe also Tana… After all, they need a chance to swing their tails on occasion."

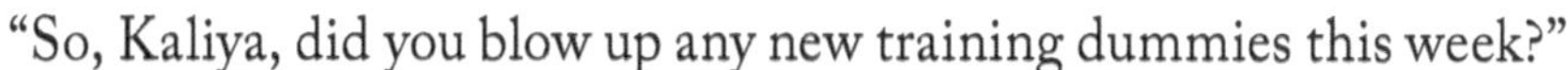

"So, Kaliya, did you blow up any new training dummies this week?"

"Ha ha… Very funny, Haran," she retorts. "I told you, that was a very embarrassing moment. I broke the first rule of mage craft, I lost control. If I were in any other school, I'd probably be suspended for it, but fortunately this one is a lot more forgiving and encourages growth."

"Indeed, I can recall a few of my own moments from our old academy in Rolsklinde. My old masters were very strict, and quite harsh. Still, for your first application of a new spell, and to so completely devastate a field of training dummies specially designed to resist such attacks, that's truly frightening. You need to pay special mind to your strength."

"I know, and I'm putting in extra time on meditation and mental discipline."

"Some of the students are still talking about it. They say you were throwing out fireballs from both hands, and one said something about a spray, which isn't even mentioned in the lesson!"

"That's the dangerous part, to perform a casting not otherwise described in class. It must've occurred while I was recalling those visions of the orcs and the city on fire."

"I'm reflecting on my own lessons now. Even if I do go the full study of nine Circles, you might still outclass me at eight."

"Haran, I'm sure you'll do fine. Just keep up the work like all the rest and it'll come to you. As for me, I'm going to put a little time in on my combat practice today. I've been spending so much lately on the mage studies, that I need to give my body a good workout."

"Oh yes, I'm quite familiar with that. In those first days when they had me training up, I would finish the day with so many aching muscles, I felt as if I could barely walk back to my room."

"What about more recently?"

"Much better, of course, now that I've been practicing and developing a better physique, but I'm sure it's nothing compared to what you're going through."

"Yeah, you're more of a pure mage, whereas I'm training as a front-line combatant."

"I don't envy you that, Kaliya. It's a dangerous place to stand. But for all you've been practicing lately, I think the danger is more on their side rather than ours," he grins.

"How is Marelle doing in her studies? I've noticed she's been putting in time on both fields."

"Thaelyn has been encouraging her to take herself to the Sixth Circle for some reason. I think he's got something special in mind for her, but you know how he is on such matters. She's also working on light arms in combat training, which I suppose means she won't be spending as much time on the front lines, thankfully."

"You worry for her, I guess."

"Naturally, she's my sister and the only family I have left, other than for Cousin Leesa and her family."

"Has Leesa made any decisions to join up? She's of age by now, right?"

"Yes, she's twenty years old now, and a fine example of a young lady. Last I heard, she didn't have a strong interest in a military career, but her experience in those days when she was playing the spy, and then helping alongside the others during the attack and such, has inspired her for a civilian role, maybe in law enforcement and investigation."

"Sounds nice and safe, within reason."

"Unlike the rest of us, I'll say."

"What actually made you decide to serve a military career? Was it because of Marelle?"

"A little, but I didn't originally see myself as a soldier, as she was doing. On the other hand, I didn't want to be a shop clerk, like my father."

"Nothing wrong with being a shop clerk."

"No, of course not. We need those as much as we need soldiers. But I always aspired to take myself a little higher. Much like Marelle, I didn't want to spend my life stuck inside those walls."

"But you mostly did anyway, just because of the Governor and the Dean. Being part of the Order essentially makes you a soldier now. You may find yourself on the lines somewhere, even if standing behind someone like me."

"I would much rather stand behind you than in front," he chuckles.

"Are you suggesting that due to my combat skills, or maybe because I make a good shield?" she grins widely.

"I think a little of both," he laughs.

Kaliya and Haran were wrapping up their after-school chat. It was only the two of them this time as Marelle and Relissa were spending extra time on the mage field. The meeting comes to an end, and they go their separate ways, Haran to his mage practice and Kaliya to her combat training. She meanders through the corridors to the training hall, passing through to a changing room on the other side.

She sets down a bag she was carrying with her training uniform inside, unpacks it and changes from her usual cadet uniform to the new one. She then stows her bag in a locker and proceeds out into the training hall.

After checking in with the Sergeant to clock her time, she finds a convenient position near a set of exercise equipment, including bars for performing chin-ups, although in her case she already stood at level with the bar, and weights for strength training.

She begins with a few stretching and limbering exercises, then prepares to work out with a punching bag, performing a variation of kickboxing as part of her martial arts training. The bag was a standard fare as used by all the students, and it hung from a heavy crossbeam on a sturdy chain.

She began her workout, first with punching and blocking, followed by a few side and round kicks. As part of her conditioning, she had to envision the bag as her opponent, and they were locked in mortal combat. Discipline is as important here as it is on the mage field, but at least here she wasn't in danger of blowing anything up. She intensified her approach, throwing harder punches and solid high kicks. The bag was swinging wildly from her assault, and as it returned, she would hit it again.

She could feel her body burning from the vigorous play, timing her actions with that of her adversary, striking whenever she would see an opening in his defense. She struck him hard with a forward kick, then dodging to the side as he made his return, jabbing him in the flank with a reverse elbow swing. She jumps back and steps in again with another side kick. Her opponent was dazed and wobbling, unable to stand up under her vicious assault. He tried circling around her, but her highly refined reflexes had her ducking to one side and laying down a series of low punches, followed by a knee to the lower gut and a roundabout kick.

He was just about ready to make one last desperate charge when she saw her killing shot. She altered her stance and lunged at him with a powerful roundhouse kick to the chest.

A prominent ting echoes through the room as the supporting chain snaps. The punching bag is sent flying into the nearby wall, knocking over a rack of practice weapons, and dislodging a row of shelving.

The other students in the room halt their practice to observe the destruction, glancing up at the broken link still dangling from the eye hook at the top, and then at the bag settling onto a mound of debris on the floor. The Sergeant struts over to examine the damage.

"Great cu'Nar," Kaliya mumbles. "When I asked for strength before, I didn't quite mean this."

She pulls herself nervously to attention as the Sergeant walks up next to her. He studies her, and then the bag on the floor.

"Sergeant, my apologies," she begs. "I guess my training has improved my strength more than I was previously aware."

"So it would seem, Cadet."

"I'll offer myself for reparation if you require it."

"No need, Cadet. From time to time we do find ourselves in need of occasional maintenance, and since this is a combat hall, this equipment takes a lot of abuse."

"Yes, Sergeant…although I have my doubts it involves anything like me," she chuckles faintly.

"Indeed," he nods. "Instead, I have something else for you. We have been working on a new set of training equipment specially designed for you and your kin, since you do bear a considerable amount of strength. This is being organized outside, though I think it is not quite ready. But I will have you move out there for your future practice."

"Thank you, Sergeant. It seems I'm becoming rather dangerous these days."

"Indeed, you are. I heard about that little incident out on the mage field."

"You and the entire academy by now," she sighs.

"Cadet, I would actually say you should feel honored that you are developing so nicely. Keep it up! Meanwhile, I will have you practice more on your staff exercises. And I think it's time for us to promote you to a new line."

"Sergeant? What do you mean?"

The Sergeant walks over to a cabinet near his desk. He pulls out a unique instrument of a design Kaliya had never seen before. It bore the appearance of a staff with a shallow crescent-shaped blade running the full length of it. The staff portion had leather grips interspaced along its length between the four mounting points of the blade.

"Cu'Nar help us, what is that?"

"This will be your specialty, Cadet. The blade is not sharp on this one, but be aware of the points on the ends, as they can still be dangerous for the manner of which you will be wielding it."

"What's it called?"

"This, young lady, is called a sword-staff. A delicate and graceful weapon used by only the most gifted of warriors. And in your case, you will learn to use this in such a way that it will be as a part of your own body, like a katana would be to a kensai."

"But this is only a practice weapon, right? May I ask what the final example will look like? It will look the same, I suppose, but sharpened?"

"I don't have the final word on this, but essentially yes. Further, as with most of our weapons, it will also be enchanted to some degree. I would guess, due to your special status, it will make a very handsome example. For now, however, you must work on your technique. I will assign a special trainer to show you how. But for this, you will go…outside!" he winks as he points into the field.

"Yes, Sergeant! Of course…"

✦✦✦✦✦

"Ankhia, how are the results of our outpatient experiment coming along today?"

"So far, Likha, it's looking good. The numbers are within the markers of our lab results, and the recent images sent back are showing the same deterioration of the entity as what we had before."

"I just hope it all goes according to our expectations. The only wildcard is the effect on the brain. Do we have any new developments as to her apparent behavior?"

"The first couple of weeks showed only negligible effects, but this past week the results seem to be accumulating. She mentioned a few times what I'm interpreting to be a tingling sensation, so I'm going to assume this to be a kind of progress note on the entity's control coming under attack internally and being disrupted."

"My biggest fear is the effect on her most critical organs. If it simply lets go, everything might fall back to a natural rhythm. But will her brain function resume without interruption, or might it cause heart failure along the way?"

"That's what we're watching for, Likha. I guess we'll know the answer in another week or so. Suli and her people have been watching over her diligently. Up until now, it's mostly been a waiting game, but this next week is the one when we start pulling our horns out."

The medical trial on Tyanna was proceeding along as expected. Sulíma, Túfula, and Captain Lapäli were paying close attention and feeding daily reports to the team at the Naarg uy'Sodrad. Tyanna had been continuing her work as best she could during this time, but those around her were beginning to notice an obvious change in her concentration, coordination, and ambulatory capacity.

Sulíma and Túfula were taking the most interest in her, with Tana stepping in to cover for their rest periods. The Captain was also doing his best to watch out for Tyanna's health, but he found himself divided between that and his other duties in the city. Therefore, the girls devoted themselves as Tyanna's personal health care workers and babysitters. It was going into the fourth week, and the situation had been growing incrementally more worrisome.

"Túfu," Sulíma asks. "Have you seen how's she's moving so much slower today?"

"She didn't move very quickly before this. It's almost enough to put a person to sleep just watching her."

"I know, and I'm wondering something. We still have a few days left to go, if Ankhia's estimates are correct. So, we need to pay extra special attention to her during this time."

"I just hope we're awake for it. What if it happens one night when we're asleep?"

"Tana's helping during our rest periods, but maybe we can recruit some more people to take a night shift and watch her."

"That's a good idea. We already have her sleeping in one of the back rooms here, just so we can keep a close eye on her."

"Right, and that makes it so much more convenient if we need to give any emergency aid or to quickly send her through the conveyor."

"That…thing…on her back, I thought it was awful when it was healthy. I really hate to think of what she's feeling right now with it just drooping off her like it is."

"I shudder to think. Please don't mention that, Túfu."

"Sorry, Suli, but you just can't help wondering. And the next thing is what happens after it dies."

"I, for one, would not wish to be in the surgery room trying to peel it off. I don't know if my stomach could handle that."

"I guess we're fortunate in that regard, as the surgery room is on another planet. But I feel for your sister for this part."

"So do I."

✦✦◆✦✦

"Hey, Kaliya!" Marelle shouts as the team meets up again in the guild courtyard. "I see where they patched the hole you made in the wall last week."

"Are you going to razz me for that one now? Cu'Nar's pity! First, I blow up the mage field, then I rip apart the combat hall. I wonder what comes next. Maybe I'll tear a whole in space and the whole universe gets sucked in."

"Wow, I hope not! But if you do, try to make sure it's not in THIS universe."

"I'll do my best. So, what are we conspiring to do this afternoon?"

"They have me working hard on my new mage practice. I'm just going over my lessons before I make my next session. Thaelyn said he's working on a special training course for me, but it's not ready yet."

"Did he say what kind? I'm wondering why he would ask you to go to the Sixth Circle. You weren't originally thinking of going very far in your mage studies, so this is an interesting turn of events."

"No, nothing yet out of him," she sighs. "But I'm not going to argue. He always knows what's best, so I'll go along with it."

"And Relissa, I see you still out there on occasion."

"Aye, even though I'm deep in the ranger training by now, they're suggesting I keep up the mage class for a few more years, if I can hold my eyes open long enough."

"Until what Circle?"

"They're saying to the Seventh, then I can mark runes and carry people all around the place, a bit like we saw from those first few scouts when they came out of those rocks and pestered us with the worry of a new invasion."

"I remember that…" she recalls fondly. "And here it was Thaelyn and his people just arriving in our world. A skill like that would be handy to have."

"And believe it or not, I'm actually getting into the liking of it. Who would've thought one day I'd be as much a scabby finger-wiggler as this old mug over here," she thumbs at Haran.

"Excuse me, Relissa," Haran declares haughtily. "But to be a part of the mage craft is a highly esteemed profession. And I, for all my scabby finger-wiggling, am very proud of it."

Relissa rubs his shoulder teasingly.

"Kaliya," Marelle continues. "Did I hear they have you working on a new kind of weapon training?"

"Yeah, and it's going to be my specialty. I don't really know what the final result will be, but working with this new one is a dream. I'm remembering a little of my gymnastics training from my old school, and some of the acrobatics I would perform with my batons, although this is a two-handed item, mostly."

"So, it's not the same as using a staff?"

"Not nearly... The staff gave me the basics of handling the long stick, but this involves much more grace and style. It's like an extension of my arm, and unlike a staff, where you're mostly just standing still with relatively little body movement, this one is much more like a dance."

"Nice, I can't wait to see you in action. But then again, maybe I can, because from the sound of it, you'll be slicing and dicing your way through their ranks leaving nothing but body parts in your wake."

"I'm actually hoping it won't be as bad as that. Keep in mind, we're hoping to save lives, not make mincemeat out of them. But yeah, whatever I use it for, there won't be much left of it by the time I'm done."

✦✦◆✦✦

"Suli, I'm very worried. Have you noticed how she's been stumbling around this morning?"

"How could I not notice, Túfu? It's been this way since we woke up. I have a bad feeling about this."

"Should I pull out the field kit and have it ready?"

"It might not be a bad idea to keep it on the table over here. What did the last set of readings say?"

"A lot of fluctuating rhythms... Things were still working, but not very well."

"Dammit, Túfu, why didn't she choose to go to Ankhia when she had the chance? I'm standing here wondering how we're going to push her through the conveyor if she collapses on us."

"Do we have anything to lay her on, like a gurney, or even just a sled?"

"I had some people cobble something together," Sulíma recalls. "It's not very professional, but it might work. The trouble is, I wonder what will happen as we try pushing her head-first into the conveyor.

She looks heavy, and the sled doesn't slide very smoothly. In the time it'll take us to push her through, her head will be arriving on the other side while her hooves are still over here. What does that do to a person?"

"Well, I suppose she'll be a lot taller in the end," Túfula muses timidly.

Sulíma glares at the girl for the awkward suggestion, but finds she can't hold back at least a small grin for the comical image it conjures up.

Tyanna was clearly struggling with herself today. She had been staggering around the building, attempting to steady herself on walls and furniture, occasionally bumping into chairs and knocking against tables. She barely spoke a word. Her eyes were droopy, and she hunched forward. Sulíma and Túfula had been watching her since sunrise. Captain Lapäli kept one eye on her while the other tried to focus on his own work. This day was becoming very nerve-racking for all of them.

The unfortunate woman had been trying to stack some books on a side table and return to her desk, when she stumbled. She twisted and awkwardly reached out to catch herself as she fell, but she missed and crashed to the floor.

"Túfu!" Sulíma shouts. "Get the kit, and the monitors!"

Túfula runs to a nearby cabinet and grabs the field kit and a heart monitor. The Captain notices the commotion and rushes over to help.

"Captain," Sulíma urges. "Send word over there, now! Tell them we have a problem."

"Right away," he responds to the young girl.

He quickly returns to his desk, scribbles out a note and rolls it up, securing it with a small metal clip. He then runs outside and around the corner of the building to toss it through the conveyor they set up a month ago.

"Túfu," Sulíma urges. "Get that thing over here. Put the mask on her."

Túfula dashes back across the room, opens the kit and pulls out a breathing mask. She hooks up the hose to an oxygen tank and places the mask on Tyanna's face, turning the valve of the tank to allow the gas to flow. As she holds the mask in place, Sulíma picks up the heart monitor and sets it on Tyanna's chest to take a reading.

Tyanna was clumsily thrashing about on the floor. Her movements were slow and uncoordinated. Her eyes appeared glazed over and she was making dull burbling sounds, like that of a baby unable to speak.

The room became the center of attention as the shouts called in other officers and several of the scouts, including Tana.

Sulíma studied the heart monitor. It showed an irregular rhythm. She tried looking into Tyanna's eyes, but they appeared unfocused.

"Tyanna," she calls gently. "Can you hear me? Can you say something? Try to talk."

The woman doesn't seem to understand or respond to the request, only to continue thrashing weakly with one arm as she lay on the floor.

✦

"General! This just came in from Portal One!"

"Give it here, page."

A page had just arrived in the strategy room at the WIC building in Rolsklinde. He carried the note from the Captain on Ruuki uy'Daan. The General takes it and examines it briefly, and on seeing it was written in the Daanen-Aryku native language, he passes it to Kailen.

"Commander, here... Take a look at this."

Kailen takes the note and reads it. His reaction to the message is clearly marked on his face.

"We need to assemble our people immediately. My mother has gone down."

He pulls out his trans-com and dials up a number.

"Medical Ward, Med-tech Tad'vaal here."

"Ankhia, get your people over here, quickly! She's collapsed!"

"Oh dear cu'Nar, I hope this isn't critical. I'll be right there."

"Page!" the General orders. "Fetch His Lordship...and Kaliya.

560

Get help if you need it. Bring them both here at once, Kaliya in her projected form."

The page bows and runs outside, calling another along the way to follow. The two of them exit the building and split off, with one heading over to the parliament building to find Thaelyn while the other continues on to the guildhall.

Kaliya was still enjoying her meeting with Relissa and friends in the guild courtyard when the page arrived panting from his run.

"Kaliya, you're needed…now! Get to the WIC building."

"Projected?" she replies nervously.

"Aye! It's about a note from Ruuki uy'Daan."

"Oh dear cu'Nar above, no!"

Kaliya twists in all directions, trying to decide which way to go. Her pleasant mood from her earlier conversation had shattered. Now she felt panic.

"Kaliya, what's wrong?" Marelle asks imperatively. "I mean, I know what's wrong, but with you?"

"I don't think I can do this! Suddenly, I'm too upset. I don't think I can focus!"

"Girl, you need help," Relissa suggests. "Maybe a priest… Or better yet, Aerlie! Call her to meet you here. You can do the telepathy bit now, ay?"

"Yeah, but can I do it like this?"

Kaliya strains to focus her thoughts on a telepathic line, having been practicing for several months along with the other Daanen'kai trainees in the new study course given by Aelwyn.

Aerlie was in her office when the flustered sensation came through. The thoughts were only barely constrained enough to form a message. She recognized the voice in her head as being Kaliya, as they had been practicing together on a few occasions, but this instance was deeply troubling, and she suspected she knew why.

She lurches out of her chair and through the door, hurrying across the temple and into the street. She places her attention on the grounds just outside the guildhall front gates, which was line-of-sight from her location. She circles her fingers as a bullseye to her target and waves the other hand in a sweeping motion towards her objective.

Her form is suddenly whisked away as a wisp of light, zipping through the air over the rooftops of the nearby buildings and across to the hillside where the avenue led up to the guildhall gates. The ball of light angled downward to impact on the roadway, forming an ascending column and coalescing back into her natural form. From there, she ran through the gates to find the group inside the courtyard.

"What is it, Kaliya?" she demands.

"It's my mother, I just know it!" she sobs. "Something's happened and I need to get to her, but I can't focus like this!"

"All right, sit here and I'll help."

Aerlie sets the grief-stricken girl on the bench and leans her back. She moves around behind her and begins a soothing massage on her temples and brow, calling a peaceful chant to aid in the girl's relaxation.

Kaliya tries to center herself on her meditation so she can project. Relissa and the others sit and wait, keeping silent to allow her time to settle.

Aerlie's expert aid at her relaxation technique helped Kaliya bring herself under control, and although the process involved this secondary step, the girl just barely managed to find her composure again. She continued to draw her attention to releasing herself and proceeded with her usual practice of stepping outside her body.

The others watched and waited as Aerlie continued her chant and their tall friend seemed to descend into a deep meditative trance. As they continued to study her, they finally saw Kaliya's spirit projection emerge into the local space.

"Jiggers," Relissa whispers. "I've never actually seen her do it before."

"Yeah," Marelle follows. "And it's even creepier than I thought. Now, what do we do with her body sitting here?"

"Can we poke it with a stick, just to see if she feels it?" Relissa snickers.

"You better not, Relissa!" Kaliya answers as she picks up on the conversation. "And Haran, you keep your hands to yourself. I still recall how you wanted to 'science' me during my examination."

"But Kaliya," he smiles innocently. "How else are we to, ahem, learn anything around here?"

"Uh huh. Relissa, Marelle, watch him while I'm gone."

"Aye," Relissa nods humorously. "But do we just leave you sitting here?"

"I'll be alright for now. My concerns are more for my mother… if this really is the issue. And Aerlie, thanks for the help. I need to get to the WIC center now."

Kaliya redirects her thoughts and vanishes away from the scene.

✦✦✦✦✦

"Suli, what's her condition now?" the Captain urges, just returning from outside after sending the note through.

"Her heart is beating. It was erratic at first, but I think it's slowly settling itself, which is a good thing…maybe."

"You should be a little more precise than just maybe."

"Sorry, Captain, I never attended medical school. I only know this much from what Ankhia told me."

"All right, but can we move her? Where's that sled?"

"Over here, Captain," Tana announces as she hauls a makeshift stretcher out of storage.

Tyanna's thrashing had slowed, and she appeared dazed. Her eyes had not changed since she went down, and she still could not talk. Túfula continued to hold the mask over the woman's face while Sulíma tried once again to incite a response.

"Tyanna, can you hear me? Are you able to talk yet? Try to say something."

The girl's attempt only resulted in more gibberish. It was spoken faintly, but it seemed as though Tyanna was at least aware of someone making the effort. She swings one arm lazily at the girl, bumping into her knee. Sulíma takes it in her hand.

"I wish Kali were here right now," she moans. "Should we just send her through like this, or wait? Is this just a reaction or something more serious?"

"I don't think it's wise for us to wait too long, Suli," the Captain admits. "We should see about moving her to the sled."

"Dammit, I know you're right, Captain, but I can't think of what to wait for on the other side. Kali! Damn you! If you don't get your tail over here, I'll jump through that conveyor myself and drag you by the horns halfway across the universe for this."

"Easy does it, Suli," Túfula offers. "I don't know if they gave her the message or if they're simply expecting us to pass Tyanna through. But I think if she's aware of it, she's probably also in a panic. Wouldn't you think?"

"Yeah, sure she would be. I'm sorry, Túfu."

"Suu…lii…" comes a rasping voice.

"Tyanna? Can you talk? Please say something!"

"Suu…lii…" she announces again.

"Yes, I'm right here. I'm holding your hand. Can you feel it? Just try to hold on, we're going to send you to Ankhia. You're very sick and need help. No more talk about what you look like, do you hear me? I'm angry and I'm worried."

"Yesss… Wait…"

"No more waiting!" she shrieks. "Get that thing over here!"

Tana dragged the sled next to Sulíma and Tyanna and they tried to reposition themselves to lift her onto it, unsure at first how to grip the woman for the sagging and delicate appearance of the organism.

"Maybe if we use a blanket," Túfula offers. "Or a sheet or something."

"Do we have one?" Sulíma wonders.

"Su--li…" Tyanna moans softly. "Moo--ving… Every--thing… moo--ving… Please…wait…"

"Moving?" she blasts. "Cu'Nar's pity, Tyanna, we need to get you to Ankhia!"

"Yes… I…under--stand. No…more…fighting. Just…give me…a moment."

"I don't think we can wait that long... Hold on a second," she pauses. "What did you just say?"

"I said... Wait...a moment. It's...coming...back..."

"Túfu, are you listening to this?"

"Suli, how can I not listen to it? Tyanna, try to speak some more. How do you feel right now? We really need to know."

"Slowly... My head... Feels like..." Tyanna holds her statement momentarily. "Feels like...a comet impact..."

"Really!" Túfula intones inquisitively. "Um, Suli?"

"Yeah, I heard it. Looks like one, too. Captain?"

"What are you asking me for?" he retorts. "I'm just an old soldier. What about the monitor readings?"

Sulíma checks the heart monitor again.

"It reads as a stable rhythm now. Thank the cu'Nar for that!"

"You should thank...more than...the cu'Nar...Suli," Tyanna states.

Sulíma looks into the woman's eyes again. They appeared to be focusing better, and the glazed condition was dissipating.

"Tyanna, come on, keep it coming. What else can you say? Keep up the dialog."

"Everything...is ringing. It feels like...being squeezed."

Sulíma decides to try a few simple tests, recalling them from her childhood when Ankhia would play doctor with her back home.

"Tyanna, can you see my hand?" she asks as she holds it in front of the woman's face. "How many fingers am I holding up?"

Tyanna tries to focus on the girl's hand. Her vision was still blurred.

"Three...maybe. Still...a little...unfocused."

"Tyanna, are you listening to yourself?" Túfula asks. "Do you actually hear what you're saying? You're talking! And not that broken half-minded nonsense from before."

Tyanna tries to analyze her feelings as a new rush of sensations now fills her mind. A strained smile forms across her lips.

"Cu'Nar be blessed... I think this heathenish beast is dead!"

Sulíma begins to break down. She turns and lays her head on the

Captain's shoulder as he was kneeling next to her. He wraps his hands around her, patting her on the back and trying to ease her distress.

"Tyanna," Túfula continues, struggling to contain herself. "Other than that, can you tell us anything more about how you feel?"

"Maybe… What actually happened to me? I'm on the floor. Did I fall? I suppose I did."

"You didn't just fall. All day you've been behaving like you were in your last moments."

"Probably so. Trust me, Túfu, I wouldn't want to go through it a second time."

Kaliya arrives on Ruuki uy'Daan outside the Sentinels HQ, having briefly stopped by the WIC building in Rolsklinde for instructions. She surges through the doors and into the main office.

"What happened!" she pleads. "Where is she? Oh dear cu'Nar…" she whines as she notices the gathering on the floor.

Túfula and Sulíma were helping the elder woman to a seated position as Kaliya arrived. Tana was kneeling next to the sled, as it didn't seem to be needed by now. Tyanna's focus was much better, and her speech had cleared substantially.

"Túfu…" Sulíma mumbles as she observes the woman. "Look at that! Her eyes…"

Túfula studied Tyanna's eyes carefully, blinking once to make sure she understood what she was looking at.

"The blessing of the cu'Nar, it's returning to her."

"Suli! Túfu!" Kaliya shouts. "What happened? Mother! Are you alright? Say something!"

Kaliya drops to her knees by the others in the group and frantically glances over her mother's body, then into her face, only to halt her motion as she sees the glow returning to the woman's eyes.

"Cu'Nar be blessed…" she emits breathlessly.

"I already called that one, Kali," Tyanna declares gently. "You'll need to think of another."

Kaliya rolls back, nearly falling over at the sound of her mother's natural voice. Her panic had transformed into a gush of elation. The upsurge of emotion was so powerful, it even reflected back along her link to her physical body.

Relissa, Marelle, and Haran were still watching over Kaliya's body in the courtyard, when they began to notice a single tear emerge from her eye and run down her cheek.

"Is that good or bad?" Marelle asks.

"Buggers," Relissa mutters. "Should one of us run over there and see what we can find out?"

"I'm afraid to, really."

"Aye, me too, but we're not going to get anything out of it sitting here. At least not till she pops back into her body. I'll go."

"All right, Relissa, we'll stay here and babysit."

"Now, Mother," Kaliya commands. "You're not going to argue with me on this again, are you? We need you to go to Ankhia to get this thing removed from you. We can't just let it…hang like this."

"Yes, Kali, I'll go," Tyanna relents. "But I do ask you to try to keep me away from our people, so they don't see me as I go in. Maybe, if you can wrap me in a blanket or something."

"Fine, I'm sure we can do that much. Now, listen to me. I need to tell you how this works. In your condition before, I can't be sure how much you actually understood."

Tyanna nods in agreement, waiting for her daughter to continue.

"First, are you able to walk?"

Tyanna tests her legs and tries to stand up. She is wobbly, but Sulíma and Túfula support her from the sides.

"This may be tricky," Kaliya observes. "We'll see how well you're able to move around in a moment. For now, listen. You'll pass through a conveyor just outside here. This will take you to an outpost we have on the other side. From there, they'll forward you to a city we occupy. Ankhia and her team are waiting for you."

"Is this the city where you live now?"

"Actually no, it's a city we liberated during our war against Darumon and his goons a few years ago. He toasted the city with a little farewell gift, and we've been trying to rebuild it ever since.

The city actually belongs to a race called Humans, one of the races we found on that world who were under siege by his military."

"Then where is it you actually live?"

"I'm currently living on a world called Tae'Eladar, in the capital city called Bya'an Tamoranth. That's where I'm attending the academy."

"And this is where you're learning all these incredible new skills? I would dearly love to see that place."

"Don't worry, Mother, there's plenty of time for that. The only thing I ask is for you to speak with Kailen, and probably also Thaelyn before you go out and start talking to the Council or anyone else. There are a lot of security issues going around and the Council has voluntarily stepped out of the picture to help us keep it that way."

"I still find this hard to believe. This is simply not the way of our people to leave out the Council from the most crucial aspects of our work together."

"I know, but it's actually because of this where we have this security issue. Darumon was spying on us, impersonating one of our Council members."

"What? You didn't mention this before…I don't think. How was he able to do this, and who was it?"

"We think it was Drescuul, and Darumon is what we call a shapeshifter. He can alter his appearance, so he could look like anyone or anything, which is bad enough in itself."

"I don't recall that from our encounter on Azgarén. But then, we didn't stay long enough to discover it."

"This is also the reason we were found each time. We think he simply followed along and called in our position each time we settled."

"In the cu'Nar's name, that's sinister," she frowns. "So, this is to say we never really had a chance of escaping."

"Probably not, but enough for now, let's get you going. How do your legs feel?"

Tyanna checked her legs again, which were feeling a little stronger now. Kaliya assisted and led the team through the doors and outside to the conveyor. They circled around the building in front of the unit, where Kaliya motioned them to hold their position while she moved forward and made several curious gestures at the apparatus.

"Um, Kali," Sulíma wonders. "What are you doing?"

"The other side of this conduit opens up with a virtual image of what's on this side. They can see whatever is standing directly in front of the conveyor. So, I'm using a form of sign language to tell them to expect my mother to pass through, and to assist if she has trouble."

"You mean they can actually see us? So, as we pass by, they see what's happening over here?"

"Yeah, the image of this place passes through from this side and displays on the exit aperture like a portrait on a window."

"Wow! So, if I wanted to, I could stand here and make funny faces at them?"

"You could..." Kaliya grins. "But just remember, one of these days you might meet them face-to-face."

"Suli," Tyanna notes. "Did you ever actually grow up?"

"What's the fun in that? I like who I am," she giggles.

"Are we ready?" Kaliya solicits. "Mother, you need to recall the textbooks on nether-space travel here. It's basically the same thing, but without the ship carrying you. The passage from one side to the other might represent a long tunnel. It's quick, but time seems to play with the senses on the inside. And you need to watch your step as you come out."

Tyanna nods as she makes one last check of herself. She pulls together whatever strength she has available as Kaliya motions her to go forward, and the woman makes a brave leap through the portal.

"All right, the rest of you," Kaliya concludes wearily. "I want to thank you from the top of my horns to the bottom of my hooves for all that you've done. I'll let you know how things turn out, but for now I think we can go back to normal, if such a thing is possible."

She gives a hug to each of her friends and to the Captain before flashing out of sight.

Marelle and Haran waited. To say they waited patiently would be far from the truth, but they waited, nonetheless. Kaliya's body still seemed at rest. Relissa had departed some time ago to visit Rolsklinde, but no word had come through as to the result. Then a flash formed in front of them. Kaliya had reappeared in the courtyard and was moving to join them.

"Kaliya?" Marelle mutters urgently.

Kaliya smiled gently and nodded, and gestured a pause.

"We're alright. Give me a moment."

She then stepped back into her body.

"If you say so," Marelle sighs.

Kaliya reunited herself in body and spirit, shortly after to awaken. She looked at peace, but worn from stress.

"All right, now can you talk?" Marelle asks. "What actually happened over there? We saw you crying on this side."

"Crying?"

"Well, we saw a tear rolling down your cheek. I have no idea what that means."

Kaliya tried wiping her cheeks, discovering one of them was wet.

"Fascinating, a psychosomatic reaction from my projection," she muses.

"Fine... Psycho...whatever... What's the final result?"

"It's alright, she's alive and apparently the entity is dead. She collapsed, but probably from a shock reaction. Now she's on her way to Rolsklinde, and Ankhia is there waiting for her. By the way, where's Relissa?"

"In Rolsklinde... When we saw that tear, she decided to go over there to see if she could get an answer."

"Good little Relissa."

"Aerlie also left, saying she was going to gather up some people and head over there to offer medical support."

"Good. It's nice to have so many people working the problem. I need to go there now. Do you want to come along?"

Marelle and Haran share a quick glance and they all get up together.

Tyanna was arriving in Rolsklinde in the upper plaza district as Relissa was passing through the hub gate. Thaelyn, Kailen, and the other officers were emerging from the WIC building to meet with the new arrival. Ankhia was waiting outside near the portal arrival zone when the woman stumbled into view.

"Grace of the cu'Nar!" Tyanna exclaims. "How in all the nether-space do they make a conveyor out of a piece of rock!"

"Welcome home, Tyanna," Ankhia announces. "Or at least what we might call home these days. Remember me?"

Tyanna studies the younger woman in her well-appointed medical uniform.

"Ankhia! Oh, how I missed you! And look at you…a full medical chief now?"

"Yes, things changed a bit after we arrived here. And Tyanna, we all missed you, more than you can imagine."

Tyanna notices the approach of several new figures walking across the plaza, one of them very familiar.

"Ankhia, please, I do not wish everyone in the city to see me like this."

"Don't worry, we'll take care of you. The most important thing is you're here with us and free of this awful little bug."

Kailen steps up to the assembly and gazes longingly at the disfigured woman. His professional countenance had finally broken down due to his stress. Tears were welling up in his eyes.

"Mother…" he calls softly with his voice trembling.

"Kailen, my dear!" she reaches out to him.

They grip each other in a delicate embrace, and she pats him on the back to comfort him through his distress.

The General was walking alongside Thaelyn as he observed the scene.

"That just doesn't seem right, for some reason," he muses humorously. "The size differential between the two of them. He stands head and shoulders above her, with a torso twice or more her dimension, and yet, to see her coddling him like a young child…"

"Indeed," Thaelyn chuckles gently. "But then, I suppose, despite the physique, we are all the same on the inside."

Tyanna pulled away to examine her son, as he also studies her.

"How do you feel?" Kailen asks.

"Much better, even though this horrid little creature is still attached to me. Already, I can feel it pulling away, and not only on the outside. By the way, where is Kali?"

"I would imagine she'll be arriving any moment now. She usually does her projection from a quiet room inside the guildhall in B.T."

"B.T.? Oh, wait, would that be the city she mentioned on that world...Tae'Eladar?"

"Yes, that's the short form we often use. Those of us here have gotten used to it."

"It reminds me a little bit of our old home on Azgarén."

Tyanna looks over at the other officer standing nearby. Kailen follows her gaze to find Padriyl.

"Do I know you?" she asks. "Forgive me, but so long a time in my condition, and I find I must relearn a few faces."

"Yes ma'am. I'm Lieutenant... Well, actually you might not remember me as a lieutenant. Padriyl Lapäli. The last time we met, I would've been a cadet training for the Sentinels."

"Ah, yes... Tudorin's boy! My, you've grown, and now a Lieutenant!"

Thaelyn steps around into view, joined at his side by Relissa.

"Looks like we have a happy ending here," she observes. "We were getting a mite worried back there."

"Indeed, I think we all shared in that," Thaelyn agrees. "Thankfully, we seem to have a victory in this battle."

He approaches to make his introduction, having to speak in the Daanen-Aryku language for their new visitor.

"Madam Nazég, I bid you a pleasant greeting and welcome to our fair city of Rolsklinde. I am Lord Thaelyn, King of the world we call Tae'Eladar," he offers a bow. "As well as some portions of this one, by now."

"A...king? Oh my..." she hesitates, discreetly rolling her eyes at her disfigured form. "Kailen!" she whispers urgently. "I'm a wreck!"

Tyanna attempts a bow, even though her condition makes it rather uncomfortable.

"Do not concern yourself with your appearance," Thaelyn soothes. "Considering all you have been through; we are overjoyed enough that you are alive and standing amongst us. Everything else is secondary."

"You are most gracious, Your Majesty. But as a woman of breeding, this condition of mine is most disquieting. It cannot be soon enough to see it fully removed."

"Of course. And after, perhaps you would join us in a more pleasant circumstance. There is much that needs to be brought forward to our modern day. In fact, as I am presently sensing, my wife may wish to offer her services to assist the Med-tech here in your recovery."

Thaelyn turns to spy Aerlie and her entourage of priests coming into view out of the city hub center, followed shortly after by Kaliya, Marelle, and Haran. Tyanna recognizes her daughter right away, but gazes in awe at the extraordinary, winged form arriving at Thaelyn's side.

"Blessed cu'Nar, what..." she catches herself in her wording. "Rather, I should ask, who is that?"

Aerlie steps forward to make her introduction.

"Good greetings to you, I am Lady Aerlie, wife and Queen to this man," she finishes by laying a hand on Thaelyn's arm.

"Incredible. Please forgive my surprise, but you look nothing the same as he. Is this some curious form of dimorphism within your race?"

"Actually, no, although that would be a most interesting suggestion. Instead, I am a member of a race called Tel'Quessir, and in my case, a particular clan we call Aril. But I am also a Celestial, meaning to say I am ascended from the more common example, the same as he is from his. In this form, I would be described as Eladrin, whereas he would be called Aasimar, better resembling of humans," she waves at Marelle and Haran as examples.

"Ascended? What does this actually mean?"

"In our cases, we are a hybridization with a much higher form of life we call the Estelar."

"A hybridization," she muses. "Such a fascinating form of

interaction. Is this a common practice? And then the interbreeding between the two of you. Would this mean you are all biologically compatible with each other?"

"Humans and elves, as my people are commonly known, are compatible, and may often find partnerships. But the hybridization aspect is rather unique, and not typical at all. However, it might come into play for some rather extraordinary occasions and demands. Ours was to unite our world in harmony, and direct it on a path of enlightenment. As for the Estelar, they are a very different variety, and largely incompatible for direct interaction. Combining anything with them more often requires an artificial effort to imbue certain elements into the result."

"Really! This is a very interesting manner of conduct. I would be eager to learn more about how this works for you. I was once a professor in our old university. Psychology was my specialty, but I always found it fascinating to study other cultures."

"Yes, Kaliya has told us a few things about you. I would enjoy sharing a pleasant conversation with you, but of course we should first attend to your physical condition."

"Yes, I would very much desire this."

Tyanna finally turns to Kaliya, seeing for the first time her adult daughter in the flesh.

"Kali..." she calls warmly. "Just look at you, so prim and proper in that uniform. My little girl, who once was an honor student, a star athlete, such a graceful delight on the gymnastics floor...and let us not forget...our precious savior. Many people owe you more than we can repay. If it were not for you, we would be lost forever, and here you found us."

Kaliya feels a warm blush coming over her as she considers the words.

"The lost will be found..." she mumbles reflectively and glances at Kailen.

Kailen smiled and returned the gaze.

"Those cu'Nar..." he accedes.

"And Adalon..."

Tyanna was oblivious to the mention, not having any knowledge of the prophecy.

"Huh? What are you two talking about?" she inquires.

"Father was given another prophecy shortly after we arrived here," Kaliya admits. "It involved a number of details we're starting to see occur around us, like me finding all of you on Ruuki uy'Daan. But apparently, Mother, the cu'Nar aren't the only ones behind things."

"They aren't? Who else is?"

"First of all, they're messengers and spies for a member of this society Aerlie mentioned, the Estelar, a race of godlike beings who want to see Sargeras destroyed. We ran right into them here on this world when we met Thaelyn and Aerlie."

Tyanna's eyes bulged and her mouth dropped open as she made the connection.

"Are we speaking of those friends you mentioned once?"

"Yeah, that's who they are, old rivals of Sargeras and Darumon. That word, Titan, is known to these people."

"Oh dear cu'Nar…and literally so. What have we gotten ourselves into."

"Before we try answering that," Ankhia urges. "Do you think we can get on to removing the entity before it falls off by itself?"

"Yes! Please, Ankhia, I would be very grateful for it. I can feel it tugging at me, and it is not at all pleasant. I hope we can successfully dispose of it."

"We'll take it one step at a time. I have a little experience at this already with Banni, so we should be ready for it."

"Banni? Who is Banni?"

Ankhia slaps a hand over her face and sighs deeply, realizing she will need to go through this one more time.

Chapter 9

COMING OF AGE

"Now remember, we didn't tell him in order to keep him calm. He's not as young as he used to be, and the pressure of the war, among so many other things, has worn badly on him."

"I understand, Kailen. I'll wait outside for you to announce me. Do you actually worry so much about his health?"

"Mother, when we first crashed here, many were killed, and many others took injury from the impact. Fortunately, most recovered, but the emotional and psychological harm of being stranded on a foreign world, and the devastating losses on Ruuki uy'Daan, took a huge toll on us, especially him, as he blamed himself for most of it…which is nothing new, as he blamed himself for so many things along the way…"

"Yes, I recall this, and I as well in some ways, even though we could not accurately say we were responsible for any of it."

"True. And then, of course, we had Kaliya. The trauma she suffered was especially hard on us."

"Yes, from the stories you and she have been telling me, it seems this was perhaps the worst incident of all during our long trek."

"We think it's likely due to Darumon getting ready to dispose of us anyway, as we were just a game for him, and he's probably coming close to his goal of revenge on the Estelar."

"That, in itself, is perhaps the most despicable, on both counts. It's one thing that he treats so many others as toys, but when his kind finally meets with a form of justice, they simply reject all notion of it. And you think this might also relate to Kali and her Prodigy Gift, and his displeasure that she may be developing something?"

"Yeah, his kind wouldn't care for it. This would also be the reason for the original Prodigy Children on Azgarén."

"I swear, it's no wonder the cu'Nar told us to run away."

"And then there was you being lost to us, which only made things worse, as now Father was alone. And that's not a good thing for an elder."

"I can certainly appreciate that much," Tyanna nods solemnly. "I was the same on Ruuki uy'Daan. And worse was the deformity I had to suffer. There were many times when I had thoughts of suicide, but I could never bring myself to it. It was as though there was a tiny voice inside my head telling me to wait, that one day someone will come and help. Although it seemed hopeless to assume this much."

"A little voice?" he muses. "I wonder whose voice that was, because I doubt it could be your imagination at this point."

"Yes, I must ask the same now. It certainly wasn't mine," she chuckles faintly.

Tyanna had been released from the medical ward after many long hours of surgery to remove the organism. Ankhia and her team, along with Aerlie and a selection of her priests, worked laboriously to ensure every strand of alien tissue had been successfully extracted and the puncture wounds closed. Now, Tyanna was trying to reacquaint herself with the Naarg uy'Sodrad and the remains of her people, starting with her husband.

Kailen led her up to the door to Velen's study, where the Master Elder spent so much of his time in deep thought. He buzzes the announcer before entering, while Tyanna held back, giving him time to soften the blow.

Velen had long known of the situation on Ruuki uy'Daan since the early days when Kaliya returned from her accidental projection and visitation. This naturally included the fact that Tyanna was still alive, though she suffered as a victim of the orcish attack. He realized the time may come when she might return, but he had not been told of her decision to volunteer for the curative treatment. This was a safety measure due to his weak health.

"Father?" Kailen calls softly as he enters the room.

Velen was sitting in his favorite chair, which was conveniently turned away from the door. He stirs at the summons and turns to greet his visitor.

"Kailen, my son," he replies in a weary voice. "Please come in."

"How do you feel today?"

"Well enough, all things considered. I am pleased to see our people moving forward so nicely with the aid of His Lordship out there. Perhaps, on this occasion, we may have a chance for ourselves."

"I see the construction efforts outside have begun to take shape in the form of a quaint little village."

"Yes, and I'm hearing word that our people are inspired more and more each day, as they continue to interact with our new neighbors. So, what is it that brings you here, Kailen? Your work has been keeping you so busy that I rarely see you inside the ship anymore."

"Sorry Father. As you know, the war is far from over, and most of our work is being coordinated now from the new military building in Rolsklinde. But this is a special occasion. You have a visitor. I just wanted to make sure you're in good enough condition to accept her."

"Of course, I am always willing to entertain guests. Who is it?" he asks while glancing back towards the door.

"I'll go get her. Just try to keep yourself calm."

"Kailen," he smiles. "I may be old, but I am not on my deathbed yet."

"Yet..." Kailen winces briefly as he walks back over to the door. "Still, you've seen better days, I'm sure."

Velen lethargically pulls himself out of his chair, taking his long walking staff in hand for support. Kailen strolls across to the open door and waves for the visitor to come inside. Tyanna makes a cautious appearance and enters the room.

"Hello, Velen," she announces soothingly.

Velen gazes at the elegant form standing on the other side of the room. He seems frozen in his steps and speechless. He tries calling to her, only to stammer the words. He totters, bumping into the side of his chair as he grapples to catch himself.

Kailen rushes over to help stabilize him, bringing the elderly man upright again.

"Tyanna?" Velen murmurs. "Is it you?"

The woman saunters up to him, reaching out to take his arms.

"Velen, my dear... The years have not been good to you."

"Not simply years, by now," he mumbles softly.

She moves in for a deep embrace, wrapping her arms around him and pulling him close to her.

"Just take care not to squeeze too hard," she cautions. "Although Ankhia tells me I should be strong enough to haul this wreck out of this hole it dug, I think it wise to take things slow."

"But how? What are you doing here? And your injury..." he examines her at length. "You look the same as I always remembered you."

"These people worry about your health, and since the procedure they were using was still a little experimental, they chose to keep the results hidden until they could be sure."

"But why you, Tyanna?"

"And why not?" she returns intrepidly. "Are you going to argue the same as all the others?" she raises her brow and gazes at the two men. "I already went through this with Kali. I hold just as much responsibility as the rest. Do you think I would send another in my place? And besides, someone needs to tend to the work around here," she states as she looks around the room at the bare shelving and poor accouterments. "Who decorated this place? Dear cu'Nar, I'm absent for a few centuries and look what happens."

"That's my mother," Kailen admits. "Give her half a chance and she'll turn this place inside-out."

"It's already inside-out! It needs my touch to set it right again!"

"My dearest Tyanna," Velen sighs with a reassuring smile. "How I missed you."

"And I missed you as well, Velen, as I did Kailen and Kali. I kept photos in the family room back home, those that were still intact. It was all I had to remind me. I was in so much depression, I nearly lost my mind on many occasions. I recall when Kali came to visit that first time. I thought I was delusional. Up until that time, all I could do was to sit in the bedroom and hide from the orcish patrols that would sometimes pass through the city. When she came in, it gave me new hope."

"But your injuries… I was told you had been hit by the orcs with that mutation weapon."

"I was, and it was awful. I'd really rather not remember the occasion. It was the worst experience of my life, and considering my years, that's a lot to reflect upon. I am still amazed at how Ankhia developed such a remarkable solution to it, and more so at the efficiency of the treatment given to me by her team in combination with that Lady Aerlie. I was asleep for the procedure, of course, but as I woke up, I expected to see myself stitched together like an old rag doll. But look at me! Not a mark on me."

"Yes, I see, and this is even more to my surprise. How is it possible?"

"They explained how Lady Aerlie is some sort of priestess, and she carries what she describes as a gift of divine healing, which is apparently a donation by these beings they interact with called the Estelar. She can close an injury with the touch of a hand. I've never heard of such a thing, but then with what Kali has been telling me about her so-called mage studies, I'm wondering what manner of wisdom these people truly have."

"I have only heard a few small mentions from this side. I know many of our people are fascinated by this magic of theirs, which is clearly more advanced than what the orcs were demonstrating to us. From what I've heard, they've apparently solved many of the same technological issues that took us so long with our science, and in only a fraction of the time."

"Yes, and I hope to speak with Lord Thaelyn and Lady Aerlie more on this later. Kailen and Kali are encouraging me to participate in a group discussion with them about what's happening around here, and why the Council is stepping out of these affairs."

"If you wish to do this, I won't get in the way, but you should also know they informed us of a critical flaw in how we manage ourselves that could be used against us."

"Right, Kali told me about this. I'm not part of the Council, so I probably wouldn't be a focus for this point. Nevertheless, I realize that if I involve myself to any level of detail, I will need to be aware of the risks."

◆◆◆

"Kali! We've been waiting for you to show up again!" Sulíma shouts.

"Suli, I was under a lot of stress and other emotions yesterday. But I'm feeling better now, so I'm here to give you an update."

"It's about time! So…what was the final result?"

Kaliya was making a follow-up visit to Ruuki uy'Daan at the Sentinels building. She needed to deliver the news on the procedure to remove the organism from her mother's body, as well as some new instructions for the rest of the victims.

"We were successful at removing the organism. The procedure was long and difficult, but they got it all out. Mother is as healthy as a hill ox, and she's already giving the crew a hard time, from what I hear."

"Oh, thank the cu'Nar for that…well, not for giving everyone a hard time, but you know. We were worried about her. That thing looked so horrid on her body. Are there any aftereffects?"

"It doesn't seem that way. So, here's the plan for the rest. In order that we don't overload the medical staff, we'll be calling them a few at a time on a weekly basis. It'll take time to process them all, but our team has only so many hands to work with. Ankhia and her team, and Lady Aerlie with her people, will all coordinate to see this through as efficiently as possible."

"Lady Aerlie? Isn't she that Queen you mentioned from that other world? What's she doing in a medical ward?"

"She's a priestess, among other things, and on Tae'Eladar the priesthood serves their medical needs. They have some very special techniques which can be useful here."

"Such as?"

"Well, first, their ability to heal injuries and cure illness is a divine gift, a type of laying-on-hands treatment."

"Sounds like faith healing, more of that mysticism like the orcs were said to use."

"Remember what I said about that word, Suli. In this case, they offer their worship to these Estelar I told you about. This is a kind of give-and-take relationship, and they also combine this with a scientific approach, so it's a combination of things."

"That sounds a little strange to me, but I'll go with it for now."

"In addition to this, Thaelyn and Aerlie also brought some of their advanced knowledge to the world to help invent some very useful medicinal agents, including one that helps to regenerate damaged tissue."

"That sounds nice. So, what's next?"

"Next, we start selecting candidates to send through in groups. We'll follow the same process as with my mother, but this time under supervision of our medical team. No offence, Suli, but this last episode was a little nerve-racking."

"Don't worry, Kali, I'm happy to have them go to the Ward for this, rather than mope around here. But what about the rest of us, when do we get to go?"

"I'm working on it, maybe another year or so, depending on how things progress. I'm moving through the Fifth Circle now, and in a few more months I start the Sixth. Once I get into the Seventh, we'll start working on a way to bring all of you home."

"You know, technically we could just jump through the conveyor here."

"Yes, that's true, but not until we have a chance to bring our people here to relieve you. You just need to be patient a little longer."

"And how is it you'll bring them here again? You use some kind of magical portal thing? Is this anything like the conveyor over here?"

"A little bit, but the theory of operation is based on a different form of science. The trouble is, much the same as with our conveyors where you need to locate and calculate the coordinates for the exit point, the rune stones they use need to be physically present in the location where you want the exit portal. Also, the mage casting the enchantment on it needs to hold it in his hand while he channels the energies. My problem is I won't be physical, so I can't channel the energies the same way, which means we'll need to experiment a little to see what works best."

"And then you bring in those people to take over the place, and we can go home."

"Basically. We'll probably set up a garrison outpost, maybe in the field just outside the city, and if they work their usual practice, they'll also construct a gateway node at the same time."

"A gateway node?"

"A magical version of our conveyor… The only difference is it doesn't need a fusion reactor to power it."

"How in all the nether-space do you power a conveyor without a fusion reactor?!" she shrieks.

Kaliya lets out a rowdy laugh.

"Well, Suli, if you want the answer to that, you'll need to stick around and watch."

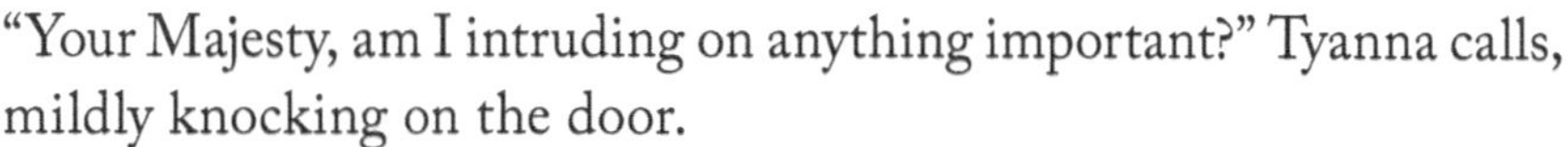

"Your Majesty, am I intruding on anything important?" Tyanna calls, mildly knocking on the door.

"Of course not, come on in, Madam Nazég."

"Please, if you like, you may simply call me by my given name. There is no need for such formality, as we seem to have been developing such a close relationship, your people and ours."

"Very well, and thank you, Tyanna. What can we do for you at this time?"

"If it is not too much trouble, may I ask for a few simple moments to help me settle my mind on something?"

Tyanna was visiting the WIC strategy room where Thaelyn and his officers were gathered for their daily review and planning. The affairs of her return and medical restoration had relaxed by this time. Now she was working with others at the Naarg uy'Sodrad to give aid to the mutation victims being imported from Ruuki uy'Daan.

During this time, she held lengthy conversations with both Kaliya and Kailen on the affairs of the war since the time of the attack on Ruuki uy'Daan, including the sabotage of the Naarg uy'Sodrad, the redirection and marooning on Therinë, the pressures of the Suuden-Aryku and Darumon on their people during the occupation, and the atrocities committed to the other local races.

Her briefing also included the details involving the junior school going into shelters, the principles behind the orcish attack and how it related to Darumon owning them for a much longer period of time, and finally the evolutionary influence Darumon apparently had on the Suuden-Aryku. It was also necessary to fill her in on those portions of Adalon's prophecies leading up to this point. Needless to say, she felt overwhelmed.

"Your Majesty," she begins. "With all that has happened in this time, and these revelations that have been discovered, I feel as if we owe you a great deal for opening our eyes to a much greater conspiracy. However, this truly does not bring with it any solace that we may one day find peace. If anything, it only makes matters worse in my mind, and as a mother I worry for my children."

"I am sure you are not the only one, and more so that many of you have already lost children, as others have lost parents. There is no cure for this, no way to go back and right those wrongs. But at the same time, we must also recognize that without action, more may be lost, and not only for you, but many we cannot even number."

"I understand. Kali tried to explain this to me. I am not a soldier, and I cannot abide the wanton destruction of life and property for any reason, most of all that which Kailen here was explaining about Darumon and his actions. Where does such a fiendish creature as this come from? And what right does he have to preside over the life and death of those around him?"

"These are good questions, Tyanna. Unfortunately, there are those who consider themselves above the answers."

"So it would seem, and now both my children are engaged in this battle, and I fear for their safety. I am too old to try for another. Kali was my last, and even then, it was something of a calculated risk."

"I am told your kind can reproduce well into your late years, is this correct?"

"It is, but from a medical standpoint, it can become risky at my age. And what makes matters worse is how we are always pressed by the Suuden-Aryku each time we tried to settle on a world and rebuild. Just as we start to settle in, they come, launch a surprise attack, kill some portion of our people, and force the rest to flee. As we came to rest on the next world, we needed to restore what was lost by producing a new generation of children to replace those who were taken."

"Yes, I have heard this story before. It has become something of a habit for your people as you are driven by your enemies."

"Driven... Yes, as livestock to a slaughter," she grimaces. "Your Majesty, Velen and I are the last two original citizens of Azgarén. We were betrothed and united well before Sargeras came to our world and corrupted our people, but we did not bring forth any children immediately. It was actually not until later, shortly before they arrived, when we bore a child together...our first."

"Should I assume by your demeanor that this child is no longer with you?"

"You assume correctly, and he was not the only one. He managed to grow to maturity, became an engineer, and was working in one of our manufacturing facilities when they came at us. I think it was after our third jump. The Suuden-Aryku bombarded us from orbit on that occasion. Only a few shots, mind you, but enough to frighten us into moving again. One of them hit the facility where he was working. There was not even enough time for an evacuation order. The building was blasted away, and only a crater left behind."

"I am very sorry for your loss. Curiously, however, this reflects on this city and the bombardment he made here. It was a statement of spite against a group of locals who were making trouble for him."

"So, you think that monster did this just because my son was working there?"

"I dare not make any suggestions, but his manners do drive one to their conjectures."

"Maybe. But anyway, it was many centuries before I could bring myself to try again. Our people were in need to rebuild our numbers, and like the others, I gave of myself to bring a new life into the world, a girl this time."

"Do I dare ask what became of her?"

"As you might suspect, it was during another attack that she was lost. I realize there was probably nothing I could do to change the outcome, but I still feel the pain of it. She was working in the Council building as a political secretary. She was such a beautiful young lady, filled with so much hope. The Suuden-Aryku launched a ground attack on that occasion. We had enough time to give the order to evacuate, and I remember calling her with the news, but she didn't make it. They cut her down in the streets as she made her run, the heathens."

"Once again, firing on fleeing refugees. I spoke with that Commander Geilv about this once. I must wonder how he can justify the occasion, especially if you are not known to possess arms of any kind."

"For this point," Kailen notes. "I would probably point my finger at those chips."

"Indeed, and therefore denying them the capacity to realize their actions. But I truly feel your pain, and it is enough to burn the soul. This makes two you have lost, and the manners of which are simply criminal. It is one thing to attack an industrial building, if you think it to be a strategic target, but to fire upon a fleeing populace..." he shakes his head. "This might be more indicative of Darumon and his style of play."

"As before, I was mortified," Tyanna reflects. "It was a long time before I would try again," she pauses to look up at Kailen. "He was born on the world just before Ruuki uy'Daan, one we called Ghabeel. He was just a boy when they came, and I was bound and determined not to let him out of my sight!"

"I wasn't quite a boy, Mother," Kailen corrects pleasantly.

"Still, you were much too young to fall victim to those butchers. Again, they made a random bombardment from space taking pot shots at us, just enough to force us to move. We ran, managed to get inside the ship, and departed. It was on this occasion when the Council decided we needed to make a wild jump in an effort to evade them permanently."

"Ah yes, this famous wild jump of yours," Thaelyn smiles.

"Yes, Kali was telling me about that. Just one more count against him, I suppose. Our navigation systems were not designed for this, basing their calculations only on known celestial factors. Apparently, there was some manner of argument on whether we should make the attempt, and then someone punched in some numbers and hit the initiator. Next thing you know, we are flying almost blind until we arrived near Ruuki uy'Daan."

"Right," Kailen admits. "And here we have that extraordinary discovery of a conveniently habitable world."

"That's exactly how I felt! It was a miracle we arrived in any form of physical space at all. To find a star system with anything more than one or two hostile planets inside would be beyond astronomical… seriously!" she chuckles ironically

"An argument, you say?" Thaelyn wonders. "Was this amongst the Council members?"

"Yes. I recall Velen and Santari were involved, along with the High Commander at the time. I wasn't present in the room, but I learned of it later."

"What about Drescuul?"

"I think he was absent, having excused himself for some reason."

"How convenient… And then a navigator shows up, and so remarkably punches in coordinates to carry you to an unknown location that just happens to be the home of those orcs."

"I don't think I would buy that if my life depended on it," Kailen relents. "Not after everything else we've been learning."

"It's truly amazing," Tyanna muses. "How we were so easily manipulated by him. And so we settled on Ruuki uy'Daan, hoping we were safe at last, and as with so many times before, many of the women began bringing forth a new wave of children. I was hesitant at first, but after a while, when I felt we were indeed safe, I tried one last time and gave birth to Kali."

"And from here we can pick up with the events that followed," Thaelyn surmises.

"Yes, she grew into a beautiful young girl, very talented in school, and with such an innocent spirit. We were at fourteen centuries by this time on that world, and we felt as if there were no more threats to spoil our future."

"Tell me about when you first discovered this gift in her."

"Ah, yes," she smiles. "That was a curious moment. There had been a few occasions when she would come to me with stories of some strange dreams she had. At first, I simply considered these to be the wild imagination of a young child. At least until Ankhia called me one night and told me Kali was wandering around the medical lab unattended."

"Oh? What was the occasion?"

"It was late in the evening, and I felt sure she should be in bed by then. When Ankhia called, I went to look in Kali's room, and sure enough I did see her asleep in bed. But Ankhia was adamant that Kali was standing right next to her in the lab asking questions about her work."

"Indeed," Thaelyn grins. "Even in your culture, children must be a charm to behold."

"I suppose this might be regarded as a universal constant, Your Majesty," she smiles. "So, I asked Kailen to watch over the house while I charged down to the lab to see what Ankhia was talking about. I told her to keep this mystery child occupied until I could arrive, and she did. When I entered the lab, I found Ankhia and what appeared to be Kali playing a little game on one of the tables. I couldn't believe my eyes! Kali looked over at me, said hello, and even rushed up to give me a hug."

"That must have been a good surprise for you."

"You have no idea!" she chuckles. "It was at this moment I started to remember some of the old research done on Azgarén about the Prodigy Children. It was such a rare instance that we barely knew how to recognize it. According to Velen's early hypothesis on the subject, which unfortunately no one ever listened to, I was looking at my daughter's spirit projected outside her physical body into real space. Clearly, I needed to understand what this was, so I began a research project at the university."

"Allow me to ask you this. Did you recall those early children and the mysterious deaths they experienced?"

"Yes, I did! Velen and I spoke of this, as he had a team conducting some of the early research. But before they could find any answers, the children were found dead, and very quickly after they were first discovered. And I mean this to say, we receive a report of a discovery, we go out, look at it, take a few moments of rest, and then boom! Someone shouts in distress that the child is now dead, and from some extremely disturbing circumstances. It didn't seem physically possible for the time frame."

"If Darumon was monitoring those reports… For instance, if he had access to whatever means those reports pass through to find people like you to conduct your work, he was probably riding along with you for his own review. Are you familiar with a vampiric action, to drain a body of its life essence?"

"This sounds much more like something out of a thriller vid-com program than anything real. But there it was. And if he was watching us so closely, I guess we never had a chance to learn anything. And naturally, this frightened us for Kali. But at the same time, we began to reason it couldn't be due to any of the causes they were suggesting on Azgarén. We were simply too far removed from that for it to hold any relevance."

"Indeed, and therefore you proceeded to consider an alternate cause."

"The Prodigy Gift, yes… There could not be any other realistic explanation to allow what we were seeing other than to say she was somehow separating her spirit entity from her body, even if accidentally. One of my greatest concerns was that mysterious death syndrome, and if it could be related as perhaps losing control of the effect. My hope was to learn how she did this and to see if it could be contained, maybe even to govern it by her natural will, thereby better controlling it."

"Fascinating, but did you fully understand what it was, or only guessing at this time?"

"Guessing, mostly, but I was beginning to suspect something. Between this and studying the orcs and this thing they called magic, I began to wonder if there was a connection. We did not see them use anything like a tool when they conjured up this stuff, and since our science faction was attempting to study metaphysics, I began to suspect if the will of the mind could play a role. This then brought me to our scientific thesis."

"Ah, let me guess," Thaelyn smiles. "This statement Kaliya has so often described as the riddle of metaphysics."

"Yes!" she chuckles. "Many of our younger generations took to using that analogy. I suppose I can't blame them. Back on Azgarén, our entire faction was often ridiculed and downplayed as so much rubbish for the theories we were proposing."

"Indeed, their desire for empirical data. But Tyanna, you might have been very close to a breakthrough, as you are most certainly travelling on the right path. Magic, or as we call it, Arcane Science, does work on the power of the mind, though you need to be very careful to govern yourself. Kaliya's gift is also based on her will to project herself outward and carry her projection from place to place."

"And those early children, the poor things… A vampiric action. Yes, I suppose I can see it…if he holds such loathing of lesser beings pretending to hold such powers as these. But in all the nether-space, that beast!" she growls. "He would kill children, on top of everything else! For this point, I might actually feel the urge to go to war with him."

"And thus the reason we are here."

"Yes, so it seems. However, at the time I was observing this, I chose not to tell Kali about it, not directly, only to encourage her to experiment with a few ideas I gave during these episodes. I was afraid she might develop some unfortunate psychological aberration."

"What about your Council, how did they react?"

"Elder Vankkar, if you know his manners, began to argue about the potential security risks and the trouble this Gift could bring. As for Elder Drescuul, his reactions seemed mixed. He was interested in knowing who it was, but I wasn't about to let out any names. It would be very unprofessional for me, and since it was my own daughter, I wanted to protect her, most of all."

"Of course. Then we can assume Elder Drescuul, or rather Darumon, if he was in disguise, might not be personally aware of this child being Kaliya."

"Unless he stole the knowledge telepathically during one of these reports," Kailen suggests.

"Possibly," Thaelyn wonders. "Did you ever deliver any of these reports directly to the Council?"

"No, not personally," Tyanna responds. "Usually, they followed a bureaucratic path to their chamber. Most of my time was spent in the university research center."

"Out of reach... In any event, I suppose it might be moot at this time. If Darumon knew who it was specifically, I doubt she would be with us today."

"Unless..." Kailen offers. "Maybe he did somehow find out, and decided to take this other action anyway, either out of spite or simply for his pleasures."

"A kind of blanket effect? Since she was clearly a child, and likely attending that same school? Again, possibly. Either scenario is valid, at this point. It would certainly offer a clever cover for his reasoning."

"Yes, this is a very disturbing suggestion," Tyanna submits. "But I suppose you could be right. And now I must wonder about your plans for her. Clearly, you are training her to use this Gift, but to what end? Or is this one of those classified secrets I'm not supposed to ask about?" she smiles gently.

"I suppose the best way to answer that question, Tyanna," Thaelyn grins. "Is to also ask if you want to be inside or outside our little circle."

The months passed, and Kaliya continued to train with her new weapon. She had become very nimble by now, swinging and swirling it around her body and over her head, spinning it in one hand, clutching it in both, then twisting, thrusting, and slashing. It was a dance of metal with potentially lethal implications.

She was out on the field during her practice one day, dressed in her traditional training outfit, and limbering up for her latest workout. As she prepared herself, she first conducted a light meditation to find her center, then to pick up her sword-staff and begin the exercise.

From a walkway above, overlooking the field, an elder woman discreetly observed the young lady in her practice, as she once did long ago when Kaliya was a child in school during her gymnastic classes.

Tyanna had been watching Kaliya for weeks now, occasionally sneaking in unobserved during her combat practice, and a few times for mage practice. She had never seen the conjuring of magic before, not outside the primitive efforts of the orcs, and certainly not on the scale being taught in the academy here and the extremes of where Kaliya was taking it. The girl was now into her Sixth Circle of study, sending out blazing torrents of fire and shards of ice. The terror she was letting loose on the field was frightening, even to those upper classmen more accustomed to it.

As the school season comes to a close, she and her friends make another meeting.

"Well, girl, this is it, ay?" Relissa inquires.

"Yes, I'm signed up for the Seventh Circle," Kaliya admits. "This is the big one that takes us to Ruuki uy'Daan."

"Are you nervous about it?"

"A little… But at this moment, no more so than any other new course of study. It's just the implications of going back to my old home that gets to me now. And this means one step closer to Azgarén and Sargeras."

"Aye, just don't go running so far ahead that we can't keep up with you."

"I see where those modrons came in with the details for relocating the orcs," Haran mentions.

"Yeah," Kaliya affirms. "And Thaelyn is currently reviewing his options with Kailen and the General."

"I wonder where they'll go to find this new home of theirs."

"I don't know, Haran, the universe is a big place, and we know of two full examples. Well, outside of Tae'Eladar and whatever's left of this place."

"But this one has to be a barren example. Could it be the same one where you came from?"

"That's a good question, but personally, I hope it's nowhere near Azgarén."

In the WIC building in Rolsklinde, Thaelyn and his officers were indeed going over the reports delivered by the modrons. The selection process seemed fairly straightforward. The list involved the top ten best choices, along with some criteria for the planets in question.

Included with the other reports was Thaelyn's special request for information regarding Maker Kuroku. He was deep in study of the paper, which represented a single sheet made from synthetic fibers to simulate paper, but more durable.

The General and Kailen both sat at the table, now reviewing a series of local reports, but the General took special notice of Thaelyn as he seemed to stare blankly at this one sheet, leaning an elbow on the table and resting his head in his hand.

"My Lord, is there something disturbing you?"

"General, this report is that secondary request I made with Primus regarding Maker Kuroku."

"Right, you mentioned this to us before. Does it give you any interesting details?"

"Oh, yes, I suppose you could call this interesting. If there could ever be an occasion of censorship amongst the Estelar, this is a prime example of it."

"What do you mean?" Kailen wonders. "What were you hoping to find?"

"I was curious, mostly, to see if I could discover anything to help associate the Maker with any or all of our interests where your people or Sargeras are concerned."

"You mean, how and why she was following him, and watching him for so long? If she knew who he was, and follows the same manners as the others, she might want to keep tabs on him, right?"

"Yes, this follows naturally, and with good reason. But the question is this. Why would she, more than any other, remember him after all this time, when the others generally forgot or otherwise believe them to be dead. And then, why go to so much effort, such as with the cu'Nar, and then you and your father, Adalon and her prophecies, and whatever else she might be involved with, simply to lead us on this long escapade to seek him out."

"Well, my Lord," the General muses humorously. "Is it not said the gods work in strange ways?"

"Oh, General, you would pull that on me now?" he chuckles. "Very well, but listen to this. This one paper represents all the public information Primus is permitted to give out. For instance, she first joined the local body of the Estelar an epoch ago. No numbers, simply an epoch. If I try to interpret this with some of the stories of the Primordials, this might match up for the terminology. But the terms are indistinct, much like with the stories themselves."

"Which means," Kailen considers. "We could possibly associate a point of origin at or near the time of the Celestial War, which could then provide a link. She could've been present at the time."

"Perhaps, and this might offer a small clue for how and why she holds an interest. But, as for where she originally came from, this is classified. What name did she use previously...classified. Age... classified. Race...classified."

"Oh dear cu'Nar..." Kailen moans and covers his face.

"And then, when asked about any associations with other prominent Estelar, there was an intermittent relationship with Helm, and an intermittent relationship with Tyr, but any and all interactions are again marked as either private or classified. She is publicly known to have created the Draconic race, and this much I know from my own teachings."

"Ah, good, so we do have something on her."

"Right, but the reason for doing so is classified..." he begins laughing mindlessly. "Any associations with any Child Race... classified. Associations with Tae'Eladar...classified, other than for the restoration effort. And THEN," he raises a finger for emphasis. "She is listed as missing for an indeterminate amount of time and for no apparent reason."

He slaps the paper on the table while still laughing deliriously.

"Gentlemen," he concludes. "If ever we said she was elusive, we could not have been more correct!"

"That sounds like one of our old vid-com spy programs," Kailen muses.

"I swear," the General shakes his head. "Now we know where Adalon gets it. She probably took private lessons. So, where does this actually lead us, or does it?"

"What I can tell you of my own interpretations might be this," Thaelyn offers. "There are two possibilities that come to mind. One is she is extremely elusive, demands extreme privacy, and simply does NOT like giving out details for any reason. While I will not argue this, as she does have this prerogative, this level of privacy seems a little unwarranted."

"Maybe, but then, who knows what her reasons may be."

"Perhaps. And this is where my second thought comes in… her occupation. If we consider the Draconics being created for a reason, and we already know they are described as a guardian race of some sort, and then to combine one or more aspects of where we are with Tae'Eladar, Adalon's prophecies, and of course, Sargeras and Darumon, I might suggest she is involved in some manner of secret intelligence or a law enforcement role, and therefore must maintain a high level of security for herself. This might also correlate her relations with Helm and Tyr, where they would also fit this category."

"That sounds like a fine suggestion, but good gracious, she must be strict."

"Based on what we have, we might have an association of timing with the Celestial War, and I think this much we can assume anyway if she knows of Sargeras at all. As for the rest, I suspect she is hiding something very deep and very personal, if she is burying herself in so much intrigue. She must have known him personally, or held something close that caused her to follow him. What that is, we might not know until the very end."

"So, we just do what we do best, and wait for it as it comes to us."

"Precisely, General! We will allow her this moment and follow the clues laid out for us. Surely, if she is the one planning all these curious little sequences, she must have spent a considerable amount of time on it."

"Cu'Nar's pity," Kailen mumbles. "And just one more reason to wonder where this is going."

"Yes, but for now we have our work. And mine currently requires my attendance in B.T. Kaliya is moving into her new mage class, and we need to prepare ourselves."

Thaelyn rises from his chair and excuses himself from the meeting. He then marches outside to the local gateway hub and takes a transit back home. On his arrival at the guildhall, he called several pages from the courtyard to assemble a meeting of his higher-ranking scholars, while he diverted to freshen up briefly. He joined the others in the guild's tactical center, where he would often conduct official staff meetings and consultations.

"The time is close upon us, gentlemen," he begins. "In addition to making our move on Ruuki uy'Daan, I have also received word from Primus. A delivery was made not long ago, and I have been in discussion with the General and others on the possibilities of our choices. I bade the modrons to return when we were ready to make our advance. They will monitor our progress and contact us when we have our troops ready. In the meantime, we must discover the best manner in which to have Kaliya perform her duty on our behalf."

"My Lord," offers one of the Masters. "In her projected form, we have already discredited the notion that she could perform this function directly. In order for her to cast any form of incantation, she would first need the spell inscribed onto a scroll. But the next question is whether she could even cast it from there. She is not physical, so I am of the mind we might need to devise something special to direct her voice into it."

"Perhaps you can consult with Professor Cogswoggle for an idea. He is currently working on a project that might provide a few elements to assist."

"Very good, but then, as to the glyphs themselves. We might need to adapt some of our more recent techniques of using harmonic conceptual plates on a program board to sequence the conjuring. We could then attach this to an arcanic inductor to provide our effect."

"Excellent. Just try not to blow up the lab as you put this together," he smiles tenderly. "We will experiment with this and see if it works. But as for the actual casting, we also mentioned a need for an external focus."

"Yes, as opposed to her physical body channeling the energies. This should be fairly easy to implement. If we can fashion a portable unit for the inductor, something small that she can carry, this would serve our purpose nicely."

"Very good. Let us see to it at once. She is entering the Seventh Circle now, so we should not delay. We cannot know what Darumon is doing outside our field of view, and given his nature, I would not wish to give him so much advantage."

"Absolutely, my Lord!"

<hr>

"All right, Likha, how many does that make so far?"

"A lot, but it seems like barely a drop in the bucket compared to what's left. Ankhia, this is going to take a while. There are hundreds of victims over there. We're only taking a few each week. It could take years to process them all."

"Probably, but our staff needs rest on occasion, and these surgical procedures aren't easy. We'll get it done, it's just a matter of working the problem."

"Speaking of which, I had another thought. As we work on all these mutation victims, what about the Suuden-Aryku? Say, for instance, one day we are in a position to rescue a few. How do we handle that? Or do we even try?"

"That thought crossed my mind a few times also. If only we had a better idea of how those implants worked…at least, in a living body. The ones we studied from the bodies picked up outside seemed inactive, as if they shut down when the body died."

"That's certainly an effective way to prevent an enemy from learning anything about it."

"An enemy…from learning something…" Ankhia muses distantly. "But if Darumon is involved in their design, does he actually expect any enemies to get that close? And would he actually care? This is for HIS use to control his goons. And those goons aren't intended to be captured and examined by…enemies. Especially if they tend to blast everything out there to bits, and the only real enemies are gods who probably wouldn't do autopsies anyway."

"Um, well, all right. So, what are we saying here?"

"Well, for one thing, grab a live specimen," she chuckles ironically.

"Uh huh, sure. But that sounds extremely risky, Ankhia. I really doubt they'll go down without a fight, especially if these things control them in some way giving them a singular thought to kill whatever they see. We would need to subdue them somehow."

"I think it might go even deeper than that. There was that external device on the side of their cranium. I had a couple of engineers take a look at it and it looked like some sort of control interface, possibly with a data uplink."

"Oh wonderful! So even if we capture one, he relays his status to the others, and our efforts are blown."

"Unless we somehow devise a way to jam the signal, but to do that, we need to know the methods and frequencies used. This presents us with a little paradox."

"Yeah, how to capture a live specimen without the others knowing about it, so we can study his implants to jam the signals that otherwise tell the others we captured him. Very nice, Ankhia…"

"We'll see if we can study these old implants some more, but according to His Lordship, there should be a Suuden-Aryku outpost on Morndindor. Maybe, if we can get close enough, perhaps to bring in some scanning equipment, we can take a few readings and learn something from it. But we need to get something ready. Somehow, if that base exists, we need to capture it, either with or without its crew. Who knows how that'll work, especially if more come to investigate?"

✦✦✦

"Tanjhira," announces a smallish voice from below. "His Lordship is asking about our prototype. We need to put the finishing touches on it as quickly as our little feet can carry us."

"Feet for you, Professor, hooves for me," she responds cheerily.

Professor Cogswoggle and Chief Technician Lapäli had been working feverishly on the new armor prototype at the Bahlaie Research Center, known locally as the BRC, where the interactions between the Tae'Eladaran scientists and Daanen-Aryku researchers have been progressing at an accelerated pace in recent months to assemble the latest assortment of new technologies expected to be placed into service for the coming engagements.

On site were several large buildings designed as aircraft hangers.

Some were used as storage, where the engineers had built a set of small training vessels, a design commonly used by the Daanen-Aryku to train new pilots for such duties as scouting patrols and cargo transport. Other buildings were used for research where they had been developing several new vehicle designs.

One prototype in production was a single man combat craft. The design began with the training vessel, then expanded with a more robust framework, an advanced propulsion system, rigid structural reinforcements, and sleeker contours, as befitting Tae'Eladaran cultural standards, which should make it look sufficiently alien to the Suuden-Aryku. And of course, it also included weapons. It was intended to be quick and nimble, but as with all new designs, it needed testing.

In an adjacent building, still partially in the course of remodeling, a very unique design was taking shape. It was huge, and therefore the reason for the building remodel. Several components were being fabricated independently so far, to be assembled into a superstructure later. They resembled a skeletal framework involving a long spine and two sets of curved armatures. Another module was turning out to be much more like the bridge section of a naval vessel than the cabin space of an aircraft. A large drawing board in a planning office showed the design concept, but some elements, like the engine nacelles, were still under debate as to the final configuration.

In an open field was a testing ground, where the pitted and scarred earth marked the result of weapons testing for a new technology based on the Suuden-Aryku plasma design combined with an arcanic hybrid. The soldiers who would use these weapons would need to be practiced in the arcane arts, and this explicitly excluded the Suuden-Aryku from gaining any technical understanding of their design.

The Professor and his cohort continued their work on the prototype battle armor. They were assembling the final few pieces and running a series of diagnostics to ensure it met with their expectations. The only thing they needed after this was a willing subject to try it out.

Marelle was just arriving in the tactical office to meet with Thaelyn and Kailen. She had received a summons recently to join a conference regarding some new work ahead.

"Commander, you asked for me?" she inquires as she enters the room.

"Marelle, we're ready for you to begin your training. Since we don't have a dedicated air military base, I will assign an escort to take you to the BRC for your first lessons."

"Um, excuse me, Commander, but I think I missed a small detail here. What are you training me for?"

"Ah, I thought you might already be expecting this. This is in relation to your time piloting that heavy transport. We're teaching you to fly."

Marelle's eyes light up in excitement at the mention, and she squeals in delight. She bounces into Kailen's arms and wraps herself around in a spontaneous hug.

"Ooh! Thank you, Commander, you remembered!" she croons with a broad smile, and then pulls back to recompose herself. "And of course you too, my Lord," she continues to Thaelyn on the other side of the table.

The sudden gesture caught Kailen unaware, but he returned with a quick pat on her back and a pleasant smile. Thaelyn smiled admiringly at the scene.

"You will begin with the training simulators, Marelle," Thaelyn asserts. "This is the standard method the Daanen-Aryku use to train new pilots. From there, you will graduate to the actual vessel, although that which you will be practicing on will be considerably smaller than the one you brought home from the Dwarven enclave."

"Sounds fair enough, and maybe a little easier to get started… Can I ask a question while I'm here? Why would I need to learn the mage studies up to the Sixth Circle? You didn't mention a reason before this, and if I'm going to learn to fly, I'd like to know what my ultimate objective is here."

"Indeed. It is reasonable to say you may serve multiple functions here, and the combat vessels we are designing will use a hybrid form of weapon that will require mage studies to operate it. So far, we are still in the design stage, but it is likely you will require a healthy amount of study to qualify."

"So, is that to mean I'll be flying over their heads dropping fireballs on them?" she giggles tenderly.

"While that might conjure up a curious image," he smiles, "the weapon designs we are developing will resemble the Suuden-Aryku plasma rifles, but mounted outside and using your mage focus to fire ahead of you."

"I hope my training will include lessons on how to do that. If I'm inside the thing, I'd hate to see the result if one of them bounced back at me," she winces.

"Yes, that would be rather unpleasant," he chuckles. "But we will see to this as we move forward."

Marelle grins as she recalls the time when she flew the large Suuden'kai transport from the Dwarven enclave in the north down to Firstfall in the valley.

"We further believe," Thaelyn adds, "that this reflects on Adalon's message to you. To learn something we do not teach back home, and thus be able to go places you never thought possible."

"Oh dear gods, is THAT what it is? But what about the part where we share something together?"

"This is likely for a future moment, but you must first begin your journey with the basics."

"Right, so I have my work cut out for me, it seems. I'll spend as much time as I can on this. I'm sure it'll be a lot of work, but it sounds like you'll be sending me to war, and I need to be ready for it."

"As we all must be," he nods. "Lieutenant, will you be kind enough to show the young lady to her new assignment?"

"Yes, Your Lordship," Padriyl responds. "After the fact that she flew a complex piece of machinery for the mere pleasure of it, NOW we teach her how to do it officially," he chuckles ironically. "Marelle, will you follow me, please."

"Let us not forget your role in that little escapade," Thaelyn muses jovially.

"Oh yes! And how she twisted my horns along the way."

Padriyl and Marelle exit the building into the plaza, and disappear into the city hub center across the way.

"Now, General," Thaelyn continues. "With Marelle engaged in her practice, and Kaliya with hers, we must look forward to what may lie ahead of us once we arrive."

"Yes, my Lord, this has been on my mind of late, as well."

"We are going to make a few assumptions here, and hope we are correct in our findings. First is the conveyor from Portal Three. If that second index does indeed point to Morndindor, then we can assume we have our next waypoint."

"This is reasonable if we consider Adalon's prophecy on the matter."

"If, for some reason, we are in error, then I hope she, or some other factor, will correct us."

"I feel fairly confident in the Maker for this point. If she is watching these events unfold, I think she would see to our success."

"Very good, then we shall place our faith in her and see where it takes us."

"Excellent, but what do you suggest after? We cannot allow Darumon or the Suuden-Aryku to take notice of our arrival. This conveyor opens up to an unknown location, so our arrival must be very discreet until we can discern where we are in relation to them."

"Absolutely, General," Thaelyn affirms. "I would first wish to send a single scout through. Morndindor must surely reside within a dynamistic cloud, perhaps the same as where we are now, since the dwarves are familiar with such materials as mithril and adamantium, and we know these can only form in such an environment as this."

"Yes, and so we could perhaps behave as we first did here, to send someone across to make a quick survey and try to bring away a rune to the local area."

"Do you think we should expect an unwelcome arrival on that side?" Kailen wonders.

"This becomes problematic," Thaelyn considers. "The dwarves from up north described this invasion to originally come out of a portal, and this surely represents an unexpected arrival, to say nothing of a potentially uninvited one."

"Yes, I suppose it would."

"On the other hand, if it were me, I would not deliver an invasion force of any kind within easy view of the local population. Therefore, these orcs, and later the elves, would likely have been delivered to a remote location where they would have opportunity enough to amass themselves into a proper strike force."

"At least until the dwarves got wise to it," the General advises.

"Correct, which now leaves us to wonder what is there currently. For instance, did they erect a garrison outpost to watch for any future invasions?"

"That could be a problem," Kailen relents.

"I further recall the dwarves actually used the word portals, in plural form. Could this mean there is more than one, or could it simply be a form of propaganda by their Thane to embellish his famous stories?"

"If he follows the ways of Darumon," the General muses. "Maybe so, as he became quite famous for his own stories."

"This is true, and so far, we only know of the one conveyor with this addressing. Next is to ask about Darumon himself and where he is presently. If he was here on Therinë while this Thane was controlling things on Morndindor, does this mean we have another servant creature working for Sargeras, or someone else, perhaps a local who has been badly corrupted."

"If it's another servant creature, we will need to step very carefully. Although, was it not said, through our spy recordings of the Governor, that he was the last of his kind?"

"It was, and I suppose we might need to trust this statement, as I do not see a purpose to lie on this smatter when he was essentially confessing something to the old Dean of the academy."

"Perhaps."

"But either way, this brings yet another thought to mind, which may demand us to look at things from the other side."

"Uh oh..." Kailen moans. "All right, the other side of what?"

"If we are suggesting the Thane was fabricating so many stories relating to this invasion, but we know the real invasion was much different and not nearly as long, then what is actually on the other side of that conveyor, if the Thane KNOWS there is no invasion occurring presently?"

"You're right. Darumon only sent those elves for a relatively brief amount of time, probably just long enough to distract the dwarves from his own efforts, and then it stopped. So if the Thane, whoever it is, is in control of things over there, he probably wouldn't bother with a garrison as there's nothing else to be expected out of it."

"And therefore," the General concludes. "It might just be an open field, the original remote location where it all started."

"If this is the case," Thaelyn accedes. "We may hold a small advantage. We can establish a base, perhaps also to camouflage it to hide it from view, and launch out from there."

"Very good, but then what? We should organize our objectives for that place, one of which is clearly to find the city of Glimmerheim, and another is to find the Suuden-Aryku base."

"Yes, this much is certain. We should move cautiously to investigate the local surroundings, including any nearby cities or towns, and try to maintain a very low profile, just in case the Thane has spies, or if word might filter back up to him."

"That would cut things short for us in a hurry," Kailen relents.

"Didn't the dwarves mention another mining operation?" the General wonders.

"Yes," Thaelyn affirms. "Something to the south of the city, I believe, so this adds one more item to our list. And this does not yet consider what condition that world is actually in after Darumon had his way with it."

"I am asking myself where the best choice for that Suuden-Aryku base would be. If the Thane is pulling out work teams under the influence of this drug, I would imagine it cannot be far to travel before they are delivered into the hands of the Suuden-Aryku."

"This is a good point, and could also narrow things for us. It might be in close proximity, perhaps even within fair walking distance, if these men are simply sent out a door. We will need to consult with Chief Bronzeheart and his people to see about this, as well as any details they can provide for the lay of the land."

"Very well, my Lord," the General nods. "Once we find our way there, it seems we will already have our work for us."

✦✦◆✦✦

"Now, Kaliya, here is what we have in mind," the academy Master begins. "We have a series of scrolls here for you. First, we will have you scribe the spell in your personal tome and practice in your natural form, simply to gain some experience in casting the spell. After that, we will have you practice a few times casting it from a scroll, again for the experience. When you are ready, we will have you go into your projected form for the next step."

"Yes, Master. I'll get on this right away."

Kaliya was in session for her Seventh Circle studies. On this day, she was pulled aside for a special practice session. She was handed the spell description to scribe into her tome for the incantation to mark a portal rune. Once she had the spell properly formed in her book, she studied it carefully. She then took up a box of blank runes and marched outside to the training field for her practice.

It was a sunny autumn day, and she set her book and the box of runes on the table in front of the practice lane she was using on the lower field. It was not necessary for her to go to the upper field on this occasion, as she was not practicing any combat spells.

She retrieved a rune from the box and held it in her hand, with the forward markings oriented away from her body, as was the standard practice for marking a rune. The result would open a portal in the same orientation as the rune. She recalls the chant and waves her hand in circles over the object. As she invokes the arcane forces, the energies wrap around her body forming a spiraling vortex at her feet, which swirls up the length of her body into a funnel above her head, then twisting and spinning downwards into the rune itself, causing the stone to glow from the aftereffects of the enchantment. The surface of the rune changed its hue as an indication of her success.

The academy Master was standing off to her side on this occasion, observing her progress. He took the rune from her to examine it and gave his approval. She was then instructed to perform this process several more times to make sure she understood it well.

Once she felt comfortable with the casting ritual, she then took up one of the spell scrolls sitting near her on the table. The scrolls were a standard design and inscribed with the same incantation, but in this case, it was a self-contained item that didn't require her to channel her own energies. She would read from the scroll using relatively little of her personal effort to direct the enchantment into the rune.

She broke the seal on the scroll and unrolled it, holding it in her hand. She took up a fresh rune in the other hand, just as she did before, and began to read the glyphic inscription on the parchment.

As she read off each glyph, it glowed, until the full set on the paper was ablaze. With the pronouncement of the final glyph, the scroll erupted in a flash, vaporizing in a puff of smoke while the arcane energies began to swirl around her, forming a vortex. They spiraled up, turned, and funneled into the rune, the same as when she cast it from her own power. The Master took the latest example and approved of her success. Again, he had her practice this several times until she felt confident in her abilities.

"Very good, Kaliya," he confirms. "Now, we are going to try perhaps a few different methods to see how well this works in your projected form. I will have you retire to your room and submerse yourself, then return to me straight away."

Kaliya nods and rushes off to her room where she can meditate quietly. She returns soon after in her projected state, appearing in a puff standing on the platform near her instructor.

"Good," he affirms. "Now, we suspect you might not be able to cast from this condition directly. Nevertheless, I will have you try a few simple exercises on the field just to be sure. Let us keep this to the First or Second Circle combat grade. It does not truly matter what Circle you choose, if you can do it at all, but the lowest Circles would be the easiest."

Kaliya steps up to her stall and targets a nearby training dummy. She decides to try a simple attack spell sending out a volley of small missiles at the target. This was a very easy spell with just two spoken elements to call the arcane action. She utters the words and stretches out a hand over the alley, but to no effect. She tries it again, attempting to apply a stronger focus while speaking the words, sending out her other hand at her quarry. Again, nothing occurs.

"I'm sorry, Master. I don't feel the energies flowing through me this time."

"As we suspected, Kaliya," the Master admits. "But do not despair, as we are not so easily discouraged," he smiles.

He pulls a box over to the table from the rear of the platform. He opens it and selects a scroll from inside, handing it over to her.

"Try this. We will test to see if you can cast directly from a scroll in this condition."

Kaliya looks at the scroll and reads the name from the rolled-up flap.

"Magic Missile… The same as I was just trying on my own."

"Yes, this one is a stock item from our stores. Continue as you were, and as I am sure you have done many times before."

She breaks the seal and unrolls the new scroll. While holding it in her hand, she sets her sights on her target and tries once again to focus herself. She stretches out her free hand and calls the words on the scroll. But much like before, there is no reaction. The glyphs showed no activity from her attempt to cast the spell.

"As we thought," the Master muses. "Even though it might contain the energies within, you still need a body to impose your mental efforts into the conjuring…although not as deeply in this case. In the absence of that, your voice is simply playing out in the open without a presence to carry your commands."

"Uh oh, that doesn't sound good. How am I supposed to be able to do anything if I don't have anything to do it with?"

"Ah, but my dear young lady," he smiles. "We are not without our means."

"Yeah, I was afraid you might say that. Do I need to pull out a fresh set of horns for the occasion?"

"Well, it might not be as bad as that. Here, hand that one back and we will simply return it to the box."

Kaliya gives back the scroll as the Mage Master prepares for the next step.

"Now, listen carefully," he continues. "A group of us have considered this problem. Our first concern is that you need some manner of physical presence for the energies to pass through to your target. When conjuring any spell, you do so with your own body as the channeling pathway. Since your body is currently unavailable, we need a surrogate. Furthermore, even if casting from a scroll, you still need a physical mind and body to invoke the commands to engage the glyphs. A projected spirit essence is not tangible enough to do this. For this, we had to invent something special. And as His Lordship suggested to us, we had to do so without blowing up any laboratories along the way," he chuckles vigorously.

"Oh, gee, how considerate of him!" she smiles.

"Yes, he does contribute that occasional moment of humor. But the exercise itself was a curious one, and might even open up a new form of study for us. Take a look at this…"

He reaches into his box again and pulls out a strange apparatus. It resembled a ring of six small, imbued disks attached vertically in a wire frame, each inscribed with a softly glowing glyph, similar in nature to the disks that were often used on the gateway nodes and other arcanic devices that needed to channel energy. The wire framework was mounted on top of a short cylindrical base containing a collection of components, including several wheels and gears, along with a strange rodlike chemical power cell. The wheels seemed to turn the ring framework, as well as two counterrotating sets of crystals inside the base.

Kaliya studied a strange apparatus as the Master set it up on the table. The framework on top included a fixed mounting cradle for a rune in the center of the ring, and a slanted shelf to the rear that seemed designed to install something. The shelf had a small retaining clip at the top, but the bottom edge appeared as a slot, more like a docking port to install a component board of some kind. And just in front of the slot was a circular device vaguely reminiscent of a microphone attachment.

Kaliya gazed in awe at the bizarre otherworldly apparatus. She leaned closer to study the internal workings.

"Unbelievable! It looks partially electric, and partially mechanical… maybe also partially electronic. Almost like a mechanical channeling device."

"This unit is what we call an arcanic inductor," he directs. "It's a custom-made variation for our needs, but based on a recent study we've been making for some of our newer industry to apply certain roles where focused surges of energy are demanded."

"I haven't had much opportunity to look at your industry, I've been so busy in here."

"Yes, we have a lot of inspired minds working on a variety of devices and methods for using our arcanic sciences. Some of these require the delivery of arcanic energies, and not always by trained mages doing the work. So we are developing appliances to carry some of this for us."

"And this up here…" she points at the shelf. "What goes in there?"

"Normally," the Master begins. "If we are using a spell scroll, it is cast while held in the hand, and the mind invokes the energies as you speak the words from the glyphs inscribed onto the paper. You don't need to channel your own energies, instead simply allowing it to channel through you. But here we have a problem. In the absence of your body, we must apply a sort of effigy, an external device as a surrogate. But even at that, as we saw with your previous attempt at using a scroll, simply calling out the glyphs doesn't seem to work in your case."

"Yeah, that would sort of defeat the whole purpose of it."

"However, you DO have the capacity to speak, even if not through a natural body. Therefore, we also need to substitute that with something to capture your voice. His Lordship recently gave instructions to our research teams in the form of one of his knowledge quests to invent a type of ultra-frequency communication device. So, we are going to borrow from that to solve our dilemma here..." he points at the microphone.

"In all the nether-space, you're going to make mages obsolete with this thing," she chuckles.

"Well, I think not entirely, but the objective here is to capture your voice to invoke the incantation, even without your body to provide the impetus. But we are not finished here, as we still need the incantation itself..."

He now picks up an envelope from the box. It was large and flat, and appeared to hold something thick and solid inside, more so than simple paper. Kaliya studied him as he carefully pulled out the contents. Inside was a uniquely fashioned item resembling a large plastic breadboard, as for mounting circuit prototypes. It was roughly the same size and shape as a sheet of paper, and affixed with a series of thin mithril frames around glass plates which plugged into sockets mounted on the board.

The plates all appeared iconic. They were embedded with small crystal adornments of various shapes and sizes, molded into the glass, and inscribed with the conceptual name of the glyph along the bottom edge using a type of enamel glaze. The sockets also had connectors branching in various directions, some of which were attached to metallic conduits to form a program sequencing between the glyphs.

"This looks fancy!" Kaliya croons.

The Master inserts the board into the docking port on the device and clamps it into place.

Kaliya shook her head at the audacity of the odd invention.

"So much for the idea of Early Industrial," she emits. "I think you people just bumped it up to a new level. Where do you get these ideas of yours?"

"Some of this is borrowed from other technologies we have been experimenting with to create devices capable of harnessing certain conceptual meanings into configurable iconic applications.

Although, I will admit, this is the first time to try something like this," he chuckles.

"And did you actually blow up any labs along the way?" she grins.

"Fortunately, no. We've been playing with these for long enough now that all the original labs are in ruins."

"Oh wonderful. All right, so how do we use it and what does it do?"

"Firstly, this example uses the natural energies around us, but His Lordship once mentioned during the development stage that we should also include an attachment socket for an arcanic capacitor, just in case we might try using it in an area that is absent of the natural energies."

"Good idea, to give it a local charge."

"What you see here," he points at the breadboard, "is what we call a program board. It is configurable, depending on the need, and follows a very similar conceptual pattern as your typical spell scroll. These iconic components," he directs at the glass plates, "represent the glyphs, and the connectors here program their sequencing."

"Incredible! You know what this looks like to me? It looks like some kind of crazy printed circuit board with program instructions written on it. And this thing on the table is a type of reader device. Cu'Nar help us all! Does Chief Tech Lapäli know about this yet? This would be enough to cause another month's worth of horns to go flying."

"Not as yet, but before we go and celebrate, let us first make sure it serves our needs."

"Has it been tested?"

"We did test this configuration in one of our labs…just before it blew up…" he smirks. "But the technology itself has been serving us for a while now. However, this particular configuration is another thing. The real test is to see if YOU can do it."

"Ah, but of course."

"Now, this here…" he points at the microphone, "will capture and channel your voice into the board. Normally, the physical presence of a body while speaking carries a force through space and into the apparatus."

"This actually reminds me a little of my visit to Sigil, where speaking can carry force if you use the right words."

"Yes, and so it is here. We are borrowing a few of those same concepts. One could almost say we are inventing our own form of an early Celestial technology."

"That sounds dangerous, and your society is so young."

"So it is. But the lack of a body in your case requires us to simulate this with the microphone to capture your voice independently and channel it with a similar force, but more mechanical in this case. The harmonics will then resonate with one or another of the glyphs, engaging them in sequence as you call them out. And as the result, you will effectively activate the spell program in a manner resembling the casting procedure."

The Master now demonstrates by turning on the device with a small switch on one side. This causes the internal mechanics to come to life. The wheels begin to turn, rotating the disks in the wire frame and the crystals inside. And as the unit spun up to full power, the glass plates also came to life.

Kaliya watched in amazement as each glass plate pulsed softly with a gentle glow, being powered internally by the device. The hues seemed to resonate with the unique color arrangements of the components embedded within the glass.

"Does a person even need to be a mage to use this?" she asks. "This looks like even a novice could call this out, if only to read the thing."

"Technically, yes, although I'll also admit this is used only in those applications of qualified professionals with the appropriate ranks and permissions."

"Naturally. Now, am I supposed to try this out as it is?"

"His Lordship suggested we should apply this as if you were performing this officially. So we will disassemble it, and you will take each piece and assemble it yourself, as if to say you were relocating them at your destination for use in the field."

"All right, sounds fair."

They disengage the device and remove the program board. Kaliya then picks up the apparatus and holds it briefly, allowing it to realign with her phased condition, then sets it back on the table and reaches into her box for another rune. As before, she holds it to allow for the phase transition, then sets it into the cradle, causing it to re-phase to the local environment, just as it would if she had transported the whole arrangement to Ruuki uy'Daan. She hooks a small wire clamp at one end to secure the rune in place, then takes the program board again and attaches it as they did before.

"Are we ready for this?" she remarks hesitantly.

"I believe we can do nothing else but try. One final mention to be aware of, however. Unlike your more traditional scrolls, these glass plates tend to resonate with a slight murmuring sound as they activate. So, be aware of your focus, and do not let yourself be disrupted by the curious effect," he smiles.

"Uh huh…right."

Kaliya glances over the device one more time before gazing at the program board, preparing to call out the glyphic names. She recalls her previous experience at using the more common scrolls, and calms herself for this new demonstration. The process would follow the same, even though she is not personally channeling the energies. But she still needed to maintain her focus of mind from start to finish.

She begins speaking the words, and with each pronouncement, the glass plates altered from the soft pulsing to a bright radiance, accompanied by a tiny whisper-like echo of her voice. She struggled to keep herself from being distracted by the reaction as she continued through the incantation.

As she finished with the last of the glyphs, the full arrangement of plates was aglow. A distant hissing sound issued up as the energies were released, and the crystals inside charged with a flash of energy. Kaliya lurched back impulsively as the energies erupted in a lateral swirling action around the table, rapidly spreading outward, and then condensing back into the rune stone in the center, causing it to glow as the enchantment settled.

"Um…" she hesitates. "Is that normal?"

"Not to worry. This is what we saw in the lab."

"Is that before or after it blew up?"

The Master responds with a hearty laugh as he reaches to remove the rune from its mounting.

"Now, the true test is to see if it provides us with a proper exit point. It would not serve us to use a rune pointing to an unknown space."

"Oh, absolutely."

The Master now slides the table to one side, clearing the space of any obstructions. Kaliya steps out of the way, allowing him to work. He considers his options, finally choosing a nearby chair as his test subject. He brings the chair out along the platform, at some distance from the location where the rune was marked, and casts the enchantment for secondary transport. He touches the rune to the chair and the object vanishes in a flash, reappearing instantly in another flash at the point where Kaliya had successfully marked her rune.

"Very nicely done, Kaliya," the Master lauds with a smile. "I believe we should report to His Lordship on our success. I'm sure he will be most eager to see this through at our earliest moment."

The Master dismisses the girl as he packs up the device and the other materials to be reconditioned for another use.

Chapter 10

BREAKING NEW GROUND

"Cu'Nar be blessed! You're ready? When are you going to do it? I want to watch! In fact, I'm sure we ALL want to watch. You simply MUST give us time so we can all assemble to see it…PLEASE!! Oh Kali, I've waited for this moment for what seems like FOREVER!"

"Suli, calm down," Kaliya begs. "All right, I'll relay word on my side. They've got a few last-minute details planned for me anyway, and we need to get them organized. Since we're not technically in a state of war this time, we can be a little more relaxed on it."

"Like what?" she asks nervously. "What are they doing over there this time?"

"First of all, our research teams have been working on a prototype set of armor. It's been in development for some time and needs testing. And guess who they picked for it," she thumbs at herself. "Next, Thaelyn is giving me the honor of leading our initial expedition with a medium guard contingent."

"A medium guard?" the Captain asks. "Do you have the command rank for that, or is this a special allowance for you?"

"I don't have the rank for what he has in mind…yet. In a couple of days, however…" she grins.

"Great cu'Nar, you people move quick over there!"

"It's not actually that they move this quick with just anyone. I'm a special case, for a couple of reasons, one of which is my previous experience in the Sentinels. He'll be taking this into consideration, along with the pressing need to condition me for my future duty assignments."

"Future duty…" he shakes his head. "Kali, do you know how long it took me just to make Captain? You're not even out of training, and what are they giving you?"

"Um, Lieutenant…" she mutters timidly. "But yes, he is pushing me hard on this. Anyway, I'll bring our initial expedition in, but another officer, a Colonel, will lead a more appropriate garrison force."

"How many, do you know?"

"I believe they're preparing a moderate brigade of ground troops, plus gryphons and camp supplies."

"Gryphons… Wait, I recall you mentioned that word before."

"They're a type of flying mount they often use for scouting and sometimes for air supremacy in combat situations."

"Flying mounts for air supremacy," Túfula reflects. "I remember you talking about this. Kind of like using aircraft, but with animals, and I think I recall you once said they can fly supersonic. In all the nether-space, how does an animal handle that? I mean, the wind forces would tear it apart, wouldn't it?"

"Actually, Túfu, you're right, but the way they apply it is very clever. They wrap themselves in a type of envelope which offers protection from the outer environment, and this carries them along, slicing through the air without affecting the occupants."

"That sounds almost like a spatial inversion bubble," the Captain relents.

"General, I see our people have been assembling nicely outside. We should be on with ourselves soon. What about the wagons?"

"My Lord, the supply wagons are loaded and ready on Trader's Row. We just need to bring the runes over once the others are through."

"And the building materials?"

"Also loaded and ready. We are using trucks on this occasion since we have been advancing a few of our services in this time to use mechanical transport. That, plus work crews are all standing by at the Cormyr Military Stockpiles."

"Very good. This should make a good show for our friends over there. I simply hope we have enough cleanup crews on-hand for when their horns go flying," he chuckles. "Kaliya, the time has come. Go forward and perform your finest."

"Yes, my Lord!" she salutes proudly. "And it's my great privilege to lead our people forward on this historic day where we travel to new worlds."

"Indeed, Lieutenant! And such a curious manner in which this travel is taking place."

Kaliya was already in her projected form and carrying a bag with her supplies. They were assembled in the strategy room at the WIC building in Rolsklinde. Outside in the plaza stood almost a thousand troops, fully outfitted for battle, even though they didn't expect to see one when arriving on Ruuki uy'Daan. The parade of armor was a standard fare when deploying troops into the field. It also held a special role as a demonstration of the pride of the Order for their audience on Ruuki uy'Daan. Kaliya made one last check of her supplies before departing on her way.

Sulíma, Túfula, the Captain, and many others had assembled on the western edge of the city on the northern side. They made arrangements earlier with Thaelyn and his officers to use this space for their deployment, as it represented a vacant grassland region away from their farming efforts to the south. The fields of wild grasses had been cut to clear the way between the city and the coastline further up, and the full assembly of refugees had been gathering this morning along the outskirts of the city, keeping behind walls and filling up yard space near homes and parks.

Kaliya makes her appearance in a prearranged clearing just outside a garden wall separating the field from the northern neighborhood district. Sulíma and her friends all waved to greet the arrival as Kaliya walked over to a table they set up in the field.

Voices are heard murmuring through the crowd as she places her bag on the ground and begins carefully pulling out the unusual conjuring apparatus and setting it on the table, followed by the rune and the program board.

"All right, I need quiet, everybody," Kaliya calls to the assembly. "Even though I've practiced this a couple of times by now, I'm a little nervous this time because it's for real."

A series of shushing sounds pass amongst the audience while Kaliya calms herself, setting the rune in its cradle and installing the program board in its docking port. She closes her eyes briefly to focus her thoughts on her objective, then she begins to read.

Sulíma and the others listen intently to the strange ritual, noticing an abnormal glow emanating from the iconic glass artifacts as Kaliya progresses with the chant. Suddenly, they see the arrangement erupt in a flash of light as the crystals conduct the surge of energy. The surprise sent waves of shock through them, and they all jerked back.

A surge of swirling light spreads out around the table, expanding outward, then quickly condensing into the strange rock in the center of the device, causing it to glow briskly and then fade.

"Cu'Nar's grace," Sulíma gasps. "I don't recall anything like that out of the orcs before."

"They're nowhere near as skilled as this," Tana admits.

"But that's a device," Túfula notes. "That's not even her doing it by hand, in this case."

Kaliya smiles at her accomplishment as she repacks her bag, taking the marked rune separately in her hand, and then moving the table off to the side. She holds the rune up to the crowd and they let out a cheer, then she vanishes from view.

"Now for the fun part," Sulíma announces expectantly.

"Here we are, my Lord," she holds it up for display. "I pray it worked this time as well as it did in practice."

She sets the rune on the table, as well as her bag on the floor nearby. Thaelyn takes the rune and examines it briefly.

"Good," he acknowledges. "Now, Lieutenant, get into your body and lead us to this new world."

"Yes, my Lord! With haste!" she salutes again and disappears.

On this occasion, she reappeared in another part of the WIC building, a meeting room in this case, where she made her projection, rather than the conference room she used so often before in the guildhall. She merged with her body and awoke from her meditation, checking herself to make sure all was well.

She was already dressed for her role in the new prototype armor recently developed at the Bahlaie center. Her legs and arms were covered in plated segments, and she wore heavy boots with vulcanized rubber soles. Her midsection was encased in sectioned plates, with overlaid leafing along the abdomen to protect the vital organs, and ribbing along the spine. Even her tail was enclosed within a sleeve of segmented links composed of wide blades on the upper side and hinged joints underneath.

Her helmet fully enclosed her head and horns. A visor slid on a hinged track over her crest and mounted at a comfortable distance in front of her face to allow circulation of air and the presentation of a heads-up display. The suit was designed for extreme environments, such as exposure to space and hostile conditions, and even some limited underwater exercises. It was durable in the critical areas, but also flexible with joints made from a composite carbon fiber and a mithril studded chain mesh.

She ran a quick diagnostic on a control panel which was positioned as a cuff on her left arm. She stood up and checked her joints, testing to make sure they were limber enough for easy movement. She picks up her new weapon, which had been leaning against her chair while she rested, and fastens it to mounting clips on her back. The item was sheathed in a long crescent-shaped scabbard, to match her new sword-staff. Along the way, she closes her visor to test the environment seal and HUD systems. When she feels secure that her suit is functioning properly, she opens the visor again and returns to the strategy room.

"I'm here, my Lord. Everything appears to be working within parameters. My suit functions show nominal, the environmental regulator is operational, and the HUD system displays my statistical details. I'm ready."

Thaelyn makes a quick inspection of her armor before commencing.

"Young lady, if ever I might be worried to see such a sight as this on the battlefield, yours would be a good example," he grins. "Very well, proceed."

She turns and exits the building into the plaza, with Thaelyn and the other officers following close behind. She closes her visor once more to simulate her battle mode. As they arrive with the other troops, Thaelyn passes the newly marked rune to a mage, who then moves away and begins casting to open the portal.

"May the gods walk with you, Children," Thaelyn mutters softly as he observes the team depart from sight.

Sulíma, Túfula, and the other refugees waited for something to happen. They were anxious to see Kaliya's return, but time seemed to pass very slowly. The field in front of the group was empty. It had been several minutes by now. Then it came, a spiraling vortex of energy opening onto the field.

First to arrive was a tall figure fully covered in a glimmering metal suit, with a face mask displaying two glowing slits for eyes, and a small grill aperture for the mouth.

"Cu'Nar's grace!" Túfula gasps. "What in all the nether-space is that?"

"I'm going to make a wild guess and say that's Kali's new suit," Sulíma replies delicately.

"Where does she think she is, Capitol Prime on Azgarén?"

"Well, she did say she needed to test it, so let's not get ahead of ourselves just yet."

"What's that on her back?" Petrith asks.

"Petrith, at this moment, I haven't a clue," Túfula submits.

Kaliya charges ahead several paces, then quickly turns to direct the other guardsmen as they follow through the portal, waving them off to the side.

"Soldiers, this way, standard formation. Scouts, here!" she calls as they appear on the field.

A group of scouts line up in front of the officer and she begins giving instructions.

"I want a routine survey. We're not expecting anything, but make a circle to our west," she points in the direction of the valley across the river. "And make a quick run up through those hills. The other side of these mountains is jungle. We'll send gryphons out that way for a long-range patrol. I want another team heading east, through the city. Watch yourselves and stay low. There's a camp of orcs on the other side. Friendly, so far, but let's keep it quiet. I don't want to spoil anything with a lot of new faces."

The scouts nod in acceptance of the order, then cast haste spells on themselves and dash away in a blur.

"Suli," Túfula whines. "Did you see that?"

"Túfu, I'm not sure what I saw. It didn't stick around long enough for me to make a positive identification."

"Mages!" Kaliya shouts. "I need way-lines, two of them, ten wide each. Line up one of them across here," she directs to the location where her original portal opened up, but extending further into the field. "The other will be further aside there," she points at another location. "That one will be for the caravans. Be sure to space them apart sufficiently for the vehicles to arrive. Divide them up and get them delivered."

"Aye!" the lead mage returns.

The team of mages moves into position pulling rune stones from their belts. They cast their marking spells for the first line, and then move to the next for another batch.

"That looks like more of what Kali did," Túfula observes. "Cu'Nar's pity, how many do they need?"

The mages gather together, and one brings out a return rune.

He enchants it for each of them to touch, causing them to disappear back to Rolsklinde.

"Well, so much for them," Sulíma jests. "They're vaporized. Next?"

Kaliya stands by with her guard, keeping the space clear for the arrival of the larger contingent. A few moments later, a row of ten portals opens up right in front of her. Waves of soldiers start pouring through, spaced at three-second intervals. Kaliya moves to one side to direct the flow. An officer comes into view and approaches to meet her. She raises her visor as he arrives.

"Colonel Marlaine," Kaliya stands at attention and salutes. "The local area appears secure. I've dispatched scouts to our west and east to survey the region, but there do not appear to be any hostiles within visible range."

"Well done, Lieutenant. Not that we were actually expecting any, but you followed your protocol nicely."

"I also have a second way-line being delivered right now for the caravans. I would expect them to be arriving soon."

"Excellent, we'll get the camp set up as soon as they arrive."

"In the meantime, I would wish to ask permission to send out a gryphon team for a tour of the local surrounds."

"You know this land better than most, Lieutenant. You may do so once they appear."

"Thank you, Sir."

Captain Lapäli watched the exchange with great interest, recognizing the display from his own time in training and ascending the ranks. He could almost read their lips, even though he didn't know the language. He couldn't help but smile at their professionalism.

Rows of soldiers continued to emerge from the line of portals. The area was filling up with many hundreds of troops.

"Look, Túfu!" Sulíma motions cheerily at the mass. "We're being invaded by little people!"

Túfula glances at her friend to check the girl's mental stability after all the excitement.

"I'm simply fascinated by this display. Imagine what we're looking at, Suli. Technically, it's an invasion, and from another world directly into ours, and by people not even advanced enough to travel by interplanetary means. Even in my wildest dreams, and from the stories my father used to tell, I couldn't envision anything like this."

"You really enjoyed his stories, didn't you."

"Yeah, they were great, and they filled me with something special," she sighs.

"Take it easy, Túfu," Tana encourages. "We'll be together again soon, and maybe you can get him to tell you a few new ones."

"Maybe if they have a nice library I can visit on that new world, I can read a few of theirs."

Another line of portals opens up, this time with automotive trucks rolling through, carrying supplies and camp materials. Kaliya once again begins directing traffic to divert them into a holding area.

"In the name of the cu'Nar!" Túfula blasts. "Wheeled vehicles jumping through hyperspace? And look at them! They look like something out of an ancient history lecture."

"What's powering them?" Tana wonders. "They're mechanical, but are they powered by a combustible fuel, or electric?"

"I see a compartment in front," Sulíma asserts. "That might be the engine. But I don't hear any noise, like from something producing mechanical power. So, maybe it's electric. They have those fuel cells, and small enough that they could fit that space."

"And with wheels…travelling interplanetary… Túfu, we're in trouble, if these people only need a conveyor to move around."

"Yeah," she retorts. "And worse, we're supposed to fight a godlike creature on another world, in another universe, with THAT?"

The Colonel lines up his troops for a quick inspection, then divides them up into companies and sends them off to different areas to hold their station. As the last of the soldiers came through, they were followed by a flight of gryphons and their riders.

"Great cu'Nar above, what are those?" Sulíma shouts.

"I'm going to suggest those are the gryphons Kali was talking about," Túfula mutters. "And cu'Nar help us, they look a lot worse than that animal Tana mentioned once."

"Yeah," Tana reflects. "And these are real this time, MUCH bigger, and with people riding them!"

"Gryphon scouts, over yon!" Kaliya calls, directing the team into a clearing.

"Aye, where do you need us, Lieutenant?"

"To our north we have this sea. Not much out there, so let's make a nice leisurely circle along the coastline to the west and southward past the hills. One of you will take that route while a second flies eastward across this bay and up the other side. Continue around to the far coastline before making your return. Mark your runes in the sky above us here," she orders, giving a thumb sign to start them on their way.

"As for the rest," she continues. "One will make a quick pass due east, this side of the mountains. The others will make a staggered run to the south, sweeping east over four major rivers, and meet back here when you're done."

"Aye!"

The gryphons each charge away across the field, taking flight when they have enough momentum. They rise in the air and sweep around in the direction of their assigned course.

"Look at the power of those creatures, Suli," Túfula observes.

"I'm actually a little more concerned about those claws. They look sharp enough to rip a person in half."

"Yes, but clearly these are trained as mounts."

"Mounts, yes, but for soldiers... So, are those animals trained to attack?"

"I suppose they might be. Kali did say they used them on occasion for air supremacy."

"Air supremacy is one thing...and that's in the air. What about down here?"

"I don't know, but if they're part of a military body, they might serve multiple roles."

The girls watch as the large, winged beasts rise in the air, some turning off to follow the coastline, others swinging back inland.

"My guess," Petrith suggests. "At least on this occasion, they're making a scouting run. We shouldn't have anything to fight around here."

"All right, Petrith," Túfula agrees. "But it looks like a very relaxed run so far. Didn't she say something about supersonic?"

The gryphons leveled out and their riders angled their driving lances in the mounting cradles on the collars. They then began a chant to engage the transport spheres. A moment later and the beasts flash away into the distance, leaving behind a thunderclap striking the ground, and causing the people below to cringe at the sudden disturbance.

"Does that answer your question, Túfu?" Sulíma shrieks.

"That is simply amazing," Túfula mutters. "Early Industrial, with animals doing at least some of the work, and yet they can travel supersonic in the air, and dash away at high speed on the ground. Why do they even need machines at all?"

Kaliya continued directing the caravans to one side. Sulíma and her friends studied the assortment, which included the same types of building materials Thaelyn once imported to establish his camp at Firstfall.

"I wonder how all that will appear once it's set up," Petrith wonders.

"I don't know," Túfula responds. "The whole sight of it is a little hard to believe. When you consider the stories of the Suuden-Aryku and the weapons they used on us, and then look at this…"

"But according to Kali, they apparently chased that Marshal Darumon away, so that must say something in itself."

"They chased him away as much with the threat of these Estelar as anything else."

"Yeah, that's right, but I think Kali's been holding back on us a little. If these people are so daring that they would actually chase after him, they can't be as simple as they appear."

"All right, so are you going to say a society in their Early Industrial is brazen enough to take on a society in its advanced Space Age?"

"Túfu," Tana offers. "If it includes magic, I think they might hold a few secrets on their side. We, just like the Suuden-Aryku, don't know the first thing about what this stuff can do, other than maybe to start a campfire. But if it can carry you to new worlds and send animals at supersonic speed, I think we should take a moment and ask ourselves what else it can do. Kali said it's based on the power of the mind, remember?"

"Yeah, that old riddle of metaphysics…"

"Right, and our science needs numbers before anything will work for us. The mind doesn't need anything but the imagination. I've spent some time thinking about this ever since she showed us that little trick once."

"Have you tried inventing anything new out of it?"

"So far, I'm taking her advice. I've practiced making fire on a stick several times by now, enough to get the idea in my head that I shouldn't play with it any further than that without someone guiding me."

"All right, I'll hold my comments for a while longer until I can get over there, and maybe we can see about a training course or two."

They continued to watch as the vehicles passed through the portals, now followed by passenger cars loaded with groups of laborers.

"Well, you have to admit," Petrith muses. "Conveyors or otherwise, they at least travel in style."

"But they're all so short!" Sulíma yips.

"Suli, maybe it's not that they're so short, but that we're so tall."

"I don't know, Petrith. I've never seen anything other than the orcs, so I really don't know how we compare to anything else."

More vehicles come into view, some now pulled by horses, including flatbed wagons, where one is carrying a large flat concrete platform, and others with curved spires wrapped in silvery metallic jackets.

"These are pulled by animals now," Tana notes. "So, not everything is converted to automation yet."

"Fascinating," Túfula mutters privately. "Still in the early stages of it. We're looking at a form of transition of a society as it evolves."

These newest arrivals were also accompanied by a crew of exceptionally short workmen in overalls and hard hats.

"Dear cu'Nar, they just keep getting smaller!" Sulíma winces.

"Be careful where you step out there, girls," Petrith teases.

"Lieutenant!" calls the gnomish foreman. "What a jing-dingally fine day it is today!"

"Indeed it is, Professor," Kaliya replies. "And welcome to Ruuki uy'Daan…what's left of it. Are your people ready to set up the gate?"

"We're ready on this side. Where do you want it?"

Kaliya studies the area and tries to visualize the lay of the camp.

"It looks like we'll be using this area out here for the camp buildings, and with the city off to that side, maybe if we place the gate just there between us and that wall, it might serve a nice intermediate role."

"Ooh, what a fantabulous suggestion! We'll get right on it."

The gnomes begin directing their crew to the assigned space as Sulíma and her friends watch. They pull aside wagons with sections of a crane and start unloading.

"They're so cute!" Sulíma croons. "Like little dolls with tool bags."

The last of the wagons finally comes through and the portals close again. Kaliya takes a quick glance around at the workers as they start leveling out foundations for the buildings and unloading supplies. The scene was a flurry of activity.

Several moments pass, and another portal opens allowing Thaelyn, Aerlie, General Gabarleine, and the Daanen-Aryku officers to arrive.

"Look at that one!" Sulíma coos. "She's got wings!"

"Just how many races are involved in this society?" Túfula relents.

"My Lord," the General considers as he examines the activity. "It would seem our young protégé has her affairs well in hand here."

"She is a credit to her training as well as her breeding," Thaelyn nods.

Captain Lapäli perks up as he sees the High Commander enter the scene. He stands up from his position behind the wall and begins marching out onto the field to greet the newest arrivals. Sulíma, Túfula, Petrith and the others all advance behind him. As they approach, the Captain offers a traditional Daanen'kai military salute.

"Commander Nazég," he announces. "Greetings and welcome…

Although I'll admit, it feels a little strange addressing you as the HC. You're barely half my age."

"I know, Captain," Kailen responds. "But this is where we are now. Anyway, you've done a fine job for us over here. We're looking forward to your return. I'm sure the Council will have something special in mind for you when you arrive, and His Lordship has also expressed a desire to commend you for your service."

"I'm deeply honored, Sir. It's been a long hard tour. A soft bed and a good meal would suit me just fine."

The Captain now turns to Padriyl standing next in line. He steps around to examine the young officer.

"And what do we have here, I wonder," he states in a haughty tone of authority. "The last time I saw this face, he was nothing more than a wet-nosed velvet horn with dreams of serving the Sentinels. Now look at him, a Lieutenant, is it?"

Sulíma and Túfula both stand back to observe the interaction, quickly recognizing the Captain's obvious demeanor. They share a grin as they watch.

Padriyl rolls his eyes briskly as he comes to attention at the authoritative address, holding his posture stoically while the Captain makes a cursory inspection.

The Captain makes a pass around the young officer, then comes forward to address him again. His face softens as he looks into his son's eyes.

"Would it be too much for a father to ask his only son for a sturdy hug after three and a half centuries of absence?"

"Not at all, Father," Padriyl affirms. "Mom and I missed you terribly during this time."

The two leaned in for a strong masculine embrace, with the Captain patting his son on the back.

"Speaking of which, how is she? Is she coming here, or is she going to make me chase her halfway across the universe to see her?"

"Some of us suspect it's only halfway across the galaxy, but she's been very busy lately, so she's hoping to meet up with us tomorrow. My understanding is these gnomes should have the gate up by then, and everyone here can step through to Rolsklinde, where we're building a similar gate as a dedicated access."

"So, we'll have a new conveyor to that other world? Is this simply to leave Ruuki uy'Daan, or can we come back?"

"It'll be bidirectional, at least until we can better establish ourselves and build a more permanent unit inside the city."

"Wow, we'll get our own conveyor after this?" Sulíma asks.

"Not only that, but you'll have two other worlds to explore if you like. The one where we live, and Tae'Eladar where His Lordship and his people come from," he turns to call Thaelyn's attention to the meeting.

Thaelyn and his group were casually touring the construction sites, joined by Kaliya as she saw them come in. They chose to make this tour first, allowing Kailen and Padriyl to meet with their people. When Padriyl announced his call, Thaelyn diverted his attention to the meeting.

"Father," he declares. "This is Lord Thaelyn and his wife, Lady Aerlie, the King and Queen of Tae'Eladar, as well as territories on Therinë. And next to them is General Gabarleine."

"Suli," Túfula whispers imperatively. "That's them. Bow and show your respect. You too, Petrith," she jabs him with her elbow.

"I greet you, Your Majesties," the Captain offers with a bow. "We all owe you and your people a great debt. I hope one day we will find a way to repay you."

"The burdens of war, Captain, are upon us all," Thaelyn admits. "Let us strive to see it through as a combined effort. That will offer payment enough."

"Why couldn't we have found people like this several worlds ago?" Sulíma wonders quietly.

"May I ask what your immediate plans are while you're here?" the Captain continues.

"In the short term," Thaelyn affirms. "We must establish a foothold. I would also wish to take a closer look at that conveyor you found representing Portal Three on our side. If that secondary index is of any value at all, we must investigate where it leads and what waits for us there."

"And what about us? What do we do in the meantime?"

"For now, Captain, I would suggest you find some rest. You have surely earned it by now. We will take charge of the issue of security from this moment, and until the foreseeable future. My association with the Commander provides us with a well-coordinated effort between our forces. Therefore, if you should wish to continue your service, I would recommend you confer with him initially. In addition, our people speak a different language from yours, and many of his troops are already trained in this regard."

"So, if we want to interact with any of your people," Túfula considers. "We need to study your language. Is there some place we can go to learn this?"

"Indeed there is. We offer language courses in our schools back home on Tae'Eladar."

"Would these courses be available to us? That is, we don't really have anything like money in our situation here."

"Not to worry. This particular course is freely available. We had a rush on the classes in recent years as we acquired a large flood of new citizens on Therinë at the close of the war there. But by this time there should be adequate openings for you and yours. Kaliya could assist if you like."

"Does this use that strange blue elixir stuff again?" Tana asks.

"It does, as does most of our education system back home."

"I'm really very excited to see this world of yours," Sulíma offers. "Kali told us a few stories about it, and what she's been studying there."

"I'm still trying to get over what she's wearing right now," Túfula recounts. "Kali, is that really you inside that metal shell?"

Kaliya had been standing behind the others when Túfula called her name. She steps up to the group and glances over her glimmering armored suit.

"Yes, Túfu, it's me," she responds. "The real me this time, not a projection. You should've seen me when they first brought this contraption out of the lab. I was expecting some kind of armor, but this went a little outside my imagination."

Sulíma and her friends circled around to study Kaliya's form. They examined the control cuff on her arm, the flexible joints and hard plates, and several embedded elements that resembled sensors.

"What's this thing made of?" Sulíma asks. "This isn't any kind of metal I recognize."

"Keeping in mind, this isn't the finished product. It's just a prototype to test the design and technological features. The larger plates are adamantium, and this chain mesh is mithril."

"That doesn't actually mean anything to me."

"Yeah, our science wouldn't know about these. It's a special kind of magical metal you can find on certain worlds, maybe like the one we're on now."

"You mean we might have this here?"

"It's possible, but you need a lot of background knowledge to use it. It forms on worlds like this that have the magical energies present."

"And you're fully encased in it?" Túfula adds. "How does that feel?"

"A little strange as compared to what I'm used to. I'm wearing a pressure suit inside here."

"A pressure suit! Why do you need one of those?"

"This is powered battle armor, Túfu. Fully self-contained, environmentally sealed, and able to withstand atmospheric pressures from the vacuum of space, up to a heavy or ultra-heavy planetary environment...at least in theory. It's still experimental, and with lots of room to grow, but so far it looks good."

"Great cu'Nar," Sulíma gasps. "Full military battle armor?"

The girl makes a close examination of the layers of armor plates. She lifts one of Kaliya's arms and tests the joints, then circles to study the ribbing on the spine, and back again in front. She further examines some of the sensors embedded within the plates.

"What are these?" she points at the small devices.

"Those are sensor arrays. They're calibrated to detect objects in my environment and give me a tactical readout on a HUD inside my visor."

"You have a HUD inside there? And this control device on your arm, it looks like some kind of informational interface, but what is this..." she points to a round pad attached to the interface midway on the forearm, and displaying a dragon shield emblem on it.

"That...well, maybe if I can demonstrate..."

Kaliya glances at Thaelyn for the suggestion. He smiles and nods, and she steps back a few paces, then reaches for the shield emitter control. She takes up a defensive stance as she taps the emblem, and the device comes alive with a sudden crackle of energy, causing Sulíma and the others to jump back. A large energy barrier resembling a tower shield instantly formed on Kaliya's arm, the same effect as used by the Infinity Shield in the old fortifications that once stood around Firstfall. It moved with her arm, forming a protective wall that was virtually weightless. Sulíma and the others gazed at it.

"Can I touch that?" she wonders. "Or will I lose something."

"Go ahead."

Sulíma reached out carefully to lay her hand on it. As she does, she feels the impossibly solid surface of what appeared to be a nearly transparent energy field.

"It's solid! How in all the nether-space do you make a solid thing out of energy?"

Túfula and Tana now reach forward, soon followed by Petrith.

"Túfu," Petrith admits. "If you had any doubts about their technology versus the Suuden-Aryku, I think you need to reconsider some of that."

"Yeah," she admits. "Maybe you're right."

"How does this work against any kind of weapons?" Sulíma asks.

"Impenetrable," Kaliya replies. "Even if you drop an atomic on it..."

"What?!" she shrieks.

"Of course, this one doesn't give me full coverage, so I would need to use an umbrella field in that case."

"Dear cu'Nar, you'll be unstoppable! What's this on your back?"

Kaliya now turns off the shield emitter and reaches over her shoulder to pull out her new weapon. She slides it out and twirls it in her hands, spinning in a pirouette, then gripping it with one hand and aligning it with her body in a presentation stance.

The three girls each stepped back at the ominous display.

"Great cu'Nar above!" Túfula yelps. "I thought you said you were hoping to save some of those people. What do you plan on using that on?"

"We do hope to help them," Kaliya admits. "But we still need to prepare for war. Remember, they're likely under the control of those devices, and we might not have any choice but to defend ourselves. Besides, it might not be limited to the Suuden-Aryku. We could find ourselves travelling to other places one day, and as a soldier, if we ever get into trouble, I may be fighting on the front lines using melee combat techniques, since I'm trained to use martial arts, as well as rifles. And this is my weapon."

"That's one thing I think I do NOT want to touch," Sulíma whines. "But is it my eyes, or is that thing glowing…among other things," she emits softly.

Sulíma and the others looked at it closely. This was no ordinary piece of metal attached to a wooden staff. It glowed with energy, seemingly vibrating with electrical impulses. In addition, it also emitted a condensed mist of cold air.

"It is," Kaliya affirms. "This is called a sword-staff," she holds it out for display. "This one was specially made for me since I'm pioneering a new field of training in the academy. We have a number of people currently in training as a combined force, and we'll probably end up as a special unit of some sort."

"A special unit?" Petrith wonders.

"When you combine our skills at magic, our specialized training, and a few other unique talents we're learning right now, it'll be one for the books. We were given a suggestion by Adalon once in her prophecies that we might end up as a Special Ops force of some kind, but we're not sure how that's going to pan out yet. As for the glow, this is due to an enchantment."

"An enchantment," Tana considers and leans in for a closer look. "Is this more of your magic?"

"The material in use here is mithril, which carries its own magical aura, as does adamantium. The metals can also take strong enchantments, which essentially enrich them with some form of magical augmentation. In this case, we're drawing from the air and water schools of magical study, which associate as lightning and ice enchantments, respectively. What this means is, if the razor-sharp edge doesn't cut you in half, you'll also suffer electrocution and freezing aftereffects."

"Isn't that a little like overkill?" Petrith winces.

"Some things out there are a bit harder to kill than your average Suuden'kai trooper."

"I don't think I want to meet any of those," Tana shudders. "If it requires this much, it sounds a LOT worse than that tiger or those gryphons of yours."

"Yeah, this goes well beyond my father and his stories," Túfula reflects. "He would tell me stories of knights and such, but we never had magic in any of that, although we did have our fantasies."

"You had knights at one time?" Thaelyn asks. "How long ago was this? It could not be any sort of recent history, is it?"

"Oh no, this was a long time ago. My father is Elder Vankkar, and he was a historian before he took his seat on the Council. When I was little, he would tell me stories based on some of our old history. We're talking about our medieval days, which were something like a thousand millennia ago."

"This is indeed a fair amount of time. How curious. To have knights would suggest a moment where you must have had a more militaristic environment than where you stand now as a society of scientists. How did this actually occur? Was there some manner of transition?"

"As I understand it, it was a period where we were once ruled by a powerful king. This is why I keep reminiscing whenever I hear stories about you and your people, and then watching all this out here," she waves at the assembly of soldiers. "He was said to have once united our full world, a lot like you apparently did on yours, using his army of knights who travelled out on crusades to bring the people together."

"Túfu," Kaliya wonders. "Is this where that old saying, 'and here comes the knighthood...' comes into it?"

"Yes, actually, but this is so old by now, a lot of people don't even remember the actual origin. Although, it's my understanding, this time period has often been romanticized for one thing or another."

"Crusades..." Thaelyn muses thoughtfully. "Yes, a bit like I did at one time. So, you were a fragmented society before this?"

"Yes, apparently we had a lot of small kingdoms and other nations, some of them peaceful, others not."

"That sounds a lot like Tae'Eladar in those early days," Aerlie reflects.

"It does," Thaelyn admits. "But now I am wondering how this might fit with the other pieces..."

"Uh oh... Other pieces, like with Adalon and what she tells us?"

"Although I truly hate to spoil this young lady's romance, if Darumon was in control of things over there, raising them as a new minion species, would he even allow them to divert themselves into so many rivaling nations?"

"Perhaps he was looking for more of his entertainment along the way? Or do you think it got out of hand for a time?"

"If his ultimate goal is revenge against the Estelar, entertainment or no, he would surely not find much success if they spent most of their time infighting."

"True."

"And therefore, this remarkable king arrives to set things straight again. What was this king's name, Miss Vankkar?"

"His name was King Saakerav," she replies uncertainly. "So, what is it you're thinking? I'd hate to think this was Darumon playing more of his games on us."

"And I would similarly hate to disrupt your stories, but I must ask myself these questions. It would be far more beneficial to Darumon to have your full society united behind one rule, rather than a hodgepodge assemblage of feuding rivals spending so many of their resources against each other."

"Cu'Nar's pity," Kailen moans. "I hate to say it, but you're right. So he comes in, creates this king image, and then a military body that goes out on a crusade of some sort. And then, here we are, I suppose, romanticizing over it."

"Thank you, Kailen," Túfula moans. "Like I needed that…"

"I'm sorry, Túfu, but we have too many controversies circling around us with that guy."

"This king image…" Thaelyn considers. "A romance? Yes, I think it would be! How else do you motivate a society that may not be inherently militaristic to bring a world together, whether politely or otherwise? If your society broke into smaller segments, I might suggest it is likely due to a migration effect from his original culture, spreading out to conquer the land. Then, those individual tribes began developing independently beyond his direct supervision. Perhaps even he cannot be in all places at once. Therefore, to advertise this crusade as a romance the people would want above all other things. And then, in the modern day, you still romanticize over it as such a wondrous thing he did. I must now ask myself if he uses this in any way, perhaps to motivate them again for this new effort."

"You know," Túfula notes. "For a guy who didn't want to spoil my childhood fantasies, you're doing a fantastic job at it," she chuckles ironically.

"I am sorry, but I suppose it is unavoidable by now. And so, we have this king image, and likely during a time when your society is better able to manage itself over a broader area of land. He sends out these crusades, collects everyone together, probably tells a few fanciful stories to bind them into a new social order, and converts these once-rival nations into a collected body, maybe also redirecting them into these new developmental venues, like science and research."

"Non-militaristic ones, by the way," Kailen adds.

"Indeed! And ultimately, with the potential to lead him here."

"Yeah, well…" Túfula huffs. "There goes that one. So, here we are now. We have this wonderful story which I grew up with about the Stormhooves, and…”

“Stormhooves?” Kailen utters abruptly.

“Stormhooves?!” Kaliya yips suddenly.

“Stormhooves!” Thaelyn and Aerlie emit simultaneously.

“Ugh… Stormhooves…” Kailen repeats while covering his eyes and subtly shaking his head.

Túfula’s voice catches and her eyes bulge as she darts them around the group. She begins creeping backwards towards Petrith, inching her way behind him to take shelter.

“Hey!” he protests. “Why are you hiding behind me?”

“Because you’re the big strong man,” she replies tepidly. “And if you want any part of this tail, you’re going to protect me, right?”

“Excuse me, I grew up watching this guy when he was in that strength training program of his. Those arms could probably twist me in half.”

“Actually,” Kailen corrects. “I haven’t been involved in that since the attack, so it’s probably only a third by now,” he grins.

“Miss Vankkar,” Thaelyn issues. “What is this mention of Stormhooves?”

“That’s the name King Saakerav used for his order of knights.”

“Indeed!” he intones strongly. “Aerlie?”

“Yes, I remember it,” she recalls. “Um, let’s see… Children of Breed, who walk in their sleep, a slumbering gift possessed; their Hooves of Storm will rise anew, and the turn of battle blessed.”

“Huh?” Túfula blurts. “What do you mean?”

“She’s speaking of Adalon again,” Kaliya replies. “One of her more recent prophecies we’re looking at right now that speaks of something using a metaphor. She apparently does this often to hide things until some specific moment when it’s ready to come out. According to a woman we know back home who studies this, these sometimes involve private knowledge that someone, somewhere, would know about. Adalon is an exceptionally cryptic individual, and we believe she’s following a kind of script, planning each of these moments where we discover things we need to know as we move forward towards Azgarén. And now here you are with this."

"So you're saying, I actually held some important piece of something to fill in a missing part of a prophecy...but why? And Kailen, you should know about the Stormhooves, right?"

"Actually," he nods bashfully. "I do have those lessons from my old history studies, but it didn't click until just now. Sorry, but I don't think as much about that time period as some impressionable young women I know."

"Oh! Thank you, Mister High Commander of the Sentinels. But what relevance does an ancient king and his knights have to do with us, the Suuden-Aryku, Azgarén, or...anything?"

"This is who we are, Túfu," Kaliya affirms. "We just didn't know the name until you came along. Our Special Ops unit is turning out to be a small army of people with some very unique talents, so don't lose hope on your romance. We're going to reinvent it."

✦ ✦✦✦ ✦ ✦

Sulíma was perusing the bustle of the newly forming camp after a restless night. Several of the smaller structures were in their final stages already, and the finishing touches were being put into place on the large platform resembling an oddly mysterious interpretation of a conveyor.

The circular aperture was assembled, and the little men were now making their final adjustments to the control unit on the side. Sulíma watched as they diligently labored on the project with the efficiency of a well-oiled machine. It appeared as a practice that was well-known to them in their native environment. But try as she may, she could not interpret one item out of the odd selection of components making up the unit.

"Suli?" calls a voice off to the side.

She turns to see Túfula approaching from the housing district, freshly out of bed in the early morning light.

"Túfu, you're awake finally?"

"What do you mean, finally? How long have you been up?"

"I had trouble sleeping last night. I would lie there listening to the sounds, and all the shouts out here, and asking myself: What are they doing this time?"

"Yeah, same here, actually, until I forced myself to close my eyes and try to get some rest. Did you get any sleep at all?"

"I think I dozed off after a while. Then I woke up early and couldn't stand it anymore, so I came outside to see how things were going."

"Looks like they've been busy. What's this thing here, some kind of conveyor unit?"

"It looks that way, but in all the nether-space, I have no idea how it works."

"What's inside that box, do you know?" Túfula asks, pointing at the control unit.

"I looked inside several times as they were assembling it. I saw a few crystal thingies, some metal whatsits, a couple of round doohickeys, and several rectangular thingamajigs."

"Such an amazing analytical assessment, Suli," she grins. "I'm truly impressed. No wonder you couldn't fix that old nano-rearticulating unit back at the mining camp."

Sulíma gives a gentle shove on Túfula's shoulder at the teasing gesture.

"Túfu," she offers. "Have you eaten yet? They have a kitchen over there serving up some of their food for the troops here."

"I'm not one of the troops, Suli."

"I don't think it matters, whether one of them or not, they're feeding everyone. I came in and smelled the food, so I took a closer look just to see. Next thing you know, someone is waving at me to come closer. They gave me a plate and started loading it up."

"Did they say anything about what it was?"

"Most of them don't speak our language. I learned some of these little fellows can speak it, apparently because they're some kind of scientists working with our own engineers from the Naarg uy'Sodrad.

I asked them what it was and...well, I didn't recognize the names, but after experimenting a little, I discovered I liked it."

"Well, I am kind of hungry, and I have to admit, it smells good, I think."

"Come along and I'll show you how it goes."

Sulíma brings Túfula over to the kitchen area where she hands the girl a plate and leads her across the bar past the various food dishes. Túfula attempts to ask about each item, but Sulíma simply hushes her and instructs the attendants to load up a similar fare to what she enjoyed earlier. They next turn to find a suitable table.

"All right, Suli," Túfula insists. "Before I poison myself on any of this, you'd better tell me what it is."

"Fine, this stuff here is a kind of meat they call ham. It comes from an animal called a pig, but I really don't know what that is. It must be native to their world. Then we have some bread, some white mushy stuff they call porridge, and these other things are eggs."

"Eggs?!" she shrieks. "Like from birds? Unborn avian embryos? Ew!"

"Túfu, I felt the same at first, but these aren't apparently the fertilized kind. So there aren't any...um...body parts involved. Just try it, it's apparently a staple item in their culture, and although I felt a little repulsed at it, they suggested if I dip the bread into the yellow part, it actually tastes very good. Trust me. I ate the same, and I'm still alive. In fact, I have to admit, it was very satisfying, probably the best meal I've had for a long time."

Túfula eyes her friend suspiciously for a moment before tenuously sampling some of her food. After a few bites, she felt confident that it wasn't toxic, and she might actually survive the alien cuisine.

The two of them sat there while Túfula continued her meal. Eventually, Petrith arrived, along with Tana, and Sulíma helped them with their plates. The group sat down and carried on their conversation while observing the activity of the camp.

The gnomes were preparing to mark the first of three runes for the gate. They only had the intention of using one rune in this case, linking it to a sister unit in Rolsklinde as a single dedicated bridge.

The other two runes would be used as spares, a precautionary measure commonly practiced for safety reasons.

A shout ushers up from the gnome standing near the control unit as he places the first rune in the U-shaped mounting slot. The other gnome throws a lever behind the unit and the portal aperture comes to life in a brief flash.

"Whoa!" Sulíma yips. "What was that? The thing just sparked and blew out again."

"Maybe it shorted?" Petrith suggests.

The gnome removes the first rune and replaces it with another, then repeats the process. Sulíma and her friends continue watching the affair from the table. The gate flashes again as it marks the second rune with the gate's dimensional index.

"That looks intentional," Tana muses.

"Well, whatever it is they're doing," Sulíma observes. "They seem to be using up those little rock thingies."

"Did anyone mention what those…rock thingies…were, Suli?" Petrith asks.

"I didn't ask, actually."

"It looks a little like that thing Kali used to establish that portal of hers," Tana considers.

The gnomes reset for the third rune and go once again. They pull it out and hand all three to a man in an ornately adorned robe. He steps away, placing the runes in a pocket, pulls out another one and enchants it for his departure. The gnomes finally place one last rune in the slot and close up the unit.

"I really have no idea what it was we just saw," Túfula suggests. "But I think I might go with Tana's idea. They did something to those three rocks, and that man just took them away in one of his magical portal spheres. But now, what's the new one they put in there?"

"They look to be packing it up now," Petrith considers. "Does that mean it's ready?"

"If we reflect on Kali yesterday," Tana suggests. "She had to mark an index of some kind, and then she took her…rock thing…back home. This might be the same idea, but for the apparatus instead."

"Fair enough…"

"Look at that one," Sulíma notes of a gnome moving another control lever.

The gnome engages the gateway node with the new rune in place. Sulíma impulsively gets up from the table as she observes the action and moves in front of the unit at distance to study it. The other members follow close behind.

The circular structure begins to glow as the glyphic disks in their jackets come to life, and a spiraling vortex ripples into view within the aperture.

"Suli," Túfula murmurs. "Other than for those little conveyors, I have never before seen anything like this, not even as a child watching the old vid-com shows."

"That's got to be impossible!" she responds. "Everything I ever heard of technology like this tells me you need at least a fusion reactor to power it. But here, they're just using more of those fuel cells like we saw before," she points at a series of boxes and tanks behind the assembly.

"Remember," Tana offers. "It's also powered by these magical energies, and they must be doing most of the work here, which means they must be really potent."

They continue to study the anomaly within the ring-like structure when another sight begins to form before their eyes. At the center of the rippling vortex, a dot appears, rapidly expanding to fill the space, opening the portal as a fully bidirectional conduit to the other side, the result of the mage delivering the runes to the sister unit in Rolsklinde. The four bewildered friends simply stared in awe at the image of a modest city, fully populated with people strolling through what appeared to be a busy town plaza at near midday local time.

"Cu'Nar's eyes, everyone," Sulíma mumbles with her voice trembling from the shock. "That's a whole other world we're looking at, and it's only one step away, if I'm interpreting this correctly."

Thaelyn and Kailen come into view in the window, apparently

inspecting the work. One-by-one they step through, disappearing for a brief instant from the image and reappearing on the near side of the portal.

"Suli," Túfula whispers imperatively. "Did you see that? How they vanished, and then reappeared? I've never had the chance to see it before, but that's how they describe the transition through nether-space, or whatever it is these people call it."

Sulíma shakes her head in amazement at the mention.

"Professor," Thaelyn announces to the gnomish foreman. "You have done well, as is customary to your creed. We shall store the additional runes for safekeeping, and work to solidify our foothold on this world. I believe your work here, for the moment, is complete."

"Right-a-diddly-do, my Lord! I'll have my team pack up and head back to Tae'Eladar to join the others on those big projects. We can't let a moment pass by without figgledy-gidgeting some new dinky-doodle along!"

"Indeed, and I do so love it when you bring forth such colorful phrases."

Kailen steps forward from the platform, noticing Sulíma and her group standing spellbound at the scene.

"The way is open for you now," he announces. "You may step through whenever you're ready to leave and rejoin the others. Suli, I know your sister is waiting patiently, or maybe not so patiently. Ever since we first made contact, she's been driving me crazy over how much she wishes she could hold her baby sister in her arms again. Last night was especially intense. I almost ran down to the medical ward to grab a hypo-spray sedative just so the two of us could find some rest."

"Kailen, don't you dare hurt my sister, you big meanie!" she jeers.

He shares a laugh with the group and turns to the others.

"Túfu, I think it goes without saying, your father is a little, um, anxious. You too, Petrith, with your mother, so you should both get your tails over there as soon as you can. And let the others know about it, as well."

"Yes Sir," Petrith replies.

"Commander," Tana asserts. "What about my mother? She's supposed to be in training, so where do I find her?"

"She would be in the dorms on Tae'Eladar, so you and your father will need to travel there. I may need to find an escort for you, so you don't get lost."

"Kailen," Túfula asserts. "Is this to say we'll be relocating over there? What about the city? It's our home, isn't it? Or are we just abandoning it, like all the rest?"

"At the present time, Túfu, the priority is to reunite our people together in one place so we can reestablish our society, whatever is left of it. The condition of the city here is such that it would take nearly as much effort to rebuild as it would to build a new one on Therinë, with the exception that we have help over there from Tae'Eladar."

"But with this conveyor thingy here up and running," Sulíma offers. "Couldn't that same help just come over here and…?"

"While you are generally correct," Thaelyn interjects. "We do not wish to spread ourselves so thin, and on so many projects, that nothing ever gets accomplished. Therefore, we have decided to leave this be until we can better stabilize our efforts in one place. The Commander and I have conferred on this many times. When considering your population numbers, even with the inclusion of those of you here, you are rather sparse to be dividing your attention on so many projects at once. I suspect, at some time, we will return to reclaim this space, but the society we are building together on Therinë offers the benefits of community and association that work well to create a world together."

"All right," Túfula submits. "But what about some of the salvage we have here? There's some old industry we were hoping to reclaim, and some of the machines might still be useful to us. Rather than rebuilding everything from scratch, couldn't we try refurbishing some of this? I mean, with the conveyor, it's not that much to send work crews here to reengage the industry and still return home for everything else, right?"

"This does indeed make a good point. Perhaps we can send some people across to investigate the possibilities, and for those occasions where the work is within reason, we can make the effort. Many of our people from Tae'Eladar are offering volunteer efforts to assist with the construction on Therinë, and I think we could probably ask some to further assist in the cleanup here. But more importantly is to focus ourselves on the work that is most imperative to our immediate cause, and that is still the war."

"Of course, maybe I'm just jumping ahead. I'm feeling a little anxious to get my hands into something to make myself useful."

"Your ambition is a valuable quality. I would be more than happy to find a useful purpose for you, and any others who would join along. But if memory serves, your primary education was interrupted, and with all the new developments occurring around us, it would be a far more valuable service for you to complete some portion of that before you jump on the labor wagon."

"You're right," she sighs heavily. "Back to school…"

"Do not despair, young one, for we can teach you many things, and do so quickly. If we combine some of ours with what you still have of yours, we can perhaps fill in many of those gaps. And if to use the Elixir of Visions, time will pass swiftly, thus allowing you to move into the higher studies much more rapidly."

Sulíma turns up a bright grin at the notion. She nudges Túfula, trying to get her response. The girl looks up at her, and reluctantly smiles and nods.

"But are we speaking of a civilian course, or military," Petrith wonders. "For instance, if Kali was able to get in, does that mean any of us could follow?"

"We do hold certain policies and entrance requirements, some of which are academic in nature. With Kaliya, we had to fill in a few educational demands for her to qualify, although this was an easily resolved issue. But the most important is what we call the Spirit test, which is a special measurement to determine the purity of your spiritual energies."

"How do you do that?" Túfula asks. "And why is it needed?"

"This is something I brought with me as I arrived on Tae'Eladar and began to establish myself and my military Order. It uses an application we are familiar with in the Outer Planar domains where we have a much more intimate understanding of the nature of spiritual energies and how to classify them for their polarity and character. As a Celestial, I represent the Positive side of the planes, so I would prefer those who follow me to conform to this as best they can. I can be rather particular as to whom I offer my gifts and teachings, as I want to be sure they are used appropriately," he smiles.

"Ah, well, all right. So, do we need to do something to prepare ourselves for this?"

"Generally speaking, you are what you are, so there is no real form of preparation. But this is only required if you wish to join our military forces. There are a good many civilian studies that are not as demanding. Although I should temper this if you should ever desire to go into any advanced technical studies that involve higher ranking skills, as these might then require special qualifying, and this again means the test."

"To ensure no one blows up any laboratories, I guess," Sulíma giggles. "This seems fair. I'm sure we can associate with some of our own high security procedures."

"Petrith," Kailen intercedes. "Are you thinking you would like to join His Lordship's military rather than the Sentinels?"

"With all due respect, Commander," he responds. "I appreciate the Captain, and I was happy to serve with him, but...well, if you would excuse my words, my impression of the Sentinels is that it's little more than a civil defense militia, not a full and proper military. We've been shoved from one world to another. Now it's time to start shoving back...Sir."

"I understand, and you're not alone with this opinion. There are a lot of people back home who feel the same. We may not be a naturally militaristic society, but even a bunch of pacifists need to understand when enough is enough. If this is truly how you feel, then I wish you good fortune in your efforts to serve. So far, we have some of our people working in tandem with His Lordship's forces in a combined training effort. At the very least, you might find this of interest."

"What about this magic of yours?" Sulíma continues. "What kind of training do you have for that? Kali mentioned lots of people use it on your world."

"Indeed," Thaelyn responds. "It is a part of our academic studies, for both military and civilian use. If your interest is to apply yourself in this area, you could find occupation in many of our industries and other fields. On the other hand, as your sister is involved in the medical sciences, one such as you might find interest in our related practice."

"But yours is a kind of priesthood, not a medical science like ours. How does that actually work?"

"For this, I might wish to direct you to my wife, Aerlie. She would be the best to explain how our interaction with the Estelar behaves. Essentially, your worship of your chosen god or goddess grants a connection with that deity. Our relationship with the Powers is a rather unique one, as compared to most other societies. Ours is more intimate where we hold a deeper interaction with them, one society to another."

"So," Túfula surmises. "It's not like you're calling up to some mystical being as part of a ritualistic sermon. You're actually negotiating with a higher form of life and bargaining for something."

"Very much so. Most often, they tend to behave as a parental body leaving their Children to grow and mature. But in our case, we have more of a give-and-take relationship, where we can call on them from time to time for some special service. One aspect of this is to share some small part of their strength. Our priests offer their worship, which we could describe as a form of offering in exchange for a return of some gift or ability. Very often, we use this in the healing practices, or perhaps on a field of battle to augment our troops."

"Kind of like holy warriors...sort of," Túfula mutters.

"That sounds a little scary, actually," Sulíma winces. "But I suppose it doesn't hurt to ask, even if it's not my final decision."

"Absolutely," Thaelyn affirms. "Knowledge is the most valuable commodity one can afford."

"Personally," Túfula resumes. "I never really considered myself for military service. In fact, I originally saw myself following my father in the historical studies. But for all the things I've been hearing from Kali, and then watching your people here, I'm asking myself what else is out there. I mean…" she titters. "Just sitting here watching these little guys putting this thing together," she waves at the gateway, but then pauses with a curious stare. "What in the cu'Nar's name are those?!" she shrieks.

The group turns to witness a fantastic display appearing on the opposite side of the portal. A parade of metallic beings had arrived and began marching through the aperture. The lead unit resembled a multi-faceted polyhedral form with innumerous sides leading others with seemingly similar designs, though technically of subordinate levels in their native hierarchy. The lead unit steps onto the scene and turns to approach Thaelyn, directing the next unit to usher in the remaining mass through the portal into the field.

"Celestial entity Thaelyn," it announces in a subtly mechanical voice. "We have observed your progress and have returned in accordance with our agreement to continue our service in the directive of constructing a mecha-arcanic door to the chosen destination prime material solid body. We request further direction specific to the regional vector coordinate location of the construction objective."

"Great cu'Nar above!" Sulíma yelps. "Do you people actually have robots, on top of everything else?"

"Túfu," Petrith intones warily. "Your earlier suggestion of their technological state is becoming more and more indistinct."

"Yes, Petrith," she replies timidly. "I hear you loud and clear. Now help me and Suli pick up our horns before we lose them."

"Welcome, associate modron," Thaelyn answers to the inquiring unit. "We have a fair amount of open space here, but we would wish to keep it within close proximity of our camp. The field just off to the side there," he points to an area away from the local bustle. "That should do nicely. Use your best judgment for the placement so as not to interfere with our other activities."

The unit turns to examine the area and selects a suitable location. It then gives orders in an indecipherable language to the others to deliver the supplies they were importing. The small army of mechanical beings continued to pour through from Therinë, having just arrived with tools and component parts for their own design of a portal to the world that would ultimately serve as the new home for the orcish population.

Sulíma and Túfula gawked at the display, finally to find their voices again to inquire as to what was happening.

"Your Majesty," Túfula begins. "What in all the nether-space are those? Are they yours? Do you actually have robots on your world?"

"In truth, no. These entities are called Modrons, a race of living machines from a dimensional realm we call Mechanus."

"Living machines?!" she screeches, feeling faint from the implication. "I… In all the… Oh dear cu'Nar, what else waits for us out there?"

"What are they doing?" Sulíma asks tenderly.

"If you recall," Thaelyn responds. "We were searching for a potential new home for the orcs. I visited Mechanus a while back to confer with Primus, which is a godlike entity in machine form… their leader, if you will. Think of it as a master computer of immense proportions and with knowledge that spans the breadth of virtually all Creation."

"I can barely even conceive of that. I feel so small now."

"The result of my inquiry provided me with several promising choices, of which I selected one and informed the modrons that when the time was right, they should return to assist in the construction of what they call a mecha-arcanic door. Essentially their own brand of portal device. Their technology is very unique, as I am sure you will discover if you should decide to stay and watch. The end product will serve as a portal for the orcs to use to depart this world to their new home."

"Where is this new home, can you tell us?"

"I think it would be impossible to describe it to you in reasonable terms. It is not located in this universe, as we need it to exist outside an arcanic cloud. This is to limit their ability to use magic, and therefore open any new portals. Furthermore, I requested a few other important criteria, such as limited proximity to other inhabited worlds, and thus affording them a measure of isolation. This is both for their benefit and others, to keep any early interactions at bay. Hopefully, this will allow the orcs privacy and the chance to grow, perhaps even to evolve to a more prestigious form."

"I would love to understand your mind," Sulíma winces. "But I think it would short mine out in the process."

Thaelyn grins at the suggestion.

"Patience, young one, there are many possibilities in front of you. And if you should desire to take any of our courses on Tae'Eladar, you can gain a small glimpse of it in the form of my work."

"Careful, Suli," Túfula warns teasingly. "I think he's flirting with you now."

"But now should be the time for us to make some of our own progress," Thaelyn concludes. "I will ask you to relay word to your fellows about the availability of the gateway so that they can rejoin with the rest. We must also send word to the orcs, telling them the time has come for them to find their new home. They should pack everything they can carry, but leave a few hands free as I wish to offer them additional tools and supplies to aid them in the beginning. We also have seed and a collection of livestock to send along."

"You are extremely generous, Your Majesty. So much offered to what was originally a hostile race."

"We are a prosperous society, Miss Vankkar. This is considered a small thing, and I would feel remiss in the ways of my own teachings should I send these beings forward into unknown territory without a fair chance of survival. The lessons they have learned from us to teach them how to live and survive in civilized fashion may carry them far, but that first step will be difficult. And finally..."

Thaelyn pauses to survey the continued activity of the camp, which was now compounded by the mass of metal bodies industriously laboring on a stack of strange mechanical parts.

"I want to see that conveyor of yours, the one you found in Camp Three, with the unknown destination index. We should set it up post-haste and see where it leads us. If we are right, this will take us one step closer to our goal. But here is where our most difficult objectives will begin, and I need information."

✦✦✦

Work was underway to reassemble the conveyor from Portal Three. The unit had been pulled out of storage and brought onto the field just on the edge of the new outpost. One of the mini fusion reactors was reassembled, along with its support equipment, and using a water supply from the nearby river passing through to the shoreline. While they waited for the work on the conveyor, Thaelyn oversaw the completion of the mecha-arcanic door from the modrons, and the remainder population of orcs called out of their jungle encampment.

The orcs travelled through the city and into the fields to meet with their benefactors, where they checked their belongings one last time, picked up the new supplies, donned backpacks provided by the Tae'Eladaran forces to help carry the load, and took up leashes attached to the animals. Slowly, they filed through the strange contraption that looked like a hodgepodge of clockwork gears and hammers, glowing cylinders, and bobbing disconnected spheres.

The orcish shaman waited for his people to pass through before taking his turn. He wanted to offer a final few parting words before joining them.

"The blue-skins, their friends and their gods, have been good to my people," he notes as he gives his final goodbye. "We will sing songs to you for all the gifts you give to us. I will teach our young ones the story for many seasons."

"Perhaps the time will come when your people and our people may meet again," Thaelyn suggests.

"We will wait for that day, and try to remember this day. We will try to prove ourselves worthy in the eyes of your gods for what we make until then."

"Work hard and take care of your people, shaman of the Ur'nuk tribe. Share your teachings with many, that more like you can rise up. I wish a good life to you."

The orcish shaman bows his head and turns to pass through the portal.

With the orcs successfully removed from the equation, all focus could now be placed on the future movements of the war, beginning with Morndindor.

The next morning, Thaelyn and his team of officers reconvened in the strategy room at the WIC building. They were reviewing several ideas on how to proceed on the initial survey of Morndindor, should the conveyor function as desired leading them to a new world.

"Kailen!" Sulíma shouts as she storms into the room. "What did you do to my sister, you big meanie!"

"Suli, what are you talking about this time?" he replies from the table.

"You know darn well what I'm talking about! I swear, I leave you two alone for a few centuries and look what you do!"

The young girl struts up to the officer and sneers in his face, then softens and throws her arms around him in a big bear hug.

"You're going to have a baby!" she yips.

Thaelyn and the General glance at each other, then back at the duo.

"Commander," Thaelyn contemplates jovially. "I am trying to comprehend the mental integrity of this young lady, perhaps you could enlighten me?"

"Your Lordship, Suli has always been like this. It's just her way, ever since we were young back home."

"He's right, Your Majesty," she concedes. "We're a bit like brother and sister, without the brother and sister part, if you know what I mean."

"I may need to spend some time deciphering that phrase," he smiles. "But yes, perhaps I can see it. And if I am correct in this, you are the same age as Kaliya, around four centuries...hmm. Now I see why it takes so long for your kind to mature," he grins.

"Aw, come on, I'm not that bad. I like who I am."

"Indeed, Miss Tad'vaal, I know of whole societies like you... light-minded and free-spirited. You would fit in quite nicely."

"Hmm, I'm not sure how to interpret that, so I'll take it as a compliment."

"Precisely as I might hope you would."

"Well, I'm sorry for interrupting your meeting. I just had to congratulate Kailen. I was talking to Ankhia, and she told me the news. In just under a year, I'll have a little niece or nephew to play with, not sure yet which."

"She's not the only one, Suli," Kailen admits. "With our new-found reprieve from the Suuden-Aryku, many of the women are taking up their roles to bring forth a new wave of children to get us started again."

"Again…and again, and again… It just keeps going around in circles, doesn't it!"

"Yes, but this time is different. We found what brought us out here in the first place, and now there's hope for us, if only we can finish this war with His Lordship's help. Now we know who we're fighting and what we're fighting for, and with the blessing of the cu'Nar, and of course all the Gods of Tae'Eladar, we may finally see it through."

"And I want to be a part of that help somehow…though I'm not sure how since I don't really want to be in the military, but maybe something will come along where I can help. But not the baby part, I'm not quite ready for that yet. Unless you think…I mean, with our numbers so low right now…"

"No, Suli, give yourself another few centuries. I think we'll have time for it."

"All right, Kailen. I'm going back to the ship and see what kind of trouble I can find for myself. Maybe Ankhia can put me to work on something. I'm also hoping to visit Tae'Eladar soon, maybe look around a bit and see if I can speak to Lady Aerlie a little, if she's not too busy. And I wanted to ask around about the guildhall and how that works."

"A little anxious, are we?"

"You bet I am! Do you think I'm just going to sit around on my tail waiting for the next surprise attack?"

Sulíma makes a quick wave and bounces out of the room.

"Your children must be quite the experience, Commander," Thaelyn notes as he watches the girl leave.

"You think Suli is bad, you should've seen Kaliya when she was young. And then the two of them together..." he shakes his head and grins.

"And one of your greatest gifts is that you have such an extended period in which to enjoy them."

"Gifts?" he snickers. "You might want to ask our parents about that one."

"Indeed, but now..." he returns to a report in his hand. "General, we discussed before how we should send just a single scout through on this occasion. We have our assumptions that this portal exits to a remote area as a staging point for the original invasions. The scout will bring a return rune back to our new outpost, to provide a fast turnaround in case we need to take any quick corrective actions to any sightings on the other side."

"A wise idea," he agrees. "And thus staving off any leakage of details concerning our arrival."

"I would further suggest, as a precaution, he should equip a scroll for the return, just in case we find ourselves in an arcanic dead-space."

"A good point... We do not wish to take any chances here."

"He should also carry the standard fare of potions, for haste and cloaking, in case he finds himself in the midst of trouble and needs to make a quick exit."

"Of course, my Lord."

"And lastly, as is the usual practice whenever we find ourselves travelling to a new location, he should mark one of our own runes for the area, to provide a link for our future use. We could then use this to import troops and supplies, just as we did here and on Ruuki uy'Daan."

"Very good, and if the area is indeed clear of any observers, this should not be a problem."

"Next, I would wish to begin moving troops through to establish a foothold as soon as possible, assuming the local area provides the security for it. It will make our scouting runs that much more efficient. After that, it is just a matter of time and a lot of ground to cover. We will confer with Chief Bronzeheart to see what he and the others can provide in relation to the local landforms and general placement of cities and towns, but orienting ourselves will be the first goal. We will go from there."

"Good enough to start. I'm fairly sure Captain Hagmaert has been itching for some work. Perhaps we could have him lead the expedition."

"Excellent, General. Indeed, I have seen him on several occasions partaking of the local tavern. We certainly cannot have that sort of behavior when there is work to be done!" he smirks.

✦ ✦ ✦ ✦ ✦ ✦ ✦

It was early morning the next day, and Captain Hagmaert had been assigned a detachment of troops in preparation for an incursion through the conveyor. Thaelyn and a gathering of his officers, including Kailen, and both Padriyl and his father, Captain Lapäli, were in attendance to oversee the operation.

A scout had been prepared with a rune recently marked for a return zone within the new camp on Ruuki uy'Daan. Tensions were moderate and expectations were high that this journey could take them to their intended destination, but nothing would be known until that first step was made. In fact, nothing could be truly known until some form of confirmation could be established with the discovery of a known element in this next world to identify it as Morndindor.

"I would like everyone's attention for a moment," Thaelyn calls to the assembled mass. "On this occasion, we are entering unknown territory that is potentially hostile, but at the same time we must consider there may be friendly factions that are unaware of their own predicament and therefore potentially hostile to ours. If this world is indeed Morndindor, there should be dwarves present. We will consider them friendly, but uncooperative at this time, until we can learn more of the local situation."

He glances at the scout standing next to him as he continues.

"Our first objective is to investigate the local terrain immediately surrounding the exit point of this conveyor. If it appears secure, we will send our incursion force. If there are hostiles, we must contend with them quickly, in order to secure the area for our own occupation. If there are friendly forces present, we may need to take measures to secure an agreement, or simply go dark to escape the local area and find another."

He next turns to Captain Hagmaert while continuing his announcement.

"Our incursion force will take and hold the area, and from there begin a series of sweeping patrols of the region to find the evidence we need, first to confirm our suspicions of where we find ourselves, and second to locate our primary objectives. These objectives are the dwarven city of Glimmerheim, a suspected mining operation being conducted by their Thane, and we hope to find a Suuden-Aryku command base. In the meantime..."

He makes a cursory pass around his assembled officers.

"We must also try to understand the general situation on that world, and what has been occurring for what we suspect to be four centuries of occupation. If our dwarven friends from the mines north of Rolsklinde were so oblivious to the situation of the Suuden-Aryku, I must wonder what history that world has endured, especially as we look at Therinë and what occurred there. For this, we need a careful review of the land and possibly to infiltrate their cities and settlements to listen in on their local gossip."

He looks back at the scout again before wrapping up.

"Morndindor is suggested to be a world with a heavier form of gravity than what we have here, meaning you will feel heavier on your feet than normal. This will create additional wear on our people, causing them to tire more easily. The air may also be heavier and difficult to breathe, as is the story passed along by our dwarven friends on the invasion of the elves. For this reason, we are choosing human and dwarven troops to make this operation. We may experiment with our own elves later, as we find opportunity, but I think the more robust bodies of the others would make the best choice for our initial invasion."

He steps over to look at the conveyor, which had been set up and appeared to be operating normally using the unknown destination index discovered by Kaliya and her friends when they first installed it.

"Scout, you will go in and make a quick survey of the area. If all appears clear, you will mark a rune in a convenient location and return. I would recommend you apply a strength augment before departing, to give you a slight boost for that first step. Watch yourself and be safe."

The scout nods and casts a chant on himself to magically boost his physical strength, then lines up with the conveyor and leaps through it.

He travels through the trans-dimensional conduit, taking notice of the usual display of odd glows and swirls, streams of energy, and the passage of unfamiliar objects in the distance outside. The travel time seemed longer than it actually was, until he found himself approaching the membrane of the dimensional sphere where the conduit reentered real space.

He emerged from the portal exit and immediately felt the burden of a heavy draw on his body pulling him to the ground. At the same time, he noticed the thick air pressing on his lungs, making his breathing uncomfortable. He stumbled to the ground, catching himself with his hands until he could stabilize his footing and pull himself upright again. His strength augmentation allowed him to stand fully upright with relative ease.

It was dark, though he could not immediately tell if it was early dawn or late dusk. He could see sunlight just barely on the horizon. He made a quick glance around his immediate area. The land appeared empty...fortunately.

He had arrived in what appeared to be a modest hillside canyon gorge opening up to a large plain. The darkened sky occluded much of his view at distance, but it resembled a dry savannah with only a sparse scattering of trees. The line of hills behind him was a smooth rocky outcropping, lightly covered with dry grasses and scrub.

He moves a few steps to one side, offset from the conveyor exit point, and begins marking his new destination rune. He calls the chant, and the typical display of swirling light envelops his body and accumulates into the rune. He then puts that one away and pulls out another for his return trip.

Thaelyn and the others waited patiently and with great anticipation for the scout's return. The camp was dead silent. All eyes watched for the return of the scout in the arrival zone. It had been only a few minutes, but it seemed as if much more time had passed since his departure.

A flash erupts within the marked circle designated as the exit point for the return rune. The scout steps through, appearing relieved for the stress he just incurred.

"Scout, are you alright?" Thaelyn asks on seeing his condition. "And do you have favorable news for us?"

"Aye, my Lord, on both accounts. First, I'll say you should watch that first step. There is indeed a heavy power tugging at you when you first enter, and the air is just as heavy on the lungs."

"This would certainly suggest we were right in our assumptions, but I would wish something more precise if we are to say this is Morndindor, as there may be other worlds out there with such qualities. What else can you tell us? Did you see anything of critical import?"

"Nothing at close range, no sign of civilization, no camps or outposts, the area appears clear and safe for our people to enter. It was dark, though I can't be sure if it was dawn or dusk, but the sun was just barely in view."

"A nighttime arrival would work well for us to make our incursion, using the cover of darkness to establish our camp. Although we still need to wait for daytime if we wish the best results for our scouting. Dwarves are not commonly known to conduct spell-craft, so using an invisibility cloak will work well for us on that world. What about the terrain?"

"Just as you thought, we seem to be secluded in a nice little nook at the base of some hills in a gully. Only one side of it opens up to view, and it looks to be a large barren with barely a spotting of trees here and yon."

"Very nice! Perhaps we could borrow from the trick we used on the dwarven miners with their prison setting to conceal ourselves in that place using false cover to match the local terrain. Did you mark a rune for us?"

"Aye, here you are, my Lord," the scout replies and hands over the rune he made.

"Most excellent. We should see about moving our people and supplies to that world as quickly as possible in order to secure a place for ourselves."

Thaelyn gives the rune to a mage standing nearby. He and a group of others join Captain Hagmaert and his team, ready to establish a way-line at the destination, and later to return to Tae'Eladar to meet with a waiting caravan of wagons.

"For the moment," Thaelyn considers. "We will keep this conveyor open for our people to move easily from here to there, and using our own runes for their return. Once we have our own gate ready, we will pack this up and store it again. Commander, perhaps you would like to have some of your people make a close inspection of these conveyors to see about their design concept, especially as we once suggested Darumon's possible use of…proprietary technology… to make them work with such limited parameters."

"Yeah, I'm sure Chief Tech Lapäli will appreciate yet another set of horns gone missing," he chuckles. "But it could also give us a chance to study whatever Darumon has been doing over there in this time. And I know the Chief Tech expressed an interest in those mini fusion reactors, also."

Thaelyn turns around to Captain Hagmaert, who was waiting expectantly for his next order, along with his troupe.

"Captain, the time has come. Pass through and secure an area for us. We will send camp supplies and building materials shortly thereafter. Prepare your scouts for a quick run through the local region and survey the area. You may report back using our traditional methods of rune messaging to the WIC center in Rolsklinde. I shall return there to plan our next move."

Thaelyn pauses in thought briefly before offering further advice.

"And another thing… Considering we are moving into a region of heavy gravity; we should take extra care on our men until they can become accustomed to it. You should delay your usual timing through the portal for a slightly longer duration to offer the men time to pull themselves upright on entry," he grins. "Otherwise we might have a rather unfortunate pile-up on the other side."

"Aye, my Lord!" he affirms solidly. "Not to worry, I'll make sure these lazy scoundrels keep to their toes."

"And remember to keep out of sight of the locals until we can gain a better understanding of the situation."

The Captain makes a proud salute and begins ordering his troops through the conveyor. Thaelyn watches the line of soldiers depart, and finally makes his own return to Rolsklinde.

✦ ✦ ◆ ✦ ✦

Somewhere across a broad and desolate valley, roughly south and east of the incursion point of Thaelyn's troops, within a row of mountains, was an old and seemingly abandoned mining camp. And within this remote mining settlement, a beleaguered dwarven worker wends his way through the passageways to his home in a quaint row of housing carved out of the rocks of a large artificial cavern. It was a journey he made often, as he, and others, struggled to survive in cramped spaces and with limited resources.

He trudges up to his home and steps inside to be greeted with the smells of cooking, though only just barely. The faint aromas were wafting out from the kitchen where a feminine voice ushers up to welcome him.

"Belrum, be that ye a-comin' through the door?"

"Aye, lass, 'tis only me, returnin' from the run again…"

"Why ye have t' make that run, I don'na know. There be nothin' t' see out there but wasteland an' rubble."

"Friah, me love. Ye know why. By the tales of our fathers an' their fathers, that wasteland was once our home. An' we need t' keep lookin' out for the beasties that blasted it t' the All-Father an' beyond."

"D' ye think they truly ever be a-comin' back, Belrum? How long has it been by now, an' with nay as much as a whisper out there since?"

"Aye, ye may be right, but don'na forget the Adamant mine we found that time. It be out there, an' they still be a-workin' it, the poor sods."

"But can it be verily the work of those beasties, or be it by some other foulness? The thoughts circlin' here were they be a-comin' out of Glimmerheim for it."

"Ye're right," he agrees wearily. "But we have'na seen a sole come out of there since the day. Some think they dug deep t' escape the pummeling, while others think it got blasted the same as the rest."

"But if it got blasted the same, where d' ye think those poor sods be a-comin' from then, ay? Nay from here, an' nay from the other camps we've found."

"Aye, 'tis true, the outer city was blasted t' dust, along with half the mountain above. There nay be a way in or out that we can see from the barrens. An' let us nay forget that time..." he cautions.

Belrum shifts his position in the chair for better comfort.

"D' ye recall when we first saw those fiendish mounds of festerin' death?" he continues. "They come back now an' again t' the mine. Only the All-Father knows what they be a-makin' out there, but ye an' I can both guess it must be t' haul off the Adamant those workers bring up."

"An' it be for this reason ye think they be a-servin' up t' them?"

"Lass, I don'na know what they be a-servin'. Their eyes are as empty as a poor man's cup, an' they speak nay a word, nay even if ye lay a hard one across their chin."

TO BE CONTINUED

www.ingramcontent.com/pod-product-compliance
Lightning Source LLC
Chambersburg PA
CBHW032058310726
48972CB00001B/13